George Sikes

The life and death of Sir Henry Vane

A short narrative of the main passages of his earthly pilgrimage

George Sikes

The life and death of Sir Henry Vane
A short narrative of the main passages of his earthly pilgrimage

ISBN/EAN: 9783337225360

Printed in Europe, USA, Canada, Australia, Japan

Cover: Foto ©Raphael Reischuk / pixelio.de

More available books at **www.hansebooks.com**

Sir Henry Vane
Knight. of Raby castle.

THE
LIFE
AND
DEATH
OF
Sir Henry Vane, K^t.

OR,

A short *Narrative* of the main *Passages* of his
Earthly Pilgrimage; Together with a true Account
of his purely Christian, Peaceable, Spiritual, Gos-
pel-Principles, Doctrine, Life, and
Way of Worshipping God, for which he
Suffered Contradiction and Reproach from all sorts
of Sinners, and at last, a violent Death, *June* 14.
Anno, 1662.

To which is added, His last Exhortation to
his Children, the day before his Death.

Printed in the Year, 1662.

The LIFE and DEATH of Sir *HENRY VANE*, Knight.

Christian Readers,

PRepare your Faith. The enfuing Narrative concerns a perfon, who for his unweariednefs in doing well and fuffering ill, together with the ground and fpring of his deportment in both, doth in very truth exceed the fingle reception of humane underftanding.

He was partaker of the Divine Nature, (2 *Pet.* 1. 4.) 'tis paft the skill of humane nature to interpret him. His attainments were too big for the tongue of Men and Angels. Divine Life muft have divine words, words which the holy Ghoft teacheth, to give its own Character. All other will be fwallowed up of matter.

He had the *New Name*, which no man knowes but he that hath it. A Riddle therefore he was to man in his New Birth, Nature, Life, Principles, Ways, Actions. He was full of Faith and of the holy Ghoft. Who can expound *Sampfons* typical Riddle, unlefs he plow with his Heifer? The things of God knoweth no man but the Spirit of God and he that hath it, 1 *Cor.* 2. Can any give a true account of things he hath neither heard nor feen? Can any fee or hear Spiritual things without Spiritual Senfes, or have fuch Senfes without Spiritual Life, the *New Name?*

He was, but affected not to be Myftical. He fighed after, he longed for the manifeftation of the Sons of God. He defired godlinefs might put off its myftical drefs, lay afide its fackcloth; that they that are all glorious within, (*Pfal.* 45.) might be fo without too: they who are the Sons of God, might appear to be fo; 1 *John* 3. 2.

When the feventh Angel begins to found, *Time fhall be no longer*; to wit, for godlinefs to be a myftery; The myftery of God fhall be finifhed, *Revel.* 10. 7. This Angel is ready to come forth. Then Godlinefs will be manifeft and triumphant. While that is a Myftery, Iniquity is fo to; during which, *he that will live godly, muft fuffer Perfecution*, 2 Tim. 3. 12. *He that departs from evil maketh himfelf a prey, and there is no Judgement*; Ifa. 59. 15. Men hear

of

of the Divine Life in a difguftful found of words, that lie crofs to their defigns, and hate it. It difparages, it difcountenances the whole Scene of things feen, fpeaking of them, as of things that are not. What can they think of this, that fee no other? It judges, condemns the World, the God, the Spirit, the Religion of this World. It fpares not the very goodlinefs of flefh, the wifdom, the glory, the righteoufnefs of Man; It declares all to be vanity that man puts value on: yea man himfelf, and that at his beft eftate, altogether vanity; a goodly, flourifhing, but a corruptible, vanifhing thing. The day *Adam* finned, he died: Loft the life, glory, wifdom, and righteoufnefs he was created in, and fo his communion with God in fuch fhadowie manifeftations and refemblances of divine glory, as were fuited to the difcerning, and made up the happinefs of that condition. 'Tis fad tydings to all thofe whofe **Life** is but of the firft-creation-ftrein, lies in things feen, to hear that all they have, are, or aime at, is lefs than nothing and vanity, *Ifa.* 40. 17. Who can bear it? Yet the defign is honeft and full of kindnefs. 'Tis to rid our hearts of things feen which are temporal, and make room in them for things not feen, eternal, 2 *Cor.* 4. 18.

While the Believers *Life is hid with Chrift in God,* and he fpeaks at this rate of all the vifible glory and righteoufnefs of man, and much more yet, againft the fhameful, apoftate and unrighteous ftate of Man, what entertainment is he like to find?

There are two forts of Princes in this World, that are on horfeback by turns; he is againft them both, and goes on foot, till his great mafter come upon his white Horfe, with his heavenly Armies on the like, *Rev.* 19. 11, 14.

There are inward and outward Princes of this World; Princes over themfelves, and Princes over others. The former have their rational Powers reftored into Dominion over their fenfual, whereby they become workers of righteoufnefs, in the renewed Spirit of a man. Such Princes, (reigning as Kings, 1 *Cor.* 4. 8.) were fome of the Priefts, Scribes, Pharifees, and profeffing *Jews,* who yet knew not, and therefore crucified the Lord of glory, 1 *Cor.* 2. 8. becaufe both in his example and doctrine, he gave forth the proper character and difcovery of a more excellent way.

The latter fort of this Worlds Princes, are fuch as do fit upon vifible Thrones of Judicature, furnifhed with Crowns, Scepters and other pompous Badges of Soveraignty and Dominion over others. Thefe are often fuch as have no Dominion over themfelves at all,

the

the basest of men. *Nebuchadnezzar* himself, the golden head of the four worldly Monarchies (*Dan.* 2. 38.) was so, and accordingly handled; followed not the light of his reason, and therefore was turned to graze among the very beasts of the field, *Dan.* 4. 32.

The true spiritual watchman of God, is to warn both these sorts of Princes, and all others, the righteous and the wicked; the one that he turn not from his righteousness, or rather that he seek the righteousness of God in the true regeneration, which cannot be turned from : The other, that he turn from his wickedness and work righteousness, *Ezek.* 18. and *Chap.* 33. Will men bear this ? Can he that is a man of a marred visage (one in whom the glory, wisdom and righteousness of man, is daily passing away, spoil'd and triumphed over by the cross and spirit of Christ) give this twofold witness against these two sorts of Princes and their Nations (called *Revel.* 13. *two Beasts*) in all their flourish and ornament of things seen, and will they not stone him ? will they not be ready to tear him in pieces ? Divine Life, together with the Wisdom and Words of it, seems such foolishness, and is so distastful to man, that let the person of the true spiritual watchman be cloathed (as *David*) with the outward Pompe of Thrones and visible Scepters, this shall not secure him from the ill word of the Judges, or from appearing so contemptible, as to become the song of drunkards; *Psal.* 69. 12.

'Tis the divine Life men chiefly hate and strike at, all along from *Cain* downwards, but can hit onely the humane, the Woman that brings it forth; The natural man of the Saint is persecuted into a desolate, wilderness condition; but his spiritual part, the Man-child is caught up to God, and secured from the persecuting Dragon, *Rev.* 12. 5, 6. He that is begotten of God, keepeth himself, and that wicked one toucheth him not, 1 *John* 5. 18. That which the Believer hath in common with his Persecutors, (*flesh and blood, that cannot enter into the Kingdom of God*) is all that Divels or Men can touch. And this, no farther, nor till such time as God permits, which never is, till he hath served his Generation, done his Work, and it be great gain to him to be stripped of his mantle, that he may come fully to experience (what he hath been long obscurely guessing at, amongst his fellow mortals) *Mortality swallowed up of Life,* 2 *Cor.* 5. 4.

Spiritual or divine Life and the things of it, the wisdom, righteousness, glory, and all concerns thereof, have more of essence and so

of

of intelligibility in them, than any first creation Life or things. They are therefore in themselves more intelligible, though less, yea, not at all understood by man, 1 *Cor.* 2. 14. What's the matter? where lies the fault? In man's understanding. The objects are too dazling and bright for it; over-master, over-set it. That is not all. They are quite out of its reach; shut up in an utter invisibility. It can receive no notice of them, but in a type, and if this condiscention be made for the expression of them, it decries allegory, runs away with the shadow and rejects the substance.

But if God please to enlighten and raise mans understanding in some hopeful measure, towards its first-created capacity; will that do it? No. There is utterly a fault, an inability in it at its best, to take the immediate view of these things. This seems a hard saying. But God himself who pronounced of every thing in the first creation, *that it was very good,* (*Gen.* 1. 31.) doth yet comparatively find fault with the very best things in it, Heavens, Angels, & Men, and that at their best estate. 'Tis written, *His Angels he charged with folly,* Job 4. 18. *The Heavens are not clean in his sight,* Job 15. 15. and, *Every man at his best estate, is altogether Vanity,* Psal. 39. 5.

The first Covenant, or first state of Life in man, and communion therein with God, was faulty, comparatively with the new-creature-state of man, and the new and everlasting Covenant-communion with God, that he forms and sets up the Believer in, by true Regeneration. Think we what we will, if God say so, shall we contradict and blaspheme? He tells us, *If the first Covenant had been faultless, there had been no place for the second,* Heb. 8. 7. and Gal. 3. 21. If there had been a Law, or a ruling power of Life given, and set up in man at first, or renewed since, that could have given Life, (or have carried us through, for eternal life) everlasting righteousness and Life should have been by that Law; there would have needed no other by a new creation. God will not do any thing that is impertinent or redundant. So *Rom.* 11. 6. *If eternal Life be by Grace, or by the Law of the Spirit of Life* (Rom. 8. 2.) brought into man by a new creation; *then it is no more of works,* proceeding from the utmost activity of the Law, or ruling power of natural Life and perfection, set up in man at his first creation.

What shall we say to these things? How is man out in his divinity? *God's thoughts are not as our thoughts, nor his ways as our ways, they are everlasting,* (Isa. 55. 8, 9.) *his footsteps are not known.* To be sure, *his ways are equal, ours unequal.* He will be Judge. *Every way of man is right in his own eyes, but the Lord pondereth the hearts.*

Shall

Shall not the Judge of all the earth do right? **Can he do wrong? God is not**
a man that he should lie. He giveth not account of any of his matters, (Job
33. 13.) *neither is there need; for he will not do wickedly, or pervert
Judgement; he will not lay upon man more then right, that he should enter
into Judgement with God,* Job. 34. 12. *and* 23.

But the person here character'd, as he affected not to be mystical in
his person, so, nor obscure in his language. 'Tis the fleshly veil on
mens understandings, as to his matter, that makes them carp at his
expression, and cry, *obscure, obscure;* doth he not speak parables? *Ezek.*
20. 49. The mystical reach and significancy of Scripture, as exhibit-
ing the peculiar form of new-creature Life, (under the letter or most
significant figures thereof, that are to be found in the first-creation)
by a sound of words, lies so remote from the veil'd understandings of
men, that they make nothing on't. They are willing to be blinded
and deceived as to Gods Truth, that they may more securely please
themselves in their own lie (2 *Thes.* 2. 10, 12.) and the old Serpent,
the God of this World, is as ready and willing to beguile and blind
them, that the light of the glorious Gospel of Christ who is the Image
of God, may not shine unto them, 2 *Cor.* 4. 4.

In this discouraging posture of the present World, did this believing Pilgrim wade through it, waiting on the Lord, and seeking out
such acceptable words for the explicating of Divine Oracles, as were
most exactly calculated and accommodated to the understandings of
men, so as to unlock, insinuate into, and gain them by a holy guile, into the entertainment thereof, upon convincing demonstration of their
grand concern therein. He did most industriously set himself to bring
forth the most inward thoughts of his heart, in characters to be
seen and read of all, as to the Life hid with Christ in God, experienced in his person, and held forth in the Scriptures of Truth. This was
his essay in his [*Retired man's Meditations*] even to present to our
view this mystical life, in the most intelligible form, language, or
certain sound of words, he could any wayes hit upon, which yet how
subject they have left him to misconstructions through the ignorance
and presumption of his confident undertakers, is sad to see, in their
most groundless calumnies of his Person, and gross mistakes of his
Doctrine and Principles.

To obviate such causeless misprisions of him, I shall briefly present
you with some chief Remarques of his Life.

He was born a Gentleman. My next word is so much too big for
that, that it may hardly seem decorous to stand so near it. *He was a
chosen Vessel of Christ, seperated* (as Paul) *from his mothers womb,*
though

though not actually called, till 14. or 15. Years standing in the world, ('twas longer ere *Paul* was called) during which time, such was the complexion and constitution of his Spirit, through ignorance of God and his wayes, as rendred him acceptable company to those they call good fellows, (yet at his worst, restrained from that lewdness, intemperance sometimes leads into, which he hath been oft heard to thank God for) and so long he found tollerable quarter amongst men. Then God did by some signal impressions and awakening dispensations, startle him into a view of the danger of his condition. On this, he and his former jolly Company came presently to a parting blow. Yea this change and new steering of his course, contracted enmity to him in his fathers house, (*Mat.* 10. 36, 37.)

It was also suggested by the Bishops to the then King, concerning him, That the heir of a considerable family about his Majesty, was grown into dislike of the Discipline and Ceremonies of the Church of *England*, and that his Majesty might do well to take some course about him. On this, the then Bishop of *London* took him to task, who seemed to handle him gently in the Conference, but concluded harshly enough against him in the Close.

In fine, seeing himself on all hands in an evil case, he resolved for *New-England*. In order to this, striking in with some *Non-conformists* which intended that way, his honourable Birth, long Hair, and other Circumstances of his Person, rendred his fellow-travellers jealous of him, as a Spye to betray their Liberty, rather than any way like to advantage their design. But he that they thought at first sight to have too little of Christ for their company, did soon after appear to have two much for them. For he had not been long in *New-England*, but he ripened into more knowledge and experience of Christ, than the Churches there could bear the Testimony of. Even *New-England* could not bear all his words, though there were no Kings Court or Kings Chappel, *Amos* 7. 10, 13. Then he returns for *Old-England*. Shortly after, the leading and preparatory passages to the Long Parliament and the late great publick changes, drew on. From the beginning of that Parliament, he became such a drudge for his Countrey, so willing on all accounts, both in Person and Estate, to spend and be spent (in his chargable circumstances and unwearied endeavours for the publick Good, and just Liberties of men as men, as also for the advance of the Kingdom of Christ in these Nations) as I know not any former age or story can parallel.

His Principles, Light, and Wisdom were such, that he found the bare mention of his utmost aimes amongst his fellow labourers, would

(in

(in all probabillity) so expose him to censure from all parties and sizes of understanding, as would disable him for doing any thing at all. He was therefore for small matters rather than nothing, went hand in hand with them, step by step, their own pace, as the light of the times would permit. He was for quitting still the more grofs disorders in Church and State, (corruptions in Courts of Judicature, Popish and Superstitious formes in Religion, and wayes of Worship) for what he found more refined and tollerable. But he ever refused to fix his foot, or take up his rest in any Form, Company, or Way, where he found the main bulke of Professors avowedly owning, but such inward Principles of Life and Holinefs, as to him evidently lay short of the glory, righteousnefs, and life hid with Christ in God. He was still for pressing towards the mark, *Phil.* 3. 14. He was more for Things than Persons, Spirit than Forms.

This carriage of his, all along in *New-England* and in *Old*, exposed him as a mark for the arrow, from almost all sorts of People, rendring him a man of contention with the whole earth ; Yet was he all along a true Son of Peace ; a most industrious and blessed Peace-maker, to the utmost of his power, for the reconciling all sorts of Conscientious men, (whatever variety of Perswasion or Form he found them in) to one another, and to Christ.

He never affected any military employment. He was in a litteral sense, free from the blood of all men, as well as in a spiritual, by his faithful performance of the duty of a Watchman, not shunning to declare unto all men the whole counsel of God, *Ezek.* 18. and 33. and *Acts* 20. 27. They that call him a man of contention, what would they have said of *David* ? He (though a man after God's own heart) had so abundantly shed blood in his great warrs, that it was objected as a reason against him, why he should not have the honour of building a house unto the Name of the Lord his God, 1 *Chron.* 22. 7, &c. Yea, he left order with his son *Solomon* on his death-bed, to take such course with *Joab* and *Shimei*, that their hoary heads might be brought down to the grave with blood, 1 *Kings* 2.

He was no humoursom conceited maintainer of any perverse or irrational opinions, but a most quiet calme, composed speaker forth of the words of Truth and soberness, at all seasons, upon all occasions, and in all companies. He was full of condescention and forbearance, hating nothing more in his very natural temper, than brangling and contention. He would keep silence even from good, (though his sorrow was stirred by it, and the fire burned within, while he was mu-

B
sing,

ling, *Psal.* 39. 1, 3.) in cafe that either wicked, or but fhort-fighted good men were before him, that he perceived could not bear more fpiritual and fublimated Truths, *John* 16. 12. *He became all things to all men, that he might by all meanes fave fome,* 1 Cor. 9. 22. His heart was of a right Scripture latitude, ftood fair and open for any good, but no evil. All forts of confcientious inquirers after Truth, found a friendly reception with him; yea, he was in a conftant readinefs to perform any warrantable civilities to all men. Any thing that was good he owned, and cherifhed in the honeft moral Heathen, legal Chriftian, or fpiritual Believer; and fo, fought opportunity by honeft infinuations to catch them with guile, and lead them forward into more excellent Truths, 2 *Cor.* 12. 16.

But more particularly yet, to undertake that general Reproach that was caft upon him, to wit, *That he was a man of Contention from his Youth up,* where ever he came or had to do, *in* New-England, *or in* Old.

He was a true Believer, that's enough, if ye knew all, to fet all the World againft him. He was not of the world, and therefore hated by it, *John* 15. 18, 19. He was partaker of God's holinefs, (*Heb.* 12. 10.) had eternal Life abiding in him; ftood poffeffed of the Wifdom and Words of that Life which the holy Ghoft teacheth (1 *Cor.* 2. 13.) and he could not but fpeak forth the things he had heard and feen. Then there's no dealing for him, *Rev.* 13. 17. Divine Truth feems moft frightful and contrary of all other, to men; puts all men to a gaze; renders the witnefs bearer thereof, like *Jeremiah,* a man of contention with the whole earth. He needs no other occafion of controverfie; the meer and fingle declaration of this truth will do it. Here's the ground of the quarrel with him; for this, every one will curfe him, *Jer.* 15. 10.

This was *Paul's* cafe, even amongft the profeffing Churches of Chrift, converted by his Miniftry, that were yet but in their own legal fhort-fighted-fpirit, they were ready to have pluck'd out their eyes, and have given them to him, while gratified by him in the firft branch of his Miniftry, for renewal of the Law, or the ruling activity of their own rational powers, in them; But let him fpeak a word of the divine Life, (broadly and plainly, in its diftinction from their prefent attainment) that is to be propagated in them by another birth, he is prefently looked upon as an enemy.

There are two births or formations of Chrift in the fouls of men. Thofe that ftay with unwife *Ephraim* in the firft, (which is but that state or place , whence the true Heavenly Seed and Children of God, do break forth, *Hos.* 13. 13.) refusing to be born of God, (*John* 1. 13.) Of the will of God, (*James* 1. 18.) By the new second, and more excellent Birth , will in fine appear in their colours, false brethren, that will hate and slander their own Mothers Son, *Psal.* 50. 20. In order to this second birth, under the metaphor of a Mother, *Paul* saith, *He travelled with* the Galatians *again*, *till Christ*, in his second, more excellent appearance and communicable life, *be formed in them*, Gal. 4. 19.

Veritas odium parit, (Truth brings hatred) is a Proverb that holds too true, in all sizes and kindes of Truth. Let a man take upon him the boldness to exercise but his Moral-Philosophy-Principles, in giving check to the open Enormities of his time , drunkenness, beastliness, swearing, and the like, he makes himself a prey. *He reproves a scorner, and gets himself a blot*, Prov. 9. 7. This is his portion from the lewd multitude, that will but attempt so much as with the *Pharisees*, to wash the outside of the dish and of the cup ; to circumcise and lop off the wild excrescencies, and exuberant superfluities of naughtiness. Sir *Thomas Moore*, *Overbury*, and many others, for their faithful counsel on such accounts, have been cut off.

If *Socrates* a heathen Philosopher, through the sublimity of his speculation, cannot own the Magistrates Religion, but give his Testimony against *Polytheisme* or a plurality of Gods, he must die for it without remedy. If *Seneca* and other Stoicks declare against the corrupt manners and bruitish practises of the generation amongst whom their Lot is cast, they are not like to scape much better.

The main bulk of mankind is so plunged and lodged in wickedness, or the wicked one, the Devil, 1 *John* 5. 19. and *Chap.* 3. 12. that they'l not endure a word against downright Bruitism. But for the true Believer that comes forth in and with the Spirit, Testimony, and everlasting Gospel of Christ, he must expect to become hatred , even in the house of his God, (*Hos.* 9. 8.) As it fared with *Paul*, in the Church of *Galatia*, *Gal.* 4. 16. Yea, *Paul* himself, when an eminent practitioner in the righteousness of the Law, or of Man, was the hottest and maddest persecutor the spiritual believer had, and verily thought that he ought to do what he did therein, (*Acts* 26. 9. 11.) as Christ had foretold in like case, (*John* 16. 2.) *They shall put you out of the Synagogues, yea, and whosoever killeth you, will think he doth God service.* Your brethren that hated you, that cast you out for my Names sake, said, *Let the Lord be glorified*, (we doubt not but we glorify God herein, by punishing and excommunicating such Here-

ticks

ticks and Blasphemers) but God himself takes up the Controversie very short, telling his out-casts, he will appear to their joy, and their enemies shall be ashamed, that cast them out, *Isa.* 66. 5. *Paul* saw this bitter ignorant zeal in the professing Churches at *Jerusalem*, which he had had experience of both wayes ; in himself towards other Saints, and in other *Pharisaical sticklers*, lately towards him. He therefore chose rather to cast himself upon the Heathen Magistrate for his tryal, than be returned to them ; and *Festus* answered, unto *Cæsar* shalt thou go, *Act.* 25. 11, 12. He did make the better choice, for the *Jews* were ready to destroy him immediately, without a hearing, (*Act.* 23. 12, 15.) *Cæsar* gives him a breathing while ; He scapes his Sword two whole years, what ever more, *Act.* 28. 30, 31. Yet suffers at last under that Lyon *Nero*, whom he had for a season been delivered from, 2 *Tim.* 4. 17. Tyrannical Magistrates are so metaphor'd in Scripture, as also by others, Beasts, Birds, and Fishes of prey, the most potent and ravenous Creatures in Air, Earth, and Water ; Eagles, Dragons, Lyons, Unicorns, Bears, Wolves, Foxes, the Leviathan or Whale, &c. But God hears, that is delivers, his humble broken-hearted Saints, from the hornes of such Unicorns, saves them from the Lyons mouth, (*Psal.* 22. 21.) **that is,** from the pow**ers of the** darkness of this World, (Devils, or Men by them influenced) **till** they be enabled to triumph over death, and conquer them by dying.

Satan is called, *The God of this world, the great red Dragon,* (of a bloody, murtherous colour) the *root, father, and spring of all corrupted worldly Magistracy, and arbitrary domination. Pharaoh* is called, *a Dragon,* (*Ezek.* 29. 3.) And it is written, *As a roaring Lyon and a ranging Bear, so is a wicked Ruler over the poor people,* Prov. 28. 15. *Her Princes are like Wolves, ravening the prey, to shed blood, destroy souls, and get dishonest gain,* Ezek. 22. 27. *Her Judges are evening Wolves, they gnaw not the bones till the morrow,* Zeph. 3. 3. In Herod, they are termed *Foxes, Luk.* 13. 32. Such *Foxes* (amongst others) are taken notice of, as *spoilers of the Vines,* (Cant. 2. 15.) Wasters of the true Churches and People of Christ, by their sacrilegious intrusions, and magisterial lording it over those, *that after the way which men call Heresie,* are rightly *worshipping the God of their Fathers.*

What a world is here for a Believer ?

To the generality of brutish men, an honest moral Heathen will be reputed a Phanatick. The Legal Christian, with his Ordinances, and imputed righteousness of Christ for his Justification and acceptance with God, (though but upon the tearms, and in the renewed

Princi-

Principles of the first Covenant) will appear so, to the honest Heathen. The spiritual Man, as born of the will of God, partaker of the Divine Nature, (the proper New-creature Principle of eternal Life, that quallifies him for the steady, Sonly obedience, in the spirit and way of the new and everlasting Covenant) he appears a Phanatick to them all; a Fool, a Mad man ; *The Prophet is a Fool, the Spiritual man is Mad*, (Hos. 9. 7.) *Yea, he is reputed so in the house of his God*, vers. 8. *amongst his mothers children*, Psal. 50. Thus the *Jewes*, Christ's own People, said of him ; *He hath a devil, and is mad; why hear ye him ?* Yea his very friends go about to lay hold on him, for, said they, *he is besides himself*, Mark 3. 21. The Servant is like to find but harsh entertainment where the Lord is thus handled. The bruitish party of men is incomparably the greatest and will carry it by Vote. The honest Heathen, and the Legal Christian, will all joyn with them, to call the Spiritual man *mad*. The very Christ, Christ in Spirit, the very Christian, the Spiritual man, he is cast out of all their Synagogues. *Away with him, away with such a fellow from the earth* (say they) *it is not fit that he should live*, Act. 22. 22. We find the *Jewish* religious party that served *Paul* thus, striking hands with a profane Interest, Act. 17. 5, 7. Through envy at the spiritual believers Faith and Testimony, *they call to their assistance certain lewd fellows of the baser sort, set all the City in an uproar, assault the house of* Jason, *dragging him and other brethren before the Rulers of the City, and crying, These that have turned the World upside down, are come hither also ; and do contrary to the Decrees of* Cæsar, *saying, there is another King, one Jesus.*

This is the charge at all adventures ; they matter not much for proofes, while they can find stones, as they served *Steven*, Act. 7. The World is turned upside down indeed. But understand how, *O ye bruitish among the People ; ye fools, when will ye be wise ?* The honest Heathen is soberer than you ; the legal Christian is soberer than he ; the spiritual man is the soberest of all, and he is reckoned the most disordered. He speakes forth the words of greatest truth and soberness.

The case then is this ; when the World is in a mad, bruitish, disordered-hurly burly, they that attempt to bring righteousness a-floate, are accused of turning it up side down. Setting all to rights, is reckoned the greatest Confusion. The Rights of the Kingdom, are reckoned the Wrongs of the King ; and many, with whom the true native Rights of an earthly Kingdom will down, are ready to startle at and resist the rights of Christs Kingdom, in the Spirits and Consciences of men. Even they will be ready to say of the Assertors of such Rights, that *they are no longer fit to live in the World* ; that's man's judgement.

The

The World is no longer worthy of them; that's God's, *Heb.* 11. 38. 'Tis plain, God and men **are** of exceeding contrary Judgements concerning the true believer. 'Tis as plain, *We muſt all appear at laſt before the Judgement ſeat of Chriſt, for our final ſentence.* 'Tis plain alſo, *that we ought to obey God rather than Men,* Act. 5. 29. And *not to be the ſervants of Men in things pertaining to God,* 1 Cor. 7. 23.

From the croſs conſtitution then which this world is generally found in, to all Truth, but moſt of all, to the Spiritual and Sublimeſt ſort of Truth, it may appear, what a hard time a Believer is like to have of it, if he ſtand up for the Cauſe and Intereſt of God againſt the Devil, who is called *the God of this world,* 2 Cor. 4. 4. Here is the grand competitor of Chriſt, that ſtruggles for the Soveraignty, *the great red Dragon,* Rev. 12. 3. This is he that muſters up, animates and influences the ſons of men, to fight againſt God, that he may exalt **himſelf** in them, *above all that is called God,* (2 Theſ. 2. 4.) *Working in the children of diſobedience at his pleaſure,* Epheſ. 2. 2. Do you ſee your General, O ye ſons of men? will ye ſtill fight under his Banner? Conſider the main Impoſtures of this ſelf-transformer, whereby you are beguiled into his Intereſt.

Firſt, He ſeduces your Underſtanding into this moſt **falſe** perſwaſion, That he is the higheſt rational Being, to whom doth of right belong the Legiſlative Authority and Supream Magiſtratical Dominion over the whole earth, as God of this World, under whoſe influence and dictates, all earthly Thrones and Benches of Judicature, ought to proceed in judgement. Under this pretended and aſſumed Title of the higheſt rational Being, he expects to be owned and ſubmitted to, as requiring no allegiance or obedience from his Subjects, upon any other tearms, than as he approves himſelf to their Conſciences, to mannage his Government exactly according to the Principles of humane Nature and Rules of right Reaſon.

Secondly, He aſſumes and challenges to himſelf, the Authority of the higheſt Spirit of Truth, boaſting himſelf, as the infallible Teacher and Guide in matters of Faith and divine Worſhip, in all things pertaining to the good and ſalvation of Souls. Having thus aſſumed to himſelf theſe two grand prerogatives of Chriſt's Crown, as the Supream Head, (not under but above Chriſt himſelf, yea, in direct contradiction to him) in all Cauſes, and over all perſons, as well Eccleſiaſtical as Civil, 'tis obvious to imagine, what Titles Chriſt and his followers are like to have from this Dragon and his.

Firſt,

First, They will boldly and openly affert, that that which is indeed the fpirit of Chrift, in him and his, is an irrational, Fanatick fpirit, deftructive to all natural Order, and good Government, in humane Society.

Secondly, That it is a deceitful deluding Spirit, deftructive to all found Doctrine, divine Inftitutions, Church Order and Rule.

In thefe four things, this grand Antichrift is the liar, *that denies Jefus to be the Chrift*. Under which Generals are comprehended multitudes of Particulars in his skilful methods of delufion, needlefs here to be enumerated. He that hath once gained thefe four points in the generality of men, will eafily out-vote and cry down Chrift and his, for Blafphemers and Difturbers of mankind, and accordingly handle them. He prevailed even with the learned & Religious *Jewes*, to ferve Chrift thus. Yea, he attempted to feduce Chrift himfelf to his party, **to own him** for God, fall down and worfhip him. **Chrift refufes** ; He therefore fteers another **courfe** ; fets the *Jewes* upon **it, to** call him *Blafphemer, and fay, he hath a Devil*. This is one ftep towards the accomplifhing of his defign ; when he hath once engaged men to fay of Chrift and his followers, that *they are Blafpemers and Devils* ; he that thus makes them liars will make them Murtherers too ; they will foon cry, *Crucifie them, Crucifie them*, right or wrong ; *Away with **them from** the earth, it is not fit that they fhould live*. Chrift hath told us thefe things before hand, (*Joh*. 15. and *Chap*. 16. 1, and 4.) that we fhould not be offended or furprifed, when they really come upon us. If they *have done thefe things to the green tree, what will they do to the dry*? Luke **23**. 31. *The Servant is not greater than his Lord*, Joh. **15**. 20. *If the Mafter be called* Beelzebub, *how much more fhall they call them of his houfhold*? Matth. 10. 25. Satans followers have the ftart of Chrift's for number, they out-vote them clear. He ha's four hundred lying Prophets againft one true, 1 *Kings* 22. 6. and *verf*. 20, 23.

I fuppofe you may difcern by this time, whether this Sufferer or his Enemies were in the fault, that he was reckoned *a man of Contention*. But peradventure this may yet grow clearer, by confidering his Principles.

He fpake much of Principles. What meant he ? Some Fundamental Truths, worded and propounded in a Book, as *Perkins his Six Principles*, or the like ? He meant inward ruling Principles, or Springs of Life and operation in men. By taking a little freedom in handling this Point, I fhall give you aim at his Principle, in its proper Character of diftinction from all other Principles. 'Twill be requifite here to take notice of all the Principles of Life and Operation, Man is

capable

capable to be found in, or does actually live and come forth in the exercise of.

That Nature, that gives the distinguishing Form or Character to any Creature, and is the immediate spring of all its operations, is the proper Principle of its Life ; be it divine, angelical, humane or sensual Nature. The Faculties or Principles of operation, scituated, founded and rooted in each Nature, to wit, the discerning and desiring powers, called (in Men and Angels) Understanding and Will, do receive their respective denominations from the Nature they are seated in and belong unto, and so are tearmed divine, angelical, humane or sensual Principles of operation.

For instance, The Understanding and Will of participated divine Nature, in the true heirs of God, are divine, spiritual, heavenly and high.

The Understanding and Will of meer humane Nature, at best, are but natural, fleshly, earthly, and comparatively, low ; holy flesh is but flesh, *Jer.* 11. 15. Renewed, refined, adorned Nature, is but Nature ; a goodly, beautiful, but a perishable thing, *as the flower of the field*, *Isa.* 40. 6. *As the man is, so is his strength*, so are his works. The righteous works brought forth but in the ruling activity of renewed humane nature, entring into competition with the righteous works, duties and ordinances, observed and performed in the Life and ruling activity of participated divine Nature, become more loathsom to God than all the debauchery and shame of polluted Nature, that is but the result of *Adams* first transgression, and not of the reiterated and more fatal Apostacy in our own persons, after a revival from our native death in trespasses and sins.

Those that bring the righteousness of man (or the righteous works, performed in the single power of renewed humane nature) into a self-exalting preference to the righteousness of God (or the righteous works and duties performed in the ruling power of participated divine Nature, taking the humane into a subordinate co-operativeness therewith) may find what entertainment they are like to meet with from Christ, in the case of the foolish Virgins, and of those that cast out Devils, or preach down the corruption that the devil brought into our Nature, *Mat.* 25. 12. *and Mat.* 7. 22, 23. *Depart from me, I know you not, ye are workers of iniquity.* That's the answer to both, plead while they will, or say what they can.

Casting out Devils, preaching the corruption of Nature down, the righteousness of it up, so as to render men wise, strong and honorable in Christ, (1 *Cor.* 4. 10.) Is this offensive ? No; But the telling them,

this

this is the place or state of their Rest, concerning which the Master saith, *Arise, depart, let us go hence, this is not your rest*, Micah 2. 10. Joh. 14. 31. You are liable here, to return with the dog to the vomit, draw back to perdition, to be afresh invaded and finally triumphed over by sin and Satan, as is expressed, 2 *Pet.* 2. 20, 22. *Heb.* 10. 39. and implied, *Rom.* 6. 14. You must therefore quit this first-creation-state and forme of life, at best, by way of sacrifice, (*Rom.* 12. 1, 2.) or you will never come to the Father, whither Christ is gone to prepare Mansions for those that follow him whithersoever he goes. No man can be thorowly happy and at rest, till this corruptible be dead, in and with the Lord, by which meanes onely we may come to inherit incorruption. Here's the highest sense of *Ante obitum nemo, &c.* No man can be blessed till he die ; He that is made willing thus with Christ to lose **Life**, shall **find** it, and whosoever will save his Life shall lose it, and **never attain** the Life that is unchangable and eternal, *Mat.* 16. 25.

The corruptible frame of man at his best estate, was never intended or warranted by God, either in the primitive purity or greatest possible renewals thereof, to be the place of God's rest, or the state that Man should rest in. One crucified, broken-spirited man, that's made willing to be taken in pieces, and be so joyned to the Lord as to become one spirit with him, is more valuable to him, than all men and angels, or whatever glory and excellency is to be found in the whole first-creation, *Isa.* 66. 1, 2. *The Heaven is my throne, the Earth is my foot-stool, but where is the place of my rest ? All these things hath mine hand made*, in the first creation. I look for regenerated, transformed new-creation things, in order to which, the old fabrick or tabernacle must be taken down ; *To this man will I look* (or have respect) *even to him that is of a poor and contrite spirit ;* This is the place of my rest, so *Isa.* 57. 15.

Man in his first-creation frame, or in whatever renewal of it since the Fall, is but the house on the sand, founded on the mutable, wavering Principles of humane Nature. Many that pretend to be great master-workmen in Divinity, warrant this for the right building on the rock, that will stand it out in all stormes ; the true spiritual building, (1 *Pet.* 2. 5.) into which they need never fear Satans return, (as *Mat.* 12. 44.) or any fresh Invasions and Revolutions of their old sins into the exercise of dominion over them again. They cause their hearers and followers to hope that they will confirm this word, *Eze.* 13. 6. But the walls of this building are faulty as wel as the foundation. They daube up all with the untempered mortar of refin'd

C   humane

humane Nature ; nothing of the divine Nature, wisdom and righteousness of God, will be admitted into their building. Building therefore and builders will all tumble together, when the storm comes;and
then also will the sandy foundation thereof be discovered, *verf.* 13,
16. **Blind** leaders and blind followers will both into the ditch together, *Mat.* 15. 14.

Both these buildings *(Mat.* 7. 24, 27.) had their beauty, their glory while both stood. To man's eye, that with the sandy foundation
and untempered walls, generally carried it. The more visible, literal
natural godliness in their renewed flesh, or humane Nature and Principles, look'd fairer to man, (that judges by outward appearance)then
the spiritual, mystical, hidden Life and Godliness, in the house upon
the rock, which has nothing but the broken, crucified, transformed
Principles, and more undiscerned cooperations of humane Nature, to
set off its self by, to man's judgement.

The Children of the first house or kingdom of Christ, *shall be cast into utter darkness,* and many heathens, publicans, sinners, and *Mary
Magdalenes* shall be taken over their heads, and caused to sit down
with *Abraham, Isaac,* and *Jacob,* in the spiritual house, (1 *Pet.* 2. 5.)
the building on the rock, (*Mat.* 7. 24.) the second and more excellent kingdom, that cannot be shaken, *Mat.* 8. 11, 12. *Heb.* 12. 26,
28. *Esay* is reckoned very bold for saying this, (*Rom.* 10. 19, 21.
Isa. 65. 1, 2.) which *Moses* said before him, (*Deut.* 32. 19, 21.)
and Christ after him, *Mat.* 9. 12, 13.

Cleansedness from the pollutions of the World, corruption of Nature, revival from their death in trespasses and sins, hinders not but
Satan may re-enter, old sins recover dominion, and so the members
of that building on the sand, that kingdom or heaven that may be shaken, (*Heb.* 12. 26, 27.) may come to be trees twice dead, fit only to
be plucked up by the roots, cast into the fire and burned, *Jude* 12. and
Heb. 6. 8. 2 *Pet.* 2. 20, 22. *Mat.* 7. 22, 27. and *Chap.* 12. 43, 45.
Ezek. 16. 38. And as it is not the present freedom from natural pollution, so neither is it the ornament of excellent gifts, supernatural
or infused humane learning, (much less, natural parts, and acquired
humane learning) the tongue of men and angels, (all dexterity of
expressing, their conceptions either intuitively or by a sound of words,
incident to those two choicest ranks of creatures, in their first crea-
tion-capacity) that can secure them from being *but as sounding
brass or tinckling cymbals,* 1 *Cor.* 12. 31. and 13. 1. *Ezek.* 16. 1, 15.
A great noise they may make, a great repute they may have, as the
onely compleat interpreters of the Oracles of God, yet all amounts
but

but to an indistinct, uncertain sound. No man can tell thereby how to prepare himself to the battel, (1 *Cor*. 14. 7, 8. and *Ezek*. 33.) what weapons or what armour to provide. They give no right character of those spiritual weapons, mighty through God, for the pulling down of strong holds in our selves and others, (2 *Cor*. 10. 4.) or of that whole armour of God (*Ephes*. 6. 11.) wherein alone the true belie-ver is able to wrestle it out, not onely against flesh and blood, but a-gainst Principalities, Powers, Rulers of the darkness of this world, and spiritual wickedness in high places, *vers*. 12.

The onely new-creature spirit in man, that is greater than he that is in the world (1 *John* 4. 4.) is set at naught by those that warrant the first building secure; is contradicted, blasphemed, called the de-vil. The wisdom of God is by them tearmed the wisdom of the Ser-pent. Did not matters go thus between Christ and the Master-build-ers in Religion amongst the *Jews* ? They *reject the chief corner stone*, (*Psal*. 118. 22. *Mat*. 21. 42.) and how is their house like to stand ? it may indeed be emptied of filth ; swept, cleansed, garnished with excellent gifts and ornaments, (*Mat*. 12. 44. 2 *Pet*. 2. 20. 1 *Cor*. 12. 31. *Ezek*. 16. 9, 13.) Yet in all this flourish, there may be a deep unsuspected ignorance, or inadvertency of the more excel-lent way, the way of love, or state of divine Life, wherein the stones of their building, members of their Churches are capable to be brought forth, by being broken and formed up anew, into an unchangable har-mony and indissoluble union of spirit with the Lord, 1 *Cor*. 6. 17. If this be gain-said, the onely spirit and spiritual harness that accom-modates men for a successful contest with the devil and all the pow-ers of darkness, is wholly laid aside. How then shall we fight the bat-tels of the Lord, when that very faith is decried as a diabolical ficti-on, that is the onely principle of Life in men, whereby to undertake, resist, conquer, triumph over the devil, and swallow up death it self into victory ? Let us no longer be flattered by our crafty over-reach-ing adversary, into a security and satisfaction in such armour and weapons as he knowes he can strip us of at pleasure, and re-enter.

The renewed spirit of man, (however accomplished and adorned with spiritual gifts) the wisdom, the righteousness of man, are not the spirit, the weapons, the armour of God, nor can secure any man from the most fatal and irrecoverable apostacy. Many stars of the first magnitude, as to all this glory and ornament, have often been known to fall from this kind of Heaven, or Kingdom of man's righteousness. Besides all the sad instances in former ages for this, have not the late years of *Englands* deliverance, brought upon this stage of ours, and

exhibited

exhibited to our view, multitudes of teachers and profeffors, who have notably fhined forth in this glory, wifdom and righteoufnefs, through the knowledge of Chrift after the flefh, accompanied with excellent gifts, and yet through a fpirit of enmity and contradiction, (a root of bitternefs fpringing up in them, *Heb.* 12. 15. againft the more excellent way, the Life of Faith, the Crofs of Chrift, the true Circumcifion, which worfhip God in the fpirit, *Phil.* 3. 3.) have moft evidently apoftatized from, and loft even that they had, yea and have been the meanes of betraying the whole Nation afrefh, and rolling all back again into more infufferable bondage than ever? We may fay and hear this with weeping. And moreover do we not yet daily experience an inftability in fuch principles, ornaments, weapons, armour? Are not multitudes of profeffors at this pafs ftill, yea and nay, off and on with God, and fo with fin and fatan to? And will it alwayes be fo well? Will thefe wavering Principles, this unftable kind of life and righteoufnefs (if not quitted for a better) be ever able to fecure us from a final parting with God, and entire clofing with the devil, as one fpirit with him? The unftable nature of man's firft-creation, at beft, muft either afcend into a fixed union with Chrift in fpirit, and fo contract an everlafting difability to any thing which is evil, (2 *Cor.* 13. 8.) or elfe it will defcend into a fixed union with the devil, and thereby contract an everlafting inability to any thing that is good. The firft created freedom of man's will to good and evil, the liberty of the fons of men, however renewed again by Chrift, will be finally fwallowed up, either into a diabolical freedom to evil onely, and not at all to good, or into a divine freedom to good onely and not at all to evil, which is *the glorious liberty of the fons of God, wherewith Chrift makes thofe that receive him, free indeed,* John 1. 12. *and* Chap 8. 36.

Let us then put off the armour of man, even of the renewed old man, (as *David* did *Sauls*) *and put on the whole armour of God,* the new man, *which after God is created in wifdom, righteoufnefs and true* (or everlafting) *holinefs,* Ephef. 4. 24. Then the fpiritual *Goliah* will certainly fall before us. 'Tis the divine new-creature-Life onely, with fpiritual weapons, can over fet all his power of darknefs, and detect all the crafty ftratagems and methods of delufion, to the laft period of his myftery of iniquity.

Profeffors in the firft-building, flourifhing in the wifdom, glory and righteoufnefs of the Law, or of the ruling activity of renewed humane Nature, and rectified rational Powers, (though received from Chrift himfelf, as no mean fruit or benefit of his death) if they oppofe, contradict and blafpheme the true fighting, conquering and reigning

prin-

principle of divine Nature in the second, they do thereby become worse than those foolish and contemptible sinners of the *Gentiles*, that never yet peeped out of the bondage of sensual Lusts. Men of this spirit in Religion, stand every moment liable to be run a ground by Satan, into the most dangerous and remediless posture of all, a latter end worse than their beginning, a state of sin and sorrow, unchangeable.

This we are still to have in our eye. Where ever two or more natures meet together in any creature, 'tis the true interest and concern of that creature, to yield up the Scepter and Government over all other nature, life and operation in it, to that which is in it self superiour to all the rest, and best able with safety to manage the whole person. Divine nature, that is the highest Principle of Life and operation communicable to man, will upon no lower tearms enter as an ingredient into his constitution, than to be king. 'Twill be *Cæsar* or nothing. 'Tis man's interest, priviledge, security, it should be so. *'Tis not in man that walketh*, at his best estate, with stability, certainty and continuance, *to direct his steps*, Jer. 10. 23. He is therefore (in a sort) under the curse of the Law, even whilst he is working the righteousness of it, because not in the continuing principle. For 'tis said, *Cursed is every one that continueth not in all things which are written in the book of the Law to do them.* *Paul* alledges this as a warning-piece to those that were of the works of the Law, or that were working righteousness but in the single activity and ruling power of their own renewed, enlightened, cleansed spirit, and humane principles, *Gal.* 3. 10.

The question is, Whether God's Spirit or our own be best at working righteousness, steering our course, directing our steps? whether Law or Grace, Old or New-creature Life, the Soveraignty of our own or God's Spirit in us, be fitter to undertake the work, keep off Satan from re-entry, sin from returning into dominon? *Paul* warrants us not safe from the most dangerous apostacy, under the Law or ruling power of our own renewed mind, but under grace onely, the Law of the spirit of Life, or ruling authority of participated divine Nature.

Men are ready to say here, as *Pilate* to the *Jewes* in a different case concerning Christ's person; *What, will ye crucifie our King?* Strike down the ruling authority of the Law, or soveraignty of our own renewed mind, for the directing of our steps? Yes; 'Tis best for you to let this king, this spirit be taken to task in you, bruised, sacrificed, crucified, triumphed over, and brought into an everlasting captivity

and

and most desirable subjection to a better king, a better spirit, that can wilde the scepter of righteousness in you, with a more steady hand against all enemies. Men should take heed indeed of yeilding up the Scepter out of their own hands, to a worser spirit, the devil, who will not fail to use all his wiles, engines, and glittering flourishes as transformed into an angel of Light, to impose himself upon us, as our *Baal* or *Moloch*, our Lord and King. Such error may involve us in a more dangerous, hardened, fixed enmity to all farther visits or approaches of the Redeemer, than ever, and in a remediless deprivation of all further benefits of his sacrifice and death.

It was the refusal to surrender up the ruling power of their own renewed spirit, to be bruised, crucified, and triumphed over by the fire-baptism of the spirit of Christ upon it, that made the Princes of this world, the Priests, Scribes, Pharisees, and other professing Jewes, (1 *Cor.* 2. 8.) that were reigning as Kings, as to the righteousness of the Law, (1 *Cor*. 4. 8.) cry out so eagerly and prevailingly to *Pilate*, that Christ himself might be crucified. He that is not made willing by the second, divine, new creature-birth of Christ in him, to have the first birth of a renewed humane life and Principle in him, thus handled, will be sure to prove a spiritual Idolater at last, become a member of mystical *Babylon*, *trample under foot the Son of God, count the blood of the Covenant, wherewith he was sanctified,* in the first birth, (as it is offered in a farther, and greater benefit thereof, for the working this spiritual new-creature-form and more excellent spirit in him) *an unholy thing,* a diabolical figment, *doing thereby despight to the spirit of grace,* which is the sin against the holy Ghost, *Heb.* 10. 29. *Mat.* 12. 31, 32.

'Tis better to be servants and subjects under God's spirit, then Rulers in the soveraign authority and uncontrolled activity of our own. God's service is that perfect freedom wherewith the son makes us free indeed, our soveraignty leaves us liable to eternal bondage. 'Tis better in this sense also to obey God rather than men, his spirit in us, than our own ; yea, to bring our own, with all that before it was Ruler of, into pure and everlasting subjection to God's ; we shall otherwise be sure to find our selves at last, under the dominion of sin again.

Let as many natures as will, be in man, that nature or principle of Life and operation in him, that rules, denominates the person. If sensual nature in its operations, desires and delights, bear sway in a man, over the head of his own rational powers, (causing them to truckle under it, and become serviceable in their witty pleadings and devisings

to

to gratify and humour that, over which they should be rulers) that man is a beast. If rational powers bear sway over sensual, he is a man ; If spiritual, a Saint. The participated divine nature is the onely spring of the power of godliness in man, and sure foundation of eternal Life ; *The grace of God, that bringeth salvation, teaching* effectually *to deny all ungodliness,* open and mystical to, *Tit.* 2.

How apt are men to give up the scepter and soveraignty over themselves, into the hands of the basest principle of Life in them, sensual ? and how apt is that to catch at the scepter, as the basest of men have been usually catching at visible Thrones and Soveraignty over others that are Princes in understanding, a hundred times more men than themselves? Such Princes are oft walking as servants upon the earth, when servants are upon horses; It is an evil, an error which proceedeth from the Ruler, to set folly in great dignity, and let the rich sit in low place, *Ecclef.* 10. 5, 7. Those men that are willingly subject to the basest lusts of sensual Life in their own persons, are willing to set up the basest of men on outward visible Thrones, over them, (*Dan.* 4. 17.) that they know are in bondage to the same inferiour lusts with themselves, and therefore such under whom the godly man ceaseth, and the vilest men will be exalted, *Psal.* 12. 1, 8. What amounts all this to, without us and within us, but a most irrational yeelding up our selves into captivity, under the soveraign authority of the bramble? as in *Jotham's* Parable, *Judg.* 9. 7, 15. In such case, the bramble, when once it finds it self secure in the Throne, will not fail to domineer over the other trees, fig-tree, vine, olive, or whatever else, as if it were really the best of them all, and no man must say to the contrary. Yea, to such unimaginable degrees of folly and presumption are the souls of men liable to be baffled by the devil and their own hearts, as 'tis not altogether improbable, men of debauched consciences and bruitish conversations, may think the superiority and dominion over men of Principles and Conscience, was theirs of old, and though now and then interrupted, will be returned back into their hands again, as their right.

Man, that is called *a little World,* may receive instruction from what is observable to him in the greater, for the giving of him aim how much he is concerned to be yeelding up all inferiour Life and operation in him, to the sacrificing knife and transforming activity of the divine Nature, or heavenly manhood of Christ, in order to be reduced into an absolute harmony with & subjection thereunto. By this change he receives his own again with usury. He loses the good, holy, but corruptible, vanishing Life, liberty and righteousness of the Sons

of

of men, and findes in the room thereof, the more excellent, most holy, incorruptible marvellous light, life, wisdom, righteousness and glorious liberty of the sons of God. He findes himself enabled to do all things for the Truth, in the power of God's spirit, and disabled to do any thing against it, in his own ; disabled to sin against God and wrong his own soul ; such weakness is his strength ; such captivity is his glorious liberty ; Thus *Paul* was made weak in Christ, when others were strong and reigning as Kings, in the single activity of their own renewed spirits, which they also had from Christ, 1 *Cor.* 4. 8. 10. But his weakness was better than their strength ; his seeming folly and despicableness, better than all their wisdom and glory.

That the life, righteousness, glory and freedom of man at his best, are but corruptible things, all the World are my experimental witnesses, say what they will to the contrary. They are therefore to be accounted but as dung and loss, for the excellency of the knowledge of Christ after the spirit ; for the wisdom, righteousness and Life hid with Christ in God, the glory that excels. Let us turn over and read the book of the visible creation, and see what occurs there, conducible to this purpose. The elements are content to loose their own single natures, essences, properties, formes and qualities, and run together into a quintessential compound, distinct from them all. The Earth parts with its vigor, for the production of vegetables. These again do readily surrender their life, without resistance, to feed the beasts of the field, and thereby find their own life again with usury, by way of resurrection, in subjection to and association with the sensual life of the Beast. The beast again looses its life, becomes a sacrifice to man, finding its own sensual life again with usury, by way of resurrection, in conjunction with and subjection to the rational life of man. This rational life of man, being yet but a corruptible, first-creation-thing, is by all this significant instruction from the very book of the Creature (as also from Christ himself, and his great Apostle, *Mat.* 16. 25. *Rom.* 12. 1, 2.) abundantly informed, that it is its true interest to be given up in sacrifice to the divine life, and find its own again with usury by way of resurrection, in the life hid with Christ in God. All the former sacrifices, deaths and resurrections of inferiour creature-natures, to one another and to man, (as also the subjection of vegetal and sensual powers in man, to rational) are but typical significations and teaching resemblances of this last and greatest of all, beyond which there is no other. Those that will not adventure to offer up this holy and reasonable sacrifice, their rational Life (*Rom.* 12. 1.) in hope of the better resurrection, (*Heb.* 11. 35.) but chuse to remain

main in the single glory and soveraign activity of renewed humane nature, the great master of the family himself intimates to them, that this is but the state of servants, that abide not in the house for ever, whereas those that are made willing to resign the life and soveraignty of their own nature and principles, and become willingly subject to communicated divine life, and God therein, are the true sons that abide in the house for ever, *John* 8. 35.

But between the natural, first-creation Life of man, and the spiritual or divine Life by the new-creation, the great deceiver, (as transformed into angel of Light) when he sees us gazing after this superiour dispensation, is ready to present himself to us, as Christ in spirit, or the holy Ghost, and obtrude upon us angelical Nature of the first-creation-frame onely, to keep us yet short of the divine. In this posture, (finding men dissatisfied in their natural and legal attainments) he makes the same demands that Christ himself makes ; requires the intire resignation of their wills and understandings unto him, so as not to think their own thoughts, speak their own words, do their own works, or find their own pleasure, but wait in a passive silence for his dictates and inspirations, and speak onely such oracles as his beguiling serpentine wisdom teacheth. The condition they are brought into by this imposture, is so much the more dangerous, by how much the more secure and confident they are under it, as cherished and pleased with some delusive raptures of joy from this flourishing deceiver. By this means he labours to gain more and more upon them, till they resign themselves totally up to the conducting influence of angelical nature. This is that voluntary humility and worshiping of Angels, *Col.* 2. 18. The devil attempted to bring the humane nature of Christ himself to his lure, in this main point of all ; even to worship him, or become subject to his influence *Mat.* 4. *Luke* 4. This last and great deceit of the adversary, (together with the false mortification of things seen, attending it, where he prevails) is notably charactered, *page* 340, and so on to the 350th *page* of [*The Retired man's Meditations.*]

All first-creation Nature, sensual, humane or angelical, comparatively with divine, spiritual, new-creature Life, is but shaddow, letter, or significant figure and resemblance. Any of these therefore terminated or rested in, (whatever it be, from the lowest shrub of sensual, to the tallest Cedar in the first-creation, angelical nature) so as that man resolves to sit down under the ruling influence and protection thereof, as the highest principle of Life he will ever be induced to own, this will appear in conclusion to be down-right idolatry.

D

All

All obedience also to the Commands of God in the Scriptures, performed onely in the ruling activity of any first-creation nature in us, humane or angelical, is but serving of God in the oldness of the letter of the first-creation, not in the newness of the Spirit of the second.

It were well therefore, if all Controversies in Religion were reduced to this main Querie.

What is that Divine Nature, Man is capable to partake of, in the prevailing activity whereof he may be enabled to follow God fully, resist the devil stedfastly, and live in the certain assurance, and clear evidence of eternal Life?

By the divine Nature which a chosen generation are made partakers of, (2 *Pet.* 1.4.) we are to understand the humane or creature-nature in Christ's person, called divine, by a communication of properties. In this blessed Mediator between God and man, *it pleased the Father all fulness, or perfection should dwell*, creaturely, and divine, *Col.* 1. 19. *In him dwelleth all the fulness of the Godhead bodily*, Col. 2. 9. In him also dwels all the fulness of the creature spiritually, or in its most heavenly, spiritual, sublimated capacity, and incorruptible form. Christ that is perfect man, is also perfect God, very God of very God, the very form or invisible image of God, (so some render *Col.* 1. 15.) which seperately considered, in distinction from all creature-nature in him, is meerly and singly the object of God's own uncreated understanding, absolutely uncommunicable, invisible, or undiscernable to any meer creature capacity, natural or spiritual, for ever.

The highest Nature or Principle of Life in any person, does by way of prerogative give the denomination and derive its title to the whole person and all that is in him, when compleatly subjected to its ruling influence. Thus all that is in Christ, who is a person undisputably Divine, is also called divine. So where the Principle of new-creature Life, or Life of Faith, is sown by Christ in any man, though it be but as a grain of mustard-seed (*Luk.* 13. 18, 19.) it will spring up into such a prevailing exercise of its spiritual senses, over all fleshly, first-creation Life and principles in him, that his whole person may thence be called a spiritual man. *David*, on this account, was called a man after God's owne heart, (1 *Sam.* 13. 14.) though he had such a remainder of his fleshly nature yet about him, as did lust and strive against the Life and operation of his spiritual form, so as that after this choice Character of his person from God's own mouth, it carried him by a kind of violence into some particular enormities, more gross than many heathens

thens were ever guilty of, from their Cradles to their Graves, in a longer life upon earth, than *David* lived.,

But the solution to the above mentioned Querie, requires at least a glance farther upwards, into some brief contemplation of the Trinity, from such proper language and expression as they are exhibited to us in, by the holy Ghost, 1 *John* 5. 7. and *Col.* 1. 15 .19.

In the former of these Scriptures it is written, *There are three that bear Record in Heaven, the Father, the Word, and the holy Ghost ; and these three are one.* In the latter, we find these three expressions concerning Christ ; *Image of the invisible God, First-born of every Creature, and First-born from the dead.*

From these two Scriptures duly compared and explicated, we might doubtless receive very considerable information touching the mystery of God, and of the Father, and of Christ, *Col.* 2. 2. In the former we find the *three that bear Record* ; In the latter, the Record that is born by all the three ; the Witness or Testimony, Image, Name, Glory, manifestation or threefold personal appearance they give of themselves, in Christ. In the former is exhibited to us God as the head of Christ, in his threefold essential property or spring of operation. In the latter is represented Christ as the express Character, threefold glory or personal appearance of the three that are one, brought forth by the operation of the said three essential properties in the Godhead. And as the three in the first consideration, are one God and father of our Lord Jesus Christ, so are the three in the second consideration, one Christ, Image or personal appearance of God. Father, Word, and Spirit, that manifest themselves in Christ, are one. Christ that is the Father, Son, and holy Ghost in personal appearance, Name or manifestation, is also one. God in Christ and Christ in God, are all one pure, uncompounded, infinite, eternal God, blessed for ever. God in Christ is not three persons, as three distinct individual men are, (for so there would be three Gods) but may more fitly be resembled to our capacity, by a threefold personal appearance of one and the same man ; his personal appearance in the body to his fellow mortals ; his personal appearance in the spirit, to angels, when his body is laid down ; and his personal appearance in both together, in the rarefied and incorruptible state of both, meeting together in the Resurrection. God then as head of Christ, is three and yet one, in an absolute impersonallity or invisibility. God as giving forth a threefold personal appearance of himself, in Christ, is three persons ; yet so, as that he may also be said to be one person. Christ and the Father are one ; *John* 17. 22. To say God the Father and Christ, is in summe, to say

all

all that is to be said of God, if the apostolical form of sound words may find place with us, 1 *Tim.* 1. 2. 2 *Tim.* 1. 2. *Tit.* 1. 4. 2 *Thef.* 1. 1, 2. and *Chap.* 2. 16. In the second Epistle of *John verf.* 3, and 9. it is said, *He that abideth in the doctrine of Chrift, hath both the Father and the Son.* And he that hath them, hath all; even Father, Word, and holy Ghost, revealed in and by the Son. *No man hath seen God the Father at any time,* nor ever can, any otherwise than as declared by the onely begotten son, *which is in the bofom of the Father,* Joh. 1. 14. and 18. So Mat. 11. 27. *No man knoweth the Father save the Son, and he to whomsoever the Son will reveal him.* God and the Mediator are so one, that there's no right receiving or owning them apart. He that denieth the Son hath not the Father, and he that acknowledgeth the Son, hath the Father also, 1 *John* 2. 22, 23. *Antichrist is a liar, he denies the Father and the Son.* The true believing **Christian** receives and ownes both, and both are one. God ha's abundantly warn'd and prohibited all men, in the Scriptures, that they neither make nor take to themselves any single creature-formes, as Images of him, by or through which to worship him, but onely such as he ha's given of himself in Chrift, before whom was no God formed, or nothing formed of God, neither shall there be after him, *Efay* 43. 10. The Scriptures are plentiful in this testimony concerning God, under these expressions, *God and Chrift, Father and Son ; God considered absolutely, as in himself, and God considered as the Mediator, God our Saviour,* 1 Tim. 2. 3. The Head of Chrift, God the Father, is three and one, and in God the Son he appeares or shewes himself to be so. *I am in the Father, and the Father in me,* sayes Chrift, *John* 14. 11. and *John* 17. 21, 22. He prayes for the like indissoluble union of his Saints with him, as he ha's with the Father, *That they may be one, as he and the Father are one, by his being in them, as the Father is in him, that they may be made perfect in the one Mediator,* verf. 23.

 These things premised concerning the Trinity in their impersonality, and the same Trinity, as in their threefold personal appearance, God and the Mediator, Father and Son, which are one, we may, I hope, with better success descend into and re-assume the consideration of the various creature-capacity in the same person of Chrift, who is also God, and of the derivation and communication thereof to the particular persons of men and angels, who in Scripture phrase, are thereby asserted to be partakers of the divine Nature.

 Chrift, as *he is the living WORD, express Character or Image of the invisible God,* (Col. 1. 15.) brought forth from Eternity by the peculiar operation of the Father, yet not without the joint concurrence of the other two, is the personal manifestation of the Trinity, in a form purely divine, very God, and singly as so, is difcernable to God alone, not at all to angels or men, in any capacity that ever they are to be brought forth in, natural or fpiritual.

The fame bleffed Mediator, as brought forth in his twofold creature capacity, by the peculiar operations of the fecond and third in the Trinity (not without the joynt concurrence of all the three in each) is the immediate reprefenter of God, the root and parent to both worlds, and the immediate fatisfying object of enjoyment to the natural and fpiritual capacities of angels or men.

In a fhadowy refemblance of Chrift in this twofold creature-capacity and right ftated fubordination of the natural to the fpiritual, was man at firft created male and female, in the fame perfon, (*Gen.* 1. 27.) before we hear of *Eve* (unlefs by anticipation) *Gen.* 2. 22. Rational and fenfual nature, the Angel and the beaft were married together in *Adam*, on thefe tearms and with this **Law**, that the rational was to keep its ground and rule as Lord and Husband, (till a higher Lord came, to which that alfo was to become fubject) and the fenfual to obey and continue fubject, in his individual perfon. So ought matters to go in every one of his pofterity, and then their houfe, or firft-creation-building would be in order; but this ftill, at beft, is not the new creature. The new creation, by way of fire-baptifm, purifies and ftrips this natural, firft-creation form of man, of its mortality, changeablenefs, corruptibility, and brings it into an incorruptible form, an unchangable life of righteoufnefs, true holinefs and glory everlafting. This is the leaft fruit of the new-creation. Over and above all this, it brings upon a more peculiar fort of everlaftingly faved men, a diftinct fuperiour forme of manhood and more excellent glory, (in affociation with the fpiritual and moft exalted capacity in Chrift) taking in and comprehending alfo the inferior, in the fame perfons.

But by what in Chrift, is this transforming, new-creation work, performed upon the firft-created formes and perfons of angels and men?

By the higheft, moft excellent, and fpiritual-creature power in the perfon of this Mediator. As the natural root and head of the firft-creation, was Chrift himfelf willing to become *a Lamb flain*, under the fire-Baptifme-activity of his fpiritual and more excellent creature-form, (brought forth in him as a peculiar emanation from the third in the Trinity) which was originally unchangable, and in an indiffoluble

union

union with the living *WORD*, or Image of the invisible God. The duty and great concern of angels and men, *is to follow this Lamb, whithersoever he go*, in that transition which he was content to make under the fire-baptisme, once *in the beginning of the world*, and again, *in the fulnes of time, when made of woman*, Rev. 13. 8. Heb. 9. 26. 'Twas the sin and fall of angels & men at first, that they refused to follow this head of the first creation, in that transition he was willing to make by way of death & resurrection into the unchangable state & life thereof. On the contrary tis said of the good angels, that were content to have this fire baptism pass upon their first-creation state and glory, that whithersoever this spirit or head of the first creation looked, they looked ; and whither he went, they went ; *they turned not as they went*. This we find in that commonly reputed uninterpretable vision of the Wheels, *Ezek.* 1. 20. and *Ch.* 10, 11. By the way give me leave to ask, what can *the four living creatures* be, (*Chap.* 1. 5.) that are called also, *one living creature* ? verf. 20, 21, 22. and *Chap.* 10. 15, and 20. What, but Christ, as the Spirit and Creator, Head and Ruler of the first Creation ? And what signifies the *letting down of the wings of this living creature*, (*Chap.* 1. 24.) but the cessation from the voice of speech, from the noise of his first ministry , the dispensation of the Law, given forth by the disposition of Angels, (*Acts* 7. 53.) for the government of this first world. This letting down the Wings, was his becoming *the Lamb slain*, in order to come forth a better comforter, in the more excellent way and dispensation, upon the Throne, and that as a man, *Ezek.* 1. 26. and *John* 16. 7. And what are or can be the Wheels, (called also, *one Wheel*, *Ezek.* 1. 15. and 10. 13.) *moving up and down with the living creature*, Spirit and Head of the first creation, but the angelical attendance and retinue of Christ in his first-creation Government and Ministry ? Some of these pass along with him under the fire-baptism, into the more excellent glory, while others (with *Lucifer*, their head) apostatize into a fixed and everlasting enmity against him.

How familiarly are angels in their Ministry and Magistratical government of this World, represented by Charets and Wheels? It is written, (*Psal.* 68. 17.) *The Charets of God are twenty thousand thousands of angels ; the Lord is amongst them as in Sinai. Thousand thousands of them also continue to minister before him, when upon the Throne.* Dan. 7. 9, 10. Some of these good angels were the Charet and Horses of fire, that translated *Eliah* from the Earth, and delivered *Elisha* in Dotham from the *Syrian* army, 2 *King* 2. 11. 12. and *Chap.* 6. 17. What all humane forces, charets and horses have amounted to, when they
have

have come to grapple with the angelical hoft, hath fufficiently appeared. To this effect, above feven years ago, have I heard this vifion of the Wheels expounded by this bleffed Martyr, with abundance of fatisfactory evidence and fpiritual demonftration, together with many rich, fruitful and comfortable obfervations thereupon, for relief of God's people (when all vifible means fail) by the angelical hoft; the next difpenfation.

But to recover our felves out of this digreffion; The devil and his angels (as we find in this vifion) turned away from Chrift their natural head, refufing to adventure the exchange of their firft-creation glory and Life, through unbelief of the gain and ufury thereby attainable, even the fixednefs and unchangablenefs of what they already had, in the greater and more excellent glory, of the refurrection. By this not yeilding to the conditions of paffing along with their head, into the more excellent ftate and unchangable form of their very natural Beings, they loft even that they had, their firft creation glory, righteoufnefs, and the Life of communion with God in Chrift, marageable therein. *Jude* tells us (*verf.* 6.) what befel them hereupon. *The angels which kept not their firft eftate, but left their own habitation, or* head, Chrift; choofing their diftinct oppofite *Luciferian* head, the devil and fatan, *are* (with this their chieftaine) *referved in everlafting chaines under darknefs, unto the judgement of the great day.*

When *Lucifer* had drawn to himfelf and engaged a numerous party of angels with him in his apoftacy, by attempting to affert, maintain, and exalt the leffer natural glory of the firft creation, into a competition with, yea, a preferrence and oppofition to the new-creature ftate of Life and glory in the fecond, which excels; his next bufinefs was, to feduce our firft Parents, and in them all their pofterity, into the fame oppofition to new-creature Life and Glory, the true myftical Sabbath ftate, *THE SAINTS EVERLASTING REST.* This moft defireable Reft is attainable only by our being made willing to enter into a conformity with Chrift in his death, through a furrender of the fingle and ruling activity of our firft-creation principles, at their beft, and giving up our felves wholly into a pure fubjection to what we meet with that's more excellent in the fecond.

Angels fell more knowingly than man, (who was lower than they in underftanding and ftrength) and therefore irrecoverably. Man fell fomewhat ignorantly, (as over-reached through the woman, his weaker part, by the beguiling infinuations of the Serpent) fo he and his are again fet upon their feet, in fome degree or other, by the mighty Redeemer, to try them over again in their own perfons, how they will be mean themselves, in this great fundamental point, about yeilding to the tearms of a transition out of the corruptible state of the life, glory, and righteousness of their first-creation, the house upon the sand, into the incorruptible and unchangable life, glory, and righteousness of the second, the house founded upon the rock, Christ in spirit. So, *The soul that sinneth* again, after the similitude of *Adams* first transgression, after all fair warning, *it shall die* for its own personal transgression, and not for the *fathers having eaten sower grapes,* Ezek. 18. 1, 4.

In order to this new creation, Christ, in the single or double portion of his spirit, is given forth, received and owned by the sons of men, either in the unchangable, spiritualized state of his natural manhood, or also in the more exalted capacity of his spiritual, each of which gifts do baptize and transform the corruptible state of their natural man, into an incorruptible life and unchangable union with the natural or spiritual man in Christ's person, by the new and everlasting Covenant, established in all things, and sure.

The twofold creature-nature in Christ's person, (as the former and inferiour is transformed and brought forth by the latter and more excellent, into an unchangable state of Life and union therewith) is called the *WORD of God, that abides for ever, in them that receive it ; the spirit of God, Christ in spirit , the Son of man in heaven* (Joh. 3. 13.) *that overshadowed the Virgin,* and formed for himself a fleshly tabernacle in her womb. The clothing of himself herewith for the Redemption of man, was a greater condescention than his actual coming forth in the Life, and capacity of the first-born of every creature, for the Creation of the World. Redemption is a greater work than Creation, and requires greater condescention in the undertaker. As first-born of every creature, he was in a superiority of headship to all the angels, as the works of his hands therein, the highest ranck of meer created Beings, in the first world. But when this *WORD,* (which was God, and the twofold original spring of all creaturely life and perfection also) *was made flesh, took on him the particular nature of man,* (not angels) *he became little lower than the angels for a season,* (Heb. 2. 7. and 16.) and not onely so, but was content also to suffer the *visage of* **this** *flesh to be marred more than any man, and to be humbled and abused therein,* **even to** *the death upon the Cross,* Esay 52. 13, 14. and Chap. 53.

The creature-nature in Christ is so enfolded together, and hypostatically united with his purely divine form, that it receives the denomination from that supream form of all.

(　33　)

He is therefore called *Michael*, Gods equal, and the man his fellow, *Zech.* 13. 7. The whole perſon of Chriſt, as comprehending all fulneſs of perfection, creaturely or divine, is very God. But the perſons of men and angels, that are brought into an everlaſting union and aſſociation with Chriſt, in one or both of his creature forms, are not God nor Chriſt. For the higheſt denominating form in their perſonal conſtitution, is but creaturely, yet ſpiritual and divine, in diſtinction from the natural, corruptible form of men or angels, received at their firſt creation. The everlaſting ſecurity of elect angels and men lies in their inſeparable union with their head, the Mediator, in whom alone both creature capacities are in perſonal union with God.

The exalted creature nature in Chriſt, is divine, altogether lovely, (*Cant.* 5. 16.) the true Vine, (*John* 15. 1.) that cheareth the heart of God and man, as in *Jotham's* parable, *Judg.* 9. 13. It is the Spirit of God, the immediate womb, parent, & fountain-head of all new-creation life and principles in men or angels, by the fire-baptiſme. An inferior work to this, is alſo thereby performed upon and in the ſons of men; to wit, all that gradual revival of rational light & life in the moral heathen, or legal Chriſtian, that is very obvious and familiar to obſervation, all the world over. The legal Chriſtian experiences ſuch an operative, actuating influence from this ſpirit, as revives, enlightens, cleanſes, renews & reſtores him to ſome good meaſure of firſt-creation Life & righteouſneſs. As for the flawes & deficiencies yet incident to his perſonal operations, God imputes to him or puts upon him that perfect righteouſneſs of the Law (called *Gods comelineſs, Ezek.* 16. 14.) which Chriſt himſelf performed and had in his fleſhly manhood, rendring it applicable to men, through the merit of his death therein. This whole work of Chriſt in men, inwardly waſhing & ſanctifying them by his blood, as alſo juſtifying them by the imputation of the perfect righteouſneſs of the law to them from his own perſon, amounts but to their practical and experimental knowledge of him after the fleſh (2 *Cor.* 5. 16.) and a proſpering onely into that Kingdom or heaven, that may be ſhaken; *Heb.* 12. 26. Yea, though they receive withall, the baptiſm of gifts from this ſpirit of Chriſt, and in that ſence, be made partakers of the holy Ghoſt, yet they may prove at length to be but briars and thorns to this very ſpirit of Chriſt, from whom they receive all, and to thoſe true believers, in whom the very ſeed of this ſpirit is ſpringing up, as a well of living waters into everlaſting life, *Joh.* 4. 14.

The ſingle Baptiſm of Gifts, ſupernatural Ornaments, and the tongue of Men and Angels, all this amounts not to the Baptiſm with the holy Ghoſt and with fire, *Mat.* 3. 11. The partaking of the holy

E　　　　　　　　　　　　　　　　　　　　Ghoſt

Ghoſt in the ſingle baptiſm of gifts, without the very ſeed of ſpiritual, eternal Life ſown in the heart, does not mar the viſage of the natural man, does not ſacrifice and offer him up, but more abundantly adorn, beautifie and ſet him off. Thoſe that have the glory of their earthly man, but thus higher advanced by ſupernatural gifts and accompliſhments, are liable to play the Idolaters againſt the glory that excels, the Life hid with Chriſt in God, and (finally refuſing the ſuperior diſpenſation and thoſe that own it) return with the dog to the vomit, upon the loſs of what they have already received, *Ezek.* 16. 1, 15. 2 *Pet.* 2. 20, 22.

MORE in his *MYSTERY*, holds that the Fall of the Angels came by their refuſal of the divine Life, and giving themſelves wholly up to the animal ; and that ſatans kingdom of darkneſs extends to and comprehends all the intereſts and advantages of whatever Life, excluding onely the Divine. The ſame Author exhibits a new and unanſwerable charge againſt *Paganiſm*, that by whatever ſlights of wit the beſt of them all may ſeem to wipe off the imputations of *Polytheiſm*, or Idolatry, aſſerting themſelves to be the adorers of one eternal Deity in his various manifeſtations, yet they worſhipped God in ſuch appearances onely as related to and concerned but the animal Life. 'Tis to be feared, this charge will reach a great way into Chriſtianity, abundance of the profeſſors whereof, are followers of Chriſt onely for loaves, ſuch cleanſing gifts and ornaments as do but gratifie and advance their earthly, firſt creation ſtate. Speak but a word of the croſs and fire-baptiſm of the ſpirit, that's to come upon all this glory and goodlineſs of fleſh, (in order to a more excellent birth and knowledge of Chriſt after the ſpirit in them) you become an enemy preſently if you tell them this truth, *Gal.* 4. 16. If matters be well ſcann'd and weighed in the ballance of the ſanctuary, abundance of Religion and Profeſſors will be found no currant and well tried Gold, (*Rev.* 3. 18.) that will paſs for the Kingdom of Heaven.

The Scripture latitude of the animal or natural man is comprehenſive of all that is to be found in mans firſt-creation ſtate and life, in diſtinction from the ſpiritual, new creation man. The natural body or animal man is interpreted by the apoſtle to be of the ſame reach and ſignificancy as the living ſoul of the firſt *Adam*, at beſt, as the ſpiritual body or man is comprehenſive of that new-creature Life and perfection that's recieved from the indwelling preſence of the quickning ſpirit of the ſecond *Adam*, 1 *Cor.* 15. 44, 46.

Thoſe Chriſtians that are brought into communion with God, but
in

in the renewed activity of the natural body or living soul of the first *Adam*, (taking the renewed old man for the new : Restauration, for Regeneration)are apt to grow so conceited & confident therein, that they wil not lend an ear to the tydings of any superiour dispensation and more excellent way. Man, in whatever possible refinement and glory of his first-creation state, is yet but that natural man, in whose mind there is so vast an asymmetry and incongruity to spiritual, divine things, *the New Name, the Life hid with Christ in God, the Wisdom and Righ-teousness of God, that shines forth in the New Creature*, that he knows not what to make of them, *they are foolishness to him*, 1 *Cor.* 2. 14.

Nothing less than the very seed of spiritual, new-creature Life from Christ, will find or make its way through all possible obstructi-ons from within man, or from without, and prosper into that king-dome of grace and glory, that cannot be shaken. This will spring up in the soul and declare it self King, take the Scepter and ruling power out of the hands of our first-creation spirit and principles, and will safely steer our course, direct our steps, and enable us to work righte-ousness in the way everlasting ; *Psal.* 139. 24. Sensual Life gene-rally rules at first in children. When Reason springs up, and begins to shew it self, that takes (or should take) the Scepter, curbes the in-solencies and exorbitancies of the Sensual powers, and governs the whole person. If there be a seed of grace or spiritual Life sown in him, when that springs up into exercise, it will take the Scepter out of the hands of humane Reason and Wisdom, and govern the whole person in the Divine, Spiritual Reason and Wisdom of God.

The receivers of the spirit of Christ, (the seed of spiritual wisdom and divine Life) are of two sorts ; either such as receive the single, or such as receive the double portion thereof. They that receive but the single, will thereby be brought into the incorruptible form of the na-tural man, which renders them fit associates for the elect angels, to stand about the Throne as friends of the Bridegroom and the Bride. They that receive the double portion of the spirit, in the sense above expressed, are the very Bride her self, the Lambs wife, that sits down upon the Throne with him, in a more exalted state of Glory, for ever.

The Mother of *Zebedee's* Children desired of Christ, *That her two sons might sit, the one on his right hand, and the other on his left, in his kingdom*, Mat. 20. 21. There may seem to be a right and left hand scitu-ation or state of glory for ever, in the kingdom of Heaven. The double portioned Saints are they that sit on the right hand ; the single, on the left. Christ tells her and her sons, *they know not what they ask*, if they would have either of these advancements on this side the Cross, the

grave

Ghost in the single baptism of gifts, without the very seed of spiritual, eternal Life sown in the heart, does not mar the visage of the natural man, does not sacrifice and offer him up, but more abundantly adorn, beautifie and set him off. Those that have the glory of their earthly man, but thus higher advanced by supernatural gifts and accomplishments, are liable to play the Idolaters against the glory that excels, the Life hid with Christ in God, and (finally refusing the superior dispensation and those that own it) return with the dog to the vomit, upon the loss of what they have already received, *Ezek.* 16. 1, 15. 2 *Pet.* 2. 20, 22.

MORE in his *MYSTERY*, holds that the Fall of the Angels came by their refusal of the divine Life, and giving themselves wholly up to the animal; and that satans kingdom of darkness extends to and comprehends all the interests and advantages of whatever Life, excluding onely the Divine. The same Author exhibits a new and unanswerable charge against *Paganism*, that by whatever flights of wit the best of them all may seem to wipe off the imputations of *Polytheism*, or Idolatry, asserting themselves to be the adorers of one eternal Deity in his various manifestations, yet they worshipped God in such appearances onely as related to and concerned but the animal Life. 'Tis to be feared, this charge will reach a great way into Christianity, abundance of the professors whereof, are followers of Christ onely for loaves, such cleansing gifts and ornaments as do but gratifie and advance their earthly, first creation state. Speak but a word of the cross and fire-baptism of the spirit, that's to come upon all this glory and goodliness of flesh, (in order to a more excellent birth and knowledge of Christ after the spirit in them) you become an enemy presently if you tell them this truth, *Gal.* 4. 16. If matters be well scann'd and weighed in the ballance of the sanctuary, abundance of Religion and Professors will be found no currant and well tried Gold, (*Rev.* 3. 18.) that will pass for the Kingdom of Heaven.

The Scripture latitude of the animal or natural man is comprehensive of all that is to be found in mans first-creation state and life, in distinction from the spiritual, new creation man. The natural body or animal man is interpreted by the apostle to be of the same reach and significancy as the living soul of the first *Adam*, at best, as the spiritual body or man is comprehensive of that new-creature Life and perfection that's recieved from the indwelling presence of the quickning spirit of the second *Adam*, 1 *Cor.* 15. 44, 46.

Those Christians that are brought into communion with God, but

in

in the renewed activity of the natural body or living soul of the first *Adam*, (taking the renewed old man for the new : Restauration, for Regeneration) are apt to grow so conceited & confident therein, that they wil not lend an ear to the tydings of any superiour dispensation and more excellent way. Man, in whatever possible refinement and glory of his first-creation state, is yet but that natural man, in whose mind there is so vast an asymmetry and incongruity to spiritual, divine things, *the New Name, the Life hid with Christ in God, the Wisdom and Righteousness of God, that shines forth in the New Creature*, that he knows not what to make of them, *they are foolishness to him,* 1 *Cor.* 2. 14.

Nothing less than the very seed of spiritual, new-creature Life from Christ, will find or make its way through all possible obstructions from within man, or from without, and prosper into that kingdome of grace and glory, that cannot be shaken. This will spring up in the soul and declare it self King, take the Scepter and ruling power out of the hands of our first-creation spirit and principles, and will safely steer our course, direct our steps, and enable us to work righteousness in the way everlasting ; *Psal.* 139. 24. Sensual Life generally rules at first in children. When Reason springs up, and begins to shew it self, that takes (or should take) the Scepter, curbes the insolencies and exorbitancies of the Sensual powers, and governs the whole person. If there be a seed of grace or spiritual Life sown in him, when that springs up into exercise, it will take the Scepter out of the hands of humane Reason and Wisdom, and govern the whole person in the Divine, Spiritual Reason and Wisdom of God.

The receivers of the spirit of Christ, (the seed of spiritual wisdom and divine Life) are of two sorts ; either such as receive the single, or such as receive the double portion thereof. They that receive but the single, will thereby be brought into the incorruptible form of the natural man, which renders them fit associates for the elect angels, to stand about the Throne as friends of the Bridegroom and the Bride. They that receive the double portion of the spirit, in the sense above expressed, are the very Bride her self, the Lambs wife, that sits down upon the Throne with him, in a more exalted state of Glory, for ever.

The Mother of *Zebedee*'s Children desired of Christ, *That her two sons might sit, the one on his right hand, and the other on his left, in his kingdom,* Mat. 20. 21. There may seem to be a right and left hand scituation or state of glory for ever, in the kingdom of Heaven. The double portioned Saints are they that sit on the right hand ; the single, on the left. Christ tells her and her sons, *they know not what they ask ,* if they would have either of these advancements on this side the Cross, the

E 2 grave

grave, the fire-baptism, the strait gate, that excludes flesh and blood, all that is corruptible from the Kingdom of God. *Can ye* (faies he) *drink of the Cup I shall drink of, and be baptized with the baptism that I am baptized with ? They answer, We are able.*

The single portion of the Spirit, where it is received as a feed of new Life, will not fail to perform that transforming fire-baptism, in and upon the souls of men, that will purifie them, not onely from corruption, (the utmost extent of the inward water-baptisme and circumcision of the heart, in the Letter) but from corruptibility, gradually fetching them up into the glory of the resurrection, till their mortality be quite swallowed up of Life. It will make them of the same mind that was in Christ, willing so to suffer in the flesh under the power of his spirit, as to cease from sin, or from that state that can return back into sin again, 1 *Pet.* 4. 1. This incorruptible form (atteinable onely by the fire-baptism, performed upon the natural man at his best, by the single portion of the spirit of Christ) is called spiritual, and denominates the whole person a spiritual man, though yet in the mortal body, in distinction from those who have but only the renewal of their first-creation form by the influence and gifts of the same spirit.

All that these receive is but the goodliness of flesh ; renewed, adorned nature, which is decried and blown upon by a second vice, a superior dispensation and ministry of the same spirit, as a perishing vanity, after the first voice has done its work, made a straight path for God in the desert, by rectifying the rational powers in bewildred man, *Esay* 40. 3, 8.

Our corruptible tabernacle is to be taken down. This mantle, this filthy garment, this vile body, flesh and blood at its best, is *to be changed into the likeness of Christs glorious body*, his heavenly man, *by the mighty power and transforming operation of that spirit, whereby he is able to subdue all things to himself,* Phil. 3. 21. We must *put off the old man at best, and put on the new, which after God is created in righteousness and true holiness,* Ephes. 4. 22, 24. Col. 3. 9, 10. That Image of God received by the first-creation, and all the wisdom, glory, and righteousness thereof, is but shadow, to what is to be received by the new creation. 'Tis but self-glory, self-wisdom, self-righteousness, and when these are opposed to the wisdom, righteousness, and glory of God in the new creation, they are Idols ; shadows preferred to substance ; the Law or ruling Principles of our first creation Life, to grace and truth in the second.

Some few Results or Corollaries of what hath been said in this matter, take as followeth.

1. The Spirit of God, the holy Ghost, the divine Nature, which the Scriptures do evidently affert and declare to be communicable to men, exceeds not in its reach and fignificancy, the natural and fpiritual creature capacity in the perfon of the Mediator, whereby individual angels and men are brought into an everlafting union with him, in one or both, as he is one with the Father, *John* 17. 22.

2. Where-ever the Seed of eternal Life is fowne, by Chrift's caufing himfelf to be received in the fingle or double portion of his Spirit, it will mar the vifage or wifdom of man, it will take him off from his way of working righteoufnefs, and worfhipping God in the oldnefs of the letter of the firft creation, and enable him to perform all in a more excellent and acceptable way, in the newnefs of the fpirit of the fecond. *Paul* in his own perfon, gives us notice of this diftinction which he ftood in, from thofe youthful, flourifhing profeffors that were reigning as Kings at the righteoufnefs of the Law, performable in their own fpirit, 1 *Cor.* 4. 8. 10. With fuch he faid he durft not compare himfelf, (2 *Cor.* 10. 12.) who pleafing themfelves and applauding one another in a way of mutual felf-deceivings and commendations, are not thofe whom the Lord commendeth, as he rather defired to be, *verf.* 18. They have but the inward heart-circumcifion in the letter of the firft (not in the fpirit of the fecond creation) *whofe praife is not of men*, as is implied, *Rom.* 2. 29.

'Tis worth obfervation, that even in the ancient Hieroglyphical divinity of *Egypt*, no fervice or worfhip of God was accounted acceptable and well-pleafing, but what was performed by fome divine power of God himfelf in them.

3. There are two diftinct forts of everlaftingly faved men ; fuch as receive the fingle, and fuch as receive the double portion of the fpirit. Both pafs under the fire-baptifme. The former are exalted into affociation with the elect angels, and have for the immediate and adaequate object of their fruition and converfe, God, as fhining forth to them in the incorruptible form of Chrifts natural Manhood. The latter and more exalted fort of Saints, are taken into affociation with the fpiritual manhood in Chrifts perfon, and have for the immediate and adaequate object of their fruition and converfe, God, as fhining forth to

them

them in that highest and most exalted creature form, in Christ's person. And by and through these (who do properly constitute the *general assembly, and Church of the first-born*) the *spirits of just men, and the holy angels*, even those *principalities and powers in heavenly places*, do (as at second hand) receive that manifold wisdom of God, that shines forth more immediately upon the Church, *Ephes.* 3. 10.

4. The highest sort of these Saints, are not Christ or God ; much less, the lower. Christ is the head, root and parent to both these sorts of glorified men , in his twofold creature capacity or manhood, natural or spiritual. And Christ, as he is the purely divine form or image of the invisible God, is head to both these creature-headships in his own person ; and God is the head of Christ, considered as in his purely divine form. 1 *Cor,* 11. 3.

5. Christ in his creature-capacity, is the maker, redeemer and heir of all things in both worlds ; as all things were created by him so for him, *Col.* 1. 16. *Heb.* 1. 2. and *Rom.* 11. 36. *Of him, through him, and to him, are all things.*

6. Men, that in their first creation were made little lower than the Angels, (*Psal.* 8. 5.) are in the second or new creation made equal to the elect angels ; and all those of the double portion, are advanced quite over the heads of all the angels, into an immediate association with Christ in his most exalted creature-capacity, on the Throne of his glory, even in that more excellent creature name than the angels have, *Heb.* 1. 4.

Behold then the heavenly order in the whole family of God.

First, God himself, the head of Christ, and that, as Christ is the Image of the invisible God, very God.

Secondly, Christ himself, as thus considered in his capacity purely divine, head to his twofold creature-headship, the natural and spiritual man in his own person.

Thirdly, Christ in his twofold creatureship, as the immediate head to all spiritual and natural men and angels, in his heavenly family, his members, his body mystical.

Fourthly, Behold these also in their two grand distinctions of superiority and subordination, spiritual and natural.

Fifthly, There may seem also to be intimated in the Scriptures, a gradual difference of capacity in the individuals of either of these two

ranks

ranks of everlastingly glorified men ; *Dan.* 12. 3. and 1 *Cor.* 15. 41. *There is one glory of the Sun, another of the Moon, and another glory of the Stars, and one Star differeth from another Star in glory.*

Variety of intellectual light or discerning is resembled in Scripture by the variety of figurative light in the outward visible creation. Christ is called, *The Sun of Righteousness*, Mal. 4. 2. Angels, *Stars*, Job 38. 7. And the Spirit of Man, *The candle of the Lord*, Prov. 20. 27.

To wind up all then, and secure our selves from the mistake of the **German** Divinity ; The servants that stand about the Throne, are not the Bride that sits upon it. The Bride is not the Bridegroom. The Bridegrom himself, in whatever creature-state he is married to men or angels, by the new and everlasting Covenant, is yet but as the Bride to himself in his purely divine form ; and as so, yet, he is not the Father, but as the Bride of the God-head, the express character, or personallity of all the three, as Image of the invisible God. The Bride the Lambs Wife, Angels or Men, are all gathered up into one common Interest ; all do live in the beatifical Vision and enjoyment of God in Christ, in their several intellectual distances, ranks, and capacities, and may all be said to partake of the divine nature. But more peculiarly, (next to the living creature that is under the God of *Israel*, in personal union with God, *Ezek.* 10. 20.) the superiour and more excellent sort of Saints are partakers thereof, being actually brought forth in the highest kind of creature capacity, that is next to the purely divine form.

See all summ'd up together, *Heb.* 12. 22, 24. *Ye are come unto Mount Sion, and unto the City of the living God, the heavenly Jerusalem, and to an innumerable company of Angels, to the general Assembly and Church of the first-born, which are written in heaven ; to God the Judge of all, and to the spirits of just Men made perfect, and to Jesus the Mediator of the New Covenant.* Here we have a distinct expression of the heavenly Orders.

1. *An innumerable company of Angels, and spirits of just Men made perfect.*

2. *The general Assembly and Church of the first-born,* that have the double portion of the Spirit.

3. *Jesus the Mediator of the new Covenant.*

4. *God the Judge of all.*

Will any now say, *What signifies this prolixe Discourse of Principles to the present undertake.* 'Tis answered, Much every way, in case what

hath

hath been said, be true, and intelligibly expressed. For it most exactly suits with what is engaged for in the Title Page. He lived in the Spirit and walked in the Spirit, *Gal.* 5. 25. 'Tis this Life, *hid with Christ in God*, I principally intend the character of, the Life of Faith, which now with him is turn'd to sight, being absent from the Body and at home with the Lord, 2 *Cor.* 5. 6, 7. This Life is no way explicable but by considering his Gospel Principles, Doctrine, and Way of Worshipping God, in spirit and truth. And what signifie all his publick and outward actings in Church or state, but as issuing from and reducible to this his new-creature Life and the Principles thereof ? This discourse therefore is principally directed to Christian Readers, who are furnished with the spiritual discerning of Faith, which can take in the evidence and demonstration of things not seen to any other eye in man, things eternal, *Heb.* 11. 1. *2 Cor.* 4. 18.

This Pilgrim quitted *the broad way that leads to destruction*, and took the *narrow path that leadeth unto Life, which few there be that find, Mat.* 7. 14. His lot was to be upon the earth, while the Church was in her Wilderness condition, in her sackcloth. Briars and Thornes were with him all along : he dwelt among Scorpions, *Ezek.* 2. 6. *Many archers shot at him ; they did shoot forth their arrows, even bitter words ; they smote him with the tongue,* and at length with the hand ; *but his Bow abode in strength, his Armes were made strong by the hands of the mighty God of Jacob.* Gen. 49. 23, 24. *His enemies encouraged themselves in an evil matter : they communed of laying snares privily, that they might shoot at him in secret ; their teeth were spears and arrows ; they did whet their tongue like a sword, to wound him. But God shall shoot at them, with an arrow suddenly shall they be wounded,* Psal. 64. and 57. 4. *He will whet his sword, and ordain his arrows against the Persecutors,* Psal. 7. 12, 13.

But where may it appear that this sufferer was of the opinion, that there are two distinct sorts of everlastingly saved men? In his general Epistle to the Church of Christ upon earth, which is like to be exposed to publick view before this. Not long before his death I received express notice in a Letter concerning these two Witnesses of Christ, both of them coming forth in the self-evidencing power, and demonstration of the single or double portion of his spirit. He took rise for his conceptions herein, from such irradiations of divine glory as he received in the contemplation of these following Scriptures, with many others.

‘ *First,* Revel. 11. 18. *The Nations were angry, thy wrath is come,* ‘ *and the time wherein thou shouldest give reward unto thy servants the* ‘ *Pro-*

' *Prophets, and to the Saints, and to them that fear thy Name, small and*
' *great.* There is (said he) intended here by the holy Ghost a con-
' siderable difference between those called Chrifts servants the pro-
' phets, and the rest that are named saints, all being such as are said to
' fear God's Name, great or small, and are declared to be objects of
' Chrifts reward, who hath one kind of reward for the prophet, and
' another for righteous men, saints, just men made perfect. These, as
' faithful servants, are to abide in the house for ever, friends to the
' Bridegroom, that rejoyce at hearing of his second voice, which they
' have but at second hand, through the Bride. But those more excel-
' lent sort of servants, the prophets, that are the very Bride, they have
' their peculiar priviledge above the other, personally to possesse the
' Bridegroom, as his Name is the *WO R D of God* ; a Name, (*Rev.*
' 19. 12, 13.) which no man knows, (nor angel) but he himself, and
' they to whom the Son will reveal it. In this sence is that to be
' understood, which is testified by Christ himself, *Luk.* 10, 22. *No*
' *man knowes who the Son is, but the Father, and who the Father is, but the*
' *Son, and he* (or they) *to whom the Son will reveal him. This is the*
' *Name that Christ by inheritance hath obtained, more excellent than the*
' *Angels, the Name above every Name, that at the manifestation thereof*
' *every knee should bow, and tongue confess, to the glory of God the Fa-*
' *ther.*

 ' After this Name it was, *Jacob* was so inquisitive (*Gen.* 32. 29.)
' *saying, tell me, I pray thee, thy Name.* And he came afterwards to un-
' derstand, it was the face of God, or sight of God face to face, in his
' very similitude, which it is not permitted in so ful and intimate a
' manner for every saint to have. Upon this, *Jacob's* name was chan-
' ged to *Israel,* and he became a Prince or chief prevailer with God
' and with Man.

 ' Agreeable to this distinction does the Prophet *Esay* describe *Isra-*
' *el,* Chap. 41. 8, 9. *Thou Israel my servant, Jacob whom I have cho-*
' *sen, the seed of Abraham my friend, unto whom I have said, thou art my*
' *servant ; I have chosen thee and not cast thee away.* Here, the holy seed
' or divine birth of God's Image, that makes the true *Israelite* by faith,
' is described to be of a nature and quality that is incorrupti-
' ble, securing him in whom it is, whether *Jacob* the chosen servant,
' or the seed of *Abraham* the chosen friend, as well as chosen servant,
' from ever being a castaway. Hereby is intimated, what it is to be the
' chosen, faithful servant and no more, and what it is over and above,
' to be the chosen and intimate friend, that is called and admitted
' to see God face to face, as friend speaks with friend. Thus of *Aaron*

                         ' it

‘ it is faid, (*Exod.* 4. 15, 16.) *That Mofes fhould fpeak to him and put*
‘ *words in his mouth, and* (faies God) *I will be with thy mouth, and with*
‘ *his mouth, and will teach you what ye fhall do. And Aaron fhall be thy*
‘ *fpokefman unto the People, he fhall be to thee inftead of a mouth, and thou*
‘ *fhalt be to him in ftead of God.* Confider how interpretable this is of
‘ the fon of man glorified, the great Prophet of all, in the perfon of
‘ the bleffed Mediator, fet down on the right hand of the Majefty on
‘ high, who ftill reteins the form of a fervant, or perfection of his na-
‘ tural man in its incorruptible form, with which as with a mouth,
‘ (typified by *Aaron*) he comes forth as a head to the holy Angels,
‘ and *Jacob* his chofen fervant, in a fuitable way of converfe and frui-
‘ tion, to their capacity, fpeaking therein to the body of the People,
‘ whilft at the fame time he is in his fpiritual manhood, exalted to an e-
‘ quality with the eternal *W O R D,* as the man God's fellow, admit-
‘ ted to a communication with God, face to face, as friend fpeaks with
‘ friend. In this glory, he is more properly the very mouth of God,
‘ (typified by *Mofes*) in a capacity and fitnefs for converfe with
‘ the Bride, the Lambs Wife, as head to the general Affembly of the
‘ firft-born, who are a fort of faints, of greater dignity and prehemi-
‘ nence, by whom the manifold Wifdom of God, or fecret Name, his
‘ *W O R D,* fhall be made known to principallities and powers,
‘ *Ephef.* 3. 10.

‘ The loweft fort of all thefe heaven-born Saints, that have but the
‘ fingle portion of the fpirit, have not onely by the external influence
‘ of Chrifts heavenly Nature, fuch a change as the legal or firft Co-
‘ venant Saint has, (from the polluted to the cleanfed and reformed
‘ ftate of the natural man, which make but a member of the myftical
‘ earthly *Jerufalem,* that may become the fpiritual *Sodom*) but by the
‘ very feed of Chrift's heavenly nature fown in them, they have an in-
‘ ward real partaking of the divine nature, or that new principle of
‘ Life which baptizes the natural ftate into a conformity with, and fub-
‘ jection thereunto, advancing it thereby for ever into a fublimated &
‘ incorruptible form. It is in his Light onely (with whom is the foun-
‘ tain of all Life and perfection) that we can fee Light, *Pfal.* 36. 9.
‘ In the fpiritual, new-creature difcerning onely of a divine commu-
‘ nicated underftanding and fuperinduced form, can we fee that ob-
‘ jective, light or unveiled glory of God, that renders the true heir e-
‘ verlaftingly bleffed. But even amongft the children of the heavenly
‘ kingdom, the children of the Refurrection, there are fome of a firft
‘ and others of a fecond Refurrection, into a more exalted ftate of Life
‘ and glory. Yet all the Veffels of glory, great and fmall, will be fil-
‘ led

' led from the Ocean of those unutterable riches of divine Glory, that
' are in Christ, which no natural eye can see. There will be no want,
' or envying one another there.

Concerning ORDINANCES.

HAving already spoken joyntly concerning this Sufferers Principles and Doctrine, I come now to mention his way of worshiping God, and what his Judgement and Practice was, as to Ordinances.

After that way which men call Heresie did he worship the God of his believing Fathers, *Abraham* and the rest, *Acts* 24. 14. He was for worshipping God in spirit and in Truth ; *such the Father seeks to worship him,* Joh. 4. 23. He lived, walked, worshipped, prayed, spake in the spirit, and so, as the oracles of God, (1 *Pet.* 4. 11.) ministring as of the ability that God gave him, that God in all things might be glorified. This language and way of Worshipping God, that is so despicable to man, is that onely which hath the praise of God. He kept the true mystical Sabbath, not thinking his own thoughts, &c. *Esay* 58. 13. He was baptized with the holy Ghost, and with fire. He did in such sort eat the flesh and drink the blood of Christ, that he was thereby brought into a conformity with Christ in his death, and had eternal Life abiding in him, *John* 6. 54. This is satisfactory to God in this point ; that that answers his well pleasing. What further shall be said, shall not be in order to please, but instruct, convince and stop the mouthes of gainsaying men, *Tit.* 1. 9.

He that worships God in the power of the single or double portion of the spirit of Christ, does undeniably worship him in spirit and truth. The power of godliness comes in with this new creation Spirit. All Worshp, Righteousnes, Ordinances, or whatever, performed but in the renewed, reformed, enlightned, gifted, adorned state of our first-creation spirit, amounts but to the form of godliness, that saith that may be shipwrack'd, that interest in Christ, and that good conscience that may be lost, 1 *Tim.* 1. 19. They that have not the divine nature, in the sence above expressed, (2 *Pet.* 1. 4.) *are blind and cannot see afar off,* (*verf.* 9.) they discern not the land of distances, the new *Jerusalem.* They may have great illumination, excellent gifts, and in the confidence of these they say, they see, what get they by that ? *Therefore their sin remaineth,* (*John* 9. 41.) that is, is unpardonable ; there remaineth no more benefit of Christ's sacrifice to them. *There remaineth onely* at last, (upon final refusal and resistance of the

new

new-creature life, spirit, and way of worship) *nothing but a certain fear-ful looking for of judgement and fiery inignation, which shall devour the ad-versaries,* Heb. 10. 27. and *Chap.* 6. 4, 8. Their light, their seeing, takes away all cloak for their sin, *John* 15. 22, and 24. The warning which the true spiritual watchman gives them, if neglected and de-spised by them, does dangerously set forward this work, (through their miscarriage under it, and becomes a savour of death to them, (*Act.* 13. 40. 41.*) but even so, a sweet savour to God, as prospering in the thing whereto he sends it, and accomplishing his pleasure, 2 *Cor.* 2. 16. *Esay* 55. 11.

These keen concisionists, that cannot afford a good word for the true circumcision, that worship God in the spirit, and have no confi-dence in the flesh, or in the knowledge of Christ after the flesh, they are hot about the outward circumstances of worship, time, place and the like. Christ reproves them in his answer to the woman of *Sama-ria,* at *Jacobs* Well ; *Neither in this Mountain, nor at Jerusalem, shall ye worship the Father, but in spirit and truth,* Joh. 4. 23. Neither in this Form nor that, but excluded out of all Synagogues has the true Church and Spouse of Christ been worshipping God this twelve hundred Years and upwards, in her mourning persecuted wilderness-conditi-on, out of which she is shortly to appear and speak for her self. By this Sufferers reckoning *the time, times and half a time,* or, *three years and a half,* are very near expired, those *forty two moneths, and one thou-sand two hundred and sixty days,* prophetical for years, all which do cha-racter and point out the same *Epocha* in *Daniel* and the *Revelation,* for the Churches abode in the Wilderness from the time of her flight, mentioned, *Rev.* 12. 6. She will very shortly be called up out of the wilderness, by the name of *Shulamite,* which comes from the same word that *Solomon* and *Salem* do, signifying *Peace.* This true peace-able *Pilgrim and Spouse of Christ,* that in her Life and Testimony hath been so distasteful to this world, out of which she is chosen, (as to be reputed by all the Inhabitants of the earth a wrangling Heretick, a Blasphemer, and one that turns the World upside down) will shortly come up out of her political grave, or exclation from all authority or allowance in Church and State, into the exercise of true Christian Po-lity in both, in association with the holy Angels, who with the risen Witnesses will make up the two hosts, before whom no opposite power of contradicting man wil be able to bear up. See for this, *Cant.* 6. 13. *Return, return, O Shulamite, return, return, that we may look upon thee: what will ye see in the Shulamite ? as it were the company, or dance of two Armies, Mahanaim ;* relating to *Jacobs two hosts of Angels and Men,*

when

when he was to meet *Esau*, (*Gen.* 32. 1, 2.) and importing the victory these two obtain over all their enemies, as also their dance, or triumphant rejoycing after the victory. And all this yet amounts but to the preparatory work, for the second coming of Christ, by plucking up every thing that offends, so as at last there may be nothing to hurt in all the holy mountain, *Mat.* 13. 41. *Esay* 11. 9.

But how shall the risen Witnesses handle their enemies, when spirited and set upon their feet, as a Nation born at once, and in one day? *Esay* 66. 8. *Rev.* 11. 11. 'Tis answered, fire shall proceed out of their mouth to devour any that would hurt them, and in this manner must they be killed; that is, at the desire of the believing, risen witnesses, angels that are a flaming fire, (*Psal.* 104. 4.) will destroy any men that oppose them. Fire goes out of the saints mouth, that is by prayer to God, on which the angels are commissioned to do execution immediately and irresistibly, without more ado. Thus *fire went out of Elias his mouth, to devour the two Captains and their fifties*; Angels were the executioners, 2 *King.* 1. 9, 12. Those acts of *Elias* were but Types and shadows of what will be done in the end of the world, at the winding up of all dispensations, towards the highest, even the personal coming forth of Christ with all his *New-Jerusalem* Armies following him, *Rev.* 19. 14. As to what will be performed by the risen Witnesses, relation is had to *Elias* and to *Moses*, *Rev.* 11. 6. Where 'tis said, *They shall have power* (as *Elias* had) *to shut heaven that it rain not, and to smite the earth with Plagues, as often as they will, as Moses did in Egypt* It may appear what work one Angel can make with whole Armies of men ; *a hundred fourescore and five thousand Assyrians were slain by an angel in one night, in the Leagure before Jerusalem*, 2 King. 19. 35.

But to return from this Contemplation of the true *New-Jerusalem* spirited Church and Spouse of Christ, and what she will do when she comes out of the Wilderness, consider we a little the general posture of all visible Churches, even at this day, as this Sufferer hath left it represented to us, in writing.

' There are many Churches in the World, that make a profession
' of the Name of Christ, under several Forms and Denominations,
' according to the variety of Judgements, and Interests of the Ru-
' lers & Members thereof. There is a Church called Catholick or Uni-
' versal, headed by the Pope, who pretends to be Christs Vicar. There
' are also National Churches, headed either by a Civil Magistrate,
' as the Church of *England*, or by general Assemblies, as the Church of
' *Scotland* hath been, with other Reformed Churches. There are also
' particular

'particular, Independant, Congregational Churches, diftinguifhing
'themfelves into variety of Sects, and diverfity of Judgements and
'Opinions, as well about the way and order of the word in matters of
'worfhip, and the fervice of God, as in what they hold Fundamental
'in matters of Faith. Thefe all make up one Body, as to the owning
'and upholding a Church in fome outward vifible Form, who not-
'withftanding all their differences and proteftings againft one ano-
'ther, do generally agree together in one mind, as to the preferring
'of the Church in Name, Shew, and outward Order, before what it
'is in Spirit and Truth, as it is the real and living Body of Chrift.

'Hence it is, that the true Church indeed, the very living, real,
'fpiritual members of Chrift's Body, have been for many hundred
'years a difperfed, captivated people, under all worldly powers, ci-
'vil or Ecclefiaftical, and never been fuffered to ufe or enjoy a free-
'dom in their Communion together, and the purity of God's Ser-
'vice and Worfhip, but are upon one pretence or other, reftrained by
'Humane Lawes, and fupprefied as Hereticks, Schifmaticks, Fana-
'ticks, and fuch as turn the World upfide down, while thofe that have
'the repute and credit to be the Church, or Churches of Chrift, under
'fome one of the Formes, and outward Orders before mentioned,
'have the Powers of the World on their fide, and are contending one
'with another, who fhall be uppermoft, and give the Rule of Con-
'formity in Doctrine, Worfhip, and Church Order, to all the reft, by
'Compulfion and Perfecution. But the dayes are now haftening a-
'pace, wherein the living Members of Chrift's Body fhall be made
'manifeft, in diftinction from all thofe *that have the Name to live but*
'*are dead.*

Thus in brief you fee his Judgement concerning the Church.

Concerning *BAPTISM, he writes thus.*

'There are feveral Baptifmes fpoken of in the New Teftament,
'and the Doctrine concerning them hath been fo dark and my-
'fterious, that there is little yet extant in the Writings of men con-
'cerning the fame, that carries with it fatisfaction.

'There are two general tearms, under which all Baptifmes menti-
'oned in the New Teftament, feem to be comprehended; that is to
'fay, *Of Water, and of the holy Ghoft and Fire.*

'*Water Baptifm* is twofold, and fo alfo the *Baptifm of the holy Ghoft,*
'There is a figurative outward *Water Baptifm*, and a real or inward.

'In

' In the firſt ſenſe, it is an Inſtitution which doth appoint the outward
' man to be waſhed in Water, thereby to ſignifie the proper effect
' and operation of that waſhing with Water by the Word, which cau-
' ſes a renovation or reſtauration of man by his repentance from
' dead workes, and return to the ſervice of the living God, in amend-
' ment of Life.

' By this inward *Baptiſm* and real work of the Spirit on the hearts
' of men, they are but cleanſed from the filthineſs and pollution of
' their corrupted Nature, not regenerated and altered from their firſt
' make and conſtitution, that is attended with inſtability and liable-
' neſs to apoſtacy.

' There is alſo a twofold outward *Water Baptiſm* mentioned.

' 1. *John's Water Baptiſm*, which was the onely outward ſign that
' accompanied his Miniſtry, the Ordinance of that time and ſeaſon, to
' prepare the way for Chriſt's coming in the fleſh, and to ſignify the
' proper effect which his firſt appearance, as God manifeſted in fleſh,
' was to have upon the hearts and natures of men, conſiſting chiefly
' in theſe two particulars, *Repentance from dead Works, and Amend-*
' *ment of Life.*

' 2. The ſecond outward *Water Baptiſm*, was that which Chriſt him-
' ſelf inſtituted and committed to his diſciples in his Life time, as the
' outward ſign that was to accompany their firſt miniſtry, when he
' employed them much in the ſame nature as *John* was, ſending them
' before his face, as labourers into the harveſt, to all places whither
' he himſelf afterwards intended to come.

' Both theſe Adminiſtrations had their Known Adminiſtrators, and
' were diſpenſations, proper to that ſeaſon they were ordained in, to
' prepare the minds of People to receive Chriſt in his firſt appear-
' ance, or coming in the fleſh, and the fruits flowing there-from, in *a-*
' *mendment of Life.*

' The inward or real *Water Baptiſm*, conſiſting in the waſhing of
' man's nature by the Word, *unto Repentance and Amendment of Life*,
' is capable of being adminiſtred three wayes, or by a threefold
' hand.

' 1. By the Miniſtry, Hand, or Tongue of Men, as by *John Baptiſt*,
' through the preaching of the written Word.

' 2. By the Word as ſpoken by Angels, whereby inward abilities
' and diſpoſitions are wrought in the minds of men, in ſome ſort an-
' ſwerable to what is required by the Law of the firſt Covenant. *Thus*
' *the Law is given by the diſpoſition of Angels.*

' 3. By the Word, as ſpoken by the Son himſelf, in his firſt-appear-
ance,

'ance, *Heb.* 1. 2. which is yet but the preparatory work to the *Ba-*
'*ptifm of the holy Ghoſt and of Fire.*

' The *Baptiſm of the holy Ghoſt* is either, a *Baptiſm of Gifts* onely, or
' alſo *of Fire.*

' 1. The firſt is that wherewith the earthly man is capable to be
' *Baptized,* through the *pouring out of the Gifts of the holy Ghoſt.*

' 2 The ſecond is that whereby the natural or earthly man is *Ba-*
'*ptized into conformity with* Chriſt *in his death,* and is made to grow up
' into the incorruptible form of heavenly manhood.

Of theſe four *Baptiſms,*

' The two *Water Baptiſms* have ſerved their ſeaſon, and are gone off
' the Stage.

' The ſingle *Baptiſm of Gifts,* or firſt *Baptiſm of the holy Ghoſt,* hath
' been of late ſomewhat remarkable amongſt us ; and the *Baptiſm of the*
' *holy Ghoſt and of Fire* is haſtening upon us, as a general diſpenſation ,
' wherein the Viſion of God will be ſo plain, that he that runs may
' read it.

' The declining of the two *Water Baptiſms,* deprives not the Saints
' of theſe times of the true uſe of that Ordinance, which is kept up in
' the third, and comprehends all that is now uſeful in the other two,
' in a more heavenly and Spiritual way, leading us yet forward to the
' end they all aim at, which is the very thing it ſelf, contained in the
' fourth and laſt *Baptiſm,* that of *Fire.*

So much in brief of his Judgement as to *Baptiſms.*

He was for *Breaking of Bread* in a way of Chriſtian communion,
and any other uſeful Obſervations, could he have found them practi-
cable in the Primitive Apoſtolical purity, ſpirit, and way, which what
hopes he had of, in any viſible Form allowed by man, while the true
Church is in the Wilderneſs, cannot be difficult to conjecture.

Such Meetings as he found to approach neareſt to the Apoſtolical
Order, (as to liberty of Propheſying one by one, &c. 1 *Cor.* 14.31.)
he moſt approved, and frequented.

Concerning the SABBATH.

HE accounted the *Jewiſh Sabbath* Ceremonious and Temporary,
ending upon the coming of the Son of man, who was *Lord of*
the

the Sabbath day, Mat. 12. 8. And if he had thought that which is commonly observed in the room thereof, to be rather a Magistratical Institution among Christians, in imitation of the *Jewish*, then that which hath any clear appointment in the Gospel, the Apostle would not have him judged for it. *One man (saies he) esteems one day above another: another esteemeth every day alike. Let every man be fully perswaded in his own mind. He that regardeth a day, regardeth it unto the Lord, and he that regardeth not the day, to the Lord he doth not regard it,* Rom. 14. 5, 6. This I can say, he usually took the opportunity of spending more time in exercise and prayer in his family, or other Christian Meetings on that day, than on any other.

And will any yet say he was a Sabbath breaker ? If they do, see what company we may find for him under that imputation, *John* 9. 16. *The Pharisees said, this man is not of God because he keepeth not the Sabbath day.* So *Joh.* 5. 16. *The Jewes did persecute Jesus and sought to slay him, for curing the impotent man at the Poole of* Bethesda, *and bidding him take up his bed and walk, on the Sabbath day.* Yea, with this they joyn another 2d charge, as they reckon, that he had not onely *broken the Sabbath, but said also that God was his Father, therefore they sought the more to kill him,* vers. 18. And John 19. 7. *They answer Pilate, we have a Law, and by our Law he ought to die, because he made himself the Son of God.* What strange work do the Sons of Men make with the Sons of God, with the spirit, wisdom, righteousness, glory and kingdom of God? It was the religious professing *Jew* that Crucified Christ, and persecuted *Paul* where ever he came. *Pilate,* the *Roman* Magistrate would have acquitted Christ; and *Paul* rather appeals to *Cæsar's* Judgement seat, than appear before the *Jewish* Consistory, *Act.* 25.

The true spiritual Sabbath is to be continually kept, as it is charactered by *Esay, Chap.* 58. 13. consisting in a cessation from the single activity, thoughts, words and ways of our spirit, which is but letter, and in the performance of all duty, by power of the communicated spirit of the new creation, springing up in us, which alone is worshipping God in spirit and in truth, after his own heart.

He was for taking all opportunities of *assembling our selves together, to instruct and exhort one another, and so much the more, as we see the day approaching,* (Heb. 10. 25.) *Looking for and hasting unto the comming of that day of God, wherein the Heavens will be dissolved, and the Elements will melt with fervent heat,* 2 Pet. 3. 12.

He was such a right spirited *Latitudinarian* as Paul was, (1 Cor. 9. 20.) *became all things to all men, that by all means he might save some.*

He was against the exercise of a coercive Magistratical power in

Re-

Religion and Worfhip ; and for the fingle Rule, Power, and Authority that Chrift himfelf claimes, as his peculiar prerogative in and
over the hearts and confciences of all men. How grofly inconcin-
nous muft it needs appear even to the common reafon of all mankind,
that fuch as take upon them to be Magiftrates and Rulers, whether the
People will or no, as it often falls out, yea, or though freely chofen,
fhould give the Rule to all others Confciences, in point of Religion,
when they many times have no Religion at all in themfelves, nor any
other Confcience but a dead or feared one, hardened in the moft brut-
ifh vileneffes, that the bafeft of men can be guilty of ? But if the
Magiftrate do plaufibly pretend to fomething of Religion, what a
changable thing will Religion be at this rate ? as fickle as the Magiftrates Judgement, at leaft as his perfon, for the next Ruler may be
of another perfwafion, as this Nation hath experienced off and on, between Popery, and the Proteftant profeffion, in *Hen. 8. Ed. 6.* and the
two Queens, *Mary* and *Elizabeth.*

Concerning PREACHING and PRAYER.

Firft, I ask, are all Preaching and Praying amongft thofe that call
themfelves Chriftians, Ordinances and Inftitutions of Chrift ?
Then the Popifh Mafs, and Jefuites and Friers Sermons are his Ordinances. The Ordinances of Chrift are to be diftinguifhed from all
counterfeit imitations of them, by the fpirit and way of performance,
and by the matter that's delivered, as carrying its own evidence in
the Confciences of the hearers, to be the very truth of God, 1 Cor.
14. 25. 2 Cor. 4. 2. and 5. 11. Satan will be found at laft to have
had the greateft hand in all fuch Ordinances, Praying, Preaching,
and what ever elfe, that for fpirit, manner and matter, are performed
in a way of enmity and contradiction to the true fpiritual believer and
his more excellent way.

The ufual practife of this Sufferer was to fpend an hour or two every evening with his Family, or any other that were Providentially
there, and as much both morning and evening on the firft day. He
was of that truly bounteous, princely, communicative fpirit, noted
in the Spoufe, *Cant. 7. 1. Rich in good works, ready to diftribute, willing
to communicate,* (1 Tim. 6. 18.) to make manifeft the favour of the
knowledge of Chrift (that himfelf had deep and large experience of)
in every place, 2 Cor. 2. 14. His gravity, purity, and chaftnefs of
fpirit was very exemplary. He held out in the mideft of all the late

Apoftacies

Apoſtacies and Changes. He was ſtedfaſt and unmovable, alwayes a-
bounding in the work of the Lord, and his labour was not in vain,
as he well knew, 1 *Cor.* 15. 51. So aſſiduous was he in continual
ſearching of the Scriptures, waiting upon the Lord in Faith and Prayer, for more full diſcoveries of his mind therein, that it was ſaid of
him, *Put him where you will, if he may have but a Bible, he is well enough* ;
as *Janſen*, (of whom the *Janſeniſts* in *France*) reckoned himſelf with
Auſtin.

But what can be ſaid for his Allegorizing the Scriptures ? Here's
another Branch of this Sufferers Charge from men, wherein he ſhares
with the learned *Origen.*

The Charge againſt Allegoriſts, uſually runs at this rate ; *That by
Allegorizing the Scriptures, they carry them quite out of their native ſignificancy and intendment, wreſting and forcing all to their own purpoſe and
conceit, and ſo frame Divinity Romances, what Concluſions, and Bodies
of diſcourſe they pleaſe.* To this miſcarriage, men of the moſt ſoaring,
curious and ſearching capacities are reputed moſt liable. Jeſuite, maſ-
ked Papiſt, no title is thought bad enough for ſuch men, by their ignorant adverſaries, in their blind zeal.

We have but fragments of *Origen*, (that famous Allegorizer, and
diligent Searcher of the Scriptures) and thoſe, tranſlated out of Greek
into Latin, and handed to us by his enemies ; ſo that it may ſeem
dubious, when we read the ſmall remains of his thouſands of Books,
whether we read the genuine Iſſues of his Contemplation, or the ſpu-
rious Interpolations of ſome other man. 'Tis agreed on all hands
by friends and foes, that he was a perſon of more than ordinary tall-
neſs in Underſtanding, and that he did fairly offer at a more pertinent
diſquiſition into the whole bulk of intelligibles, Divine or Philoſophi-
cal, than was uſual. And how was he handled ? what ſaid they of
him ? That he was a temerarious, daring Fanatick, quitting the plain
truths of Scripture, and bewildring himſelf and followers in diabolical Phantaſms, being perverted through his great learning, on which
account he was oft perſecuted and dragg'd along the ſtreets.

Concerning Allegories and Allegorizing the Scriptures.

WHen one thing is ſaid, as Type, Letter, or ſignificant Figure,
through which another, farther and more excellent thing is
meant, and to be underſtood, that is an Allegory, which he that ex-

pounds

pounds, muſt Allegorize. Whether then there be not as much need of Allegorizing the Scriptures as of underſtanding them, or whether there be any other poſſible way of interpreting them, ſo as to diſcover the whole counſel of God therein, detect Satans whole myſtery of iniquity, and render men wiſe unto Salvation, ſhall appear by and by.

There are two ſorts of Allegories in Scripture, perfect and mixt. Perfect are purely alluſory, when all the expreſſions are naturally ſuited to the perſon or thing firſt ſpoken of; but much more accurately, to ſome more excellent perſon or thing that is to be underſtood thereby. An Allegory mixt or but partly alluſory, is when ſome one of the expreſſions onely are applicable to the type, ſome inferiour perſon or thing, and ſome onely to the antitype, quite over-reaching and leaving behinde them the natural or hiſtorical ſhadow, and pitching ſingly and expreſly on the ſpiritual and myſtical ſubſtance, the more excellent perſon or thing that is to be underſtood. Of this ſort we find many Allegories in Scripture, where Chriſt is typified and repreſented by other perſons, who when they are ſpoken of in that capacity and intendment, ſome of the expreſſions out-pace the ſhadow, and are not at all applicable, ſave meerly and ſingly to the very perſon of the Maſſiah. Thus (amongſt others) *Melchizedeck*, (who met *Abraham* returning from the ſlaughter of the Kings, *Chederlaomer* and the reſt) *is ſaid to be without Father, Mother, or deſcent, having neither beginning of dayes, nor end of Life, but made like unto the Son of God, a Prieſt for ever, or of the everlaſting Order*, Heb. 7. 1, 3. This points us back to *Pſal.* 110. 4. and that yet more backward, to *Gen.* 14. 17. If *Sem* here were the type, (as many *Jewiſh* Rabbins aſſirm) thoſe expreſſions, *without Father, Mother, Deſcent, or beginning of dayes*, are not at all applicable to him, but ſingly to Chriſt himſelf. *Sem* was the moſt righteous Son of *Noah*; a Teacher of *righteouſneſs* as *Noah* was, called therefore properly *Melchizedeck*, that is, *King of righteouſneſs*, and *King of Salem*, that is, *Peace*; from the place he was chief Governour of, afterwards called *Jeruſalem*, from *Jireh* and *Salem*, (the place where *Peace* ſhall be ſeen, as tyre of the heavenly *Jeruſalem*) occaſioned by *Abraham's* offering *Iſaac* here on Mount *Moriah*, where *David* ſaw the Angel by *Araunah's* threſhing-floor, and *Solomon* built the Temple, *Gen.* 22. 14. 2 *Sam.* 24. 16, 17. 2 *Chron.* 3. 1. *Sem*, on the accounts mentioned, might fitly be called, *King of righteouſneſs*, and *King of peace*, (Heb. 7. 2.) but much more fitly yet may Chriſt be ſo called, in whom all the righteouſneſs of the firſt Covenant and all the peace that's to be found in the ſecond, kiſſed each

other

other in the second, and were the summe of his Ministery, *Psal.* 85. 10.

But to proceed, shall I ask a bold question ? *What else can the whole Scripture be, as to the saving truths and doctrine thereof, but an Allegory , in case it be presumed to speak intelligibly to humane understanding ?*

The main things signified in Scripture are things spiritual and eternal, things not seen, (2 *Cor.* 4. 18. *Heb.* 11. 1.) not at all immediately and in themselves discernable to meer humane understanding. *The natural man receiveth not the things of the spirit of God : they are foolishness to him ; neither can he know them, because they are spiritually discerned,* 1 Cor. 2. 14. What then is to be done ? Either Christ in his own personal discourses, as also by his Prophets, Apostles and Evangelists, must condescend to gratifie the capacities and understandings of men, by representing spiritual and heavenly things to them, through such natural, earthly Mediums, as are suitable and adæquate objects to humane understanding, or else 'tis as if nothing were said. What is no wayes intelligibly spoken, is as not spoken. Spiritual things in their own naked essence and properties are uncapable of expression by a sound of words. Words, that are the meanes of humane converse, even at their best, and in the original language, are but the proper signifiers of natural things.

Adam by giving Names to the Creatures, *Gen.* 2. 19, 20. discovered his compleat Philosophical prospect into and knowledge of them in their hidden qualities essences and properties, which the dim sighted reason of fallen man, hath since been a pittiful bungler at. *Solomon's* Physicks, and his book of Plants and the three sorts of Animals in air, earth, and water, (Birds, Beasts, and Fishes 1 *King.* 4. 33.) were it yet extant, (as some think it is, in *Presbyter John's* Library at *Amyra*) would doubtless appear a great masterpiece in that kind, transcending all the Wisdom and disquisitions of the learned *Greeks.* *Hebrew* words were fitted to the things they signified. There was a certain connexion between things and words. All other words, as they come less or more near to the *Hebrew,* do more or less significantly represent the things meant by them. The more any Language recedes from the *Hebrew,* the more it is confounded by humane changes and additions, the more obscure and difficult means are the words thereof for conveying the knowledge of things to us. *Homer* and other *Greek* Poets and Philosophers set themselves therefore to Etymological learning, by reducing the primitive words in other languages to their *Hebrew* roots, and then the Derivatives to those Primitives.

This

This they laboured in, as the moſt notable means conducible to the knowledge of things. Then *Chryſippus, Demetrius,* and abundance of others, writ Books of Etymologie. Then the *Latins,* receiving Learning as well as the Empire from the *Greeks,* ſteer the ſame courſe, in order to Etymological diſcipline as the choiceſt means to lead men into the knowledge of things. *Cato, Varro,* and other antient and famous Latines writ many Volumns to this purpoſe. Of later times, on the ſame account, did *Julius Caſar Scaliger,* compoſe a hundred and ten Books *de Originibus.* Then *Joseph Scaliger,* (Son of *Julius*) *Lipſius, Caſaubon,* and many others ſteered the ſame courſe.

But when all comes to all, were we reduced and advanced into the perfect knowledge and exerciſe of the Original Tongue, what then ? All the words thereof at beſt, are but the adæquate ſignifiers of natural, firſt-creation things. All theſe things and words too, are but the types, letters, ſhadows, reſemblances, rhetorical figures, and ſignificant expreſſions of ſpiritual, heavenly, new-creation things. If this be true, what can the main bulk of Scripture be, but an Allegory? Spiritual things expreſſed and ſignified by Natural, and the words thereof from the beginning of *Geneſis* to the end of the *Revelation,* and that in the typical hiſtories, & perſons, as well as in the ſacrifices, ceremonies and parables thereof? What jejune and feeble Interpreters of Scripture then muſt they needs be that cannot Allegorize it, nor therefore endure that others ſhould ?

The whole firſt Creation, without humane words, is a piece of dumbe but ſignificant Rhetorick, to expreſs the ſecond, and things thereof. *The heavens declare the glory of God, and the firmament ſheweth his handy work,* Pſal. 19. *The inviſible things of God from the creation of the World, are ſo intelligibly repreſented and expreſſed to humane underſtanding, by the things that are made, as to leave men without excuſe for neglect of their duty towards God.* Rom. 1. 20. *Raymund, de ſabunde,* ſeems to have ſpoken notably towards the expoſition of this creature Book.

As the firſt whole creation in general, is letter, ſhadow, and expreſſion of the ſecond, ſo more particularly, is the firſt *Adam* in his primitive natural perfection, type, letter, or figure of the ſecond, and of what he himſelf was capable to be made and in all probability was made by a new creation in, the ſecond.

Paradiſe, Canaan, the earthly *Jeruſalem, Mount Sion,* &c. all are Types, Letters and ſignificant Figures of the heavenly. The three ſtories in *Noah's* Ark, (*Gen.* 6. 16.) as alſo the three diſtinct places in *Moſes* his Tabernacle and *Solomons* Temple, *the outward Court, the Holy,* and then *the moſt Holy Place* (or *Holy of Holies*) as they are

Types

Types of Chrift, fo of his followers too, as to the three parts of their compofition, Body, Soul, and Spirit, 1 *Thef.* 5. 23. Man is the Tabernacle of God, the Temple of the Holy Ghoft, 1 *Cor.* 6. 19. His Body is the outward Court, what's done in that, is expofed to the common view of all. His Soul is the holy place, furnifhed with the lamps of the fpirit, excellent fpiritual gifts, (for the raifing and enlightening of humane underftanding) refembled by the feven lamps that ftood over againft the twelve fhew-bread Cakes, (*Exod.* 25.) which fignified the light of the Law, or ruling power of enlightened humane Underftanding, in which the twelve Tribes of *Ifrael* were to walk, who were fhewed, reprefented or propounded before God in the Temple, over againft the Candleftick, but without the *Holy of Holies.* Thofe twelve Cakes (laid on the Table, frefh every week) were therefore called the bread of propofition, and fhew-bread. But the Spirit of Man, or rather, the fpiritual mind is to be the moft holy place, for God himfelf to dwell in.

This is the new-creature principle of marvellous light and eternal Life, by which the Lamp or Candle of fingle humane Underftanding is put out, fwallowed up, and transformed into a better and more excellent, the Light of the Sun. The Lamp of Man's Underftanding, till transformed, has nothing to do within the Veil. The *New-Jerufalem* ftate of Life is fo far from needing Man's intellectual Candle-light, that angelical ftar-light, yea the fun-light of Chrift's own natural perfection is out-fhined there, by the light of his Spiritual form, which is fevenfold brighter. There's no need there of man's Candle, or of the Light of the Sun, or Moon, for the glory of God lightens it, and the Lamb is the light thereof, *Rev.* 21.23. and 21.5.

What are (in general) all the Sacrifices and Ceremonies in the Old Teftament, but fignificant Types or Expreffions of what we are to be or do in the New? The Sacrifices, Beeves, Sheep, and Goats, taught and declared primarily the Sacrifice Chrift was to make in his own perfon; and fecondarily alfo the facrifices, that all his true followers are to make in their perfons; *that holy and acceptable facrifice of our rational Life and powers thereof,* at beft, under the fire-baptifm of God's fpirit, required, *Rom.* 12. 1, 2. *that fo we may be transformed and grow up into the fpiritual powers of eternal Life,* hid with Chrift in God, (as our true intereft and grand concern) without which we cannot be faved.

For perfons; *Adam, Enoch, Noah, Sem, Abraham, Ifaac, Jacob, Jofeph, Mofes, Jofhua, Sampfon, Samuel, David, Solomon,* and many others, were they not Types, Letters, or fignificant Figures of Chrift?

Cain

Cain and *Abel*, *Ishmael* and *Isaac*, *Jacob* and *Esau*, were Letters and Types of two Seeds or Births of Christ in Men; one after the flesh, for the cleaning them from the corruption of Nature; another after the spirit, which delivers them by degrees from corruptibility, as before from corruption, *till mortality be swallowed up of Life*.

Do not the Typical signifiers of Spiritual things, in *Moses* and the Prophets, hold on all along to the very end of the *Revelation*? What's the *New Jerusalem* character'd by at the very last, but by the twelve precious stones in the High Priests Pectoral, which also signified the twelve Tribes of *Israel*? Are any so bruitish as to imagine that those glittering trifles of the East, the *Jasper*, *Saphire*, *Emrald*, *Chrysoprase*, and the rest, are litterally and really to be found in the heavenly *Jerusalem*, *Rev.* 21?

Does not *Paul* Allegorize the history of *Abraham*, *Sara*, *Hagar Ishmael* and *Isaac*, as representing Christ, the true Father of the faithful, and as a twofold Husband to a first and second Covenant-Spouse, which bring forth two sorts of Children, one after the flesh, another after the spirit? The former of these Children (arriving onely at the practical and experimental knowledge of, and conformity with Christ in the flesh, or in his fleshly, changable manifestation) persecutes the other, the true *Isaac*, the spiritual circumcision, that's born of Christ after the Spirit, and brought into a likeness and conformity with him in his unchangable creature state, *Gal.* 4. 22, 31. *Rom.* 8. 1. Christ is that twofold Husband, (mentioned, *Rom.* 7. 1, 2, 3.) married first to a first-Covenant-Spouse; then dies. Unless that first Spouse be content to pass with him under the fire-baptism, drink of his cup, taste of his death, in order to be brought into conformity with him therein, she never meets with him or sees him more, to her comfort. Her Husband is dead, but alive again, *and lives for ever more*, *Rev.* 1. 18. The Wife also must die with him, or she cannot come to live with him for evermore, *2 Tim.* 2. 11. How die, or to what? To the Law, or in the Ruling power of our own natural, first-creation Spirit, activity and principles, however renewed or adorned, that so we may come to live under grace, the law of the spirit, or spiritual, eternal Life, in the ruling activity and principles of that more excellent spirit we receive from Christ, as a transcript of his heavenly manhood in us, by the new creation. This is that onely, under the Government whereof, *Paul* dares warrant us safe from sins ever recovering dominion again, *Rom.* 6. 14. This is that state of Life onely, in which, as married to him that is risen from the dead, we may bring forth fruit unto God, in the newness of the Spirit of our new creation,

not

not in the oldness of the Letter of our first-creation Spirit, as is signified, *Rom.* 7. 4, 5, 6.

The cleansed state of our first-creation Spirit, amounts but to the renewed old man, not the new : but to the circumcision of the heart, in the letter of the first-creation, (not by the spirit of the second) *whose praise is of Man, not of God, Rom.* 2. 29. This makes but the concision, that are of a diminutive, narrow, dogged, snarling nature towards the true spiritual circumcision, or *circumcision of the heart in the Spirit, whose praise is not of men, but of God,* Phil. 3. 2, 3.

There may be a little dark interval in the passage the first wife of Christ adventures to make through death and the grave, in order (and with full assurance of hope) to meet with him again in the better Life of the Resurrection. But she will soon find her own again with usury ; the quitted and resigned activity, and ruling authority of her own corruptible spirit, (which brings her into the true mystical grave and conformity with Christ in his death) in the raised and advanced condition of the same spirit, into harmony with and subjection to Christ, in her superinduced, incorruptible new-creation form and Life. This is the mystical Resurrection the spiritual believer has real fellowship with Christ in, even while yet in the mortal Body. Such fellowship of Christs sufferings, conformity with him in his death, and power of his resurrection, *Paul* lived in the experience and longed for the full accomplishment of, *Phil.* 3. 10, 11.

This passage out of the Life of our first-creation spirit and form, into that of the second, being gradual and leisurely, and the tempter laying all his engines of battery against those that are attempting this way, and Christ for a little moment hiding his face, or withdrawing that kind of comfortable presence, he had afforded the soul in his first-marriage-union with her, that after a little while he may with everlasting mercies have compassion upon her, in the second ; these things considered, 'tis no wonder she sits for a little season, as a disconsolate, fruitless Widow. *But God bids her be of good cheer, for more shall be the Children of the desolate Widow, than of the first married Wife,* Esay 54. 1. And Christ gives that long and most solemn exhortation to his Disciples in the 14, 15, 16, and 17 Chapters of *John,* to this very purpose, to establish and support their hearts in this passage (so dark and dismal to flesh and blood) into the Life and glory of the Resurrection. Upon his fleshly departure and disappearance, as their Bridegroom in that first way, he knew they would have a little mourning season of it, *Mat.* 9. 15. and therefore sets himself to comfort them before hand with the expectation of what was

H

to follow. *You shall have another Comforter*, saies he, meaning himself in the spirit and glory of the Resurrection. *I will not leave you comfortless*, Orphans and Widows, *I will come to you, after a little while*, *Joh.* 14. 16, 18. To the very same purpose is that, *Esay* 54.7, 8. *For a small moment have I forsaken thee, or withdrawn my self from thee*, as to my fleshly and first kind of manifestation to thee, which looks like wrath, *but with great mercies, and everlasting kindness will I gather thee up to my self in my second and more excellent glory, and become thy husband in the new and everlasting Covenant, saith the Lord, thy Redeemer.*

Both these Dispensations are on foot still, Christ yet communicates himself to the souls of men in his fleshly way of manifestation, bringing them into conformity with that holy state of his earthly manhood, which makes the legal Christian, first-covenant professor and Wife of Christ, on this side the cross, the grave, the crown. His withdrawing from them as to this appearance and the fruits of it, is of the same import, as his withdrawing from his disciples when he was actually & personally in the flesh. He was then litterally in the flesh in his own person, but he was even then but mystically in the flesh as to the persons of his disciples, as God manifested in their flesh; & so he is in all that thus experimentally know him but after the flesh now. Their so being in Christ Jesus, knowing of him, and walking in him but after the flesh, does not free or secure them from apostacy, (2 *Pet.*2.20,22.) or condemnation, (*Rom.*8.1.) but the knowing of him, & walking in him after the spirit, as he is the new-Covenant Bridegroom and better Comforter. In this state, they are married to him that is risen in the other, to him only that was made flesh, & with whom they in that fleshly glory, even from him received, must be crucified. How else can they be brought into conformity with him in his death ? It was holy flesh, the natural man in its greatest purity, that was offered up and slain in him. This at the best then, renewed by himself in us, is also to be slain and offered up, under and by the fire-baptism of the new-creature spirit, or spirit of Christ, that performes the new-creation work in man. It must be the holy, reformed, natural state, that must be offered as the true Christian sacrifice, *Rom.* 12.1.2, By this means as we come to be married to Christ in the Resurrection, so we come to be children of the Resurrection, begotten by the force, influence, and benefit of Christ's Resurrection, into a meetness of spirit to be married to him that is risen from the dead, *Luke* 20. 36. 1 *Pet.* 1.3. Such marriage there is even in the Resurrection. Such a state of the resurrection there is while we are yet in this mortal body. The spiritual man, who lives in the spirit, knowes Christ in spirit, and walks

after

after the spirit, (*Gal.5.25. Rom.8.1.*) is really and actually, thou[gh] but gradually, in this myſtical and beſt kind of Reſurrection, while ye in the earthly body. The new creature, he that lives the life, and in the ſpirit of the new creation, lives in the Reſurrection.

The Reſurrection of our Bodies (after the death of them) at laſt is not to be put in the ballance with the priviledges of this ſpiritual Reſurrection, while we are yet in the earthly body. The ſpiritual, new-creation Life we are riſen into, is eternal Life. But millions of men will find their bodily riſing to be but a Reſurrection into eternal death, and ſhame, everlaſting puniſhment and contempt, *Dan.* 12. 2, *Mat.* 25. 46.

But let's take a little further view of Chriſt's firſt-Covenant Wife and Children, what they may do, and what may become of them ? They may play the harlot with that very beauty and comelineſs, that very firſt-creation kind of glory and perfect righteouſnes of the Law, that Chriſt has put upon them, called God's comelineſs, and yet their own beauty, becauſe it beautifies and adorns but that ſelfiſh ſtate of the firſt-creation, *Ezek.* 16. 14, 15. What comes of them for playing the harlot with this, and oppoſing thereby the more excellent diſpenſation and glory, that comes from the ſame Redeemer in his new-creation work ? They muſt be judged by Chriſt as thoſe that ſhed blood and break wedlock are judged, as Murtherers, and Adultereſſes *verſ.* 38. This they come to.

Not unlike to this, is that, *Eſay* 63. 8, and 10. *He ſaid, ſurely they are my People, Children that will not lie, ſo he was their Saviour. But they rebelled, and vexed his holy ſpirit : therefore he turned to be their enemy, and fought againſt them.* There are a People, a Wife, Children, Members of Chriſt after the fleſh, that ſtand liable to forfeit all their priviledges and intereſt in him, by apoſtacy, and then Chriſt becomes their enemy. *As he delighted before, to deliver and ſave them, rejoyced over them to do them good and multiply them ; ſo now he will rejoyce over them to deſtroy them, bring them to nought, and root them out of the land he gave them,* Deut. 28. 63. If the tranſgreſſion, the apoſtacy be general, ſo will the Judgement be too; *That which he hath built, he will break down; that which he hath planted he will pluck up, even this whole land,* Jer. 45. 4.

This was the caſe between God and thoſe religious *Jews*, that lived and walked but in the wavering principles of the firſt-covenant. They would be ever and anon ſtarting aſide, like a deceitful Bow. They were not of the right, or new-covenant heart : Their ſpirit was not ſtedfaſt with God ; and when they failed of their duty, he let looſe one enemy or another ſtill upon them. *Then they remembred that God was their Rock, and the high God their Redeemer. Nevertheless they did but flatter him with their mouth, and lied unto him with their tongues, for their heart was not right with him, neither were they stedfast in his Covenant ;* or they were not in that new, stedfast Covenant with him, *that is established in all things and sure.* And *God will not be mocked ;* he knows how to handle them. All this over and over, and much more is to be seen, *Psal.* 78. 8. 35. 36. 37. and 57. *verses, &c.*

And *Jer.* 3. 14. The same People in the same breath, are reckoned both the Children and Wife of Christ, though back-slider ; *Turn again, O back-sliding Children, saith the Lord, for I am married to you.*

The Children that are born but of that changeable seed of the first-creation in Christ, hate and persecute them that are born after the spirit, (or of the incorruptible seed of Christ in spirit, as he is head of the new-creation, in which he becomes, that word or image of God, that lives and abides in them for ever) and then they backslide and lose what they have in the first-covenant, *Mat.* 13. 12. 1 *Pet.* 1. 23, 25. *Esay* 40. 6, 8. These two Seeds, Births, Children, as they are typified by *Ishmael* and *Isaac, Gal.* 4. so by *Cain* and *Abel, Esau* and *Jacob,* and other pairs of brothers. *Aaron* and *Moses* rather typify the natural and spiritual Saint in the glory of the Resurrection, in the new and everlasting Covenant, as above described. But *Cain* and *Abel, &c.* signifie the fleshly, or first-Covenant worshipper, of the one party, and both the spiritual, new-covenant worshippers (whether of the single or double portion) on the other.

Cain and *Abel, &c.* may be Allegorized into this spiritual significancy and reach, as mystically indigitating and presenting to us the distinction of the fleshly and spiritual Worshipper, the reformed natural, and the transformed, or spiritual man; the first and second Covenant Saint. The elder often turns malignant, envies, hates, persecutes the younger ; he after the flesh, him after the spirit. They may with good warrant also be Allegorized into a narrower compass yet, as typifying the natural and spiritual man, flesh and spirit, in the same individual Saint, that is born of Christ after the spirit, and yet not quite rid of flesh, which will be lusting against the spirit in him, that is his sin ; as the spirit also will be lusting against that flesh, which is his duty, *Gal.* 5. 17. Not onely corrupt nature, filthy flesh, but renewed nature, holy Flesh, goodliness of flesh, that that was born of Christ after the flesh, will be envying and lusting against, striving and contesting with that in man, that is born of the same Christ, after the spirit, *John* 3. 6. What struggle they for ? what's the matter, that enlightened reason and the marvellous light of Faith, the renewed

old

old man and the new, nature and grace can't agree? They have the
same Father, Chrift; they tumble in the fame womb, the foul of man.
This is it; they ftruggle like *Jacob* and *Efau* in the fame womb, in
the fame perfon, for the dominion, the Scepter. The queftion in debate between them is, who fhall be king? The renewed enlightened
natural mind (which yet is but flefh, though holy flefh) thinks it felf fit
to rule and give Law to the whole perfon; would keep all under the
dominion of the Law of the firft creation. The fpirit of the new creation claims all this as its right, though the latter and younger birth,
(as reafon alfo had been to fenfe) yet the true heir of the crown, and
the elder muft ferve or become fubject to this younger. The renewed
firft-creation fpirit and ftate of life, glory, and freedom in man, finally
refufing, refifting and perfecuting the more excellent, new-creature
Life, fpirit, and glorious liberty of the fons of God in the fecond,
amounts to no lefs than the fin unto death, the fin againft the Holy
Ghoft, or Chrift in Spirit.

This fame myftery is typified, and by no other way but Allegorizing, is to be fetched out of the hiftory of *Hagar* and *Sarai*. *Hagar* has
the ftart of *Sarai* at fruitfulnefs, fhe is firft with Child, *Sarai* is yet
barren. But *fing O barren,* (faies Chrift in this fenfe) *that didft not
bear, more fhall be thy Children, greater thy fruitfulnefs at laft.* God
fwore to *Abraham upon his offering up Ifaac, and not with-holding his
onely Son, that bleffing he would blefs him, and multiply his feed as the ftars
of Heaven, and as the fand on the Sea-fhore; and that in his feed fhould all
the Nations of the earth be bleffed,* Gen. 22. 16, 18. and Gen. 15. 3,
6. This promife relates to *Ifaac,* not *Ifhmael*; and to *Sarai,* not *Hagar*; and to *Abraham* not *Abram.* *Ab-ram* fignifies *high Father.*
This was all the name he had while he had but *Ifhmael* onely, (Gen.
16.) but when *Ifaac,* the promifed Seed is coming, the fyllable *Ha,*
or letter *H,* (being the fift fyllable or letter of *Hamon,* a multitude)
is added to *Abram* and *Sarai,* fo he is called, *Abraham* (Gen. 17. 5.)
fhe *Sarah,* v. 15. *Abraham* by this addition, fignifies *high Father of a
multitude* (of nations.) and for *Sarah,* as type of the *New-Jerufalem*
Spoufe of Chrift, fee her numberlefs Children, her *Ifaac's,* Rev. 7.
4, 9. We find here firft, *a hundred forty four thoufand fealed ones; that
are the peculiar Bride and fpoufe of Chrift,* refembled by *Sarah, and then
a numberlefs multitude,* of the lower rank of everlaftingly glorified
men, *that ftand about the Throne, Children of the Bride-chamber, and
friends of the Bridegroom and the Bride.*

But lets review, that Allegory, firft in Hiftory, then Myftery. *Sarai* gives her maid *Hagar* to *Abram* to be his wife, Gen. 16. 3. *Hagar*

con-

conceives, and presently the fruitful servant despises her barren mistress, *verf.* 4. *Sarai* complaines of her to *Abram*. *Abram* bids her handle her as she pleased. *Sarai* deales hardly with her, and she flies for't, *verf.* 5, 6. The Angel of the Lord finds her and advises her to return and submit her self under her Mistresses hands, *v.* 9. Here's the History. Deny Allegorizing, and there will be no Mystery in it, and then what an insignificant story may this seem ? Did not all these things happen for ensamples? were they not written for our admonition, upon whom the ends of the World are come ? 1 *Cor.* 10. 11. Is not *all Scripture given by inspiration of God, for doctrine, reproof, correction, instruction in righteousness ?* 2 *Tim.* 3. 16. What doctrine, reproof, or instruction can we receive to any purpose, from this, and abundance of like Scriptures, if Allegorical interpretation be carped at and exploded, and insipid litteral glosses, owned and adhered unto, as the onely sence, reach, and intendment thereof ?

With your leave then, let us try by the Allegorizing engine, our spiritual discerning if we have it, to give birth to the mystical sence and rich significancy which this history carries in the womb of it.

As soon as *Hagar* saw she had conceived, the next news we hear, is, her Mistress is despised in her eyes. Behold here the proper Character of the first-covenant wife of Christ. She is warm, flourishing, prosperous and fruitful in a way of outward Ordinances, and also in working Righteousness, in the goodliness of Flesh, in a wisdom, glory and comeliness, that Christ himself hath wrought in her, and put upon her. She is wise, strong, and honourable in Christ, and makes no scruple but this will alwayes hold, thinks her mountain so strong that she shall never be moved. On this account, the true new-covenant spouse of Christ, the right new-spirited Saint is despised and slighted, as a weak, foolish, contemptible thing, no body at Ordinances and righteousness in her way, which she experiences to be the way of Christ, finding the fruits of his presence in it. Thus was it between *Paul* with others, and some of the *Corinthian* Church. Both were married to, and interested in Christ, but by different Covenants. *We are fooles,* (faies he) *for Christ's sake, ye are wise in Christ. We are weak, ye strong : Ye honourable, we despised,* 1 *Cor.* 4. 10. and 2 *Cor.* 10. 12. We dare not make our selves of the number, or compare our selves with such as commend and compare themselves with one another of the same principles and persuasions, and so applaud themselves in one another, by their mutual self-deceivings. The true spiritual Elder, *Paul* the aged, he is in body with this flourishing,

youth-

youthful, warm, legal-spirited generation. The main business he has to say for himself, is *a Life hid with Christ in God*, and worshipping God in spirit and truth. This they reckon as nothing but discourse, fiction, foolishness. But be it known, those that with *Paul* are weak, foolish, and despised for Christ, are better than such as he there implicitly reproves and taxes with folly, that yet he acknowledges were wise, strong and honourable in Christ. Such foolish, weak, despised ones of Christ, as *Paul* was, are they that will quite confound the wise, the mighty, the honourable. The things that are not, shall bring to nought the things that are ; and no flesh with all its ornament, righteousness, and wisdom, shall enter into Christ's kingdom, or glory in his presence, 1 *Cor.* 1. 27, 29. And as the spiritual saint is thus handled by the fleshly, so is the spirit or spiritual part in the same saint dealt with by the fleshly. Holy flesh, the renewed natural mind, will be despising the feeblness of the spiritual (while weak and low) and jusling it out of the Throne, as to its interesting it self, as the ruling Principle at working righteousness and worshiping God.

Having thus in *Hagar* taken notice of the malapert, proud, insulting carriage of the first-covenant Wife or Spirit, in different saints, or in the same, against the right spirit of the second, through confidence in the works of the Law, (or works performed in the ruling activity of their own renewed mind) let us proceed to other branches and observables in the said Allegory before us. *Abram* as a type of Christ, delivers up *Hagar* into *Sarai's* hand; *Sarai* dealt hardly with her, so she should. *Hagar* fled ; 'twas her sin. What signified *Sarai's* hard dealing with her ? Persecution ? No ; the Spirit of Christ, the fire-baptism, the strait gate, that will not suffer flesh and blood to enter into the kingdom of God, this it signified. *Hagar's* flight then imports the declining and refusal of all these. The legal spirited professor, confident in the works of the Law, will endure none of these things. They are all a sad story, a hard saying to him. His usual way of waving them, (if urged and hard put to't) is to call them Blasphemy, and the Witnesses thereof Blasphemers ; and on he goes very secure in his doatage. But say or think man what he will, this is Christ's way, he gives up the fleshly worshipper, and the fleshly part in the true spiritual worshipper, to the spiritual, to be humbled and abased, broken and subdued, hardly dealt with, crucified, slain and offered up in sacrifice, under the power of the Cross of Christ or fire-baptism of his spirit, typified by *Sarai*. There's no entring into the kingdom, but we must pass thorow this fire, this tribulation, this bruising of the inmost part of the natural man, his very spirit and rational powers, whatever

ever becomes of his outward, as to persecution from the world. *Hagar* despised *Sarai*, *Ishmael* mocked *Isaac*, (*Gen.*21.9.) this was persecution. Usually, those that are taken out of the world, (or worldly, first-creation constitution and frame of spirit within them, by the fire-baptism) do so differ even from the professing part of the world, in their very religion or union with God by another Covenant, and in their more excellent way of worshipping God, in spirit and truth, not letter and form, that they seldom or never scape the external branch of the cross and baptism of blood, through the rage & enmity of man against this new-creature marvellous light and life, that is springing up in those whom God is transforming into another nature. But let men take it how they will, the cross, the fire-baptism, we must come to, within us, first or last, or we cannot be saved.

The fleshly worshipper either yields to this fiery doctrine, ministry and way, or resists, or flies. If He get the magistrates sword, on his side, (as if *Hagar* could have got *Abram* to side with her against *Sarai*) then he'l make the messenger of such tydings fly, *Sarai* must fly or suffer under *Hagar*. Men decry it for heresie, blasphemy, and persecute him that talkes at such a rate. Thus Christ himself was served by the zealous, legally religious *Jew*. 'Twas the religious, professing party of the *Jewes* that crucified Christ, and would take no answer, hear no reason or argument from *Pilate*, the Heathen Magistrate, to the contrary. But if the sowre Legalist neither will yeild, nor can brutishly resist this hard doctrine by outward force or persecution, then he takes *Hagars* course, flies it. And what then? He every where decries this spiritual doctrine of the cross and fire-baptism, for heretical, dangerous and seductive, wishing all to beware how they meddle with such books, converse with such persons, or listen to such dangerous suggestions. While toleration lasted, I have experimented this to be the too general frame of spirit amongst professors in this nation, who have evidently chosen rather to venture a persecution of their own doctrine and persons, than endure this and the assertors thereof. Here's the mystery of *Hagars* flight. The Angel of the Lord advises her to return, and submit her self to her Mistris. In her, all these timerous, fugitive, envious, legal-spirited Christians, that are leavened with the leaven of the Pharisees, are admonished to entertain better thoughts of the *New-Jerusalem* Spouse, resembled by *Sarai*, and submit themselves to her doctrine and more excellent way: to the cross, the fire-baptism, the spirit of Christ, the covenant of grace, *Sarai*. This is the doctrine, the reproof, the correction, the instructi-

on

on in everlasting righteousness, which that History, that Allegory is pregnant with.

Christ with both his Covenant Spouses and Children, are allegorically expressed by Husband and Wife, Father and Children, Head and Members, with the like. Such expressions are interpretable into mystery, by a due considering the duties and offices of such Relations in the letter. And as Christ himself, so *Paul* and others, are (in way of Allegory) called Fathers of such as by them *are begotten to Christ, through the Gospel,* 1 Cor. 4. 15. and *verf.* 17. he calls *Timothy, his beloved Son;* so 1 *Tim.* 1. 2. 2 *Tim.* 1. 2. and 2. 1. They are also called *Pastors, Mothers,* and *Nurfes* to both the Seeds or Children of Christ, in their kind, 1 *Thef.* 2. 7, and 11. *Gal.* 4. 19. In another respect, every true believer, as he becomes the Child, so is the Mother of Christ, as with pangs and throw's towards the new birth, (so the loss, and at last, death of the single activity of his fleshly mind and heart) Christ in spirit be formed and brought forth in him, by him.

Then comes the Life of Faith, the true reigning, *New-Jerusalem* Principle, (in which reason has its resurrection) the kingdom of heaven within him. He ownes Christ in his heavenly headship, as his Lord and King, expressed (*Cant.* 3. 11.) by setting the Crown upon his head, owning a willing subjection to the Law of the Spirit of Life, in this day of espousal to him, which is a day of gladness to Christ, good men and angels, *Luk.* 15. 10. The believer is the wise Virgin, who becomes at same time the Mother and Spouse of Christ, brings forth her own Lord and King in Spirit, as the Virgin *Mary* brought him forth in Flesh. In the very day that Christ is thus brought forth in and by the believer, they are espoused together by the new and everlasting Covenant. The believer owns Christ, as Head, Husband and King. Upon this, Christ rejoyces, Angels rejoyce, the Believer himself rejoyces, *with joy unspeakable and full of glory.* 'Tis a solemn thanksgiving day, a day of gladness of the heart unto them all. Thus in a various sence is Christ Father and Son of the Spiritual believer, and the believer the Mother and Child of Christ. Christ is Head, Lord, King, Husband, Brother, Son, Fellow-heir to believers. They are Body, Subjects, Wife, Children, Members, Fellow-heirs to him. All these expressions are Allegorical, borrowed from natural Relations to signify spiritual Mysteries of love, union and converse between Christ and his Church ; One thing is said, and a farther, more excellent thing meant. The Apostle having spoken of the duties of Husbands and Wives towards one another, winds up all into this, as his main intendment, the spiritual marriage-union between Christ and his

Church.

Church, This (faies he) is a great myftery, or myftically fignifies a far greater thing, *concerning Chrift and his Church, Ephef. 5. 22, 23.*

The *Revelation*, in a manner all along, is a defcription of heavenly things by fuch earthly Mediums, fuch Allegorical types, and expreffions as are borrowed out of *Mofes Pentateuch*, in the Tabernacle and Temple-worfhip. And of Chrift himfelf tis faid, *that without a parable,* (a fimilitude, an allegory) *he fpake not unto the people, Mat.* 13. 34. *Mark.* 4. 34. Muft not he then that truly expounds thofe parables, allegorize them ? But how muft he do it ? Parable in the *Hebrew* is a word that fignifies fharpnefs, as proceeding from a fharp wit, and needing the like to interpret it. That fharp wit muft be no lefs than fpiritual difcerning, and that ftrong and well exercifed too, or Scripture Riddles will be too hard for it. One or two more of thefe, let us take notice of. *Sampfons* typical Riddle together with the *Philiftines* expofition, does yet want an expofition. Out of Chrift, the ftrong Lion of the tribe of *Judah*, (as the eater, or facrificer of the natural man in himfelf and us, by the fire-baptifm) comes the choiceft meat, the fweeteft hony-comb of all ; that that feeds and brings us into a conformity with him in his death and refurrection. Chrift ha's left his own interpretation of the parable of the Sower and Seed, of the Tares, and the like, upon record in Scripture, and yet who underftands them ? how much do men yet need an expofition of thofe very expofitions ?

Paul tells us *Hagar* and *Sarai* are an Allegory, two Covenants, *Gal.* 4. 24. Then he myftically expounds *Ifhmael* and *Ifaac* into two Seeds of Chrift, (the true antitypical Father of the faithful) in both Covenants. He declares moreover, that he that's born of this Father, but after the flefh, will perfecute him that's born of the fame Father after the fpirit : Even fo it is now , *verf.* 29.

Notwithftanding this Allegorizing expofition given by *Paul*, how little does the felf-confident, legal Chriftian hold himfelf concerned in the character of him that is born after the flefh ? How verily does he conceit himfelf to be the other, that's born after the Spirit ? Hereupon he juftles out the fpiritual man indeed, for a Fanatick wrangler, a fool, a madman, a blafphemer, any thing, that he lifts to call him, *Hof.* 9. 7. At laft, he comes to this downright wilful refolution, (as *Efau* againft *Jacob*, and as the profeffing religious *Jewes* againft Chrift, in the very fame cafe) *Come, this is the heir, let's kill him, and the inheritance fhall be ours.* They imagine this vain thing, even to take the kingdom of Heaven by force, from the right owner. But if this eager-fpirited generation would but give themfelves leifure to con-
                                                                    fider

fider this and the like Scriptures, they might see, that they that are
charactered here by him that's born after the flesh, are a holy seed of
Christ, that have Covenant interest in him, and actual communion
with him. They are Children of *Hagar*, or the first Covenant. One
would wonder how they should miss this. But they shuffle it off upon
the *Jews*, that were under the ceremonious dispensation of the Law,
and so rid their hands of it. Is there no legal Christian then? is there
no danger of the leaven of the Pharisees under the outward dispensa-
sation of the Gospel? Yes, say they, but that lies onely at their door,
who depend upon their own personal operations for their acceptance
and communion with God, not on the imputed righteousness of the
Redeemer. I interrogate, When *Paul* describes his Pharisaical state,
he tells us, *he was, touching the righteousness which is in the Law,
blameless.* Could this be, unless by the comeliness of God put upon
him, or perfect righteousness of that kind, from Christ imputed to
him? *Ezek.* 16. 14. Was he a legal *Jew*? was he any more than a
moral Heathen else? But if what is abovesaid will not help to rectify
this mistake, I shall be somewhat hopeless of being instrumental to
your relief, in this point.

'Tis sad to see the self-pleasing interpretations of this and the like
Scriptures, all along the Bible, so universal and unscrupled, amongst
all sorts of Professors; an epidemical mistake. How to lift them out
of the mire of these their own self-bewildring imaginations, who
knowes, but Christ? *Flesh, and the carnal mind that's enmity to God,*
(*Rom.* 8. 7.) must never be of any larger compass, or farther significan-
cancy with them, than corrupt, polluted, debauched, degenerate nature, *dead in trespasses and sins*; or at best, but the moral heathen, with
some glimmering revivals and sparklings of rational Light and Life.
But as for their part, they are in Christ, they experience actual communion with God; and once in Christ, for ever in Christ. A company
of such false Maxim's I have too often heard in discourse with them,
gleaned up from mis-interpreted Scriptures, in which they are so confident and secure, that there's no speaking to them to the contrary.
They have not a hearing ear, to listen to the voice of any spiritual charmer, charm he never so wisely. The cunning old serpent rings another bell in their ear, that deafs them to the voice of the true watchman, whose business is to warn these legally righteous Christians as
well as the prophane Heathen, of the danger of their condition, *Ezek.*
18. and *Chap.* 33. 13, &c. Men that are righteous, and that in Christ,
will not dream that this warning concerns them. As they serve that
Allegory, (*Gal.* 4.) so other Scriptures of like import, as *John* 3. 6.

That

That which is **born of the** *flesh, is flesh ; and that which is born of the spirit, is spirit.* Flesh here, with them must be nothing but the corrupt nature, the polluted natural condition ; by which shift, renewed nature must pass for spirit, and the spiritual man indeed must be excluded out of every Synagogue for an Apostate , a spiritual wanderer from the plain Truths of the Gospel ; so they call the greatest Mysteries.

The Gospel and things of it, spiritual things, are utterly unintelligible and undiscernable to the natural understanding, which, of what extent it is, hath bin described. Yet I have oft heard men of very inferior natural capacities, with great confidence assert, *That the main Truths of Gospel, are familiar, plain, easie, obvious things to common ununderstanding* ; I grant, they must be so indeed, if they understand them.

Does not Christ plainly signify, that *one sort of branches in him the true Vine, may be cut off, and cast into the fire, Joh.* 15 .6. and that after high illumination, and partaking of the Holy Ghost, in the gifts thereof ? *Heb.* 6. 4, 8. Does not the great Apostle preach the same doctrine at large, *Rom.* 11 ? We find there, that the natural branches, that had one sort of Being and Life in the good olive tree, (Christ) partaking of the root and fatness thereof, were yet broken off among the *Jewes*, and sinners from among the *Gentiles*, renewed in the principles of natural perfection, and put in their room ? These among th *Gentiles*, that have but this kind of engrafture into this good Olive tree, are warned of the same liableness to apostatize and be cut off, as the *Jewes* were, in *verf.* 17, 21. The natural branches among the *Gentiles* make but the mystical earthly *Jerusalem* which may come to be the spiritual *Sodom*, and *Egypt*, the very same kind of cross spirited generation as those were, amongst whom as our Lord was crucified long since in his own person, so will he again be crucified signally in his two Witnesses, *Revel.* 11. 8. at the close of the persecution day.

The main ground for that most false Maxime, *Once in Christ and for ever in Christ*, (which must, by the way, needs argue that there is no such thing as apostacy) so far as I could ever hear from the deluded assertors of it, is 1 *Cor.* 5. 17. *If any man be in Christ, he is a new creature* ; *old things are passed away, all things are become new.* The legalist so triumph in this Scripture, that he can hardly tell what ground he stands on. He stands on the sand, and thinks he is on the rock. Let the words be well eyed in our common *English* translation, and you'l find [*be*] and [*he is*] in different Characters, which intimates them to be but the Translators superadditions and glofs. Strip

the

the Text of these Redundancies, and the words run thus. *If any man in Christ a new creature, old things are passed away*, (or the old man, flesh and blood at its best, is put off) the ruling activity of first-creation Principles, however renewed, ceases. Some render it thus; *If any man be in Christ, let him be a new creature* ; let him be sure he has that second, more excellent, new-covenant birth and being in Christ, that constitutes and makes him a new creature, and not onely the renewed old creature, the natural or first-creation man. The words to me seem to carry this sence, *If any man in Christ be a new creature, all things are become new.* This implies a being in Christ, that does not amount to the constitution of the new-creature, but only to an experimental knowing of him after the flesh, not after the spirit, as is also implied, *Rom.* 8. 1. which secures not from apostacy or condemnation, 2 *Pet.* 2. 20, 22.

One Scripture Allegory more I will mention, because 'tis prophetical, and more nearly concerns the present season, than is commonly believed, *Cant.* 3. 6. *Who is this that commeth out of the Wilderness, like pillars of Smoke, perfumed with Myrrhe and Frankincense, with (or above) all the powders of the Merchant?* In the *Jewish* Worship *Myrrh* typified *death and resurrection*; *Frankincense, Mediation.* The Question is put by strangers, enemies, or else by some friends and well-wishers, daughters of the heavenly *Jerusalem,* (though hitherto somewhat captivated to the formes and wayes of the earthly) who seem to stand gazing and admiring at this new unthought of Church , consisting of the risen Witnesses, (*Revel.* 11.) when they shake off their mourning guise, put off their sackcloth, and begin to stand upon their feet, in the unresistible power and wisdom of Faith. Pillars of smoke ascend from them through the fire-baptism, whereby they are a sweet favour to God, as perfumed with the Mediation of Christ, and with conformity to him in his death and resurrection. The earthly *Jerusalem professors* will be amazed at this, their hearts failing them for fear of that which they never would before be induced to regard or own. Then will those expressions in the book called, *The Wisdom of Solomon* be suitable for the hitherto deluded inhabitants of the Earth, (of all sorts) to take notice of, *Chap.* 5. 1, 9. *Then shall the righteous man stand in great boldness before the face of such as have afflicted him, and made no account of his labours. When they see it, they shall be troubled with terrible fear, and amazed at the strangeness of his Salvation, so far beyond all that they looked for. Then they shall repent, and groan for anguish of spirit, and say within themselves, this was he whom we had sometimes in derision. We fools counted his Life madness, and his end to be without honour. How is he numbred among the Children of God, and has his lot among the Saints?*

Saints? Therefore we have erred from the way of truth. We have wearied our selves in a way of wickedness and destruction. What hath pride profited us, or riches which our vaunting brought us? All these things are passed away as a shadow.

I cannot willingly let go this business of Allegories, till I have told you that all mankind, considered as in their first-creation make and constitution, are an Allegory. They and all they have, at best estate, are but type, shadow, figure of the spiritual man, that is of the new-creation frame. Their glory, wisdom, righteousness, are but shadows of his, and to be done away. Their, goodness is but a morning cloud, and as the early dew it goeth away, *Hos. 6. 4.* Their wisdom is comparatively but foolishness, and their lesser shadowy glory of the Law, (or ruling powers of their first-creation state) is to be done away, as no glory, by reason of the glory that excelleth, in the spiritual man, *2 Cor. 3. 10. Every man at his best estate,* (renewed, enlightened, gifted man) *is altogether vanity.* He was so in his first-creation, he is so in his greatest renewal. Nothing below the new-creature, the spiritual man, is exempted from this title, in Scripture. Vanity is of larger extent than sin. Any thing that will vanish, that is corruptible and perishable, is vanity. The whole first-creation is vanity, and was sowne in corruption, that is, was a corruptible, not a corrupt thing. Angels and Men, the choicest flowers in it, have withered and corrupted their way before God, and so lost that life of communion with God, wherein they were created. The natural body, that's interpreted to be the first *Adam* at best, with his living soul, (*1 Cor. 15. 44, 45.*) is but the vile body, or inferiour, first-creation state of man, that is to be transformed into the likeness of Christ's glorious body, in the new-creation, *Phil. 3. 21.*

How too generally and universally are professors (in all variety of form, judgement and way) lodg'd in a kind of invincible conceitedness, that the revival of first-creation principles and life in them, towards a conformity with *Adam* in innocency, or Christ in the flesh, is the only attainment beyond which they are not concerned to look? All this is but the natural or vile body. Yet how strangely are men captivated to this day, under this embondaging and incorrigible dotage? Every thing that they are, have, see, or desire, while in this case, can be no other than vanity. Their wisdom, glory, righteousness, all are vanity; vanishing things. Men that are vanity, love vanity; outward, visible vanities, that gratify sense; inward vanities that gratify reason. Man's reason is vanity. How oft have we heard and seen mens reason to vanish, before their bodies? All the inmost
thoughts

thoughts of mans heart, all the more overly imaginations of his fancy, all the reasonings and desires springing from both, are vanity. There is nothing man is or does, till he come within the sphere of the spiritual world, the new creation, but it's vanity. Outward visible Thrones, Crownes, Scepters, great Revenews, and all possible flourishing accommodations of bodily life, amounts but to the more glittering, splendid sort of bruitish vanities, and often fall to the share of beasts, the vilest & most bruitish men. Rational parts, together with their advance and ornament by acquired and infused humane Learning, Arts, Sciences, excellent Gifts, the tongue of Men and Angels, these are far choicer, and more eligible things, than the above mentioned Lordly circumstances of bodily or bruitish Life, and yet these all fall within the compass and sphere of vanities, vanishing things, *as sounding brass and tinckling Cymbals.* Nothing below the very seed of spiritual, new-creation Life, gets out of the sphere of vanity. Those that have all possible outward and inward gallantry too of the natural man or vile body, are exhibited to us, as to their duration and continuance, under the allegory or parable of a green bay tree. They may be in great power, spreading themselves like a green bay tree, but they soon pass away and are not; we may seek them while we will, their place can no more be found.

What a stage of the choicer sort of vanities, (glory, righteousness, wisdom of man, excellent gifts, high illuminations, dexterity of expression, tongues of men and angels) has *England* been these twenty years? We have seen a praying Ministry, Parliament, Army, going forth in a way of Righteousness, in Covenant with God, and no weapon that was formed against them could prosper. No Army, no Counsel could stand before them. All opposition proved a feeble, infatuated thing. What is all come to ? *They were not stedfast in the Covenant, they started aside like a deceitful Bow. Their righteousness vanished as a morning cloud, an early dew;* and the bodies of the chief Leaders in that Ministry, Parliament, and Army, are in their graves. All is vanished, save a few faithful, chast-spirited men, who for being true to their trust, stedfast in their Covenant and undertake, have been and are daily delivered up *as Lambs for the slaughter,* by their apostatized friends. What a Scene of vanities and shadows is this earth at best ? how little worth minding ? *Things seen, things temporal, are the things that are not. Things eternal, things not seen, are the onely things that are.* Man thinks quite otherwise. That matters not.

Did we truly know our selves, we might the more easily be perswaded in another sence, not to know our selves. If we knew but the vanity of our whole first-creation state, & the goodliness thereof, comparatively with what we are capable to be made in the second, we would not know our own souls, no though we were perfect, yet would we despise our life, *Job* 9.21. All the wisdom, righteousness, thoughts, reasonings, imaginations and desires thereof, are vanity. Did we thorowly know this, we would be content to resign all ; *not think our own thoughts, speak our own words, do our own works, find our own pleasures, and so enter into the true mystical Sabbath, and rest of God, in the new creation.* If we lose the temporary life and righteousness of our first-creation, we shall find it again with usury in the eternal Life and everlasting righteousness of the second. If not, we shall lose it for ever, in the eternal or second death. If we lose our litteral, shadowy Life and Image of God, received in the first creation, we shall find it again with usury in the mystical substance, spirit and truth of the second. Then, let the letter and figure of Scripture be interpreted into spirit and truth, we shall know what to make of it ; not before. Could man be content to be baffled out of himself, allegorized out of his first-creation shadow, into spirit and truth ; he would be content, Scripture should be so allegorized too, out of its letter and shadow, into spirit and truth.

The true allegorizing interpreter of the Scriptures, does and must expound them into things not seen, things eternal, into a sence, quite out of the reach and discerning of all the sense and reason in mankind. Spiritual things, things eternal, are discernable onely to the eye of faith, the spiritual discerning, the hearing ear. He only that hath this ear, will hear *what the spirit saith unto the Churches,* Heb. 11. 1. *Rev.* 2. 29. 1 *Cor.* 2. 14.

Men then do seem concerned in this point ; for the allegorical sence of Scripture, leaves them quite at a loss. If they will not therefore be content to lose their sense and reason, with a full assurance and stedfast perswasion that they shall find them again with usury, in conjunction and harmony with the new-creature Life of saving Faith ; let them make their best of them for their defence in this case. Let them produce their strong reasons, let them come forth in the greatest pomp of Argument and Eloquence they can, against allegorizing. Unless they can afford more pertinent interpretations of the 'bove mentioned Scriptures and in any others, without allegorizing ; what they say in this matter is not much to be valued. They will find themselves as far wide from understanding the Scriptures, in any other way, as *Jobs* three friends were from understanding his case : and my answer to such colourable reasonings, shall be that which *Job*
has

has furnished me with; *How forcible are right words? but what doth your arguing reprove?* Job. 6. 25.

This yet must be granted; that the devil (who is a most dextrous and skilful imitator of Christ in all his dispensations, by feigned resemblances of truth) will also strike in at this allegorizing way of interpreting the Scriptures. He will labour hereby to the utmost, to confound and bewilder both teachers and hearers, that take and own this course. He will (if possible) run them all a ground in a thousand mistakes, and false conclusions. But he never puts himself to this trouble, till he finds men will be allegorizing; as neither will he make use of the choicest flourishes of his transformed angelical appearance to impose himself on men, as Christ in spirit, till nothing but that will serve their turn. Then he perremptorily commands them (under this disguise of an angel of light) out of their own senses, wills, and understandings, into a pure subjection to his dictating and ruling influence, as the onely superiour dispensation and attainment, to what they ever yet experienced. And allegorizing of Scripture in his way, he finds to be a very apposite means to nourish and keep them safe under his wing, in that his highest dispensation, his mystical sabbath, a rest from their labours, under his angelical steerage. These, with all other his inferiour crafts and designs above mentioned, does this perillous Impostor mannage upon the various tempered and differently enlightened inhabitants of the whole world, every moment of time.

But it is one grand piece of his mystery of iniquity, to keep men quite off (if he can) from allegorizing of the Scriptures, and consequently from all the spiritual sence and mystery of them, throughout. He perswades by all means, that men would stick in the letter, as the onely course *to hold fast the form of sound words;* and that they would quit mystical sence in the Scriptures, and so, the mystery of Godliness in their persons. He would never have them own *the Life hid with Christ in God.* That's the onely Life he fears. Those that rest in the letter of Scripture and deny the mystery, will easily be induced to rest *in the form of godliness, and deny the power thereof; from such turn away,* 2 Tim. 3. 5. They cry out against the Allegorist, call him blasphemer, say he has a devil, as the *Jews* served Christ, and *Luther Swenckfeld,* in that general answer to his puzzling Letters, *The Lord rebuke thee, Satan.*

So much for Allegory.

BY way of Recapitulation then, and as deducible from, or at leaft in exact confonancy with the divinity part of this Sufferers Doctrine and Character, take thefe following Conclufions.

1. God in Chrift, as Chrift is the purely divine form of God, is abfolutely unmovable, incommunicable; in a capacity too high for the creation of either world, natural or fpiritual.

2. Had **God,** remaining purely in the divine nature, (without affuming Creature-nature into perfonal union therewith) produced or created this firft world, it muft needs have been created in a violent, inftantaneous manner, without any progreffive motion, as in the fix dayes, *Gen.* 1. And when created, Angels and men, fo made, muft needs have been everlaftingly miferable, unlefs reduced to their primitive nothing again. For God that is the onely Fountaine of all happinefs and fatisfaction, had remained in an utter uncommunicablenefs, and been fhut up in abfolute invifibility to them, for ever.

3. God therefore in Chrift, condefcended to cloth himfelf with a twofold creature-forme, natural and fpiritual, through the peculiar operations of the fecond and third of the three that are one, (1 *Jh.* 5.7.) in order to capacitate himfelf for the creation of both worlds, as alfo for the communication of himfelf to his creatures, when created.

4. This twofold creature-nature, as in perfonal Union with God in Chrift, may (by communication of Idioms, and denomination of the whole perfon from the purely divine nature and form) be called God. God is faid (*Acts* 20. 28.) *to have purchafed the Church with his own blood.* 'Tis a Maxime in School divinity, *Whatfoever is in God, is God.*

5. This twofold creature-nature of Chrift, as tranfcribed and copied out by him, in the perfons of elect angels and men, may be called divine, (fpecially the fuperiour and more excellent kind of it) but not God : neither are the perfons of angels or men, by being but thus partakers of the divine nature, either Chrift or God.

6. That being which angels & men received in their firft creation, and that Image of God that was then ftamped on them, was in the life, glory

glory and righteousness of it, but a shadowy, corruptible or changable thing. It was the Image of the Mediator, considered as in that changeable state of creatureship, wherein he became *the Lamb slain from the foundation of the world*, and again in the fulness of time; the image of the first *Adam*, in Christ; that that is to be crucified in us as well as in him; otherwise, how can we be brought into conformity with him in his death?

7. Angels and the souls of men, as having but **this mutable** Image of God in them, received in their first-creation, **are mortal, as to** the glory and life of their Beings, **in communion with God, and** in the way of righteousness. The angels that fell, and man when he fell, died the death, as to this Life; that is, lost that Life of communion they had with God, in the righteousness and glory of their first-creation. Thus in the day *Adam* did eate the forbidden fruit, he died; yet lived in the body, many hundred years after.

8. All mankind fell in *Adam*, the tree out of which we spring as branches. In him we all died. Christ comes to give a general revival, general redemption, out of this dangerous fall; *Rom.* 5. 12, 19. and 1 *Cor.* 15. 22. *As in Adam all die, even so in Christ shall all be made* **alive.** *It shall not be said, our first parents eate the sowre grape, and our teeth are thereby set on edge*, but all souls are redeemed and recoverable by Christ. (if they stubbornly refuse not) into the life, light and liberty of their understanding and will, the proper principles of their first-creation. *The soul then that sinneth*, (either by willful refusal of this renewal, or the loss of this life again when renewed) *it shall die.* 'Tis a tree twice dead, dead first in *Adam*, then after **a personal** revival, dead again by a wilful sinning after the similitude of *Adams* transgression, (knowingly refusing the same more excellent **life and glo**ry of the new creation, that he did, by preferring the lesser glory of the first, thereunto) **and so is pluck'd up by the roots and burned,** *Jude* 12.

9. Angels and the soules of men are immortal as **to** being, if we mean by immortal, everlasting. Angels will remain a flame of fire, and man will consist of body soul and spirit, all the essentials of their first-creation constitution, for ever. But what then? is this their advantage? would it not be a great gain to them to lose themselves by annihilation, rather than be eternally miserable? They are stripped of all righteousness, glory, comfort, deprived of all communion with God, and in their single, meer naked beings, exposed to everlasting

K 2   punish-

punishment, in the pouring forth of his fierce wrath and displeasure upon them, *Mat.* 25. 46. Does not Christ say of *Judas, it had been good for him, if he had never been born?* Mat. 26. 24. 'Tis not proper to say that wicked men and angels, when under the paines, or in the state of eternal death, (eternal *a parte post*) are immortal, but everlasting, unless it be proper to say, immortal death.

10. 'Tis observable, that which is said, 1 *Cor.* 15. 46. *First that which is natural, and afterwards that which is spiritual.* This holds true of the different creature-capacity and form, in head and members, root and branches, in Christ, angels and men. The natural creature-form in Christ, as a peculiar product or emanation from the second of the three that bear witness, (capacitating him for the creation of the first world, and to exhibite the Image of the three that are one, to the creatures natural understanding, when made) is to be considered by us in a priority to that spiritual and more exalted creature form, brought forth in Christ, by the peculiar operation of the third in the Trinity, by which the natural form is baptized into its unchangable state of Life and Union with God. By this twofold creature-form in Christ, are the three that are one, everlastingly exhibited to the view and enjoyment of men and angels, in a suitableness to what ever capacity, natural or spiritual. This is the beatifical vision God gives of himself in Christ. Will any here or any where else in this discourse, cry Tautologie? 'Tis answered once for all, the same things are oft said in scripture by several persons; yea by the same, on several occasions, and sometimes scarcely that; as is to be seen in the *Psalms*, and *Proverbs*, &c.

11. As tis said of the natural and spiritual form in Christ and his members, *first that which is natural, then that which is spiritual*, so is it said of them, in another scripture, by way of allegory, in *Jacob* and *Esau, The elder shall serve the younger*, Rom. 9. 12. The natural or elder creature-form is to be so handled by the spiritual or younger, as to be through the fire-baptism transformed out of its changable capacity, and captivated into everlasting subjection to and unchangable harmony with the spiritual. This holds true in Christ and his members also. The whole rank and order of angels and men, that are about the Throne, in their incorruptible natural form, are as servants to the Bridegroom and Bride that sit upon it, in the spiritual. The natural form also of Christ and all those peculiar Saints that constitute his heavenly Bride, is subject to the spiritual, in the same persons.

12. These

12. These two creature forms, natural and spiritual, in Christ and his members, are resembled to us by the two olive trees, candlesticks, and two annointed ones, that stand before the Lord of the whole earth. This may appear by comparing *Zech.* 4. 11, 14. where they are peculiarly applied to Christ, with *Revel.* 11. 4. where the true Saints, that receive this twofold oyl or spiritual anointing with the heavenly name or nature of Christ, (and thereby become the two Witnesses, or Witnesses of his twofold **creature-glory** and perfection, shining forth in their persons) are also called the *two olive-trees and candlesticks, standing before the God of the whole earth.*

13. Those that are truly anointed with both or either of these names or formes of Christ, natural or spiritual, by the new and everlasting **Covenant**, are such onely as can most properly be said to affemble or be gathered together in his Name, that is, in the power and exercise of the new name and nature of Christ, communicated to them, *Mat.* 18. 20. Such meetings Christ **promises** to be in the midst of, engages to hear all their prayers, and to grant all things whatsoever they ask, *John* 14. 13, 14. How can it be otherwise ? for whatsoever they ask in that spiritual **new-creature** name, in the desire of that new Spirit and Life in them, *that is born of the will of God,* (Jam. 1. 18.) must needs be according to God's will ; and (saies the same Apostle, 1 *John* 5. 14, 15.) *If we ask any thing in or according to his will he heareth us. And if we know that he hear us, whatsoever we ask, we know we have the petitions that we desired of him.* Meeting *in the name of Christ, in the fellowship of the spirit, in the communion of the holy Ghost,* (*Phil.* 2. 1. 2 *Cor.* 13. 14.) are all the same thing.

14. Christ has excellent gifts to bestow upon *the rebellious also,* (*Psal.* 68. 18.) upon a sort of People, *that* for a while *are in Covenant with him, married to him, and made comely, through one sort of comeliness from him, put upon them,* Ezek. 16. 14. *They are his Children, wholly a right seed, children that will not lie, branches of the true Vine, who are yet liable to be turned into the degenerate Plant of a strange Vine unto him,* (Jer. 2. 21.) *to rebel against and vex his holy spirit, so that he may turn to be their enemy,* Esay 63. 8. 10. This sort of Saints or People of Christ, who may again *become no People,* (Hos. 1. 9.) make up his first-Covenant Spouse, resembled by *Hagar.* His Children they are, but they stay in the place, rest in that state of their first-creation Life and Glory with unwise *Ephraim,* and the foolish Virgins, whence the true Children that have the seed of the new and everlasting Covenant-

venant-Life in them, do break forth, *into the wisdom, glory and righteousness of the new-creation,* Hos. 13. 13. Those that thus stay in that place or state of Life, that is neither God's nor the creatures true Rest, will at length set themselves to vex and persecute the spirit of Christ in them that quit that place and state for the more excellent way, the true Rest, and so as downright enemies to Christ, will make use of those very natural parts, or spiritual gifts he has bestowed upon them, to decry, vilifie and persecute him in his true spiritual seed. Who are these?

Those that are made Eunuchs, as to any ability to bring forth fruit unto Christ in the way of their first-Covenant Life and Principles, being brought to keep his true mystical Sabbath, in the exercise of their new-Covenant, spiritual Life, by which means they come to have *a name and place in his house for ever, better than the name and place of those sons and daughters by the first Covenant, an everlasting name that shall not be cut off, or blotted out of the book of Life,* as the others may, *Esay* 56. 4, 5. *Revel.* 3. 5. Those first-covenant sons and daughters that swel and are puffed up with the towring imaginations and self-exalting thoughts, that by Satans suggestion and their own ready compliance are apt to spring up in them (from a confidence in what they have already received) against the more excellent way, are with *Capernaum, exalted unto heaven,* in righteousness, Ordinances, excellent Gifts, high Illuminations, and ready utterance, but *must be brought down to hell* for this mistake and presumption. Yea, *'twill be more tolerable for Tyre and Sidon* or the very litteral *Sodom in the day of Judgement, than for this mystical, spiritual Sodom,* in which the Lord and his true spiritual, heaven-born Saints are still crucified, *Mat.* 11. 23, 24.

15. The meer natural state and frame of man, considered either in its first-creation or as renewed since, is a comprehensive Epitome of the first world. All sort of Being and Life that's to be found in the first creation, is summ'd up and put together, in every particular individual man. He has being, with the visible heavens, Sun, Moon, Stars, Elements, and all inanimate compounds; vegetable Life, with Plants and trees; sensual, with beasts; rational, with angels; add spiritual, with Christ in God, by the new-creation, and then he is the compleat Epitome of both worlds, natural and spiritual too. In this sence, man is called a *Microcosme,* or little World. Angels in their first-creation frame, are not so, nor yet in the second, their new-creation,

ation, or refurrection ftate. They do not formally contain and comprehend in their very perfonal beings, all inferiour nature in the firft world. But they have that that is the man in man, reafon, in a fuperiority to man himfelf, as appears by the over-reaching exercife of it in the devil, to the deceiving of man in his Paradifical, primitive, and beft eftate. Yea 'tis faid of Chrift himfelf, as a man in flefh, *that he was made lower than the angels*, Heb. 2. 7. Angels then, though they do not formally contain all inferiour nature in their perfonal conftitution as man does, yet do they eminently coprehend it all. And they have originally a more quick, active, and vigorous natural underftanding, that does more fully pierce and pry into the hidden fecrets and myfteries of nature, than man. Their thoughts run to and fro, as a flafh of lightning. With one glance of their intellectual eye, they can take notice of all that's to be found in the firft-creation. *They excel man in ftrength alfo*, Pfal. 103. 20. They have alfo the ftart of man, for reprefenting all firft-creation glory, as eminently comprehended in their own perfons. Thus the devil reprefented to Chrift, in a flourifh of his transformed appearance, *all the kingdoms of the world and glory of them*, all the defirable excellencies of the firft creation, *Mat.* 4. 8. He is called *The God of this world*. All his flourifhes in firft creation light and glory, are with defigne to dazle and affect mens eyes and hearts with the appearance of tranfient vanities, fo as to keep them from ever looking after the marvellous light and more excellent glory of the fecond; to keep off the Light of the glorious Gofpel of Chrift, that that may not fhine upon them, or be taken any notice of by them, 2 *Cor.* 4. 4.

He that is called *God of this world*, has doubtlefs a vaft, univerfal underftanding and infight into all firft-creation nature and things. How elfe can he make the beft of every thing, for the tempting, feducing and enfnaring of men ? He made the utmoft ufe of all, to Chrift, this way, when he *prefented him with all the kingdomes and glory of the firft-creation*. This bait could not catch him. Far lefier catch other men ; little parcels of creature-contentments, delights of the fons of men. His Table is fpread with all variety of firft-creation things, for the entertainment and feduction of man. Here's the duft, this lying old ferpent feeds on, (*Gen.* 3. 14.) and couzens others with, natural things, things feen, gloffed over by him, to carry on his work. The generallity of men are fatisfied with the crums that fall from this ferpents Table, the moft inferiour fort of contentments that humour and gratify but their bruitifh lufts. They tumble in fenfual pleafure, like fwine in the mire while that holds, while provifions

fions come in, to keep that on foot, they reckon all well with them. Horfes, afles, and the reft of the bruitifh rout of animals, have fully as good a time on't as they, in this world, and in this confideration a better, no akings of heart about a world to come and an irrevocable fentence of condemnation to everlafting and unexpreffible punifhment. If men do peep out of this bruitifh ftrain of Life, (the prevailing difpenfation of the devil in *England*, at prefent) through fome awakenings of Confcience, and begin to look after a little moral righteoufnefs in their perfonal operations; the old ferpent can apply himfelf to them, as their Tutor, Influencer, and Inftruftor herein; has diet at his board, that will fit their palate. Yea, he can accommodate the Legal Chriftian, with the appearances and exact refemblances of all that he is for. If the Legallift be unfatisfied, and will be looking after Chrift in fpirit, he puts in with his utmoft flourifhes and appearances of angelical glory, to fatisfie him in that point alfo. He has before him, all firft-creation things, from the loweft part of the duft of the world, bruitifh fatisfactions, to the higheft part of the duft of this world, angelical glory, and he has the utmoft imaginable skill and dexterity to ufe and improve all, for the feduction of men. He puts the moft taking, infinuating gloffes upon every thing, prefents every man with objects fuited to his palate, capacity, light and attainment. Thus does this grand deceiver of all the Nations of the world, practife his witchcrafts and forceries on the fenfes and imaginations of men, by prefent or abfent objects, and by his immediate influence labours to kindle and ftir up their flefhly affections and defires, to meet with and entertain thofe trifling vanities he has infatuated and bewitched their imagination to put fuch a value upon. The *Galatians Paul* found bewitched with no lefs a matter than the glory of the Law, the righteoufnefs of man, *Gal. 3.* Others are bewitched with the glory of angelical nature, higher duft than the glory of man; the generality, with fmaller matters, bruitifh toyes.

The Devil then, that's called *the God of this world*, (together with his fallen angels) knows exactly what this world amounts to; knows all inferiour nature, humane amongft the reft, through and through. He can tell where to have man, and fit him at every turn. He thorowly knows all the things he is to tempt him with, and he thorowly him that he fets himfelf to tempt; and fo is compleatly accomodated for his feducing work, in all points. And this will be his courfe, till he be fealed up in the bottomlefs pit, which will be Synchronal with Chrift's coming forth to reign, *Rev.* 20.   tuB

But if once man become a new creature, by receiving either the single or double portion of the spirit, he passes out of the devils hands. This manchild is quite out of his reach, *Revel.* 12. The spiritual believer, that is partaker of the divine nature, (in the sence above expressed) is partaker of the wisdom, holiness, and righteousness of God. Then he is wiser than the Devil, if the wisdom of God be superiour to the wisdom of that Serpent. This is a thing one did once spitefully tax this Sufferer with, as boasting that he was wiser than the Devil, because on some occasion that was offered ; he replied, *He was glad he lived in a spirit the Devil was so little acquainted with.* Sure he that lives in the spirit of God, lives in a spirit that is superiour to the devil, and that he is little acquainted with. The lowest degree of wisdom, light, life and glory in the new creation, is above the highest excellencies and glory of any nature or creature in the old. He that has but the single portion of the spirit, and that but in seed, will be too hard for that roaring and devouring Lion, will resist him effectually, and finally, in the stedfast faith of God's elect, 1 *Pet.* 5.8,9. Even babes and suckling in the Life of grace, shall be able to still that enemy and avenger, with all his shews and flourishes in Natures excellencies, first-creation power or things, *Psal.* 8. 2.

16. 'Tis observable from the sentence passed upon the Serpent, that the devil and his angels are yet alive. He with *Adam* and *Eve* are summoned to appear before Christs Tribunal, to answer what each of them had done in that business of the fall. His sentence runs thus, *Because thou hast done this, thou art cursed above all cattel, and above every beast of the field ; upon thy belly shalt thou go, and dust shalt thou eate all the dayes of thy Life.* Angels, and men, the highest ranks of Creatures in the first world, are (comparatively with the new-creature state of men and angels in the second world) reckoned but as cattel, the choicer sort of the beasts of the field. Satan with his retinue of fallen angels does yet live. His diet is dust. As God of this world he has all sorts of beings, and excellencies of the first creation before him. This is the dust he feeds on, and feeds others with. This diet he offered to Christ himself, when he was hungry. His trade of seducing mankind, managable by these things, he has been at, well towards six thousand years. 'Tis a *Rabbinical* observation, that these six thousand years of the worlds labour under this seducing work of the devil, as plunged in that wicked one, were resembled by the six dayes works, in the creation of it, *a thousand years being with the Lord as one day.* The

L

seaventh

venth thousand, the *Jewish* doctors held to be typified by the Sabbath day, in which the world should rest from this bondage under the God of this world. They observed also that the Sabbath is not described as the other six dayes, by an evening and morning, as having no darkness at all in it, that so it might more fitly represent to us the perpetual joyes and light of the *New-Jerusalem*, or World to come.

During the six thousand years of the Worlds miserable thraldom and labour under the Satanical yoke, righteous men are perpetually oppressed from *Abel* downwards, and there is no judgement for them to be had in this world. But in the seventh thousand year, the seventh day of the world, they will be in their proper Sabbatical state, *and nothing shall hurt in all the holy Mountain, or kingdom of Christ* The light, glory and wisdom of the first creation, when men or angels are deteined and held by them, from entring into the more excellent glory of the second, are but as chains of darkness upon them. When Satans time is come to be sealed up in the bottomless pit, at Christs coming forth to reign, this yet does not absolutely and finally strip him of his first-creation flourish, but onely suspends his exercise of it, as to his former deceiving of the nations thereby, till the thousand years be fulfilled, and then he comes forth again for a little season, to deceive the nations, and engage his whole party of angels and men, in order to the giving his final & utmost assault to the *New-Jerusalem* camp of Christ and all his Saints, the beloved City. So far he will be permitted to proceed herein, as to besiege it, with a kind of seeming hopefulness to outvie it in a flourish of spirituality and in the state of the resurrection, in order yet to carry the Kingdom and dominion from Christ and all his saints. Then fire comes down from God out of Heaven upon him and his (on the *New-Jerusalem's* ascending into their utmost glory of the resurrection, and full vision of God for evermore, and then nothing but torment wil be their portion for ever and ever, when perfectly stripped of all first-creation glory, & enjoyments and tied in the second death, however he cozen men with conceits even to this day, that those torments shall have a period, and all shall be saved. In *Rev.* 20, we have an account of these particulars.

17. What are the Old and New Testament, as written Books, representing the mind of God in a sound or sight of words, but Letter, Shadow, significant Figure of natural and spiritual-creature perfection in Christ and men; in men, as natural and spiritual properly distinguish old and new creation Life in them.

Men of a first-Covenant, old Testament, old *Adam*, natural or legal
                                                                  spirit

spirit are all one thing. So are men of a new Covenant, new Testament, second *Adam*, new Creature, or truly evangelical Spirit, the same. In the former is the Life of the Law, or the ruling activity of rectified humane first-creation Principles : In the latter, the Life of the Gospel, or the ruling activity of the new-creature Spirit and principles. One is the Legal professor, the other the Spiritual believer. One is under the Law of Nature or the first Covenant, the other under Grace, the Law of Faith, spiritual Life, or the new and everlasting Covenant.

18. The Law of Nature and of the first Covenant are the same thing in man, but as to the perfection of them in or upon man, this difference is observable. Man in his first creation as he came out of the hands of God, had the Law of Nature or the ruling powers of natural Life, in full perfection, inherent and operative in his own person. The same Law of natural or first created Life and perfection, is renewed by Christ in men, as to kind, so as also to be inherent and operative in them, in some degree ; but the deficiencies of inward personal sanctity and of inward and outward operations, are made out by the compleat righteousness of the Law, as wrought by another person for them, and imputed to them for their justification before God, upon the tearms of the first Covenant, qualifying them for communion with God therein. In this sence, *Paul* was according to the Law blameless ; to wit, under this comliness of God put upon him. In the other sence, as to inherent personal perfection, 'tis said, 1 *John* 1. 8. *If we say, we have no sin, we deceive our selves, and the truth is not in us.*

19. As to the whole bulk of the written Oracles of God, there is frequently given the proper character both of the Law and Gospel Principle or state of Life, in the old Testament as well as new ; but of the latter, more eminently and plentifully in the new.

20. There were true spiritual Saints both before and under the outward dispensation of the Law, *Enoch, Noah, Sem, Heber, Abraham, David* and many others; and there are sowre, narrow, Pharisaical, legal-spirited Christians, under the outward dispensation of the Gospel, at this day.

21. Even the first Covenant or Legal state of first-creation Life and Principles, renewed in men, comes to them in the way of Gospel, or

through

through the glad tydings of the mighty Redeemer, who was promised to *Adam* under the name of *the womans seed, that should bruise or break the Serpents head, Gen.* 3. 15. This he did by dying; *through death destroyed him that had the power of death, that is, the devil,* Heb. 2. 14. Thus Christ died for all, (2 *Cor.* 5. 14, 15.) to recover all again out of that dead sleep in trespasses and sins, into which they were cast by *Adams* first transgression, and to set them upon their first-creation feet again, in order to a new trial of their personal demeanour in that great point, *Adam* first miscarried in, as to the loosing the Life, quitting the righteousness, wisdom, and lesser glory of their first-creation, for that which excelleth in the second; *the tree of Knowledge, that puffeth up, for the tree of Life, that edifieth.* Thus was Christ *a propitiation, not for the sins of his elect onely, but of the whole world,* 1 *Joh.* 2. 2. Here's all the general Redemption the Scripture holds forth.

22. If these things be so, what signify all the voluminous Controversies of the *Pelagian* and *Antipelagian, Arminian* and *Antiarminian, Supralapsarian* and *Sublapsarian,* about Free-will, general Redemption, and the Like ? What Free-will is it, the one pleads for, the other denies ?, Only such as *Adam* was created with; the wavering Liberty of the sons of men, the object whereof, is natural good and evil. As for spiritual, new-creation things, they were in themselves, in their own naked essence, clear out of sight to *Adams* discerning at best, which was but natural. They were onely representable and understandable to him, in a riddle, through some first-creation shadow, the Tree of Life. Neither of the above mentioned parties, in all their warm digladiations and pickerings, once dream of a distinct superiour state of Life and Liberty, that should swallow up all that of the first creation into victory, & bring it forth again with usury and great gain, by way of resurrection, *in the glorious Life and Liberty of the sons of God,* the spiritual, eternal Life and Freedom to good onely, and not at all to evil. But whoever returns not into the exercise of his rectified first-creation Principles and Liberty, as a general fruit of Christ's death, 'tis his own voluntary default. *He sins against God and wrongs his own soul; he hates Christ and loves death,* Prov. 8. 36. He refuses the righteousness and glory of his own humane nature, and chuses to be a beast.

23. But what lies in man to do towards the superiour and more excellent dispensation and way, by which he should be led forward into *the glorious Liberty of the sons of God,* and *eternal Life* ?

'Tis

'Tis anfwered, He hath power in the right ufe of his natural free-dom, not to refift it ; but upon experience of the infufficiency of the felfifh fpirit and wavering Principles of his firft creation, to fubmit all the Life and glory thereof to the fire-baptifm, in order to the be-ing brought forth in a more excellent ftate, that is unchangable.

'Tis not in man to do any thing towards his new creation, as nei-ther did he contribute any thing towards his firft make. But God makes fuch propofal and offer of this new-creation work to all man-kind, as not one man failes of being made a new creature, but it will be moft righteoufly interpreted by God to have befallen him through his own voluntary default, in neglecting, refufing, and refifting that offer. Where comes in the difference then ? *A remnant according to the election of grace obtain it, the reft are voluntarily blinded and fall fhort,* Rom. 11. 5. 7. That faying of *Auftin* is not amifs ; *God will not fave* *any man whether he will or no, but he will make that man willing to be fa-ved, that he refolves to fave. He may do what he will with his own.* Mans firft-creation Liberty mifufed in this great point, brings forth this fad truth ; *Thy deftruction is of thy felf, O man.* And Gods referving fingly to himfelf the forming up of the new creature, and the prerogative-Liberty of effectually and irrefiftibly difpofing of this great favour, where, when, and to whom he pleafes, brings forth that excellent truth, *That our falvation is onely and meerly of God,* as Sir *Francis Bacon* obferves in his Confeffion of Faith. Who then maketh men to differ, one from another, the new creature from the old ? Man makes him-felf to differ from the new creature or fpiritual man, by his volunta-ry rejecting and defpifing this more excellent Life : but God alone makes him that is a new creature, to differ from the old. And this in-deed is the proper meaning of difference in fuch cafes. To differ is to excel, Phil. 1. 10. *That ye may approve things that excel, or differ.* So 1 Cor. 15. 41. *One ftar differs from, or excels, another ftar in glory.*

Thou wilt fay, if the cafe be thus, *Why doth God yet find fault ? For who hath refifted his will ?* Thofe that he hath elected, and is refolved to fave, he will effectually and irrefiftibly make willing to be faved, and they will certainly be faved, and no others. *Nay, but O man, who art thou that replieft againft God ? Shall the thing formed fay to him that formed it, why haft thou made me thus ?* He may make veffels of honour or difhonour as he pleafes, amongft *Jewes* or *Gentiles* all the world over, Rom. 9. 19, 24. *God that is infinitely juft,* and can be no otherwife, *is not bound to give an account of any of his matters,* Job 33. 13. *Why therefore do ye ftrive againft God,* while ye put forth this querulous demand, *who*

hath

hath refisted his will? Will you caſt all your ſins and deſtruction too, upon God's final rejection of you as reprobate ſilver? *Jer. 6. 30.* God ſtrives by his Spirit with men to bring them to himſelf, *Gen. 6. 3.* to which *Peter* refers, *1 Pet. 3. 19, 20.* Men ſtrive and fight a-gainſt God, are diſobedient and rebellious. If God ſuffer men to pre-vail, in a final reſiſting of his ſpirit that ſtrives with them, they are undone for ever. If they be conquered, they are ſaved. If they loſe their mutable Life, they find it again in that which is unchangable. If they keep it a while in oppoſition to the more excellent Life, they loſe it at laſt, in eternal death. Theſe are the Goſpel riddles, which the very diſciples ſcarcely underſtood, while Chriſt was with them in the fleſh, nor we while we have but the like knowledge of Chriſt after the fleſh, as they then had. Knowingly to reſiſt and hate the new-creature Life, and words thereof, is to do *deſpite to the ſpirit of grace,* to ſin againſt the Holy Ghoſt. *He that hath an ear to hear, let him hear.*

'Tis in vain for man to quarrel. *God will be juſtified, when he judges, Pſ. 51. 4.* He will at laſt bring forth the grounds of all his diſpenſations towards man and proceedings with him, in ſuch a demonſtrative and undeniable conſonancy to the very reaſon of man, *that every mouth ſhall be ſtopped.* Yea, there is enough ſaid already in his written Ora-cles, to ſtop every mouth.

24. We may take notice from what hath been ſaid, who thoſe *poor, mourning, meek-ſpirited men, thoſe merciful, pure, peace-making, yet per-ſecuted Children of God are, that Chriſt pronounces bleſſed, Mat. 5. 3, 11.* We may alſo come thereby to know on the other hand, what Chriſt meanes by that *rich, full, laughing ſort of people,* to whom he cries, *wo, wo, wo, Luke 6. 24, 25.*

The poor in ſpirit are they that are willing to be broken and emptied of the activity, life, righteouſneſs, glory, wiſdom, reaſonings, deſires, thoughts and wayes of their own mutable firſt-creation ſpirit, in order to be filled with the ſpirit of Chriſt, the wiſdom, and righteouſneſs of God, in the new creation. Thus with *Steven* they come *to be ful of faith and of the Holy Ghoſt,* (*Act. 6. 5.*) *rich in God, or rich towards God, Luk. 12. 21.* That righteouſneſs that is imputed to, or inhe-rent and operative in the new creature, is called the *righteouſneſs of God.* All the fruits of ſaving faith, all the works that are performed in the operative principle of new-creature Life, are the righteous works of God, who by his indwelling ſpirit, *worketh all ſuch works in us,* Eſay 26. 12. On the other hand, all the righteouſneſs, imputed to, or in-

herent

herent and operative in the first-Covenant Saint, is called *the righte-*
ousness of man, such righteousness as Christ had and wrought in his
changeable fleshly manhood, which he *imputes to them that are sanctifi-*
ed through his blood, into an experimental knowledge of him, and conformi-
ty with him, in the flesh. This imputed comeliness or righteousness, is
called both God's and Man's, in a breath, *Ezek.* 16. 14, 15. Men
come too often to trample the blood of this Covenant under their
feet, after they have been so sanctified, (*Heb.* 10. 29.) and to play the
harlot with that sort of righteousness imputed to them, after they have
been so justified.

The first-creation state of Life in man, by being broken and crucified under the second, comes into a peaceable, everlasting harmony with God. This makes a true son of peace, as well as of righteousness, answering his father *Melchizedeck's* constitution, who is
both *king of righteousness and king of peace*. Such sons of peace are commonly reckoned *men of contention*, though the only true peace-makers
the world has in it, that desire and labour to bring others also into the
same state of peace, harmony, and everlasting union with God, as one
spirit with him, the state of love, charactered, 1 *Cor.* 13. Is not God
himself reckoned a God of contention, for striving with men by his
spirit, in order to conquer them into a state of salvation, deliver them
out of their own hands, take them out of their own dispose, by be-
reaving them of their own liberty and power of sinning against him,
and wronging their own soules? And is not Satan, the God of this
world reckoned the God of peace, that speaks smooth and pleasing
things to flesh and blood, by all his various instruments from amongst
men, even by those whom he transformes into the very likeness of
the Apostles of Christ? 2 *Cor.* 11. Do not men generally approve
of and like the doctrine of him and his ministers best, as orthodox and
found, that advises men not to gaze after or listen to those spiritual
wanderers, that speak of an attainment beyond the righteousness and
glory of our first-creation? This doctrine of his runs through all forms
of professing Christians at this day, and the spiritual man is reckoned
mad for contradicting it. Is not Satan reckoned the God of order,
that is for one man's continued speaking onely in a Pulpit, accounting it a breach of the peace, punishable by the Magistrates sword, for
any other to speak there, though all that his pulpit man does, is but to
shut up the kingdom of Heaven, and in effect to charge men that they
look not after it, that is, not listen to those, *who after the way which*
they call Heresy, are worshipping God in the spirit? Is it not the business
of those authorized deceivers, to open their mouthes in blasphemy a-
gainst

gainst God, to blaspheme his Name, his tabernacle, and them that dwell (or have their conversation) in heaven? *Rev.* 13. 6. *Phil.* 3. 20. And is not God himself reckoned the author of disorder and confusion, for saying, *If any thing be revealed to another that sitteth by, let the first hold his peace ; for ye may prophesy all one by one, that all may learn and be comforted?* 1 Cor. 14. 30, 33.

Thus Satan and men nestle warm together, in the first creation; and no right tidings or character of the second will be listened to. That crafty Serpent has *blinded their mindes, and stop'd their ears, least this light of the glorious gospel should shine unto them, or find any entertainment amongst them.* The Things, the Persons, the Churches, that this strong man thus fraudulently possesses, are in peace, till Christ the stronger than he cometh to force him out. He is coming.

25. Those rich, full, old, foolish kings, as to the righteousness of man, (1 *Cor.* 4. 8.) That will no more be admonished or warned by the wise child in the true regeneration, (*Eccles.* 4. 13.) those flourishing, legal-spirited Christians, that laugh, are warm and confident in their present attainments, their renewed flesh, they are of the *Laodicean* temper, *neither hot nor cold,* Rev. 3. 16. They are not hot enough for the spiritual believers company, under the fire-baptism, nor cold enough for the dissolute rabble of mankind, that are wholly given up to vile affections and sensuality. They think they have need of nothing, because they see the bestial multitude under their feet, to whom they say, *stand by, we are holier than you.* Yet are they (as to eternal Life) *wretched, miserable, poor, blind and naked,* Rev. 3. 17. They have no exercise of true spiritual discerning or Life in them. When this sort of professors are hard beset with the spiritual believers testimony, rather than endure that, they will venture (if there be no other remedy) to piece up with any prophane Interest ; as *Act.* 17. 5. The issue oft is , they are ruined for their paines, by those they call in to their assistance. Rich they are , wise , strong , and honorable in Christ , by a knowledge of him after the flesh, while *David, Paul* and others of their spiritual constitution, are poor, needy, weak and despicable, as to that selfish, Life, wisdom and righteousness of man , 1 *Cor.* 4. 8. 10. *Psal.* 109. 22.

Will any here Object, *That the same Scriptures are oft quoted, the same expressions oft used, and the selfe-same things unnecessarily repeated ?*

The

The Answer is, To me this course of writing the same things, is only not grievous; but to the observant Reader it may prove safe, *Phil.* 3. 1. As for others that *Diotrephes* like, *love to have the preheminence amongst men,* and gratifie their own ambitious humour, by preferring their preconceived notions at all adventures hereunto, (without any regard had to the beguiling projects of the devil upon them and their hearers all along) to me 'tis a very small thing to be censured by such men, 1 *Cor.* 4. 3. Is not their censure and reproach in this case rather to be interpreted a ratification of the things here said, than any wayes an invalidating thereof? Will they prate against these things with malitious words, *not receiving them themselves, and forbidding those that would,* as he in the 3 Epistle of *John* v. 9. 10 ? Let them. Will any that pretend to be onely teachers of the Law, *understanding neither what they say nor whereof they affirm,* (1 *Tim.* 1. 7.) out of hatred to the main things here treated of, bark at some circumstantial infirmities in the delivery thereof, contracted from the earthliness of the vessel, through which they are handed to publick view ? Let these take their course also; I shall hold my self little concerned to heed what they say. Christ pronounces *wo to those that all men speak well of*; *for so* (says he) *did their Fathers to the false Prophets,* Luk. 6. 26. That spirit in man that seeks or regards the praise and commendation of men, is never right, never has the praise of God, *Rom.* 2. 29. 2 *Cor.* 10. 12. 18. What is more familiar to observation in teachers amongst us, than that spirit of the Scribes and Pharisees that would be *shutting up the kingdom of Heaven against men, neither going in themselves, nor suffering others to go in?* Mat. 23. 13.

26. God in the first creation gives us our selves : In the second, himself. All the righteousness, wisdom, and works, as well as the very being of man, is from God, as made by him; but are called the righteousness, wisdom and works of man, or self-wisdom, self-righteousness, which he that so worketh, is under the Law or Covenant of works. If man himself may be called self, such works at best are but self-righteousness. Men grosly deceive themselves in limiting self to the corrupt nature onely. The ridding us of that, is onely the casting out of the devil, or of that which the old serpent by his first suggestion to *Eve,* brought into our nature. Those Ministers and Pastors of Churches, that are really serviceable to their hearers in this work, will find cold entertainment from Christ, if they proceed not with *Paul* to a second and more excellent birth of Life in them, *Mat.* 7. 22, 23. The fruit of their Ministry amounts but to the constituting of *the house*

upon

upon the fand, (renewed nature, the *House, empty, swept, and garnished*, that Satan can re-enter) not *the House upon the rock*, that fpiritual houfe, (1 *Pet.* 2. 5.) that is partaker of the divine nature , againft which, *the gates of hell fhall not prevail.*

All that man is, has, or does within the compafs of his firft-creation frame of mind and heart, atbeft, hath SELF ftamped upon it, fo indelebly and by fuch undeniable evidence from the fcriptures of truth, that all the fhifts and wit of man will never be able to wipe it out. That that is made or renewed by God **in the firft** creation, is of **the earth, earthy.** That that is born of God **in the fecond, is from heaven ;** and **the** righteoufnes, wifdom, and glory thereof is called the righteoufnefs, wifdom and glory of God, which they fall fhort of, that ftay in the firft. There is no eternal Life to be had, but in the glory that **excels,** 2 *Cor.* 3. 10.

There is a glory and a glory : a leffer glory that is to be done away, becaufe comparatively 'tis no glory, by reafon of the glory that excelleth, and is to remain. Reformation brings the leffer glory, the glory of man a frefh upon him. But it **muft** be Transformation by which we are changed into and brought forth in the glory of God, *verf.* 18. tis not a gradual progrefs and proficiency in the fame life, glory and righteoufnefs, that is here meant, but a total change out of one kind of glory into another ; a paffing out of the glory of the firft-creation into that of the fecond, from the changeable Life, glory, and righteoufneffe of man, into the unchangeable Life, glory, and everlafting righteoufneffe of God. The Apoftle ufes the fame word to expreffe this great change or metamorphofis of fouls, that is abfolutely neceffary to falvation, which the Poet prefixes to his fabulous transformation of the bodies of men into the fhapes of other kinds of creatures. We are metamorphofed, changed or transformed from glory to glory. Spiritual, new-creature Life only is unchangable and therefore eternal.

27. This then is the fum of man's duty ; *Offer the facrifices of righteoufnes, and put your truft in the Lord,* Pfal. 4. 5. The *Chaldee* renders it, *Subdue your lufts, and it fhall be accounted a facrifice of righteoufnefs.* Be content to quit and offer up the firft-creation ftate, at beft, *in facrifice to God, and put your truft in the Lord,* who by his fpirit given forth to you in the new-creation, will work all your works in you and for you, after a more excellent way. In the prieftly office and power of your faith, *prefent your bodies a living facrifice, holy, acceptable to God, which is your reafonable fervice ;* or is that facrifice of your reafonable

powers,

powers, your rational principles at beſt, that God will accept, and thereupon transform into an abſolute com, liance and unchangable harmony with his will, *Rom.* 12. 1, 2. *Crucifie the fleſh with the affections and luſts. Put off the old man.* Theſe and many other Scriptures of like import, do all together and each of them apart, compendiouſly imply the whole duty of man, even all that God requires of him, which is to humble himſelf under the croſs of Chriſt and walk, for ever with the Lord. So *Pſal.* 50. 23. *whoſo offereth praiſe, glorifieth me* : So the *Septuagint* render it in *Greek.* In the *Hebrew* 'tis, *whoſo ſacrificeth confeſſion* ; which the *Caldee* renders, *whoſo ſlayeth his evil* (or fleſhly) *concupiſcence*, that is, *the fleſhly or natural mind.* The renewed mind of man is but a labile, wavering, corruptible thing. This is not onely to be confeſſed, but the confeſſion or thing it ſelf that is confeſſed thus to be, is to be ſacrificed and offered up to God, by a living active faith. If not, it will reſiſt the ſpirit of God, refuſe his new-creation work, ſeek to ſave its own life, keep it ſelf whole and **unbroken, and** ſo will evidence it ſelf in concluſion to be that carnal mind, *that's enmity to God, and works eternal death to man*, Rom. 8. 6.

To come roundly and freely off with the ſacrifice of ſelf, in the full Scripture latitude thereof, by a thorow ſelf-reſignation, is the great duty of man, and the onely true and acceptable offering of praiſe to God. Truly and ſubſtantially to praiſe God, amounts to no leſs than this offering. Lets not pleaſe **and** delude our ſelves with a noiſe, a ſound of words, ſhadowes, for things, ſubſtance, truth.

28. *Know then, O vain* **man,** *that without works thy faith* **is dead,** Jam. 2. 20. What works ? the works of an active, ſaving **faith ; the** fruits that flow from the proper ſpring and principle of 'new-creature Life in man. One great work of this faith, is **to lay** hold on the unchangeable and everlaſting righteouſneſs of **God** in Chriſt's perſon.

Another great work of it, is to crucify the fleſhly **mind, or** principles **of** humane nature however renewed, ſo as for **ever** to diſable them either for working **ſin** or righteouſneſſe, in the ſingle firſt-creation activity or Life thereof.

A third work of it, is to enable man to worſhip God in ſpirit and truth, and to perform all righteous works towards God and men, **in a** more excellent and acceptable way, and with more ſteadineſs and certainty, than ever the renewed natural mind, with all its ornament and furniture, could perform ſuch things. Without ſuch a faith and the workings of it, *it is impoſſible to pleaſe God*, Heb. 11. 6. Thus by being

diſabled

disabled to perform one tittle of the Law in the single activity of our corruptible (though renewed) mind, we come so to fulfil the whole Law in the continuing and incorruptible principle of new-creature life, that against us there is no Law, that has any thing to say, *Gal.* 5. 23. *Do we then make void the Law through faith ? God forbid : yea, we come by this means onely, to establish and fulfil the Law,* Rom. 3. 31. Mat. 5. 17. They that believe in God, must be careful to maintain such good works, to wit, the works of faith, *Tit.* 3. 8. This is the *letting our light so shine before men, that they may see our good works, and glorifie our father which is in heaven,* Mat. 5. 16. We shew hereby that God's spirit which is set up in man by the new creation, is better at working righteousnesse, than mans spirit that was set up in him by the first-creation.

Any works we do, as born of God in the new-creation, are better on all accounts, than what we can do, as made of God in the first. whatever work is good in the honest Heathen or legal Christian, shall be owned and out-done by the spiritual believer, in his more excellent principles and way. The highest Principles of Life in man, include, ratifie, and out-do all that righteousnels that is performable in the lower

In such Principles was this Sufferer a worker of righteousnels, such a worshipper of God as the Father seeks and approves of; such a true Son of peace, & such a peacemaker as hath bin described, but reckoned a man of contention, for that very reason. He was content with *Paul* to be a fool for Christ, despised for Christ, the poor and needy man, with *David.* As a true Embassador of Christ, and minister of the everlasting Gospel, he warned and besought the sons of men, to consider their own true interest, in becoming not onely almost but altogether such as he was, except his bonds. His Life was not like other mens, nor his Ministry. His wayes were of another fashion, as they reason, (*Wisd.* 2. 15.) therefore have I writ his Life after another fashion than mens Lives use to be written, treating mostly of the principles and course of his hidden Life amongst the sons of God, that the sons of men may the better know and consider what manner of man it was they have betrayed, persecuted and slain. For this, read on from *verf.* 15, to 23, of *Wisd.* 2. (which I quote not as Scripture, but as a notable character of mens rational conviction and acknowledgements, together with their false reasonings, and most perverse deductions therefrom, in the present case) *We are esteemed of him as counterfeits, or hypocrites ; he abstaineth from our wayes, as filthyness. He maketh his boast, that God is his Father. Let us see if his words be true. If he be the*
Son

Son of God, he will help him and deliver him from his enemies. Let us examine him with despitefulness and torture, that we may know his meekness and prove his patience. Let us condemn him with a shameful death, for by his own saying he shall be respected. Such things they did imagine, and were deceived; for their own wickedness hath blinded them. As for the mysteries of God, they knew them not, nor discerned the reward of blameless soules.

Thus, not owning any need of an Apology for having been so large in the exposition of his divine Life, Principles, and Doctrine, (save onely this, that I have spoken these things, rather as an instruction to the living than an Apology for the dead) I return to the more publick and overt acts of his humane pilgrimage and conversation amongst men, having mentioned the private passages thereof in the beginning.

Would you know his **Title** in reference to his countrey ? He was A *Common-Wealths-Man*. That's a dangerous Name to the Peace and Interest of Tyranny.

I have lately met with two new State **Paradoxes** in Print, which speak ruine to all that own that Title.

1. *That the Common-Wealth is not safe, while Common-Wealths-Men are alive.*

2. *That the Lawes are not safe, while they are alive that every day call for the aid of the Law.*

These Assertions carry with them such an appearance of contradiction, to say no more, that I am not so much an *OEdipus* as to unriddle them.

The Character of this deceased Statesman, (with whose Principles those two sayings carry little harmony) I shall exhibite to you in a paper of Verses, composed by a learned Gentleman, and sent him, *July* 3. 1652.

V A N E, young in years, but in sage counsel old,
   Then whom a better Senatour ner'e held
   The helme of Rome, *when Gowns not Arms repell'd*
   The fierce Epeirot *and the* African *bold.*

Whe'her to settle peace or to unfold
   The drift of hollow states, hard to be spell'd,
   Then *to advise how war may best, upheld,*
   Move *by her two main Nerves, Iron and Gold.*
In all *her Equipage : besides to know*
   Both spiritual power and civil, what each meanes,
   What severs each, thou hast learn't, which few have done.
The *bounds of either Sword to thee we owe ;*
   Therefore on thy firm hand Religion **leanes**
   In peace, and reckons thee her eldest Son.

In the former part of these verses, notice is taken of a kind of angelical intuitiveness and sagacity he was furnished with, for spying out and unridling the subdolous intentions of hollow-hearted States, however disguised with colourable pretexts of Friendship. This rendred him a choice Senator, an honourable Counsellour for publick safety. The Widow of *Tekoah* said to *David, My Lord is wise, according to the wisdom of an Angel of God, to know all things that are in the earth ;* 2 Sam. **14. 20.** Will you say, this was a fluttering hyperbole ? What think you of that in *Amos, Surely the Lord will do nothing, but he revealeth his secrets unto his servants the Prophets ?* Amos 3. 7. The king of *Syria* took counsel, saying, *In such and such a place shall be my Camp against Israel. Elisha* sends to the King of *Israel,* saying, *Beware thou pass not such a place, and the King of Israel sent to the place the Seer of God warned him of, and saved himself there,* not once nor twice, 2 Kin. 6. 8, 10. On this, the King of *Syria* suspects that some about him discover his projects to the King of *Israel. No, my Lord, O King,* (saies one) *Elisha the Prophet that is in Israel, tells the King of Israel the words thou speakest in thy bed-chamber,* vers. 11, 12. Hereupon the King sends a great Army of *Syrians* to apprehend the Prophet. *They come to Dothan, where he is.* But by the assistance of an angelical host in the Mount, he baffles out all their Forces, as before their Counsels, and secures *Israel* from their Incursions ; for *the bands of Syria came no more into the Land of Israel,* vers. 13, 23. So *Ezekiel,* when in *Caldea,* was present in spirit at the City Council of five and twenty at *Jerusalem* ; took exact notice of their Deportment, Debates, and Resolves, (in direct contradiction to God's messages by the Prophets, himself, *Jeremy* and others) and what befel them thereupon. *He saw Pelatiah the Chair-man or some chief*
mem-

member of the Council, fall down dead, Ezek. 11. 1, 13.

A Statesman of such a spirit, (that can at whatever distance, know the Debates and Resolves of the enemy, as if he sate in Council with them) might advise and contrive things with best advantage to his Countrey, without such a company of chargeable wast-pipes of Spials at home or Correspondents abroad, as is usual. But was this deceased Statesman a Prophet? All Futurities are treasured up in God, but does every one that sees God, see these? The Schoolmen acknowledge, that all the most contingent and voluntary actings of the Creatures, with all future events whatsoever, have bin eternally present to God's intuition, whose understanding is infinite, *Psal.* 147. 5. They hold him also to be *Speculum voluntarium,* a voluntary Mirror, so as not all that see him, see future events, or the present actings of their fellow creatures, at a distance; but onely such angels and men, unto whom he is pleased to make a particular discovery thereof, for the managing of his designes in the World. Let this be granted: yet, whoever is partaker of the divine nature or spirit of Christ, though but in the single portion thereof, lives undeniably in a spirit and discerning, superior to what is to be found in any first-creation nature whatsoever, humane or angelical. He that lives in this spirit, knows not onely this or that man by personal converse, but humane nature, mankind, what it amounts to, how 'twill act, where it will be next. He comprehends it, knowes the most curious and otherwise imperceptible motions of every wheele in it. Many believed in Christ; but he knew what kind of Faith they had, a temporary one, that onely that cast out the devil, and made them men again, wash'd their humane nature, not baptized them into the divine. He would not therefore trust them, for he knew all men; he knew what was in man, *John* 2, 23, 25. He knew they had but the faith that might draw back to perdition, which soon after appeared, for when he came closse to them in the testimony of spiritual or eternal Life, which is the free gift of the Father, issuing out of his discriminating love, these disciples went back and walked no more with him, *Joh.* 6. 65, 66.

The true Divine is a man of another, a more excellent spirit than other men, with *Caleb, Daniel,* and Christ himself. He sees the whole frame, course and way of man, in Sanctuary Light; weighs him in the ballance of the Sanctuary, knows what he will do, and what will become of him, notwithstanding any present flourishes. He knows he has but a slippery standing, will be brought into desolation in a moment, and utterly consumed with terrors, *Psal.* 73. 17, 19. The perfon here treated of, was (with *Noah*) a preacher of righteoufnefs ; with *Abraham*, one that did command his Children and houfhold after him, that they fhould keep the way of the Lord. His Life and Doctrine feemed to carry much of demonftration in them, that he was one of the peculiar Favourites of Heaven, had that double portion , which prepares and qualifies men to fit down (in due feafon) with Chrift upon the Throne, in a fuperiority to the elect Angels ; the fingular prerogative and reward of Chrift's Servants the Prophets, beyond what falls to their fhare, who yet are his true Saints and everlaftingly faved People, that fear his name, *Rev.* 11. 18.

This Prophet or Seer of God, in the midft of the greateft fuccefles in the late war, when the Churches, Parliament, and Army reckoned their work done ; thought their mountain fo ftrong that they fhould never be moved ; faid the bitternefs of death and perfecution is over, and that nothing remained, but (with thofe felf-confident *Corinthians*) *to be reigning as Kings*, (1 *Cor.* 4. 8.) he difcovered himfelf to be of another Spirit, with *Paul*. He could not reign with them. When they thus mufed and fpake, *We fhall fit as a Queen, we fhall know no more forrow*, he would be continually foretelling the overflowing of the finer myftical *Babylon*, by the moft grofly idolatrous *Babylon*, and the flaying of the true Witnefles of Chrift between them both, as the confequent of fuch inundation. Has not he had his fhare in the accomplifhment of his own prediction ? Have not they, by their pride, apoftacy, and treachery, been the occafion of his and their own fufferings, who would not believe him, when he prophefied of fuch a fuffering feafon ? Have not floods of *Belial*, Judges, Counfellors, Witnefles, Jurors, Souldiers of *Belial* compaffed him about ? (*Pfal.* 18. 4.) Did Scripture, Law, or Reafon fignify any thing with them ? So the Waters went over his foul ; they took away his Life from the Earth. Yea, the rage and violence of bruitifh men followed him clofe at the heels, to his very execution-ftroke. But however it was with him, as to a certain fore-fight of particular events, yet that he could conjecture and fpel out the moft referved confults and fecret drifts of forreign Councils againft us, (which they reckoned as *tacita*, concealed till executed) the *Hollander* did experience to their coft.

The next branch of his publick ufefulnefs in a political capacity, was his moft happy dexterity at making the beft of a war. Armies are to fmall purpofe abroad, unlefle there be fage Counfel at home. He heartily laboured to prevent a War with *Holland*, but the fons of *Zerviah*, a Military party, (that too much turned War into a Trade) were too many for him, in that point. He therefore fet himfelf to

make

make the beft of a War, for his Countries defence. In this War, after
fome dubious Fights, (while the immediate care of the Fleet was in
other hands) he with five others were appointed by the Parliament, to
attend that affaire. Hereupon he became the happy and fpeedy contri-
ver of that fuccefful Fleet that did our work in a very critical feafon,
when the *Hollander* vapoured upon our Seas, took Prizes at pleafure,
hovered about our Ports, and were ready to fpoil all. His report to
the Houfe, as to the War-Ships by him recruited, ordered and fent
forth in fo little time, to find the enemy work, feemed a thing incre-
dible.

In the beginning of that expenfive War, (as unwilling to make a
prey of his Countries neceflities) he refigned his Treafurer-fhip for
the Navy, caufing the cuftomary dues of that Office to be converted
into a Salary of a thoufand *per annum*. The bare poundage of all ex-
pences that way, which in times of peace came to about three thoufand, would have amounted to neer twenty thoufand by the year, during the war with *Holand*. Were his perfonal circumftances and the
condition of his Family-affaires at that feafon and fince, well known,
it would render this piece of felf-denial the more memorable. Some
inconfiderable matter, without his feeking, was allotted to him by the
Parliament in lieu thereof. He had alfo long before this, upon the
Self-denying Ordinance, (little obferved by others) refunded five and
twenty hundred pounds, for publick ufes, being the moiety of his Re-
ceptions in the faid Office, from fuch time as the Parliament had
made him fole Treafurer, who before the War was joyned with another perfon.

As for the keeping of his hands free from all maner of Bribes, or what
ever might be fo interpreted, all the while he was engaged in publick
action, I refer you to his own folemn appeal on the Scaffold, to the
great God of Heaven and Earth, and to all that great Affembly round
about him, or any other perfons, on that account, which none could
contradict. He openly challenged all men, to fhew wherein he had
defiled his hands with any mans blood or eftate, or that he had fought
himfelf in any publick place or capacity. Such were his abilities for
difpatch of a bufinefs if good, or hindring it if ill, that had his hand
been as open to receive as others to offer, in that kind, he might have
treafured up filver as duft. Many hundreds *per annum*, have been offered to fome about him, in cafe they could but prevail with him, only not to appear againft a propofal. On the leaft intimation of fuch a
thing to him, he would conclude it to be fome corrupt felf-interefted
defign, and fet himfelf more vigilantly and induftrioufly to oppofe

N   and

and quash it. That *Greek* Magistrate left the best Name behind him, who (having been often in publick place, and of general fame for abilities and honesty) when he came to die, left his family so bare, though he had lived frugally, that portions for his Children were issued out of the publick Treasury. This Patriot, for his many years faithful serving of the publick, has endured several tedious imprisonments, at length lost his Life, and hazarded his own estate, that should pay his great debts, and supply his family with such honourable maintenance as becomes their birth and education. Here's his reward on Earth ; *but great is his reward in heaven.*

The latter part of this Sufferers Elogy in the 'bove-mentioned Verses, concerns his skill in distinguishing the two Swords or Powers, Civil and Spiritual, and the setting right bounds to each. He held that the Magistrate ought to keep within the proper sphere of Civil Jurisdiction, and not intermeddle with mens Consciences by way of Imposition and Force, in matters of Religion and divine Worship. In that *Healing Question*, for which he was wounded by the late Protector (so called) he did sufficiently manifest this to be as well the Magistrates true Interest, as the Peoples just Security. 'Tis observed by *MORE* and others, on various accounts, that the *Romane* Emperors owning and incorporating Christianity with the Laws of the Empire, strengthened the Interest of the formal Christian, and drave the true Spiritual Worshipper into the Wilderness. While Magistrates pretend, and (it may be) verily think they are doing Christ a high piece of service by such fawning and formal compliance, they are directly involved in the Antichristian Interest, for the persecuting of Christ in his true spiritual members : That men, yea religious, holy men, may be so mistaken, see *Joh.* 16. 2. *Acts* 26. 9, 11.

This lover of his Nation, and assertor of the just Rights and Liberties thereof unto his death, was also for limiting the civil Power, delegated by the People to their Trustees in the Supream Court of Parliament, or to any Magistrates whatsoever. He held, *That there are certain Fundamental Rights and Liberties of the Nation, that carry such a universal and undeniable consonancy with the light of Nature, right Reason, and the Law of God, that they are in no wise to be abrogated or altered, but preserved.* What less than this can secure Peoples Lives, Liberties and Birth-rights, declared in *MAGNA CHARTA,* and ratified by two and thirty Parliaments since ? Let but once this truth be exploded and blown away, all the Rights and Liberties of the Nation will soon go after it, and arbitrary Domination and Rapine may securely triumph over all. Deny that there are any Fundamental,

unre-

unrepealable Laws, and who can be secure as to Life, Liberty, or E-
state ? For if by an over-ruling stroke of abused Prerogative, a majo-
rity in Parliament can be procured, that will pull up all the antient
Laws Rights and Liberties of the Nation by the Roots, and establish
mischief by a new Law ; (make Reason and Duty Treason, and that
post factum too) in this case, he that did things most rational and justifiable by unrepealed or unrepealable Laws, yesterday, may be condemned by a Law made *post factum*, and executed too morrow. By this
meanes Judges may be put into a most unhappy capacity of *justifying
the wicked, and condemning the righteous,* under colour of Parliamentary authority, *in both which things they are an abomination to the Lord,*
Prov. 17. 15.

' *Count* Gundamore *observed it to be no uneasie thing to procure a Par-*
' *liament that would gratify a self-interested party, and abuse the People. A*
' *corrupt sort of Gentry, that have many Tenants and Dependants, (who to*
' *please their Landlords would betray their Country and Religion too) could*
' *easily procure themselves to be chosen (saies he) for the County. And*
' *for Corporations, whose Burgesses fill the far greater number of Seats in*
' *that House, their obligations for some enlargement of their Charters by*
' *Royal Grant, rendred them compliant in their choice.* He farther obser-
' ved, *That the King, as sole Judge of Chivalry, created new Lords, that*
' *could in voting, out number the antient Barons by Tenure, who purchased*
' *the ratification of the antient fundamental Rights and Liberties of* En-
' gland, (*specified in* Magna Charta) *with their Swords,* in Henry the
' Third's time. *All these things put together, he reckoned Prerogative*
' *to have such a ruling influence in the election and constitution of* English
' *Parliaments, that notwithstanding their great fame abroad, they served*
' *for little other use than to empty the Peoples purses. Yet* (as fearing what
' an *English* Parliament may come to do in time) one chief service
' he boasts of to his Countrymen, was *the working a dislike between the*
' *King and the* Lower House, *so that* (saies he) *the King will never en-*
' *dure a Parliament more by his good will, but rather want than receive*
' *conditional relief from them. Some free minds* (he said) *there were amongst*
' *the People, that laboured to preserve their just Liberties from Soveraign*
' *invasion, calling out for the due course of their Common Law ; but other*
' *Time-servers cryed the Laws down, Prerogative up, to shelter their own*
' *arbitrary domination, in preying on the Subject ; and are hated by the op-*
' *pressed Commons for their pains.* All this kind of discouraging practice
' that tended to enfeeble, emasculate, and dis-spirit the *English* Nati-
' on, he tells the *Spanish* Council, *he forwarded to the utmost.* He fur-
' ther declared, *how he had under-wrought that admirable Engine ,* Sir

' Walter

' Walter Rawleigh, *and overthrown his Voyage, which threatened dan-*
' *ger to them : that upon his disgraceful return, by him caused, he had*
' *pursued him to Execution, had not his Commission for stay in England,*
' *bin at its period ; but he had left a sure Agent behind him, that saw it*
' *done. Thus* (saies he) *by punishing him for his daring attempt upon us,*
' *I laboured to quench the Valour of the* English *Nation, that none might*
' *be so bold as to venture upon the like again. All those* English *Papists*
' *that were of the* Spanish *Faction, thorowly Jesuited, were ready* (saies
' he) *to be my bloodhounds, to hunt him or any such to death. They hate*
' *the Prosperity, Valour, Worth and Wit of their own Nation, in respect of*
' *our Catholick Cause.* He also had perswaded King *James* to let his
' *Fleet* remain unman'd and unvictualled, *least his Master should be jea-*
' *lous of some intendments to his prejudice, and so break off the* Spanish
' *Match. Now therefore* (said he) *is a fit opportunity to Invade* En-
' *land, never the like.*

' *They might probably have made better work of it at that season than in*
' 88, *but that other cross blows prevented them, as the apprehending of* Bar-
' nevelt, *and the detection of their Catholick design in these parts of Eu-*
' *rope, towards the reducing all the Kingdomes of the World, Protestant,*
' *Popish, Mahumetane, or what ever else, into subjection to the* Spanish
' *King, as the natural Head, Lord and Soveraign over all, by the Popes free*
' *donation and appointment, on condition that he bring him into the exercise*
' *of his Headship in Spirituals, as fast as he gets his own in Temporals.*
Thus they pleased themselves in their own Imaginations, to divide
the World between them ; but the World will not be so served.
These things with many other in *Gundamores* Narrative, came to light
amongst us, by Sir *Robert Cotton,* (as 'tis said) that great Treasurer
of learned and pertinent rarities.

By these observations & practises of the politick *Spaniard,* it may appear, his Reason pitched on the same conclusion with *Solomon, Pro.* 11.
14. That *in the multitude of Counsellours there is safety;* and that for any
State to refer matters too much to the single understanding and will of
some one person, may expose all to forreign invasion and ruine. Can it
then appear unreasonable, in any State, specially, when there is no single
person in possession, to offer such a proposal to free debate amongst
the Peoples Trustees, whether or no it be convenient to admit a single person to the Legislative or executive power over them ? The
Romans nipp'd Tyranny in the bud, executed their Founder and first
King, *Romulus,* to preserve their Foundations, the Laws, which he
neglected. They banished proud *Tarquin* their seventh and last, on the
same account. Whatever any may think they have to say against those

two

two popular actions, there may seem not to be the least colour of reason to alledge against one that had no hand or consent in the execution of the one, or expulsion of the other, (this Sufferers Case) to offer such a proposal to the People or Senate; Whether some other form of Government might not be more conducible to the publick Interest? Such Questions were propounded and debated amongst those old *Romanes*. They did use their just natural Liberty, as men, in considering what might most make for publick safety, (the main end for which there are any such things as Governments or Governours at all) and concluded upon two yearly Consuls, that were limitted by many Senators, as they also, afterwards by popular Tribun's, and sometimes a Dictator, till all were swallowed up again into an Emperour. The successe was this. Their Dominion while under Kings, extended about fifteen miles from *Rome*.. Under Consuls, their territories were enlarged to about fifteen thousand miles compass. Under some of their bruitish and Tyrannical Emperors, they lost ground again, faster than ever they got it.

The *Lacedemonian Ephori* and such like popular Superintendents in other *Greek* Common-wealths, that were authorized to curb, restrain, depose their Kings, and something more, in case of such exorbitances and misgovernment as deserved it, who knows not? 'Twas ordinary amongst them, not onely to change their Governours, but Government also. If one race of Kings be lawfully deposed, they are not wronged by change of Government, and who else can be? 'Tis so natural and fundamental a Right in People to have & use such a Liberty, that we may do wel to consider whether they have any right to give it out of their hands, unless it be lawful to contradict the Law of Nature, the true end of all Government in humane Societies, turn their own Reason out of Doors, and so turn beasts for their Governours to ride on. That the *Jews*, *Greeks*, and *Romanes*, (the wisest States in the world) have over and over used this Liberty of Changing their Government, as they saw occasion, and that often with very good successe, is undeniable.

Were it unlawful for a State, in any case to depose and remove Kings, what Titles have any Monarchs now upon earth to their Crowns, that are descended of those, who were elected into the room of such as the people deposed?

How bruitish then and destructive even to the Interest and Title of the present Kings (that he sought to gratify and flatter) is *Belloy's* Assertion, *That a Family once setled in the Crown, though they prove never so wicked, vitious and abominable, yea, though they go about to de-*
stroy

ſtroy the Common-wealth, muſt yet be ſacred to us, and permitted to keep their Seat, without any direction, reſtraint or puniſhment from the Common-wealth, but from God onely? At this rate, all the *Carlees* in *France* were Uſurpers, becauſe *Pepin* (the firſt of that Race) came to the Crown upon the depoſition of *Childeric* the Third, and ſo wiped out the *Merovees* or *Pharamonds* Line. The like is to be ſaid of the *Cape-vingiens*, who have now ſate in the *French* Throne almoſt ſeven hundred years, ſince the depoſition of *Charles* of *Lorain*, laſt of *Pepins* race, into whoſe room *Hugh Capet* was elected by the People. The ſame thing is to be ſeen in the *Spaniſh* Hiſtories, and where not? Four Races of Kings have been there ſince the expulſion of the *Romans*. The firſt was from the *Goths*. The ſecond from *Don Pelago*. The third from *Don Sancho Mayor*. The laſt, from the Houſe of *Auſtria*. *England* has had more changes of this kind, than both theſe neighbour Monarchies together, in the ſame ſpace of about twelve hundred years. They all three got looſe from the *Romane* Yoke, ſo long ago.

This bleſſed Witneſs and Aſſertor of the Fundamental Rights, Truths, and Liberties of Chriſts Kingdom, as alſo of the Common-wealth of *England*, and that has ſealed his Aſſertions in both kinds, with his blood, was not onely well ſkilled in ſetting the right bounds to civil and ſpiritual Power in the outward government of Worldly States, but he did yet more cloſly diſtinguiſh between natural (whence civil ſprings) and ſpiritual Power, as to the inward regulation of particular perſons.

You may take a glance into his larger Diſcourſes on this Subject, by a ſhort gloſſe on the two Trees in *Eden, that of Life*, and *that of the Knowledge of good and evil*. Theſe two Trees were the firſt ſignificant Types in and by which man was inſtructed in this doctrine, which *rightly divides the word of Truth* (Chriſt the living, and Scriptures the written Word of God) between the natural and ſpiritual man, alotting unto each their proper portion and character. One of theſe *Adam* might, yea, ought to have fed upon, the *Tree of Life*, the other not. By the Devils ſuggeſtion to the Woman, and hers to him, he made a contrary choice. He did eat of that he ſhould not, to the loſs even of that he thought to gratify himſelf in, his temporary Life of righteouſneſs and communion with God; and neglected to eat of the other, and ſo of Chriſt in ſpirit, the Antitype thereof, for the feeding and building him up into eternal Life, and true bleſſedneſs.

Theſe two Trees were an Allegory, of like ſignificancy with *Sarai* and *Hagar, Iſaac* and *Iſhmael*, Old and New Teſtament or Covenant, &c.

&c., One of them fignified the firft *Adam* with his *living Soul*, and freedom to good and evil : the other, the fecond *Adam* with his *quickning fpirit*, and freedom to good onely, which he communicates and builds men up into the life and exercife of, in fellowfhip with himfelf. *Adam* chofe to gratify his primitive natural conftitution and freedom to good and evil, which together with the things that feed it, were typically ftated and reprefented in *the Tree of the knowledge of good and evil*. The new-creature Life, and the glorious Liberty of the fons of God, together with the things thereof, (not feen to man, in the former capacity) things eternal, were typically ftated and reprefented to *Adams* natural difcerning, in *the tree of Life*, with inftruction what was his concern to do or not to do, as to that or the other. But although thefe Types were given, and expounded alfo by Chrift unto *Adam* before hand ; yet was there room left, after his fall, for the exercife of a diftinguifhing difpenfation of mercy towards him and his pofterity, from that of feverity, which was forthwith put in execution againft the apoftate angels, excluding them from any poffibility of ever entring into Gods Reft. This argues, that the Angels *who excel in ftrength, and are higher than man*, had a clearer underftanding in that point, as to the requifitenefs of a tranfition for themfelves and for men, out of the mutable ftate of life and righteoufnefs, received in their firft creation, into the unchangable Life and everlafting righteoufnefs of the fecond. Their fall therefore was more knowing, wilful, fatal and irrecoverable upon any tearms whatfoever.

That which *Paul* faid of himfelf, may be faid of *Adams* firft tranfgreffion, comparatively with the firft fin of the Angels, *that he did it ignorantly, and fo obtained mercy*. 1 Tim. 1. 13. But let man, after renewed and revived, look to it ; for if after all this warning, *he fin again after the fimilitude of Adams tranfgreffion*, he becomes a *Tree twice dead, and will be pluckt up by the roots*. This fecond fall of man is as fatal and irrecoverable as the Angels firft. *Adam's* eating the forbidden fruit, imported no lefs than a pleafing himfelf in the fingle Liberty, Righteoufnefs, Life and Enjoyments of his firft-creation ftate, in preference to what was attainable for him in the fecond. He preferred the creature, or glory of man in the firft, to the glory of God, that refts upon men for ever in the new-creation ftate. He preferred the Law of works, or the natural power of working righteoufnefs, fet up in him by the firft creation, to the Law of Liberty, Grace, Faith, that heavenly power of working righteoufnefs, that is fet up in man by the new creation, which can do all good and no evil, *fo that against fuch there is no Law, Gal. 5. 23.* This is *the glorious liberty of the fons of God*,

God, *Jam.* 1. 25. and 2. 12. To prefer the lesser glory of the first creation, the glory of man, to the greater glory of the second, the glory
and righteousness of God, *is to worship, serve, and value, the glory of
the Creature, more than that of the Creator, who is blessed for ever,* Rom.
1. 25. They that prefer the lesser glory to the greater, the righteousness and glory of man's first-creation to that of the second, will prove
hypocrites and persecute. A hypocrite is not onely he that makes a
shew of righteousness and has none, but that has the righteousness
and glory of man really in and upon him, and in the credit and flourish of this, would personate and pass for that which he is not, the
true spiritual heir, that has the glory and righteousness of God in and
upon him ; and then the next news is, he falls to persecuting of him
that indeed is the true heir, saying to his fellows in spirit and principle, *Come, this is the heir, lets kill him, and the inheritance shall be ours.*
A hypocrite is one that personates and would pass for that which he
is not. If he be stark naught, he would pass for that which is good. If
good and righteous in one kind, he would pass for that that is better
and more excellent in another. Such an hypocritical spirit is a persecuting spirit. He thats born of Christ after the flesh, and will go no
farther, will persecute him that is born of the same Christ after the
spirit : will hate his Brother, *slander his own Mothers Son,* Psal. 50.
20. To this effect did this Sufferer use to Allegorize, the two Trees
in *Eden,* and other Scriptures in exact analogie and harmony therewith.

But come we now to consider the method of his sufferings ; how
this meek, dove-like, harmless person has been handled by the injurious, wolvish spirit of this world, that has affronted contradicted and
blasphemed his principles and doctrine, and at length killed his body, as a contentious wrangler and a malefactor. Christ was so served.
He went about doing good and suffering ill to the last. This eminent
disciple and follower of his, hath waded through all those injurious
reproaches and mis-interpretations men have put upon his most innocent and useful words and actions, in that thank-worthy and acceptable imitation of him, which *Peter* represents to us under the similitude of good servants, *that can suffer patiently for well-doing, committing themselves to him that judgeth righteously,* 1 Pet. 2. 18, 23.
*He considered him that endured such contradiction of sinners against him-
self, and did not faint in his mind, but striving against sin and sinners of all
sorts, by his faithful witnef-bearing, resisted unto blood,* Heb. 12. 3, 4.
But be it known that amidst the personal sufferings of Saints, 'tis not
onely lawful but their duty, *to pray that God would awake to their judgement,*

ment, even to their CAUSE, which is his CAUSE, that *all those may yet come to shout for joy that favour their righteous CAUSE; and that the enemy may not rejoyce over them, as if he had swallowed them up, though they abuse and kill them all the day long, as sheep appointed for the slaughter,* Pſal. 35. 23, 27. *Some of you* (ſaies Chriſt) *they shall put to death: but not a hair of your head shall perish,* Luk. 21. 16, 18.

This worthy Patriot was freely choſen, without any ſeeking of his, to ſerve as Burgeſs for the Town of *Kingſton* upon *Hull,* in that Parliament which ſate down *November* 3. 1640. About thirteen years did he indefatigably labour therein for his Countries relief, againſt manifeſt Oppreſſions and publick grievances that were upon it. And well nigh ten years more he hath patiently ſuffered, as either a uſeleſs or pernicious perſon, becauſe of his deſtructive conſtitution to the Peace and Intereſt of Tyranny. During the long Parliament, he was uſually ſo engaged for the Publick, in the HOUSE and ſeveral Committees, from early in the morning to very late at night, that he had ſcarce any leiſure to eat his bread, converſe with his neareſt Relations, or at all to mind his Family affaires. Were I indeed furniſhed with the tongue of the learned, the pen of a ready writer, I ſhould think it adviſeable to let the uſefulneſs & ſucceſſe of his publick Actings all along that Parliament till forcibly diſſolved, ſpeak for themſelves. That race of action being run, (not without much ſtruggling, contradiction, and miſ-reports all the while) he comes to his ſuffering Scene. He was for ſeveral years rejected, perſecuted, & impriſoned by his apoſtatized friends (that had gone to the houſe of God in company with him) who at length to compleat their perſecuting work upon him, delivered him up, to be hunted to death by his profeſſed foes, enemies of all righteouſneſs, Gods and mans too.

First, his falſe Friends that had ſat in Council with him, (and who owed, in great meaſure, their very Lives and ſucceſs to him, under God) *they faſted for ſtrife and debate,* kept a mock faſt, to draw ſuch as durſt give them faithful counſel and warning, into a ſnare. Upon their apoſtacy, when brought into diſtreſs through forreign diſappointments, they (ſomewhat *Jezebel*-like) proclaimed a faſt, publickly declaring their willingneſs to receive information from any hand, as to what was amiſs in the Government, that might be the ground of God's not going forth with their Armies as he was wont. He laid hold on this publiſhed offer, and as a faithful watchman and able Patriot, exhibited his thoughts to them in a *Healing Queſtion,* on which he was ſhortly after ſent for by the Council, from the place of

O   his

his refidence at *Belleau* in *Lincolnfhire*, proceeded againſt as ſeditious, and impriſoned about four moneths at *Caris-brough* Caſtle in the Iſle of *Weight*. Thus the *Jews* ſerved *Jeremy*, Jer. 42, and 43. They deſired him to enquire the mind of the Lord, as to their intended journey for *Egypt* , and ſolemnly engaged they would obey the meſſage, calling God to witneſs between them and him. He ſeeks the Lord, and after ten dayes receives and faithfully declares the word of the Lord, which was, *That if they went to Egypt, the ſword they feared at home, ſhould meet with them there ; and if they tarried in their own land, they ſhould be preſerved*. They proudly rebelled againſt this word, and not onely ſo, but forced *Jeremy* along with them to *Egypt*, to bear a ſhare in their ſufferings, though not in their ſin, as the wiſe Servant was handled by his fooliſh Maſter in *Ariſtophanes*, and as is frequently the caſe amongſt mortals. God the great diſpoſer of all the kingdoms of men, gave *Egypt* to *Nebuchadnezzar* and his Army, as wages for their hard ſervice in pulling down proud *Tyre*, (whoſe Merchants were Princes, *Eſay* 23. 8.) where every head was made bald, and every ſhoulder peeld with long and exceſſive labour in a thirteen years ſiege and filling up a channel of the ſea, in order to their approaches, *Ezek.* 26. 9. and *Chap.* 29. 18, 20. Thus *Nebuchadnezzars* ſword, that the *Jews* feared in their own Countrey, (upon the killing of his Deputy Governour, *Gedaliah*) meets with them amongſt the reſt, in *Egypt*, the character and ruine whereof we have, *Ezek.* 29. 30. 31. and 32. Chapters; as of *Tyre, Chap.* 26. 27. and 28.

Thus treacherouſly was this ſteddy Witneſs of the true Liberties of Chriſts Kingdom, and his native Countrey, handled by thoſe that for many years had joyned with him in the profeſſion of the ſame righteous C A U S E, againſt ſacrilegious and tyrannical domination in Church or State. What was his crime ? He was ſtedfaſt in the Covenant : they turned aſide like a deceitful Bow. The criminous party had the Sword, and innocency ſuffered. Even ſo it is now. To omit his rejection and confinement by the Long Parliament, after their return to take their Seats afreſh in the H O U S E, 1659. his laſt Scene of Sufferings was under the preſent Powers.

Under this variety of Perſecutors and Perſecution, he notably experienced the truth of that Apoſtolical Argument for the Reſurrection : *If in this Life onely, we have hope in Chriſt, we are of all men moſt miſerable*, 1 Cor. 15. 19. He took that courſe in the face of all affronts and contradictions of ſinners, (of one kind or other, from firſt to laſt) which ſhewed the invincible ſteaddineſſe and chaſtity of his ſpirit. What he vigorouſly proſecuted when he was active, he ratified and
ſealed

sealed with his blood, (and all the tendencies thereunto, by *witnessing a good Confession*) since he was passive. He stood up for the defence of the Lives and Liberties of his Country-men, and lost his own Liberty and Life for his paines. As a true lover of his Nation, he boldly asserted the Rights thereof at the last push, to the faces of those that have sufficiently declared themselves enemies thereunto, in condemning him. What he could do or suffer more for his Countrey than he did, is somewhat difficult to say.

His two years imprisonment under this power, was by meer will and pleasure (no particular crime being laid to his charge) in direct contradiction to the fundamental Laws and Liberties of *Englishmen*, stated in *MAGNA CHARTA*, *Chap.* 29. *Festus* a heathen Judge, deemed this unreasonable in *Paul's* case, *Act.* 25.27. *It seemeth to me unreasonable* (saies he) *to send one as a Prisoner, and not withal to signify the crimes laid against him.* 'Tis against the Law of nature, the conscience and common light of Reason in all mankind, that any man should be so dealt with. For their most injurious underhand-dealing, in picking up a charge (while he was kept two years close-prisoner) and procuring Witnesses against him by threats or promises, together with their proceedings about him at the Grand Jury and Kings Bench, I do once for all refer you to the Narrative of his Tryal. I reserve onely a liberty of speaking something in general, as to the difficulty of his circumstances in the tryal, and for particulars, to lay before you the main passages of the *Jews* proceedings with Christ, trusting them and you together, to make the application. I take hint for this latter branch of my liberty, from one of his occasional speeches recorded in his Tryal. Mention being made by a Friend, of the cruel proceedings against him; *Alas,* said he, *what a-do they keep to make a poor creature like his Saviour?*

He was an able *Common-Wealths-Man* and a *true Believer*; two dangerous qualifications to Church and State, as this world goes. He had remarkable insight in the Politie of the true Common-wealth of *Israel,* the *Holy Jerusalem that will shortly come down from God out of Heaven,* Rev. 21. This gave him no small aime at what he ought to be doing in the Common-wealth of *England,* as preparatory thereunto. What was done in the day of small things, (when the Nation was delivered from its taskmasters) was not despicable in its season, though a cloud be now drawn over it. 'Twas a usual saying with him, *Come what would, every thing was upon the right Wheel, in the wise contrivement of God, for the accomplishing of his righteous designs in the world.* But considering matters betwixt man and man; that expostulation,

Eccles.

Ecclef. 2.15. (*Why was I then more wise ?*) may seem to be fairly interpretable into this fence ; That true wifdom is a great difadvantage to a man in this difordered world, where 'tis the fashion for luft, will, and pleafure to bear fway, againft Scripture, Law, and Reafon. Perfons of the beft rational abilities and moft confcience, have ufually been deftroyed in Courts of Judicature (fo called) throughout the world, in all times. A man of Reafon and Confcience, called forth to declare his mind, cannot afford to gratifie the corrupt humors & lufts of men (*that put good for evil, and evil for good, light for darknefs, and darknefs for light,* (Efay 5.20.) much lefs, become one in pirit and principle with thofe that fo do) and then he muft die. *When truth failes, and every thing is called by a wrong name, good evil and evil good, men abhor him that fpeaketh uprightly ; they hate him that reproveth in the gate,* Amos 5. 10.

If the foundations be deftroyed, what can the righteous do ? Pfal. 11. 3. Yea, or what can he fay ? when the Soveraignty and infinitely moft Supream Legiflative power of God and Chrift himfelf is fet at naught; there's the main Foundation gone, as to the righteous man's defence amongft his fellow mortals. If Judges that have no fear of God before their eyes, be on the Bench, then long fchrowls of I know not what muft be formed up and read againft the moft faithful Patriots and choiceft Chriftians, as not having the fear of God before their eyes, and fentence accordingly muft be pronounced againft them by one ruful wight or other, that's an enemy to all true Law and right Reafon. This fort of Cattel have not been wanting in any place or time. Queen *Jezebel* could find them in *Jezreel* ; Judges and witnefles of *Belial* againft *Naboth,* and away goes his Life, and fhe (not long after) to the Dogs, 1 *King.* 21. and 2 *King.* 9. Such Judges as have no fear of God before their eyes, what will they ftick at ? All inferiour and fubordinate Foundations of the righteous mans fafety, all the Laws, Rights, and Liberties of any Nation will fignify little with Judges fo qualified and fitted to abufe and murder any righteous men that are brought before them. See the boldnefs of the Kings, Rulers and People of the earth, not onely in flighting but down-right bidding defiance to the Soveraignty of God and Chrift, Father and Son, with the Laws of both, *Pfal.* 2. 2,3. *The Kings of the Earth fet themfelves, and the Rulers take Counfel together, againft the Lord, and againft his Chrift* ; there's their Soveraignty affronted. Then they fay, *verf.* 3. *Let us break their bands afunder, and caft away their cords from us* ; there are their Lawes rejected. Then, if the antient fundamental Lawes or Liberties of any Nation be flighted, laid afide, or pull'd up

by

by the roots, and mischief established by some new one ; with this advantage, the basest of men may gather themselves together against the soul of the righteous, and condemn innocent blood, *Psal.*94. 20, 21. If over and beyond all this, there be such wicked Judges to be found, that neither fear God, nor regard that which is the man in man, Reason, but onely that corrupt State Reason that lies in point blank contradiction thereunto ; if such be to be found, who will venture by their superadditional glosses to stretch a mischievous new Law beyond the proper significancy of its words, to serve their present purpose ; yea, or if they dare, even beyond all this, lay down their meer arbitrary assertions, (that have not the least hint for them in such a new made Law) which will pass with Jurors for a legal ground of taking away ones Life ; A righteous man in these circumstances has an exceeding hard time on't. Beyond all this yet, if a proviso-Foundation for securing an innocent persons Life, any voluntary unsought for grant, (made upon a supposal that all other Foundations of his security should fail him) if this also be laid aside and slighted, (though the word of a King, in answer to the Petition of a Parliament, amounting in effect to an Act of Parliament) where's the righteous man then ? gone, without remedy ; But whither ? from earth to heaven. A sad loss to us, a great gain to him. Sure something will come down from heaven amongst us er'e long for such doings. A righteous man in a case so circumstanced, (which I have thus taken Liberty according to my word, to speak a little to in general) what can he say in his just defence, that his Accusers and Judges will not call Treason, and be ready to form up a new Charge against him for, if commanded? Thus the *Jews* served Christ ; (and so I pass to the other branch of my reserved liberty, the consideration of particulars, in the case of the leading Sufferer.) *Ye have heard the blasphemy,* (saies the high Priest) *he hath spoken blasphemy, what further need have we of Witnesses ? What think ye ?* The Jewry-men never study the point; they have their Verdict ready at their fingers ends ; *he is guilty of death,* Mat. 26. 65, 66. Quick work. But what was the crime ? *He denied not but that he was the Son of God.* For Christ or Christians to be in the highest sence what they should be, & own it; this men (yea, the very high Priests, Archbishops, that pretend to be the chief watchmen over souls) are ready to call *Blasphemy.* If they can but get any the least intimation of such a thing out of them by interrogating, they reckon they have enough to take away their Lives. They *that are of their Father the Devil* (as Christ told these *Jews*) can't endure to hear any own themselves to be the *Sons of God.* What a world is this for Christ and his followers ?

The

The chief Priests, Elders and all the Council sought false Witnesses a-gainst Jesus to put him to death. They tamper with many, yet for a good while find none but such as are insufficient to do their work, either through the invalidity of the matter testified, or inconsistency of their testimony, for they agreed not. To murder him they were resolved. all they sought for was a colourable pretext. *At length come two false witnesses* (well paid, 'tis like, for their pains) *which say; this fellow said, I am able to destroy the Temple of God and build it in three dayes;* whereas his words were (*Joh.* 2. 29.) *destroy ye this Temple,* his Body, (so they did) *and in three dayes I will raise it up;* so he did. But what a feeble testimony was here to go about to take away a man's Life upon, in case it were true, that he spake these words, and that, in their sence, concerning the material structure of the figurative Temple? They lie at catch therefore for some word from his own mouth at the bar, to carry on the work. Very little 'twas he spoke there. He lets the false witnesses pass uncontrolled; *answers not a word,* though deminded by the high Priest, *Mat.* 26. 61, 63. Then the high Priest falls to interrogating, tries what new matter for a charge he can get out of him by Questions. Yea, *he adjures him to tell them whether he be the Christ, the Son of God.* Christ denies it not. Now they reckon they have enough. They slight their false witnesses. They are now Judges and Witnesses too, themselves, and that in a matter of far greater consequence, *blasphemy; he makes himself the Son of God,* say they. Then they hurry him away before *Pilate* the *Romane* Deputy, where the chief Priests and Elders that sat as his Judges in the other Court, turn his Accusers, vehemently urging and witnessing many things against him before *Pilate,* and he lets all pass, *answers not a word.* Yea, though minded of it, and urged by *Pilate* to speak for himself, not a word could they get of him, say or do what they would. He's a Mute. It seems their Testimony, in *Pilates* judgement, amounted to very little; for after all, he asks them, *What evil hath he done?* Their answer is, *Let him be crucified.* Bruits! Oh, but (say they) *we have a Law, and by our Law he ought to dye, because he made himself the Son of God.* 'Tis a dangerous thing amongst men, for Christ or his fellow-heirs, to own themselves to be *the Sons of God, Heirs of the heavenly Kingdom,* though they give no disturbance or just occasion of offence to any Kings in their worldly Thrones. Men will be laying their heads together, to frame some mischievous Law against them, to call them *Blasphemers,* & then put them to death for it. They will call that *Heresy,* which is the only right way of *worshipping the God of our Fathers,* & then punish them for it. What goodly work are Magistrates with some new

upstart

upstart Lawes, like to make on't at Religion and Worſhip? If there be any that do what they ſhould in either, of all others they muſt be ſure to go to wrack.

But *Pilate* yet ſeeks to releaſe Chriſt. All that is ſaid yet, will not do it with him. 'Twas a cuſtom to deliver ſome one Priſoner at the Feaſt; he asks them therefore, *Shall I deliver Chriſt or Barabbas? Now Barabbas was a robber and a Murtherer. They cry out all at once,* like mad men; *away with this man, and releaſe unto us Barabbas.* Men will rather favour Murderers and Robbers than Chriſt and his follow-ers. *Pilate willing yet to releaſe Jeſus,* (Chriſt had the better on't of our Priſoner, as to the Lord chief Juſtice that ſat upon him) ſpeaks once again to them of it. But they hold to their old tone, cry *crucifie him, crucifie him.* He replied yet again, *Why? what evil hath he done? I find no cauſe of death in him. But they were inſtant with loud voices, re-quiring that he might be crucified. Pilate ſayes to them, What? Shall I crucify your King? The chief Prieſt anſwered, we have no king but Caſar.* And here they take hint for a new charge againſt him, that it will high-ly concern *Pilate* to take notice of. *If thou let this man go,* (ſay they) *thou art not Caſars friend. Whoſoever maketh himſelf a King, ſpeaketh a-gainſt Caſar.* Then *Pilate* complies with them. The voices of the People, and the chief Prieſt prevailed; ſo he paſſes ſentence, that it ſhould be as they required.

'Tis the legally religious party all along, that accuſe, proſecute and deliver up Chriſt and his followers into the hands of ſinners among the *Gentiles,* and ſo, have the greater ſin, as Chriſt told *Pilate.* But *Pi-late* alſo, however he may flatter himſelf and waſh his hands of it, he can't waſh his heart, or render himſelf guiltleſs of the blood of that *juſt Man,* as his Wife, (being admoniſhed in a dream) warned him to keep himſelf. 'Tis ſaid, both by *Romane* Hiſtorians and *Greek* Wri-ters of the *Olympiads,* that *Pilate* was accuſed by the *Jews* to the *Ro-mane* Senate, and ſo continually vexed by the Emperour *Caius Caligu-la,* that about the Year 39, being five or ſix years after the Paſſion, he killed himſelf with his own hand.

But what truth had that laſt charge in it, *that he made himſelf a King,* or had ſpoken any thing againſt *Caſar?* Theſe very *Jewes* themſelves would fain have had him owned himſelf as their temporal King, to de-liver them from the *Romane* Yoke; ſo indeed, they were the Traytors, if any body. *Pilate* himſelf had been pulled off the bench, if that could have bin. But Chriſt would not accept the offer, though as the Son of *David* in a direct line, the temporary Soveraignty might ſeem to be his right. He perceived they would take him by force, to make him a
King

King, and away went he to a mountain himself alone, *Joh.* 6. 15.
And in his answer to their ensnaring question about tribute, he quite
non-plust and silenced them. *Give* (saies he) *unto Cæsar the things
that are Cæsars,* Mat. 22. 15, 22. Be subject to his jurisdiction in
temporals , the outward actions and concerns of your bodily
life ; yea, though fore'd by the *Romane* sword to promise allegiance
to him. *Jeremy* tutored the *Jews* to like effect ; to submit to *Nebuchadnezzar,* though a forreign Prince and Conquerour. And God himself espouses *Nebuchadnezzars* quarrel against *Zedekiah*, calling the
engagement he made with *Nebuchadnezzar, HIS Covenant,* and *HIS
Oath,* and holding himself concerned in point of honour, to recompense the breach of it upon *Zedekiah's* head, *Ezek.* 17. 11, 21. *Zedekiah* signifies, *the righteousnes of Jah or Jehovah.* This name was given him by *Nebuchadnezzar,* to intimate to him, that if he broke Covenant, the righteousnes of the Lord would not suffer him to scape
unpunished. Accordingly it came to pass. He is taken by the *Caldean*
Souldiers, brought to the head Quarters at *Riblah,* a place between
Jerusalem and *Tyre,* where *Nebuchadnezzar* lay to hear the news from
both his Leagures before those famous Cities. There a Council of War
sits on him ; the sentence is, *That his sons be slain before his eyes; then,
that his eyes be put out, and that he be carried prisoner to Babylon,* where
he died not long after. This he got by breach of Covenant, 2 *King.*
25. 1, 7.

Christ advised the *Jews* to keep their Covenant with *Cæsar,* (as
Jeremy with *Nebuchadnezzar*) he paid him tribute himself, *Mat.*
17. 27. If *Cæsar* will have more than his due, if he will invade Gods
Prerogative ; venture out of the proper sphere of worldly Magistracy,
which relates but to the bodily actions and concerns of this mortal
Life, (1 *Cor.* 6. 3, 4.) if he demand those things that peculiarly belong
to God ; that other mens Consciences and Light, as to Religion and
divine Worship, be levelled, squared and regulated by his, (who it
may be has none at all) then *Cæsar* himself is to blame, as a sacrilegious intruder into the proper Rights of Christs Kingdom ; see he so
that. They are commended of God, that conscientiously deny him
obedience therein, as most justly refusing *to become servants of men in
things perteining unto God,* 1 Cor. 7. 23.

It was suggested, *The King could not be safe while V A N E was alive.*
Why ? what would he do ? No man more disswaded from popular tumults , (even against this power that God hath permitted to be
brought over us) then he. His demeanour in this point was much
like that of *Jeremy* amongst the *Jews,* who disswaded them from con-
spiracies

spiracies with *Egypt*, or infurrections againft the King of *Babylon*.
But why was not care taken to remove all finifter and prejudicial reports, as to this matter, from the chief in power ? I anfwer; why
did not Chrift anfwer a word to the *Jewes* fierce accufations of him before *Pilate*, but let *Pilate* take it as he would ? If his actions would
not fpeak for him, he was content. Was this a crime in Chrift ? Is
there not rather an emphafis laid upon this regardlefnefs of a felf-de-
fence, (while his heart was fixed upon a publick good) as a fingular
ingredient into the excellency of the fufferings of *that Captain of our
Salvation*? And fhall the fame deportment be reckoned culpable in
his followers ? No man could take away Chrift's Life from him :
Were *Pilate* and the *Jews* then guiltlefs in fhedding his innocent
blood ? No. Is Chrift a *felo de fe*, a felf-murderer, becaufe he laid
down his Life of his own accord? Neither. *Gods hand and counfel
had determined it fhould be fo*, Act. 4. 27,28. The *Jews* were moft ex-
ecrable murderers of the Lord of glory for all that, and refponfible
for it. *Pilate* had his fhare in it too, by yeilding up his own reafon
and confcience, either to the violent importunities and moft irrational out-cries of the *Jews*, (who faid, *away with him, away with
him, let him be crucified*) or to their moft falfe and flanderous infinuations of Treafon, charactering him as an enemy to the Crown and
dignity of *Cæfar*, which they could make no proof of.

Were all the affronts and injuries that were put upon this truly
Chriftian *Common-Wealths-Man* (who was indeed, for what others
talked of, the Liberty of Men as Men, and Chriftians as Chriftians)
well and orderly fet together, it would be difficult to find a *Parallel
proceeding for Injuftice*, next that againft Chrift, in all Hiftory, humane
or divine. *VIOLENCE and WRONG in ftead of RIGHTEOUSNES
and TRUTH, were weighed out to him by thofe that pretended to hold the
Scales of Juftice in their hands*, Pfal. 58. 2. *But Judgement fhall return
to Righteoufnefs*, Pfal. 94. 15. Righteoufnefs will come at laft to have
Judgement paffed on its fide. They feem to be parted, *while wicked
men are juftified and the righteous condemned*. This Sufferer did ufually
difcourfe of and expect a failer of all vifible reliefs to good men, when
others little dream't of it. But has the righteous man no remedy in
fuch a feafon ? He would familiarly invite others with himfelf to caft
their thoughts upon what is fignified, (*Ecclef.* 5. 8. amongft many
other Scriptures) in way of refolution to this Querie. *If thou feeft
the oppreffion of the poor, and violent perverting of Judgement and Juftice in a Province, marvel not* (or be not difmaied) *at the matter: for he
that is higher than the higheft, regardeth, and there be higher than they.*

P

Angels are higher than the highest powers amongst men, in the Magiftratical Government of this world, and God and Chrift are higher than they. This, with many like Scriptures, points us upwards, to a higher creature Magiftracy than man's; and yet higher to the original fpring and eternal root of all juft Magiftracy, in Chrift and God.

The holy angels will not fail to exercife their Magiftracy in an exact fubferviency unto and confonancy with Chrift. When the Monarchy of this world, lodged for a feafon in the hands of men, is degenerated from the *golden head* of it in *Nebuchadnezzar*, to the *iron leggs and feet of it, part of iron, part of clay,* fo as that it is become extreamly, univerfally, & remedilefsly oppreffive to righteous men, then is the feafon for thofe angelical powers (that put feven years interruption even to the golden head) to come forth in a general difpenfation of juftice, to pluck up by the roots every thing that offends Chrift and his followers, all the world over. Thefe Principalities and Powers, thefe invifible Thrones and Courts of Judicature, have from the beginning, and all along this worlds duration, been in the exercife of a fuper intending Magiftracy over the higheft powers amongft men. In purfuance of the decrees of thefe watchers, (*Dan.* 4. 17.) Thefe obfervers of the wayes of men, (as *Hefiod* calls them) in fubferviency to Chrift, have particular Angels been fent forth and commiffioned to punifh the proud infulting Monarchs, and bruitifh People of this world, and to minifter for the heirs of falvation, *Heb.* 1. 14. The *Sodomites,* when they affaulted *Lot,* were fmitten with blindnefs by two Angels that Chrift fent that way, while he tarried with *Abraham, Gen.* 18. 22. and *Chap.* 19. 11. So were the *Syrian* Army before *Dotham* ferved by the like angelical powers, at *Elifha's* prayer, 2 *King.* 6. 18. By thefe were the two Captains and their fifties flain at *Eliah's* prayer, 2 *King.* 1. 9, 12. Seventy thoufand *Jews* were flain by the Angel that *David* faw by *Arannah's* threfhing-floor, 2 *Sam.* 24. 15, 17. An Angel meets with *Balaam* to ftop him in his covetous and ambitious defign, for the effective curfing or contriving mifchief to thofe whom God had bleffed. He caufed the very dumb Affe, by fpeaking with man's voice, to reprove the madnefs of the Prophet, 2 *Pet.* 2. 16. An Angel in one night executes one hundred eighty five thoufand *Affyrians* before *Jerufalem,* 2 *King.* 19. 35. An hoft of Angels appears at *Mahanaim* to *Jacob,* to relieve him againft *Efau, Gen.* 32. 1, 2. King *Herod* in all his flourifh of outward pomp, making an eloquent Oration to them of *Tyre* and *Sidon,* and owning that flattering fhout and acclamation of the People, *it is the voice of a God and*
not

not of a Man, was immediately smitten by an Angel, because he gave not God the glory, and was eaten of worms, Act. 12. 20, 23. Many things of like nature have been oft performed by Angelical powers, in a way of difcountenance to corrupt worldly Magiftrates, & for the protection of good men, heirs of falvation. They are the higheft meer creature Powers, unto whom Chrift has put this firft world in fubjection, as is implied, (*Heb.* 2. 5.) where tis faid, *That he hath not put the world to come in fubjection to them.* There, that lower fort of glorified men above charactered, that have but the fingle portion of the fpirit, are equal to them ; and thofe that have the double portion, will judge them, (1*Cor.* 6. 3.) or be fcituated in a fuperiority of life and difcerning to thofe *Principallities and Powers in heavenly places,* Ephef. 3. 10.

These miniftring Spirits (we fee) have often come forth to preferve the bodily Life of Saints from the rapacious talons of corrupted worldly Magiftracy, at fome certain critical feafons and junctures of time, that the main defignes of Chrift in the world required it. But this has been but checker work, a white and a black. The fame perfons that have been relieved at one time, have been left expofed at another, to the rage and violence of their fellow mortals. *Eliah* had Angels at hand to deftroy the Captaines and their Companies, that came to apprehend him: another while, upon *Jezabels* menaces, he flies and hides for his life. And many thoufands of Saints have been abufed and loft their lives under the tyrannical powers of this world, which Satan is called the God of. But when the time draws near for him to be bound and fealed up in the bottomlefs pit, the good angels will come forth in a more general, vifible, and univerfal difcovery, and exercife of their magiftratical power, in affociation with the rifen Witneffes, and at their prayer of Faith, will do execution fpeedily and irrefiftibly, on any that fhall affront their perfons or teftimony, (*Rev.* 11.) as is above fignified. This they will do, in the preparatory work to Chrifts perfonal coming forth to reign. And when he comes himfelf, thefe are that *flaming fire,* in or by which *he will take vengeance on them that know not God and obey not his everlafting Gofpel* ; and fo will it be all along the thoufand years Reign. The like miniftry fhall then be exercifed by the new *Jerufalem* Saints to the righteous inhabitants of the earth, (admonifhing them of the requifitenefs of their pafs by the crofs of Chrift and fire-baptifm of his heavenly fpirit, out of the glory of their earthly and natural ftate, into the glory of the refurrection) to that which Chrift (when new rifen) exercifed towards the two difciples in the way to *Emmaus, Luk.* 24. 13, 31. He appeared and converfed with them, and then difappeared ; fo fhall the Saints

in

in the thousand years reign, acting and being as in or out of the Body, at their pleasure; appearing & preaching to mortal men, & then vanishing out of their sight. The devil & his angels will be all fast sealed up and bound, that they can't seduce or hinder men from obeying this everlasting gospel-ministrey of the *New-Jerusalem* Saints. Then will be experienced what humane nature, at its best, amounts unto, as to eternal life, after the fairest play that can be given it, no tempter, no adversary being left upon the Stage to seduce or disturb it, and all the warnings of its miscarriage in former instances, set before it. Yet if many of them shall not refuse to obey the *New-Jerusalem* Gospel-ministry, what need can there be of the flaming angelical ministry, in subserviency thereunto, to do execution upon the resisters thereof? Those that obey it, will soon grow to a fitnesse to be translated in a moment out of their mortal state, into the *New-Jerusalem* society, as *Enoch* and *Eliah*, and ne'er see death at all; This is the mystery *Paul* tells us of, (1 *Cor.* 15. 51) and that *Enoch* the seventh from *Adam*, was both a type of, in his own translation, and foretold the season of, to wit, *when the Lord cometh with thousands of his Saints, to execute judgement on wicked men,* (Jude 14, 15.) which, (say the *Jewes*) will be the seventh thousand year of the world. The first coming forth of this angelical magistracy into a publick discernableness, to secure the Saints in the undisturbed exercise of their Religion and Worship, preparatory to the coming forth of Christ himself, may seem together with the risen witnesses to be represented by *the little Stone cut out of the Mountain*, that will make sad work and that irresistibly with all worldly, corrupted magistracies and people. The coming of these same angelical powers, as immediate attendants on Christ and his heavenly bride, when he comes in person, seems to be signified by the great Mountain which this stone grows to, so as (on the demolishing of all opposite Powers, every thing that offended having been pluck'd up in the preparatory dispensation) it comes to fill and possess the whole earth. The meek followers of the Lamb are to inherit the earth.

The first coming forth of this angelical magistracy, (which will be the onely suitable magistracy to the Church State of the risen witnesses, or Church that's to come up out of its Wildernesse condition and mourning apparrel) will put a period to Saints troubles and cast tribulation the other way, on those that troubled them. *It is a righteous thing with God* (saies the Apostle) *to recompense tribulation to them that trouble you, and to you that are troubled, rest with us, when the Lord by his mighty angels, who are a flaming fire, shall take vengeance on all enemies and obstructers of the Gospel,* 2 Thes. 1, 6, 10. Then there shall

be

be righteous judgement, (*verf.* 5.) now ther's none to be had for them. Now they are defpifed and Chrift in them; but at that day, Chrift will be admired in them, and furnifh them with power to deal with their affailants, as they pleafe. And after this, he will come yet more to be admired and dreaded in his own perfon, with all his heavenly Armies following him, (*Rev.* 19. 14.) and thoufand thoufands of Angels miniftring to him. Thus you fee the Believers hopes and expectations of relief, where they are placed, while he is crufhed and abufed under corrupt Rulers in worldly States. But what is his duty while the night of Sufferings and fackcloth is yet upon him ? *He is to be preparing for and hafting to the coming of this day of God* (2 Pet. 3. 12.) on which man's judgement or man's day will ceafe. In another fence, *he that believeth will not make hafte,* (Efay 28. 16.) not grow impatient at Chrift's patience and long fuffering towards his enemies ; not antidate his feafon, but quietly wait till the fet time for *Sions* deliverance be come, through the State-miniftry of the mighty angels and Church-miniftry of fpiritual believers.

Peter was too hafty in this point, when he drew his fword againft thofe that offered violence to his mafter. Chrift checks him for ufing a wrong weapon, that that will never work any full and final deliverance from the tyrannical Powers of this world. *I could* (faies he) *at my prayer, have prefently more then twelve Legions of Angels to refcue me; But how then fhould the Scriptures be fulfilled, that thus it muft be ?* Mat. 26. 53, 54. So, after his refurrection, *Ye fools and flow of heart* (faies he) *to believe all that the Prophets have fpoken; ought not Chrift firft to fuffer, and then enter into his glory ?* Luk. 24. 25, 26. *And ought not his members alfo to fuffer with him,* (*till fuch time as the afflictions of Chrift which are behind in their flefh, be accomplifhed*) *and fo enter into glory alfo?* 1 Col. 24. *Muft they not dye with him, if they will live with him, fuffer with him, if they will reign with him ?* 2 Tim. 2. 11, 12. *Muft they not go the fame way he went, if they will come to the fame place, the heavenly manfions that he is gone before to prepare for them in his Fathers houfe ?* John 14. 2. I am confident, could this choice Martyr have procured at his prayer, twelve legions of Angels, to have laid all his bruitifh adverfaries on the Scaffold and round about him, dead at his foot, he would have forborn to defire it, till the proper feafon for that difpenfation be come, which he reckoned to be very near. This is the difpenfation, by which God will decide the controverfie betwixt his people and enemies, in the Valley of *Jehofhaphat,* Joel 3. 12. The Hiftorical type of this, relat d to in *Joel,* we find, 2 Chr. 20, *A great multitude of Moab, Ammon and mount Seir come againft Jeho-*
fhaphat ;

in the thousand years reign, acting and being as in or out of the Body, at their pleasure; appearing & preaching to mortal men, & then vanishing out of their sight. The devil & his angels will be all fast sealed up and bound, that they can't seduce or hinder men from obeying this everlasting gospel-ministrey of the *New-Jerusalem* Saints. Then will be experienced what humane nature, at its best, amounts unto, as to eternal life, after the fairest play that can be given it, no tempter, no adversary being left upon the Stage to seduce or disturb it, and all the warnings of its miscarriage in former instances, set before it. Yet if many of them shall not refuse to obey the *New-Jerusalem* Gospel-ministry, what need can there be of the flaming angelical ministry, in subserviency thereunto, to do execution upon the resisters thereof ? Those that obey it, will soon grow to a fitnesse to be translated in a moment out of their mortal state, into the *New-Jerusalem* society, as *Enoch* and *Eliah*, and ner'e see death at all ; This is the mystery *Paul* tells us of, (1 *Cor.* 15. 51) and that *Enoch* the seventh from *Adam*, was both a type of, in his own translation, and foretold the season of, to wit, *when the Lord cometh with thousands of his Saints, to execute judgement on wicked men*, (Jude 14, 15.) which, (say the *Jewes*) will be the seventh thousand year of the world. The first coming forth of this angelical magistracy into a publick discernableness, to secure the Saints in the undisturbed exercise of their Religion and Worship, preparatory to the coming forth of Christ himself, may seem together with the risen witnesses to be represented by *the little Stone cut out of the Mountain*, that will make sad work and that irresistibly with all worldly, corrupted magistracies and people. The coming of these same angelical powers, as immediate attendants on Christ and his heavenly bride, when he comes in person, seems to be signified by the great Mountain which this stone grows to, so as (on the demolishing of all opposite Powers, every thing that offended having been pluck'd up in the preparatory dispensation) it comes to fill and possess the whole earth. The meek followers of the Lamb are to inherit the earth.

The first coming forth of this angelical magistracy, (which will be the onely suitable magistracy to the Church State of the risen witnesses, or Church that's to come up out of its Wildernefs condition and mourning apparrel) will put a period to Saints troubles and cast tribulation the other way, on those that troubled them. *It is a righteous thing with God* (saies the Apostle) *to recompense tribulation to them that trouble you, and to you that are troubled, rest with us, when the Lord by his mighty angels, who are a flaming fire, shall take vengeance on all enemies and obstructers of the Gospel*, 2 Thef. 1. 6, 10. Then there shall be righteous judgement, *(vers. 5.)* now there's none to be had for them. Now they are despised and Christ in them; but at that day, Christ will be admired in them, and furnish them with power to deal with their assailants, as they please. And after this, he will come yet more to be admired and dreaded in his own person, with all his heavenly Armies following him, *(Rev. 19. 14.)* and thousand thousands of Angels ministring to him. Thus you see the Believers hopes and expectations of relief, where they are placed, while he is crushed and abused under corrupt Rulers in worldly States. But what is his duty while the night of Sufferings and sackcloth is yet upon him ? *He is to be preparing for and hasting to the coming of this day of God* (2 Pet. 3. 12.) on which man's judgement or man's day will cease. In another sence, *he that believeth will not make haste,* (Esay 28. 16.) not grow impatient at Christ's patience and long suffering towards his enemies ; not antidate his season, but quietly wait till the set time for *Sions* deliverance be come, through the State-ministry of the mighty angels and Church-ministry of spiritual believers.

Peter was too hasty in this point, when he drew his sword against those that offered violence to his master. Christ checks him for using a wrong weapon, that that will never work any full and final deliverance from the tyrannical Powers of this world. *I could* (saies he) *at my prayer, have presently more then twelve Legions of Angels to rescue me; But how then should the Scriptures be fulfilled, that thus it must be?* Mat. 26. 53, 54. So, after his resurrection, *Ye fools and slow of heart* (saies he) *to believe all that the Prophets have spoken; ought not Christ first to suffer, and then enter into his glory?* Luk. 24. 25, 26. And ought *not his members also to suffer with him,* (*till such time as the afflictions of Christ which are behind in their flesh, be accomplished*) *and so enter into glory also?* 1 Col. 24. *Must they not dye with him, if they will live with him, suffer with him, if they will reign with him?* 2 Tim. 2. 11, 12. *Must they not go the same way he went, if they will come to the same place,* the *heavenly mansions that he is gone before to prepare for* them *in his Fathers house?* John 14. 2. I am confident, could this choice Martyr have procured at his prayer, twelve legions of Angels, to have laid all his bruitish adversaries on the Scaffold and round about him, dead at his foot, he would have forborn to desire it, till the proper season for that dispensation be come, which he reckoned to be very near. This is the dispensation, by which God will decide the controversie betwixt his people and enemies, in the *Valley of Jehoshaphat,* Joel 3. 12. The Historical type of this, related to in *Joel,* we find, 2 Chr. 20. *A great multitude of Moab, Ammon and mount Seir come against Jeho-*

*shaphat. God takes the battel out of Jehoshaphat's and his Armies hands;
tells them, they shall not need to fight, but stand still and see the Salvation of
the Lord,* verf. 17. and verf. 22,23. *The Lord sets ambushments against
their enemies, and causes them to destroy one another. Jehoshaphats Army
has nothing left them to do, but to take the spoiles of their enemies, which
they were three dayes in gathering, it was so much,* verf. 25.

Farther notice is given of this last kind of undertaking the enemies
of God and his People, *Joel* 2. 1, 11. *Blow the Trumpet in Zion :
Sound an alarme in my holy Mountain. Let all the inhabitants of the Land
tremble ; for the day of the Lord is at hand. A great people and a strong
are his Army ; (even Angels that excel in strength) a fire devoures
before them, and behind them a flame burneth. Nothing shall escape them.
The appearance of them is as the appearance of Horses and Horsemen. Like
the noise of Charets on the tops of Mountains shall they leap : Like the noise
of a flame of fire that devoureth the stubble, as a strong people set in battle
array, before whom all their enemies faces shall gather blackness. They
shall run like mighty men and not break their ranks. They are an invulnera-
ble Army. When they fall upon the Sword, they shall not be wounded. The
Earth shall quake before them, the Heavens shall tremble, the Sun and Moon
shall be darke, and the Stars shall withdraw their shining. This day of
the Lord will be very terrible : who can abide it ? Mens hearts will fail
them for fear, and for looking after those things which are coming on
the earth ; for there shall be signs in the Sun, Moon and Stars, and upon the
earth distress of Nations with perplexity, the Sea and the Waves roaring,
Luk.* 21. 25, 26. All this that is so terrible to the Inhabitants of the
Earth, is good news to those that are in the Wilderness, Pilgrims and
Strangers in the Earth. *They are bid to look up and lift up their heads,
when these things begin to come to pass, for their Redemption draweth
nigh,* verf. 28. *The Lord shall utter his voice before his Army, his Angelical Camp, which is very great,* Joel 2. 11. There will be no standing
for men before them. Then will be brought to passe those sayings indeed, (*Psal.* 149.) which some made use of in the late war, that
was but a shadow to what this Angelical host and their performances
upon the enemy will amount unto. *The Saints shall sing aloud upon their
beds, and have the two-edged sword in their hands.* The Faith and Prayer
of these chosen ones will have Angels ready to do execution upon all
enemies. *Fire thus will go forth of their mouthes to destroy them,* Revel.
11. *They shall execute vengeance upon the heathen and punishments upon
the people,* even upon both those sorts of enemies that took counsel together against them, whether the prophane or but legally religious
party, *Psal.* 2. 1, 2. Both the Heathen, that are no People of God at
all,

all, and such a People of God as may apostatize & become no people again, they shall all go to wrack ; *their Kings shall be bound with chains, and their Nobles with fetters of iron.* All this shall be performed by the faith and prayer of Believers in association with the holy Angels, *Such honour have all his Saints.* This concluding Battel, that is to make a clear riddance of all the wicked tyrannical Monarchies and Powers of this world, is else where expressed thus ; *Not by might, nor by power, but by my spirit, saith the Lord of Hosts,* Zech. 4. 6.

But the greatest conquest that can be attained over enemies, while tis yet but a suffering season, is by Death. This Martyr followed his great Master herein, *Who by Death overcame him that had the power of Death, the Devil,* Heb. 2. 14. He that conquers by killing, overcomes but men, he that conquers by dying, overcomes the Devil. His false friends conquered their enemies by killing them : he tried another and the surer way of Conquest, (though mystical) to conquer them by being killed by them. He has more advantaged a good C A U S E and condemned a bad one, done his honest Countrey-men more service, and his enemies more disservice by his death, (as *Sampson* served the *Philistines*)then before in all his Life, though that also were very considerable. If death were not the noblest, most excellent and certain way of conquest, would the great *Captaine of our Salvation* have led us that way ? Are we followers of that Captain, unless we go the same way he went ? They that conquer by killing others, are still subject to death themselves ; Yea, to be killed by some remainders of those they conquered. They that conquer by dying, are no longer subject to death. *'Tis appointed unto man once to die.* No rage or power of man can take away this Martyrs Life the second time.

'Tis true ; Christ himself *offered up supplications with strong crying and teares, unto him that was able to save him from death, and was heard in that he feared,* (Heb. 5. 7.) that is, was delivered from the fear of Death before hand, and out of the jawes of it after, *for it was not possible he should be holden of it,* Act. 2. 24. This disciple of his, prayed for the same thing, and he did experience and say, Death shrunke from him, not he from it. He had experienced the good hand of God in delivering him from Deaths oft, and when the season was come, he found that Death it self would prove the greatest deliverance that he ever had in all his life. So he experienced the delivering hand of God from Death oft, and by Death once, which was the accomplishment of all his former deliverances. He did look Death in the face with a true chearful boldness, not in a transport, or dissembled courage, (as is usual) but in a fixed composure and full vigor of all his natural senses.

To

To be thus delivered from the fear of Death, is more then to be delivered from Death. So to be delivered from all inordinate love of our natural Life and the concerns thereof, is a greater mercy then to be gratified with a confluence of all worldly defirables. All the Crowns and Scepters of this world are fhort of this frame of mind, crucified to things feen. *Alexander* put fo great a value upon a fhadow of this, in *Diogenes*, that he faid, *Were he not Alexander he would be Diogenes.* The Conqueror accounted a deadnefs to the whole fcene of outward Vanities, the beft condition, next to the having all at command. Had he not been partial he might have reckoned it better. He foon after loft his world and himfelf together, in a drunken fit at *Babylon*, the common Rendevouz for bruitifh pomp under three of the four worldly Monarchies, *Affyrian*, *Perfian*, and *Greek*.

The love of this world is enmity to God, and breeds in us the fear of man, that can deprive us of what we love ; and the fear of man brings a fnare ; will keep us from witneffing a good confeffion as Chrift did. *If we fear them that can kill the Body*, we fhall never be bold in a good caufe before wicked Judges.

This Patriot feared not Death, and therefore did as boldly, fully, and clearly affert his Countries Rights and Liberties at their Bar, as he had before for many years together, on all occafions, in the Parliament Houfe. His ftedfaftnefs in the Faith, in the Covenant ; his conftancy for the publick Intereft, rendered him very unfolicitous as to his own perfonal concerns or Life. And what muft all this be tearmed by his enemies ? This Readinefs and boldnefs of fpirit in afferting the Caufe of God and thefe Nations to the Death, which is highly efteemed of God and all good men, is by his bruitifh adverfaries called, *an impudent defence of his Treafon.* He was well fteeled and made of God with *Jeremy*, as an iron pillar and brazen walles againft any impudence or treafon that others could affront him with, under a face of authority. He evidently preferred the Lives and Liberties of all the knowing honeft-hearted people in the Nation, to his own. He was couragious therefore in the defence of them. What thought his enemies of this ? Ready they were to charge him with fuch deportment in his Trial and on the Scaffold, towards them and the king, as *Job* was truly charged with by *Elihu* againft God, (*Job* 34. 37) He addeth rebellion to his fin, he clappeth his hands amongft us, and multiplieth his words againft the King. What were the words ? can any tell ? They multiplied their words againft God, the Laws of *England* and him. He refifted them unto blood. This was the higheft demonftration of his fincerity that was poffible to be given, and the

greateft

greateſt victory over all his enemies that was poſſible to be obteined. *Cromwels* victories are ſwallowed up of Death : he has ſwallowed up Death it ſelf into victory, and is gone in the Charet of ſalvation to receive his Crown from the hands of Chriſt, (2 *Tim.* 4. 7, 8.) which no man by any treachery or force can ever take from him. He let fall his mantle, left his body behind him, that he had worn nine and forty years, and is gone to keep his everlaſting Jubile in Gods Reſt. 'Tis all *D A Y* with him now, no night or ſorrow more, no priſons or death. He is gone from a place, where ſo much as the righteouſneſs of man can't be endured. He is gone to a place where the righteouſneſs of God is the univerſal garbe of all the inhabitants. He is gone to that better City, the *New-Jeruſalem*. He had ſerved his generation in his mortal Body, done his work, and was glad to fall a ſleep, and go look for his reward ſome where elſe. You ſee what this ingrateful world has afforded him for all his kindneſs ; reproach, priſons, and death ; he had need have other returns ſome where. *Great is his reward in heaven*. He was a burning and ſhining light, he burned hotter and ſhined brighter in heavenly life and light under all the injuries of this perſecuting world, ſo that his laſt works were his beſt. So death was to him a great gain. If any ſit down by the loſs, 'tis we that ſurvive him. But he left this comfortable word behind him ; *God would never want inſtruments to do his work*. Yet we may ſay ; *The honourable Counſellour is taken from thee (O England) this day, whoſe worth few knew. A famous Maſter in our Iſrael, is taken from our heads, and who laies it rightly to heart ? His enemies were afraid of him, as Saul of David, becauſe the Lord was with him* ; 1 Sam. 18. 12. *Pharaoh*, though but a heathen Prince, was of another mind concerning *Joſeph*. He adviſed with his Council about appointing ſome diſcreet, wiſe man over the Land of *Egypt* ; and of *Joſeph* he ſaith, *Can we find ſuch a one as this, a man in whom the ſpirit of God is ?* So *Joſeph* became chief Ruler in *Egypt*, under ſeveral Kings fourſcore, years together, from the thirtieth to the hundred and tenth year of his age. The like great authority fell to *Daniels* ſhare, (as a man of this more excellent ſpirit) in *Babylon*, under ſeveral *Aſſyrian* or *Babyloniſh*, and *Perſian* Monarchs.

'Tis a ſign Monarchy is notoriouſly degenerated, that perſons of *Joſeph's* and *Daniels* ſpirit are for that very reaſon hated and ſlain, for which they were advanced even in heathen States. The enemies of this *Engliſh Joſeph* and deliverer, were of the right Satanick ſpirit ; hated him only for following the thing that good is. *They that render evil for good are mine adverſaries*, in the original 'tis, *are Satan*, Pſal 38. 20.

Q

Men

Men of the excellent spirit, do now find sad entertainment. People flock together, and every one is ready to act his part, towards the shedding of their innocent blood; Judges, Jurors, Witnesses, Counsellors. No time must be granted, all must be huddled up in a trice, when they are making haste to destroy them. And they are ready to say (as the *Jewes* of Christ) *His blood be upon us and on our children.* It is not like to be alone upon them, they must take a heavier load with it. Upon the abettours and contrivers of this murder (if they repent not) will come all the blood that has been shed upon the earth, from the blood of righteous *Abel*, to the last drop of the innocent blood that they have or shall farther spill. *Precious in the sight of the Lord is the death of his Saints,* Psal. 116. 15. God will be soundly payd for their blood. He will not fail to encrease his wealth by their price, *Psal.* 44. 12.

One main ground of the unjust proceedings of worldly Powers against righteous and conscientious men, is *Reason of State;* which usually brings the most signal desolation upon them, by that very means whereby they thought to prevent it. With what a vengeance this thing called *Reason of State* has been repayed, we may observe in all times and places.

Pharaoh for *Reasons of State* murthered the Male-Children, and sought to suppress the *Hebrews* by cruel bondage. No messages from God, though accompanied with Prodigies, could stop him in his course, till he was payd home, once for all, in the *Red Sea.*

Reason of State made *Saul* seek the ruine of *David*, *Absolon* lie with his Fathers Concubines, *Jeroboam* seek the establishment of himself by his Calf-worship, thereby distinguishing his people in Religion from the *Jerusalem*-Worship under another King. *This* made *Herod* seek Christ's life, and destroy the male Children about *Bethlehem.* *This* made the *Jews* and *Pilate* crucifie him, least *Cesar* should destroy their Nation, whereas for that very thing they came to be destroy'd by *Cesar*; and what end all the other, with many like examples came to, I refer you to the Scriptures, and other authentick Histories, to enquire.

Caiaphas said of Christ, *It was expedient that one man should dye for the people.* The like was urged against this follower of Christ. Here's another *Reason of State*. And he declared himself content to be any thing God should permit them to make of him : to be handled as *Paul* was, reckoned *as the filth of the world, the off-scouring of all things,* 1 *Cor.* 4. 13. The word there is περικαθάρματα, which relates to the heathenish custome of culling out slaves or other contemptible persons,

sons, to offer up to the devil, as expiatory sacrifices to purge from some National guilt they had contracted, and so deliver them from some National judgement they lay under.

Be the adversaries *Reasons of State* what they will, they have done all they can do to this lover of his Countrey and the Laws thereof. But I would willingly have their understandings disabused in one point. Let them not think they have conquered him. They knew him not. He judg'd his Judges at the Bar. He triumphed over his executioners on the Scaffold, *R.* and the rest. Such a publick execution was more eligible then to have lingred out some small time in a prison, as a condemned person, liable to any arbitrary afterclaps, or any future motion or pretence of motion in our troubled Sea. He had more ease, God more glory, the honest party of the Nation and their just CAUSE more advantage, and why may I not say, his most intimate friends and dearest Relations more comfort in this way of his deliverance, once for all ?

He did fully comply with that rational notion of the heathen Philosophers, concerning his mortal body, *That it was one of his prisons, from which he could receive no final discharge* (as he might from others) *but by death*. Right joyful he was to lay aside this burthensome weight and go to his Father. *His heart was fixed, trusting in the Lord. He was not therefore afraid or any way startled at evil tydings, but did sing and give praise, that his full redemption drew so near*, Psal. 112. 6, 7. and 108. 1.

When the Sheriffs Chaplain came very gravely to him at the midnight before his execution, (the most dismal, unseasonable, and unusual time for such messages) he told him he was come to bring him, as he called it, the fatal message of Death. On this, the Lord presently cast into his mind that which is written (*Zech.* 3.4.) to intimate to him, *That he was now taking away his filthy garments, with intention to give him change of raiment, that his mortal might put on immortallity. Thus his Mortallity came to be swallowed up of Life, and Death and the Grave into Victory.*

Presently after his receit of that message of Death, *he laid him down and slept, for the Lord sustained him*, Psal. 3. 5. When his Relations and Acquaintance came about him in the morning, he told them he did not look upon that message of Death, as having any thing at all of dismalness in it.

The World was no longer worthy of him. He is therefore gone from the earth. But his Person and righteous Testimony *shall be had in everlasting remembrance*, Psal. 112. 6. *His eye was fixed upon a better*

Coun-

Countrey, the Saints everlasting Rest. There the wicked cease from troubling, and the weary are at rest. Those that have been made Prisoners and out-casts in this world, as the off-scouring of all things, shall rest together there They shall no more hear the voice of the oppressor, Job 3. 17, 18. The present enjoyments and blessedness of this deceased Saint, do set him clear out of the reach of his enemies malice or my pen. He steaddily sees and unchangeably enjoyes what *Paul* (before quite rid of his mortal body) had but the transient view of, in a short rapture, *when caught up to the third heaven*, (1 *Cor.* 12.) or into that vision of God in Christ, that is exhibited to the double-portioned Saint, that sits on the Throne with Christ. 'Tis the favourable presence of God in Christ onely, that makes heaven to angels or men. God's threefold various presence with his Church, in and through Christ, makes the three heavens. That presence that is afforded in the adæquate intelligible form to the highest life and discerning of the double-portioned Saint, the Bride the Lambs Wife, makes the third heaven. That which is given forth in the adæquate intelligible form to the elect Angels and Spirits of just men made perfect, as the sutable immediate object of their discerning, makes the second heaven. That presence of God, (together with the fruits of it) that in Christ is afforded to Saints on earth, makes the first. They have their conversation in this first heaven, **Phil.** 3.20. or lowest kind of presence and converse of Christ in spirit. They do live in the exercise of that spiritual seed and those principles, which when fully awakened in the resurrection, will render them fit inhabitants of the second and third heavens. *Paul* in the short glance he had of that most excellent glory of God in Christ, that is intelligible or discernable to the most exalted sort of Saints, tells us, *he heard unspeakable words, (or saw unspeakable things) which it is not lawful or possible for a man to utter.* Here then I must take off my hand, and leave you to make the best you can of it, in silence and wonder.

Thus have I cast in my small mite towards the vindication of the Person, Doctrine and Way of this choice anointed one of the Lord, and faithful assertor of his Countries Liberties unto Death, from the groundless aspersions, causeless hatred, misprisions, and injuries that have fallen to his share, in this world. There are two sorts of enemies, who in the rage and vain imaginations of their hearts, have reproached, blasphemed, assaulted, affronted, resisted and persecuted Christ in him. They are both deciphered, (*Psal.* 2. 1.) under the titles of *Heathen* and *People.* I have a word or two to divide between them, and speak to each of them apart.

My

My firſt word is to a People of God, who (in whatever variety of form, perſwaſion or way) have all of them (with one conſent) ſeparated from *Rome*, as juſtly loathing and nauſeating her moſt groſs, viſible Idolatries and abominations. They have alſo ſeparated from the dry impertinent formality of a meer outward profeſſion of Proteſtantiſme under a ſuperſtitious Epiſcopacy. Theſe they have ſeparated from on the left hand ; it was their duty ſo to do. But they have alſo ſeparated from, or rather caſt out the ſpiritual Believer and true heir of the everlaſting Kingdom, on the right hand. This is their great ſin, that has brought a prophane, heatheniſh, ſuperſtitious, idolatrous Intereſt over their heads again, and run all a-ground. They have demonſtrated themſelves to be of that ſpirit that *Paul* reproved in ſome of the *Corinthian* Church, *that would be reigning as Kings* in the but renewed principles of humane nature, and righteouſneſs of man, **1** *Cor.* 4. 8. When therefore this true heir ſounded his trumpet in his *RE-TIRED MEDITATIONS*, and proclaimed another ſort of Saints, men of another ſpirit, other principles, and a more excellent way of life, to be the onely true heirs of the Kingdom, and poſſeſſed of the true reigning Principle, they could not bear it. They have choſen rather to give the Scepter back again into any hand, then the true heir of the heavenly Kingdom ſhould wield it ; I mean not a Perſon onely, but a People, a People prepared for the Lord.

Whoever you be that have thus demeaned your ſelves, and ſinned away twenty years Mercies and Deliverancies, (whatever your Judgment, Form or Way be, as to this or that particular Doctrine or Ordinance) if you yet lodge but in the renewed old- *Adam* ſtate of life, or firſt creation ſpirit and principles, (as you have ſeen them above-charactered) to you it is I direct this word. You that are in ſome good meaſure and degree, inwardly cleanſed from the pollutions of this world, the corruption of nature, give me leave to tell you ; you may be thus waſh'd and baptized by the word of truth, into a practical, experimental knowledge of Chriſt after the fleſh, and conformity with him, as he was found in the fleſh, (*born of a woman, made under the Law*). for your ſanctification. Let me tell you further : you may be made comely through his comelineſs or righteouſneſs (of that ſort) put upon you or imputed to you, for your juſtification. You may over and above all this, be adorned with many jewels and bracelets, excellent gifts, *and the tongue of men and angels*, and yet fall ſhort of the glory and righteouſneſs of God in the new and everlaſting Covenant, and ſo may prove to be at laſt *but ſounding braſs or tinkling cymbals*, Ez. 16.

Ez. 16, 11, 12. 1 *Cor.* 12, 31. 13, 1. All your fanctified, juftified, beautified and adorned ftate, in which you flourifhed, was but the reƈtified, adorned , firft-covenant natural man, and you took all to be fpiritual, new-covenant Life and ornament. This is one of the faddeft miftakes mortal men are fubjeƈt to, and is like to coft them deareft. Their difappointment is fatal and irrecoverable. **Their work is** exceeding dangerous in *kicking againft the pricks*, perfecuting of **Chrift** in the true fpiritual believer. But their cafe is not remedilefs, as they may fee in *Paul*, till they knowingly and malitioufly fay; *Come, this is the heir, let's kill him, and the inheritance fhall be ours.*

There are thofe from amongft thefe Legal fpirited profeffors, both Paftors and People, that have had their fhare in betraying this juft man ; in blafpheming his Principles and Doƈtrine ; in cafting reproaches upon him while living, and pleafing themfelves to think that they are now well rid of him, his Doƈtrine and Way, by his Death. Deceive **not** your felves. His teftimony has received a more fignal ratification by his Death then **in** all his Life. He warn'd you of many things. In reference to one of his warning-pieces, as to the making clean riddance of Antichrift from amongft us, I fhall ask you a Queftion.

Do you imagine that you have banifhed Antichrift out of your coafts, your Churches, by excluding the Romifh beaft, the heathenifh part of the Antichriftian Church ?

Jewel, Reynolds and *Whitaker,* (againft *Harding, Hart* and *Bellarmine*) as alfo other famous and learned Writers of the Proteftant intereft, *White, Mede,* and many more, have from the Quiver of common reafon and humane Writers, drawn out and fhot fuch arrows at that Beaft, that her wounds are incurable by any other Engine, fave the Sword and Belluine force.

What will you fay, if the very Proteftant Churches in what ever variety of Judgement, as to this or that particular, (fo far forth as they have miftaken the *One thing neceffary,* the great fundamental Point, or different foundation of the two Houfes Chrift mentions, *one on the fand, the other on the rock,* Mat. 7. and have refted and gloried wholly in the leffer glory of renewed, adorned man, that's to be done away) fhould at length prove the Myftical *Babylon,* however confidently they have paffed for the true heavenly Spoufe and People of Chrift ? Under this conceit of your being the true everlafting Spoufe of Chrift , how confident have you been, that the Kings of the earth fhould joyn intereft with you, and efpoufe your quarrel, in order to pull down and tear in pieces the beaftly Idolatrous Antichrift of *Rome* ? What a

crofs

cross blow would it be to your expectations in this kind, what a sad and amazing disappointment, if it should fall the other way ? If the Kings of the earth, in the most bruitish, degenerate state of worldly Monarchy, should strike in with *Rome* against you, and accomplish that prophesie upon you, as the genuine intendment thereof ? *Revel.* 17. 16.

Shall I ask you another Question, with some tendency towards a disquisition into this Riddle ?

Do or can you imagine the Popish party and Religion, in the posture it has stood these many hundred years, can in her Spirit, Doctrine and Principles, be that glittering Strumpet, which for inward Ornament, holiness, and exceeding likeness to the true heavenly Spouse of Christ, did so dazle Johns eyes in Patmos, (amidst all his ravishing Visions of God) as that he wondred with great admiration to hear her tearmed by the Angel, MYSTERY, BABYLON *the* GREAT, *the* MOTHER OF HARLOTS *and* ABOMINATIONS OF THE EARTH? Rev. 17. 5, 6.

MEDE, and many others have evidently and undeniable demonstrated that Popery is the very sink of all the old *Gentile* Theologie of Dæmon Gods, in their worshipping and praying to Angels and the souls of deceased men. Some great Authors or Patrons and advancers of their most ridiculous Idolatries, they have formally canonized for Saints, and do pray to their departed Souls, as *Heroe's,* a rank of Demi-Gods, inferiour to Angels. If any were more notoriously vile in their idolatries, & more eminently serviceable in the propagating & advancing thereof, & so more useful to *Demetrius* & his subordinate Shrine-makers, and Image-mongers, (*Act.* 19.) they have been advanced in their *Apotheoses,* after the manner of old heathenish *Rome,* into the very order of Dæmons or Angels, and so their prayers to them as well as to fallen Angels, come properly under the title of Dæmonolatry, or worshipping of Devils. Yea the most superstitious abominations and gross bodily whoredoms that ever were found scatteredly up and down in any the most bruitish heathen States since the world began, are pack'd up all together, in the Papacy. They may set up a *Pantheon,* a Temple for the Catholick or universal Worship of all the old heathen Gods, in all Nations, as old *Rome* did. Here's their Catholick Religion, *They fall down to Stocks and worship Stones, graven and molten Images, the works of their own hands.* They are sadly derided for it, with the rest of their old brother-heathens, by God himself, at large, *Esay* 44. *They take a piece of wood, with part whereof they rost their meat and warm their hands, and the residue they make a God. Horace,*
a heathen

a heathen Poet, scoffs at the same folly, bringing in an Image that applauds it self for its good hap, that when it was a rude mishapen piece of wood, the Carpenter was thinking to put it to some inferiour use, but all upon a sudden it came into his head, to make it a God. Yea, the very *Turks* abhor the Popish Imagery and Image-worship, as more against the Common light of Reason, than any thing they have in their *Mahumetane Mosch's* or Parish Meeting-places. If *John* then should have wondred to hear that such a heathenish Church as the *Romane* now is, and has long bin, (when represented to him in the Spirit, Principles, and gross Idolatries thereof) should be called *the Whore of Babylon*, might not all the world wonder at *John* for his paines? He might indeed in such a case, have wondred the other way; that that should at all be called Mystical *Babylon*, as having so much creditable resemblance of the true Spouse of Christ, as to pass for it. There is no such thing as gross whoredom of body or soul, in Religion or Conversation, in the whole World, if it be not in the apostate *Romane* Church, in a transcendent manner.

'Tis certainly then some clearer, finer-spirited Church, which *John* wondred should be called *The Mother of Abominations*; some such Church as he was ready to think, if Christ hath any such thing as a chaste Spouse upon earth, that will keep close to him and never apostatize, this is she. Thus *Samuel* said of *Eliab*, *Jesse's* eldest son, *Surely the Lords anointed is before him*, 1 Sam. 16. 6. 'Tis answered there, *The Lord seeth not as man seeth*, vers. 7. That that man admires and praises, God regardes not; and that which man regards not, is of highest esteem with God. *Paul* was no body with those that were wise and honourable in Christ, as to the glory of man, by him renewed in or put upon them, but mean while was he whom the Lord commended, 1 *Cor.* 4. 10. 2 *Cor.* 10. 12. 18.

But to help open your eyes, you see Popery is such a mass of gross Idolatries and commonly discernable Abominations, that the very present Magistracy, whom you are apt, it may be, to have some hard thoughts of, would seem so resolute against it, as to make it criminous for any to blemish their repute with such slanderous imputations, as if they had the least intendment that way.

If you chance to object; *How comes it to pass then, that all the more refined sorts of Christian Meetings are disturbed, killed, imprisoned, hurried up and down from post to pillar, grosly abused and injured before their Judgement seats, and the Mass onely quiet, and what is next it, the dry, impertinent publick Assemblies under Episcopacy? If you say further, what mean they to force those Oathes upon us that were originally intended*

for

for the keeping of Papists quiet? Why may we not expect *England* should shortly be made a Shambles, when some moderate Papists themselves bolt out something that's hatching, which they reckon too black for them to act a part in, and so quit their ground before hand? If you ask me such questions as these, I shall referre you for an answer, to those whom it concerns. If you further expostulate, and say, though we may not say Popery is intended, may we not think so when we see all this? What must we do with our eyes then? No great matter what become of such eyes as could not see all this before hand. Some *Cassandra's* amongst you did, but the credulous multitude thought otherwise, and carried it. *Presbyterians* and Tradesmen thought to have made a fairer game of it, then it proves. I am neither. But I know Trading is dead, and *Presbyterianisme* seems to be somewhat near giving up the Ghost; scarce a stone is like to be left upon a stone in our mystical earthly *Jerusalem*, or Church-formes, any more than once in the litteral City and Temple.

I'le tell you my mind in short; I reckon the *Romish* party but the tail of that second Beast, *that had hornes like the Lamb*, (Rev. 13. 11.) if any part thereof at all. It may rather seem to be the head or most flourishing appearance of the first, the heathenish *Romane* Monarchy, guilded over with nothing but the meer Name and Title of Christianity. And so all those Kings of the earth, that side and strike in therewith, are together with this palpable *Romish* strumpet, but of the same nature and mettal with the old heathen Monarchy of *Rome*, resembled by the *iron part of the feet and toes of Nebuchadnezzars* Prophetical *Image,* as the elder heathen *Rome* was resembled by the *iron legs,* Dan. 2. 33. The *clay* represents mystical *Babylon,* or that softened, reformed Church-state, of such a People in Covenant with God, as may again become no People. These two parties shall labour to mingle together and cleave one to another, in order to keep out the true spiritual worshipper, who has been in the Wildernes above this twelve hundred years, excluded out of both their Synagogues, and is now upon a return into power. But these two parties, resembled by *iron* and *clay,* though they assay to mix and cleave together, can't hold so long, and when they clash, guess which is like to have the worst on't, *iron* or *clay.*

From amongst you, O professors, have there been, that have sate with those now returned into power, as at one table, to consult and contrive how you may both rid your hands and the world of the spiritual worshipper and true heir. The hearts of the Kings or chief Leaders amongst you both, have been set to speak lies and do mischief to him,

R

him, becaufe he has been the rebuker of you both, (*Dan.* 11. 27.) of the one, for not looking after a more excellent ftate of righteouf-nefs; of the other, for abiding in a ftate of downright wickednefs; as an enemy to all righteoufnefs. *Paul*, in all the glory and righteouf-nefs of man, was the moft enraged perfecutor of the fpirit and righte-oufnefs of God in the true faints, the world had in it ; yet had in him the feed of that very fpiritual life he perfecuted, though unawakened unexercifed, till Chrift met with him in the way to *Damafcus* ; fo may fome, may many of you ; I wifh all had.

You once made full account you had for ever fhaken hands with Popery and prophanefs, fo as never more to enter again into any cor-refpondence with either. Has not your blind zeal and enmity againft the fpiritual believer and his Teftimony, fo far transported you, as to make you forfeit all your former difcretion, and refolution, and ad-venture the fhaking hands again with both in a kind of amity, like *Herod* and *Pilate*, to work jointly, what prejudice you can to the true heir of the heavenly kingdom ? are not you the two diftinct branches of Antichrifts Kingdom, refembled by the *iron* and *clay*, that though you would never fo fain, yet cannot mix or piece up together, fo as to hold long, but will clafh and deftroy one another, and fo make way, by the moft wife providence of God, for the coming of the true heir over both your heads ? *Dan.* 2. 43, 44. Are you not almoft rea-dy to go to work for the accomplifhing of what this deceafed Patriot has foretold you of, in his *MEDITATIONS*, about the clafh of the two branches of Antichrifts kingdom, the finer and courfer parts of *Ba-bylon* ? See elfe. But who hath believed his report, or regarded it ? They onely, to whom *the arm of the Lord hath been revealed.* How too gene-rally is that Teftimony of his difregarded, that of any I know extant, next the Scriptures, gives the faireft aim to *England*, truly to under-ftand its cafe and the ftate of the controverfie between God and it ; and what the true ground is, that all its moft fuccefsfully acquired Li-berty fhould be ready to be compleatly fwallowed up again into down-right heathenifh Idolatry and prophanefs ? Where's the man that wil fuffer his underftanding to be queftioned as any way faulty, that he gives no entertainment to a right report of thefe matters ? All the heavy load muft be caft upon the relator, as but cloudily or not at all making out what he fpeaks of, or that the matter of his meffage is at bottom no better then Popery ; yea it has been called masked Pope-ry, and publickly fet at defiance by a frequented Teacher in our Re-formed Congregations, as that which is far lefs to be tollerated by the Magiftrate then the open bare-fac'd Idolatries of *Rome.* What work

does

does the blind, ignorant zeal of the legalist make with the spiritual mans Testimony? What stupenduously false deductions and conclusions do they form from it, and then decry it? The sun rising is not so far distant from its fall as this deceased believers Testimony and Doctrine is from Popery. Fire is not more contrary to Water then his Doctrine to theirs. 'Tis amazing to me, to think which way such imaginations should come into their crowns. He has plainly declared to you how matters stand, had you the hearing ear or seeing eye. You either wonder at, or despise it; if you go on at such work, you will perish too. This 'twil certainly come to, *Act.* 13. 41. Through this one fatal mistake about the spiritual man and his Doctrine, the most accomplished person for *Englands* deliverance from devils and men, hath been by you betrayed and delivered up into the hands of the *Gentiles*, to be so handled as you have seen. But their case that crucified Christ himself was not remediless, till on a fair and plain declaration how matters stood, they did resolutely and peremptorily persist in their error, contradicting and blaspheming. *Then Paul waxed bold and resolute on the other hand; seeing* (saies he.) *that you put this word or warning away from you, thereby judging your selves unworthy of everlasting life; lo, we turn to the Gentiles,* Act. 13. 45, 46.

The foundation of all Controversy with the spiritual believer, the ground of all the contradicting and blaspheming his Testimony meets with, what is it? This. *The natural man perceiveth not the things of God, because they are spiritually discerned.*

Spiritual things are not at all the suitable, intelligible objects to the natural understanding. But will self-confident man ever suffer this to become the Question, *Whether the fault lye in him, that he perceives not what is said by the spiritual watch-man?* By no meanes; specially if this natural man be renewed, cleansed, enlightened, adorned with excellent gifts and the tongue of men and angels, so that he is in one kind, wise, and strong, and honourable in Christ, a Prince at working righteousness, reigning as a King; 1 *Cor.* 4. 8. You may sooner remove a mountain, then get this man, so accomplished and qualified, once to suffer his understanding and reception of things to be scrupled or questioned, as insufficient for these things. Then there's no remedy, but if the spiritual believers Testimony be not received, the fault must be laid at his door, *That he daringly asserts many things, but clears nothing, proves nothing.* Thus the *Pharisees* serv'd Christ. *Are we blind also?* Do you think that if you talk'd any thing that has Sence, Reason, or Scripture in it for its evidence, we could not see what 'tis you drive at? *John* 9. 40.

Let's

Let's confider whether thefe learned felf-confidents, with the reft of the *Jewifh* Rabbies, were blind or no, as to the true reach and fig- nificancy of thofe very Oracles they were generally reputed the onely Interpreters of, in *Mofes* and the Prophets. *Paul* being fet down in the *Jewifh* Synagogue at *Antioch* in *Pifidia*, upon inti- mation from the Rulers thereof, to fpeak a word of exhortation, (a thing not admitted in our Synagogues) infifts upon this very point. *They* (faies he) *that dwell at Jerufalem, and their Rulers, becaufe they knew not Chrift, nor yet the voices of the Prophets, which were read every Sabbath day, they have fulfilled them in condemning him. And though they found no caufe of death in him, yet defired they Pilate that he fhould be flain,* Act. 13. 27, 28. They are faid therefore *to have done it igno- rantly.* The Princes of this World, that is, the *Jewifh* Priefts, Scribes, Pharifees, &c. that were Princes in underftanding and at working the righteoufnefs of the Law, *they yet knew not Chrift, for had they known him, they would not have crucified the Lord of Glory*, 1 Cor. 2. 8. 'Twas well for them, their murdering of him was capable of fuch an interpre- tation, for this keeps the door yet open for falvation, through Chrift crucified, to be preach'd even to them that crucified him. *Men and brethren, children of the ftock of Abraham, to you is the word of this falva- tion fent,* Act. 13. 26.

What a marvellous thing may it feem, that the very learned Rulers and onely reputed expounders of the Law and the Prophets, fhould crucifie Chrift, and in all the circumftances of their proceedings with him, fulfil all that was foretold of him in *Mofes* and the Prophets, and yet not know all along what they were doing? They thought, and fo our Rabbies think they underftand the Scriptures, but did they or do we? What though men have been reputed famous expounders of the letter of Gofpel, thirty or forty years together, may not they yet be ignorant of Chrift in fpirit, or the Spiritual man and all his concerns, and fo with great confidence cry him down for a Blafphemer, and per- fecute him? No doubt. Is not Chrift in Spirit, and in the ap- proaches of his fecond coming, as like to be decried, blafphemed and perfecuted by the onely reputed expounders of the Gofpel, as Chrift in the flefh was by the onely reputed expounders of the Law? His fecond coming, both in his Saints, (the true fpiritual believer) and in his own perfon, is as fairly foretold in the New Teftament, in re- ference to his reign, as his firft coming in the flefh was foretold in the old Teftament, in reference to his Sufferings. And of the two, men will be more fhort of guelling right at the predictions that concern his fecond coming, then thofe that concerned his firft. It lies more re- mote

mote by far, in all the circumstances and things of it, from humane understanding, then the first did.

Christ makes this dealing of God with men, the ground and matter of a solemn thanksgiving to his Father, *I thank thee, O Father, Lord of heaven and earth, because thou hast hid these things from the wise and prudent, and hast revealed them unto babes*, Mat. 11.25. And 1 Cor. 1. 26. *Not many wise men after the flesh, not many mighty, not many noble are called.* See the self-confident reasonings of the *Jewes* against the reception of Christ or his Doctrine. The Officers that went to apprehend Christ, *are astonished at his doctrine, and durst not lay hands on him.* What (say the Priests and Pharisees that sent them) have ye not brought him ? *Oh,* say they, *never man spake like this man.* Then answered the Pharisees, *are ye also deceived ? Have any of the Rulers or Pharisees believed on him ?* But this people that knoweth not the Law are cursed. *He onely deludes a company of poor fishermen , and the silly, credulous multitude, that know nothing.* Here is their Verdict of Christ. Why should his true followers expect other from the learned Rabbies and onely reputed expositours of Scripture, in any succeeding generation, amongst whom their lot is cast ? This is the way of man. God's way and his reasonings are quite contrary. The poor onely, those that are emptied of all their *Laodicean* riches, and self-confidences, they are the fitly disposed persons to receive the gospel, in God's esteem. These are they, he puts value on. That passage in *Acts* 13. about the *Jews* crucifying Christ and not being aware what was the matter, though the very Scriptures (which they were reckoned the only interpreters of that the world had in it) foretold and charactered the birth, progress, and death of him, in all the circumstances thereof; I say, the serious weighing of this, one would think should encline men, amidst all the repute they have, and pleas: themselves with, as to the interpreting of the Scriptures, to reflect upon and call themselves in question, whether they do yet know any thing at all of them, as they ought to know. If not ; then all the question they put to the spiritual believer, is still, *How do you prove it ? how do you make out this from Scripture ?* They'l not admit the least scruple but that they can discern it, if it be proved. They will not suffer it to be questioned, whether they have the hearing ear, and seeing eye, to discern what the spiritual man sayes to the Churches.

Men that have not this eye and ear, and yet reckon they have, and will not be beaten out of it, the true believer were almost as good speak to stones as them. These old foolish kings at knowledge and righteousness, in first-covenant principles, they will not endure to be

admonish-

admonished, or told any thing, of new-covenant light and righteousness, *Ecclef.* 4. 13.

Let a skilful Mathematician mention some obscure proposition in the Mathematicks to an unlearned man, or at least unveried in his Art ; He demands a demonstration. *How do you prove this saies he ?* the other gives an exact demonstration, but he through ignorance of the very rudiments and principles of Mathematick learning, receives not the demonstration, as any satisfactory account of the proposition to him, at all. He is as far to seek as ever. What then ? where lies the fault ? In the pretended demonstration, he will say. He will by no means suspect his capacity. The defect lies wholly in his understanding, and he laies it all upon the demonstration, saies nothing is proved. Let a skilful Artist hear the matter, he presently grants the demonstration to be as clear as the Sun. This may be the case, where the subject matter of the discourse is properly within ken to meer natural reason, as the suitable and intelligible object thereof. How much more difficult is the case with the true spiritual Believer, and his Gospel doctrine, in case he discourse with one that is confident he wants not for discerning, and yet sees nothing at all as he ought to see ; has no discerning at all of spiritual things, or of the spiritual sence, reach and significancy of the Scriptures ? He has no eye at all, suited to such matters ; yet none more confident. The true spiritual watchman were as good meet a Bear robb'd of her whelps, as talk with such a man about spiritual things. He is absolutely unreasonable as to such things, that faith only sees. *Paul* prayed to be delivered from such cattel, and desired others to pray for him on that account, as the most irksome thing in the world. *Finally brethren, pray for us,* (saith he) *that the word of the Lord may have free course, and that we may be delivered from unreasonable men ; for all men have not Faith ;* 2 *Thef.* 3. 1, 2. He that has not faith or the spiritual discerning, is perfectly unreasonable as to spiritual things. You were better talk to a tree, if he be confident, for that will make no noise to trouble you ; he will. Men are still for *How do you prove it ?* They never question but they can understand and receive it, if rightly evidenced. Did not Christ himself speak with evidence, *as one having authority beyond all the teaching of the Scribes ?* Mat. 7. 29. Yet how was he and his doctrine rejected by the Scribes and generallity of the religious party amongst the *Jewes,* and received only by some poor fishermen, and common sinners ? where was the fault that Christ's doctrine was not received ? Did not he give the demonstration right ? how often is it said in Scripture, *He that has an ear to hear, let him hear ?*

hear ? The grand obstruction to the propagating of the Gospel , is the want of the hearing ear. Till there be this, we speak to deaf men. The old serpent has deaf'd and stop'd up their ears, *that they will not listen to the* spiritual *charmer, charme he never so wisely.* And what then ? why, then they fall to disputing and cavilling with him ; *How do you prove this, and how do you prove that ? You assert many things; but what ground do you shew for all ?* The disputer of this world is set at naught by the Holy Ghost ; *Where is the wise ? where is the disputer of this World ? hath not God made foolish the wisdom of this world ?* 1 Cor. 1. 20. These disputers are not to be gratified in their way. If there be a spiritual discerning, spiritual things which carry their own evidence in them, need onely to be asserted ; and prove while you will, discourse a whole year together with one in whom is no such discerning, he never will own that any thing is proved; but holds fast his own conclusions still. The way of Christ himself was not to dispute, but assert ; and *he that hath an ear to hear,* (saies he) *let him hear ; if you will receive it, receive it.* The true believer is to wave those unprofitable janglings, by which contentious , self-confident men would labour to confound all , 1 *Tim.* 1.

The *Jewish* teachers put this question to Christ himself ; *Art thou the Christ ? tell us. He said unto them, if I tell you, you will not believe ;* Luk. 22. 67. When Christ preach'd, how many contradicted and blasphemed ? was the fault in him ? Speak who will, *Paul,* an Angel from heaven, or Christ himself, and let the hearing ear be wanting, what can be done ? The very disciples, when they were coming down from the Mount where Christ was transfigured before them, he lets fall a word about the Resurrection, and they are all in a puzzle, to think what rising from the dead should mean. *Why say the Scribes that Elias must first come,* say they ? *Elias is come* (saies he) *and they have done to him what they listed,* (*Mark* 9. 9, 13. and *Mat.* 11. 14.) speaking of *John Baptist. If ye will receive it, this is Elias which was for to come.* The last word of prophesy in the Old Testament, pointed at *John,* the immediate preparatory Minister to the publick and general dispensation of the Gospel, upon Christ's coming in the flesh. *Mal.* 4. 5, 6. *If ye will receive it, receive it. He that hath an ear to hear, let him hear;* that is, he that has a spiritual understanding and discerning, will take it. They did so. But what would the disputer of this world have said to him ? *Sir you assert that John Baptist was that Elias, but how do you prove it ?* So when the Apostle *John* saies of false or short-sighted teachers ? *They are of the world, therefore the world hears them* ; They

have

They have populous Congregations, all the world goes after them, and admires this man, and the other man. *But we* (faies he) *are of God : He that knoweth God, heareth us : Hereby know we the spirit of truth, and the spirit of error,* 1 Joh. 4. 5, 6. Would not the disputer of this world be out of all patience to hear a man assert at this rate, and (as he reckons) prove nothing ? Let him be what he will, this (we see) is the way of Christ and his Apostles. If there be a spiritual ear, this doctrine is received, if not, will any elaborate discourses or demonstrations ever bring to pass, that *the natural man shall receive the things of God ?* What will become of that Scripture then ? 1 *Cor.* 2. 14. Demonstrate while you will, if there be not the right reception, the hearing ear, all's a case ; you are where you began. The vain, jingling, disputative way of foolish man is not at all to be gratified in the declaration of the mysteries of the kingdom of God. Will you yet cavil and dispute (O professors) will you yet contradict and blaspheme ? *Lo, then I turn to the Gentiles.*

My second Word is to you, O *Gentiles.*

Be wise O Kings ; be instructed O ye Judges of the earth. Serve the Lord with fear, Psal. 2. 10, 11. The Signs and Wonders of God are coming thick upon you. *While it is yet called to day, harden not your hearts* against the God of Heaven, and against the Saints of the most High. Practise not thus against them, nor think to change the times and the Laws, *Dan.* 7. 25.

Will you (O Rulers) be paid in your own coin ? You have taken away a famous man in our *Israel,* this day, upon some dark *REASON of STATE,* against all the Laws of *England,* and against the common light of Reason in all mankind. Will you hear a *REASON of STATE* that might have moved you to the contrary ? Though it be too late, as to his Life, because his blood that you have spilt, cannot be gathered up again, (as the wise woman of *Tekoah* told *David*) yet it may happily be somewhat preventive to your further proceedings that way, against others. Remember then what is recorded of *Aan de Burg,* burnt in *France,* 1559. The Death and Constancy of a man so conspicuous, made many curious to know what Religion that was, for which he had so couragiously endured punishment. By that means great numbers of people were baptized into his perswasion. *Trust me,* (faies one) *you have gotten nothing by these spectacles. Men return from them more confirm'd in their detestation of you, than terrified from any of their purposes towards you. Their*
names

names will be recorded amongst those who have died out of debt to their country, by having paid the utmost they owed it. Their worth will be remembred. Their children and kindred will alwayes be looked upon as descendants from the Liberatours of their Country, and esteemed accordingly.

I wish heartily for your own fakes and ours too, that this REASON of STATE had come into your mind, and had prevailed against any other, before you ventured to embrue your hands in the blood of so deserving a subject. But proceed no farther to lift up your selves thus against the Lord of heaven; for when ye have done all, the meek ones of Christ must inherit the earth; *when the wicked are cut off, they shall see it,* Psal. 37. 34. *The Saints of the most High shall take and possesse the kingdom for ever and ever, do what any can to hinder them,* Dan 7. 18. Quarrel not at these things, but, *like noble Bœreans, search the Scriptures and see whether they be so or no.* Do not put far from you the evil day. It never was nearer. Hinder not Saints assembling together. 'Tis their duty so to do; and that so much the more, as they see the day of Christ's heavenly appearance approaching, *Heb.* 10. 25. Praying persons, praying People, that have an interest in God, are the main bulwark and security of any Nation. Ten righteous, praying persons had saved all *Sodom* and the neighbour cities, *Gen.* 18. 32. The *Sodomites* vilify and assault *Lot,* and he is the onely man that stands betwixt them and the storm of fire and brimstone that was coming upon them. *God bids him haste away, for he cannot do any thing till he be got to some place of security.* Gen. 19. 9. 22. 'Twas a Proverb in *Israel, Without standings the world could not stand;* that is, without prayers; the posture was put for the duty. Would you rid your hands and the world of Saints, praying Persons, and Meetings? Then the world will stand no longer; and where then will your standing be? what should the world stand for, when God has no share or portion in it? What mean you then, O Rulers? Are Protestants murder'd and hurried up and down for meeting to worship God, and the service of the Devil in the abominable Idolatries of the Mass, wink'd at or countenanc'd? Nothing hardly of Protestantisme scapes your censure, but what's to be found in the publick Assemblies, into which you have returned an insipid, frothy, Episcopal Ministry, whose Divinity amounts not to so much as found and well managed moral Philosophy. Their words have no power to awaken Consciences, or authority in Consciences that are already awakened. I doubt they aim at no such thing; but onely, to lull awakened Consciences into a deep sleep againe, and those that are so,

S to

to keep so still. 'Tis an enlightened, knowing People, that are the only burdensome stone to them. Do you think *England* can away with such work as this, that have flourished of late years, in Light and Liberty, beyond any Nation round about her ? Do you imagine that the Mass, or a barren Episcopal Ministry with an Organ and a Common-prayerBook will down with a Nation that has such light stirring in it, as not only the Presbyterian, but, in a manner all the variety of Congregational Churches, yea the very Fift-Monarchy-men (so called) will hardly bear ? Will you pull out all our eyes ? will you stop our mouths with gags and handkerchiefs, because you have no Law or Reason to stop them with ? Do you think the righteous man has no remedy left him ? *The Lord is, in his Temple : his Throne is in heaven. His eyes behold, his eyelids try the children of men. The wicked and him that loveth violence, his soul hateth. Upon the wicked he shall rain snares, fire and brimstone, and an horrible tempest,* Psal. 11. 4, 6. *God is angry with the wicked every day. If he turn not , he will whet his sword, he hath bent his bow, and made it ready. He ordeineth his arrows against the persecutors. He hath prepared for them the instruments of death. Their mischief shall return upon their own heads, and their violent dealing shall come down upon their own pates,* Psal. 7. 9, 16. Is not here enough for you ? If you persist in your way, every syllable of this will be accomplished upon you. There's no flying from God's presence or escaping his hand. No visible confidencies, bulwarks, forts, armies, treasure, or whatever else, can secure you from men, much less from angels, and much less yet from God. *'Tis a fearful thing to fall into the hands of the living God.* He is the transcendently highest over-ruling Magistrate of all. He is the great General of all the armies in heaven or earth, Angels, stars, men, and all inferiour creatures. His host of angels relieved *Elisha* against the *Syrians. The stars in their courses fought against Sisera,* Jedg. 5. 20. Yea, to shew the contemptible folly of self-exalting man, God can so animate an army of frogs, locusts, lice or flies, as to appall the proudest Tyrant, and make him buckle, and acknowledge that he has sinned against the Lord in abusing his people, and desire them to pray for his deliverance, as we see over and over in *Pharaoh's* case, *Exod.* 8. 9. 10. How oft have rich and potent kings bin dragg'd out of all their visible supports, taken by force out of their ablest troops and choisest armies, and carried up and down to be laughed at by their enemies ? how many signal instances for this do we find in *Jewish*, *Assyrian*, *Persian*, *Greek*, *Romane*, *Turkish* and other Histories, the *English* not excepted. Queen *Jezebel* with all her pomp and retinue can't secure her body from being dogs meat. Have you killed, and also taken possession ?

seſſion ? Remember her. Remember *Ahab. Where dogs lick'd* **Na-**
boths blood, *they lick'd his,* 1 King. 21, 19. and *Chap.* 22. 38.

If any Magiſtrates yet ſtout it out in their cruel and oppreſſive
courſes, whereinſoever they deal proudly, God will be above them,
Exod. 18. 11. They are nothing in his hands. They are but little in
an Angels hands ; And not much in man's. You were but little, you
know, in the hands of men. Thoſe whom you have valiantly executed after they had layne a good while in their graves, together with
thoſe whom you have killed and cut in pieces, ſingle, were two hard
for you when they were alive and together. There is a generation a-
mongſt us, oh how lofty are their eyes ? (*Prov.* 30. 13.) but what have
they done ? The honeſt party of *England* are (as 'twas once ſaid of *Ger-*
many) triumphed over but not conquered. Well, you have been but
little in the hands of men, that's undeniable. You are as nothing in
the hands of an angel. *You are accounted as leſs than nothing to God.*
Eſay 40. 17. What may be performed upon you by the inviſible
ſtrokes of angels, you may learn from what is recorded for your inſtruction ; 1 *Kings* 19. *One hundred eighty five thouſand were ſlain by an*
angel in one night, in the camp of the Aſſyrians. Some prodigious alarms
of their approach to undertake you, on the behalf of betrayed, abuſed
Saints, have of late been given.

What ever you have heard of in former times, as to the exploits of
Angels in this kind, you will find to have been but type to what God
will perform by thoſe angelical hoſts, in the laſt dayes, when all viſible reliefs fail his praying People.

See (*O King*) the honeſt and juſtifiable boldneſs, plainneſs and
freedom of ſpeech, that *Daniel* and other Prophets have uſed to greater Monarch's. *O thou King,* ſaies *Daniel* to *Belſhazzar, the moſt high*
God gave thy Father a Kingdom and glory and honour. But when his heart
was lifted up, and his mind hardned in pride, he was depoſed from his king-
ly Throne, and they took his glory from him. And thou, his Son, O Bel-
ſhazzar, haſt not humbled thine heart, though thou kneweſt all this ; but
haſt lifted up thy ſelf againſt the Lord of heaven, and abuſed (his Saints)
the Veſſels of his houſe ; and the God in whoſe hand thy breath is and all
thy wayes, haſt thou not glorified. Then he interprets M E N E
M E N E   T E K E L   U P H A R S I N ;   God has numbred thy
kingdom and finiſhed it, &c. Dan. 5. 18, 28. *Daniel was highly honour-*
ed by the King for thus dealing with him, verſ. 29.

See the commendable ſtoutneſs as well as honeſt boldneſs of Saints,
in their conferences and parting-blows with Kings. *Pharaoh,* in a
fume, bid *Moſes get him gone, and take heed to himſelf, for in the day he*

ſaw

saw his face again, he should die. Well, saies *Moses*, Ile see thy face again no more. Who had the worst on't? The King would need *Moses* help before he the King's. He had sent for him with all speed before, time and time, in several distresses, under the plagues that were upon him and his People. *Moses* needed nothing that he could do, but that that would be done whether he would or no, *Israels* deliverance from bondage. *All these thy servants*, saies *Moses*, *shall come and bow themselves to me, saying, Get thee out and all the people that follow thee; and I will go out : And he went out from Pharaoh in a great anger. Pharaoh* was wickedly and proudly angry and stout, in ridding his hands of *Moses*; and *Moses* was meekly and justly angry and stout in a resolved quitting of *Pharaohs* company, for ever, *Exod.* 10. 28, 29. and *Chap.* 11. 8. The Oracles of God, delivered by *Moses*, though accompanied and ratified with miracles, were called by that vain King, *vain or lying words, Exod.* 5. 9. Those Kings that will do as *Pharaoh* did, refuse all Messages from the Lord, delivered to them, scoffe at and persecute the messengers, must look for *Pharaoh's* wages, and that, dispensed to them from such a hand, as *can tear them in pieces, so as none can deliver*.

Kings have usually had a great antipathy to true Prophets, and their messages, but, bin very kind and friendly to false, flattering Prophets, who speak smooth, pleasing things. About four hundred false Prophets, with one mouth, encourage *Ahab* to go to *Ramoth-Gilead*, a City of *Israel*, and recover it from the *Syrian*. They saw he had a mind to it, and they all prophesied success and Victory. At *Jehoshaphat* the king of *Judah's* motion, *Michaiah*, a true Prophet is called in. *Ahab* had no mind to him. *I hate him* (saies he) *for he does not use to prophesie good concerning me but evil*; that is, did not use to gratify his present humour and lust, as the others did. He deals truly with *Ahab*; warnes him, that if he go, he dies for't; and so it fell out. The false Prophets, no doubt, had incouraging rewards. *Michaiah's* recompense is a Prison, and the bread and water of affliction. But the Kings following the pleasing counsel of the false Prophets was his ruine, and the listening to *Michaiah* had been his safety. Who were the Traitors, the four hundred false Prophets or the one true?

The true **Prophet and** Subject is handled as the Traitor, and the false Traitors go currant away with gratuities and favours. Why do not Kings consider such instructing paterns? It highly concerns them, both in point of honour and safety, *1 King.* 22.

Nebuchadnezzar sets up a stately piece of Popery, an Image of gold, thirty

thirty yards high. The Princes, Governours, Captaines, Judges, Treasurers, Counsellours, Sheriffs, & all the Rulers of Provinces, &c. come to the dedication of it. A Herald solemnly proclaims, That when they hear the sound of the Cornet, Flute, (Organ) Harp, Sackbut, Psaltery, Dulcimer, and all kinds of Musick, they must all fall down and worship the Image; and that those who refuse, are to be cast into be midst of a burning fiery furnace. The generallity of the Governours and People obey the Decree. *Shadrach*, *Meshach* and *Abednego*, are traduced before the King, as Rebels and Hereticks, for slighting his Commands, not serving his God's, nor worshiping the golden Image which he had set up. The King in a fury sends for them, tells them he will try them once more, and if they refuse the second time, to the fiery Furnace they go. They tell him, he need trouble himself no further about trying them, they are resolved what to do. *We are not careful, O King, (say they) to answer thee in this matter. God will deliver us out of thy hand, O King, Or if he will not, yet be it known to thee O King, we will not serve thy Gods nor worship thy golden Image.* Then his fury is exercised upon them for a while, till he sees their executioners fall down dead upon the place, while they scape. This quite **turns** his mind, and he makes a Decree, *That if any speak against the God of Shadrach, Meshach and Abednego, they shall be cut in pieces, and their houses made a dunghil, because there is no other God that can deliver after this sort.* Dan. 3. Yet it appears not that *Nebuchadnezzar* himself worshipped this true God, or forsook his false.

A while after we find him boasting and vaunting, as if there were no other God but he, *Dan.*4.30. What a fickle thing is that Religion that depends upon the Magistrates Decree ?

Darius the *Mede*, when he comes upon the Stage at *Babylon*, he is flattered by his corrupt Courtiers to turn Pope, take upon him to be the holy Father; all must pray to him for thirty dayes, and not ask a petition of any other God. If they did, they must to the Lions den. *Daniel* is charged with slighting the King and his Decree. The King set himself to deliver him, but could not. An Angel did, by stopping the Lyons mouths. Then his accusers with their wives and children were cast to the Lyons, and were torn in pieces immediately, before they came to the bottom of the Den, *Dan.* 6. What looking-glasses are here for Kings, to give them aim what persons to put most value on, Idolatrous flattering Courtiers, that counsel them to their dammage and disherison, or true Prophets and faithful Subjects that advise them for the safety of their Crown and Dignity. True, they *know not to give flattering titles to men ; for in so doing, their maker would soon take them away,* Job. 32. 22. They fear him more than men. 'Tis the true advantage of Kings to be plainly dealt with by them. Flatterers ruine them. They are the Traitors, as has appeared in all ages.

Believe it, O ye Rulers and Judges, if you go on at the rate you have begun, should all the Angels in heaven, and Men on earth, lay their understandings together, to demonstrate the requisiteness yea absolute necessity of having made a Parliamentary and popular defence against such corrupt sticklers for prerogative and arbitrary domination, when got into armes, (1641.) 'Tis hard to imagine how they should mend that which your selves have given by your most injurious and oppressive practices, since your return. What should we mince the matter for? The world is almost at an end ; *The Devils rage is great because he knows he has but a short time.* It highly concerns us to deal plainly with one another, lest that great deceiver of the Nations cozen us all.

If men do as wickedly as they can, and make a law that no body must tell them of it ; must every body therefore hold their peace, and let them go on? What can the Devil desire more? Must God and his Messengers have no hearing with you? What do you imagine will become of you then? Will ye change Religion and the Laws, and must no body dare to say so? But they will, you see. Will you put out the eyes of all the good People of *England*? They have eyes and will use them too, do what you can, as long as their heads are on. With these eyes they see clearer what you are about, then (it may be) you are aware.

The Lord in the late War was a Rebuker of you all, in many pitch'd Fields and a continued series of disappointments for many years together.

If you would but mend the matter as to what this Nation felt when it groaned under the Tyranny of your apostate Conqueror, this yet were something. Many of the same persons that he abused and oppressed, you have slain, and so finished his work upon them. You should let the oppressed go free, ease those heavy burdens that he put upon the People, and you encrease them, so that the Nation languishes under a general discouragement, as to Trade, and almost every thing else.

What work God will suffer to be made by any instruments of cruelty amongst us, that are profound to make slaughter, though unfit to
fight,

fight, he himself best knows. But that God will send deliverance in the close, and preserve a remnant in the scramble, I am as confident, as that there is a God that judgeth in the Earth, who will make himself known by the Judgements which he will execute upon all wicked Opposers of him and his People. Freely I have received, and I freely give you such portion as the Scripture allots you.

Yet say not, (O Rulers) there is no hope ; we will therefore fill up the measure of our wickedness ; and then let God strike. Say not thus. There is yet hope. You may repent of the evil of your doings, and quite lay aside all your mischievous and destructive intendments towards this peeled People, and you and we together may be a flourishing Nation. If the King say as the King of *Nineveh*, *Let every man cry mightily unto God, let them turn every one from his evil way, and from the violence that is in their hands* ; *who can tell but God may turn away from his fierce anger, that we perish not ?* Jonah 3. **8, 9.**

FINIS.

Some Notes of Sir *Henry Vane's* Exhortation to his Children and Family, (brokenly and imperfectly taken) *June* 13. 1662. being the day before his Execution.

Genesis 18. 17, 18, 19.

And the Lord said, Shall I hide from Abraham that thing which I do, seeing that Abraham shall surely become a great and mighty Nation, and all the Nations of the Earth shall be blessed in him? For I know him, that he will command his children and his houshold after him, and they shall keep the way of the Lord, to do Justice and Judgement; that the Lord may bring upon Abraham, that which he hath spoken of him.

WE have here a description of God's reasoning within his own mind, concerning the open-heartedness he would use towards *Abraham,* who is called his Friend (*Isa.* 41. 8.) for the eminency of his Faith, by which he was made *one spirit,* and of *one mind with the Lord,* so as he could instantly surrender and perform whatever God called for from him, or required of him, however hard or contrary to the desire, eye and reasonings of flesh and blood.

The greatest tryal of his Faith, and the most signal manifestation of it, was the offering up his only begotten son, the son of promise, **of** whom it was said, *In Isaac shall thy seed be called.*

This Typical Father of the Faithful, behaved himself **but as a** pilgrim and stranger, even in the earthly Land of Promise, seeking yet *a better Country, a heavenly,* Heb. 11. 12. He came off readily with this greatest offering of flesh at its best, in his *Isaac,* the figure of Christs offering ; so, as by the transforming Baptism of the Spirit, to grow up into **a** perfect harmony with the will of God, *Rom.* 12. 1, 2. Hereupon he is termed the *Father of the Faithful* ; and hereby *Isaac* also became a *Son of the Resurrection,* as he was also before, in a figure, *Heb.* 11. 12, & 19. as springing up from *Abraham's* body and *Sarah's* womb, when both of them were as good as dead.

The present occasion admits no long insisting on this, being, together with the care he had of his Family, but the introductory consideration with God (*who revealeth his secrets to his servants the Prophets,* Amos 3: 7. *and them that fear him,* Psal. 25. 14.) for the

discodifcovering unto *Abraham* that exemplary vengeance he then refolved to pour out upon *Sodom* and the neighbouring Cities, for their wickednefs.

Abraham, by the offering up of *Ifaac*, did certainly perform the choiceft, higheft, and moft acceptable Sacrifice and Service that is required of God, or performable by the Faith of Gods Elect. Nothing was fo dear to him as the Will of God ; and God thought nothing too much to give him. He muft become a great and mighty Nation ; yea, all the Nations of the Earth muft be bleffed in him. Moreover, he will not withhold his fecret counfels and refolutions from his friend *Abraham*. If he intend to execute his Judgements in the Earth, he will unbofom himfelf to *Abraham* before-hand, and fo afford him the opportunity of trying the utmoft that may be done by his interceffion, on behalf of the Generation amongft whom his lot was caft. The fervant knows not what his Lord is about to do ; but the Friend, the Son, all muft be difcovered to him. The Friend will readily do whatfoever the Lord commands, (*Joh.* 15. 14, 15.) will follow the Lamb whitherfoever he goes, (*Rev.* 14. 4.) therefore is the Lord willing to difclofe to him, whatfoever he is going about to do. The Son that abideth in the houfe for ever, is open-handed, free and univerfal in his love and refignation of all he is or hath, unto God ; and God is as free and open-hearted unto him, knowing that he will make a right conftruction and improvement of his difcoveries.

Obferve, firft, then ; *That the life of Faith is the moft excellent life, and that thofe therefore that live by Faith in the higheft operation of it, are of higheft efteem with God.*

This is apparant in *Abraham*'s cafe, here before us. He was a Believer of the higheft rank, and therefore the choice Friend of God, the *Father of the Faithful, in whom all Nations are to be bleffed.* He is thought fit for moft intimate bofom-familiarity and converfe with God. 'Twas a more excellent operation of the Faith that faves, and is Eternal life in the Believer, which *Abraham* did experience and walk in ; in diftinction from, and fuperiority to, the elect Angels, and an inferiour fort of everlaftingly faved Men, that fhall ftand about the Throne, on which *Abraham* (with others of his more fublimated fpirit and higher participations of Chrift) fhall fit, as the Bride, the Lamb's Wife.

From the fingular notice God here takes of *Abraham*, and the peculiar friendlinefs he fhews, in revealing to him alone, (of all mankind) his prefent intendment towards *Sodom*,

Obferve,

Obſerve, ſecondly, *That as it is the Duty, ſo is it the great Pri-*
viledge and advantage of Believers, highly to value, and carefully to
improve Divine Diſcoveries.

Why did God ſhew this ſecret to *Abraham*, more than to any man
living, but becauſe of the ſingular good uſe he knew *Abraham* would
make of it ? He knew he would inſtruct and command his Children
and Family after him, to keep the way of the Lord, and to worſhip
him in Spirit and in Truth, though a way, by men called Hereſie.
God thinks he can never be open enough to a tryed Believer, a known
Friend.

Uſe 1. How ſhould this encourage us to give up all our *Iſaacs* to
him, to do with us, and all we are or have, whatſoever pleaſes him ?
How willing ſhould this render us, to have our Sacrifices faſt bound
to the horns of the Altar, with the threefold cord of God's love to us,
man's enmity to us, and our love to God ? Whatever we ſurrender
and part with, in obedience to the Will of God, we are ſure to receive
again with Uſury ; *to die, is gain.* To loſe life, is the way to find it
eternally. A Believer draws forth the choiceſt communicable Excellencies and boſom-ſecrets of Chriſt. God puts a great value upon
every motion of his believing Friends. Much tribulation they meet
with, in this Vale of tears ; many affronts and cruel mockings from
contradictious men ; yea, bonds, impriſonments and cruel deaths. But
the Lord ſtands by them, to aſſiſt and give them peace in the midſt of
all, to make them ſtedfaſt and unmovable in the work of the Lord,
and in their ſufferings for ſuch work. He raiſes in them, ſuch raviſh-
ments of joy, through the manifeſtation of the glory that follows, that
they chuſe rather to be tortured and ſlain, than to accept of deliverance, in order to obtain a better reſurrection, than their deliverance
from priſons and death, would amount unto. They abide ſtedfaſtly
with God, unto a temporary death ; and he then ſets upon their heads,
the Crown of eternal life. Conſider; was not Chriſt, the great Captain of our Salvation, made perfect through ſufferings ? did not he paſs
this way to the Crown, and muſt not he that will live godly, ſuffer perſecution, and through much tribulation, enter into the Kingdom of God ?
The Apoſtle bids us conſider Chriſt, *who quietly endured ſuch con-*
tradiction of ſinners, against himſelf, leſt we be wearied and faint in
our minds. I am now going, through the grace of God, *to reſist man*
unto blood, as knowing *that I ought to obey God rather than men.*
I am ready to follow the Lord whitherſoever he goes and calls me after him. Reſt aſſured of this ; However diſmal and ſad the Believers

work

work and condition appears to men, God will give (besides a holy triumph of rejoycing in the way) an expected end ; an end, that will answer, and over-answer all the desires and expectations of his soul. Whoever is able throughout to mark the perfect man, and to behold the upright in heart, will find, *that the end of that man is peace :* such peace, and so given, not as the world giveth, but so, as no man can take it from him.

Objection. *But what peace is this, Believers have ? Is it not their usual lot here, to be delivered into the hands of sinners ? doth not God permit the men of this world, the inhabitants of the earth, to trample upon and insult over them ? yea, even to ride over their heads,* (Psal. 66. 12.) *so that they are forced to lay their bodies as the ground and as the sheet, to their oppressors that go over them,* Isa. 51. 23. *Doth he not suffer the Devil by wicked men, to proceed further against them for the tryal of their Faith, than he had commission to proceed against* Job, *for the tryal of his patience ? even to the touching and taking away their very lives, and that with all manner of lying aggravations, centring in this, to fix the black and infamous character of the greatest malefactors upon them, and then cry, Crucifie them, crucifie them, away with such people from the earth, it is not fit they should live any longer ?* Act. 22. 22.

Answ. To this I answer. Thus Christ himself was served ; and therefore (all this notwithstanding) they may have peace ; Yea, they have the only *true peace, which passeth understanding.* In the midst of all the tumultuous confusions and insurrections of the workers of iniquity against them, they have a steady composure, and un-interrupted serenity of mind, through an unshaken submission to, acquiescence in, and conformity to the will of God, in all occurrences. In the greatest storms, the sharpest and most fiery tryals that can befal them; when they see the flames of man's wrath, the floods of *Belial* (or wicked men) devouring on all hands, and overwhelming all considerations or appearances of true outward peace, equity or order, they have the inward peace and joy unspeakable and glorious, which such strangers cannot intermeddle with, or interrupt. A perfect calmness and serenity, both in spirit and outward deportment, may be the Believers portion and ornament, in such a season, and such circumstances, *when the vilest of men are exalted, and the wicked walk on every side.* When the world is in the most injurious career against the Saints, then doth Christ more intimately imbrace them, and more abundantly manifest to their Faith, the riches and glory of the world to come.

Use 2.

Use 2. for your instruction. These things I leave with you, as the words of one in my place and circumstances, that ought to have weight with you that are young and liable to be misled. Learn hence to put value upon the priviledge of believing Saints. Be the daughters and children of *Abraham* and *Sarah*, in all modest, chaste and holy conversation. Quit the broad way and beaten Road that leadeth to Destruction, and be for the narrow path that leadeth unto Life, the way everlasting, *Psal.* 139. 24. Let not your care be spent in outward adorning, but in adorning the hidden or inner man of your hearts, with that which is not corruptible. Get the ornament of a *meek and quiet spirit, which in the sight of God is of great price.* With all your getting, *get divine wisdom and understanding,* Prov. 4. 7. Be as circumspect and curious as you can in these heavenly ornaments, watching alwayes to cast and keep out every thing that defiles, that you may *possess your vessels in sanctification and honour, as becomes the temples of the holy Ghost, glorifying God with your bodies and with your spirits, which are his.* After this manner, holy women that trusted in God, did in old time adorn themselves, whose daughters ye are so long as ye do well, and you will find no need to be afraid with any amazement : For, (keeping alwayes by this means, *a good conscience, void of offence towards God and towards man*) when men *shall speak evil of you, as of evil doers, the shame shall be their own ;* It will appear, 'tis only your chaste and good conversation in Christ, they persecute and accuse you for. This is the ground of all their malice and reproaches. Christ hath chosen you out of the world ; be ye followers of him out of it, in the peculiar distinguishing spirit and conversation of pilgrims and strangers. But then know, the inhabitants of the earth will hate you. Let this common lot and portion of Believers from this world, be expected by you, and rendred familiar to you, that when you come indeed more eminently under the experiences of it, you may not look upon it as any new, strange, or unusual thing, that happens to you above all other Believers. But, when such things come to pass, rejoyce, *in as much as ye are made partakers of Christs sufferings, that when his glory shall be revealed, ye may be glad also, with exceeding joy.* If ye be reproached for the Name of Christ, *if ye suffer for Righteousness sake, happy are ye ; for the Spirit of Glory and of God resteth upon you. Be ye not therefore afraid of their terrour, neither be you troubled, but sanctifie the Lord God in your hearts, by your stedfastness and boldness.* It may be ready to startle you, to see a Believer thus handled as you see me now, to end his

mortal

mortal dayes by the hands of violence, though not without the free and willing surrender of his Life, in compliance with the divine hand and determinate counsel of God, herein. This is the way which the Lord himself, the great Captain of our Salvation, went before us in. Let not this way of the Lord be evil spoken of by you. Let not the least prejudice or thought arise in your hearts against it, on this occasion; but rather let it serve for the increase and strengthning of your Faith, as it ought.

Use. 3. That which hath been said and observed concerning *Abraham*, (as to God's taking such peculiar notice of him, and making such peculiar discoveries of his secrets to him) should serve to instruct, inform and mind us of the great benefits and glorious advantages attainable for us, by abiding and increasing in the spirit and faith of our father *Abraham*. It will meet with glorious Returns from God. The Spirit of Glory will rest upon such, as do thus improve the example of *Abraham*. The secrets of the Lord are with them that fear him: The Angels of the Lord encamp round about them, and deliver them; yet, not alwayes from a violent death, by the hands of men. Christ himself, would not imploy the Angels in this service, though he could have had more than twelve legions of them for his rescue, at his desire. The followers of Christ then, are not altogether delivered from death, but from the fear, the sting, the power of death, and so are made to conquer and triumph over death it self, and him that hath the power of death, by dying; as Christ did, who was thus heard in what he feared, *Heb.* 5. 7.

Live then in the Spirit, and walk in the Spirit and Faith of our Father *Abraham*. Listen to the Experiences of your Father, in this dying hour and season of darkness, who can and doth here give a good report of that heavenly and better Country, he is now going to the more free and full enjoyment of. In the midst of these his dark circumstances, his enjoyments and refreshings from the presence of the Lord, do more abound than ever. I can truly say, that as my tribulations for Christ have risen higher and abounded, my Consolations have abounded much more. My Imprisonment and hard usage from men, hath driven me nearer to God, and more alienated and disentangled my mind from the snares and cumbrances of this mortal life.

You have no cause to be ashamed of my Chain; or to fear being brought into the like circumstances I now am in, so it be on as good an occasion, for the *Name and Cause of Christ*, and *for his Righteousness sake*. Let this word abide with you, whatever befalls you;

Resolve

Refolve to fuffer any thing from men, rather than fin againft God: yea, rejoyce and be exceeding glad, when you find it given to you on the behalf of Chrift, *not only to believe in him, but to fuffer for his Name*. *Stand faft in one fpirit, with one mind, ftriving together for the Faith of the Gofpel, and be in nothing terrified by your ad-verfaries, but go on in your courfe of well-doing, without any amaze-ment*. Sufferings for well-doing, patiently born, are acceptable with God. A quiet rejoycing deportment in fufferings, will be to your adverfaries, an evident token of their Perdition; but to you of Salva-tion, and that of God. To him that thus overcometh in the Faith and Spirit of Chrift, (the true *Abraham*) *he will give to fit with him on his Throne*, and to inherit all things.

Let the like Spirit of Faith be in you, that was in *Abraham*, and you will never reft till you come into his bofom. You will be but pilgrims and ftrangers here: Your eye, your heart and expectations will be upon that better Country. Such a frame of mind and heart God is fo well pleafed with, that he will not fail to make more rich and full difcoveries of himfelf to you daily, for the building and ga-thering of you up, nearer and clofer unto himfelf, till he be the whole defire of your foul, the only defirable, who is altogether lovely.

Tex*. *I know Abraham* (fayes God) *that he will command his Children and houfhold, &c.*

Obf. 3. **Obferve hence,** *That it is the duty of every believing Fa-ther, not only to teach his Children and Family, for the keeping them in a good converfation while he is prefent with them, but to leave inftructions with them, and charge them after him, that they may know how to deport themfelves both in their inward and outward man, when he is gone.*

Thus it was with *Abraham*. He inftructed or **catechized** them, (as the Original imports) laid the foundation for a future growth and progrefs in the fame Faith with him, whereby they alfo might be enabled to communicate it, and fo lay the like foundation in others, and *build up one another in the fame moft holy Faith*: which charge is alfo implyed and fuppofed to have been infifted on, and with all earneftnefs preffed upon them, as being unfpeakably moft carefull and concerned in the propagating of his believing Seed to the worlds end. Thus *Abraham* alfo, (as others in like cafe) will have his great perfonal advantage, by the bountiful communicating and in-

filling

ftilling the fpiritual and heavenly Doctrine of the Gofpel, into the hearts of as many as he can, fpreading abroad amongft others, the precious favour of that grace of God, that he had fo plentifully been enriched with, and tafted of, in his own experiences all-along.

This heavenly Life and marvellous Light of the Faith of the Son of God, is of that nature, that the more it is diffufed by way of communication unto others, the more it encreafes in the Difpenfer thereof, redouading to his advantage, as well as theirs that receive it. The fruit of his doings (*Jer.* 17, 10.) fpring up from fuch foundations of Holinefs, as by his inftruction were minifterially laid ; The works that naturally flow from that Doctrine, follow them, after they are gone hence ; *Rev.*14.13. The Church in the *Canticles* (chap. 7. 1.) is defcribed by him that beft knew her temper, to be of this noble, princely, communicative difpofition. *Freely ye have received, freely give,* fayes Chrift ; and by giving, they receive more abundance. The fruit of fuch labours will be reckoned on their account. This is a great encouragement for men to abound in the work of the Lord, forafmuch as they know, *that their labour is not in vain in the Lord,* 1 *Cor.* 15. 58.

Let it be your conftant care then, to multiply fuch fruits as may abound to both our accounts, in purfuance and imitation of that Faith which by word and deed ye have heard and feen in me, all the time that God hath pleafed to continue me with you. It will be both yours and my great gain, if you be careful to glorifie your heavenly Father, anfwerably to the many feafonable inftructions, directed to you in the Word of the Lord, by my Miniftry.

This was *Abraham's* faith, way, life and practice, who being dead yet fpeaketh to the whole Family of Faith, throughout the whole world, unto this day.

While he was prefent with his Family, he taught them in word and deed, by what he faid in his Miniftry, and by what he did, in all other holy converfation and godlinefs.

Firft, by the things he did, as a pattern of Faith, Holinefs and Sobriety, in his converfation ; and then by what he faid, in giving daily inftructions to them, to follow his fteps, walk honeftly, as in the day, in the Spirit, worthy of God, by the fame Rule they obferved him to walk. *For they ought fo to walk, even as he walked, abiding in his words,* 1 Joh. 2.6. Thus *Abraham's* Family had his pattern and inftruction in the Faith of God's Elect, for their direction, while he was converfant amongft them.

Secondly,

Secondly, He gave forth command, and instructed them in the Name of the Lord, that when he, their believing Father, should be gone from them into a more exalted state of life, (to them invisible and undiscernable, as to any further personal converse with him in his former way) they should be as careful still, as ever, to walk in the steps of his Faith, bringing forth the fruits thereof unto holiness, if not more than ever before, while he was with them. Christ himself, the most true and absolute Father of the Faithful, took this course a little before his death; gave that large and most admirably significant Instruction to his Disciples, recorded in the 13, 14, 15, 16, and 17 Chapters of *John*, to strengthen and establish their hearts in the present Truth they had been taught and were possessed of, (whatever hatred, persecution, or cross blows they should meet with from the world) as also to beget in them an assured expectation of his Return to them in a more excellent way of converse, than ever they yet experienced. On this account, he told them (that how sad and troubled soever they may be, through mistake of his departure, and of the sharp and bitter way of it) it was expedient, even for them as well as for himself, that he should go away, forasmuch as he would then return to them, in a more excellent estate, a better Comforter, a better Counsellor, that would tell them more excellent things, things they could not yet bear, to the fulfilling of their joy.

Use. Let me then direct unto you a word of Exhortation, by the example of *Abraham* and *Christ* himself, in my present circumstances, in the near approach of my dissolution and parting with you. Be not disheartned in the way of the Lord, be not discouraged in the way I have gone before you in, and am yet going, drawing near now to the finishing of my course with joy. The God of Heaven hath set his seal to it in my heart, that it is the very way of Truth, the choicest and best way you can go : the way, that not only will have the most comfortable close, by ending in everlasting joy, but that hath also the most solid foundation of inward rejoycing, all-along attending it, even in this world. Though there be sorrow and death to the flesh in this way, there is life and joy in the Spirit. The Believer, the true spiritual Circumcision rejoyces in Christ Jesus, having no confidence in the flesh, nor mattering much how it goes with that : So he may win Christ, and know him in the power of his Resurrection, he is willing also to know him in the fellowship of his Sufferings, and in being made conformable unto his death. There is no other way to the eternal Crown. *If we suffer with him,* (who before *Pontius Pilate,*

V   witnessed

witnessed a good Confession, 1 *Tim.* 6. 13.) *we shall also reign with him* : If we deny Him and his Cause before men, through fear of them that can but kill the body, and have no more that they can do, he that can destroy both body and soul in Hell, will deny us before the Angels of God.

Whatever frightful appearance the present tribulations may have, this remains sure, *Light is sown for the Righteous, and gladness for the upright in heart.* My harvest is at hand, the season for me to reap the good fruit of the incorruptible seed of eternal life, that hath been sown in me many years ago, by the good hand of the Lord. I have so much already of that fruit, as makes me set very light by the present tribulations, that are but for a moment, and are not to be compared with the glory that follows. I have sown in tears and am now going to reap in joy, where all tears shall be wiped away, for ever. There shall be no more sorrow, crying, or hearing the voice of the oppressor.

I charge you therefore, *be ye followers of me, as I am a follower of Christ.* Walk in that Faith ye have seen me to walk in, and be not dismayed. Observe what I now say to you, and the Lord will bless you; yea, you shall be encouraged and commended by him as a choice pattern of obedience unto others, like the sons of *Jonadab* the son of *Rechab*, who were commended for performing the words of their father that he commanded them. and were therein propounded as an imitable pattern to the men of *Judah* and inhabitants of *Jerusalem*, who did most perversly refuse to obey the Commands of God himself, in the Messages he sent to them by the ministry of the Prophets. Encline your ear therefore, and hearken unto me now, in this parting Instruction ; Listen to my command, and obey the words I speak to you in the Name of the Lord. I charge you to walk in the Faith of our Lord Jesus Christ, and that with all stedfastness and constancy, as not (in the least) discouraged by what you see now to befal me and other his servants and followers, in this evil day. *The servant is not greater than the Lord.* He went this way, and hath warned us, *that through much persecution and tribulation we must strive to enter into the Kingdom of God* Walk then in the Spirit and Faith of *Abraham* ; in that immutable frame of spirit, that feeds upon that which is incorruptible, whereby you will be nourished up into eternal life, and carried on through all difficulties and oppositions, to the compleat, full, and certain saving of your souls. Be bold, confident, stedfast, and undaunted herein, though bryars and thorns be with you, and you dwell among Scorpions. Be not afraid of their big words, or stout looks, though
they

they be *a rebellious house*, (Ezek. 2.) *not having the fear of God before their eyes*, and therefore lifting up themselves Belshazzar-like against the Lord of Heaven, and practising to destroy the People of the Most High, till the Antient of dayes come and set them upon their feet ; at which time, Judgement shall be given to the Saints of the most High, and they must possess the Kingdom. Who are you then, (if you live and abide in the Faith of *Abraham*) that you should be afraid of a man that shall die, and be made as grass ? *Isa.* 51. 12. All the Nations of the World are less than nothing before Him, in whom is your help, *Isa.* 40. 17. Stay your selves then upon God, in the greatest outward confusions or alterations of Government or Governours, that possibly can befall ; though the Earth be removed, and the Mountains be carried into the midst of the Sea. Be of good courage, take to you the whole Armour of God, fight the Battels of the Lord, the good fight of Faith, and he will make you more than Conquerors.

Let these dying words of your Father never be forgotten. *Be strong in the Faith of Abraham.* He that now speaks to you, hath for many years proved and tryed what this amounts unto ; he sees great cause to recommend it to you, upon that Experience he hath had of the support and relief it carries with it, in all occurrences ; as also, how bold, stedfast and comfortable it renders the possessors thereof, against all possible affronts, contradictions and oppositions of sinners. When you can no longer enjoy the bodily or visible Presence of your Father with you, live more in the Faith of your Father, that he that is my heavenly Father, may discover himself more and more to be yours also, as you shew your selves more to be his Children, (which will highly concern you) *that through the more plentiful communication of his grace and spirit amongst you and in you, you may be more strengthened with his might and glorious power in your inward man, unto all patience and long-suffering with joyfulness ; and be able to stand it out, in this evil day.*

This is the last opportunity I am like to have of this kind. The Lord set my words home upon your hearts. Be glad and rejoyce thus to be minded of your duty, and charged by me. And what greater cause of rejoycing can your Father have, than that his Children walk in the Truth ? See then *that you alwayes keep your Consciences void of offence, towards God and towards men.* Hate and decline *every unrighteous way, and whatever is contrary to the Gospel of our Lord and Saviour, Jesus Christ.* Put one another in mind of these things, that

your

your Father thus minds you all of, in this his laſt Charge and Inſtructi-on, which he leaves with you : *Provoke one another unto love and good works. Exhort one another ſo much the more, as you ſee the day ap-proaching.* Shew forth your Faith in the workings of it, by which you may glorifie your Father which is in Heaven. *Thoſe that believe in God, will be careful to maintain good works,* Tit. 3. 8. Conſider, *what manner of perſons it concerns you to be, in all holy Converſation and godlineſs, ſeeing that all theſe things that now are, and which ye ſee, are very ſhortly to be diſſolved,* (ſooner it may be, than you can yet believe) even *the Heavens and Earth that now are,* the whole out-ward face of things in Church and State, the world throughout, 2 *Pet.* 3. 7, 11, 12. Live then as thoſe that wait for their maſters coming ; for the *new heavens and new earth, wherein dwelleth righteouſneſs :* Live in the pure Spirit of this tried Faith of *Abraham,* largely experienced by your Father, and by him now recommended unto you. Keep the way of the Lord, to do juſtice and judgement, that he may fulfil unto you all the rich and precious promiſes of the Goſpel, belonging to *A-braham* and his believing *ſeed,* the ſeed of Promiſe, that are found walking in his wayes.

Obſerv. 4. Fourthly, and laſtly, obſerve ; *That it is a duty, incumbent on believing parents, to mind their children and houſhold, of walking in the faith, and keeping in the way of the Lord, doing that which is juſt and right. So alſo is it the duty of children to obey ſuch charge, and be found ſo living and walking in the ſpirit and way of the Lord, as they expect the bleſſings of Gods Covenant with Abraham, to be made good unto them.*

But here this *Query* may be offered ; *How did Abraham walk and worſhip ?*

The anſwer is ; In a Family-way ; 'twas Family-worſhip. There were, in his time, no formed Churches or Societies of a larger kind, made up of divers families, embodying themſelves and walking in com-munion together. That which he was capable to do, he did. He cate-chized and inſtructed his Relations, ſpreading abroad amongſt them the favour of the riches of that Grace, which (through mercy) he was partaker of. This was the ſtate of the true Church then, as to its outward form. If larger viſible Societies, and collective Bodies, or Churches of Saints be now interrupted, this Family-way of Religion and Worſhip may be kept up, and ſo things return to their primitive way again, as in the dayes of *Abraham.* To this *Joſhua* profeſſes he will have re-courſe, when the purity of publick Worſhip fails, (*Joſh.* 24. 15.) *If,*

faith

saith he, *it seem evil to you to serve the Lord*; if you be for other gods, or other wayes of worship than God requires, I will quit your publick societies; *as for me and my house, we will serve the Lord.*

Use 1. My word of *exhortation* then to you, is; When publick worship is to be had in purity, without defiling of your Consciences, use and frequent that. But if that bedenied, or is not to be found, frequent private and family worship; yea, however it be as to the publick, let these be kept on foot with all diligence. Be found still in the way of the Lord; own that, where ere you see it, and joyn in it, as the Lord shall please to open the way for you, and give opportunity. Whatever you do, be not conformed to this world, in the spirit, way, principles, affections, no nor religion thereof. Quit those worshippers, that are confident in a spirit and way that is liable to apostacy, calling that heresie, which is the only true way of worshipping the God of our Fathers.

Amidst the great variety of Churches and ways of Worship, that this world abounds with, be not by any means induced or forced to observe and become subject to the ordinances of man, in things pertaining unto God. *Give unto God the things that are Gods: Give also unto Cæsar the things that are his.* If he unlawfully require more, you may lawfully refuse to obey him; let him take his course: wherein any deal proudly, God will be above them. If one Church say, *Lo, here is Christ*; another, *Lo, there*; and the trumpet that's blown in both, give but an uncertain sound, look up to Christ himself with the Spouse in the *Canticles*, and say, *O thou whom our souls do love, tell us where thou feedest and makest thy flock to rest at noon,* under the scorching heat of mans persecuting wrath. He will discover to you the false *Babylonish spirit*, that lurks in such Churches and Teachers, as (to the deceiving of themselves and others) are but transformed into the likeness of the Apostles and Churches of Christ, 2 *Cor.* 11. And he will by his Spirit (if rightly sought to, and waited on) infallibly direct you to the true shepherds tents, those spiritual pastors and assemblies, that walk in the footsteps of his ancient flock, even in the faith, spirit and way of *Abraham, Isaac, Jacob* and their families (who are now in the kingdom of God) and in the way, doctrine and spirit of the Evangelists and Apostles.

And as I would have you to quit all *false Churches,* and reject the *Babylonish spirit,* whatever curious dress, insinuating appearance, or refined form she shines forth in; so, much more yet, would I have you to loath and depart from all manner of prophaness and common debauchery, whatever countenance or encouragement it may have

round

round about you in the Land of your nativity. Do but keep in *the Way*, live and walk in the *Faith* and *Spirit* of *Abraham*, and all is done.

This your Father hath found joy and comfort in upon very large and plentiful experiences; but most remarkably, in his Prison-state. As troubles and straits from without have encreased upon me, I have been more enlarged within. The more I have been shut up on earth, and from earthly Relations and enjoyments, the more have the Heavens opened upon me, and let down to me the larger sights and tasts of the glory and enjoyments of the world to come.

Use 2. Lastly, I charge you, (as the utmost desire of my soul to God on your behalf) be obedient to the Lord, walk humbly with him, and keep close to him. Let your heart be right with him: *Be stedfast in his Covenant, not turning aside like a deceitful Bow.* Be not off and on with him, yea and nay, but in Christ, yea only; and then all the Promises of God in Christ to you, will be, *Yea, and Amen*, to the glory of **God the Father.** Then, *if any of you lack Wisdom* (or particular direction in any difficult circumstances) *ask it of God, who giveth liberally, and upbraideth not, and it shall be given you.* But then, *ask in Faith,* the stedfast Faith of *Abraham,* nothing wavering; for he that wavereth, must not think or expect to receive any thing of the Lord, *James* 1. 5, 7. Christ hath assured you, that *whatsoever you shall ask in his Name, he will do it; and the Father will do it,* (*Joh.* 14. 13, 14. and *chap.* 15. 16.) that is, whatsoever ye shall ask in the power and exercise of a living saving Faith, or of the heavenly Anointing and new Name of Christ, in and upon you, it shall be done unto you: For whatsoever ye thus ask, will be asked by you, in the *will of God that ye are begotten of,* (Jam. 1. 18.) or, according to the will of your heavenly Father; *And this we know, that whatsoever we ask according to his will, he heareth us,* 1 John 5. 14, 15. Yea, though ye be but young, and weak in this Faith, and in the expression of it, if *as new-born babes ye* do but *truly desire the sincere milk of the Word,* and brokenly stammer and lisp forth such desires to God, ye will find acceptance with, and answer from him, not only according to, but abundantly *above all that you are able to ask or think* No Mother can have so tender a regard to the cry of her sucking Child, as he will have to you, in this case, *Isa.* 49. 15. *Wait on the Lord then, be of good courage, and he shall strengthen your hearts: wait, I say, on the Lord, Psal.* 27. 14. *Wait on the Lord, and keep his way, so shall he*
exalt

exalt you to inherit the Land, and verily ye shall be fed. The true believing Seed of *Abraham* shall (in the close) possess the gates of their enemies. *The meek shall inherit the Earth, and delight themselves in the abundance of Peace : But the transgressors shall be destroyed together. The end, hope, and expectation of the wicked shall be cut off.* Know this for your comfort, though the Lord be pleased to take your Father from your head this day, you have other wayes and means to learn and be built up in the mind of the Lord, in your most holy Faith. Never cease to beg of the Lord more abundant communications of his Spirit of Grace, *till you be strengthened with all might in your inward man, that ye may be able to serve God acceptably, and resist the Devil effectually and finally.* Remember, it hath been the prayer of a poor worm on your behalf, that ye may so pray, and be so answered by your heavenly Father, that your joy may be full.

See and consider the gracious design of God towards you, in this very dealing of his with you, by taking me away from you. Is it not that ye may be brought more singly and immediately to rely upon his Influence, that he may bring the Blessings of *Abraham* more plentifully upon you ? Once more, I say, be not discouraged ; Regard not the reproaches that are fallen on your Father. Say or do men what they will, *Abraham's* Faith will find the Blessing *Abraham* found, in whomsoever it is. As for me, I can truly say with *David, The Reproaches, O Lord, of those that have reproached thee, are fallen upon me, Psal, 69. 9.* And he will (in his due time) take off all such unjust Reproaches from himself, from me, and all his faithful hidden ones, and will make himself known by the Judgments that he will execute in the Earth, so that it shall be said ; *Verily, there is a reward for the Righteous ; verily, he is a God that judgeth in the Earth.*

God seems now to take all our concerns wholly into his own hands. You will be deprived of my bodily presence, but *Abraham's* Blessing shall come upon you. If you be under *Abraham's* Covenant, all that's therein promised, will be made good to you, as well as to him, or me. The Lord revive and cause to grow up and flourish whatever is of that Faith of *Abraham* in you, that is in your Father ; and grant it may more and more appear in my Family, after I am gone hence, and no more seen in my mortal body.

Certain

Certain PASSAGES in a *Letter*, sent from a Friend out of the Country, to one that accompanied Sir *Henry Vane* to the SCAFFOLD.

My loving and worthy Friend,

Didst thou stand fast by my worthy Friend, and bear him company? Did thy soul suffer with him and rejoyce with him, riding in his Chariot of Triumph, to the Block, to the Ax, to the Crown, to the Banner, to the Bed and Ivory Throne of the Lord God thy Redeemer? Didst thou stand by, to see all these put upon him in the day of his Espousals, in his solemn Nuptials? Was he not (my Friend) most richly trimmed, adorn'd, deck'd with all manner of fine Linnen, curious Embroyderies? Did not the Perfume of his Garments give a good smell to all the Room and Company? Was he not like the Lord's, the Lamb's Bride, made altogether ready? Was not his Head richly crown'd, and his Neck like the Tower of David? Didst thou see the Chain about his Neck of one Pearl, dazling the Beholders? Were not his Eyes like the pure Dove's, fixed above upon his Mate, single and clear? Was not his Breast-plate strong like Steel? Did the Arrows, the sharp Tryals and cruel Mockings pierce it? Did not his Shield cover him like the Targets of Solomon? was it not beaten Gold? When it was tryed, did it yeeld to the Tempter? O precious Faith! Tell me, my Friend, how did he weild his glittering flaming Sword? Did not it behave it self valiantly, conquering, and turning every way, to preserve the Way of Truth, Liberty, Righteousness, and the Cause of the Lord and his People? Was not his whole Armour very rich? Was it not all from the Sanctuary, for beauty and strength? Oh mighty Man of Valour! thou Champion for the Lord and his Host, when they were defied! How hast thou spoyled them? The Goliah is trodden under foot. The whole Army of the Philistims fly. Is He fled? Is He gone from amongst men? Was not this Earth, this Kingdom worthy of Him? Wast thou upon the Mount of Olives with him, to see how he was lifted up,
glorified,

glorified, advanced? Didst thou see him ascend, and Chariots and Heavenly Hosts, the Glorious Train, accompanying Him to his Chamber, to the Palace of the great King, whither he is gone, we gazing below after him? But, will he not come again? Will not the Lord his Bridegroom bring him, when He shall come to reign, and his Seints with Him? Make ready then, my Friend; Gird up thy loins; Ride through gloriously, for the Day is a great Day of Battel. And he that, overcometh, shall sit down with Abraham, Isaac, Jacob, the Prophets, the Apostles, and our late Friend VANE, *in the Kingdom of* Heaven, *whither I shall ever long to be prepared to set forward with the first, and to meet thee, Friend, ascending into the Heavenly Place.*

A LETTER from a Person of Quality, to a Relation of Sir *Henry Vane*, about a week after the Execution.

MADAM,

IF *I do later than others,* give *you an account of the share I have, in the losse of your generous Kinsman, it is, because I would not rudely disturb the Motions of so just a Sorrow; but I hope, that you are assured, I have so real a concern in all that relates to you, that it was not necessary, by an early haste, to send you an Information of it. I have (*Madam*) whilst I own a love to my Country, a deep Interest in the* Publick *Losse, which so many worthy Persons lament. The World is robbed of an Unparallel'd Example of* Vertue *and* Piety. *His great Abilities made his Enemies perswade themselves, that all the* Revolutions *in the last Age, were wrought by his Influence, as if the World were onely moved by his Engine. In him they lodged all the dying hopes of his Party. There was no Opportunity that he did not improve for the Advantage of his Country. And when he was in his last and much*

X   *deplored*

deplored Scene, he strove to make the People in love with that Freedom, they had so lavishly and foolishly thrown away.

He was great in all his Actions, but to me he seemed greatest in his Sufferings, when his Enemies seem to fear, that He alone should be able to acquaint them with a Change of Fortune. In his lowest condition, you have seen him the Terrour of a great Prince, strengthened by many potent Confederates and Armies; you have seen him live in high Estimation and Honour, and certainly he dyed with it. Men arrive at Honours by several wayes. The Martyrs, though they wanted the glittering Crowns, the Princes of those Ages dispensed, have Rich Ones in every Just man's esteem. Vertue, though unfortunate, shines in spite of all its Enemies; nor is it in any Power, to deface those lasting Monuments your Friend hath raised of his, in every heart that either knew him, or held any Intelligence with Fame. But, Madam, I trespass too long upon your patience. This is a subject I am apt to dwell on, because I can never say enough of it. I shall now onely desire you to make use of that Fortitude and Vertue, that raised your Friend above the malice and power of his Enemies; and do not by an immoderate Sorrow destroy that which was so dear to him, your Self; but live the lively Representation of his Vertue, the exercise of which, hath made you alwayes, the admiration of

Your humble Servant, &c.

The 22d *June*,
1 6 6 2.

F I N I S.

PAge 5. line 4. for *grazs*, reade *grasse*. P. 7. l. 9. f. *obscure*, r. *obscure*. P. 8. l. 27. f. *two* r, *too*. P. 12. l. 15. f. *others, beasts*, r. *other beasts*. P. 16. l. 7. f. *sounded*, r. *founded*. P. 22. l. 2. f. *wilde*, r. *weild*. P. 23. l. 6. f. *to*, r. *too*. P. 25. l. 31. f. *of*, r. *to*. P. 29. l. 30. f. *capacity*, r. *creature-capacity*. P. 37. l. 24. f. *not*, r. *but*. P. 50. l. 20. f. *Popist*, r. *Popish*. P. 60. l. 9. f. *back-slider*, r. *back-sliders*. P. 61. l. 36. r. *resembled also*. P. 62. l. 41. f. *in*, r. *no*. P. 66. l. 5. r. *Pentateuch, the Tabernacle, or*. P. 68. l. 37. f. *triumph*, r. *triumph's*. P. 70. l. 3. f. *which*, r. *with*. P. 71. l. 6. f. *amounts*, r. *amount*. P. 80. l. 37. r. *thorowly knows*. P. 99. l. 8. f. *too*, r. *to*.

There are also several mistakes in the pointing, Comma's and other points are wanting in some places, redundant in others, which obscure the sence ; but the ingenuous and unprejudiced Reader will easily mend all.

THE
TRYAL
OF
Sir Henry Vane, K^t.

AT

The KINGS BENCH, *Westminster*,
June the 2d. and 6th. 1662.

Together

With what he intended to have Spoken the Day of his
Sentence, (*June* 11.) for *Arrest of Judgment*, (had
he not been interrupted and over-ruled by the
Court) and his *Bill of Exceptions*.

With other Occasional SPEECHES, &c.

Also his SPEECH and PRAYER, &c. on the *Scaffold*.

Printed in the Year, 1662.

The TRYAL of Sir *Henry Vane* Knight, at the Kings Bench, *Westminster*, June the 2d. and 6th. 1662.

R E A D E R,

THou *shalt not be detained with any flourishing Preface. 'Tis true ; whether we consider the Person or Cause, so much might pertinently be said, as (were the Pen of some ready Writer imployed therein) a large Preamble might seem to* need but a very short *Apology, if any at all. Yet, by that time we have well weighed what this Sufferer hath said for himself, and left behind him in writing, it will appear, that there needed not any tongue of the Learned, to form up an Introduction thereunto, but meerly the hand of a faithful Transcriber of his own Observations, in defence of himself and his Cause. Rest assured of this, thou hast them here fully and clearly represented.*

The necessity of this course for thy information, as to the truth of his Case, be pleased to consider on these following accounts. He was much over-ruled, diverted, interrupted, and cut short in his Plea (as to a free and full delivery of his mind upon the whole matter at the Bar) by the Judges of the Kings-Bench, and by the Kings Counsel. He was also denyed the benefit of any Counsel to speak on his behalf.

And what he did speak at the Bar and on the Scaffold, was so disgustful to some, that the Books of those that took Notes of what passed all along in both places, were carefully called in and suppressed. It is therefore altogether unpossible to give thee a full Narrative of all he said, or was said to him, either in Westminster-Hall, *or on* Tower-Hill.

The Defendant foreseeing this, did most carefully set down in writing, the substance of what he intended to enlarge upon, the three dayes of his appearance at the Kings-Bench Bar, and the day of his Execution. Monday June 2. 1662, *was the day of his Arraignment. Friday* June 6. *was the day of his Tryal, and the Jurors Verdict. Wednesday* June 11. *was the day of his Sentence. Saturday* June 14. *was the day of his Execution on* Tower-Hill, *where limitations were* put

put upon him, and the interruptions of him by many hard speeches and disturbing carriages of some that compassed him about upon the Scaffold. as also by the sounding of Trumpets in his face to prevent his being heard, had many eye and ear witnesses.

Upon these considerations, I doubt not, it will appear undispersably necessary, to have given this faithful Transcript of such Papers of his, as do contain the most substantial and pleadable grounds of his publick actings, any time this twenty years and more, as the only means left of giving any tolerable account of the whole matter, to thy satisfaction. Yet such Information as could be picked up from those that did preserve any Notes, taken in Court or at the Scaffold, are here also recorded for thy use. and that, faithfully, word for word.

Chancellor Fortescue doth right worthily commend the Laws of England, as the best now extant and in force, in any Nation of the world, affording (if duely administred) just outward liberty to the People, and securing the meanest from any oppressive and injurious practices of Superiours against them. They give also that just Prerogative to Princes, that is convenient or truly useful and advantagious for them to have; that is to say such as doth not enterfere with the Peoples just Rights, the intire and most wary preservation of which, as it is the Covenant-duty of the Prince, so is it his best security and greatest honour. 'Tis safer and better for him to be loved and rightly feared by free Subjects, than to be feared and hated by injured slaves.

The main fundamental Liberties of the free People of England, are summed up and comprehended in the 29th Chapter of Magna Charta. These be the words;

No freeman shall be taken or imprisoned, or be disseized of his Freehold, or Liberties, or free-customs, or be out-lawed or exiled, or any otherwise destroyed. Nor will we pass upon him, or condemn him, but by lawful Judgement of his Peers, or by the Law of the Land. We will sell to no man, we will not deny or defer to any man, either Justice or Right.

Lord Chief Justice Cook observes here nine famous branches of the Law of England, couched in this short Chapter, and discourses upon them to good purpose. He saith also, that from this Chapter, as out of a root, many fruitful branches of the Law of England have sprung.

As for the very leading injury to other wrongings of the Subject, (to wit, the restraint or imprisonment of his person) so curious and tender is the Law in this point, that (sayes Cook) no man is to be attached, arrested, taken, or restrained of his liberty, by petition or
                                                                    sug.

suggestion to the King or to his Council, unless it be by Indictment or Presentment of good and lawful men (of the neighbourhood) where such deeds be done.

This great Charter of **Englands** Liberties, made 9 Hen. 3. and set in the front of all succeeding Statute-Laws or Acts of Parliament, (as the Standard, Touch-stone or Jury for them to be tryed by) hath been ratified by about two and thirty Parliaments, and the Petition of Right, 3. Caroli.

The two most famous Ratifications hereof, entituled, Confirmationes Chartarum, & Articuli super Chartas, were made 25 and 28 of Edw. 1.

All this stir about the great Charter, some conceive very needless, seeing that therein are contained those fundamental Laws or Liberties of the Nation, which are so undeniably consonant to the Law of **Nature**, or Light of Reason, that Parliaments themselves ought not to abrogate, but preserve **them**. Even Parliaments may seem to be bounded in their Legislative Power and Jurisdiction, by divine Equity and Reason, which is an eternal and therefore unalterable Law. Hence is it, that an Act of Parliament that is evidently against common Right or Reason, is null and void in it self, without more ado. Suppose a Parliament by their Act should constitute **a** man Judge in his own cause, give him a meer **Arbitrary power** ; such Act would be in it self void.

This is declared to be the ground of that exemplary Justice done upon Empson and Dudley, (as acting contrary to the Peoples Liberties in Magna Charta) whose Case is very memorable in this point. For, though they gratified Hen. 7th in what they did, and had an Act of Parliament for their Warrant, made the 11th of his Reign, yet met they with their due reward from the hands of Justice, that Act being against Equity and common Reason, and so, no justifiable ground or apology for those infinit Abuses and Oppressions of the People, they were found guilty of.

The Statute, under colour whereof they acted, ran to this effect. Be it enacted, that the Justices of the Assizes, and Justices of the Peace upon Information for the King, before them to be made, have full power and authority by their discretion, to hear and determine all offences and contempts. Having this ground, they proceeded against the People, upon meer Information, in the execution of Penal Laws, without any Indictment or Presentment by good and lawful men, but only by their own Promoters or Informers, contrary to the 29th of

Magna

Magna Charta, *which requires, That no free-man be proceeded against, but by lawful Judgment of his Peers, or by the Law of the Land.*

Secondly, This Act allowed them to hear and determine arbitrarily, by their own discretion, which is not according to the Law and Custom of England. *And* Cook *sayes, 'tis the worst (and most aggravated) oppression of all, that is done under the colour of Law, or disguise of Justice.*

Such a Statute or Act of Parliament, is, not only against the light of Reason, but against the express letter of unrepealed Statute-Law; 42. Edw. 3. 1. *It is assented and accorded,* That the great Charter, and the Charter of Forest be holden and kept in all points, and if any Statute be made to the contrary, that shall be holden for none.

This also is consonant to the first chapter of the great Charter it self, made 9. Hen. 3. We have granted to all the free-men of our Realm, these Liberties under-written, to have and to hold to them and their heirs, of Us and our Heirs, for ever.

But what if this great Charter it self had never been made ? had England *been to seek for righteous Laws and just Liberties? nothing lesse. The same Liberties and Laws were ratified before that, in the great Charter made the seventeenth year of King* John, *and mentioned (among others) by* Matthew Paris.

And to what yet amounted the matter of all these Grants, but what the Kings themselves were bound before to observe, by their Coronation Oaths, as the antient fundamental Laws or Customs of this Land? This we may find in Mr. Lambard's *Translation of the Saxon Laws, from the time of King* Ina, *who began anno* 712; *to* Hen. 1. *who began* 1100. *Amongst the Saxons, King* Alfred *is reputed the most famous and learned Compiler of our Laws, which were still handed along from one King to another, as the unalterable Customs of the Kingdom. In the* 17th *chapter of* Edward the Confessor's Laws, *The mention of the duty of a King (which, if not performed,* nec nomen Regis in eo constabit) *is remarkable. And Mr.* Lambard *tells us, that even* William the Conqueror, *did ratifie and observe the same Laws that his kinsman* Edward the Confessor *did, as obliged by his Coronation Oath.*

So then, neither the great Charter in King John's *time, nor that of* 9. Hen. 3. *were properly a new Body of Law, but a Declaration of the antient fundamental Laws, Rights and Liberties of this Nation, in* British, Saxon, Danish *and* Norman *times, before. This.* Cook *in his Proem to the second part of his Institutes, observes ; where he notes also, that this Charter is not called great, for quantity of words,*

(a sheet

(a sheet of Paper will contain it) but for the great importance and weight of its matter.

Through the advice of Hubert de Burgo *Chief Justice* of England, Edward *the first*, *in the eleventh year of his Reign*, did, *in a Council held at* Oxford, *unjustly cancel this great* Charter, *and that of Forest:* Hubert *therefore was justly sentenc'd according to Law, by his Peers, in open Parliament.* Then, 25 Ed. 1. The *Statute*, called, Confirmationes Chartarum *was made*, *in the first chapter whereof*, *the* Mag. Charta *is peculiarly called the Common Law.* 25. Ed. 1. cap. 2. Any Judgment given contrary to the said Charter, is to be undone and holden for naught. *And cap.* 4. Any that by word, deed, or counsel, go contrary to the said Charter, are to be excommunicated by the Bishops; and the Arch-Bishops of *Canterbury* and *York* are bound to compel the other Bishops to denounce sentence accordingly, in case of their remisness or neglect.

The next famous sticklers *to* Hubert de Burgo, *for Arbitrary Domination, were the two* Spencers, *father and son, by whose rash and evil counsel* (*sayes* Cook) Edward *the second was seduced to break the* Great Charter, *and they were banished for their pains.*

By *these passages we may observe, how the People would still be* strugling (*in and by their Representatives*) *for their Legal Rights and* Just Liberties ; *to obviate the Encroachers whereof, they procured several new Ratifications of their old* Laws, *which were indeed in themselves unrepealable, even by* Parliaments, *if they will act as men, and not contradict the Law of their own Reason, and of the common Reason of all mankind.*

By 25 Ed. 1. cap. 1. Justices, Sheriffs, Majors, *and other Ministers, that have the Laws of the* Land *to guide them, are required to allow the said Charter to be pleaded in all its points, and in all causes that shall come before them in Judgment.*

This *is a clause* (*sayes* Cook) *worthy to be written in letters of gold*; That the **Laws** are to be the Judges guides, (*and therefore not the* Judges, *the guides of the* Laws, *by their arbitrary glosses*) which never *yet misguided any that certainly knew and truly followed them. In consonancy herewith, the* Spaniard *sayes, Of all the three learned Professions,* The Lawyer is *the only letter'd man, his business and duty being to follow the plain literal construction of the* Law, *as his guide, in giving* Judgment. *Pretence of mystery here, carries in the bowels of it, intents, or at least a deep suspition of arbitrary domination. The mind of the* Law *is not subject to be clouded, disturbed or perverted*

by paſſion or intereſt. 'Tis far otherwiſe with Judges ; therefore 'tis
fitter and ſafer the Law ſhould guide them, than they the Law. Cook
on the laſt mentioned Statute affirms, That this great Charter, and
the Charter of Foreſt, are properly the Common Law of this Land, or
the Law that is common to all the People thereof.

2 Ed. 3. cap. 8. Exact care is taken, that no Commands by the
Great or Little Seal, ſhall come to diſturb or delay Common Right.
Or, if ſuch Commands come, the Juſtices are not thereby to leave to
do Right, in any point. So 14 Ed. 3. 14. 11 Ric. 2. 10. The Judges
Oath, 18 Ed. 3. 7, runs thus :

If any force come to diſturb the execution of the Common Law,
ye ſhall cauſe their bodies to be arreſted and put into Priſon. Ye ſhall
deny no man Right by the King's Letters. nor counſel the King any
thing that may turn to his dammage or diſheriſon.

The late King in his Declaration at Newmarket, 1641, acknowledged the Law to be the Rule of his Power. And his Majeſty that
now is, in his Speech to both Houſes, the 19th of May laſt, ſaid excellently, The good old Rules of Law are our beſt ſecurity.

The Common Law then, or Liberties of England, comprized in the
Magna Charta and the Charter of Foreſt, are rendred as ſecure, as
authentick words can ſet them, from all Judgments or Precedents to
the contrary in any Courts, all corrupting advice or evil counſel of any
Judges, all Letters or Countermands from the Kings Perſon, under the
Great or Privy Seals ; yea, and from any Acts of Parliament it ſelf,
that are contrary thereunto. As to the Judges, no queſtion, they well
know the ſtory of the 44 corrupt Judges, executed by King Alfred, as
alſo of Treſillian, Belknap, and many others ſince.

By 11 Hen. 7. cap. 1. They that ſerve the King in his Wars, according to their duty of Allegiance, for defence of the King and the
Land, are indempnified ; If againſt the Land, and ſo not according to
their Allegiance, the laſt clauſe of that chapter ſeems to exclude them
from the benefit of this Act.

6 Hen. 8. 16. Knights and Burgeſſes of Parliament are required
not to depart from the Parliament, till it be fully finiſhed, ended or
prorogued.

28 Ed. 3. cap. 3. No man is to be impriſoned, diſherited, or put
to death, without being heard what he can ſay for himſelf.

4 Ed. 3. 14. and 36 Ed. 3. 10. A Parliament is to be holden every
year, or oftner if need be.

1 Ric. 3 cap. 2. The ſubjects of this Realm are not to be charged
with any new impoſition, called a *Benevolence*.   37 Ed.

37 Ed. 3. c. 18. All those that make suggestions against any man to the King, are to be sent with their suggestions before the Chancellor, Treasurer, and his grand Council, and there to find surety that they will pursue their suggestions; and are to incur the same pain, the party by them accused should have had, if attained, in case the suggestion be found evil, or false.

21 Jacobi, *cap.* 3. All Monopolies and Dispensations, with Penal Laws, are made void, as contrary to the great Charters.

These quotations of several Statutes, as Ratifications and Restorers of the Laws of the Land, are prefixed to the following Discourses and Pleas of this Sufferer, as certain, steady, unmovable Land-marks, to which he oft relates. The rouling Seas have other Laws, peculiar to themselves, as Cook observes (on that expression, Law of the Land) in his Comment on the 29th Chapter of Magna Charta. Offences done upon the High Sea, the Admiral takes connusance of, and proceeds by the Marine Law.

But have those steady Land-marks, though exactly observed and never so pertinently quoted and urged by this Sufferer, failed him, as to the securing of his Life? 'Tis because we have had Land-floods of late; Tumults of the People, that are compared to the raging Seas, Psal. 65. 7.

The first Paper of this deceased Sufferer, towards the defence of his Cause and Life, preparatory to the Tryal, (as the foundation of all that follows) before he could know how the Indictment was laid, (and which also a glance back to any crime of Treason since the beginning of the late War, that the Attorney General reckoned him chargeable with, shews to be very requisit) take as followeth.

Memorandums touching my Defence.

THe Offence objected against me, is *levying War*, within the Statute 25 *Ed.* 3. and by consequence, a most high and great failer in the duty which the Subject, according to the Laws of *England*, stands obliged to perform, in relation to the Imperial Crown and Soveraign Power of *England*.

The crime, if it prove any, must needs be very great, considering the circumstances with which it hath been accompanied: For it relates to,

and

and takes in a series of publick action, of above twenty years continuance. It took its rise and had its root in the Being, Authority, Judgment, Resolutions, Votes and Orders of a Parliament, and that, a Parliament not onely authorized and commissionated in the ordinary and customary way, by his Majesties Writ of Summons, and the Peoples Election and Deputation, subject to Adjournment, Discontinuance, and Dissolution, at the King's will; but which by express Act of Parliament, was constituted in its continuance and exercise of its Power, free from that subjection, and made therein wholly to depend upon their own will, to be declared in an Act of Parliament, to be passed for that purpose, when they should see cause. To speak plainly and clearly in this matter; That which is endeavoured to be made a Crime and an Offence of such an high nature in my person, is no other than the necessary and unavoidable Actings of the Representative Body of the Kingdom, for the preservation of the good People thereof, in their allegiance and duty to God and his Law, as also from the imminent dangers and destruction threatned them, from God's and their own Enemies.

This made both Houses in their *Remonstrance* (*May* 26. 1642.) protest; *If the Malignant spirits about the King, should ever force or necessitate them to defend their Religion, the Kingdom, the Priviledges of Parliament, and the Rights and Liberties of the Subjects, with their Swords; The Blood and Destruction that should ensue therupon, must be wholly cast upon their account, God and their own consciences telling them, that they were clear; and would not doubt, but that God and the whole world would clear them therein.*

In his Majesties *Answer* to the *Declaration* of the two Houses, (*May* 19. 1642.) he acknowledgeth his going into the House of Commons to demand the five Members, was an errour : And that was it, which gave the Parliament the first cause to put themselves in a posture of defence, by their own Power and Authority, in commanding the Trained-Bands of the City of *London*, to guard and secure them from Violence, in the discharge of their Trust and Duty, as the two Houses of Parliament, appointed by Act, to continue, as above-mentioned.

The next cause was, his Majesties raising Forces at *York*, (under pretence of a Guard) expressed in the humble Petition of the Lords and Commons, (*May* 23. 1642.) wherein they beseech his Majesty to disband all such Forces, and desist from any further designs of that nature, otherwise they should hold themselves bound in duty towards God, and the Trust reposed in them by the People, and the Fundamental

Laws

Laws and Constitutions of this Kingdom, to employ their care and utmost power, to secure the Parliament, and preserve the peace and quiet of the Kingdom.

May 20. 1642, The two Houses of Parliament gave their Judgment, in these Votes.

First, *That it appears, that the King (seduced by wicked Counsel) intends to make War against the Parliament, who in all their Consultations and Actions have proposed no other end to themselves, but the Care of his Kingdoms, and the performance of all Duty and Loyalty to his Person.*

Secondly, *That whensoever the King maketh War upon the Parliament, it is a breach of Trust reposed in him by his People, contrary to his Oath, and tending to the dissolution of this Government.*

Thirdly, *That whosoever shall serve or assist him in such Wars, are Traytors by the fundamental Laws of this Kingdom, and have been so adjudged by two Acts of Parliament, and ought to suffer as Traitors.*

Die Jovis, Octob. 8. 1642, In the Instructions agreed upon by the Lords and Commons about the Militia, They declare, *That the King (seduced by wicked Counsel) hath raised War against the Parliament, and other his good Subjects.*

And by the Judgment and Resolution of both Houses, bearing date *Aug.* 13. 1642, upon occasion of his Majesties *Proclamation* for suppressing the present Rebellion under the Command of *Robert* Earl of *Essex*, They do unanimously publish and declare, *That all they who have advised, declared, abetted, or countenanced, or hereafter shall abet and countenance the said* Proclamation, *are Traytors and Enemies to God, the King and Kingdom, and guilty of the highest degree of Treason that can be committed against the King and Kingdom, as that which invites his Majesties Subjects to destroy his Parliament, and good People, by a Civil War ; and by that means, to bring ruine, confusion and perpetual slavery upon the surviving part of a then wretched Kingdom.*

The Law is acknowledged by the King, to be the *onely Rule*, by which the People can be justly governed; and that, as it is his duty, so it shall be his perpetual, vigilant care, to see to it : Therefore he will not suffer either or both Houses by their Votes, without or against his Consent, to enjoyn any thing that is forbidden by the Law, or to forbid any thing that is enjoyned by the Law.

The King does assert in his Answer to the Houses Petition, (*May* 23. 1642.) *That He is a part of the Parliament, which they take* upon them to defend and secure ; and that his *Prerogative is a part of, and a defence to the Laws of the Land.*

In the Remonstrance of both Houses, (*May* 26. 1642.) They do assert ; *That if they have made any Precedents this Parliament, they have made them for posterity, upon the same or better grounds of Reason and Law, than those were, upon which their Predecessors made any for them;* and do say, *That as some Precedents ought not to be Rules for them to follow, so none can be limits to bound their Proceedings, which may and must vary, according to the different condition of times.*

And for the particular, with which they were charged, of setting forth Declarations to the People who have chosen and entrusted them with all that is dearest to them, if there be no example for it in former times ; They say, *it is because there never were such Monsters before, that attempted to disaffect the People towards a Parliament.*

They further say; *His Majesties Towns are no more his care than his Kingdom, nor his Kingdom than his People , who are not so his own, that he hath absolute power over them, or in them, as in his proper Goods and Estate ; but fiduciary, for the Kingdom, and in the paramount right of the Kingdom.* They also acknowledge the Law, to be the safeguard and custody of all publick and private Interests. They also hold it fit, to declare unto the Kingdom, (whose Honour and Interest is so much concerned in it) what is the Priviledge of the great Council of Parliament, herein ; and what is the Obligation that lies upon the Kings of this Realm, as to the passing such Bills as are offered to them by both Houses, in the name, and for the good of the whole Kingdom, whereunto they stand engaged, both in Conscience and Justice, to give their Royal Assent.

First, *In Conscience* ; in respect of the Oath that is, or ought to be taken by them, at their Coronation, as well to confirm by their Royal Assent, all such good Laws as the People shall chuse, (whereby to remedy such inconveniencies as the Kingdom may suffer) as to keep and protect the Laws already in being.

The form of the *Oath* is upon Record, and asserted by Books of good authority. Unto it relation is had, 25 *Ed.* 3. entituled, *The Statute of Provisors of Benefices.*

Hereupon, The said Commons prayed our said Lord the King, (sith the Right of the Crown of *England,* and the Law of the said Realm, is such, that upon the mischiefs and dammages which happen to this Realm, he ought and is bound by his Oath, with the accord of of his People in Parliament, to make Remedy and Law, for the removing thereof) That it may please him to ordain Remedy.

This Right, thus claimed by the Lords and Commons, The King doth not deny, in his Answer thereunto.

Secondly, *In Justice* the Kings are obliged as well as in *Conscience*, in respect of the Trust reposed in them, to preserve the Kingdom by the making of new Laws, where there shall be need, as well as by observing of Laws already made ; a Kingdom being many times as much exposed to ruine for want of a new Law, as by the violation of those that are in being.

This is a most clear Right, not to be denyed, but to be as due from his Majesty to his People, as his Protection. In all Laws framed by both Houses, as *Petitions of Right*, they have taken themselves to be so far Judges of the Rights claimed by them, That when the King's Answer hath not been in every point, fully according to their desire, they have still insisted upon their Claim, and never given it over, till the Answer hath been according to their demand, as was done in the late *Petition of Right, 3. Caroli.*

This shews, the two Houses of Parliament are *Judge* between the King and the People in question of Right, as in the Case also of *Ship-money* and other illegal Taxes ; and if so, why should they not also be Judge in the Cases of the Common Good and Necessity of the Kingdom, wherein the Kingdom hath as clear a Right to have the benefit and remedy of the Law, as in any other matter, saving Pardon and Grants of Favour ?

The Malignant Party are they, that not only neglect and despise, but labour to undermine the Law, under colour of maintaining it. They endeavour to destroy the Fountain and Conservators of the Law, the *Parliament.* They make other Judges of the Law, than what the Law hath appointed. They set up other Rules for themselves to walk by, than such as are according to Law ; and dispence with the Subjects obedience, to that which the Law calls Authority , and to their Determinations and Resolutions, to whom the Judgment doth appertain by Law : Yea, though but private persons, they make the Law to be their Rule, according to their own understanding only, contrary to the Judgment of those that are the competent Judges thereof.

The King asserts, That the Act of Sir *John Hotham* was *levying War against the King*, by the letter of the Statute, 25 *Ed.* 3. cap. 2.

The Houses state the Case, and deny it to be within that Statute; saying, If the letter of that Statute be thought to import this ; That

no

no War can be levied against the King, but what is directed and intended against his Person; Or, that every levying of Forces for the defence of the King's Authority, and of his Kingdom, against the personal Commands of the King, opposed thereunto, (though accompanied with his presence) is Treason, or levying War against the King;
Such Interpretation is very far from the sense of that Statute, and so
much the Statute it self speaks, beside the authority of Book-cases. For
if the clause of levying War had been meant only against the King's
Person, what need had there been thereof, after the other branch in
the same Statute, of compassing the King's death, which would necef-
sarily have implied this? And because the former doth imply this, it
seems not at all to be intended, at least, not chiefly, in the latter branch,
but the levying War against his Laws and Authority; and such a levying War, though not against his Person, is a levying War against
the King; whereas the levying of Force against his personal Commands, though accompanied with his Presence, and not against his
Laws and Authority, but in the maintenance thereof, is no levying of
War against the King, but for him, especially in a time of so many
successive plots and designs of Force against the Parliament and Kingdom, of probable Invasion from abroad, and of so great distance and
alienation of his Majesties affections from his Parliament and People,
and of the particular danger of the Place and Magazine of *Hull*, of
which the two Houses sitting, are the most proper Judges.

In proclaiming Sir *John Hotham* Traitor, they say, The breach of
the Priviledge of Parliament was very clear, and the subversion of the
Subjects common Right. For though the Priviledges of Parliament
extend not to these cases, mentioned in the Declaration of Treason,
Felony, and breach of the Peace, so as to exempt the Members of
Parliament from Punishment, or from all manner of Process and Tryal, yet it doth priviledge them in the way and method of their Tryal
and Punishment, and that the Parliament should first have the Cause
brought before them, that they may judge of the Fact, and of the
grounds of their Accusation, and how far forth the manner of their
Tryal may or may not concern the Priviledge of Parliament : Otherwise, under this pretext, the Priviledge of Parliament in this matter,
may be so essentially broken, as thereby the very Being of Parliaments may be destroyed. Neither doth the sitting of a Parliament
suspend all or any Law, in maintaining that Law, which upholds the
Priviledge of Parliament, which upholds the Parliament, which upholds the Kingdom.

They

They further assert ; That in some sense, they acknowledge the *King* to be the only person, against whom Treason can be committed, that is, as he is *King*, and that Treason which is against the **King-dom,** is more against the *King*, than that which is against his Person ; because he *is King* : For Treason is not Treason, as it is against him *as a man*, but *as a man that is a King*, and as he hath, and stands in that relation to the Kingdom, entrusted with the Kingdom, and discharging that Trust.

They also avow, That there can be no competent Judge of this or any the like case, but a *Parliament* ; and do say, that if the wicked Counsel about the King could master this Parliament by force, they would hold up the same power to deprive us of all Parliaments, which are the ground and pillar of the Subjects **Liberty,** and that which only maketh *England* a free Monarchy.

The Orders of the two **Houses** carry in them *Law for their limits, and the Safety of the Land for their end.* This makes them not doubt but all his Majesties good Subjects will yeeld obedience to his Maje-sties Authority, signified therein by both Houses of Parliament : for whose encouragement, and that they may know their Duty in matters of that nature, and upon how sure a ground they go, that follow the Judgment of Parliament for their guide ; They alledge the true mean-ing and ground of that Statute, 11. *Hen.* 7. *cap.* 1. printed at large in his Majesties Message, *May* 4 ; This Statute provides, that none that shall attend upon the King and do him true service, shall be at-tainted, or forfeit any thing.

What was the scope of this Statute ?

Answ. To provide, that men should not suffer as **Traitors** for ser-ving the King in his Wars, according to the duty of their Allegiance. But if this had been all, it had been a very needless and ridiculous Statute. Was it then intended (as they seem to make it, that print it with his Majesties Message) that those should be free from all crime and penalty, that should follow the King and serve him in War, in any case whatsoever, whether it were for or against the Kingdom or the Laws thereof ? That cannot be : for that could not stand with the duty of their Allegiance, which, in the beginning of this Statute, is ex-pressed to be, *to serve the King for the time being in his Wars, for the defence of him and the Land.* If therefore it be against the Land, (as it must be, if it be against the Parliament, the Representative Body of the Kingdom) it is a declining from the duty of Allegiance, which this Statute supposes may be done, though men should follow the Kings

C

Person

Person in the War. Otherwise, there had been no need of such a *Proviso* in the end of the Statute, that none should take benefit thereby, that should decline from their Allegiance.

That therefore which is the Principal Verb in this, is *the serving of the King for the time being*, which cannot be meant of a *Perkin Warbeck*, or any that should call himself *King*, but such a one, as (whatever his Title might prove, either in himself or in his Ancestors) should be received and acknowledged for such, by the Kingdom, the Consent whereof cannot be discern'd but by Parliament; the Act whereof, is the Act of the whole Kingdom, by the personal Suffrage of the Peers, and the Delegate Consent of the Commons of *England*. *Henry* 7th therefore, a wise Prince, to clear this matter of contest, happening between Kings *de facto* and Kings *de jure*, procured this Statute to be made, *That none shall be accounted a Traitor for serving in his Wars, the King for the time being*; that is, him that is for the present allowed and received by the Parliament in behalf of the Kingdom. And as it is truly suggested in the Preamble of the Statute; It is not agreeable to reason or conscience, that it should be otherwise, seeing men should be put upon an impossibility of knowing their duty, if the Judgment of the highest Court should not be a Rule to guide them. And if the Judgment thereof is to be followed, when the question is, *who is King?* much more, when the question is, *what is the best service of the King and Kingdom?* Those therefore that shall guide themselves by the Judgment of Parliament, ought (what ever happen) to be secure and free from all account and penalties, upon the ground and equity of this Statute.

To make the Parliament countenancers of Treason, they say, is enough to have dissolv'd all the bands of service and confidence between his Majesty and his Parliament, of whom the Law sayes, a dishonourable thing ought not to be imagined.

This Conclusion then is a clear Result from what hath been argued; That in all Cases of such difficulty and unusualness, happening by the over-ruling Providence of God, as render it impossible for the Subject to know his duty, by any known Law or certain Rule extant, his relying then, upon the Judgment and Reason of the whole Realm, declared by their Representative Body in *Parliament*, then sitting, and adhering thereto, and pursuing thereof, (though the same afterwards be by succeeding Parliaments, judged erroneous, Factious and unjust) is most agreeable to right Reason and good Conscience; and in so doing, all persons are to be free and secure from all Account

and

and Penalties, not only upon the ground and equity of that Statute, 11 *Hen.* 7. but according to all Rules of Juſtice, natural or moral.

The day of Arraignment, being Monday June 2. 1662.

Reader, The beſt account thou canſt yet be furniſhed with, as to this dayes proceedings in Court, is, as followeth.

SIR *Henry Vane* was the laſt Term, indicted of High Treaſon, before the *Middleſex* Grand Jury, and the Bill being found by them, he was upon Monday the ſecond of *June* this Term, arraigned, to this effect.

That you as a falſe Traitor againſt his moſt excellent Majeſty King Charles *the* ſecond, *your ſupream and* natural *Lord,* not having the fear of God before your eyes, *and withdrawing that your duty and allegiance,which a true Subject ought to have and bear to our ſaid Leige and ſovereign Lord,* thirteenth of May, *in the eleventh year of our ſaid ſovereign Lord the King, at the Pariſh of St.* Martins in the fields *in the County of* Middleſex, *did compaſs and imagine the Death of our ſaid ſovereign Lord the King, and the ancient frame of Government of this Realm, totally to ſubvert and keep out our ſaid ſovereign Lord from the exerciſe of his Regal Government ; and the ſame the better to effect, the ſaid Sir* Henry Vane *the ſaid thirteenth day of* May, *in the ſaid eleventh year, &c. at St.* Martins *aforeſaid, together with other falſe Traitors, to the Jurors unknown, did traiterouſly and maliciouſly aſſemble and ſit together, and then and there conſulted to bring the King unto deſtruction, and to hold him out from the exerciſe of his Regal Authority, and then and there uſurped the Government, and appointed Officers, to wit, Colonels and Captains of a certain Army, raiſed againſt the King, againſt the Peace of our ſovereign Lord the King his Crown and* Dignity, *and contrary to the form of the Statute in that caſe made and provided.*

* *And the better to effect this, the twentieth of* December, *in the ſaid eleventh year, with a multitude, to the number of a thouſand perſons, to the Jurors unknown, in warlike manner aſſembled, and arrayed with Guns, Trumpets, Drums, &c. did levy War againſt the Peace, &c. and contrary to the form of a Statute.*

Which being read, he prayed to have it read a ſecond time, which was granted him. He then prayed to have it read in Latine, which

all

all the Court denyed, and *Keeling* the King's Serjeant said, That though all Pleas and Entries are set down on Record in Latine, yet the agitations of Causes in Court, ought to be in English.

The Prisoner moved several Exceptions to the Indictment, as that the 25. *Ed. 3.* is not pursued ; that he had levied no such force as amounted to a levying of War ; Also, the place in which, persons with whom, are both uncertain ; and the particular acts of levying War, being not set forth, he thought therefore the Indictment was *insufficient*. Also, he said, here is a long time of Action for which I am charged, and I may be concern'd for what I acted as a Member in that sovereign Court of *Parliament*, and if any thing concerns the Jurisdiction of that Court, I ought not to be judged here ; at which the Court and King's Counsel took great offence.

He said also ; There hath been an Act of General Pardon, since that time, whereby all Treasons are put in utter oblivion, and though Sir *Henry Vane* were excepted, yet none consent that he was that Sir *Henry Vane*. But the King's Counsel said, If he would plead that Plea, they would joyn that Issue with him, if he pleased, which if it should be found against him, it would be too late to plead, *not guilty*.

But the Court said, in favour of life, a man may plead a double Plea, and give in his Exception, and plead over to the Felony or Treason, *not guilty*.

But as to the Exceptions taken to the Indictment, they gave little heed to them, but pressed him to plead or confess.

Whereupon he pleaded, *Not guilty* ; and had four dayes, to wit, till Friday next, for his Tryal.

From another hand, take, as followeth.

The Prisoner did much press for Counsel to be allowed him, to advise with about any further Exceptions to the Indictment, besides those by him exhibited, and to put all into form, according to the customary proceedings and language of the Law, as also to speak to them at the Bar, on his behalf, he not being vers'd in the punctilio's of Law-writings and Pleas. He further said, That the Indictment, which so nearly concern'd his Life, being long, and his memory short, it could not well be imagined that he should upon the bare hearing it read, be able in an instant to find out every material Exception against it, in form or matter. He pleaded a good while on this account, but Counsel was finally denied him till he should plead *guilty* or *not guilty*, unto which,

which, being a third time urged, he pleaded *Not guilty*; The Court having assured him beforehand, that after pleading, Counsel should be assigned him, which yet never was performed.

Here followeth a Transcript of the Prisoners own Papers, containing certain *Memorandums* pleadable upon his Arraignment.

Memorandums for, and towards my Defence.

Upon hearing the Indictment read, and before pleading.

First, To lay before the Court the impossibility that he humbly conceives, is already in view, as to the having any such indifferent and equal Tryal, as the Law intends him, and doth require and command on the behalf of all the free-People of *England*. The Rise for this Conception he takes from what hath been already done in relation to the Prisoner himself, unheard, unexamined, and yet kept close Prisoner for near two whole years. This he shall leave to the Judgment of the Court, after that he hath made known the particulars thereof unto them, as necessary to precede the thing demanded of him, in pleading *guilty*, or *not guilty*.

Secondly, What is the indifferency which the Law requires and appoints throughout, as well in matters that go before the Tryal, as in the proceedings at the Tryal it self?

Before the Tryal, and in the first step to it, which is the keeping and securing his person, *Magna Charta* is clear, and gives this Rule, cap **29**. *Nullus liber homo capiatur, &c.*

No free-man shall be taken or imprisoned, or be disseised of his freehold or liberties, or free-customs, or be outlawed or exiled, or any otherwise destroyed : Nor we will not passe upon him, nor condemn him, but by lawful Judgement of his Peers, or by the Law of the Land : We will sell to no man, we will not deny or defer to any man either Justice or Right.

Out of this Chapter, as out of a root (saith Sir *Edward Cook*) do many fruitful branches of the Law of *England* spring. It contains nine branches; some whereof I shall insist upon in my Case.

First, That no man be taken or imprisoned but *per Legem Terræ*, that is, by the Common Law or Custom of *England*; which words, *per Legem Terræ*, though put last, refer to all the precedent branches.

Secondly, The Goods of any Offender cannot regularly be taken

and

and seized to the King's use before Conviction, nor be Inventoried, nor the Town charged therewith, before the owner be indicted of Record.

Thirdly, **No man shall be exiled or banished** out of his Country, nor be in any sort destroyed but by the verdict of his Peers.

This appears by *Bracton* and other ancient Writers, quoted by *Cook*, in the third part of his *Institutes*, fol. 228.

Upon the whole matter saith *Cook*, these two Conclusions are manifestly proved.

First, That before Indictment, the Goods or other things of any Offender cannot be searched, inventoried or in any sort seized, nor after Indictment, seized, removed, or taken away, before Conviction or Attainder.

Secondly, That the begging of the Goods or Estate of any Delinquent, accused or indicted of any Treason, Felony, or other offence, before he be convicted and attainted, is utterly unlawful ; *Stat. Ri. 1. cap. 3.*

And besides, it maketh the prosecution against the Delinquent, more precipitant, violent and undue, than the quiet and equal proceedings of the Law and Justice would permit : Or else, by some under-hand Agreement, stops or hinders the due course of Justice, and discourageth both Judge, Juror and Witness to do their duty.

Thirdly, The Judges are not to give so much as their Opinion before-hand, concerning the Offence, whether it prove that Offence in that Case.

Cook in the chap. of *Petty Treason*, fol. 29. expresly saith ; *And to the end the Tryal may be the more indifferent, seeing the safety of the Prisoner consists in the indifferency of the Court, the Judges ought not to deliver their Opinions before-hand. of any Criminal Case, that may come before them judicially.* And he there cites *Humphrey Staffords* Case that Arch Traitor, in which *Hussey* Chief Justice, besought *Hen.* 7. not to demand of them their Opinions before-hand. And in the 4th of his *Institutes*, in the chap. of the *High Court of Parliament*, fol. 37, he fully shews the evil of asking the Judges Opinions before-hand.

But instead of this, The Judges being assistant in the Lords house, when all Acts of Parliament passe, and whose Advice is taken in them, have (as appears by what is declared in the said Acts) prejudg'd by their Opinions and the Opinions of the Parliament before-hand, the merit of the Cause that now appears to be put upon the Issue in my Tryal,

Tryal. Hereby the Judges are rendred *ex parte*, and the indifferency the Law requires, impoffible to be afforded.

Nor is this all ; but by the Rules declared in the *Act of Indempni-ty*, all are difenabled to plead, or make ufe of the Ordinances, Orders and Votes of both, or either Houfes of Parliament, that may have occafion thereof; and then by excepting the Prifoner and his fellow out of the faid Act, and all benefit thereby, a door is left open to Arraign, bring to Tryal and Sentence the whole Caufe from the beginning to the ending, in the perfon of the Prifoner, and at the fame time, deprive him of all means and poffibility of Juftification and Defence.

Fourthly, It is obfervable how early hard meafure appeared in the way wherein the Prifoner became excepted out of the Act of Indempnity, when the Commons, his proper Judges, declared him in their thoughts, not fit to be endangered in the point of Life ; yet unto the Judgment of the Lords, (that ought not to judge Commoners, unbrought before them by the Commons, much lefs, in oppofite Judgement to the Commons) The Commons were neceffitated to yeeld, left otherwife the Act of Indempnity to the whole Nation fhould ftop upon this difpute and effential difference between the two Houfes ; A Competition, eafily over-ruled ; although (as it proves by the fequel) That Act of *Indempnity* is like to become *felo de fe*, or a deftroyer of it felf, if your Lordfhips fhall conceive your felves at liberty, (notwithftanding that Act) not only to bring anew into memory upon the ftage, the ftate of all the paffed differences, from firft to laft, but to try and judge the merit of them in my perfon, and therein call in queftion the validity of that whole Act, and make void the benefit intended by it, in cafe the War undertaken and managed by both or either of the Houfes of Parliament, be judged unlawful, and within the Statute of 25. *Ed.* 3. For this adjudges all the People of *England* morally guilty of the evil of a fin and offence againft the Law of Nature, which once done, what ever promifed Indempnity be granted for the prefent, the Evil of the Action remaining upon Record ; not only to the Infamy of the whole People of *England*, but their future danger, upon pretence they have forfeited the very Indempnity granted.

Fifthly, The length of time taken to fearch out matter againft the Prifoner, and the undue practices and courfes to find out Witneffes, do further evidence how unlike the Prifoner is to have an equal and indifferent Tryal. He doubts not, this will appear in his two years clofe Imprifonment, (fix months whereof was Banifhment) during which

time,

time, he was never so much as once examined, or had any question put to him, whereby he might conjecture wherefore he was committed to Prison, any further than was expressed in the Warrants of Commitments.

Now these were so general, that nothing certain or particular could be gathered out of them. But upon the received opinion, that he was excepted out of the Act of Indempnity, and in the sence of both Houses, a great Delinquent, his Estate was attempted to be inventoried, his Rentals demanded, his Rents were actually seized in the Tenants hands, and they forbidden to pay them. His very Courts were prohibited by Officers of great Personages, claiming the Grant of the Estate, and threatning his Officers from doing their duty. By these kind of undue proceedings, the Prisoner had not wherewithal to maintain himself in Prison, and his Debts, to the value of above ten thousand pounds, were undischarged, either Principal or Interest. The hopes of private lucre and profit hereby, was such, in the Tenants and other persons, sought out for far and near, to be Witnesses, that it is no wonder at last, something by way of Charge comes to be exhibited.

And as this is the Case of the Person before his appearance at this Bar, with respect to the foresaid unequal proceedings towards him, and the great disadvantages put upon him, and all these as it were, in a continued series of Design ; so, the matters and things themselves with which it now appears he is charged in the Indictment, make his Case still very extraordinary and unusual, involving him in difficulties that are insuperable, unless God's own immediate Power do shew it self in working his deliverance.

The things done, are for many years past, In a time of Differences between King and Parliament, and Wars ensuing thereupon. Many extraordinary Changes and Revolutions in the State and Government were necessitated in the course of God's Providence, for wise and holy ends of his, above the reach of humane wisdom.

The Authority by which they are done, is prejudged. The Orders, Votes and Resolutions of Parliament are made useless, and forbidden to be produced. Hereby, all manner of defence is taken away from the Prisoner ; and that which was done according to Law, as the Laws of those times were, is endeavoured to be made unlawful, and so the persons, acting according to such Laws, are brought to punishment.

The Judges (as hath been shewed) are forestalled in their Judgements, by the declared sence of Parliaments, given *ex post facto*.

The

The Jurors are put upon difficulties never known before, for twelve Commoners to judge the Actions of all the Commons of *England*, in whom they are included, as to whose Judgment is the right, the one or the others; and whether their Representatives be trusty.

The Party indicted is under an incapacity to bring Witnesses, as well from the nature of the place wherein the things were done, within the Walls of the House, as from the shortness of time, having heard nothing of his Charge, and being kept a close Prisoner, to the last day. His Solicitors and persons imployed in his Law-businesses, were also restrained from him.

It is also most evident, that the matters for which he is questioned, being the Product of so many years Agitations of Parliamentary Counsels and Arms, cannot be of a single concern, nor be reputed as the actions of a private man, done of his own head, nor therefore come within any of the six Classes of Treason, contained in 25. *Ed.* 3.

It is a Case most unusual, and never happening before in this Kingdom; yet it is alledged in the Indictment to be a levying War within that Statute, and so comes to have the name of *High Treason* put upon it, thereby (if possible) to deprive him of the use and benefit of Counsel, as also of competent time to prepare for his Defence, and all fitting and requisit means for the clearing of his Innocency. Unto this, unless some remedy be afforded by the justice, candor and favour of this Court, it may be better for the Prisoner (for ought he yet knows) to be immediately destroyed by special Command (if nothing else will satisfie) without any form of Law, as one to whom Quarter, after at least two years cool blood, is thought fit to be denied in relation to the late Wars. This may seem better, than under a colour and form of Justice, to pretend to give him the benefit of the Law and the King's Courts, whose part it is, to set free the Innocent, upon an Equal and Indifferent Tryal had before them, if their Cause will bear it: but it is very visible beforehand, that all possible means of Defence are taken and withheld from him, and Laws are made *ex post facto*, to forejudge the merit of the Cause, the Party being unheard.

And when he hath said all this, that as a rational man, does occur to him, and is fit for him to represent in all humility to the Court, he craves leave further to adde; That he stands at this Bar not only as a man, and a man clothed with the Priviledges of the most Sovereign Court, but as a Christian, that hath Faith and reliance in God, through whose gracious and wise appointment, he is brought into these circumstances, and unto this place at this time, whose Will he desires to be

D   found

found refigned up into, as well in what He now calls him to *suffer*, as in what He hath called him formerly to *act*. for the good of his Country, and of the People of God in it. Upon this bottom (he bleffes the Name of his God) he is fearlefs, and knows the iffue will be good what ever it prove. God's ftrength may appear in the Prifoner's weaknefs ; and the more all things carry the face of certain ruine and deftruction unto all that is near and dear to him in this world, the more will divine deliverance and falvation appear ; to the making good of that Scripture, That *he that is content to lofe his life* in God's Caufe and Way, *fhall fave it*, and *he that inftead thereof goes about to fave his life* upon undue terms, *fhall lofe it*.

Far be it therefore from me, to have knowingly, malicioufly or wittingly offended the Law, rightly underftood and afferted ; much lefs, to have done any thing that is *malum per fe*, or that is morally evil. This is that I allow not as I am a Man, and what I defire with ftedfaftnefs to refift, as I am a Chriftian. If I can judge any thing of my own Cafe, The true reafon of the prefent difficulties and ftraits I am in, is becaufe I have defired to walk by a juft and righteous Rule in all my Actions, and not to ferve the lufts and paffions of men, but had rather die, than wittingly and deliberately fin againft God and tranfgrefs his holy Laws, or prefer my own private Intereft before the Good of the whole Community I relate unto, in the Kingdom where the lot of my refidence is caft.

Here follow the chief Obfervables (as to matter of new Argument) on the day of his Tryal, being Friday June 6. 1662.

ON this day, the Sheriff returned forty eight Freeholders of the County of *Middlefex*. After thirty two were challenged by the Prifoner, he had a Jury of Twelve men fworn, to wit. Sir *William Roberts*, junior. Sir *Chriftopher Abdy*. *John Stone*. *Henry Carter*. *John Leech*. *Daniel Cole*. *Daniel Browne*. *Thomas Chelfam*. *Thomas Pitts*. *Thomas Upman*. *Andrew Bent*, and *William Smith*.

The Attorney-General's Speech to the Jury.

The Indictment is, *for traiteroufly imagining and intending, &c. the Death of the King*. This very imagination and compaffing, *&c.* is Treafon. Yet, forafmuch as the intentions of the heart are fecret ; the Law cannot take notice of them, till they are declared by Overt Act. Therefore we fhall give in Evidence, That for the accomplifhing

of

of these Intentions, the Prisoner sate with others in several Councils, or rather Confederacies, incroached the Government, levied Forces, appointed Officers, and at last, levied open and actual War, in the head of a Regiment. If any of these crimes be proved, it is sufficient to make him guilty within this Indictment. And the open levying of War, and appearing in the head of a Regiment, is not only a Treason of it self, but an evidence of all those other Treasons he stands charged with in the Indictment.

These things happening before the Act of Oblivion, you will take notice of that Act, and that the Prisoner being excepted by name from the benefit of that Pardon, though he be chargeable for any crime of Treason since the beginning of the late War, yet we shall confine the Facts for which we charge him, to the Reign of his now Majesty.

After the House had voted the late King's Concessions in the Isle of *Wight* to be a good ground for Peace, many of the Members were kept out by force, others turned out; the Peers laid aside, and at last, the King murdered. The first thing then that we shall lay to the charge of the Prisoner, is, That that very day, wherein that horrid Act was committed, we find his hand and seal to a Warrant to the Officers of the Navie, to issue out Stores for a Summers Guard of the *Narrow Seas*. This was the first day of the Reign of his now Majesty; and so he enumerated all the Particulars which he intended to charge him with, and proved them, as followeth.

1. The Warrant of the 30th of *Jan.* 48, was proved to be the hand of Sir *Henry Vane*, by *Thomas Lewis* and *Thomas Turner*, as they believe, neither of them affirming that they saw him write it, but knowing his hand, believed it to be so.

2. *Ralph Darnel*, an Under-Clerk of the House of Commons, proved the Journal Book of the House, and said, though he will not take upon him to say, when Sir *Henry Vane* was there, and when he was absent, yet he said positively, that at what time soever he is set down in the Journal, to have acted or reported any thing, he was there. In which Book, *Febr.* 7. 1648. fol. 653, was the Order to set up a *Council of State*.

Fol. 684. 13th *Feb.* were the Instructions presented to the House, upon which the Council of State was to act.

1. The first was, *That you, or any four or more, are to suppress all and every person and persons pretending Title to the Kingly Government of this Nation, from or by the late King; Charles Steward, his son; or any claiming from or by them or either of them, or any other Single Person whatsoever.*

This

This the Attorney said, was in the first part of that Instruction, to destroy the King's Person, and in the second part, the Kingly Government.

2. *That you, &c. are appointed to direct the Forces of this Commonwealth, for the preventing and suppressing of Tumults and Insurrections at home, or Invasions from abroad ; and for these ends, to raise Forces, &c.*

3. That Febr. 14. 1648. fol 695 ; Sir *Henry Vane* was chosen a Member of the Council of State, and acted upon these Instructions, which they proved thus ; To wit,

First, That Sir *Henry Vane*, as (fol. 893) 23d of *March* 1648, Reported from the Council of State, an Estimate of the number of Ships for the Summers Guard of the *Narrow Seas*.

Secondly, *March* 30. 1649, Sir *Henry Vane* reports from the Council of State, That ten thousand pounds, parcel of the twenty thousand pounds, assessed upon *South Wales* for their Delinquency, be allowed towards the setting out of this Fleet, for the service of the Parliament ; which was Ordered accordingly, and to be paid to Sir *Henry Vane*, as Treasurer of the **Navie.**

Thirdly, That Sir *Hen. Vane* usually sate in Council, but this Deponent, being never admitted to go in, after the Council was sate, proves, that he often saw him go in at the fore-door and back-door, and often continue there all the time the Council was sitting.

William Dobbins and *Matthew Lock* say, That they several times saw Sir *Henry Vane* sit in a Committee of the Council, in the years 1651 and 1652, which consisted only of Members of the Council, and particularly at the Committee for Scotish and Irish Affairs, where Sir *Henry Vane* was often in the Chair, and produced several Orders of that Committee.

Fourthly, *Febr.* 12. 1649, A new Council of State was chosen, of which Sir *Henry Vane* was one, fol. 720.

Feb. 13. 1649, All the Instructions of the former year were read and assented to.

Feb. 22. 1649. fol. 760, Sir *Henry Vane* reported the form of an Oath of *Secresie* to be administred to every of the Members of the Council, which was, to keep all things which should be transacted in Council, *secret*, and to be true and faithful to their *Instructions* ; which the Attorney said, (since their first Instruction was, *to suppress all persons pretending Title from the King*) was in effect, an Oath of *Abjuration*.

Fifthly,

Fisthly, *Anno* 1652, Sir *Henry Vane* was Prefident of the Council of State, and feveral Warrants were produced, to wit, *May* 20.
1652, and 22d of *May* —52; to deliver to Major *Wigan*, two hundred Firelocks, and ten Drums. The other, for the delivery of five
hundred Foot-Arms, for Recruit of Col. *Ingoldsbyes* Regiment ; and
thefe were fubfcribed by Order of the Council, *H. Vane*, Prefident.

April 2. 1653. A Warrant of that date was produced by the
Commiffioners of the Navy, of which he was one, for furnifhing out
the *Hampshire* Frigat, with Provifions and Ammunition for the ufe of
the State.

From this time to 1659, they charge him with nothing, and then
the Journal-Book was produced and attefted by *Ralph Darnel*, wherein, *May* 7. 1659, an Order was made for appointing a *Committee of
Safety* (whereof Sir *Henry Vane* was one) *That they, or any four or
more of them, fhould take care of the Safety of this Commonwealth*,
and they to fit for eight dayes and no longer, fol. 36.

Die Ven. May 13. 1659, Sir *Henry Vane* reported, That they
had conferred with all the Foreign Ambaffadors. That the Common-
wealth is in Amity with all Foreign Princes, but *Spain.*

Refolved, That Ch. Fleetwood, J. Lambert, J. Disbrough, Jam.
Berry, Arthur Haflerigg, Edmund Ludlow, *and Sir* Henry Vane *be
Commiffioners to nominate Commiffion-Officers for the Army of this
Commonwealth.* By vertue hereof they proceeded, *June* 17. 1659, to
nominate Commiffion-Officers, appointed *Robert Moffe* a Colonel,
prefenting a Lift of his Commiffion-Officicers ; and *John Mafon* to be
Governour of *Ferfey.*

Die Ven. May 31. fol. 158. Sir *Henry Vane* reports, concerning
affairs between the two Northern Kings, in the *Zound,* wherein the
affairs of this Commonwealth are concerned.

Die Ven. Sept. 2. 1659. At the Committee of State at *White-hall,*
An Order was produced for the redelivery of the City-horfes to their
refpective owners, Signed, *H. Vane*, Prefident.

A Warrant was produced under the hand of Sir *Henry Vane*, proved by *Thomas Lewis* and one *Falconer,* for fo many Hangers to Col.
Tompfon, as he fhall require for his Regiment.

Three feveral Letters, to deliver 1200 Arms for the ufe of my
Regiment ; to wit, To *Sam. Linn* my Capt. Leiutenant, 30 Arms for
my Company ; To Maj. *Tho. Shurman,* Major of my Regiment, four
or five barrels of Powder.

Then one *Marfh* was produced a Witnefs, who proves, That Sir
Henry

Henry Vane proposed the new Model of Government, *Whitlock* being in the Chair, in these particulars;

1. That *the Supream Power, delegated by the People to their Trustees, ought to be in some Fundamentals not dispensed with.*

2. That *it is destructive to the Peoples Liberties (to which by God's blessing they are restored) to admit any earthly King or single person, to the Legislative or Executive Power over this Nation.*

3. That *the Supream Power delegated, is not entrusted to the Peoples Trustees, to erect matters of Faith or Worship, so as to exercise compulsion therein.*

Tho. Pury proves, That he was at the debating of the two last of these Propositions, and believes they were proposed to the Chairman *Whitlock*, by Sir *Henry Vane*; but affirms confidently, that Sir *Hen. Vane* gave Reasons to maintain them.

Tho. Wallis produced, proves Sir *Henry Vane* and Col. *Rich* in the head of a Company, in *Winchester* Park in *Southwark*, and that the Capt. Leiutenant *Linn* said to the Souldiers, that Sir *Henry Vane* had given them five pounds to drink; that the said *Linn* sent home a key to his wife, to lend him four pounds out of his trunk, to give the Souldiers.

John Cook deposeth, That he was sent to the *Horseshoe-stairs*, to meet Sir *Henry Vane* and Col. *Rich*, and that Sir *H. Vane* delivered five pound to Capt. *Linn*, to reward the Souldiers. This was all the Evidence given by the King's Counsel; To which, Sir *Henry Vane* was required to make his Defence; and to go through with his Case all at once, and not to reply again upon the King's Counsel, who resolved to have the last word to the Jury.

Sir *HENRY VANE.*

Cook in his *Pleas of the Crown*, fol. 6. saith, *King* is to be understood of a King regnant and in actual possession of the Crown, and not of a King when he is onely *Rex de jure*, and out of possession. Now an *interregnum* is confessed by the Indictment. All ensigns of Authority and badges of Government, were visibly in another name and stile; the King's best friends suing, and being sued, in another name.

The Court told him, He should first make his Case out in point of Suit, and it would be then seasonable to stand upon matter of Law; for (said they) it is a good Rule, *in facto jus Oritur*, and enjoyn'd him to call his Witnesses, if he had any.   To

To which Sir *Henry Vane* desired Process of Court, to summon them; and a further time, to answer the Charge. But it was told him, The Jury were to be kept without meat, drink, fire or candle, till their Verdict was delivered in; and therefore that could not be granted.

He then cited the 4th part of *Cook's Institutes*, concerning the Priviledge of Parliament, and that many of these things, being transacted there——

The Court here interrupted him, and said; If the things charged, were done; justifie them: if not, excuse them. So he went to give answer to the Fact.

And as to the first Warrant, *Jan.* 30. 1648; He said, that his hand had been oftentimes counterfeited, and amongst other occasions, for two great sums, to the value of ten thousand pounds; and that he had great reason to believe, that this Warrant was forged, and produced two Witnesses to prove it.

Then said *Windham*, Justice; It may be your hand may have been forged for receiving of Money, but it is not to be conjectured that it should be forged to set Ships to Sea; and directed to the Jury to consider of the circumstances.

Sir *H. Vane.* Neither of the Witnesses ever saw me set my hand to either of these Warrants or Orders, nor doth one Witness prove that he ever saw me sit in the Council of State: He further said, That he absented from the House from *Decemb.* 3. 1648, till *Febr.* 7. That he was chosen a Member of the Council of State without his consent and knowledge; and being demanded to take an Oath of Approbation of what had been done to the late King, he refused, and caused it to be expunged. That these Actings in Council, (if any were) were by Authority of Parliament, of a Parliament constituted in an extraordinary manner, made indissolvable but by Act of Parliament. He insisted much on the Preamble of that Act, so as that Parliament being co-ordinate with the King. (for the Government was in the King and the two Houses) whatever he acted by Them or their Authority, cannot be Treason within the Statute of 25 *Ed.* 3.

He cited an Ordinance of Parliament in 1642, and said, That he hoped these things had been laid asleep by the Act of Oblivion, and if they should now rise in Judgment against him, he feared they would shake that Security which the People promised themselves under that Act. But if he should be now called in question for those things which were transacted in that Parliament, of which he was a Member, he shall have the comfort and peace of those Actions to support him in his

greatest

greateſt ſufferings. He added, That if he were excepted, then muſt he be judged for the crime of the whole Nation, and that crime muſt be ravelled into through him. That the Caſe is ſuch, as never yet fell out, to wit, that the Government being entruſted to three Eſtates, they ſhould ſo fall out among themſelves, as the People cannot tell which to obey; That where theſe great Changes fall out, it is not poſſible for any man to proceed according to all formalities of Law. That there was a Political Power by this Act of 17. *Caroli* co-ordinate with the King; and where theſe Powers are not in conjunction, but enmity to each other, no Court inferiour to the Parliament, by whoſe Authority theſe things were acted, ought to be Judges of this Caſe, which certainly never happened before.

He farther ſaith, he was not the firſt mover in theſe actions, and that he ſhould be called in queſtion for theſe matters, by a King that was out of poſſeſſion at the time when theſe things were acted, would be inconvenient, to ſay no more; That when the three Eſtates were diſjoyned, he thought it the beſt policy, to preſerve the Government in its root, to wit, the *Commons*; by whom it was preſerved and at laſt reſtored to its former courſe. That as to the Regiment that paſſed under his name, he diſown'd it. That Reports of Meſſages are not the fault of the Reporter, for his judgment does not always go along with them, but he is bound to deliver his Meſſage. That he alwayes loved the Government, as it is ſet forth in our ancient Law-Books; and that that *Parliament* (ſo much decried) at laſt reſtored affairs to the poſture in which they now are.

As to the Warrants ſigned by him, he ſaid, they appear to be ſigned in the Name and by Order of the Council, and his hand that ſubſcribes, is not ſo much active as paſſive, to the Commands of the Council. If the Council, who commanded the ſigning, were unwarrantable, The Parliament who appointed the Council, muſt be much more unwarrantable.

And here he offered theſe points to be conſidered, and pray'd earneſtly to have Counſel aſſigned him, to ſpeak to them;

1. *Whether the collective body of the Parliament can be impeached of High Treaſon.*

2. *Whether any perſon acting by Authority of Parliament, can (ſo long as he acteth by that Authority) commit Treaſon?*

3. *Whether matters acted by that Authority, can be called in queſtion in an inferiour Court?*

4. *Whether a King* de jure, *and out of poſſeſſion, can have Treaſon* com-

*committed against him, he not being King de facto, and in actual pos-
session ?* and pray'd it might be argued by Counsel.

5. *Whether matters done in* Southwark, *in another County, may
be given in evidence to a* Middlesex *Jury ?*

As to the last Exception, the Court said,

That he was indicted for compassing and imagining the King's
Death in *Middlesex,* and any overt act, to prove this Imagination, may
be given in evidence wheresoever it be acted. To which Sir *Hen.
Vane* prayed the benefit of a Bill of Exception, upon the Statute of
Westminster 2. cap. 31. and prayed that the Justices might seal it,
which they all refused, and held, it lay not in any case of the Crown.

The King's Counsel desired he might call his Witnesses, (if any he
had) for if they once came to reply to him, he must then be silent, and
consented, that (if it would aid him) they would allow his Actings
to be in the Name and by the Authority of the Council of State; and
the Actings of the Council of State to be by Authority of what he called a Parliament.

Sir *Hen. Vane* replyed ; Then what I acted in the *Council of State,*
and *Committee of Safety,* constituted by the Parliament to endure for
eight dayes, you will allow me. Then you must prove that I ever
acted in the other Council of State, after the Parliament was turned
out.

Then the King's Counsel produced a Warrant, dated *Novemb.* 3.
1659, which was sent in pursuance of an Order of the *Committee of
Safety,* by Sir *Hen. Vane,* as Treasurer of the Navie. This Warrant
was, for the sending of divers Arms Northwards, after Mr. *Lambert,*
who was gone down to oppose the now Duke of *Albemarle.*

Sir *Hen. Vane* produced *Will. Angel, Brisco, Middleton,* &c. Officers of that Regiment which went under his name, who having re-
course unto him for Orders, about *Octob.* 1659, he bad them desist,
and declared his dis-satisfaction in their proceedings ; and this, after
their several importunities to have Orders from him. And thus he
closed his Defence.

FYNCH, Sollicitor.

As to pretence of the power of Parliament, It is to be known, that
it was not the eighth part of the House of Commons, such as were let
in to do all that hath been complained, and the acting under Authority of such an End of a Parliament, under such a Violation, was no
Excuse, but an Aggravation; but that the Parliament was in Law,

E   ended,

ended, by the death of the late King, notwithstanding that Act of 17. *Caroli primi*, appears thus ;

First, The King's Writ for a Parliament is *ad tractandum nobiscum*; which is intended as well of the natural capacity of the King, as of his politick.

Secondly, 'Tis absurd to say, that the Acts of Parliament of King *Charles* the first, should be his Acts, in the time of King *Charles* the second.

Thirdly, A Commission of Sewers, enacted to be on foot for ten years, expires by the death of the King , and the authority of the Commissioners is at an end.

Fourthly, It is not possible for one King to impose a Parliament upon a successor. So much for his acting by colour of authority of Parliament.

And as to the Question, *Whether an House of Parliament can commit Treason ?* If they depart from that Allegiance which they have sworn, at their first meeting, they are impeachable for it.

As to a Co-ordination in the Parliament, he denied it.

As to the Question, *Whether the King being out of actual possession, can have Treason committed against him ?* he affirmed it : And said, otherwise, if Rebellion should be so prosperous, as to depose or oppress the King in Battel, the Offenders are not to be called in question, because they prevailed. He said, it was the Plea of *Watson* the Jesuite, who, being Indicted for compassing the death of King *James*, in *Scotland*, after he was declared King of *England*, and before his actual entring into this Realm, made this Defence ; That the King was never in possession of the Crown.

Windam Justice. As to the Act of 17. *Caroli*, and the Preamble of that Act, so much insisted upon by the Prisoner. 1. He held that the Parliament had not greater Authority by it, but were onely made more durable than other Parliaments have been ; but he held, that the Parliament was absolutely dissolved by the death of the King ; and put this case : If it should be enacted that such a Marriage should continue, till it was dissolved by Act of Parliament, If one dies, it is a determination of it in Fact, so as no man can say, but it is absolutely dissolved. 2. It must continue in the degree and dignity of a Parliament If the House be under a force, and some kept out, some let in, to serve a Turn, what-ever they act is a Nullity in Law. For Freedom is the principal essence and honour of a Parliament ; yet though the House be under a Force, the House is not dissolved by such Force, but

but the proceedings are to be suspended, till it require its former Liberty ; and this as well by the Common Law, as by the Civil and Canon Laws of all other Countries. 3. The Parliament is the King's great Council, The Peers are *Consiliarii nati* ; If they be forc'd away, or laid aside, as here they were, all the rest is but *Magni Nominis Umbra*.

Twisden held the same opinion, That it is not the sitting of a few Members within those Walls, that will continue it a Parliament.

And though another Parliament, a great many years after the Kings death, declared it to be at an end, yet that Act was but Declaration, it was at an end before.

Whether a Parliament may commit Treason, is not the Question ; but, Whether a few of the House, shutting out their Fellows, and usurping the Government, were not Traitors ?

Foster held the same opinion, and said, The distinction between the Politick and Natural capacity of the King , was the Treason of the two *Spencers* ; That Priviledge of the Parliament is no shelter for breach of the Peace, much less for Treason.

Twisden added, That to compass the Death of the King as a natural person, was Treason ; to compass his Death in his Politick capacity, as to depose him, was Treason, and both provided for by the Act of 25. *Ed.* 3. That in the same instant the late King expired, in the very same his now Majesty was King *de facto*, and affirmed the cases of *Watson* and *Cleark*, 1. *Jac*. If an Army be raised against the King, and the King is slain in the battel, This Treason is questionable by the Successor, as *Stonies* Case is in *Dyer*.

Thus ended the questions of Law, proposed.

The Sollicitor spake after to the Jury, concerning the Fact, which after, they withdrew to consider, and being withdrawn about half an hour, returned with their Verdict, which being delivered by the Foreman in the name of his fellows, with their consent, found the Prisoner guilty of High Treason from *Januar*. 30. 1648.

They not only found him guilty according to the Indictment, which was laid for what the Prisoner did, 1659 ; but for a long series of High Treason (as they reckon) from *Jan*. 30. 1648. By which it may appear, they were a well-prepared Jury for their work. The Judges oft, if not alwayes, pretend, that the Jury is to pass Verdict only as to matter of Fact, according to the Evidence given by the Witnesses thereof. But a general Verdict evidently involves both, that he is guilty of such fact, and that the fact is Treason, as they in this Verdict

openly

openly undertake to determine, taking in the full fence of the Indictment, and much more. Unleis a Jury diftinguifh themfelves out of this
ufually impofed fnare, by giving a fpecial Verdict concerning the Fact
only, they undeniably have a fhare with their Tutors and Inftructors
in the fhedding of innocent blood, in cafe matter of Law be wrongfully ftated.

For a Jury to refolve a Cafe of Law, that fo eminent a Subjects life
was concern'd in, and that in lefs than half an hour, which never yet
came before any Bench of Judicature in *England*, may feem a very
ftrange and bold adventure.

But *Reader*, How far this falls fhort of a full Account of all that
was fpoken by the Prifoner (though much interrupted by the *King's
Bench* and *Counfel*) in thofe ten hours, which on this day of his Tryal
he ftood at the Bar, (pleading and anfwering for his Life, and the
Caufe he had with many thoufands been engaged in) I leave to thee
to imagine, till a fuller and compleater Account thereof can be obtained, than is yet come to hand.

This was remarkable; That never being indulg'd the liberty of any
repofe to his body, all that while, (which indeed, he asked not) nor
receiving any creature-refrefhings, though fent him, for his fupport;
yea, and though after all his moft rational Plea, in his Defence, the
Jury gave their Verdict againft his Life, he came chearfully and plea-
fantly from the Bar, as thought worthy to fuffer for the Name of
Chrift; and was fo raifed and full of rejoycing that evening, at the
place of his confinement in the *Tower*, that he was a wonder to any
that were about him. This fpiritual rejoycing in Chrift Jefus, and his
heavenly raifednefs of fpirit, increafed more and more, to the very moment of his death; infomuch, that meer ftrangers to his perfon, yea,
very foreigners, wondred at his triumphant diffolution.

The true Copy of the Prifoner's own Papers, containing the fubftance of what he pleaded on the faid day of his Tryal, *June 6*.

*Memorandums as to my main Defence, in relation to matter of
Fact, and as a Narrative thereof.*

THat without any feeking of mine, I was chofen by Writ under the
Great Seal, to ferve as Burgefs for the Town of *Kingfton* upon
Hull, in the Parliament that fate down on the third of *Novemb.* 1640.
and

and having in pursuance thereof, taken my seat in the said Parliament, I was obliged by Law, to give my attendance upon the said Trust, as well as upon grounds of Duty and Conscience.

The said Parliament was not onely called and assembled after the usual manner, and had the Power and Priviledges incident to that high Court, but was by express Statute and Content of the three Estates, so constituted, as to its Continuance, Adjournment, Prorogation and Dissolution, that in none of these particulars they were subject to alteration, but by their own common Assent, declared by Act of Parliament, to be passed by themselves for that purpose, with the Royal Assent.

In the Preamble to the Act for continuance of the said Parliament, these words are contained : *Whereas great sums of Money must of necessity be speedily advanced and provided, for the relief of his Majesties Army and People in the Northern parts of this Realm, and for preventing the imminent danger this Kingdom is in, and for supply of his Majesties present and urgent occasions, which cannot be so timely effected as is requisit, without Credit for raising the said Moneys ; which Credit cannot be obtained until such obstacles be first removed, as are occasioned by fears, jealousies and apprehensions of divers his Majesties loyal Subjects, That this present Parliament may be Adjourned, Prorogued or Dissolved, before Justice shall be duely executed upon Delinquents, Publick Grievances redressed, a firm Peace between the two Nations of* England *and* Scotland *concluded, and before sufficient Provision be made for the repayment of the said Moneys so to be raised, &c.* By all which, the very work that was between the three Estates agreed to be done for the Good and Safety of the Kingdom, was in sundry particulars declared and expressed ; and not only so, but as is acknowledged by the late King himself in his Answer to the *nineteen Propositions* ; The Power which thereby was legally placed in both Houses, was more than sufficient to prevent and restrain Tyranny.

So that, by what hath been shewed, the Law it self is with me, and for me, enjoyning my continued attendance on the Trust which by this means was committed to me, and authorized me in particular to effect the things contained in the said Preamble ; and to act in all matters belonging to the high Court of *Parliament*, for the Good and Safety of the Kingdom in time of imminent danger, I had been liable to great punishment by the Law, for dis-attendance and deserting my station therein, till lawfully or by force dismissed there-from : and this,

what-

whatever occasions others might have, by a voluntary or forc'd departure from attendance upon that Trust.

The actions therefore done by me in this capacity, and according to the Law, Priviledges, Customs and Power of *Parliament*, and that, such a one as was thus extraordinarily constituted, neither are nor can be brought within the Statute of 25. *Ed.* 3. *cap.* 2. nor are to be questioned, tried, much less, judged and sentenc'd in any inferior Court. Nay, so far is it from this, that by a Declaration and Resolution of *Parliament*, *Aug.* 13. 1642, it is adjudged to be committing Treason in the highest degree, to bring both or either Houses of Parliament under that or such like Imputations.

Nor, till of late, have I ever heard but that those who took the Judgment of *Parliament* for their rule and guide, (however tortuous or erroneous it might afterwards be accounted in succeeding times) and they that acted by and under the countenance of their declared Judgments, Orders or Ordinances, (ever acknowledged binding during the sitting of the Parliament) were safe and indempnified from all punishment. And for Government-sake it self, it is requisit it should be so ; because none are Judges of the Power and Priviledges of *Parliament*, but themselves. For admit once, that their Judgment may be called in question, and disputed by private persons, or by inferiour Courts, (whose Votes are included in theirs) the *Fundamentals* of Government are plucked up by the roots. *Par in pares non habet Imperium, multò minus in eos qui majus Imperium habent* ; An Equal has no command over his Equal, much less over those that have a greater command or authority.

His late Majesty, in his Answer to the *nineteen Propositions*, **does** very briefly and exactly state the nature and kind of Government, that is exercised in this Kingdom, saying ; *The Laws in this Kingdom are made by a King, a House of Peers, and a House of Commons, chosen by the People, all having free Votes, and particular Priviledges. These three Estates, making one incorporate body, are they, in whom the Soveraignty and Supream Power is placed, as to the making and repealing of Laws. And the Government, according to these Laws, is trusted to the King, who in the Interval of Parliaments, is sole in the exercise of Government, which (the Parliament sitting) he is to exercise in conjunction with the two Houses.*

And his said Majesty asserting three sorts of Government, *Absolute Monarchy*, *Aristocracy*, and *Democracy*, does most rightly distinguish the Monarchy of *England* from all those three, and commends the

Consti-

Conſtitution of this Kingdom, as it is a mixture of all three, having the conveniencies of them all, without the inconveniencies of any one, as long as the ballance hangs even between the three Eſtates, that they run joyntly on in their proper channels, and that the overflowing of either on either ſide, raiſe no deluge nor inundation.

By the paſſing of the foreſaid Act, for the continuance of the fore-mentioned Parliament, the Intervals of Parliament were no longer, as before, at the will and pleaſure of the *King*, but the Power to continue the ſaid *Parliament*, without Adjournment, Prorogation, or Diſ-ſolution, reſided in the two Houſes with the *King*, joyntly, and in none of them ſeverally ; ſo that in effect, the Government of the Kingdom, during the continuance of that Parliament, was in conjunction of the three Eſtates, and in their common conſents and agreements among themſelves, given in Parliament, the aſſembling and meeting whereof was appointed and fixed to a place certain, by Law.

By reaſon hereof, it is not the attendance of any of the Members in Parliament (for diſcharge of the Truſt repoſed in them, confirm'd and enlarged by the ſaid Act) that is faulty or cenſurable by the Law, but thoſe that unwarrantably depart and deſert that their Truſt and ſtation, are to be blamed ; 6. *Hen.* 8. 16.

The *King* in conjunction with the *Parliament*, is *maxime Rex*, and is ſupported in the Throne and exerciſe of his Regal Power, by the joynt concurrence of both Houſes. And becauſe (as his late Ma-jeſty well obſerved) the happineſs and good of the Conſtitution of this Government, lies in keeping the ballance even between the three Eſtates, containing themſelves within the bounds of their proper channels, there-fore in attempts of either to overflow thoſe bounds, (they being co-ordinate) the Office of a *Parliament* is by the very fundamental conſti-tution of the Government, to keep this ballance well poiſed. And to that end (as was before mentioned) his Majeſties own words are in his ſaid Anſwer to the *nineteen Propoſitions* ; *That there was legally placed in both Houſes; a Power more than ſufficient to prevent and reſtrain the Power of Tyranny.* If ſo, then are they the legal Judges, when there is danger of Tyranny ; and have legal power to require their Judgment and Reſolves to be obeyed, not only when Arms are actually raiſed againſt them, but when they diſcern and accordingly declare a preparation towards it ; elſe, they may find it too late to pre-vent the power of Tyranny. There is no greater attempt of Tyranny, than to arm againſt the Parliament ; and there is no viſible way for the reſtraining ſuch Tyranny, but by raiſing Arms in their own and the

Kingdoms defence. Less than this is not sufficient, and therefore far from more than sufficient, for the punishment of Delinquents and restraint of Tyranny.

Unto the King in conjunction with his two Houses, according as is provided by the Law, in this capacity of his as *maxime Rex*, was the duty of Allegiance to be yeelded by his Subjects, during the indissolved state of that Parliament. For they were the King's great Council, and supream Court, exercising the known Power and Priviledges, that time out of mind have appertained to them, and been put forth by them, as the Exigents of the Kingdom have required, when differences have happened about the very title of the Crown, in declaring the duty of the Subject, by yeelding their Allegiance to Kings *de facto*, when Kings *de jure* have been kept out of possession. This our Chronicles, and the Histories of former times, do plentifully inform.

The causes that did happen, to move his late Majesty to depart from his Parliament, and continue for many years, not only at a distance and in a disjunction from them, but at last, in a declared posture of Enmity and War against them, are so well known and fully stated in print (not to say, *written in characters of blood*) on both parts, that I shall only mention it, and refer to it.

This matter was not done in a corner. The Appeals were solemn, and the decision by the Sword, was given by that God, who being the Judge of the whole World, does Right, and cannot do otherwise.

By occasion of these unhappy differences, thus happening, most great and unusual Changes and Revolutions, like an irresistible Torrent, did break in upon us, not only to the disjoynting that Parliamentary Assembly among themselves, (the head from the members, the co-ordinates from each other, and the houses within themselves) but to the creating such formed divisions among the people, and to the producing such a general state of Confusion and Disorder, that hardly any were able to know their duty, and with certainty to discern who were to command and who to obey. All things seemed to be reduced, and in a manner resolved into their first elements and principles.

Nevertheless, as dark as such a state might be, the Law of *England* leaves not the Subjects thereof (as I humbly conceive) without some glimpses of direction what to do, in the cleaving to, and pursuing of which, I hope I shall not be accounted nor judged an offender; or if I am, I shall have the comfort and peace of my Actions to support me in and under my greatest sufferings.

The

The Resolutions of all the Judges in *Calvin's* Cafe, entituled, *Poft-nati*, in the 7th Book of *Cook's* Reports, and the learned Arguments thereupon, afforded me inftruction even in this matter. It may be 'tis truly thence affirmed, that Allegiance is due only to the King, and how due, is alfo fhewed.

The King is acknowledged to have two capacities in him ; one a *natural*, as he is defcended of the Blood Royal of the Realm; and the Body natural he hath in this capacity, is of the creation of Almighty God and mortal : The other is a *politick* capacity, in refpect of which he is a Body politick or myftical, framed by the policy of man, which is immortal and invifible. To the King, in both thefe capacities conjoyn'd, Allegiance is due ; that is to fay, to the natural perfon of the King, accompanied with his **politick capacity, or the** politick appropriated to the natural.

The politick capacity of the King hath properly no body nor foul : for it is framed by the policy of man.

In all Indictments of Treafon, when any one does intend the death and deftruction of the King, it muft needs be underftood of his natural body, the other being immortal. The Indictment therefore concludes *contra Legiantiæ fua debitum*, againft the duty of his Allegiance, fo that Allegiance is due to the natural body.

Admitting then that thus by Law, Allegiance is due to the King (as before recited) yet it is alwayes to be prefumed, that it is to the King in conjunction with the Parliament, the Law, and the Kingdom, and not in disjunction from, or oppofition to them ; and that, while a Parliament is in being and cannot be diffolved, but by the Confent of the three Eftates.

This is therefore that, which makes the matter in queftion, a new Cafe, that never before happened in the Kingdom, nor was poffible to happen, unlefs there had been a Parliament conftituted, as this was, unfubjected to Adjournment, Prorogation or Diffolution, by the King's will. Where fuch a power is granted, and the co-ordinates thereupon difagree and fall out, fuch effects and confequents as thefe that have happened, will but too probably follow. And, if either the Law of Nature, or *England*, inform not in fuch cafe, it will be impoffible for the Subjects to know their duty, when that Power and Command which ought to flow from three in conjunction, comes to be exercifed by all or either of them, fingly and apart, or by two of them againft one.

When new and never-heard-of Changes do fall out in the Kingdom, it is not like that the known and written Laws of the Land fhould be

F   the

the exact Rule, but the Grounds and Rules of Justice, contained and declared in the Law of Nature, are and ought to be a Sanctuary in such cases, even by the very Common Law of *England* : For, thence originally spring the unerring Rules, that are set by the Divine and Eternal Law, for Rule and Subjection in all States and Kingdoms.

In contemplation hereof , as the Resolve of all the Judges, it was agreed,

1. *That Allegiance is due to Soveraignty by the Law of Nature,* to wit, that Law which God at the creation of Man, infused into his heart, for his preservation and direction, the Law eternal. Yet, is it not this Law, as it is in the heart of every individual man, that is binding over many, or legislative, but as it is the Act of a Community, or an Associated People, by the right dictates and perswasions of the work of this Law in their hearts. This appears in the Case of the *Israelites, Judg.* 20, & 21 chapters, cited in the 4th part of *Cook's Institutes,* where mention is made of a Parliament without a King, that made War, and that with their Brethren. They met as one man to do it, in vindication of that Justice, unto which they were obliged even by the Law of Nature. This is that which Chancellor *Fortescue* calls *Political Power,* here in *England* ; by which, as by the Ordinance of man, in pursuance of the Ordinance of God, the Regal Office constituted, or the King's Politick Capacity, and becomes appropriated to his natural person.

Thus Politick Power is the immediate Efflux and Off-spring of the Law of Nature, and may be called a part of it. To this, *Hooker* in his *Ecclesiastical Polity* agrees, and *Selden* on that subject.

The Law of Nature thus considered, is part of the Law of *England,* as is evident by all the best received Law-Books, *Bracton, Pleta, Lambard* upon the *Saxon Laws,* and *Fortescue* in the praise of the *Laws of England.* This is the Law that is before any judicial or municipal Law, as the root and fountain whence these and all Government under God and his Law do flow.

This *Politick Power,* as it is exercised in conjunction with, and conformity to the Eternal Law, partakes of its moral and immutable nature, and cannot be changed by Act of Parliament. Of this Law it is that *Magna Charta* and the *Charter of Forest,* with other Statutes, rehearsed in the *Petition of Right,* are for the most part declaratory. For they are not introductive of any new Law, but confirmations of what was good in all Laws of *England,* before. This agrees with that Maxime, *Salus Populi suprema Lex* ; that being made due and binding

by

by this Law, which in the Judgment of the Community, declaring their mind by their own free chosen Delegates and Trustees, in harmony with the Eternal Law, appears profitable and necessary for the preservation and good of the whole Society.

This is the Law, which is put forth by the common consent of the whole Realm, in their Representative ; and (according to the fundamental Constitutions of this Kingdom) is that, with which the Kings of this Land, by the joynt co-operation of the three Estates, do make and repeal Laws.

But through the disorders and divisions of the times, these two Powers, the *Regal* and *Political*, (which, according to the Law of *England*, make up but one and the same supream Authority) fell assunder, and found themselves in disjunction from, and opposition to one another. I do not say, The question is now, which of these is most rightly, (according to the principles of the Law of Nature and the Law of *England*) to be adhered unto and obeyed, but unto whether Power adherence is a crime, in such an Exigent of State ? Which, since it is such a new and extraordinary Case, evidently above the Track of the ordinary Rules, contained in the positive and municipal Laws of *England*, there can be no colour to bring it within the Statute of 25. *Ed.* 3. *cap.* 2. forasmuch as all Statutes presuppose these two Powers, *Regal* and *Political*, in conjunction, perfect unity and subserviency, which this Case does not, cannot admit. So exceeding new and extraordinary a Case is it, that it may be doubted whether, and questioned how far, any other Parliament, but *that* Parliament it self that was privy to all its own Actings and Intentions, can be an indifferent and competent Judge. But however, the point is of so abstruse and high consideration, as no inferiour Court can, or ought to judge of it, as by Law-Books is most undeniable ; to wit, *Bracton* and others.

This then being the true state of the Case, and the spring of that Contest that ensued, and received its decision by the late War ; The next Consideration is, how far I have had my share and part therein, that by the Laws is not warrantable , or by what appears in way of proof, to the Jury.

For the first, I shall crave leave to give you this account of my self, who have best known my own mind and intentions throughout, and would not now, to save my life, renounce the principles of that Righteous Cause, which my conscience tells me, was my duty to be faithful unto.

I do therefore humbly affirm, That in the afore-mentioned great

Changes

Changes and Revolutions, from first to last, I was never a first mover, but alwayes a follower, chusing rather to adhere to *things* than *persons* ; and (where Authority was dark or dubious) to do things justifiable by the Light and Law of Nature, as that Law is acknowledged part of the Law of the Land ; things, that are *in se bona*, and such, as according to the grounds and principles of the Common Law, as well as the Statutes of this Land, would warrant and indempnifie me, in doing them. For I have observed by Precedents of former times, when there have arisen disputes about Titles to the Crown, between Kings *de facto* and Kings *de jure*, the People of this Realm wanted not directions for their safety, and how to behave themselves within the duty and limits of Allegiance to the King and Kingdom, in such difficult and dangerous seasons.

My Lord *Cook* is very clear in this point, in his Chap. of Treason, *fol.7.* And if it were otherwise, it were the hardest case that could be, for the people of *England* : For then they would be certainly exposed to punishment, from those that are in possession of the supream power, as Traitors, if they do any thing against them, or do not obey them ; and they would be punishable as Traitors, by him that hath right, and is King *de jure*, in case they do obey the Kings *de facto*, and so all the people of *England* are necessarily involved in Treasons, either against the Powers *de facto*, or *de jure*, and may by the same reason be questioned for it, as well as the Prisoner, if the *Act of Indempnity* and the *King's Pardon* did not free them from it. The security then and safety of all the *People* of *England*, is by this means, made to depend upon a *Pardon*, (which might have been granted or denied) and not upon the sure foundations of *Common Law* ; an opinion sure, which (duly weighed and considered) is very strange, to say no more.

For I would gladly know that person in *England* of estate and fortune, and of age, that hath not counselled, aided or abetted, either by his person or estate, and submitted to the Laws and Government of the Powers that then were ; and if so, then by your Judgments upon me, you condemn (in effigies, and by necessary consequence) the whole Kingdom.

And if that be the Law, and be now known to be so, it is worth consideration, whether, if it had been generally known and understood before, it might not have hindred his Majesties Restoration.

Besides, although, until this Judgement be passed upon me, the people have apprehended themselves, as free from question, and out of danger, by reason of the *Act of Indempnity and General Pardon* ; yet
when

when it shall appear to them, that such their safety is not grounded on the Common Law, nor upon the Law of Nature, but that against both these in their actions, they are found faulty, and tainted with a moral guilt, and that as principals; also, (since in Treason there are no Accessories) what terrifying Reflexions must this needs stir up in the mind of every man, that will be apt to believe his Turn will come next, at least once in two years, as hath befallen me in my person, who (however I have been misjudged and misunderstood) can truly affirm, that in the whole series of my Actions, that which I have had in my eye, hath been to preserve the ancient, well-constituted Government of *England* on its own *basis* and primitive righteous foundations, most learnedly stated by *Fortescue* in his Book, made in praise of the *English Laws.* And I did account it the most likely means for the effecting of this, to preserve it, at least in its root, whatever changes and alterations it might be exposed unto in its branches, through the blustrous and stormy times that have passed over us.

This is no new doctrine, in a Kingdom acquainted with *Political Power*, as *Fortescue* shews ours is, describing it to be in effect, the Common Assent of the Realm, the Will of the People or whole Body of the Kingdom, represented in Parliament. Nay, though this Representation (as hath fallen out) be restrained for a season, to the Commons House, in their single actings, into which (as we have seen) when by the inordinate fire of the times, two of the three Estates have for a season been melted down, they did but retire into their Root, and were not hereby in their Right, destroyed, but rather preserved, though as to their exercise, laid for a while asleep, till the season came of their Revival and Restoration.

And whatever were the intents and designs of others, (who are to give an account of their own actions) It is sufficient for me, that at a time critical and decisive, (though to my own hazard and ill usage) I did declare my Refusal of the Oath of *Abjuration*, which was intended to be taken by all the Members of Parliament, in reference to Kingly Government, and the Line of his now Majesty in particular. This I not only positively refused to take, but was an occasion of the second thoughts which the Parliament reassumed thereof, till in a manner, they came wholly at last to decline it; a proof undeniable of the remoteness of any intentions or designs of mine, as to the endeavouring any alteration or change in the Government, and was that which gave such jealousie to many in the House, that they were willing to take the first occasion to shew their dislike of me, and to discharge me from sitting among them.   But

But to return to what I have before affirmed, as to my being no leading or first Actor in any Change, it is very apparent by my deportment at the time when that great Violation of Priviledges happened to the Parliament, so as by force of Arms several Members thereof were debarred coming into the House and keeping their seats there. This made me forbear to come to the Parliament for the space of ten weeks, (to wit, from the third of *Decemb.* 1648, till towards the middle of *February* following) or to meddle in any publick transactions. And during that time, the matter most obvious to exception, in way of alteration of the Government, did happen. I can therefore truly say, that as I had neither consent nor vote, at first, in the Resolutions of the Houses, concerning the *Non-Addresses* to his late Majesty, so neither had I, in the least, any consent in, or approbation to, his Death. But on the contrary, when required by the Parliament, to take an Oath, to give my approbation *ex post facto* to what was done, I utterly refused, and would not accept of sitting in the Council of State upon those terms, but occasioned a new Oath to be drawn, wherein that was omitted. Hereupon, many of the Council of State sate, that would not take the other.

In like manner, The Resolutions and Votes for changing the Goverment into a *Commonwealth* or *Free-State* were passed, some weeks before my return to Parliament. Yet afterwards (so far as I judged the same consonant to the principles and grounds, declared in the Laws of *England*, for upholding that Political Power, which hath given the rise and introduction in this Nation, to Monarchy it self, by the account of antient Writers) I conceived it my duty, as the state of things did then appear to me, (notwithstanding the said Alteration made) to keep my station in Parliament, and to perform my Allegiance therein, to King and Kingdom, under the Powers then *regnant*, (upon my principles before declared) yeelding obedience to their Authority and Commands. And having received Trust, in reference to the safety and preservation of the Kingdom, in those times of imminent danger, (both within and without) I did conscientiously hold my self obliged, to be true and faithful therein. This I did upon a publick account, not daring to quit my station in Parliament, by vertue of my first Writ. Nor was it for any private or gainful ends, to profit my self or enrich my Relations. This may appear as well by the great Debt I have contracted, as by the destitute condition my many Children are in, as to any provision made for them. And I do publickly challenge all persons whatsoever, that can give information of any Bribes or co-
vert

vert wayes, ufed by me, during the whole time of my publick acting.
Therefore I hope it will be evident to the Confciences of the Juiy, that
what I have done, hath been upon principles of Integrity, Honcur,
Juftice, Reafon and Confcience, and not as is fuggefted in the Indictment, by *inftigation of the Devil*, or *want of the fear of God*.

A fecond great Change that happened upon the Conftitution of the
Parliament, and in them, of the veiy Kingdom it felf and the Laws
thereof (to the plucking up the Liberties of it by the very roots, and
the introducing of an Arbitrary Regal Power, under the name of *Protector*, by force, and the Law of the Sword) was the Ufurpation of
Cromwel, which I oppofed from the beginning to the end, to that degree of fuffering, and with that conftancy, that well near had coft me
not only the lofs of my Eftate, but of my very Life, if he might have
had his will, which a higher than he hindred. Yet I did remain a
Prifoner, under great hardfhip, four months, in an Ifland, by his
Orders.

Hereby, That which I have afferted, is moft undeniably evident, as
to the true grounds and ends of my actions all along, that were againft
Ufurpation on the one hand, or fuch extraordinary Actings on the
other, as I doubted the Laws might not warrant or indempnifie, unlefs
I were inforced thereunto, by an over-ruling and inevitable neceffity.

The third confiderable Change, was the total difappointing and removing of the faid Ufurpation, and the returning again of the Members of Parliament to the exercife of their primitive and original Truft,
for the good and fafety of the Kingdom, fo far as the ftate of the times
would then permit them, being fo much as they were, under the power of an Army, that for fo long a time had influenced the Government. Towards the recovery therefore of things again into their own
channel, and upon the legal Root of the Peoples Liberties, to wit, their
Common Confent in Parliament, given by their own Deputies and
Truftees, I held it my duty to be again acting in publick Affairs, in the
capacity of a Member of the faid Parliament, then re-entred upon the
actual Exercife of their former Power, or at leaft ftrugling for it. In
this feafon I had the opportunity of declaring my true intentions, as to
the Government, upon occafion of refufing the Oath of *Abjuration* before mentioned.

And whereas I am charged with keeping out his Majefty that now
is, from exercifing his Regal Power or Royal Authority in this his
Kingdom ; through the ill-will born me by that part of the Parliament
then fitting, I was difcharg'd from being a Member thereof, about

Jan.

Jan. 9. 1659, and by many of them was charged, or at least strongly suspected to be a *Royalist* : Yea, I was not only discharged from my attendance in Parliament, but confined as a prisoner at mine own house, some time before there was any visible power in the Nation that thought it seasonable to own the King's Interest. And I hope my sitting still, will not be imputed as a failer of duty, in the condition of a prisoner, and those circumstances I then was in. This I can say, that from the time I saw his Majesties Declarations from *Breda*, declaring his Intentions and Resolutions as to his Return to take upon him the actual Exercise of his Regal Office in *England*, and to indemnifie all those that had been Actors in the late Differences and Wars, (as in the said Declaration doth appear) I resolved, not to avoid any publick question, (if called thereto) as relying on mine own Innocency and his Majesties declared Favour, as beforesaid. And for the future I determined to demean my self with that inoffensiveness and agreeableness to my duty, as to give no just matter of new provocation to his Majesty in his Government. All this on my part, hath been punctually observed, whatever my sufferings have been. Nor am I willing, in the least, to harbour any discouraging thoughts in my mind, as to his Majesties Generosity and Favour towards me, who have been faithfull to the Trust I was engaged in, without any malicious intentions against his Majesty, his Crown or Dignity, as before hath been shewed. And I am desirous for the future, to walk peaceably and blamelesly.

Whatever therefore my personal sufferings have been, since his Majesties Restoration, I rather impute them to the false reports and calumnies of mine enemies and misjudgers of my actions, than reckon them as any thing that hath proceeded from his Majesties proper inclination, whose favour and clemency I have had just reason with all humility to acknowledge.

First, with regard to his Majesties Speech made the 27th of *July*, 1660, in the House of Peers, wherein his Majesty expresly declared it to be no intention of his, that a person under my circumstances should be excepted out of the *Act of Indempnity*, either for Life or Estate.

And, secondly. however it was the Parliaments pleasure (my self unheard, though then in the Tower, and ready to have been brought before them)to except me out of the common Indempnity, and subject me to question for my actions, yet they themselves, of their own accord (admitting the possibility that in such questioning of me, I might be attainted) made it their humble desire to his Majesty, that in such case, Execution, as to my Life, might be remitted. Unto this his Majesty
readily

readily gave his Grant and Assent. And I do firmly believe, if the Houses had pleased to give me the opportunity and leave of being heard, they would never have denied me the Indemnity granted to the rest of the Nation.

That which remains of further Charge yet to me, is the business of a Regiment, an imployment, which I can in truth affirm, mine own inclinations, nature and breeding little fitted me for, and which was intended onely as honorary and titular, with relation to Volunteers, who, by their application to the Council of State, in a time of great Commotions, did propound their own Officers, and (without any seeking of mine, or my considering any farther of it, than as the use of my Name) did (among others) nominate me for a Colonel, which the Council of State approved, granting Commissions to my self and all other Officers relating thereunto. And the Parliament confirmed my said Commission, upon report thereof made to them.

This will appear by several Witnesses I have to produce in this matter, that will be able to affirm, how little I took upon me, or at all, to give any Orders, or make use of such my Commission, any otherwise than in name only.

'Tis true indeed, that at a certain time, when I was summoned to appear at the Committee of the Militia in *Southwark*, whereof I was a Member ; That which was called my own Company of Foot (from the respect which they and their Officers pretended to me) were desirous to be in a posture, fit for me to see them, and as I passed by, I took the opportunity at their desire to shew my self to them, and only (as taking notice of their respect) in some few words, expressing the reason I had to receive it in good part, I told them I would no longer detain them from their other occasions. After I was gone from them, I appointed my Capt. Lieutenant to give them from me something to drink, as might be fitting on such an occasion, which, to my best remembrance was five pounds, and he laid it out of his own money.

More than this (as I remember) was not done by me, so much as to the seeing any more, the Companies of that Regiment gathered together, or giving Orders to them, which I publickly and avowedly declined, perswading the Officers to lay down their Charges, in mine own example, so soon as I discern'd the intentions of the sitting down of the *Committee of Safety*, and the exorbitant power committed to them to exercise, and the way of proceedings by the Army, in interesting themselves in the Civil Government of the Nation, which I utterly disliked.

G   And

And although I forbore not to keep my ſtation, in reference to the Council of State while they ſate, or as a Commiſſioner of the Admiralty, during the time by them appointed to act by Parliamentary Authority ; and ſo, had occaſion to be daily converſant with the Members of the *Committee of Safety,* (whereof my ſelf, with others that would not accept, were named) yet I perfectly kept my ſelf diſ-intereſted from all thoſe Actings of the Army, as to any Conſent or Approbation of mine, (however in many things by way of diſcourſe, I did not decline converſe with them) holding it my duty, to penetrate as far as I could into their true Intentions and Actions, but reſolving within my ſelf to hold true to my Parliamentary Truſt, in all things wherein the Parliament appeared to me to act for the ſafety and good of the Kingdom, however I was miſ-interpreted and judged by them, as one that rather favoured ſome of the Army and their power.

Upon the whole matter, There is not any precedent, that ever both or either of the Houſes of Parliament did commit Treaſon. For though Priviledge of Parliament does not ſo hold in Treaſon, but that particular Members may be puniſhed for it , yet it is unprecedented, That both or either Houſes of **Parliament**, as a collective Body, ever did or could commit Treaſon.

All the Acts done in Parliaments, have been reverſed indeed, and repealed, as what was done 11 *Ric.* 2. was repealed, 21. *Ric.* 2 ; and what was done 21. *Ric.* 2. was repealed 1 *Hen.* 4. 3 ; as appears by the printed Statutes. Yet I do not find, that both or either Houſe of Parliament were declared Traitors for what they did in thoſe Parliaments ; Or that any which acted under them, ſuffered for the ſame in any inferiour Courts. And ſurely, the reaſon is obvious : For they had a co-ordinacy in the Supream or Legiſlative Power, for the making, altering and repealing Laws. And if ſo, *Par in parem non habet imperium* ; and by authorities out of *Bracton, Fleta,* and others, it may appear what Superiours the King himſelf hath, (who yet hath no Peer in his Kingdom, *niſi Curium Baronum*) God, Law, and Parliament.

And if either or both Houſes cannot commit Treaſon, Then thoſe that act by their Authority, cannot : For, *plus peccat Author quam Actor* , the Author offends more than the Actor. If thoſe that command, do not, nor can commit Treaſon, how can thoſe that act by their Authority, be guilty of it ?

Further, I muſt crave leave to aſſert, by reaſon of what I ſee opened upon the Evidence ; That what is done in Parliament, or by their

Autho-

Authority, ought not to be queftioned in any other Court. **For every** offence committed in any Court, muft be punifhed in the fame, or in fome higher, and not any inferiour Court. Now, the Court of Parliament hath no fuperiour Court, as is faid in *Cook's* Jurifdiction of Courts. And the reafon there given, that Judges ought not to give any opinion in a matter of Parliament, is, becaufe it is not to be decided by the Common Laws, but *fecundum Legem & Confuetudinem Parliamenti.* This, the Judges in divers Parliaments have confeffed. And that reafon is not to be waved, which the Lord *Cook* gives : That a man can make no defence ; for what is faid and acted there, is done in Council, and none ought to reveal the fecrets of the **Houfe** : **Every** Member hath a Judicial Voice, and can be no Witnefs.

The main fubftance of thefe Papers was read and enlarged upon by the Prifoner, this day of his Tryal. He was often interrupted, but his memory was ftill relieved by his Papers, fo as after whatever diverfions caufed by the Court or Counfel, he could recover himfelf again, and proceed. Yet the edge and force of his Plea, as to the influencing of the Jurors Confciences, may appear to have been much abated by fuch interruptions, as doubtlefs was intended, and will more at large appear, when it fhall pleafe God to afford us a full Narrative of the Proceedings of the King's Judges, Counfel and Jurors about him, and of all that he occafionally faid, upon the digreffions by them caufed.

Wednefday June 11. *being the Sentence-day.*

AFter fome little skirmifhings with the Prifoner, to dafh all the humane weapons of Law and Reafon out of his hands, by force or noife, for half an hour or more they finally refufed to hear his following Plea and Reafons for an *Arreft of Judgment*, or forbearing their fudden and rafh proceeding to Sentence. They had promifed him before Verdict, they would hear any thing in that kind he had to offer, as they had alfo before his pleading *not guilty*, promifed him Counfel, which never was granted, neither. They drew him on, ftep by ftep, firft, to plead, on his Arraignment-day, then to admit the Juries Verdict on his Tryal-day (fo called, for he never owned it for a Legal Tryal to his laft breath) and after that, out comes the Judgement or Sentence of Death againft him, (pronounced by the Lord Chief Juftice *Forfter*) and that, of the worft complexion and moft in-

famous

famous circumstances, to wit, that he should be hang'd, drawn and quartered, at *Tyburn*, the common Execution-place for Theeves and Robbers.

But in the Order for his Execution, (for reasons best known to them that made it) the manner of his death was altered, into a beheading only, on *Tower-hill* ; to which place they carried him on a Sled, drawn with horses, a circumstance very singular, and never used for those that die there, and which he was kept ignorant of till the very time; one of the Sheriffs men having that morning, a little before, told him, there was to be no Sled, but that he was to walk on foot.

Some farther Remarques of this last dayes Proceedings of the Court with him, besides what is already mentioned, (received from one that was present, and did hear and see all, being what he could best remember) take as followeth.

After the customary formalities of the Court,

The Clerk demanded of Sir *Henry Vane*, what he had to say, why Sentence of Death should not be passed upon him ?

Sir *Henry Vane* first alledged, that he had not yet heard the Indictment read in Latine. The debate upon this, took up some time. At length some of the King's Counsel desired that the Prisoner might be satisfied in that point. Sir *Henry* desired that Counsel then might also be assigned him, to make Exceptions thereto, if they found cause, otherwise he valued not the hearing of it read in Latine : This was over-ruled by the Court ; he soon therefore desisted from any further urging it.

The next thing Sir *Henry* offered in his own defence, was the Bill of Exceptions, which he brought with him ready drawn, and offered it to the Judges, desiring them according to the Statute of *Westminst.2.* 31. made 13. *Ed.* 1. to sign it. This he urged so home, that the Statute was consulted and read in open Court, running in favour of the Prisoner, to this effect, *That if any man find himself aggrieved by the proceedings against him before any Justices, let him write his Exception, and desire the Justices to set their seals to it.* This Act was " made (sayes *Cook*) that the party wronged might have a founda- " tion for a legal Process against the Justices, by a Writ of Error, ha- " ving his Exception entred upon Record in the Court where the in- " jury is done, which through the Justices over-ruling it, they could " not before procure ; so the party grieved was without remedy, for whose

" whofe relief this Statute was made : The Juftices refufing to fet to
" their feals, the party grieved may have a Writ grounded on this
" Statute, commanding them to fet their feals to his Exception. This
" Exception extends not only to all Pleas, dilatory and peremptory &c.
" but to all Challenges of any Jurors, and any material Evidence,
" given to any Jury, which by the Court is over-ruled : As in this
Prifoners Cafe, the Teftimony about falfifying of his hand to writings,
&c. was, by what was offered to the Jury by Juftice *Windham.*

Further, fayes *Cook* on this Statute, " If the Juftice (or Juftices)
" die, their Executors or Adminiftrators may be proceeded againft,
" for the injury done. And if the Judge (or Judges) deny to feal the
" Exception, the party wronged, may in the Writ of Error take Iffue
" thereupon, if he can prove by Witneffes, the Judge or Judges denied
" to feal it.

Notwithftanding all this, the Judges over-ruled this Plea alfo, by
fuch interpretation as themfelves put upon that Statute, to wit, that it
was not allowable in Criminal Cafes for Life. This makes the Law
lefs careful for the prefervation of a man's Life, than any particulars of
his Eftate, in controverfies about which, this Statute is affirmed by them
to hold ; whereas Life is the greater, and innocent Blood when fpilt is
irreverfible, as to the matter, it cannot be gathered up again ; the Eftate
is the leffer, and if an erroneous Judgment pafs about it, 'tis reverfible
upon Traverfe, Writ of Error, or otherwife.

The Reafon they alledged for their pretended Opinion, was this ;
That if it be held in Criminal Cafes for Life, every Felon in *Newgate*
might plead the fame, and fo there would be no Goal-delivery.

Sir *Henry* anfwered, his Cafe was not the Cafe of common Felons,
alledging the Grant of his Majefty to the Petition of both Houfes for
his Life, in cafe he fhould be attainted ; There is no need therefore
fure (faid he) of fearing the confequence of fpinning out the time a little
with a perfon in his circumftances. Befides (he faid) he had been a
Prifoner two years, and never call'd on to give any account of himfelf
and his actions, (fo is it not with Felons) which with other confide-
rations, may fufficiently evince, that there is no need of fuch hafting
his Death. He told them withal, that he defired not this, for his own
fake only, but for theirs, and for pofterity, that they might on a more
leifurely and unprejudiced hearing of what may be faid on all hands,
prevent the bringing of innocent Blood upon themfelves and the Land.

But being in this alfo over-ruled by the Court, (fay what he could)
He only defired, he might underftand whether they would all give it

as their Common Judgment they would ſtand to, That what he deſired was not his due by the Law ? By this means they were all put upon it, one by one, to declare themſelves in that point, unanimouſly denying him the benefit of that Act. To the by-ſtanders their chief Reaſon ſeemed to be, that it had not been practiſed this hundred or two of years.

The third thing Sir *Henry* deſired, was, That the *Petition* of both Houſes, with his Majeſties *Anſwer* thereunto, might be read in the Court, which, after ſome diſpute, was concluded to be a thing they were not bound to take notice of, not being an Act of Parliament. Yet what is any Act of Parliament, but a Bill preſented with the Petition of both Houſes to his Majeſty, with his Royal Aſſent thereto, upon Publick Record ? At length they condeſcended to reade it, and that was all.

The fourth and laſt thing Sir *Henry* offered to the conſideration of of the Bench, was this ; That in regard there were queſtions touching matter of Law, in his Caſe, which muſt receive their determination in Parliament, he deſired he might have Counſel aſſigned him, to argue them before their Lordſhips. Some of theſe points he inſtanced in, to wit,

    1. *Whether a Parliament were accountable to any inferiour Court ?*
    2. *Whether the King, being out of poſſeſſion, and the Power Regent in others*————

Here they ſtopt him, not ſuffering him to proceed, nor admitting that the King was ever out of poſſeſſion. To which Sir *Henry* replied, The words of his Indictment ran thus, *that he endeavoured to keep out his Majeſty* ; and how could he keep him out of the Realm, if he were not out ?

But when he ſaw they would over-rule him in all, and were bent upon his Condemnation, he put up his Papers, appealing to the Righteous Judgment of God, who (he told them) muſt judge them as well as him, often expreſſing his ſatisfaction to die upon this Teſtimony ; which *Keeling*, one of the King's Counſel, inſultingly anſwered, *So you may, Sir, in good time, by the grace of God*. The ſame perſon had often before ſhewed a very ſnappiſh property towards the Priſoner ; and Sir *Henry* ſometimes anſwered him according to his folly : For when he would have had the Book out of the Priſoner's hand, wherein was the Statute of *Weſtminſter* 2ᵈ. 31.

Sir *Henry* told him, *he had a very officious Memory, and when he was of Counſel for him, he would find him Books.* (Whereby was veri-
fied

fied what was said to be spoken by him, at first, in answer to one of his Brethren, on the Arraignment-day, *Though we know not what to say to him, we know what to do with him*)

After Sentence given, **Chief Justice *Forster*** endeavoured to take off the King from any Obligation by that Grant to the Petition of both Houses, saying, *That God, though full of mercy, yet intended his mercy only to the penitent.*

Reasons for an Arrest of Judgment : writ by the Prisoner, but refused to be heard by the Court.

I. I Have been denied so much as to hear the Indictment read in Latine, as it is the Original Record of the Court ; yea, so much as a Copy of it in English hath been denied me, during the whole time of my Tryal, by the sight whereof I might be able to assign the defects of Law that may be in it.

Counsel also hath been denied, not only before I pleaded, but after ; and all points by me offered in Law, to the Judges of the Court, have been over-ruled, without admitting me Counsel to argue the same, and better inform the Judgment of the Court. I have demanded, that I might put in a Bill of Exceptions, upon the Statute of *Westminst*. 2ᵈ. *cap.* 31. This likewise is denied me, over-ruled and judged, as out of that Statute. Neither will Counsel be allowed me in this, to shew cause, why it ought to be admitted as of Right. And as no Counsel was allowed, so neither were the Judges Counsel to me, as they said themselves, they would, and ought to be, but rather suffered me to wrong and prejudice my self, some of them saying, *Let him go on, the worst will be his own at last.* And they neither checked nor restrained the King's Counsel, in their high and irritating expressions to the Jury, to find me guilty, One of whom were seen to speak privately with the Foreman of the Jury, immediately before the Jurors went from the Bar, after he had spoken openly, *That the Prisoner was to be made a publick Sacrifice, in reference to the Actions done against his Majesty that now is.*

All this is very far from that Indifferency in Tryal, and from that Equality which the Law requires, and they are bound by their Oath to afford me ; besides the undue proceedings in the business of the Petty Jury. A List of forty eight persons was presented to me, who being to me unknown, and no time allowed me to gain any knowledge of of them, though I was permitted to challenge and refuse three Juries, without shewing cause, yet could not that refusal be upon such rational grounds as the Law supposes, which doubtless intends substantial relief to the Prisoner, in allowing him the liberty of such refusal: whereas, through my ignorance of the persons, I might refuse the best, and chuse the worst, as to my safety. And then, whereas the Law further allows me the refusal of any other beyond the thirty five, on just and exceptionable cause shewen ; what just exception was I capable to alledge in a sudden hurry, against persons to me altogether unknown, unless it would be taken for a just one, that they were unknown to me?

All these things, being so contrary to the Right which the Judges stand obliged to do to every one, as they are for that purpose entrusted by God and the King, is just cause for an *Arrest of Judgment* ; and a good Reason why they should yet at length allow me a Copy of the Indictment, and assign Counsel to argue for the Prisoner, against the defects in Law that may be found therein. Without this, Law is denied me, which is my Birthright and Inheritance ; the best Birthright the Subject hath, sayes *Cook* on *Mag. Charta,* for thereby (sayes he) his **Goods, Lands,** Wife, Children, his Body, Life, Honour and Estimation are protected from injury. The Life, Birthright or Inheritance we have from our parents, may soon be gone, if this Fence thereof be broken down. How great a wrong then it is for the Court to withhold it from me, is manifest. Are they not therefore in effect, chargeable with my Blood, by such unequal **Proceedings** as I have had in my Tryal ?

I I. My second Reason for an *Arrest of Judgment*, is drawn from the Issue that is joyned in my Case, which seems to depend chiefly upon matter of Law, and that in such tender and high points, as are only determinable in the high Court of Parliament.

For it is become the question, Whether I am guilty, or not guilty, according as these Propositions following, are truly or erroneously resolved ?

1. *Whether the Parliament, that began* Novemb. 3. 1640, *were dissolved by the King's Death ? and whether this Court may judge things done in Parliament ?*

2. *Whether the Powers regnant, and de facto, that successively were in being, from* Jan. 30. 1648, *to* Decemb. 20, 1659, *were such Powers* de facto, *as are the King, or* Seigneur le Roy, *within the purview of the Stat.* 25. Ed. 3. *having the exercise of Regal Power in all the particulars of it, though not the name?*

3. *Whether*

3. *Whether during that time fore-mentioned, his Majesty that now is, were properly King* de facto? *or whether he were not out of possession, and without all exercise of his Regal Authority within the Realm?*

4. *Whether the Case now in question, be a Treason literally within the words of the Statute,* 25. Ed. 3. *or at most, any other, than an interpretative and new Treason, not declared before the very time of my Tryal; and that only by the Judgment of the Court, or opinion of my Judges, eleven years after some of the things charged on me, are alledged to have been committed?*

As to the first of these; The Act for Continuance of the *Long Parliament*, is express; *That all and every thing or things whatsoever, done or to be done, for the Adjournment, Proroguing or Dissolving of that Parliament, contrary to that Act, shall be utterly void and of none effect.* I then thus argue;

The Judges do upon occasion of this Tryal, resolve, That the King's Death dissolv'd that Parliament. No Act of Parliament hath yet declared it to be so; and the Judges ought to have some Law for their guide, as *Cook* well sayes. To be sure, if in process of time, the Parliament shall expresly declare, That not the King's Death, but the Act for the Dissolution of that Parliament, did dissolve it; In such case, these Judges Resolution by vertue of such Act, is absolutely void. But innocent Blood in the mean time may be shed, and an Estate wrongfully taken away. And in case what the Judges assert herein, were Law, 'tis Law not known or declared till many years after the Fact committed. At this rate, who is secure of Estate or Life?

As to the second and third Queries or Propositions; It does appear out of the third part of *Cook's Institutes*, fol. 7. and the Statute, 11. *Hen.* 7. *cap.* 1. That Actings for the King in *Fact*, are not to be questioned by the King in *Right*. If it be said, That there was no King in this case; it may be replied, That they who had the Power and Exercise of the Royal Jurisdiction, as to Peace and War, Coynage of Money, power of Life and Death, &c. which are the highest Ensigns of Regal Authority, must needs be the Powers *regnant*, though not under the name of *King*, and are within the Statute, 25. *Edw.* 3. *cap.* 2. as a *Queen* also is adjudged, and any sovereign Prince, though under the title only of *Lord*, as was the case of *Ireland*, before it was a Kingdom. And if so, why not in more such persons as well as one, that *de facto* exercise the Royal Power and Sovereign Authority, under what name or title soever? It upon this Nicety, Judgment be

given

given against me, because the Powers *regnant* wanted the name and formality of a King, I shall doubtless have very hard measure. For the reason and equity is the same, if the Powers *regnant* had the thing, though not the Title. And where there is the same Reason, there is the same Law, as is a known Rule. Now there is the same Reason the Subject should be equally indempnified, that acteth under any Sovereign Authority that hath not the name of a King, as if it had. If there had been many Kings, as a *Heptarchy* hath been in *England* heretofore, those would have been understood to be within the Statute; and the reason and equity of the Statute is the same in all cases. For the Law is made for the benefit and security of the Subject, whom the Law requires not to examine the right of Soveraignty. Nor is the danger less under one Government than another.

The Statute is, for securing the Subject from all dormant Titles, that they may safely pay their Allegiance when they receive Protection, and that they may not be in danger of being destroyed by two Powers at the same time. For that Power which is supream and *de facto*, will be obeyed, and make it Treason to do otherwise, be it right or wrong. And if the Subject be at the same time in danger of committing Treason against the Power *de jure*, then is he in a miserable condition and state of unavoidable necessity, which is provided against by the Laws of the Land. Otherwise, if he be loyal to the King *de jure*, he shall be hanged by the King *de facto*; and if he be faithful to the King *de facto*, he shall die by the King *de jure*, when he recovers possession.

Against this it was, that the Statute of 11. *Hen.* 7. was provided, in the difference betwixt the two houses of *York* and *Lancaster*. My Case is either the same with that, and then I desire the benefit of that Statute; or else, it is new, and then I desire, as is provided, 25. *Ed.* 3. that it be referred to the Parliament. So that it is either within the Equity of the Statute, 11. *Hen.* 7. or else it is a new Case, and not to be judged by this Court.

If the Judges in the Resolves by them delivered, upon any of the particulars before alledged, have not declared that Law that ought to guide them, but their particular Judgments or Opinions, as undertaking to guide the Law, and that in points of so grand concern as touch the Subjects Life, in case their Judgments after should prove erroneous, the Verdict given upon such Errors, must needs be illegal and void. Judgment therefore ought to be suspended till such time as the truth and certainty of the Law may be fully argued and cleared, and that, in the proper Court for the hearing and judging of this Case. If this be
not

not done, but I be forthwith proceeded against (notwithstanding any thing however rationally or legally alledged to the contrary) by such undue precipitation and giving Sentence, I am (contrary to *Magna Charta*, or Law of the Land) run upon and destroyed, without due form and course of **Law**. And I am like to be deprived of Estate and Life upon no Law or certain Rule, which was declared before the Fact; no, nor before the Tryal.

Upon these Considerations, I desire an *Arrest of Judgment*, **and** that *Counsel* may be assigned me, and competent time allowed **to** make good my *Averrements*.

As an Argument to press this, I desire leave of the Court, That the *Petition* of the two Houses, and the King's *Assent* to it, may be **read** in open Court, attested by one that is present, who examined and compared it with the Book of Record in the Lords House, by which it evidently appears, that as well the King as both Houses of Parlia-ment, were agreed, that admitting I were attainted, yet Execution, as to my Life, should be remitted. And if so, there is no cause to preci-pitate the passing Sentence; especially, when also such weighty points in the Law are yet to be argued and cleared, unless the Judges will evidently charge themselves with my innocent Blood.

III. My third Reason for an *Arrest of Judgment*, is the manifest newness of this Case, being such as never happened before in the King-dom : which withal, is of so vast a consequence to people of all sorts and conditions within this Realm, as nothing more. And being so, (as I doubt not with your Lordships patience I shall make it appear) It is the known Law, witnessed by *Bracton* and antient approved Law-**Books** ; That in such Cases, the Judges in the inferiour Courts ought not to proceed, but bring it before the high Court of **Parliament.**

To prove therefore the newness of this Case, (besides what I have already alledged in my Defence, before the Verdict) give me leave to adde that, which yet further shews the newness and extraordinariness thereof. And I beseech your Lordships to let me go on without in-terruption, in my endeavouring to make it out as clearly, as God shall enable me, and as briefly also, not to spend too much of your time.

In general, I do affirm of this Case ; That it is so comprehensive, as to take in the very Interests of Heaven and Earth : First, Of God the Universal Soveraign and King of Kings ; Secondly, That of earth-ly Soveraigns, who are God's Vicegerents ; as also the Interests of all Mankind, that stand in the relation of Subjects to the one or both those sorts of Soveraigns.

This

This in general. More particularly ; within the bowels of this Cafe is that Caufe of God, that hath ſtated it ſelf in the late Differences and Wars, that have happened and ariſen within theſe three Nations, and have been of more than twenty years continuance : which for the greater certainty and ſolemnity, hath been recorded in the form of a *National Covenant*, in which the generality of the three Nations have been either implicitly involved, or expreſly concern'd, by the ſigning of their Names.

The principal things contained in that Covenant, were the known and commonly received Duties, which either as Men or as Chriſtians, we owed and ſtood obliged to perform either to God, the higheſt and univerſal King in Church and State, or to our natural Lord and Sovereign, the Kings of this Realm, in ſubordination to God and his Laws.

Again, It contains as well the Duties which we owe to every particular and individual perſon, in their ſeveral ſtations and callings, as to the King in general, and our Repreſentative Body in Parliament aſſembled. Theſe Duties we are thereby obliged to yeeld and perform, in conſiſtency with, and in a juſt ſubordination and manifeſt agreeableneſs to, the Laws of God, as is therein expreſſed : And this alſo, in no diſagreement to the Laws of the Land, as they then were.

By this *ſolemn Covenant* and *Agreement* of the three Nations, giving up themſelves in ſubjection to God and to his Laws, in the firſt place, as the Allegiance they owe to their higheſt Soveraign, (as the Creator, Redeemer, Owner and Ruler of all Mankind) they have ſo far intereſted the Son of God in the the Supream Rule and Government of theſe Nations, that nothing therein ought to be brought into practice, contrary to his revealed Will in the holy Scriptures, and his known and moſt righteous Laws.

This Duty which we owe to God, the univerſal King, Nature and Chriſtianity do ſo clearly teach and aſſert, that it needs no more than to be named. For this ſubjection and allegiance to God and his Laws, by a Right ſo indiſputable, all are accountable before the Judgmentſeat of Chriſt.

It is true indeed, men may *de facto* become open Rebels to God and to his Laws, and prove ſuch as forfeit his Protection, and engage him to proceed againſt them as his profeſſed Enemies. But (with your Lordſhips favour) give me leave to ſay, that that which you have made a Rule for your proceedings in my Caſe, will indeed hold, and that very ſtrongly, in this ; that is to ſay, in the ſence wherein Chriſt

the

the Son of God is King *de jure*, not only in general, over the whole World, but in particular, in relation to these three Kingdoms. He ought not to be kept out of his Throne, nor his visible Government, (that consists in the Authority of his Word and Laws) suppressed and trampled under foot, under any pretence whatsoever.

And in the asserting and adhering unto the Right of this highest Soveraign, (as stated in the *Covenant* before mentioned) The Lords and Commons joyntly, before the year 1648, and the Commons alone afterwards, to the very times charged in the Indictment, did manage the War and late Differences within these Kingdoms. And whatever defections did happen by Apostates, Hypocrites, and Time-serving worldlings, there was a party amongst them, that continued firm, sincere and chast unto the last, and loved it better than their very lives ; of which number I am not ashamed to profess my self to be; not so much admiring the form and words of the Covenant, as the righteous and holy ends therein expressed, and the true sense and meaning thereof, which I have reason to know.

Nor will I deny, but that, as to the manner of the prosecution of the Covenant to other ends than it self warrants, and with a rigid oppressive spirit, (to bring all dissenting minds and tender Consciences under one Uniformity of Church-discipline and government) it was utterly against my Judgment. For I always esteemed it more agreeable to the Word of God, that the Ends and Work declared in the Covenant, should be promoted in a spirit of love and forbearance to differing Judgments and Consciences, that thereby we might be approving our selves *in doing that to others, which we desire they would do to us* ; and so, (though upon different principles) be found joynt and faithful advancers of the Reformation contained in the Covenant, both publick and personal.

This happy Union and Conjunction of all Interests in the respective duties of all relations, agreed and consented to by the common suffrage of the three Nations (as well in their publick Parliamentary capacity, as private stations) appeared to me a Rule and measure approved of, and commanded by Parliament, for my action and deportment, though it met with great opposition, in a tedious, sad and long **War** ; and this, under the name and pretext of Royal Authority.   Yet, as this Case appeared to me in my conscience, under all its circumstances of Times, of Persons, and of Revolutions inevitably happening, by the hand of God and the course of his wise Providences, I held it safest and best to keep my station in Parliament to the last, under the guidance

and

and protection of their Authority, and in pursuance of the Ends before declared, in my just Defence.

This general and publick Case of the Kingdoms, is so well known by the Declarations and Actions that have passed on both sides, that I need but name it, since this matter was not done in a corner, but frequently contended for in the high places of the Field, and written even with characters of Blood. And out of the bowels of these Publick Differences and Disputes, doth my particular Case arise, for which I am called into question. But admitting it come to my lot to stand single, in the witness I am to give to this Glorious Cause, and to be left alone, (as in a sort I am) yet being upheld with the Authority before asserted, and keeping my self in union and conjunction therewith, I am not afraid to bear my Witness to it in this great Presence, nor to seal it with my Blood, if called thereunto. And I am so far satisfied in my conscience and understanding, that it neither is nor can be Treason, either against the Law of Nature, or the Law of the Land, either *malum per se*, or *malum prohibitum*; that on the contrary, it is the duty I owed to God the universal King, and to his Majesty that now is, and to the Church and People of God in these Nations, and to the innocent Blood of all that have been slain in this Quarrel. Nothing it seems will now serve, unless by the Condemnation passed upon my person, they be rendred to posterity Murderers and Rebels, and that upon Record in a Court of Justice in *Westminster-hall*. And this would inevitably have followed, if I had voluntarily given up this Cause, without asserting their and my Innocency, by which I should have pulled that Blood upon my own head, which now I am sure must lie at the door of others, and in particular, of those that knowingly and precipitately shall embrew their hands in my innocent Blood, under whatever form or pretext of Justice.

My Case is evidently new and unusual, that which never happened before; wherein there is, not only much of God and of his Glory, but all that is dear and of true value to all the good People in these three Nations. And (as I have said) it cannot be Treason against the Law of Nature, since the duties of the Subjects in relation to their Soveraigns and Superiours, from highest to lowest, are owned and conscientiously practised and yeelded by those that are the Assertors of this Cause.

Nor can it be Treason within the Statute of 25. *Ed.* 3.; since, besides what hath been said of no King in possession, and of being under Powers *regnant* & Kings *de facto*, as also of the Fact in its own nature,

and

and the Evidence as to Overt Acts pretended, it is very plain it cannot possibly fall within the purview of that Statute. For this Case, thus circumstantiated, (as before declared) is no Act of any private person, of his own head, as that Statute intends; nor in relation to the King there meant, that is presumed to be in the exercise of his Royal Authority in conjunction with the Law and the two Houses of Parliament, if they be sitting, as the fundamental Constitutions of the Government do require.

My Lords, If I have been free and plain with you in this matter, I beg your Pardon : For it concerns me to be so, and something more than ordinarily urgent, where both my Estate and Life are in such eminent peril ; nay, more than my Life, the Concerns of thousands of Lives are in it, not only of those that **are** in their graves already, **but of all** posterity in time to come. Had nothing been in it, but the care to preserve my own Life, I needed not have stayed in *England*, but might have taken my opportunity to have withdrawn my self into forreign parts, to provide for my own safety. Nor needed I to **have been** put upon pleading, as now I am, for an *Arrest of Judgment*, **but** might have watch'd upon advantages that were visible enough to me, in the managing of my Tryal, if I had consulted only the preservation of my Life or Estate.

No, my Lords, I have otherwise learned Christ, than to fear them that can but kill the Body, and have no more that they can do. I have also taken notice, in the little reading that I have had of History, how glorious the very Heathens have rendred their names to posterity, in the contempt they have shewed of Death, (when the laying down of their Life has appeared to be their Duty) from the love which they have owed to their Country.

Two remarkable examples of this, give me leave to mention to you upon this occasion. The one is, of *Socrates* the divine Philosopher, who was brought into question before a Judgment-Seat, as now I am, for maintaining, that there was but one onely true God, against the multiplicity of the superstitious Heathen gods ; and he was so little in love with his own Life upon this account, (wherein he knew the Right was on his side) that he could not be perswaded by his friends, to make any defence, but would chuse rather to put it upon the conscience and determination of his Judges, to decide that wherein he knew not how to make any choice of his own, as to what would be best for him, whether to live or to die; he ingenuously professing, that for ought he knew, it might be much to his prejudice and loss, to endeavour longer continuance in this bodily Life. The

The other example, is that of a chief Governour, that (to my best remembrance) had the Command of a City in *Greece*, which was besieged by a potent Enemy, and brought into unimaginable straits. Hereupon the said Governor makes his address to the Oracle, to know the event of that danger. The answer was ; That the City should be safely preserved, if the chief Governour were slain by the Enemy. He, understanding this, immediately disguis'd himself and went into the Enemies Camp, amongst whom he did so comport himself, that they unwittingly put him to death ; by which means, immediately safety and deliverance arose to the City, as the Oracle had declared. So little was his Life in esteem with him, when the Good and Safety of his Country required the laying of it down.

The *BILL* of *EXCEPTIONS*, translated out of the best Latine form the Prisoner could procure, No Counsel learned in the Law daring to assist him in those Circumstances, without Assignment from the Court, **which was** denied.

First, *Concerning my Imprisonment.*

(1.) I Shall here mention my entrance into this new Scene of Sufferings, under the present Power, (after my having been handled at will and pleasure, under the six years Usurpation of *Cromwel*) which I conceive not to have been at all according to the Law of the Land, as may appear by the 29th chap. of *Magna Charta*, and *Cook* upon it, with many other Statutes and Law-Books : In all which it appears, that the Law of *England* is so tender, not to say curious, in providing for the Subjects Liberty, that he is not to suffer the least restraint, confinement or imprisonment, but by the lawfull Judgment of his Peers, or by the Law of the Land : Contrary to all which, I was committed at meer Will and **Pleasure, and** have been detained close Prisoner these two years, without any cause specified, or any particular crime laid to my charge.

Secondly, *Concerning Transactions at the* **Grand** *Jury.*

(2.) The Grand Jury of *Middlesex*, without my privity, knowledge or presence, (after I had been kept a close Prisoner two full years) did meet, take the Depositions of Witnesses, and find the Bill against me, which inevitably exposed me to a Tryal at the Kings Bench
Bar,

Bar, for I knew not what; whereas Major *Rolph* and others have
had the Right of Englishmen granted them, to be present at the **Grand
Juries** proceedings; yea, and to have Counsel also present, to plead
any thing in a way of Reason or Law, for invalidating the Testimony
or disabling the Witnesses, whereby the Indictment hath been immediately quash'd, and so, the party accused, delivered from any shadow
of Infamy, by so much as appearing in the circumstances of a Malefactor at any publick Bar of Justice.

That this Prisoner had great need of that Priviledge, of being present
himself, or having Counsel and other Friends present **at the** Grand
Jury, will appear hereafter, by the subdolous and injurious handling
of matters there.

Thirdly, *Concerning the Jurisdiction of the Court.*

(3.) The Offences supposed **to be committed** by me, **are things**
done not of my own head, but as a Member of the *Long Parliament*,
or in pursuance of their Authority. The matters done by me, in the
one respect or the other, if they be deemed Offences, are punishable
only in Parliament, and I ought not to be questioned for them in any
inferiour Court; As *Cook* shews in the 4th part of his *Institutes*, chap.
1. concerning the high Court of Parliament. For the Parliament is
not confined in their Actings, by the Law which inferiour Courts are
tied up to, but in divers cases are priviledged to act extraordinarily
and unaccountably to any but themselves, or succeeding Parliaments.
Moreover, That Parliament was extraordinarily commissioned, qualified and authorized by express Act of Parliament, beyond all prece-
ding Parliaments, for the Causes and Ends declared in the Preamble of
the Act for their Establishment, accorded and passed by the joynt
Consent of King, Lords and Commons, whereby they became un-
subjected to Adjournment, Prorogation or Dissolution, but by their
own respective voluntary Consents, to be by them expressed and passed for that purpose, with the Royal Assent; which occasioned his late
Majesty in his *Answer* to the *nineteen Propositions*, to say, *That the
Power hereby legally placed in both Houses, was more than sufficient
to prevent and restrain the Power of Tyranny.*

And further, The bringing of this Case under the Jurisdiction of this
Court, or of any other, but a Parliament, may prove of very dangerous
consequence, in point of Precedent, and most disagreeing to all Rules
of Justice. For,

First, By the same reason that I am questioned in this Court, not

only

only every Member of Parliament, but the very Houses themselves, with all their Debates, Votes and Orders, may not only be questioned, but referred to a Petty Jury, and so come to be judged and sentenc'd by a Court inferiour to themselves, which Judges in all times have disclaimed and acknowledged to be out of their power, according to the known Rule, *Par in pares non habet imperium, multo minus in eos, qui majus imperium habent.*

Secondly, In such case, the Parties accused, will be debarred of Evidence or Witness for their Justification and Defence. For no Members, &c. present at Debates in Parliament, (who are the onely eye and ear-witnesses of what is said and done there) ought to discover the Counsels of the House.

Fourthly, *Concerning the Indictment.*

1. I have not been permitted to have a copy or sight of the Indictment, nor so much as to hear it read in Latine, which is the original Record of the Court, and ought to be the foundation of their whole proceeding with me. I often desired these things of the Court ; yea, or at least, to have but the Transcripts of some particular clauses in the Indictment, to enable me to shew the deficiencies thereof in Law, (all which, others in such cases have often obtained) but nothing would be granted herein.

This then was my hard lot and usage ; I was put (after two years close Imprisonment) to answer for my Life, to a long Indictment, read in English, which whether it were rightly translated how should I know, that might not hear the Original Record in Latine ? Counsel also learned in the Law, were denied me, though pressed for by me, again and again, before I pleaded. And had they been granted, what could they have said as to defects of Law in the Indictment, unless they might have a Copy of it ? What can any Counsel say to any petty business concerning any part of a man's Estate that's in controversie, unless they may have a leisurely view and perusal of the Writings thereabouts ? much more sure will it appear requisit, to the reason of all mankind, when a man's whole Estate, Life and all are at stake. 'Tis true, before I pleaded, this Court promised I should have Counsel assigned me after pleading, (*God forfend else,* said the Lord Chief Justice) but 'tis as true, I never could yet see that promise made good. All things tending to a fair Tryal, were promised me in general before pleading, but every material particular for the just defence of my Life, hath been

denied

denied me ever since. And my Tryal for Life was hudled up the next day of my appearing before you; The Jury (as was told me) must not eat or drink, till they had done their work; (so the more than forty *Jewry-men* that resolved to kill *Paul*, Act. 23. 21.) But why such haste and precipitancy for a man's Life, that's more than Meat or Estate, when you can let Civil Causes about mens Estates depend many years? and if an erroneous Judgment be passed in such matters, 'tis reversible; But if innocent Blood be spilt, it cannot be gathered up again, as the wise woman of *Tekoah* said, 2 *Sam.* 14.

2. But secondly then, As to defects in the Indictment, which I was in some measure enabled to observe from that broken hearing thereof, that was afforded me here in the Court; I say, there are many, and those very confiderable; and by the Law of *England* I ought not to have been urged to plead or make answer to such an illegal and defective Indictment.

1. There is no sufficient Overt Act therein alledged, of the Prisoner's imagining the King's Death, or that he had any the least intention that way.

2. The Levying of a War, is alledged in *Southwark*, and cannot therefore be tryed by a Jury of *Middlesex*; *Dyer*, fol. 234. and the 3d part of *Cook's Institutes*, fol. 34.

3. There is uncertainty and obscurity in the main thing alledged against me in the Indictment; to wit, *That I, together with a multitude of persons, to the number of a thousand, unknown to the Jury, &c.* whereas no Criminal Act can be tryed that is not certain; *Certa res debet esse qua deducitur in Judicium.*

4. The Treason laid to my charge, is alledged to have been committed with a multitude of other false Traitors, which were pardoned by the Act of Indempnity; such supposed crimes therefore of theirs cannot be remembred or alledged, without a manifest breach of the Act of Indempnity and Oblivion.

The Indictment is, or ought to be founded on some clause or branch of 25. *Ed.* 3. chap. 2. But no such Overt Act is alledged in the Indictment, or proved by Witnesses, as doth discover that I had any intention to kill, depose or hold out the King from the possession and exercise of his Regal Power.

Whereas I am accused of *compassing or imagining the Death of the King*; this must be understood of his natural or personal, not politick capacity; for in this latter sence, the Law sayes, *the King cannot die.*

First then, to compass only the Deposition of the King, is not within

the

the words of that Statute, (several Kings have been depofed by Parliaments fince the Conqueft) and as to my compaffing or defigning the natural death of the King's Perfon, with what colour can I be accufed of fuch intentions, in the circumftances the King at that time was in beyond the Seas?

Secondly, The affembling of men together, without any hoftility or injury offered to any perfon, but for a man's own fecurity and defence, in a time of confufion and diftraction, is not Levying War, or Treafon at the Common Law, or by that Statute. Yea, in this Cafe, and at the feafon wherein fuch an Act as this is alledged, it might be fuppofed to be done for the King's Reftoration as well as in oppofition thereunto ; and the moft favourable and advantagious conftruction ought to be made and put upon the Prifoner's actings or words, where there is ambiguity, fo that they may be taken or interpreted divers wayes. For the Law alwayes prefumeth actions to be innocent, till the contrary be manifeftly proved. However, in a time of vacancy or an *Interregnum*, when the Foundations of Government are out of courfe, by the Law of Reafon, Nature, and Common Prudence, every man may ftand upon his own guard, endeavouring his own fecurity and protection from injury and violence.

Thirdly, To be adherent to the King's Enemies within his Realm, &c. cannot, ought not to be underftood of any adhæfion to a Parliament, wherein the King by Law is fuppofed alwayes prefent, as a part thereof. Nor can the *Long Parliament* be called the King's Enemies, without overthrowing the Act of Indemnity, which the King hath declared to be the Foundation of the Nations prefent Peace and Security.

Laftly, The Treafons alledged in the Indictment, are faid to have been committed when the King was out of poffeffion ; So the Indictments runs, *to keep out the King*, &c. Now my Lord *Cook* in the third part of his *Inftitutes*, fol. 7. faith, *A King* de jure, *and not de facto, is not within this Statute ; Againft fuch a one no Treafon can be committed. For if there be a King* regnant *in poffeffion, though he be* Rex de facto, *and not de jure, yet is he* Seignior le Roy, *within the purview of this Statute ; and the other that hath Right, and is out of poffeffion, is not within this Act. Nay, if Treafon be committed againft a King* de facto, *&* non de jure, *and after the King* de jure *cometh to the Crown, he fhall punifh the Treafon done to the King* de facto.

And after, In the fame place he faith, *That by Law there is alwayes*

a

a King, in whose Name the Laws are to be maintained and executed ; otherwayes Justice would fail. The Act also of 11. *Hen.* 7. was made for security of the Subject on this behalf. The word *King* also may and ought to be taken largely for any Sovereign Power, in a King or Queen, as *Cook* in the place fore-quoted, shews ; and why not by the same reason, in a *Protector*, though a Usurper, or any other persons, one or more, in whom Soveraignty is lodged, or that have all the badges of Soveraignty, as the calling of Parliaments, enacting of Laws, coining of Money, receiving Forreign Ambassadors, &c. ? His Majesty that now is, is granted by the very Indictment to have been then out of possession : If so, then was there either some other King, or what was equivolent, some Sovereign Power in actual possession and exercise, or none. If the former, then was there a King *de facto*, so no Treason could be committed against him that was King *de jure* only : If the latter, then the Government was dissolved, no allegiance was due to any persons, and so no offence could be properly Treason, within the Statute.

But had the late *Protector* had the name and stile of a King, no Treason could have been committed against the King *de jure* only. Now God forbid that you should give away my Life upon such niceties, because a usurping Protector was not clothed with the Title as well as Power of a King. The Protector or any Usurper's taking or not taking the Title of a King, in case he have the Power, cannot alter the state of my supposed crime. You ought not to be byassed by popular Reports concerning me. 'Tis easier to be innocent, than so reported. The one is in our own power, not the other.

Fifthly, *Concerning the Evidence.*

1. No allegation was directly proved by two positive lawful Witnesses, as in this case it ought to be.

2. One of the Witnesses for the King, confessed in open Court, that to his knowledge my hand had been counterfeited, to my prejudice and dammage, in great Sums of Money ; yet Orders pretended to be signed by me, (wherein my hand may as well be counterfeited) are taken as Evidence against me.

3. The Issue of the whole Cause depended on the solution of some difficult Questions, of so high a nature and great importance, as could not safely be determined but in the high Court of Parliament ; As,

1. *Whether the Long Parliament, called in* Novemb. 1640, *were dissolved by the late King's Death ?* 2. *Whether*

2. Whether the *successive remaining Powers, that exercised the Royal or Supream Authority from 1648, to the Restoration of his now Majesty, were not within the true sense and meaning of* 25. Edw. 3. *and* 11. Hen. 7 ?

As to other pertinent Queries, thou mayest see them, Reader, in other parts of this Tryal.

That which remains, as an *Appendix to this Bill of Exceptions,* is to lay before thee the Grounds which plainly shew that there was a downright Conspiracy in Sir *Henry Vane's* Tenants and others, to prosecute him for Life and Estate, under colour and pretence of Justice.

1. Presently after I was committed to the *Tower* for High Treason, and made a Close-Prisoner, Mr. *Oneale,* Sir *William Darcy* and Dr. *Cradock* obtained an Order from the King, to seize and take into their possession, all the Estates of such persons, that were already or should be forfeited to his Majesty.

Hereupon the said Mr. *Oneale* and Sir *Will.* Darcy appointed some under them, in the Bishoprick of *Durham,* (by name, *Thomas Bowes* Esq; now deceased, and Capt. *William 'Darcy*) to joyn with the said Dr. *Cradock,* to put in execution the said Warrant, as their Deputies, who thereupon went to *Raby Castle,* and demanded the Rent-Books of *Thomas Mowbray* my Steward, offering him his place under them, which he refused.

Contrary to this proceeding, Sir *Edward Cook* expresly declares, " That before Indictment, the Goods or other things of any Offender, " cannot be searched, inventoried, or in any sort seized ; nor after In- " dictment, seized, removed, or taken away, before Conviction or At- " tainder, *Institut.* 3d part, chap. 133. concerning the Seizure of Goods, &c. for Offences, &c. before Conviction.

2. At the Instance and Prosecution of my Tenants and others, an Order was made by the House of Commons (not of the Lords) requiring the Tenants of such persons as were excepted out of the *General Pardon,* to detain their Rents in their own hands. By pretence of this Order, (though that Parliament that made it, were dissolved) The Tenants refused to pay their respective Rents, as they grew due, contrary to all Law and Equity ; and joyned together in open defiance and conspiracy against their Landlord.

3. The said Tenants, (when legally prosecuted in his Majesties Courts at *Westminster,* for the recovery of the said Rents out of their

hands)

hands) did petition the late House of Commons to put a stop to such legal Prosecution and Suits ; which Motion of theirs, put the House into a great heat and violence against me, insomuch that they had almost passed a Vote to sequester all my Estate, though unheard or unconvicted.

4. *William Watson* of *Cock-field*, and other of the said Tenants, have continued in *London* to carry on this Conspiracy against me, by whose means, with others, the King hath been importuned to send for men from the Isle of *Silly*, in order to this Tryal.

5. By common fame (which, at least, affords a strong presumption) my Goods and Estate have been long begg'd by several persons, and granted : whereas the begging of the Goods and Estate of any Delinquent, accused or indicted of Treason, before he be Convicted and Attainted, is utterly unlawful ; because till then, nothing is forfeited to the King, and so, not his to dispose of ; as Sir *Edward Cook* shews, in the fore-mentioned Chapter about the Seizure of Goods, &c.

6. I am credibly informed, that about *December* last, a certain Captain came from the Duke of *Albemarle*, to Capt. *Linn*, with threatning language, that if he would not confess things against Sir *Henry Vane*, he should be fetch'd up before the Council and made to do it. *Linn* answered, he knew nothing against Sir *Henry Vane*, nor had any Orders from him, but from the Parliament and Council.

The same Captain came again, about a fortnight after, from the Duke of *Albemarle*, with a parcel of fine words, that if he the said *Linn* would testifie, that Sir *Henry Vane* was in the head of his Regiment, and that he received Orders from him, the Duke of *Albemarle* would gratifie him with any civility he should desire. *Linn* replied, he knew no Regiment Sir *Henry Vane* had, but that it was the Parliaments and Council of States Regiment. The same Captain came again to him, from the Duke of *Albemarle*, and told him, The Duke desired him to testifie Sir *Henry Vane*'s being in the head of his Regiment, and that he received Orders from him, to fight Sir *George Booth*; *Linn* replied, he knew no such things. The Captain told him, as from the Duke, he should have any Place or Office in the Court. Be not afraid to speak, said he, I warrant you, we shall hang Sir *Henry Vane*, for he is a Rogue.

7. I am credibly informed, that one of the Grand Jury declared, that after the Bill of Indictment against me, was brought in, some from the King's Counsel came to desire them, they would please to come into the inward Court of Wards ; Upon which, one of the Jury said,

they

they were there to judge of matters brought before them, and ought not to go in thither; but if the Counsel had any thing to say, they ought to come to them. This was seconded by some; others said, They were the King's Counsel, and it was but matter of civility to grant them their Request: whereupon they went into the inward Court of Wards, where the King's Counsel were, to wit, Attorney-General *Palmer*, Sollicitor-General *Fynch*, Serjeant *Glyn* and Serjeant *Keeling*. After a while, they caused all to withdraw but the Jury. Then the Clerk read the Indictment in the usual form for Levying War from 1659. After it was read, one of the Counsel told them, It was a Bill of High Treason against his Majesty, and they were to consider of it according to their Evidence. Then they proceeded to examine their Witnesses.

Jefford said, Sir *Henry Vane* offered him a Commission to go against Sir *George Booth*; which, said Serjeant *Keeling*, was to go against the King.

Wright, being examined whether he saw Sir *Henry Vane* in the Council, said, *Yes*. The Attorney-General replied, that if he was amongst them, they might find the Bill upon that.

Upon this, the Jury withdrew, and were by themselves. Then Sir *John Croply*, the Foreman, said, *We must pass this Bill*; at which all the Jury were silent. At last, one stood up and said; *This Bill contains matter of Fact, and matter of Law. Some of this Jury, to my knowledge, were never of any Jury before, as well as I, therefore ignorant of the Law, (in so difficult and unusual a point as this is) and consequently could not give in their Verdict, as to Law, but only Fact.* Several others of the Jury seconded him in this, and protested against giving in their Verdict, as to matter of Law; notwithstanding all which, the Bill was carried up to the King's Bench.

8. On the day of my Arraignment, an eminent person was heard to say, I had forfeited my head, by what I said that day, before ever I came to my Defence: what that should be, I know not, except my saying in open Court, *Soveraign Power of Parliament*, which the Attorney-General writ down, after he had promised at my request, no exception should be taken at words. And whole Volumns of Lawyers Books pass up and down the Nation with that Title, *Soveraign Power of Parliaments*.

9. Six moderate men, that were like to consider what they did, before they would throw away my Life, were summoned to be of my Petty Jury, which the King's Counsel hearing, writ a Letter to one
of

of the Sheriffs, to unsummon them; and a new List was made, the night immediately before the day of Verdict, on purpose that the Prisoner might not have any knowledge of them, till presented to his view and choice in *Westminster-hall.* Yet one of the fourty eight of this List, (who said he would have starv'd himself before he would have found Sir *Hen. Vane* guilty of Treason) was never called, though he walked in the Hall all the while. And in that Hurry of those that compassed him about, he being alone, stripp'd of all assistance, Sir *William Roberts* Foreman, and Sir *Christopher Abdy,* were sworn by the Court before I was aware; so my challenging them, might seem a personal disobliging and exasperation of them against me, after they were sworn and fixed.

The Sollicitor also had a long whisper with the Foreman of the Jury, in the Court, before they went to Verdict, telling him, *The Prisoner must be a Sacrifice for the Nation, &c.*

Suddenly after which I am here called to receive my Sentence.

10. After the day of my Tryal, the Judges went to *Hampton-Court.*

11. None were more forward to absolve the King from his Grant about my Life, than they that had appeared most forward in promoting the Bill by way of Petition to the King, for it. This Grant, being upon Record, may seem to have the same validity that other Acts of Parliament have, which are still but the two Houses Petition to the King for his Assent to the Bills by them drawn up and passed. They used this, as a means to induce the King to exempt me from all benefit of the Act of Indempnity and Oblivion, and then at last perswade and absolve him from making good this Grant also, thereby depriving me of all visible relief for my Life. I conceived my Life as secure by that Grant, as others Lives or Estates are by the Act of Indempnity it self; for what is that, but the Bill of both Houses, with the King's Assent to it, upon their Petition?

The *PETITION* of both Houses of Parliament to the King's most excellent Majesty, on the behalf of Sir *Henry Vane,* and Col. *John Lambert,* after they left them uncapable of having any benefit of the Act of Indempnity.

To

To the King's most Excellent Majesty.

The humble Petition of the *Lords* and *Commons* assembled
in PARLIAMENT.

Sheweth,

THat Your Majesty having declared your gracious pleasure to proceed only against the immediate Murderers of your Royal Father:
We your Majesties most humble Subjects, the Lords and Commons assembled, not finding Sir Henry Vane nor Col. Lambert to be of that
number,

Are humble Suiters to Your Majesty, that if they shall be Attainted, that Execution, as to their Lives, may be remitted ;

And as in duty bound, &c.

The said *Petition* being read, it was agreed to, and ordered to be
presented to his Majesty by the Lord Chancellor.

The Lord Chancellor reported, That he had presented the Petition
of both Houses, to the King's Majesty, concerning Sir *Henry Vane*
and Col. *Lambert*, and his Majesty grants the Desires in the said Petition.

John Browne, Cler. Parliamentorum.

Concerning the Proceedings of the Court.

1. THe Judges denied Counsel to the Prisoner, on this pretext, that
they (as they were to be) would be his Counsel. They are
the King's Commissary Judges, preferred and paid for their work by
the King, who (in this case) was, through evil and false suggestions,
rendred the Prisoners chief or only Adversary, whose Death he stood
accused of imagining and compassing. What Counsel or Assistance
the Prisoner was like to have from them, let the World judge.

2. His Jury consisted of persons that had been engaged against him,
in that very Controversie and Cause for which he was tryed. A For-
reigner, in any Criminal Case amongst us, may require six of his Jurors
to be of his own Countrymen ; a French-man, six French-men ; a
Dutch-man, six Dutch-men ; &c. There was but one here (that was
suspected only to have something of an English man in him) sworn of
the Jury ; and the Lord Chief Justice sharply rebuked the Clerk of
the

the Court, alledging, that he knew not but he might have brought bread and cheese in his pocket, and would keep them all night, with other words to like purpose.

3. The Prisoner was not suffered to speak a word to the Jury, after the King's Counsel had spoken, to take off the aggravating glosses they had put upon his pretended crime : and the Judges, (that said they would be the Prisoner's Counsel) dismissed the Jury, possessed with the last exasperating charge, given by those, who were both the Accusers and professed Counsel against him.

4. The Prisoner, on his Sentence-day, challenged the Sollicitor before the Court, as to the injury done him on the day of his Tryal, by his large and bitter Invective, which he had not liberty to reply to, (for the vindicating of his own Innocency, and unprejudicing the Juries understanding) in the fittest season.

The Judges that had promised him (before pleading) they would be his Counsel (instead of relieving him herein, as in all reason they ought) afforded him no other answer, but a sharp Rebuke, for criminating and scandalizing the Court, together with some threatning expressions. But what need had he to regard their threatnings, that he saw resolved to pass a Sentence of Death upon him, say what he would ?

The main thing he charged the Sollicitor with, was his saying openly in Court, *that he must be made a publick Sacrifice,* (shewing no reason why) and of whispering to the Foreman of the Jury, in the Court, before they went to Verdict ; a thing notoriously against all Law and Reason. Amongst other things, he had also said, *What Counsel did the Prisoner think would (or durst) speak for him, in such a manifest Case of Treason, unless he could call down the heads of those his fellow-Traitors* (Bradshaw or Cook) *from the top of Westminster-Hall ?* (or to that effect) when as there were able heads in the bottom of *Westminster-hall,* ready to have spoken to his Case; if they might have been assigned by the Court. But what may not be said, when nothing may be replied ? For a person, that is designing his own Interest, Honours, Advantages and Preferments, to have the last word to the Jury, against a Prisoner that stands at the Bar in danger of his Life, (and that, a person of so generally acknowledged worth and publick concern) and to perform it with impertinent flashes of Wit, and declamatory flourishes of Rhetorick, (sending away the Jury with the fresh and last impressions of all that noise and buzze of his glosses upon the whole matter, and having with irritating expressi-

ons

ons mifreprefented and aggravated the fuppofed crimes)is a thing to be hiffed oft the ftage of this earth, by the common Reafon of all mankind.

What worfe circumftances can a Prifoner be in, than to ftand at a Bar of Juftice to be tryed, and there hear his profeffed Accufer and Adverfary, mifreprefenting, mifcalling, and aggravating the actions he is queftioned for, preffing all upon the Jurors confciences with the greateft edge and flourifh of all the Art, Wit and Eloquence he is furnifhed with (as *Tertullus* ferved *Paul*) and then be deprived of all poffible defence againft his flanderous and injurious fuggeftions ? *Paul* was not fo ferved ; he had the laft word to his Jury, when *Tertullus* had done, *Acts* 24. But the children of this world are wife in their generation ; they knew well they had to deal with one, that had been experienced for twenty years together, to be a perfon of a very happy and unparallel'd dexterity in taking oft the paint and falfe appearances that others (by premeditated Speeches) could put upon ill matters, with an extemporary breath.

If it be faid, he had fair warning beforehand, to fay all that he had to mind the Jury of, and that he was not to fpeak after the King's Counfel. It is anfwered ; Though this were hard at beft, and indeed, not at all futable to the true and lawfull Liberties of Englifh-men, yet were it more tolerable, in cafe the King's Counfel had ftarted no new thing againft the Prifoner, ufed no provoking and unworthy expreffions, or made no new and unforefeen gloffes upon the matter he ftood charged with. For then the Prifoner might be prefumed to have fufficiently obviated beforehand, any thing that would be faid by the Counfel, (had they only recapitulated) and fo (probably) might have rendred his Jury fomewhat uncapable of being prejudiced thereby againft him, unlefs they were as willing to abufe him as the Counfel. But here were many things faid at random, againft all Senfe, Law and Reafon, (as if *Tully* had been characftering a treacherous *Catiline*) and the innocent Prifoner muft be mute, and fuffer the Jury to be difmiffed, and fent to pafs their Verdict on his Life, without the leaft poffibility of Remedy.

Put this and all the reft together, (to wit, that the Jury themfelves were of the oppofit party to him in the late Wars and whole Caufe in queftion, depending before them) and it had been far better for the Prifoner, to have caft lots on a Drum-head for his Life, as a Prifoner of War, than to be fo tryed in a time of Peace, unlefs it can be reafonably prefumed, that they that would have killed him any time this twenty year in the field, fhould now be like to fpare his Life at the Bar.

Occa-

Occasional Speeches before his Tryal.

HE said, there was something in this Cause, that could never be conquered, and that he blessed the Lord, it had never been betrayed by him, or conquered in him. And before this, in a Letter from *Silly* to a Friend, he said, *God's Arm is not shortned : doubtless great and precious Promises are yet in store to be accomplished, in and upon Believers here on Earth, to the making of Christ admired in them. And if we cannot live in the power and actual fruition of them, yet if we die in the certain foresight and imbracing of them by Faith, it will be our great blessing. This dark night and black shade, which God hath drawn over his work in the midst of us, may be (for ought we know) the ground-colour to some beautiful Piece, that he is now exposing to the light.*

When he came from his Tryal, he told a Friend, *he was as much overjoyed, as a chast Virgin that had escaped a Rape : for,* said he, *neither flatteries before, nor threatnings now, could prevail upon me ; and I bless God, that enabled me to make a stand for this Cause ; for I saw the Court resolved to run it down, and (through the assistance of God) I resolved they should run over my Life and Blood first.*

June 13. being Friday, the day before his Execution.

On this day, liberty being given to Friends to visit him in the *Tower*, he received them with very great chearfulness, and with a composed frame of spirit, having wholly given up himself to the will of God. He did occasionally let fall many gracious expressions, to the very great refreshing, and strengthning of the hearts of the hearers. To wit, *That he had for any time these two years made Death familiar to him, and being shut up from the World,* he said, *he had been shut up with God, and that he did know what was the mind of God to him in this great matter ; but, that he had not the least recoyl in his heart, as to matter or manner of what was done by him ; And though he might have had an opportunity of escaping, or by policy might have avoided his Charge, yet he did not make use of it, nor could decline that which was come upon him.*

It being told him by a Friend, that his Death would be a loss to the People of God : He answered, *that God would raise up other Instruments to serve him and his People.* And being desired to say something,

thing, to take off that charge of *Jesuitism*, that was cast upon him ; He said, *That he thought it not worth the taking notice of ; for if it were so, he should never have been brought to this.* A Friend said, Sir, the Lord hath said, *Be thou faithful unto Death, and I will give thee a Crown of Life.* The Lord enable you to be faithful. He replied, *I bless the Lord, I have not had any discomposure of spirit these two years, but I do wait upon the Lord, till he be pleased to put an end to these dayes of mine, knowing that I shall change for the better : For in Heaven there is an innumerable company of Angels, the Spirits of Just men made perfect, and JESUS the blessed Mediator of the New Covenant. There are holy and just Laws, a pure Government, blessed and good Company, every one doing their duty ; herr we want all these. This is that City spoken of,* Psal. 48. 1, 2. *That strong City,* **that cannot be moved,** Isa. 26. *Why therefore should we be unwilling to leave this estate to go to that ?* And although *I be taken from hence, yet know assuredly, God will raise up unto you Instruments out of the dust.* Another said to him ; Sir, There is nothing will stand you in stead, but justifying Faith in the Blood of Jesus. To which he said, *There are some, that through Faith in the Blood of* Christ, *do escape the pollutions of the world, yet afterwards are entangled therein again ; others there* be, *that are carried through the greatest sufferings, by a more excellent, spiritual sort of* **Faith** *in the Blood of* Jesus, *and endure them with the greatest joy.*

. He further said, We were lately preaching a Funeral Sermon to our selves, **out** of *Heb.* 11. 13, 16. where those blessed Witnesses do declare themselves to be pilgrims and strangers on the Earth, and do desire a better Country, that is, a heavenly ; *Wherefore God is not ashamed to be called their God, for he hath prepared for them a City.* And if God (said he) be not ashamed to be called my God, I hope I shall not be ashamed to endure his Cross, and to bear his Reproach, even whatsoever it be that man can impose upon me, for his sake. Yea, he will enable me not to be ashamed. I have not the least reluctancy or strugling in my spirit against Death. I desire not to live ; but my will is resigned up to God in all. Why are you troubled ? I am not. You have need of Faith **and** Patience to follow the Lord's Call. This ought chiefly to be in our eye, *the bringing Glory to our heavenly* **Father.** Surely God hath a glorious Design to carry on in the world, **even** the building up of *David*'s Throne to all Generations. For he is compleating all his precious Stones, making them Heaven-proof, and then laying them together in the Heavenly Mansions, with

the

the Spirits of the Just, till it be a compleat City. When the Top-stone thereof is laid, then will he come in all his Glory.

This day, is a day wherein Christ appears in the Clouds. Oh, that every one of our eyes may see him, and consider how we have pierced him in his Members, that we may mourn! Our Lord Jesus said, *Father, I have finished the work that thou gavest me to do, and now (Father) glorifie me with the same Glory I had with thee before the world was.* Our Lord was capable of his Glory beforehand; and although we be not so capable as he, yet this we know, he wills the same to us, *that where he is, we may be also, that we may behold his Glory.* And he is our Head, in whom we are made capable, being chosen in him before the foundation of the world; and he hath set us in heavenly places in Christ Jesus. The hope of this Glory sweetens all our Sufferings.

I know, a day of deliverance for Sion will come. Some may think the manner of it may be, as before, *with confused noise of the Warriour, and garments rolled in Blood;* but I rather think it will be with *burning, and fewel of fire.* The Lord will send a fire, that shall burn in the *Consciences* of his Enemies, *a worm that shall not die, and a fire that shall not go out.* Men, they may fight against; but *this* they cannot fight against.

It being told him by a Friend, that he had delivered him up unto God as a Sacrifice, though (said he) I have day and night prayed that this cup might pass from you. He replied, *That he blessed God, he had offered himself up first to God, and it was a rejoycing to him that others had given him up also.* And why, said he (speaking before all the company) *should we be frighted with Death? I bless the Lord, I am so far from being affrighted with Death, that I find it rather shrink from me, than I from it.*

His Children being then present, to take their leave of him, he said, *I bless God, by the eye of Faith I can see through all my Relations to Mount Sion, and there I shall need none of them. I have better Acquaintance in Heaven. These Relations are nothing to those I shall meet with there.* Then kissing his Children, he said, *The Lord bless you, he will be a better Father to you: I must now forget that ever I knew you. I can willingly leave this place and outward enjoyments, for those I shall meet with hereafter, in a better Country. I have made it my business, to acquaint my self with the society of Heaven. Be not you troubled, for I am going home to my Father.*

I die in the certain faith and foresight, That this Cause shall have its Resurrection in my Death. My Blood will be the Seed sown, by which this glorious Cause will spring up, which God will speedily raise.

The laying down this earthly tabernacle is no more, but throwing down the mantle, by which a double portion of the Spirit will fall on the rest of Gods People. And if by my being offered up, the Faith of many be confirmed, and others convinced and brought to the knowledge of the Truth, how can I desire greater honour and matter of rejoycing?

As for that glorious Cause, which God hath owned in these Nations, and will own, in which so many Righteous souls have lost their lives, and so many have been engaged by my countenance and encouragement, shall I now give it up, and so declare them all Rebels and Murderers? No, I will never do it : That precious Blood shall never lie at my door. As a Testimony and Seal to the Justness of that Quarrel, I leave now my Life upon it, as a Legacy to all the honest Interest in these three Nations. Ten thousand Deaths, rather than defile my Conscience, the chastity and purity of which I value beyond all this world ; and God is not a little concern'd on my behalf. He will certainly judge my Case, wherein is the bowels of this good Cause, and in the bowels of that, the Kingdom of Jesus Christ, which will speedily be set on foot in these Nations. I would not for ten thousand Lives, part with this Peace and Satisfaction I have in my own heart, (both in holding to the Purity of my Principles, and to the Righteousness of this good Cause) and the assurance I have that God is now fulfilling all these great and precious Promises, in order to what he is bringing forth. Although I see it not, yet I die in the faith and assured expectation of it, Hebr. 11. 13. And the eternal blessedness God hath prepared for me, and is ready now to receive me into, will abundantly make up all other things. Through the power and goodness of God, I have had in this Tryal of mine, such a proof of the integrity of my own heart, as hath been no small joy to me.

The expressions of grief from his Friends, he said, were but so many lets and hindrances to him, in the view he had of that Glory he was going to possess, that heavenly City and Commonwealth, where he should behold the face of God and of his Son, in a society of Angels, and the Spirits of Just men made perfect.

Some few dayes before his Suffering, his thoughts were much fixed upon *Psal.* 118. 27. where are these words ; *God is the Lord, which hath shewed us light ; bind the Sacrifice with cords, even unto the horns of the Altar.* From this, he said, that God gives light, and is light to his People, under their darkest circumstances and sufferings ;

and when he calls them forth to suffer, he binds them as Sacrifices with cords, in three respects : First, by the Cord of his Love to us, for he loved us first. Secondly, by the Cruelty of our Enemies. Thirdly, by our Resignation-duty and love to him. These three Cords have bound me so fast, I cannot stir.

Upon Friends perswading him, to make some submission to the King, and to endeavour the obtaining of his Life ; he said, *If the King did not think himself more concern'd for his Honour and Word, than he did for his Life, he was very willing they should take it. Nay, I declare* (said he) *that I value my Life less in a good Cause, than the King can do his Promise.* And when some others were speaking to him, of giving some thousands of pounds for his Life ; he said, *If a thousand farthings would gain it, he would not give it : And if any should attempt to make such a bargain, he would spoil their market : For I think the King himself is so sufficiently obliged to spare my Life, that it is fitter for him to do it, than my self to seek it.*

He rejoyced exceedingly, that God assisted him so eminently in bearing his Testimony with faithfulness even unto Death ; and that he as willingly laid down his Life, and with as much satisfaction, as ever he went to bed. For in a natural sickness, Death seized on the body, without any consent of the mind ; but this was a free action of his mind, without any constraint upon his body.

Mention being made to him of the cruel proceedings against him ; *Alas* (said he) *what ado they keep to make a poor creature like his Saviour !* In discourse he said, *If the shedding of my Blood, may prove an occasion of gathering together in one, the dispersed Interests and Remnant of the Adherers to this Cause (of whatever differing perswasions) I should think ten thousand Lives (if I had them) well spent in such a service.*

He was much pleased in this consideration, *That he was hastening to a place where God nor none of his, would be ashamed to own and receive him. Here is nothing in this world* (saith he) *but reproaching and despising God's precious Saints ; but in Heaven there is a good reception for them, where are Mansions prepared from the beginning of the world.*

He said, *You will shortly see God coming forth with Vengeance upon the whole Earth, Vengeance upon the outward-man of his Saints, and Vengeance upon the inward-man of his and their Enemies ; and that shall perform greater execution, than was heretofore.*

After his Sentence, he said to some Friends, God brought him up-

on

on three ſtages, (to wit, before the Court) and was now leading him to the fourth (his Execution-place) which was far eaſier and pleaſanter to him than any of the other three.

Saturday June 14. **1662,** *being the day of his Execution, on Tower-Hill.*

He told a Friend, God bid *Moſes* go to the top of Mount *Piſgah,* and die ; ſo he bid him now, go to the top of *Tower-hill,* and die.

Some paſſages of his Prayer with his Lady, Children, and other Friends in his Chamber.

MOſt holy and gracious *Father, look down from the habitation of thy Holineſs ; viſit, relieve and comfort us thy poor Servants, here gathered together in the Name of* Chriſt. *Thou art rending this Vaile, and bringing us to a Mountain that abides firm. We are exceeding interrupters of our own joy, peace and good, by the workings and reaſonings of our own hearts. Thou haſt promiſed, that thou wilt be a Mouth to thy People in the hour of Tryal : for thou haſt required us, to forbear the preparatory agitations of our own minds, becauſe it is not we that are to ſpeak, but the Spirit of our heavenly Father that* **ſpeaketh in us,** *in ſuch ſeaſons. In what ſeaſons more, (Lord) than when thou calleſt for the Teſtimony of thy Servants to be writ in Characters of Blood ? Shew thy ſelf in a poor weak Worm, by enabling him to ſtand againſt all the power of thy Enemies. There hath been a battel fought with garments rouled in blood, in which (upon ſolemn Appeals on both ſides) thou didſt own thy Servants, though through the ſpirit of Hypocriſie and Apoſtacy, that hath ſprung up amongſt us, theſe Nations have been thought unworthy any longer to enjoy the fruits of that Deliverance. Thou haſt therefore another day of deciſion, to come, which ſhall be wrought by fire. Such a battel is to begin, and be carried on by the Faith of thy People, yea, is in ſome ſort, begun by the Faith of thy poor Servant, that is now going to ſeal thy Cauſe with his Blood. Oh that this deciſion of thine may remarkably ſhew it ſelf in thy Servant at this time, by his bold Teſtimony and ſealing it with his Blood. We know not what interruptions may attend thy Servant, but Lord, let thy Power carry him in a holy Triumph over all difficulties. Thou art the great Judge and Law-giver ; for the ſake of thy Servants therefore, O Lord, return on high, and cauſe a righteous Sentence to come forth from thy preſence, for the relief of thy deſpiſed People.*

*People. This, thy Servants with Faith and Patience wait for. The working of this Faith in us, causeth the Enemy to give ground already. If Death be not able to terrifie us from keeping a good Conscience, and giving a good Testimony against them, what can they do but stumble and fall backwards? The day approaches in which thou wilt decide this Controversie, not by Might nor by Power, but by the Spirit of the living God. This Spirit will make its own way, and run through the whole Earth. Then shall it be said, Where is the fury of the Oppressor? Who is he that dares or can stand before the Spirit of the Lord, in the mouth of his Witnesses? Arise, O Lord, and let thine Enemies be scattered. Thy poor Servant knows not how he shall be carried forth by thee this day, but, blessed be thy great Name, that he hath whereof to speak in this great Cause. When I shall be gathered to thee this day, then come thou in the Ministry of thy holy Angels that excel in strength. We have seen enough of **this** World, and thou seest, **we have** enough **of it**. Let these my Friends, that are **round** about me, commit me to the Lord, and let them be gathered into the Family of Abraham the Father of the Faithful, and become faithful Witnesses of those Principles and Truths that have been discovered to them, that it may be known, that a poor weak Prophet hath been amongst them, not by the words of his mouth onely, but by the voice of his Blood and Death, which will speak when he is gone. Good Lord, put words into his mouth that may daunt his Enemies, so that they may be forced to say, God is in him of a Truth, and that the Son of God is in his heart, and in his mouth. My hour-glass is now turned up, the sand runs out apace, and it is my happiness that Death doth not surprize me. It is Grace and Love thou dost shew thy poor Servant, that thou hastenest out his time, and lettest him see it runs out with Joy and Peace. Little do my Enemies know (as eager as they are to have me gone) how soon their breaths may be drawn in.*

*But let thy Servant see Death shrink under him. What a glorious sight will this be in the presence of many Witnesses, to have Death shrink under him, which he acknowledgeth to be only by the power of the Resurrection of Jesus Christ, whom the bands of Death could not **hold** down? Let that Spirit enter into us that will set us again upon our feet, and let us be led into that way, that the Enemies may not know how to deal with us.*

Oh! what abjuring of Light, what Treachery, what meanness of spirit has appeared in this day? What is the matter? Oh! Death is the matter. Lord, strengthen the Faith and Heart of thy poor Ser-

vant,

vant, to undergo this dayes work with Joy and Gladness, and bear it on the Heart and Consciences of his Friends that have known and seen him, that they also may say, the Lord is in him of a truth.

Oh that thy Servant could speak any blessing to these three Nations. Let thy Remnant be gathered to thee. Prosper and relieve that poor handful that are in Prisons and Bonds, that they may be raised up and trample Death under foot. Let my poor Family that is left desolate, let my dear Wife and Children be taken into thy Care, be thou a Husband, Father and Master to them. Let the Spirits of those that love me, be drawn out towards them. Let a Blessing be upon these Friends that are here at this time, strengthen them, let them find Love and Grace in thine Eyes, and be increased with the Increasings of God. Shew thy self a loving Father to us all, and do for us abundantly, above and beyond all that we can ask or think, for Jesus Christ his sake. Amen.

Several Friends being with him in his Chamber this morning, he oft encouraged them to chearfulness, as wel by his example as expression. In all his deportment, he shewed himself marvellously fitted to meet the King of Terrors, without the least affrightment. But to shew where his strength lay, he said, *he was a poor unworthy wretch, and had nothing but the Grace and Goodness of God to depend upon.* He said, moreover, *Death shrunk from him, rather than he from it.* Upon the occasion of parting with his Relations, he said, *There is some flesh remaining yet, but I must cast it behind me, and press forward to my Father.*

Then one of the Sheriffs men came in and told him, There was no Sled to come, but he was to walk on foot.

He told his Friends, the Sheriff's Chaplain came to him at twelve of the clock that night, with an Order for his Execution, telling him, he was come to bring him that fatal Message of Death. *I think (Friends) that in this Message was no dismalness at all; After the receipt of which, I slept four hours so soundly, that the Lord hath made it sufficient for me, and now I am going to sleep my last, after which I shall need sleep no more.*

Then Mr. Sheriff coming into the Room, was friendly saluted by him, and after a little pause, communicated a Prohibition that he said he had received, which was, That he must not speak any thing against his Majesty, or the Government. His Answer to this he himself relates on the Scaffold. He further told Mr. Sheriff, he was ready:

but

but the Sheriff said, he was not, nor could be this half hour yet ; *Then Sir, it rests on you, not on me* (said Sir *Henry*) *for I have been ready this half hour.* Then the Sheriff, at his request, promised him his servants should attend him on the Scaffold and be civilly dealt with, neither of which were performed, for (notwithstanding this promise) they were beaten and kept off the Scaffold, till he said, *What? have I never a servant here?*

After this, one of the Sheriffs men came and told him, there must be a Sled ; to which Sir *Henry* replied, *Any way, how they please, for I long to be at home, to be dissolved and to be with Christ, which is best of all.* He went very chearfully and readily down the stairs from his Chamber, and seated himself on the Sled, (Friends and **Servants** standing about him) then he was forthwith drawn away towards the Scaffold. As he went, some in the *Tower* (Prisoners as well as others) spake to him, praying the Lord to go with him. And after he was out of the *Tower*, from the tops of houses and out of windows, the people used such means and gestures as might best discover at a distance, their respects and love to him, crying aloud, *The Lord go with you, The great God of Heaven and Earth appear in you, and for you* ; whereof he took what notice he was capable in those circumstances, in a chearful manner accepting their respect, putting off his Hat and bowing to them. Being asked several times, how he did, by some about him, he answered, *Never better in all my life.* Another replied, How should he do ill that suffers for so glorious a Cause ? To which a tall black man said, Many suffered for a better Cause ; *and may for a worse*, said Sir *Henry*, wishing, *That when they come to seal their* better *Cause (as he called it) with their Blood (as he was now going to seal his) they might not find themselves deceived ; And as to this Cause*, said he, *it hath given Life in Death, to all the Owners of it, and Sufferers for it.*

Being passed within the Rails on *Tower-hill*, there were many loud acclamations of the people, crying out, *The Lord Jesus go with your* **dear** *Soul, &c.* One told him, that was the most glorious Seat he ever sate on ; he answered, *It is so indeed*, and rejoyced exceedingly.

Being come to the Scaffold, he chearfully ascends, and being up, after the crowd on the Scaffold was broken in two pieces, to make way for him, he shewed himself to the People on the front of the Scaffold, with that Noble and Christian-like deportment, that he rather seemed a looker-on, than the person concerned in the Execution, Insomuch that it was difficult to perswade many of the People, that he

was

was the Prifoner. But when they knew that the Gentleman in the black Sute and Cloak (with a Scarlet filk Waftcoat (the victorious colour) fhewing it felf at the breaft) was the Prifoner, they generally admired that Noble and great Prefence he appeared with. How chearful he is ! faid fome ; he does not look like a dying-man ! faid others ; with many like fpeeches, as aftonifhed with that ftrange appearance he fhined forth in.

Then (filence being commanded by the Sheriff) lifting up his hands and eyes towards Heaven, and then retting his hands on the Rails, and taking a very ferious, compofed and majeftick view of the great multitude about him, he fpake as followeth.

His SPEECH on the SCAFFOLD.

Gentlemen, fellow-Countrymen, and Chriftians,

WHen Mr. Sheriff came to me this morning, and told me he had received a Command from the King, that I fhould fay nothing reflecting upon his Majefty or the Government ; I anfwered, I fhould confine and order my Speech, as near as I could, fo as to be leaft offenfive, faving my faithfulnefs to the Truft repofed in me, which I muft ever difcharge with a good Confcience unto Death; for I ever valued a man, according to his faithfulnefs to the Truft repofed in him, even on his Majefties behalf, in the late Controverfie. And if you dare truft my difcretion, Mr. Sheriff, I fhall do nothing but what becomes a good Chriftian and an Englifhman ; and fo I hope I fhall be civilly dealt with.

When Mr. Sheriffs Chaplain came to me laft night about twelve of the clock, to bring me, as he called it, the fatal Meffage of Death, it pleafed the Lord to bring that Scripture to my mind, in the third of *Zechary*, to intimate to me, that he was now taking away my filthy garments, caufing mine iniquities to pafs from me, with intention to give me change of rainient, and that my mortal fhould put on Immortality.

I fuppofe you may wonder when I fhall tell you that I am not brought hither according to any known Law of the Land. It is true, I have been before a Court of Juftice, (and am now going to appear before a greater Tribunal, where I am to give an account of all my actions) under their Sentence I ftand here at this time. When I was before them, I could not have the liberty and priviledge of an Englifhman, the grounds, reafons, and caufes of the Actings I was charged

with

with duly confidered; I therefore defired the Judges, that they would fet their Seals to my Bill of Exceptions; I preffed hard for it again and again, as the Right of my felf, and every free-born Englifh-man, by the Law of the Land; but was finally denied it.——

Here Sir *John Robinfon* (Lieutenant of the Tower) interrupted him, faying, Sir, you muft not go on thus, and (in a furious manner, generally obferved, even to the dif-fatisfaction of fome of their own attendants) faid, that he railed againft the Judges, and that it was a lye, and I am here (fayes he) to teftifie that it is falfe.

Sir *Henry Vane* replied, God will judge between me and you in this matter. I fpeak but matter of Fact, and cannot you bear that? 'Tis evident, the Judges have refufed to fign my Bill of Exceptions—— Then the Trumpets were ordered to found or murre in his face, with a contemptible noife, to hinder his being heard. At which Sir *Henry* (lifting up his hand, and then laying it on his breaft) faid, What mean you Gentlemen? is this your ufage of me? did you ufe all the reft fo? I had even done (as to that) could you have been patient, but feeing you cannot bear it, I fhall only fay this, *That whereas the Judges have refufed to feal that with their hands, that they have done; I am come to feal that with my Blood, that I have done.* Therefore leaving this matter, which I perceive will not be born, I judge it meet to give you fome account of my Life.

I might tell you, I was born a Gentleman, had the education, temper and fpirit of a Gentleman, as well as others, being (in my youth-full dayes) inclined to the vanities of this world, and to that which they call *Good-fellowfhip*, judging it to be the only means of accomplifhing a Gentleman. But about the fourteenth or fifteenth year of my age, (which is about thirty four or five years fince) God was pleafed to lay the foundation or ground-work of Repentance in me, for the bringing me home to himfelf, by his wonderful rich and free Grace, revealing his Son in me, that by the knowledge of the onely true God, and Jefus Chrift whom he hath fent, I might (even whilft here in the body) be made partaker of Eternal Life, in the fiift-fruits of it.

When my Confcience was thus awakened, I found my former courfe to be difloyalty to God, prophanenefs, and a way of fin and death, which I did with tears and bitternefs bewail, as I had caufe to do. Since that foundation of Repentance laid in me, through Grace I have been kept fteadfaft, defiring to walk in all good Confcience towards God and towards men, according to the beft light and underftanding

God

God gave me. For this, I was willing to turn by back upon my Estate, expose my self to hazards in Forreign parts; yea, nothing seemed difficult to me, so I might preserve Faith and a good Conscience, which I prefer before all things; and do earnestly perswade all people rather to suffer the highest contradictions from men, than disobey God, by contradicting the light of their own Conscience. In this, it is, I stand with so much comfort and boldness before you all this day, and upon this occasion; being assured, that I shall at last sit down in Glory with Christ, at his right hand. I stand here this day, to resign up my Spirit into the hands of that God that gave it me. Death is but a little word, but 'tis a great work to die, it is to be but once done, and after this cometh the Judgment, even the Judgment of the great God, which it concerns us all to prepare for. And by this Act, I do receive a discharge, once for all, out of Prison, even the Prison of the mortal body also, which to a true Christian is a burdensom weight.

In all respects, wherein I have been concerned and engaged as to the Publick, my design hath been to accomplish Good things for these Nations. Then (lifting up his eyes, and spreading his hands) he said, *I do here appeal to the great God of Heaven, and all this Assembly, or any other persons, to shew wherein I have defiled my hands with any mans Blood or Estate, or that I have sought my self in any publick capacity or place I have been in.*

The Cause was three times stated.

1. In the *Remonstrance of the House of Commons.*

2. In the *Covenant, the Solemn League and Covenant*—— Upon this the Trumpets sounded, the Sheriff catched at the Paper in his hand, and Sir *John Robinson*, who at first had acknowledged that he had nothing to do there, wishing the Sheriff to see to it, yet found himself something to do now, furiously calling for the Writers-Books, and saying, *he treats of Rebellion, and you write it.* Hereupon six Note-Books were delivered up. The Prisoner was very patient and composed under all these injuries and soundings of the Trumpets several times in his face, only saying, *'Twas hard he might not be suffered to speak*; but, sayes he, *my usage from man is no harder than was my Lord and Masters*; *And all that will live his life this day, must expect hard dealing from the worldly spirit*—— The Trumpets sounded again, to hinder his being heard. Then again *Robinson* and two or three others, endeavoured to snatch the Paper out of Sir *Henry's* hand, but he kept it for a while, now and then reading part of it;

after-

afterwards, tearing it in pieces, he delivered it to a Friend behind him, who was presently forced to deliver it to the Sheriff. Then they put their hands into his pockets for Papers (as was pretended) which bred great confusion and dissatisfaction to the Spectators, seeing a Prisoner so strangely handled in his dying words. This was exceeding remarkable, in the midst of all this disorder, the Prisoner himself was observed to be of the most constant, composed spirit and countenance, which he throughout so excellently manifested, that a Royallist swore, *he dyed like a Prince.*

The Prisoner, suspecting beforehand the disorder afore-mentioned, writ the main Substance of what he intended to speak on the Scaffold, in that Paper they catched at, and which he tore in pieces, delivering it to a Friend, from whom the Sheriff had it as above-said ; the true Copy whereof, was by the Prisoner carefully committed to a safe hand before he came to the Scaffold, which take as followeth.

THe Work which I am at this time called unto, in this place, (as upon a Publick Theater) is, to Die, and receive a Discharge, once for all, out of Prison ; to do that, which is but once to be done; the doing or not doing of which *well*, and as becomes a *Christian*, does much depend upon the life we have been taught of God to lead, before we come to this : They that live in the Faith, do also die in it : Faith is so far from leaving Christians in this hour, that the work of it breaks forth then into its greatest power ; as if till then, it were not enough at freedom to do its office, that is, to look into the things that are unseen, with most steadfastness, certainty, and delight; which is the great Sweetner of Death, and Remover of its Sting.

Give me leave therefore in a very few words, to give you an account of my Life, and of the wonderful great Grace and Mercy of God, in bringing me home to himself, and revealing his Son in me ; that by the knowledge of the only true God, and Jesus Christ whom he hath sent, I might (even whilst here in the body) be made partaker of Eternal Life, in the first fruits of it ; and at last sit down with Christ in Glory, at his right-hand.

Here I shall mention some remarkable passages and changes of my Life ; In particular, how unsought for by my self, I was called to be a Member of the *Long Parliament* ; what little advantage I had by it ; and by what steps I became satisfied with the Cause I was engaged in, and did pursue the same.

M

What

What the Cause was, did first shew it self, in the *first Remonstrance of the House of Commons.*

Secondly, in the *Solemn League and Covenant.*

Thirdly, in the *more refined pursuit of it by the Commons House, in their Actings single* : with what Result they were growing up into, which was in the breast of the House, and unknown ; or what the *three Proposals,* mentioned in my Charge, would have come to at last, I shall not need now to say ; but only, from all put together, to assert, *That this Cause which was owned by the Parliament, was the CAUSE of GOD, and for the Promoting of the Kingdom of his dear Son,* JESUS CHRIST; *wherein are comprehended our Liberties and Duties, both as Men and as Christians.*

And since it hath pleased God, who separated me from the womb to the knowledge and service of the Gospel of his Son, to separate me also to this hard and difficult service at this time, and to single me out to the defence and justification of this his Cause, I could not consent by any words or actions of mine, that the innocent Blood that hath been shed in the defence of it, throughout the whole War; (*the Guilt and moral evil of which, must and does certainly lye somewhere*) did lye at my door, or at theirs that have been the faithful Adherers to this Cause. This is with such evidence upon my heart, that I am most freely and chearfully willing, to put the greatest Seal to it I am capable, which is, the pouring out of my very Blood in witness to it ; which is all I shall need to say in this place, and at this time, having spoken at large to it in my Defence at my Tryal, intending to have said more the last day, as what I thought was reasonable for *Arrest of the Judgment,* but I was not permitted then to speak it ; Both which may with time and God's providence, come to publick view.

And I must still assert, That I remain wholly unsatisfied, that the course of proceedings against me at my Tryal were according to Law; but that I was run upon and destroyed, contrary to Right, and the Liberties of *Magna Charta,* under the form only of Justice : which I leave to God to decide, who is the Judge of the whole World, and to clear my Innocency ; Whilst in the mean time, I beseech him to forgive them, and all that have had a hand in my Death ; and that the Lord in his great mercy will not lay it unto their charge.

And I do account this Lot of mine no other, than what is to be expected by those that are not of the World, but whom Christ hath chosen out of it; for the Servant is not greater than his Lord ; And if they have done this to the green tree, they will do it much more to the dry. How-

However, I shall not altogether excuse my self. I know, that by many weaknesses and failers, I have given occasion enough of the ill usage I have met with from men, though, in the main, the Lord knows the sincerity and integrity of my heart, whatever Aspersions and Reproaches I have or do lye under. I know also that God is just, in bringing this Sentence and Condemnation upon me, for my sins; there is a body of sin and death in me, deserves this Sentence; and there is a similitude and likeness also, that, as a Christian, God thinks me worthy to bear with my Lord and head, in many circumstances in reference to these dealings I have met with, in the good I have been endeavouring for many years to be doing in these Nations, and especially now at last, in being numbred amongst transgressors, and made a publick Sacrifice, through the wrath and contradictions of men, and in having finished my course, and fought the good fight of Faith, and resisted in a way of suffering (as you see) even unto blood.

This is but the needful preparation the Lord hath been working in me, to the receiving of the Crown of Immortality, which he hath prepared for them that love him, The prospect whereof is so chearing, that through the Joy (in it) that is set before the eyes of my Faith, I can, through mercy, *endure this Cross, despise this Shame,* and am become *more than Conquerour,* through Christ that hath loved me.

For my Life, Estate and all, is not so dear to me as my Service to God, to his Cause, to the Kingdom of Christ, and the future welfare of my Country; and I am taught according to the Example, as well as that most Christian saying of a Noble Person that lately died after this publick manner in *Scotland*; " How much better is it to chuse Affliction and the " Cross, than to sin or draw back from the Service of the Living God, " into the wayes of Apostacy and Perdition.

That Noble Person, whose Memory I honour, was with my self at the beginning and making of the *Solemn League and Covenant,* the Matter of which, and the holy Ends therein contained, I fully assent unto, and have been as desirous to observe; but the *rigid* way of prosecuting it, and the *oppressing Uniformity* that hath bin endeavored by it, I never approved.

This were sufficient to vindicate me from the false Aspersions and Calumnies which have been laid upon me, of *Jesuitism* and *Popery,* and almost what not, to make my Name of ill favour with *good men*; which dark mists do now dispel of themselves, or at least ought, and need no pains of mine in making an Apology.

For if any man seek a proof of Christ in me, let him reade it in this action of my Death, which will not cease to speak when I am gone; *And henceforth let no man trouble me, for I bear in my body the marks of the Lord Jesus.*

M 2   I

I shall not desire in this place to take up much time, but only, as my last words, leave this with you : " That as the present storm we now lie " under, and the dark Clouds that yet hang over the Reformed Churches " of Christ, (which are coming thicker and thicker for a season) were " not un-fore-seen by me for many years passed, (as some Writings of " mine declare :) So the coming of Christ in these Clouds, in order to " a speedy and sudden Revival of his Cause, and spreading his Kingdom " over the face of the whole Earth, is most clear to the eye of my Faith, " even that Faith in which I dye, whereby the Kingdoms of this world " shall become the Kingdom of our Lord, and of his Christ. *Amen.* " Even so, come, Lord Jesus.

Some Passages of his PRAYER on the Scaffold.

THe Heaven is thy Throne, O Lord, and the Earth is thy footstool, but to this man will thou look, even to him that is poor, and of a contrite spirit, and trembleth at thy Word. *Thou, O Lord, art the great God of Heaven and Earth, thou fillest all places with thy presence, art the Judge of the whole World, and dost Righteousness. We are poor unworthy sinful creatures, by nature children of wrath as well as others : We are wise to do evil, but to do good we have no knowledge. If to will be present with us, yet how to perform and go through with that which is good, and not be weary of well-doing, we find not.*

Bring us, O Lord, into the true mystical Sabbath-state, that we may cease from our own works, rest from our labors, not think our own thoughts, find our own desire, or walk in the way of our own hearts, but become a meet habitation of thy Spirit by the everlasting Covenant, the place of thy Rest. Let the Spirit of God and of Glory, that is greater than he that is in the world, rest upon us, work in and by us mightily, to the pulling down of flesh and blood, the strong holds of Sin and Satan in our selves and others, causing us so to suffer under the Fire-Baptism thereof, as that we may cease from sin for ever, or from that fleshly, mutable, & temporary state of life and righteousness, which at best is liable to roul back into sin again, to be intangled, overcome, and finally triumphed over by the pollutions of this world. Deliver us, O Lord, from the Evil One, deliver us from our selves, take us out of our own dispose, our own liberty and power, the freedom, the mutable holiness and righteousness of the sons of men, at its best, and bring us into the most glorious Liberty, the most holy immutable and righteous state of the sons of God, a freedom to Good only, and not at all to

evil,

evil, attended and accompanied with a power in us, through thy Spirit, of doing all things for the Truth, and a disability brought upon us as to the doing of any thing against the Truth, in the single power and freedom of our own spirit. Then the prince of this world coming to us, will find nothing in us ; at least, no prevailing activity of self, nature or flesh, which at best, is capable to be made by him an engin of opposition to the Kingdom of Christ, and our own true blessedness. Thou hast laid on thy Son the iniquities of us all ; by his stripes we are healed. *We must all stand before the Judgment-Seat of Christ, to give an account of what we have done in the body whether it be good or whether it be evil,* He will bring every secret counsel to light ; things that are wrought in darkness, he maketh plain and evident. *Thine eyes, O Lord, run to and fro through the whole earth.* Thine eyes do behold, thine eye-lids try the children of men. The wicked and him that loveth violence, thy soul hateth. But thou upholdest the poor and needy, him that is of a broken heart and of a contrite spirit. The humble and lowly thou wilt teach, the meek thou wilt guide in Judgment ; thou wilt beautifie the meek with Salvation. *Thou art the supream disposer of all the Kingdoms of men, giving them to whomsoever thou wilt. Whatever cross-blows thou sufferest to be given thy People for a season, thou orderest all, to thy own glory, and their true advantage. But thou hast a set time for Sions deliverance, in which the greatness of the Kingdom under the whole Heaven, shall be given unto the best and choicest of men, the people of the Saints of the most high, whose Kingdom is an everlasting Kingdom. Let the exceeding near approach of this, bear up the spirits of thy poor despised ones, in this day of extremity and suffering, from sinking and despondency. Carry them through their suffering part, with a holy triumph, in thy Chariots of Salvation. How long, O Lord, holy and true? make haste to help the Remnant of thy People. Break the Heavens and come down, touch the Mountains of prey, the Kingdoms of this evil world, and let them smoak. Let the mouth of all Iniquity be stopped. Silence every one that stands up against thee. Rebuke the debauched prophane spirits of men, that set themselves to work wickedness, running with greediness into all filthiness and superfluity of naughtiness.* They eat thy People as they eat bread. They are profound to make slaughter, skilful to destroy, though thou hast been the rebuker of them all. *But, Lord, be this dispensation of what continuance it will, for the serving of thy most gracious and wise designs, let the spirit and resolution of thy Servants be steady and unchangeable, that whether they live, they may live to the Lord, that died for them ; or whether they die, they may die to the Lord, who lives for ever to make intercession for them, that they may glorifie thee with their bodies and spirits, whether by life or by death.* Thou

Thou knowest O Lord, that in the Faith of Jesus, and for the Truth as it is in Jesus, thy Servant desires to die, walking in the steps of our father Abraham, *and for Righteousness and Judgment, following the Lord in all his wayes whithersoever he goes, worshipping the God of his believing fathers,* Abraham, Isaac *and* Jacob, *in that way which men call Heresie. In this Faith, dear Lord, I have lived, and in this Faith and Profession I die, as one that hath herein stood up for the Testimony of JESUS against all Idolatry, Superstition, Prophaness and Popery, or whatever is unsound or unfit to be brought before the Throne of so great and glorious a Majesty. 'Tis in this Faith that thy Servant dies. Now set thy Seal to it, and remove the reproaches and calumnies with which thy Servant is reproached, for thou knowst his innocency. Dear Father, thou sentest us into this world, but this world is* not our *home, we are strangers and pilgrims in it, as all our fathers were. We have no abode here, but there is a house, not made with hands, eternal in the heavens, that when this tabernacle is dissolved, we may enter into. In our Fathers house are many mansions; Oh! whatever the curses and condemnations of the Law are, be thou near to us, and spread the Righteousness of Christ over us, and we shall be safe.* Blessed is he, whose transgressions are forgiven, and whose sins are covered. *Who wil speak, who will take on him to say any thing, or to plead with Thee, upon any other terms but in the Name and Merits of the mighty Redeemer, on whom our help is laid. We desire to lie low, to be abased and take shame & confusion of face to our selves, as that which properly belongs to us, that Thou alone maist be exalted and advanced. 'Tis of meer Grace, O Lord,* that *thy Servant hath now some sign of thy special Salvation, even thy free-Grace, O God, whereby thou dost accept him in thy Son. Lay him low and humble & abase his soul for his sins, and all his unworthinesses before thee. Men cannot speak evil enough of our sins. In this perswasion, this abasement and humiliation, thy Servant desires to die. And, dear Lord, thou seest & knowst all things, and art able to witness to the truth & integrity of thy Servant. When his blood is shed upon the Block, let it have a voice afterward, that may speak his Innocency, and strengthen the Faith of thy Servants in the Truth. Let it also serve for conviction to the worst of thy Enemies, that they may say, Surely the Lord knows, and the Lord owns his Servant, as one that belongs to him. The desire of our soul is to hasten to thee, O God, to be dissolved, that we may be with Christ. Blessed be thy Name, that this great strait that we were before in, is now determined; that there is no longer abode for me in this mortal body. Our great Captain, the great General of our souls, did go in a way of affliction before us, to Heaven. Come, Lord, declare thy Will, that thy poor Servant may ma-*
nifest

nifest a readiness to come to Thee; *Prepare his heart, that in his access to Thee may, he be brought down at thy feet, in shame & confusion for all the evil it is so of hul; but Thou art his salvation.* Let thy Servant speak something on the behalf of the Nation wherein he hath lived ; *Lord, did we not exceed other Nations in our day? Great things have been done by thee in the midst of us. Oh, that thou wouldst look down in pity & compassion, and pardon the sins of this whole Nation, and lay them not to their charge; shew them what is thy good and acceptable Will, and bring them into subjection thereunto. We humbly pray thee, O Lord, look down with compassion upon this great & populous City, cleanse away the impurity, sinfulness and defilements thereof; cause their souls to delight in thy Word, that they may live. Let a spirit of Reformation and Purity spring up in and amongst them with power ; make them willing to lay down all that is dear to them for thee, that Thou mayst give them a Crown of Life ; that they may always desire & chuse affliction, and to be exposed to the worst condition & hardest circumstances, that can be brought upon them in this world, rather than sin against him that hath loved them and bought them with a price, that they might live to him in their bodies and in their spirits.*

We are assured Thou knowest our suffering case and condition, how it is with us. We desire to give no just occasion of offence, nor to provoke any, but in meekness to forgive our Enemies. Thy Servant that is now falling asleep, doth heartily desire of thee, that thou wouldest forgive them, and not lay this sin to their charge.

Before the stroke, he spake to this effect ; *I bless the Lord who hath accounted me worthy to suffer for his Name. Blessed be the Lord that I have kept a conscience void of offence to this day. I bless the Lord I have not diserted the Righteous Cause, for which I suffer.*

But his very last words of all at the Block, were as followeth ; *Father, glorifie thy Servant in the sight of men, that he may glorifie thee in the discharge of his Duty to Thee and to his Country.*

It was observed, that no signs of inward fear appeared by any trembling or shaking of his hands, or any other parts of his body, all along on the Scaffold. Yea, an ancient Traveller and curious observer of the demeanor of persons in such publick Executions, did narrowly eye his Countenance to the last breath, and his Head immediatly after the separation; he observed that his Countenance did not in the least change : and whereas the Heads of all he had before seen, did some way or other move after severing, which argued some reluctancy and unwillingness to that parting-blow; the Head of this Sufferer lay perfectly still, immediately

upon

upon the separation : on which he said to this purpose, That his Death was by the free consent and act of his mind ; which Animadversion notably accords with what the Sufferer himself had before expressed, in differencing a death by rational choice, from that by sickness, which is with constraint upon the body. He desired to be dissolved & to be with Christ.

The Names of the Grand Jury, in the Case of Sir Henty Vane.

SIr *John Cropley* of *Clarkenwel*, *London*, Knight and Baronet. *Thomas Taylor* of St. *Martins* in the Fields, *London*, Esq; *Francis Swift* of St. *Gyles* in the Fields, Esq. *Jonas Morley* of *Hammersmith*, Gent. *George Cooper* of *Covent Garden*, Gent. *Thomas Constable* of *Covent Garden*, Gent. *Edward Burrows* of *East-Smithfield*, Gent. *Michael Dibbs* of the same, Gent. *Edward Gregory* of St. *Gyles* in the Fields, Gent. *Richard Freeman* of *Islington*, Gent. *Thomas Pitcock* of the same, Gent. *Richard Towers* of *Clarkenwel*, Gent. *Robert Vauce* of *Paddington*, Gent. *Thomas Benning* of *Wilsdon*, Gent. *Francis Child* of *Acton*, Gent. *Isaac Cotton* of *Bow*, Gent. *Peter Towers* of *Mile-end*, Gent. *Thomas Uffman* of *Hammersmith*, Gent. *Matthew Child* of *Kensington*, Gent. *Bryan Bonnaby* of *Westminster*, Gent. *George Rouse* of St. *Gyles* in the Fields, Gent. Twenty one in all.

The Names of the Petty Jury.

Sir *William Roberts*. Sir *Christopher Abdy*. *John Leech*. *Daniel Cole*. *John Stone*. *Daniel Brown*. *Henry Carter*. *Thomas Chelsam*. *Thomas Pitts*. *Thomas Upman*. *Andrew Brent*. *William Smith*.

Judges of the King's Bench.

Chief Justice *Foster*. Justice *Mallet*. Justice *Twisden*. Justice *Windham*.

The Kings Counsel against the Prisoner ; (no Counsel being permitted to speak one word in his behalf, to the matter or form of the Indictment, or any thing else.)

Sir *Geoffry Palmer*, the King's Attorney General. Sir *Henneage Fynch*, the King's Sollicitor General. Sir *John Glyn*. Sir *John Mayuard*. Sir *William Wild*. Serjeant *Keeling*.

Witnesses against Sir Henry Vane.

Marsh, a Papist, 'tis said ; who witnessed what was accounted most dangerous against the Prisoner, as to change of Government. *William Dobbins*. *Matthew Lock*. *Thomas Pury*. *Thomas Wallis*. *John Coo*.

The

The Peoples Cause Stated.

HE in whom is the Right of Soveraign, and to give Law, is either so of himself, or in the Right of another, that may derive the same unto him ; which shews that there are two sorts of
Soveraigns.

A Soveraign in the first sense, none is nor can be, but God, who
is of himself most absolute. And he that is first of all others in the
second sence, is the Man Christ Jesus, to whom the Power of Soveraign, in the Right of the Father is committed, over all the
Works of Gods hands. Christ exercised the same in the capacity of
David's Root from before the beginning of the World. He ownes
himself thus to be, long before he became *David's* Seed ; This his
being in Spirit, or hidden being, even as a Creature, the first of all
Creatures in personal Union with the Word, *David* saw and acknowledged, *Psal.* 110.1. Thus Christ may be called God's Lieutenant Soveraign, or General Vicegerent of his Supremacy over
all in Heaven and in Earth. He therefore is the true Universal
King and Root of all Soveraign and just Governing Power, whether in Heaven or on Earth.

His Soveraignty is unquestionable and unaccountable, because
of the Perfection of his Person, carrying in it an aptitude and sufficiency to Govern, without possibility of Error or Defect of any
kind. Soveraign and Governing Power doth necessarily relate to
Subjects, that are to be the Ruled, and Subjects capable of such
Government. Therefore when God himself purposes within himself, to be Supream Legislator and Governour, he doth withal purpose the Being and Creation of both Worlds, as the Subject matter of his Kingdom. He propounds to Govern his Subjects by and
with their own consent and good liking ; or, without and against
it, in the way of his revenging Justice ; Governing by Laws, clearly stating and ascertaining the Duty or the Offence, as also the Rewards and Penalties.

Herein Just Government consists, or the Justice of Government ;
for he that Rules over others, must be Just ; and indeed should be
seen to be so in all his Commands : so seen, as to render the Consciences of the Ruled, and those whose duty it is to Obey, inexcusable before God and before Men, if they Dissent or Resist.

N   In-

Inexcufable they are before God, becaufe the matter Commanded is the matter of God's Law, & therefore juft to be obeyed. They are alfo Inexcufable before Men, that which is required of them being generally acknowledged and affirmed (by thofe in whom the common confent of the Subjects is intrufted to that end) to be Juft, and Reafonable, and therefore to be Obeyed. For the end of all Government, being for the Good and Welfare, and not for the Deftruction of the Ruled; God who is the Inftitutor of Government, as he is pleafed to Ordain the Office of Governors, intrufting them with Power to command the Juft and Reafonable Things, which his own Law Commands, that carry their own evidence to common Reafon and Senfe, at leaft, that do not evidently contradict it, fo he grants a Liberty to the Subjects, or thofe that by him are put under the Rule, to refufe all fuch Commands as are contrary to his Law, or to the judgement of common Reafon and Senfe, whofe trial he allows, by way of affent or diffent, before the Commands of the Ruler fhall be Binding or put in Execution ; and this in a Co-ordinacy of Power with Juft Government, and as the due Ballance thereof. The Original Impreffions of Juft Laws are in Mans Nature and very Conftitution of Being. Man hath the Law in his Mind, (or the Superior and Intellectual part of him) convincing and bringing that into obedience and fubjection to the Law of God, in Chrift himfelf. He hath alfo that which is a Law in his Members that are on the Earth, (or his earthly and fenfual part) whofe Power is Co-ordinate with the other, but fuch, that if it be not gained into a Harmony and Conjunction with its Head, the Spirit or Mind of man, hath ability to let and hinder his Mind or Ruling part, from performing and putting in execution, that which is good, juft, fit, and to be acknowledged as the righteous dictates of the Mind, which ought to be the Ruling Power, or Law to the Man. So in the outward Government over Man, the fecondary or co-ordinate Power, concurring with that which is the chief ruling Power, is effential to Juft Government; and is acknowledged to be fo, by the Fundamental Conftitution of the Government of *England*, as well as in the Legal Being and Conftitution of Parliaments, whether that which hath been ufual and ordinary, according to the Common Law ; or that which of late hath been Extraordinary, by exprefs Statute, for the continuance of the Parliament, 17. *Car.* until diffolved by Act of Parliament.

For together with the Legal Being which is given to Regal
Power,

Power and the Prerogative of the Crown, there is the Legal Power and Being reserved also unto that Body, which is the Peoples or Kingdoms Representative, who are the Hands wherein that which is called Power Politick is seated, and are intrusted with giving or with holding the common Consent of the whole Nation, according to the best of their Understandings, in all matters coming before them, and are to keep this Liberty Inviolate and Entire, against all Invasions or Encroachments upon it, whatsoever.

This second Power in the very Writ of Summons for calling a Parliament, is declared to be of that Nature, that what the first doth without obtaining the Consent and Approbation of the second, in Parliament, is not binding but ineffectual. And when the Representative Body of the Kingdom, (in and with whom, this Power is intrusted, as the Due and Legal Ballance and Boundary to the Regal Power, set and fixed by the Fundamental Constitution) is made a standing Court, and of that Continuance, as not to be dissolvable but by its own consent ; during such its continuance, it hath right to preserve it self from all violent and undue Dissolution, and to maintain and defend its own Just Priviledges, a chief of which is, to binde or loose the People, in all matters good or hurtful to them, according to their best Judgement and discretion.

In the exercise of this their Trust, they are Indempnified by Law, and no hurt ought to come unto them ; that Governing Power, which is originally in God, and flowes at first from him, as the sole and proper Fountain thereof, is brought into exercise amongst men, upon a differing and distinct account.

First, As it is a Trust and Right derived conditionally from God to his Officers and Ministers, (which therefore may be lost) who being called by him, and in the course of his Providence, to the exercise of it, are to hold it of him the Universal King, and to own themselves in the exercise thereof, as his Vicegerents, to cut off by the Sword of Justice evil-doers ; and to be a Protection and encouragement to them that do well. But because it is part of God's Call of any person to this high Trust, to bring him into the possession and free Exercise thereof, by the common consent of the Body of the People, where such Soveraign Power is set up, unless they have forfeited this Liberty. Therefore,

Secondly, God doth allow and confer by the very Law of Nature, upon the Community or Body of the People (that are re-

lated

lated to, and concerned in the right of Government, placed over them) the Liberty by their common Vote or Suffrage duely given, to be Assenters or Dissenters thereunto, and to Affirm and make Stable, or Disallow and render Ineffectual, what shall apparently be found by them to be for the good or hurt of that Society, whose welfare next under the justice of God's Commands and his Glory, is the Supream Law, and very end of all Subordinate governing Power.

Soveraign Power then comes from God, as its proper Root, but the restraint or enlargement of it, in its Execution over such or such a Body, is founded in the common consent of that Body.

The Office of chief Ruler, or Head over any State, Commonwealth, or Kingdom, hath the Right of due Obedience from the People inseparably annexed to it. It is an Office, not onely of Divine Institution, but for the Safety and Protection of the whole Body or Community, and therefore justly and necessarily draws to it, and engages their Subjection.

This Office of the Soveraign, according to the Laws, and Fundamental Constitutions of the Government of *England*, is ministred by the King in a twofold Capacity, as his Will and personal Command is in Conjunction and Agreement with his People in Parliament, (during the Session thereof) or as it is in Conjunction and Agreement with the Law, the Parliament not Sitting. But his Will and Personal Command, single, in dif-junction and disagreefrom the Parliament or the Laws, hath not the force of a Law, saith *Fortescue*, and gives the Reason of it, *Because this is a limitted Monarchy, where the King's Power (as to the exercise of it) is onely a Power Politick*.

The Obedience then which from the Subject is due to the King, and which they are sworn to perform by the Oath of Allegiance, is to him, in the ministry of the Royal Office, according to the reason and intent of the Fundamental Compact and Constitution, and according to his own Oath, which is to Govern by Law; that is, to Exercise his Rule or Royal commanding Power, in Conjunction and Agreement with the Parliament when sitting, and in Conjunction, and Agreement with the Laws of the Land, they not sitting. To exercise his Power otherwise, is and hath been always judged a grievance to the People., and a going against that which is the original Right and just Liberty of the Community, who are not to be bound to such personal Commands
mands

mands at will and pleasure, nor compelled to yield Obedience thereunto.

The contrary hereunto was the Principle at bottom of the Kings Cause, which he endeavoured to uphold and maintain, in order to decline and lay aside the Legal Restraints as aforesaid, which the Government of *England* by the Fundamental Constitution, is subjected unto, as to the exercise and ministery of the Royal Office.

From the Observation and Experience which the Pople of *England* had, and made many years together, by their Representatives in Parliament, of a desire in the King to shake off these Legal Restraints in the Exercise of the Regal Power, and on their having tried the best wayes and means that occurred to their Understandings, to prevent the same, and to secure to themselves the enjoyment of their Just Rights and Liberty, they at last pitch'd upon the desiring from the King, the continuance of the sitting of the Parliament called, *November* 3d 1640, in such sort as is expressed in that Act, 17. *Car.* wherein it is provided, *That it shall not be Discontinued or Dissolved, but by Act of Parliament.*

This was judged by them, the greatest Security imaginable, for keeping the ministry of the Royal Office within its due Bounds; and for quieting the People in the enjoyment of their Rights. But experience hath shewed, that this yet could not be done without a War, the worst and last of Remedies. For although their Continuance as the Representative Body of the Kingdom, with the Right to exercise the Power and Priviledges inherent in, and inseparable from that Supream Court and Chief Senate (whereof the King is Head, both making but one Person or Politick Body in Law) yet they themselves, as well as the King, were bound by the Fundamental Constitution or Compact, upon which the Government was at first built; containing the Condition upon which the King accepted of the Royal Office, and on which the People granted to him the Tribute of their Obedience and due Allegiance. This Condition, (as the Lawes and Experience declare) is, that the King shall exercise his Office of Rule over them according to the Laws, as hath been shewed, and as he and his People shall from time to time agree in Common Council in Parliament, for that end assembled. In respect hereof, the Laws so made, are called the Concords or Agreements passed between the King and the Subject, in the 3d part of *Cooks Institutes.*

These

These Agreements then are the Standard unto the Kings Rule and the Peoples Obedience, signifying the justice of his Commands, and the dueness of their Allegiance.

But the case so happening, that this Conjunction and Agreement which ought to be found between the personal Will of the King, and Representative Will of the Kingdom, failing, and these two Wills declaring themselves in Contrariety and Opposition, both of them becoming standing Powers, Co-ordinate and distinct parts of the Supremacy, as the two Channels wherein the Supremacy is placed and appointed to run, as to its exercise, by the Fundamental Constitution; hence sprang the War, each asserting and endeavouring to defend and maintain their own part and right, which ought not to be kept up in dis-junction and contrariety, but in Unity and Agreement each with other. These two Parties with their Adherents, in this Case, may be according to the Law, Contrarients one towards another, as the Law affords an Example, in the Preamble to *Cook's* 4th Part of his Institutes (not properly Traytors) being co-ordinate Powers, parts of the Supremacy, that are the Heads to each Party; and by consequence have a right of making a War, as their last Appeal, if they cannot otherwise agree.

Being once entred thus into a state of War and actual Enmity, they do as it were become two Nations, and cease to be under the Obligations they were in before, for during this state of War and Enmity, the standing Laws (in a sort) cease, and a new way of Rule each Party Forms to himself and his Adherents, as may best consist for each of their Safeties and Preservations.

Upon this Dis-junction of the two Wills, in the Harmony and Agreement whereof, the Supremacy is placed, these following Queries do naturally arise;

First.

To which, or Whether of these by Law is the Allegiance required as due? Is it to be yeilded to the Personal Will of the King single, in dis-junction from the Will of the Representative Body of the Kingdom, or to the Will of the People, in dis-junction from the Will of the King? Or is it to the Personal Will of the King, in conjunction with the Laws, though in opposition and contrariety to the Will of the Kingdoms Representative in Parliament Assembled? Or is it to the Will of the Kingdoms Representative, in conjunction with the Laws, though in opposition to the Personal Will of the King?

The

The Second Querie is,

In whose Judgement in this case are the People by Law to acquiesce, as to the declaring with whom the Laws are? Whether the Personal Judgement of the King single, or the Vote of the Senate, that is, the Kingdoms Representative Body?

The Third Querie is,

With whom will the Laws be found to go in this Case, so rare, unusual, and never happening before, and who is the Proper and Competent Judge? Also, whether the Laws be not perfectly silent, as never supposing such a Case possible to happen, by reason that the Power used by the one for Dissolving the other, never before suffered the Opposition to rise so high?

The Fourth Querie is,

Whether he, in this Case, that keeps his Station and place of Trust, wherein God and the Law did set him, with care to demean himself according to the best of his Understanding, agreeably to the Law and Customes of Parliament, and pursuant to their Votes and Directions, (so long as they sit and affirm themselves to be a Parliament) and uses his best endeavours in the exercise of that publick Trust, that no Detriment in the general come unto the Common-wealth by the failer of Justice, and the necessary Protection due from Government, without any designing or intending the Subversion of the Constitution, but onely the securing more fully the Peoples Liberties and just Rights, from all future Invasions and Oppressions, be not so far from deserving to be judged Criminal in respect of any Law of God or Man, that he ought rather to be affirmed One that hath done his Duty, even the next best that was left to him, or possible for him to do, in such a dark stormy season, and such difficult Circumstances?

As to the Right of the Cause it self, it ariseth out of the matter of Fact that hath happened, and by the Just and Wise Providence of God, hath been suffered to state it self, in the Contest between the Personal Will and declared Pleasure of the King, on the one Hand, and the publick Will or Vote of the People in Parliament, on the other, declaring it self either in Orders or Ordinances of both Houses, or in the single Act of the House of Commons, asserting it self a Parliament, upon the Grounds of the Act, 17 *Car.* providing against its dissolution.

This will appear with the more evidence and certainty, by considering wherein either part had a wrong Cause, or did or might do that which was not their Duty; taking the measure of their Duty from what as well the King as the Peoples Representative are obliged unto, by the Fundamental Conftitution of the Government, which binds them in each of their Capacities and diftinct Exercifes of their Truft, to intend and purfue the true good and welfare of the whole Body or Community as their End. This (in effect) is to detain the People in Obedience and Subjection to the Law of God, and to guide them in the wayes of Righteoufnefs unto God's well-pleafing : and to avoid falling out or difagreeing about the Way or Means leading to that End.

Hence that party which in his or their actings was at the greateft diftance from, or oppofition unto this end, and wilfully and unneceffarily difagreed and divided from the other, in the Wayes and Means that were moft likely to attain this End ; they were affuredly in the Fault, and had a Wrong Caufe to mannage, under what ever Name or Face of Authority it was Headed and Upheld. And fuch a Wrong Caufe was capable of being efpoufed and mannaged under the face of Authority that might be pretended unto by either part. For as the King (ftanding up on his Prerogative, and the binding force which his perfonal Will and Pleafure ought to have, though in diftinction from, and oppofition to his Parliament) might depart from the end of Government, anfwerable to his Truft, and yet urge his Right to be obeyed ; So the publick Will of the People, exercifed in and by the Vote of their Reprefentative in Parliament, afferting it felf to be of a binding force alfo, and to have the place of a Law, though in diftinction from the King and Laws alfo, (as faith the King) whatever otherwife by them is pretended, might alfo depart from the true end of Government, anfwerable to their Truft, and yet infift upon their Right to be Obeyed and fubmitted unto ; and having Power in their hands, might unduely go about alfo to compel Obedience. It is not lawful either for King or Parliament to urge Authority and compel Obedience as of Right in any fuch Cafes, where (according to the Law of Nature) the People are at Liberty, and ought to have a Freedom from yeelding Obedience, as they are and ought to have when ever any would compel them to difobey God, or to do things that evidently in the eye of Reafon and common fenfe, are to their hurt and deftruction. Such things Nature forbids the doing of, having for that very purpofe, armed Man with the defenfive Weapon of refufing to confent and obey, as that Priviledge, whereby Man is diftinguifhed from a Beaft ; which, when he is deprived of, he is made a Beaſt, and brought into a ſtate of perfect Servitude and Bondage.

Such a ſtate of Servitude and Bondage may by God's juſt Judgement, be inflicted upon man for ſin and the abuſe of his Liberty, when by God reſtored. The Liberty which man was at firſt created in, is that Priviledge and Right which is allowed to him by the Law of Nature, of not being compelled under any pretence whatſoever to ſin againſt God, or to go againſt the true good and welfare of his own Being; that is to ſay, of his inward or outward man, but in both theſe caſes, to have and to uſe his juſt Liberty, to Diſſent and refuſe to Obey.

For this every man hath that in himſelf, which by God is made a proper and competent Judge. For, as to all ſin againſt God, and the righteouſneſs of his Law, the Light of Conſcience, that is to ſay the Work of the Law, in and upon the Mind or inward Senſe, and in conjunction with it, doth lighten every one that cometh into the World, accuſing or excuſing, if it be but hearkened unto, and kept awake. And for all ſuch actings, as tend to the ruine and deſtruction of man, in his outward and bodily concerns, and as he is the Object of Magiſtratical Power and Juriſdiction, every man hath a Judgement of common Senſe, or a way of diſcerning and being ſenſible thereof, common to bruit Beaſts, that take in their Knowledge by the door of their Senſes, but is much heightned and enobled in man, by the perſonal union it is taken into, with his intellectual part, and intuitive way of diſcerning things, through the inward reflectings of the mind, compared with the Law of God. This inferiour Judgement in man, when it is conjoyned with, and confirmed by the Judgement of his Superiour part, is that which we call Rational, or the dictates of right Reaſon, that man hath a natural right to adhere unto, as the ordinary certain Rule, which is given him by God to walk by, and againſt which he ought not to be compelled, or be forced to depart from it, by the meer Will and Power of another, without better Evidence ; that is, a higher, a greater, or more certain way of diſcerning. This therefore in Scripture is called, *Man's Judgement*, or *Man's Day*, in diſtinction from the *Lord's Judgement*, and the *Lord's Day*. And this is that, in every individual man, which in the collective Body of the People, and meeting of Head and Members in Parliament, is called, *The Supream Authority*, and is the publick reaſon and will of the whole Kingdom ; the going againſt which, is, in Nature as well as by the Law of Nations, an offence of the higheſt rank,

O

amongſt

amongst men. For it muſt be preſumed, that there is more of the Wiſdom and Will of God in that publick Suffrage of the whole Nation, than of any private Perſon or leſſer collective Body, whatſoever, not better quallified and principled. For Man is made in God's Image, or in a likeneſs, in Judgement and Will, unto God himſelf, according to the meaſure that in his nature he is proportioned and made capable to be the receiver and bearer thereof. Therefore it is, that the reſiſting and oppoſing either of that Judgement or Will, which is in it ſelf Supream, and the Law to all others, (or which bears ſo much proportion and likeneſs to the Supream Will, as is poſſible for a Society and community of Men agreeing together for that end, to contrive and ſet up for an adminiſtration thereof unto them) is againſt the duty of any member of that Society, as well as it is againſt the duty of the Body of the whole Society, to oppoſe its Judgement and Will to that of the Supream Law-giver, their higheſt Soveraigh, God himſelf.

The higheſt Judgement and Will, ſet up by God, for Angels and Men in their particular beings; to hold proportion with, and bear conformity unto, (in the capacity of Ruled, in relation to their chief Ruler) ſhines forth in the perſon of Chriſt, the engrafted Word. And when by the Agreement or common Conſent of a Nation or State, there is ſuch a Conſtitution and Form of Adminiſtration pitched upon, as in a ſtanding and ordinary way, may derive and conveigh the neareſt and greateſt likeneſs in humane Laws, or Acts of ſuch a Conſtitution, unto the Judgement and Will of the Supream Legiſlator, as the Rule and declared Duty for every one in that Society to obſerve ; It is thereby, that Government or Supream Power comes to receive Being in a Nation or State; and is brought into exerciſe according to God's Ordinance, and Divine Inſtitution. So then, it is not ſo much the Form of the Adminiſtration, as the thing Adminiſtred, wherein the good or evil of Government doth conſiſt ; that is to ſay, a greater likeneſs or unlikeneſs unto Judgement and Will of the higheſt Being, in all the Acts or Laws, flowing from the Fundamental Conſtitution of the Government.

Hence it is, that common Conſent, lawfully and rightfully given by the Body of a Nation, and intruſted with Delegates of their own free choice, to be exerciſed by them, as their Repreſentatives, (as well for the Welfare and good of the Body that truſts them, as to the Honour and Well-pleaſing of God the Supream Legiſlator) as the Principle and Means, warranted by the Law of Nature and

Nations,

Nations, to give Conftitution and Admiffion to the exercife of Government, and Supream Authority, over them and amongft them : Agreeable hereunto , we are to fuppofe , that our Anceftors in this Kingdom did proceed, when they conftituted the Government thereof, in that form of Adminiftration, which hath been derived to us, in the courfe and channel of our Cuftomes and Laws ; amongft which, the Law and Cuftomes in and of the Parliaments, are to be accounted as chief. For,

Hereby *Firft*; The Directive or Legiflative Power (having the Right to State and Give the Rule for the Governors Duty, and the Subjects Obedience) is continued in our Laws, which as well the King as People are under the Obfervation of ; witnefs the **Corona**tion Oath, and the Oath of Allegiance.

Secondly, The Coercive or Executive Power is placed in one Perfon, under the Name and Style of a King, to be put forth not by his own, fingle, perfonal Command, but by the fignification of his Will and Pleafure, as the Will of the whole State, in and by his Courts of Juftice, and ftated publick Counfels and Judicatures, agreed on for that purpofe, between him and his People, in their Parliamentary Affemblies.

The Will of the whole State, thus fignified, the Law it felf prefers before the perfonal Will of the King, in diftinction from the Law, and makes the one binding, the other not. So that the publick Will of the State, (fignified and declared by the publick Suffrage and Vote of the People or Kingdom in Parliament Affembled) is a Legal and Warrantable ground for the Subjects Obedience, in the things commanded by it, for the good and welfare of the whole Body, according to the beft Underftanding of fuch their Reprefentative Body, by it put forth, during the time of its fitting.

The Body with whom the Delegated Vote and publick Suffrage of the whole Nation is Intrufted, being once Affembled, with Power not to be Diffolved but by their own confent, in that capacity the higheft Vote and Truft (that can be) is exercifed, and this by Authority of Parliament, unto *ex Officio*, or by way of Office are the Keepers of the Liberties of *England*, or of the People, by the faid Authority, for which they are accountable if they do not faithfully difcharge that their duty. This Office of keeping the Liberty, which by the Law of God and Nature is due to the Community or whole Body of the People, is, by way of Truft, committed by themfelves to their own Delegates, and in effect amounts unto this.

1. That

1. That they may of right keep out and refuse any to exercise Rule and Command over them, except God himself, who is the Supream and Universal King and Governour; or, such as shall agree in their Actings, to bear his Image, (which is, to be Just) and shew for the Warrant of their Exercise of Soveraignty, both a likeness in Judgement and Will, unto him, who is Wisdom and Righteousness it self; and the Approbation and common Consent of the whole Body, rationally reposing that Trust in them, from what is with visible and apparent Characters manifest to them, of an aptness and sufficiency in them, to give forth such publick Acts of Government, that may bear the Stamp of God's Impression upon them in the Judgements they do and execute; especially, being therein helped with a National Counsel of the Peoples own choosing from time to time.

2. They may of right, keep, hold, and restrain him or them, with whom the Coercive or Executive Power is intrusted, unto a punctual performance of Duty, according to the Fundamental Constitution, the Oath of the Ruler, and the Laws of the Land. And if they shall refuse to be so held and restrained by the humble Desires, Advice and common Consent in Parliament, and the Peoples Delegates be invaded and attempted upon by force, to deter them from the faithful discharge of this their Duty; they may, in asserting their Right, and in a way of their own just Defence, raise Armes, put the issue upon Battel, and Appeal unto God.

3. Such Appeal answered, and the issue decided by Battel, the Peoples Delegates still fitting, and keeping together in their Collective Body, may of right, and according to reason refuse the readmission or new-admission of the Exercise of the former Rulers, or any new Rulers again over the whole Body, till there be received Satisfaction for the former Wrongs done, the expence and hazzard of the War, and Security for the time to come, that the like be not committed again. Until this be obtained, they are bound in duty, in such manner as they judge most fit, to provide for the present Government of the whole Body, that the Common-weal receive no detriment.

4. In this which is the proper Office of the Peoples Delegates, and concerns the keeping and defending the Liberty and Right of the whole People and Nation, they may and ought, (during their fitting) to Exercise their own proper Power and Authority (the Exigents of the Kingdom requiring it) although the other two Estates joyntly instructed with them, (in the exercise of the Legiflative

giflative Authority) fhould defert their flation, or otherwife fail
in the Execution of their Trufts; yea, or though many or moft
of their own Members (fo long as a lawful *Quorum* remains) fhall
either voluntarily withdraw from them, or, for juft caufe become
excluded. In this difcharge of their truft, for the common welfare
and fafety of the whole, their Actings (though extraordinary and
contrarient to the right of the other two) cannot be treafonable or
criminal, (though they may be tortious, and erroneous) feeing
they are equals and co-ordinate, in the exercife of the Legiflative
Power, and have the Right of their own proper Truft and Office to
difcharge and defend, though their fellow Truftees fhould fail in
theirs. Nor can, nor ought the People, as Adherents to their own
Delegates and Reprefentatives, to be reputed criminal, or blameworthy, by the Law.

In the exercife of one and the fame Legiflative power (according to the Fundamental Conftitution of the Government of *England*) there are three diftinct publick Votes, allowed for Affent
or Difcent, in all matters coming before them; the Agreement of
which is effential and neceffary to the paffing of a Law: the perfonal Vote of the King; the perfonal Votes of the Lords in a Houfe
or diftinct Body; and the Delegated Vote and Suffrage of the
whole People, in their Reprefentative Body, or the Houfe of Commons. Unto each of thefe, appertains a diftinct Office and Priviledge, proper to them.

1. The Regal Office, and the Prerogative thereof to the
King.

2. The Judicial Office, to the Lords, as the higheft Judicature
and Court of Juftice under the King, for the exercifing Coercive
Power, and punifhing of Malefactors.

3. The Office of the Keepers of the Liberties and Rights of the
People, as they are the whole Nation, incorporated under one
Head, by their own free and common Confent.

The Regal Office is the Fountain of all Coercive and Executive
Power, purfuant to the Rule, fet to the fame by Law, or, the
Agreement of the three Eftates in Parliament.

The Rule which is fet, is that of Immutable Juft and Right, according to which, penalties are applicable, and become due, and is
firft ftated and afcertained, in the declared Law of God, which is
the fignification or making known by fome fign, the Will of the
Supream Legiflator, proceeding from a perfect Judgement and Underftanding, that is without all Error or Defect.

The

The Will that flowes from such a Judgement, is in its nature Legiflative, and binding, and of right to be obeyed for its own fake, and the perfection it carries in it, and with it, in all its actings. This Will is declared by Word, or Works, or both. By Word we are to underftand, either the immediate Breath and Spirit of Gods mouth or mind, or the Infpiration of the Almighty, miniftred by the holy Ghoft, in and by fome creature, as his veffel and inftrument, through which the holy Scriptures of the old and new Teftament were compofed. By works that declare God's Will, we are to underftand the whole Book of the Creature, but more eminently and efpecially, the particular Beings and Natures of Angels and Men, who bear the name and likenefs of God in and upon their Judgements and their Wills; their directing Power, and their executive Power of mind, which are effential to their Being, Life, and Motion.

When thefe direct and execute, in conjunction and harmony with God's Judgement and Will, made known in his Law, they do that which is right; and by adhering and conforming themfelves unto this their certain and unerring Guide, do become Guides and Rulers unto others, and are the Objects of right choice, where Rulers are wanting in Church or State.

The Rule then to all action of Angels or Men, is that of moral or immutable Juft and Right, which is ftated and declared, in the Will and Law of God. The firft and higheft imitation of this Rule, is the Creature-being in the perfon of Chrift. The next is the Bride the Lambs Wife. The next is the innumerable Society of the holy Angels. The next is the Company of Juft Men, fixed in their natural Obedience and Duty, through Faith, manifefting it felf not onely in their Spirits, but in their outward Man, redeemed even in this World, from the body of corruption, as far as is here attainable. The Power which is directive, and ftates and afcertains the morallity of the Rule for Obedience, is in the Law of God. But the original, whence all juft executive Power arifes, which is Magiftratical and Coercive, is from the will or free gift of the People, who may either keep the Power in themfelves, or give up their Subjection into the hands and will of another, as their Leader and Guide, if they fhall judge that thereby they fhall better anfwer the end of Government, to wit, the welfare and fafety of the whole, then if they ftill kept the Power in themfelves. And when they part with it, they may do it conditionally or abfolutely; and whilft they keep it, they are **bound to the** right ufe of it. In this Liberty,

every

every man is created, and it is the Priviledge and juſt Right which is granted unto Man by the Supream Law-giver, even by the Law of Nature, under which man was made.

God himſelf leaves man to the free exerciſe of this his Liberty, when he tenders to him his ſafety and immutability, upon the well or ill uſe of this his Liberty, allowing him the choice, either to be his own guide and ſelf-ruler, in the ability communicated to him, to know and execute Gods Will, and ſo to keep the Liberty he is poſſeſſed of, in giving away his ſubjection or not ; or elſe upon God's Call and Promiſe, to give up himſelf in way of ſubjection to God, as his Guide and Ruler, either abſolutely or conditionally. To himſelf he expects abſolute Subjection ; to all ſubordinate Rulers, conditional.

While mans Subjection is his own, and in his own keeping, unbeſtowed and ungiven out of himſelf, he is not, nor cannot be accountable by way of crime or offence, againſt his Ruler and Soveraign, but may do with his own what he pleaſe ; but ſtill at his peril, if he uſe not this his Liberty as he ſhould, to the end for which it is given him, which is by voluntary and entire reſignation to become an obedient Subject unto him who is the Supream Law-giver, and Rightful King, without poſſibility of change or defection.

Unto this right and the lawful exerciſe and poſſeſſion of, it this Nation did arive by the good providence and gift of God, in calling and aſſembling the Parliament, *November* 3d. 1640. and then continuing their Seſſion by an expreſs Act, 17. *Car.* with power not to be diſſolved but by their own conſent; which was not ſo much the introducing of a new Law, as declaratory of what was Law before, according to Man's natural Right, in which he was created, and of which he was poſſeſſed by God, the ſoveraign giver of all things.

But the paſſing that ſaid Act of Parliament alone, was not that which reſtored the Nation to their original Right, and juſt Natural Liberty ; but onely put them in the capacity and poſſibility of it. That which wanted to make out to the Nation a clearneſs in having and obtaining this their right, was the obligation they had put upon themſelves and their poſterities to their preſent Soveraign and his Authority, which in juſtice and by the Oathes of Allegiance they were ſolemnly bound to, in the ſight of God as well as of Man. And therefore, unleſs by the abuſe of that office of Truſt, (to that degree, as on his part, to break the fundamental compact and conſtitution

ſtitution of Government) they could not be ſet free nor reſtored to their original Right and firſt Liberty : eſpecially if together with ſuch breach of Truſt, both parties appeal to God, and put it upon the iſſue of Battel, and God give the deciſion ; and in conſequence thereof, that original Right be aſſerted, and poſſeſſion thereof had and held for ſome years, and then not rightfully loſt, but treacherouſly betrayed and given up by thoſe in whom no power was rightfully placed, to give up the ſubjection of the Nation again unto any, whatſoever.

Unto which is to be added, that how and when the diſſolution of the ſaid Parliament, (according to Law) hath been made, is yet unaſcertained, and not particularly declared : by reaſon whereof, and by what hath been before ſhewed, the ſtate of the Caſe on the Subjects part, is much altered, as to the matter of Right, and the Uſurpation is now on the other hand, there being, (as is well known) two ſorts of Uſurpers ; either ſuch, as having no right of conſent at all unto the Rule they exerciſe over the Subject ; or ſuch, who under pretence of a Right and Title, do claim not by conſent, but by conqueſt and power, or elſe hold themſelves not obliged to the Fundamental compact and conſtitution of Government, but gain unduely from the Subject, (by advantages taken through deceit and violence) that which is not their own by Law.

For a rational Man to give up his Reaſon and Will unto the Judgement and Will of another, (without which, no outward coercive Power can be) whoſe Judgement and Will is not perfectly and unchangeably good and right, is unwiſe, and unſafe, and by the Law of Nature, forbidden. And therefore all ſuch gift, made by rational men, muſt be conditional, either implied, or explicite, to be followers of their Rulers, ſo far as they are followers of that good and right, which is contained in the Law of the Supream Lawgiver, and no further ; reſerving to themſelves, (in caſe of ſuch defection and declining of the Rulers actings from the Rule) their primitive and original Freedom, to reſort unto, that ſo they may in ſuch caſe, be as they were before they gave away their ſubjection unto the Will of another ; and reſerving alſo the power to have this judged by a meet and competent Judge, which is the Reaſon of the King and Kingdom, declared by their Repreſentatives in Parliament ; that is to ſay, the Delegates of the People in the Houſe of Commons aſſembled, and the Commiſſioners on the Kings behalf, by his own Letters Patents, in the Houſe of Peers ; which two concurring do very far bind the King, if not wholly.

And

And when thefe cannot agree, but break one from another, the Commons in Parliament affembled, are *ex Officio*, the Keepers of the Liberties of the Nation, and righteous Poffeffors and Defendors of it, againft all Ufurpers and Ufurpations whatfoever, by the Laws of *England*.

The Valley of Jehofhaphat, *confidered and opened*, by comparing 2. Chron. 20. *with* Joel 3.

IT was the faying of *Auftine* ; Nothing falls under our fenfes, or happens in this vifible World, but is either commanded or permitted from the invifible and unintelligible Court and Pallace of the higheft Emperor and univerfal King, who is the chief over all the kings of the earth. For although he hath both commanded and permitted a fubordinate external Government over Men, adminiftred by man, for the upholding of Juftice in humane Societies, and for the peace, welfare, and fafety of men that are made in Gods Image ; yet, he hath not fo entirely put the Rule of the whole earth out of his own hands, but that in cafes of eminent injuftice and oppreffion (committed in Provinces, States and Kingdomes, contrary to his Lawes, to their own, and the very end of Magiftracy, which is, the confervation of the Peoples juft Rights and Liberties) *He. that is higher than the higheft amongft men, doth regard,* and will fhew by fome extraordinary interpofition of his, that *there are higher than they.*

Such a feafonable and fignal appearance of God, for the Succor and Relief of his People, in their greateft Straits and Exigencies, (when they have no might, vifible Power, or armed Force, to undertake the great company and multitude that comes againft them, nor know what to do, fave onely to have their eyes towards him) is called in Scripture, *The day of the Lord's Judgement.* Then the Battel and caufe of the Quarrel, will appear to be not fo much theirs, as the Lord's : and the frame of their heart will be humble before the Lord, believing in the Lord, and believing his Prophets, for their good fuccefs and eftablifhment.

This Difpenfation is very lively defcribed under the Type, and by the Name of *The Valley of Jehofhaphat*, as to the Seafon and Place wherein God will give forth a fignal appearance of himfelf in Judgement, on the behalf of his People, for a final decifion of the

P

Con-

Controverſie between them and their enemies. It Litterally and Typically fell out thus, as is at large recorded, 2 *Chron.* 20.

By way of alluſion to this, and upon occaſion of the like, yea, and far greater Extreamities, which God's People in the laſt dayes, are to be brought into, is that Propheſie, *Joel* 3. for a like, yea, a far greater and more ſignal appearance of God for their Deliverance and Reſcue, in order to a final Deciſion of the Controverſie, between his People and the Inhabitants of the earth, by his own Judgement. This is there called, *The Valley of Jehoſhaphat,* in which the Lord will ſit to Judge all his enemies round about. In this Battel and great Deciſion of his Peoples Controverſie, he will cauſe his Mighty Ones to come down from Heaven, to put in their ſickle as reapers in this Vintage and Harveſt, when the wickedneſs is great. Unto this, *Revel.* 14. 14, 20. refers, which doth plainly evidence, that this grand Deciſion is to fall out in the very laſt of times, and probably, is that, which will make way to the Riſing of the Witneſſes, and will be accompanied with that *Earthquake, in which ſhall be ſlain, of men ſeven thouſand, and the tenth part of the City will* thereupon *fall, Rev.* 11.

It is expreſſed, *Joel* 3. That in this day of the Lord, wherein he will be *near, in the Valley of Deciſion, the Heavens and the Earth ſhall ſhake, by the Lords own roaring out of Sion ; and he himſelf will be the Harbour, Hope and Strength of his People. The Sun and Moon* of earthly Churches and Thrones of Judicature, that conteſt with them, *ſhall be darkened, and the Stars,* (even the choiceſt and moſt illuminated gifted Paſtors & Leaders, in the earthly *Jeruſalem* Churches, with their moſt refined Forms of Worſhip, reſiſting the power of true ſpiritual Godlineſs) *ſhall withdraw their ſhining.* Even their holy fleſh will paſs off from them and conſume away upon their ſpiritual lewdneſs, and confident oppoſing the Faith of Gods Elect, *Jer.* 11. 17. *Their very Eyes will conſume away in their holes, with which they ſay, we ſee ;* and for which, Chriſt tells the *Phariſees,* in like caſe, that *therefore ther ſin remaineth.* (John 9. 41.) Or, *there remaineth no more benefit from Chriſt's Sacrifice, for their ſin ;* and therefore *onely a fearful looking for of the fiery and devouring indignation,* Heb. 10. 26, 27.

Here's that, the great confidence and boaſt of many profeſſing Churches and eminent Paſtors in the earthly *Jeruſalem* Fabrick, or Houſe on the ſand, will come to, *Ezek.* 13. and *Mat.* 7. Their very Eyes, their high enlightenings and excellent ſpiritual Gifts, their ſupernatural or infuſed humane Learning, that's admitted only

ly

ly as an adorning and accomplishment of the natural man, (unaccompanied with that Fire-Baptisme, that's performed by the unspeakable gift of the Spirit it self, for the transforming of the natural man into spiritual) even these Eyes becoming evil, (*Mat.* 6.23.)and this light, opposing and preferring it self to the more excellent discerning and marvellous light in spiritual Believers, are turned by the just Judgement of God, into the greatest and most fatal blindness and darkness of all. Their tongues also, though the tongues of men and angels, for excellency and dexterity of expressing what they see, with the forementioned eyes, will consume away in their mouth, (*Zech.* 14. 12.) and leave them exposed to become, and accordingly be dealt with, as meer *sounding brass and tinckling Cymbals*, (1 *Cor.* 12. 31. and 13. 1.) *giving no certain sound*, and right warning to the Battels of the Lord, *the good fight of Faith*.

This comes to pass through their confidence in those attainments, which may be, and oft are turned into an Idol of jealousie, and spiritual whoredom, *Ezek.* 16. 1, 15.

All these considerations of Church and State, put together, afford great ground of enquiry, as to the Condition of the times in which we live, how far the face which they bear, (and which God hath put upon them, in the course of his Providences, for some years now past) doth speak or signifie the near approach of any such extraordinary and signal appearance or day of Gods Judgement, for the Decision of his own or his Peoples quarrel and controversie with the prophane Heathen that are round about them, waiting for an advantage, utterly and universally to remove and root them out from off the face of the whole earth ?

That which hath been acted upon the Theater of these Nations, amongst us, in the true state of our Controversie, seems to be reducible to this following Querie ;

Whether the Representative Body of the Kingdom of England, in Parliament assembled, and in their Supream Power and Trust made indissolvable, unless by their own Consent and free Vote, and this by particular and express Statute, have not had a just and righteous Cause ? A Quarrel more God's, than their own ?

1. It may appear they had ; *First*, from the Ground of their undertaking the War ; Was it not in their own and the Kingdoms just and necessary defence , and for the maintaining of the publick Rights and Liberties of both ?

2. *Secondly*, Was it not undertaken upon mutual Appeals of

P 2   both

both Parties to God, defiring him to judge between them, to give the Decifion and Iffue by the Law of War, (when no other Law could be heard) as the definitive Sentence in this Controverfie, from the Court of Heaven ?

3. *Thirdly*, Purfuant to fuch Decifion, did they not recover and repoffefs the Kingdoms original and primitive freedom ? Did they not endeavour to conferve and fecure it, as due to them by the Law of God and of Nature ? For man was made in God's Image, and all *Adams* Pofterity are properly one Univerfal Kingdom on earth, under the Rule and Government of the Son of God, both as Creator and Redeemer.

By virtue of this original and primitive Freedom fo recovered, they were at their own choice, whether to remain in, and retain this their true freedom (unrefigned and unfubjected to the Will of any Man) under the Rule of the Son of God and his Lawes, or elfe to fet up a King or any other Form of Government over them, after the manner of other Nations. In this latter cafe, it is acknowledged, that when a Common-wealth or People, do choofe their firft King, upon condition to obey him and his Succeffors, Ruling juftly ; they ought to remain fubject to him, according to the Law, and tenor of the Fundamental Compact with him, on whom they have transferred their Authority. No Jurifdiction remaineth in them (after that free and voluntary Act of theirs) either to Judge the Realm, or determine who is the true Succeffor, otherwife than is by them referved and ftipulated, by their Fundamental Laws and Conftitutions of Government.

And though the righteoufnefs of this Caufe(contained in the forementioned particulars) be fuch, as carries in it its own evidence ; yet, as (as things have fallen out) it is come to be oppreffed and buried in the grave of Malefactors ; in the room of which, a contrary Judgement and Way, is vifibly owned, upheld, and intended to be profecuted to the utmoft, for its own faft-rooting and eftablifhment ; and this, by the common Confent and Affociation of Multitudes. What then remaines for the recovery and reftitution of that good old Caufe and Way, but fuch a feafonable and fignal appearance of God, (as aforefaid) in the Valley of *Jehofhaphat* ? What but the taking things immediately into his own hands, for adminiftration of Judgement, and giving the laft and final decifion? Efpecially, fince what was foretold by *Daniel*, is remarkably acomplifhed amongft us, to wit, that the vifible Power of Gods People fhould be broken and fcattered, fo as that they fhould have no might remaining

maining in and with them, to go against the Multitudes, that design and resolve their Ruine.

There is not any remedy left to them, wherein they may expect succefs, but from such a fignal day of the Lord's immediate appearance in Judgement on their behalf. *For their fakes therefore, O Lord, return thou on high, (Pfal. 7. 7.) take thy Throne of Judicature over men, from which thou haft feemed to have departed, and execute that righteous Judgement, which thou haft feemed for a feafon to have fufpended, upon wife and holy ends beft known to thy felf.*

In fuch a dark and gloomy day, thofe that truely fear the Lord, are directed and required by him, not to fear or be difmayed, becaufe he will be with them. They are encouraged in the way of Faith onely, to expect this deliverance; even to *ftand ftill*, as having no need to fight in this Battel, but onely *to fee the Salvation of the Lord*, through believing.

A Ntient Foundations, when once become deftructive to thofe very ends for which they were firft ordained, and prove hinderances, to the good and enjoyment of humane Societies, to the true Worfhip of God, and the Safety of the People, are for their fakes, and upon the fame Reafons to be altered, for which they were firft laid. In the way of God's Juftice they may be fhaken and removed, in order to accomplifh the Counfels of his Will, upon fuch a State, Nation, or Kingdom, in order to his introducing a righteous Government, of his own framing.

This may have been the caufe of our Wandrings as it were in a Wildernefs, and of God's bringing us back again into *Egypt*, after our near approach to the Land of Reft; that we have no better known, and had no more care to profecute, what he principally intended in and by all our Changes and Removes, in the courfe of his Providence. Yea we have added this alfo, to the reft of our fins, that we have improved the Gifts and Deliverances that God beftowed upon us, another way, and to another end than was by him intended, as well as Providentially intimated, by that holy Decree of his, in the Decifion, declared at the Trial in his Martial Court, with points of Swords.

Here the great Controverfie that had been depending many Ages between Rulers and the Ruled, (as to the Claimes of the one in point of Prerogative; and of the other in their Spiritual and Temporal

poral Freedoms)was after many heats & colds,many skirmishings and battels, at last decided by the Sword. This is a way of Tryal allowed by the known common Law of *England*, and the Law in force throughout all Nations. By this, the Verdict is given forth from a Court of such a Nature, as from whence there is no further appeal ; Especially since after the Tryal past, quiet possession was given to the Conquerors, and continued some years. Upon this, Reason and Gratitude to God, obliged us to such a prosecution as might answer the true end of Government ; and in especial after that manner, as might be most to God's well-pleasing.

The Powerful Being which by success of Armes, as given to the Peoples Representative Body in Parliament, did communicate to it essentiallity, according to the nature of that Being, for which it was ordained. For that Being, with Power of continuing together at their own pleasure, were as the Soul and Body, unseperated,and they might have performed things necessary at present, for the safety and preservation of the Body they represented. They might have been a good help to settle righteous Government, in a constitution most acceptable to God, and beneficial to the Governed, on the Foundation of God's Institution, and the Peoples Ordination, in consent together,laid by the Power of God and the Peoples own Swords, in the hands of their faithful Trustees.

It would imply a high contempt of God and his Dispensations, so signal amongst us, to communicate the benefit of them to his opposers. The right of choosing and being chosen into places of Trust in the Government, was returned by the Law of the Sword (which is paramount to all humane Laws) into its primitive exercise, which is warranted by the Law of God and of Nature. By that Law the most famous Monarchies of the World in all Ages were first constituted and setled ; and by it God decided our Cause, looking for an event and fruit answerable to the benefit by him given; even such a Government, as God would have given us the Pattern of (had we fought it, as was our duty) whereby Justice and Mercy should have been daily administred according to his will, to the bringing on the *new Heavens and new Earth, wherein Righteousness might dwell.*

The Vessel of this Common-wealth now weather-beaten and torn , seems to be more in danger, than that wherein *Jonah* would have fled to *Tarsus* : For though we have cast forth a great part of our goods to secure it, this has done us but small good. That Ship had but one Delinquint aboard, which occasioned the Storm ; and
his

his being thrown into the Sea, brought immediate safety. They had also many skilful Seamen to guide it, but all our Pilots are cast over-board, and none left in appearance, but guilty Passengers. Nay, admit with *Jonah*, both the Common-wealth and Cause be brought into most desperate Exigents and Extreamities, from whence there is no more appearing redemption for them, then such as they have, that go down quick into the grave and belly of the Whale ; yet they may be preserved, even by that which naturally of it self is irrecoverably destructive to them, and be employed again in service by him against whom they have been so ungratefully rebellious after former great deliverances. So infinite are God's Mercies, yea, so exceeding Merciful are the severest of his **Judge**-ments and Dispensations towards his People.

Thus may both People and Army be deprived of their Power, and another party let in to plague and root out from amongst us, such as are more wicked than themselves, and so make room for a more righteous Generation, which will begin all things anew.

By the course of things acted amongst us, God's sentence on our behalf is made void, and that seems given away for ever, which was recovered by the Sword. Our troubles are onely prorogued. No Faith or Contract is thought meet to be kept with Rebels and Hereticks, when by acquired Power it may be broken. 'Twas the great folly and self-flattery of some, to think it would be other-wise. It is most certainly true, that no Time or Prescription, is a just Bar to God's and the Peoples Right.

To murmure against God's Verdict, and resist his Doom, so so-lemnly given and executed amongst us, in the sight and concurring acknowledgement of the Nations round about, is to become adver-saries to God, and to betray our Countrey. If God then do think fit to permit such a dispensation to pass upon us, it is for the punish-ment of our sins, and for a plague to those that are the Actors there-in ; to bring more swift exemplary vengeance upon them. Such as have discharged a good Conscience in what may most offend the higher Powers, are not to fear , though they be admitted to the exercise of their Rule, with an unrestrained Power, and revengeful mind.

Though from that Mountain, the Storm that comes, will be ve-ry terrible, yet some are safest in Storms, as experience shews. Yea best therein by Gods Mercies, when their greatest enemies think most irrecoverably to undo them.

Our late Condition held much resemblance with that of the

Jewes, and we deserve as well to be rejected as they were. If Christ were in the flesh amongst us, as he was with them, we are as likely to prefer theeves and murtherers before him, and crucifie him.

The present necessity in a righteous Cause is to be submitted to, and we are not to be discouraged by the danger, which to some seems threatned us, from former or present Laws. For no man that acts for common safety, when the Sword hath absolute power, and shall also command it, can justly be questioned afterwards for acting contrary to some former Laws, which could be binding no longer then whilst the Civil Sword had Soveraignty.

What People under Heaven have had more Experiments of God's timely assistance in all their Extreamities, then *English-men*, as well with respect to times past, as within our remembrance ? Are the like Mercies recorded of any Nation ? In their times of greatest Confusion they were preserved. They were a living active Body without a Head : A Bush burning in the Flames of a Civil War, yet not consumed : A People when without a Government, not embrued in one ano hers Blood. A wonder to all Neighbours round about, and many signal Changes brought about without Blood, which indubitably evidences that God is in the Bush : and would gather us together as Chickens under a Hen, to be brooded by him, if we were not most stubbornly hardened.

Our sins have been the cause, that our Counsels, our Forces, our Wit, our Conquests, and our Selves have been destructive to our selves, to each other, and to a happy advancement towards our long expected and desired Settlement. Until these sins of ours be repented truly and throughly, all the Wisdom **and** Power upon Earth shall not avail us, but every day, every attempt, will encrease our Troubles, until there be a final extirpation of all that hinders God's Work ; When this once is, nothing shall harm us, God being a sure refuge against all evils, if we reconcile our selves to him by Faith and Repentance. Then, even those things that are most mischievous in their own natures, shall be made our advantage and security.

The Peoples Cause whom God after trial hath declared free, is a righteous one, though not so prudently and righteously managed as it might and ought to have been. God's doom therefore is justly executed upon us, with what intent and jugglings soever it was prosecuted by men.

Man's corruption makes him more firmly to adhere to that which
is

is good ; in which case, it is not many times, Virtue so much as Necessity that keeps men Constant ; having no other means of safety and subsistance for the most part.

The goodness of any Cause is not meerly to be judged by the Events, whether visibly prosperous or unprosperous, but by the righteousness of its Principles : nor is our Faith and Patience to fail under the many fears, doubts, wants, troubles, and Power of Adversaries, in the passage to the recovery of our long lost Freedom. For it is the same Cause with that of the *Israelites* of old, of which we ought not to be ashamed or distrustful.

How hath it fared with the Cause of Christ generally, for more now than 1600 years, being made the common object of scorn and persecution, not from the base and foolish onely, but from the noblest and wisest persons in the Worlds esteem! Yet, though our Sufferings and the time of our warfare seems long, it is very short, considering the perpetuity of the Kingdom which at last we shal obtain, & wherein we shal individually reign with the chief Soveraign thereof. For whereas all the Kingdoms of the World have not yet lasted 6000 years, this is everlasting and without end. They that overcome by not loving their lives unto the death, (*Rev.* 12, 11,) shall be Pillars in the House of this everlasting Kingdom, never to be removed. They shall be Kings and Priests to God, sitting with him upon his Throne, subjecting the Nations, and reigning with him for ever and ever. This is a Kingdom that consists with the Divinity of Christ, and humanity of men. Such a reign of Christ upon earth, as will not be without Laws agreeable to humane Nature, nor without Magistrates appointed as Officers under him ; in which Election, God and the People shall have a joint concurrence. God's Throne in mens Consciences must then be resigned, and his People permitted to enjoy the Liberties, due to them by the Laws of Grace and Nature. Into this, God's own immediate hand can now onely lead us, by his own coming to Judgement in the Valley of *Jehoshaphat.*

Meditations concerning Man's Life, &c. *Penned by this Sufferer in his Prison State.*

IT is a principal part of Wisdom to know how to esteem Life ; to hold and preserve, to loose or give it up. There is scarce any thing man more fails in than this. They that think nothing dearer

than

than Life, esteem Life for it self, live not but to live. Others think th: shortest Life best, either not to be born at all or else to die quickly. These are two extreams. That comes nearer Truth, a Wise Man said, Life is such a good, that if a man knew what he did in it, he would not accept, at least not desire it. *Vitam nemo cuperet, si daretur tantum scientibus.* Wise Men, in living, make a Virtue of Necessity, live as long as they should, not as long as they can.

There is a time to Live and a time to die. A good Death is far better and more elegible than an ill Life. A wise man Lives but so long as his Life is more worth than his Death. The longer Life is not alwayes the better. To what end serves a long Life? Simply to live, breath, eat, drink, and see this World? What needs so long a time for all this? Me thinks we should soon be tired with the daily repetition of these and the like Vanities? Would we live long, to gain knowledge, experience, and Virtue? This seems an honest Design, but is better to be had other wayes by good men, when their Bodies are in the grave.

None usually imploy their time so ill in this World, as Men. *Non inopes sumus vitæ, sed prodigi.* Some begin to live when they should die. Some have ended before they begin. 'Tis incident to folly to be alwayes but beginning to Live. Life is but a sorrowful state, a perpetual issue of Errors. 'Tis a Web of unhappy Adventures; A pursuit of divers Miseries enchained together on all sides. *Solum id certum, nil esse certi : Nec miserius quicquam homine nec superbius.* Vanity is the most essential and proper quality of Man's first Nature. The World is not worth that Labour and Pains Man exercises in and about it ; which caused that saying ; A wise man should do nothing but for himself. Tis not reason wise men should put themselves in danger for Fooles, much less for Knaves.

The Will onely is truly Mans own, and the considerable part of the reasonable Soul. On it depend the issues of Good or Evil, Life or Death. All the rest of a Man, his Understanding, Memory, Imagination, may be taken from him, altered, troubled by a thousand accidents. But the Will is so much in our own power, that it cannot be taken away, though its action may be hindred. 'Tis our own, till we knowingly and freely give it away, which may be. And he that hath once absolutely given up his Will to another, is no more his own man. He hath left himself nothing of his own. Tis by the Will we are good or evil, happy or unhappy.

Con-

He that gives up his Will to the Rule and Government of another, becomes subject to that other. Men that are born equal, come to be made subject two wayes; either, by the free giving up of themselves to others, or by others violent assuming and exercising power over them, because they are strangers, as *Nimrod* the mighty hunter of men, served his fellow mortals.

Government is either Royal, or Seignioral and Tyrannical, as the *Turks*. 'Tis then properly Royal, be it administred by one, by many, or by all their Representatives, when he or they that have Soveraign Power, obey the Laws of Nature, preserve the natural Liberty and propriety of the Goods and Persons of the Subjects, which no reasonable men, acted by sound judgement, will ever absolutely give away, but secure their right in, and power over, by fundamental Contracts and Agreements with their Governors.

Absolute Soveraignty is a perpetual power over all, without any restraint, limitations or conditions put upon the Soveraign. This consists in a power of giving Laws to all in general, and to every one in particular, without the consent or gift of any others, and requiring universal and undispensable obedience to all his Commands, under just penalties. This Soveraignty is proper onely to the highest Being, not at all to Creatures, though where the Government is Despotical and Seignioral, it is assumed and exercised.

But Government Royal, is that which is consonant to the immutable Laws of Nature and Dictates of right Reason, which require a conservation of the Subjects Liberty, and Propriety in their goods and persons, as well as the preservation and upholding of Empire and Authority in the Prince, and find out the Medium, through the mutual Agreements of Soveraign and Subjects, for both to consist.

In Quarrels between Subjects and Soveraigns, about the Subjects Liberty and the Kings Prerogative, 'tis seldom seen, but the Error lies on the Soveraign's part, who is apt to be flattered into the presumptuous exercise of such an absolute Soveraignty and Legislative Dominion over them, as becomes no creature, and exceeds all the bounds of that Contract he made with them, at his Inauguration.

All just Power and Authority is from God, and by virtue of his Ordinance and Institution. *He therefore that resisteth the Power, re-*

sisteth

fifteth the Ordinance of God. But all contrarient actings against the Prince, are not to be accounted a refifting of the Power ; especially, when the whole State is concerned, and the bufinefs is managed by publick Truftees, called and authorized by Law, as Conservers of the State, and Defenders of the publick Liberties and Lawes thereof. In fuch a publick capacity, to ftand in the gap, when a Breach is made, and hinder any charge or attempt that would ruinate the State, is Duty. In fuch cafe, they ought to withftand and hinder the violent proceedings of any, either by way of Juftice in a Legal tryal, or by force. For the Prince is not Mafter of the State, but onely a Guardian and Defender thereof, from injuries and evil. Yet thefe affaires, for redrefs of Grievances, in cafe of Princes failers, belong not to all, but to the Tutors and Maintainers of the State, or thofe that are interefted therein ; as Electors in Elective States, and in Hereditary States, the States General and Reprefentative Body of the Kingdom, according to the tenor of their fundamental Laws. In this cafe it is generally acknowledged lawful, to refift a Tyrant.

Under the crofs Accidents, iffuing from fuch Contefts, to which man is fubject through others arbitrary Domination, he may carry himfelf well, two wayes.

1. By a ftrong and vigorous refiftance thereof, to the laft, for diverting or blunting the point of it, fo as either to efcape or force it.

2. The other way, and that perhaps the fureft, is to take and receive thefe Accidents at the worft, let them prove what they will, though to the lofs of Life and all that's dear to him in this World. To refolve within himfelf to bear them fweetly and patiently, and peaceably to attend whatever fhall happen, without tormenting himfelf about it, or loofing the calmnefs and ferenity of his mind in going about to hinder or prevent it. He that takes the firft courfe, labours to efcape ; he that takes the latter is content rather to suffer. This many times proves the better bargain. 'Tis poffible to incur greater inconveniency and lofs in pleading and contending, than in loofing, or in flying for fafety, than in fuffering.

Concerning Friendfhip.

Perfect friendfhip is a very plain and univerfal complication or enfolding of two Soules in one, fo, that the Conjunction is moft intimate and infeparable. They can no more be divided ; nor would they, if they mi....t. *Secondly,*

Secondly, It is very free, being built upon the pure choice and liberty of the Will, without any other obligation or forreign motive.

Thirdly, Without any exception **of things**, goods, honours, judgements, thoughts, wills, Life.

Marriage it self is some resemblance of this divine knot, as saith the Apostle, who from thence mounts in his contemplation to the great mysterie of this kind between Christ and his Church. *Abraham* is called, *the friend of God*.

Concerning Enemies.

In reference to our Enemies we must take care, not to meditate Revenge. Yet in some sense we may account it an excellent and worthy revenge, to slight the worst they can do, whereby we take away the pleasure which they think to have, in vexing us. We must in suffering Injuries, have respect to our selves and to him that offends us. Touching our selves, we must take heed, that we do nothing unworthy or unbecoming us, that may give the enemy advantage against us. As to him that offends us, we should be wise as Serpents to wave his assault, till our hour is come, and we can gain and conquer by dying.

It is a weakness of mind not to know how to contemn an offence. An honest man is not subject to Injury. He is inviolable and unmoveable. Inviolable, not so much that he cannot be beaten; but, that being beaten, he doth neither receive wound nor hurt. We can receive no evil but of our selves. We may therefore always say with *Socrates*, *My enemies may put me to death, but they shall never enforce me to do that which I ought not.*

Evils themselves, through the wise over-ruling Providence of God, have good fruits and effects. The World would be extinguished and perish, if it were not changed, shaken and discomposed, by a variety and an interchangable course of things, wisely ordered by God, the best Physitian. This ought to satisfie every honest and reasonable mind, and make it joyfully submit to the worst of changes, how strange and wonderful soever they may seem, since they are the works of God and Nature, and that which is a loss in one respect, is a gain in another.

Let not a wise man disdain or ill resent any thing that shall happen to him. Let him know those things that seem hurtful to him in particular, pertain to the preservation of, the whole Universe,

verſe, and are of the nature of thoſe things, that finiſh and fill up the courſe and office of this World.

Meditations on Death.

IT is a fruit of true Wiſdom, not onely Chriſtian but Natural, to be found and kept in a frame of mind, ready for Death.

The day of Death is the Judge of all our other dayes ; the very tryal and touchſtone of the actions of our Life. 'Tis the end that crowns the work, and a good Death honoureth a man's whole Life.

This laſt act, as it is the moſt difficult, ſo but by this a man cannot well judge of the actions of anothers Life, without wronging him.

A wiſe *Greek* being asked concerning three eminent perſons, which of them was to be moſt eſteemed, returned this Anſwer, *We muſt ſee them all three die, before this Queſtion can be reſolved :* With which accords that ſaying of *Solon,* the wiſe *Athenian,* to *Crœſus,* when he boaſtingly ſhewed him his great Treaſures, *No man is to be accounted happy before his Death.*

True natural Wiſdom purſueth the learning and practiſe of dying well, as the very end of Life ; and indeed, he hath not ſpent his Life ill, that hath learned to die well. It is the chiefeſt thing and duty of Life.

The knowledge of Dying, is the knowledge of Liberty, the ſtate of true Freedom, the way to Fear nothing, to Live well, contentedly and peaceably. Without this there is no more pleaſure in Life, than in the fruition of that thing, which a man feareth alwayes to looſe. In order to which, we muſt above all endeavour that our ſins may die, and that we ſee them dead before our ſelves, which alone can give us boldneſs in the day of Judgement, and make us alwayes ready and prepared for Death.

Death is not to be feared and fled from, as it is by moſt, but ſweetly and patiently to be waited for, as a thing natural, reaſonable, and inevitable. It is to be looked upon as a thing indifferent, carrying no harm in it. This, that is all the hurt enemies can do us, is that which we ſhould deſire and ſeek after, as the onely Haven of Reſt, from all the Torments of this Life ; and which, as it gives us a fuller fruition of Chriſt, is a very great gain, that the ſooner we are poſſeſſors of, the better.

Death

Death is the onely thing of all evils, or privations, that doth no harm, hath indeed no evil in it, however it be reputed. *The sting of it is sin*, and that is the sting of Life too. There is no reason to fear it, because no man **knows** certainly what it is. This made *Socrates* refuse to plead **before** his Judges, for his justification or Life. For (saith he) *If I should plead for my Life, and desire of you that I may not die, I doubt I may speak against my self, to my loss and hindrance, who may find more good in death than yet I know. Those things I know to be evil, as unrighteousness and sin, I fly and avoid ; those that I know not to be so, as Death, &c. I cannot fear, and therefore I leave it to you to determine for me, whether it is more expedient for me to Dye or to Live.*

He can never live contentedly that fears to dye. That man only is a **free** man who feareth not Death, Life it self being but slavery, if it **were** not made free by Death. It is uncertain in what place Death attends us, therefore let us expect it in all places, and be alwayes ready to receive it. Great virtue, and great or long Life do seldom meet together. Life is measured by the end, if that be good, all the rest will have a proportion to it. The quantity is nothing, as to the making it more or less happy.

The Spirit of a good man, when he ceases to live in the Body, goes into a better state of Life, than that which he exercises in this World ; and when once in that, were it possible to resume this, he would refuse it. Yea were a man capable to know what this Life here is, before he receives it, he would scarce ever have accepted it at first. The self same journey men have taken, from no being to being, and from pre-existent being, into mortal Life, without fear or passion, they may take again from that Life by Death, into a Life that hath immortality in it.

Death is the inevitable Law, God and Nature have put upon us. Things certain, should not be feared, but expected. Things doubtful **onely are** to be feared. Death in stead of taking away any thing from **us**, gives us all, even the perfection of our natures; sets us at liberty both from **our** own bodily desires, & others domination; makes the Servant free from his Master. It doth not bring us into darkness, but takes darkness out of us, us out of darkness, and puts us into marvellous light. Nothing perishes or is dissolved by Death, but the Vail and Covering, which is wont to be done away from all ripe fruit. It brings us out of a dark dungeon, through the crannies whereof, our sight of Light is but weak and small, and brings us into an open Liberty, an estate of Light and Life, unvailed and perpetual.

petual. It takes us out of that mortality which began in the womb of our Mother, and now endeth, to bring us into that Life which ſhall never end. This day which thou feareſt as thy laſt, is thy Birth day into Eternity.

Death holds a high place in the policy and great common-wealth of the World. It is very profitable for the ſucceſſion and continuance of the works of Nature.

The fading corruption, and loſs of this life, is the paſſage into a better. Death is no leſs eſſential to us, than to live or to be born. In flying Death thou flyeſt thy ſelf, thy eſſence is equally parted into theſe two, Life and Death. It is the condition and Law of thy Creation. Men are not ſent into the World by God, but with purpoſe to go forth again ; which he that is not willing to do, ſhould not come in.

The firſt day of thy birth, bindeth thee and ſets thee in the way as well to Death as to Life. To be unwilling therefore to die, is to be unwilling to be a Man, ſince to be a Man is to be Mortal. It being therefore ſo ſerviceable to Nature and the inſtitution of it, why ſhould it be feared or ſhunned ? Beſides, it is neceſſary and inevitable, we muſt do our beſt endeavour in things that are not Remedileſs, but ought to grow reſolute in things paſt Remedy.

It is moſt juſt, reaſonable, and deſirable, to arive at that place towards which we are alwayes walking. Why feareſt thou to go whither all the World goes ? It is the part of a valiant and generous Mind, to prefer ſome things before Life, as things, for which a man ſhould not doubt nor fear to die. In ſuch a caſe, however matters go, a man muſt more account thereof than of his Life. He muſt run his race with reſolution, that he may perform things profitable and exemplary.

The contempt of Death, is that which produceth the boldeſt and moſt honourable exploits. He that fears not to die, fears nothing. From hence have proceeded the commendable Reſolutions and free Speeches of Vertue, uttered by men, of whom the world hath not been worthy.

A gallant *Romane*, commanded by *Veſpaſian* not to come to the Senate, anſwered, *He was a Senator, therefore ſit to be at the Senate ; and being there, if required to give his advice, he would do it as his Conſcience commanded him.* Hereupon being threatned by the Emperor, he replyed, *Did I ever tell you, that I was immortal ? Do you what you will, and I will do what I ought. It is in your power to put me unjuſtly to death ; and in mine to die conſtantly.* What hard dealing cannot

he

he suffer, that fears not to die ? Other designments may be hindred by our enemies, but they cannot hinder us from dying. The means whereby to live free, is to contemn Death. It is no great thing to live, slaves and beasts can do that, but it is a great matter to live freely, and die honestly, wisely, constantly. *Emori nolo* (saith one) *sed me esse mortuum, nihil estimo* ; I would not die, but to be dead, I look upon as nothing. But no man can be said resolute to die, that is afraid to confront it, and suffer with his eyes open, as *Socrates* did, without passion or alteration.

In a miserable estate of Life, which a man cannot remedy, Death is lawfully desirable, as our best retreat and onely haven from the storms of this Life ; and as the Soveraign good of nature, the onely stay and pillar of Liberty. It is a good time to die, when to live is rather a burthen than a blessing, and there is more ill in Life than good.

There are many things in Life, far worse than Death, in respect whereof we should rather die than live. The more voluntary our Death is, the more honourable. Life may be taken away from every man by every man, but not Death.

It is no smal reproach to a Christian, whose faith is in immortality and the blessedness of another Life, to fear Death much, which is the necessary passage thereunto. He ought rather to desire and thirst after death, as great gain ; *Vitam habere in patientiâ, & mortem in desiderio* ; to endure Life, and desire Death. But it is greater constancy, well to use the chain wherewith we are bound, than to break it. A man is not to abandon his charge in Life, without the express command of him that gave it him. *Sylvanus* and *Proximus*, being pardoned by *Nero*, chose Death, rather than to Live upon those terms. *Nerva* a great Lawyer, *Cato of Utica*, and others, died, as not able to bear the sight of the Weal-publick in that bad and declining state, into which by Gods Providence it was brought, in their times, but they should have considered,

Multa dies variusq; labor mutabilis Ævi,
Retulit in melius.

A man ought to carry himself blamlesly and with a steddy courage in his place and calling, against his assailants, and consider that it is better to continue firme and constant to the end, then fearfully to fly or dye. It is not a less evil to quit the place and fly, than obstinately to be taken and perish. It is a great point of wisdom to know the right hour and fit season to Die. Many men have survived their own Glory. That is the best Death which is

R   well

well recollected in it self, quiet, solitary, and attendeth wholly to what at that time is fitteſt.

But let us more particularly, and upon truly and purely Chriſtian Principles, weigh and conſider Death.

They that live by Faith, die daily. The Life which Faith teaches, works Death. It leads up the mind to things not ſeen, which are eternal, and takes it off with its affections and deſires, from things ſeen, which are temporary. It acquaints the ſoul experimentally with that heavenly way of converſe and intercourſe, which is not expreſſed by ſenſible ſignes, but by the demonſtration proper to ſpirits, whether angels, ſouls ſeparate, or ſouls yet in the body, as they live by faith, not by ſenſe. In which reſpect, the uſe of voice and mouth is attributed to God, to Chriſt, to Angels, who have that with them and in them, whereby they outwardly manifeſt what they inwardly conceive, although they expreſs not the inward word of their mental conception, by any outward voice, hand, eye, or other external ſign, but by the way of its own ſelf evidencing brightneſs, and eſſential demonſtration. Such a way of living and ſhining forth in man's naked eſſential beams, he then arrives unto, when the thick vail and wall of his fleſh is diſſolved, and his earthly tabernacle put off.

The knowledge, ſight, and experience of ſuch a kind of ſubſiſting and heavenly manner of Life, that man is capable of, is the beſt preparative, and moſt powerful motive, to leave the body, and ſurceaſe the uſe of our earthly organs. This in effect is all that bodily death, rightly known and underſtood, doth impart ; a lawful ſurceaſing the uſe and exerciſe of our earthly organs, and our willing and chearful reſorting to the uſe and exerciſe of that Life without the Body, which man is capable to ſubſiſt in, when made perfect in ſpirit, an equal and aſſociate with angels, under the power and order of expreſſing what he inwardly conceives, as they do. This made *Paul* look upon Life in the Body, and Life out of it, with no indifferent eye, but as accounting the being at home in the body, an abſence from the Lord; and ſuch a kind of abſence from the body as death cauſes, to be that which makes us moſt preſent with the Lord : which therefore we ſhould be moſt willing unto, and with greateſt longing after, deſire. The ſtrait which the Apoſtle found himſelf in, was not at all from the leaſt hæſitation in his mind, which of the two, was in it ſelf beſt and to be preferred, but by which Chriſt might moſt be magnified, and the Church benefitted, according to the will of Chriſt.

So

So then unless to live were Christ, and a real and clear magnifying of Christ in his Body, he cared not for Life, but contemned Death. He saw evidently how it was his own particular loss and hindrance, even, not to Die, since to be dissolved, to depart and be with Christ, and in the Society of the blessed Angels and Saints in Heaven, was best of all, and far more gainful and to be valued by him, than any longer continuance or abode in the flesh.

The magnifying of Christ in his Body, whether by Life or by Death, was the Consideration with *Paul*, that held the ballance, cast the scale, and that onely. So it ought to be with every true Christian.

The end of man's coming into the Body, and his temporary continuance and abode there ; according to the Law of his Creation, is the magnifying and glorifying Christ, either by his Life or by his Death, or both, the one of which if he do not, it must needs be his sin, and he is left without excuse. For none can violate or corrupt the mind of man, by the Law of Nature, nor let in Death upon his Spiritual Substance, but himself, though they dissolve his temporary abode in the flesh, break his outward case and shel ; and rather than do the one, we should choose the other, choose affliction rather than sin, the dissolution of the Body, rather than the corrupting of the Mind. In so doing and dying, Christ is magnifyed. Thus *Peter* was foretold, *by what Death he should glorify God. And to such it is given by Christ, not onely to Believe, but Suffer and Die for his Names sake*, as a transcendent priviledge and honour.

If no restraint then be upon our mind from without, what hinders that Christ is not magnified in our Body, but something within us, in our judgement, will, and affections, that are not right set and fixed, nor as yet wrought to this self same thing by God, who hath *given us the earnest of his Spirit* ?

But it may be demanded, What is it, in which this great duty of man lies, as to the magnifying of Christ in his Body by his Life, or living in the Body, which is a more difficult thing to do than to Die ? Christ himself tells us, when he saith, *Let your Light so shine before men, that they may see*, feel, and sensibly discern, *your good works ; and so, glorify your father which is in Heaven.*

There are two sorts of signs we read of, in those that believe, which justifie their Faith, in consortship (as it were) with which their Faith works and is made perfect, so as *the work of Faith is fulfilled in them with power.*

1. Signs Extraordinary, as *Mark* 16. 18. with which the Primitive

mitive Christians were well acquainted, and so may all such again, as arrive to any competent maturity in that primitive Christian Spirit.

2. Signes Ordinary, as those mentioned, *Gal.* 5. 22, 23. called, *the fruits of the Spirit in us*, that makes us *mighty in word and in deed, not onely to will but to perform that which is good ; by being filled with the Spirit in our very Bodies, made the Temples of the holy Ghost, rich in Faith and such good Works,* as are the fruit of Faith, *without which, Faith it self is dead* and unprofitable ; and by which, *Abraham justified his Faith, and was called, the Friend of God.*

It is in this sense, the Prophet urges the sanctification of our Vessels, when he saith, *Be ye clean that bear the Vessels of the Lord.* And the Apostle, when he saith, 1 *Cor.* 6. 19. *What ! know ye not that your Body is the Temple of the holy Ghost,* unto which Redemption by Christ extends , as well as to your Spirits ? *therefore glorify God in your Body as well as in your Spirit, which is God's,* and wherein he hath and challengeth a special propriety.

The Body in Scripture acceptation, signifies, not onely the material substance, from which the Soul is actually separated, when it is laid in the Grave ; but very usually the Soul it self, that is to say, that part of the Soul, which vitally unites the Body to it self, whose faculty and operation is in and by the Body, and doth properly and immediately exercise bodily Life, as that which is co-natural, and co-essential to it.

There is a higher part in man's Soul, called Spirit, in distinction from Soul and Body, expressed 1 *Thes.* 5. 23. as if the Spirit were an entire thing in it self, though it be that, in and with which, Soul and Body doth consist, as parts of the whole Man. *I pray God,* saith the Apostle, *that your whole Spirit, Soul and Body, be preserved blameless to the coming of Christ, and that you may be sanctified throughout,* or in every part of you, *in your Soul and in your Body,* which are to be esteemed but as parts, comparatively with your whole Spirit.

Man, considered as entire in his Spirit, may have and hath being, before he partakes of Flesh and Blood, as it is written, *Behold,* saith Christ, *I and the children which thou hast given me. Forasmuch then as the children are partakers of Flesh and Blood, he also himself took part of the same :* even he, who, with the children, were a mystery hid with the Father, before the World was, and had their Seminal and radical Being, in the Word of Life, the Father of Spirits. In this Word, as in the Image and Mental conception of the invisible God, the Souls of all men, even of Christ himself, as man, were

com-

comprehended, as in their original pattern and rule, in order at the time appointed, to come into flesh, and there make their temporary abode, allotted to them.

By the Condition and Law of Man's Creation, he is made a Spiritual essence, with two distinct faculties and operations, according to which he may be said to be both Immortal and Mortal, Immaterial and Material, Spirit and Body, as Body signifies man's animal rational Soul, that is to live in flesh, and hath its peculiar desire, faculty, and operation, proportioned thereunto. In all this Man bears the Image and Similitude of God the Mediator, or of the Godhead in Christ, as two Natures in him are Hypostatically united, and make but one *Compositum*, or Person. This was comprehended in that Counsel which the blessed Trinity took concerning the making of Man in their Image, and after their Similitude. He was made male and female in his very Spiritual substance.

First, with a faculty, and operation of mind, superiour, stronger and more excellent, which is free and independent upon bodily organs, exercising Life, properly and purely Spiritual and Immaterial, above and without the use of sensible, signes, or shapes.

Secondly, With that inferiour faculty and operation of mind, whose subsistence, life, being, and motion, is in, with, and by the body, and through the use of bodily organs, sensible signes, and external mediums, on the loss of which, this second faculty and operation of man's Soul, which is the weaker, inferiour, and less valuable, ceases ; at least, is for a time suspended, which in Scripture phrase is called *Death* ; even the Death of the Body. Yet the more vigorous the exercise of this latter is, and the more that thereby we are at home in the Body, the more in truth and reality we are dead ; at least, asleep in the earth, as to our more Noble and Spiritual part, in and through which, we enjoy most of the presence of God and of Christ.

Since therefore, mans constitution of Being, is such, as he cannot live both these Lives together, untill the Resurrection, but that in the one or them, he must be incompleat, have his operation much suspended, and be, as it were dead or asleep.

To resolve which of these to choose and prefer, ought not to be so difficult, as commonly it is made.

On the SUFFERINGS of the Renowned Sir H. Vane, Knight.

—GReat Soul, ne're Understood
   Until deciphered by thy Blood,
A Priest, a Prophet, and a King,
Systeme of every worthy thing.
Dying, that Liberty might Live,
The English Cause he doth retrieve;
Stating it in no formal dress,
But in the Spirit of Righteousness.
Which he from th'earth perceiving fled,
Dy'd, to Return with's from the Dead.
Persons or Forms of Government,
Did little make to his intent.
To nought was he an Enemy,
But what was fix'd in Enmity.
'Gainst which he fought with eager breath,
Became Victorious in his Death.
And this not by necessity,
It was his Principle to Dye.
Flesh will resist, but Faith can suffer,
The soft hand's gone, beware the rougher.
Th'envy and hate of every Form,
Upon his head pour'd down the Storm.
Whilst he sublim'd, and sav'd the good
O'th' lowest, and seal'd it with his Blood.
How great he was, his Enemies tell,
Who, while he liv'd, could not be well.
And in what stead his offering stood,
By resolute silence, Friends made good.
The male o'th' Flock is ta'ne, the best,
To expiate the blame o'th' rest.
What tears and prayers wanted in strength,
His crying blood brings down at length.
Groan, English Hearts! groan! help the cry,
Lord Jesus Come! I come quickly.

FINIS.

IT's very probable thou mayeſt meet with ſome faults and miſ-printings eſcaped the Corrector, which could not be avoided, by reaſon of the diſtance between the Tranſcriber and the Preſs ; thou art deſired to correct them, and paſs them by with candor. One thou mayeſt find in *page 54,* and *55,* all thoſe words within the Parentheſis, ſhould come in after the word *Penetent.* And *page 97.* in the Title to that part, read *Caſe* for *Cauſe.*

TWO
TREATISES:
VIZ. I.
An Epistle General,

TO THE
Myſtical Body of Chriſt on Earth, the Church
Univerſal in *BABYLON.*

II. THE
Face of the Times:

Wherein is diſcovered,

The RICE, PROGRESSE, and ISSUE, of the ENMITY
and CONTEST, between the SEED of the WOMAN
and the SEED of the SERPENT, *&c.*

The Deſign of it being,

To awaken up the *preſent Generation* of God's People, to
a more diligent and curious Obſervation of the *preſent*
Signs of the near Approach of the *Day* of the *Lord.*

Both written, By Sir HENRY VANE, Knight,
in the time of his Impriſonment.

Printed in the Year, 1 6 6 2.

AN
Epistle General,

TO THE

MYSTICAL BODY

OF

Christ on Earth,

THE

CHURCH UNIVERSAL

IN

BABYLON,

Who are *Pilgrims* and *Strangers* on the Earth, defiring and seeking after the *Heavenly Country.*

Written by Sir HENRY VANE, Knight, in
the time of his Imprisonment.

Printed in the Year, 1662.

t.

THE
Epistle to the Reader.

IT might be thought justly due to this *Worthy Piece*, especially being *Posthumous*, that by the Care of some or other it should not come into the World, without the attendance of some Preface or Epistle to the Reader : But there being so apposit a Letter written on the sight of it, by a Person that well knew the Author, all labour is spared the Publisher, save only the transcribing thereof, and commending it to thee, which follows in these words.

My choice Friend,

THe view I had of that General Epistle, written by that Worthy, Faithful, Dearly Beloved, and Honoured Friend of ours, I cannot passe without some acknowledgment to his Memory, whose Name lives like a Box of precious Oyntment in the House of God. Who in and through the rich Mercies of the Lord, offered up himself a living Sacrifice, holy and acceptable, in the day of Power from the Lord, and that willingly and chearfully, like a Lamb, whose great love and burning desires were after the Flock, the Sheep and Lambs of the Lord.

Who, that they might be fed and taught, spared not himself in life and death, by water and blood, to minister unto them ; yea, how did the care of all the Churches fall on him? the whole Flock, the scattered and wandring Sheep on the Mountains and Hills, solitary in the Fields, dispersed in the Woods, driven into the Wilderness.

How did his heart in this Epistle long and look after them, and call them together, under the wing of that one Shepherd ? What a blessed Example of Patience, Faith and Courage hath he left them ?

And though many Brethren knew not him, yet he knew them, and owned them. If he was rejected by many, till now by his Death many of those Vails are rent, And they mourn over him whom they pierced before : Now they see he was a Son and Heir of the Kingdom, of whom this Nation was no longer worthy.

How had God filled him with the Spirit of Wisdom, Understanding and Knowledg in all the Works & Workmanship of Gods house, through the spiritual view God had given him of the heavenly and eternal

A 2

things

things themselves, having taken him up into the Holy Mount with Himself, where he saw what he is made to testifie, that which was from the beginning, the Word of Life which he had seen and looked on, his hands handled, his heart possessed of that Eternal Love, Truth and Righteousness with the Father, which was made manifest unto him.

So he believed and bears his Record in Truth, having received Power and Wisdom to understand all Mysteries, Bezaleel-like, made able to know and search out the heights and depths, and all the several growths in God's House, to shew forth and to discover the cunning Works of all sorts, the curious workings in Gold, and Silver, and in Brasse ; As appears in his Natural, Legal, and Evangelical Conscience.

Very skilful also are his Carvings and Cuttings of Stones, to set them in Gold, knowing the value of every of the Precious Stones of Zion, their Qualities and rare Vertues, each most costly ; and to set them every one in their Order, in their Ranks, Rows and Places, fitted for each Tribe and People, (the right Stone for each Tribe) how to fix them in the Breastplate of Judgment, each in his socket of Gold, with their true and right Engravings, like a Signet ; how to call and write upon each its true Name and Work according to its Nature, (each Work of the Spirit after its kind) For the Gifts, the Operations, the Administrations of the Spirit are various and manifold, to set forth the manifold Wisdom of God.

As in the Natural Creation there are bodies Celestial and Terrestial : The Glory of the Celestial is one, and the Terrestial another; Nay, in the Terrestial there are varieties. When all the Creatures were made, they were all brought to Adam; he gave them Names according as they were, to every Creature his own Name ; to the Fishes in the Sea, to the Creeping-things and Beasts in the Earth, and to the Fowls in the open Firmament of Heaven, each in their proper places and Elements. The Earth brought forth her variety of Herbs, Plants, Fruits and Trees, every one after his kind ; all which are but the shadows of the Kingdom above, the things of higher and better natures.

As in the Paradise and Garden of the Lord, there were varieties of Fruits and Trees both for delight and shade, with the River to refresh them ; yea, the very River divided it self into four heads, to water every quarter, unbowelling it self to them in equal shares, to feed and make them fruitful.

Such

TO THE READER.

Such is the Universal Love, the Spring and Fountain of Life, in whom all live, move and have their being, to gather together all things in one, whether visible or invisible, as into their head; That as all Mankind are made of one Blood, so all Souls of one Spirit, who breathed at first the Breath of Life into them, that he that was the first may be the last, the beginning and the ending, He that was, and is, and is to come: What distance and difference soever there may seem to be here, yet all the same, to day, yesterday, and for ever, the same God, the same Father of all, the same Jesus and Saviour, the same Spirit and Comforter; yet the Appearances, Manifestations, Workings and Revelations, manifold and various: And all, to shew forth the Glory, yea, the Riches of the Glory of Him, that hath called us, and worketh all these in us and for us.

Yea, were not the works of the Tabernacle so? and yet each beautiful in its place, each work and workmanship; some works of Wood, some of Stone, others of Brass, some of Silver and over-laid with Gold, the choicest of beaten Gold; and the more holy and inward, the purer, the inmost the purest of all; each room and place as it came nearest to the living Oracle (the Mercy-Seat) the narrower, the finer, the holier: and the more and the farther any thing or place was distant from thence, the larger and courser; the more outward, the less holy.

So were the Offerings of the Lord, all pleasant, that came willingly; the skins, the Badgers skins, the red dyed Rams skins (for the Covering of the Tabernacle on the out-side) good enough, yet very course: the Boards of Shittem wood, the Curtains, the Pillars of Wood, of Brasse, of Wood over-laid with Gold, each according to its place and service in the Tabernacle, more or lesse excellent, as more or lesse inward or spiritual: So was the Linnen, the Purple, the Blue, the Scarlet, and curious Works; the most curious and pure for the Vail next the Mercy-Seat.

So was it in the Composition of the Perfume and anointing Oyl, after the curious and choice Art of the Apothecary (that no Composition or Mixture must be made like it) of the choicest Spices.

So for the Lamps of the Candlesticks to give light, and for the Altar of Incense evening and morning (Oh! great is the Mystery of Godliness in all these things) no Lights, but what was made of this pure holy Oyl, must burn before the Lord; if the Priests or Levites did burn any other, they must be cut off.

And

TO THE READER.

And so for the Incense of sweet Spices; the Lord, that Spirit, is very curious, and can soon spy and smell out the Mixtures of Flesh, or any false Compositions, and abhor them.

So in the Priests Garments for Aaron *and his Sons to minister in; the nearer the Ministration was to the Lord, the Purer and Holier, and the Garments the more curious. The imbroydered fine Linnen Coat, holy and pure; the Robe of the Ephod, of blue; the curious Ephod with the two pretious Onix Stones, and the engraving therein, set on the shoulder plates; the curious Girdle of the Ephod, with the wreathes of Gold, and the holy Brest-plate of Judgement, with the twelve pretious Stones coupled to the Ephod, and of the same curious workmanship; with the curious Girdle, the Miter, the Plate of Holiness, and the Crown for his head. For the other Priests, not so curious, nor such works, in regard their Institutions was less glorious.*

In all these things, how excellent, how skilful, and what a cunning searching Spirit of discerning and Judgement, had this wise-hearted Soul (in the Mysteries) unfolding the Riddles and hard Sayings, still opening them in Spirit, faithful in all God's House, and keeping nothing of the Counsel of the Lord back, nor hiding his Light under a Bushel, but setting it up in the Candlestick, so, that it gave light to many of the Lord's House.

I was one of the number of those, that constantly attending on his Discourses, as oft as I was in Town, knew him more in his Family Exercises and Discourses for many years than most; from whom I received more help and light in the knowledge of God, than from all the men in the World besides, and found his Ministry most searching and trying: What others took for Gold, he proved it to be but Brass; and some Doctrines that others preferred for Spiritual, he tryed, and found them Carnal.

He had such a Brest-plate of Judgement and Discerning, that he did constantly bear the remembrance of all the Tribes of Israel *on his heart before the Lord, and distinguished every Tribe after his condition; yea, he had this singular and peculiar gift of Judgement, to discern the two Natures, the two Seeds, the two Covenants, to admiration: Many a Soul he hath put upon the search, that thought he had attained and ran well, whom he found to be but in* Egypt, *or at least but departing thence.*

Shall we say he was a Scholler? Nay, but a Rabbi, *a Doctor in the knowledge of Christ, in whom a greater Fulness of the riches of Wisdom*

dom and *Knowledge* were treasured up than in most ; like that *Disciple*
that lay in *Christ's bosom : He* obtained so long a share of *his* life and
growth, having **the** true sight and measure of *every man's* state and
growth, yet himself sate on a *Rock* higher than all, and was such a
blessing in his *Witness* (and *Testimony* to the *Lord* , in his threefold
state, of Life, Death, and *Resurrection*, and so of our conformity and
likeness to *Him* therein) that no *Book* extant, but the *Scriptures*, did
ever clear so much *Truth* as his Retired Man's Meditations ; and this
blessed Epistle now of his, is as a *Key* that further opens that to the
Sons of men, and they are to be understood better in spirit, and in operation, than in words.

How did he, seeing *Truth* lay scattered, maimed, and mangled in
parts and parcels, gather it all up ? yea, and all the *Professions* **and**
Professors of it, and **made** one **whole** *Garment of Truth* amongst
them all, **and** that **without** any seam or rent ; reconciling and healing
all the *Wounds* and *Divisions* that have been amongst good *People*, from
the crown of the *Head* to the soale of the *Foot*, in the Spirit of *Love*,
Righteousness, and **true** *Judgement* ; assigning every *Profession* and
Principle, his true **and** **proper** place and state in the *Body*, whether
Natural **or** *Spiritual*.

VALE.

To

To the scattered Seed and Sheep of CHRIST *in all Nations, the true Israel by Faith, unknown for the most part to themselves, but more to the World and Worldly Christian: Yet, in this their unknown or dispersed Estate, owned of the* Lord, *as the Church that are in God the Father, truly pure, Catholick and Christian, of which Christ Jesus is the alone and immediate Head.*

Rethren and Fathers, *&c.* that in Jesus Christ are dearly beloved, and with God of great price, Grace and Peace be multiplied unto you, through the knowledge of our Lord Jesus Christ.

To you that are unknown and yet well known, it is in my heart to be representing the knowledge of Him that is invisible, and the view of your selves in your invisible state, together with those that are your known or unknown enemies; as that which may prove neither unseasonable nor unprofitable to you, in this day of *Israel's* Captivity, but approaching Redemption (which hastens fast) at which time the Sons of God shall be made manifest.

If *Paul, Acts* 17. when he passed by, and beheld the *Athenians* Devotions, with an Altar, having this Inscription [*To the unknown God*] took occasion from thence, to make him known, whom they ignorantly Worshipped; Surely, it ought not to be accounted blameworthy in any, that seeth the Worship and Devotions now in practise, in the visible Christian Church, to endeavour the distinguishing the right Catholick Church in its Purity, and way of Worship in Spirit and Truth, from them, and from their wayes of Worship (ignorantly, however zealously performed) that pass under the name of Christ's Mystical Body, and his Divine Institutions.

But you, Beloved, are of God, Elected, known as by name, having this Seal and Mark from the Lord upon you, which is your Stability and sure Foundation; the Lord knows, who are his. And, *let every one that nameth the name of Christ, depart from iniquity.*

No matter therefore, if these come to you and find you, *as to your outward estate in Babylon;* where, (according to what is *foretold* by

the

the Apostle *John, in the Revelation*) *your abode is to be, as in a wilderness* condition, for 1260 years, now near expired.

And although from that state of servitude and hard bondage, unto which you have been exposed by the Rulers, *no wrestlings or contendings by humane wisdom and power, have availed to work your deliverance, because the appointed time,* set by God, *is not come* ; Yet, this ought to be your comfort, that so soon as that time comes, there will then need very little other help than the *Grave it self to cast you forth, as the Womb doth her fruit, which it cannot longer detain.* For of this be assured, that *Christ's dead body mystical, can no more be held in its figurative grave, after the set time is come, than his natural body,* could, *in his literal grave, Acts 2, 24.* where it is said, that after Christ by wicked hands had been slain, God raised him up, having loosed the pains of death, because it was *not possible he should be held of it* ; Nor are you to be too much grieved and discouraged in this your low, depressed and dead estate, under the rage and indignation of the World and Powers of it, since to you is the promise of Life and Resurrection, and you are sure for the present to be *fed in the Wilderness,* and to be *kept green and flourishing in your inward man, by secret dew, inspired and distilled from Heaven,* whatever perishing and decays are brought upon *your outward, where you are bearing the marks of the dying of the Lord Jesus. Hearken* therefore *to the Call* that is given you, *of retiring inward into the life of your Head and Root,* the life that is *hid with Christ in God.* And, *as the means to be so with more freedom,* labour *to keep the door of your sensual part, shut,* and fast closed *about you* as much as may be, *that the noise and diversions of this sinful and unquiet World* may not *disturb* nor interrupt *you.* For though, through impatience and unbelief, you may be arguing and concluding against your selves, as the whole house of *Israel* did, *Ezek. 37. 11.* that your bones are dried, your hope is lost, and you are cut off, for your parts ; yet ye *shall know that the Lord he is God, when he hath opened, and brought you up, out of your graves, v. 13.* He will then *own you visibly, for his people, by wonderfully putting his Spirit within you,* and causing you to live ; And *when you see this, your heart shall rejoyce, and your bones shall flourish like an herb,* and the *hand of the Lord shall be known towards you, his servants,* and his *indignation towards his enemies. He hath the weapons of his vengeance* in readiness, *full Vials of his wrath, to be poured forth by his heavenly Militia and Troops, upon the Beast and his Worshippers, when all humane means fail.* This you are therefore to know, that

though

though the Saints who have adventured to oppose the Beast, and the kingdom of Antichrist (all along, contending in a good Cause) have been still crushed, and subdued, as is foretold, *Rev.* 13.7. yet the *time is coming*, yea, is even *at the very door, for God to take the business into his own hands,* and *to put forth the power of his wrath by heavenly Instruments,* forasmuch as *the earthly ones (as you have seen) have proved ineffectual.* And this ought to be a teaching to us, to depend upon God, for the avenging of his people, even, when all humane ability to perform it, is vanished ; and not hastily to run out, in the use of any indirect means, though tempted and allured thereunto.

But, to return to the things which we propound to set before you, in this Epistle ; They are reducible unto these particulars, following :

1. First, The sight and knowledge of Christ, as he is the Invisible and Holy One, from whom, as from the Head, all natural as well as spiritual good, doth flow.

2. Secondly, Christ's Headship, exercised by him, (ever since his Ascension) as he is the Son of man, glorified ; and this in the two distinct branches and administrations of it. The one, that, wherein he is the Lord and restorer of pure, incorrupt Nature, upon the Principles of the first Covenant, renewed, and confirmed in his blood. The other, that, in which he is the giver of the Holy Ghost, or, the Minister of the Spirit, and new Name, (as Ointment poured forth) which, where it is received upon the Principles of the new Covenant, never fails, but abides with such, for ever.

3. Thirdly, The true Annointed Ones, or Witnesses of Christ, according to both his before-mentioned Administrations and the Annointing, which is given, by the one and by the other.

4. Fourthly, Those that in Principles, are opposite unto these two Annointings and the effects of them, declaring their enmity, in and by the continued war they maintain against them, in the posture of open enemies, or dissembled friends, both making up, but one and the same Kingdom of Antichrist.

5. Fifthly, What Word and part of his Counsels contained in the Promises and Prophesies, (not yet accomplished) is the Lord now fulfilling, in the present dispensations of our day ?

1. To the first, 'Tis the Testimony which came out of Christ's own mouth, concerning Himself and his Father, *Luke* 1. 22. That *no man knows* who the *Son* is, *but* the *Father* ; nor who the *Father* is, *but* the *Son, and he to whom* the *Son* will *reveal Him :* which plainly declares, that the *beings* both *of the Father,* and *of the Son,* are *great*

and

and hidden Mysteries. The one as well as the other, is *mystical and invisible,* and must be *taught* and *revealed,* before it can be *truly* and *fully known* and *understood* what they are. Agreeable to this, is that, Joh. **1. 18.** *No man hath seen God at any time,* that is, *immediately,* but *by the means of the only begotten Son, which is in the bosom of the Father;* he *hath declared him.* The Son, therefore, who is the *only begotten,* is said to be the Image of the invisible God ; The first name and similitude whereby God is possible and capable to be known to others beside himself. For by and from Him, as the Head, the knowledge and fruit of the whole Deity is derived and communicated, in such fit Images and lively Representations, as He hath fore-determined within himself, to be known by, unto his whole Creation, from the beginning to the end thereof. Hence it is, that we find Christ the Mediator, by the Prophet *Isa.* 43. 10. speaking of himself after this manner, *Ye are my Witnesses, saith the Lord, and my Servant, whom I have chosen.* The Lord, *the Mediator,* hath and owns for his Witnesses, the Womans Seed, in the head, and in the members ; the promised Seed, in his Servant, the *Branch,* the chief and principal one ; and in his Brethren, the same Seed ; and who are made to bear his Fathers Name (by *Adoption*) as well as himself, and to continue it for ever ; that *one Seed,* Gal. 3. *which,* saith the Apostle, *is Christ, the mystical body,* that are *Heirs according to promise.* *Ye are my Witnesses,* sayes this only begotten, who is from everlasting , *that ye may know* and believe me, and understand *that I am he.* Or, I am the Son, that only doth or can reveal who the Father is, or who I am in mine own Person ; for, before me was no God formed, or nothing formed or to be seen of God, neither shall there be after me ; because I am his compleat Name and Manifestation, *In me it hath pleased the Father all Fulness should dwell,* and this also *bodily, in* the dispensation of the *fulness of time.* By *Christ* then (as we learn from hence) we are to understand that Person, in whom God first formeth himself, and placeth his Name, by his immediate engraving and workmanship, upon the tables of some *Creature-beginning,* some other nature begotten by him, in difference and distinction from his own; and which, as it is his *first work,* so is it his *most compleat* and *perfect work ;* that which comprehends all particulars and individuals in both creations, from first to last ; so that, as nothing is before it, to precede, so, nothing is omitted, to make new, or to come after it, that is not eminently treasured up and seated in his Person already, who is *the first-born of every creature,* he that was *before all things, and by whom all things con-*
sist,

sist, made the *Alpha* and *Omega* ; he that *was*, he that *is*, and he that *is to come*, the *Almighty*. In this state of spiritual being and hidden glory, Christ is truly and properly the *Invisible one*, which *Moses* had the sight of by Faith ; fore-seeing also his incarnation, as he was to be the great Prophet, raised up to the People of *Israel*, who when he cometh, should teach them all things, and declare the mind of God fully, receiving himself the lively Oracles immediately from God's own mouth.

From hence also it is, by reason that there is such an Invisible one, who is with God from everlasting, as his mouth, and in the Office of Mediator, that in *Moses* his Law, the first and second Commands are so positive and strict, *that we* should *have no other Gods before the Lord*, viz. the *Mediator* and *Redeemer*, that brought *Israel* out of *Egypt*, and made himself known unto them by his Name *Jehovah*, which imports the execution of his Purpose and Promise, and so, the Being he gives to what his Word hath declared. This Name will be best interpreted by the opening of another place of Scripture, which speaks of Christ in this his invisible and mysterious being, *Prov.* 8 and 9 chap. wherein the building and workmanship that Wisdom forms for her own house, (the Sanctuary wherein God records his Name) is most lively and excellently described, as that which comprehends all the fulness and perfection of all times and things, *past, present*, and *to come* ; He *that was, he that is, and he that is to come, the Almighty* ; Who, as, in one and the same Person of the Mediator, he is the God that builds all things, so he is also the Building or House it self, which is his own immediate workmanship, and, as in one total sum, contains all manner of perfection in it. For it is not the Property of the first in the Trinity, to execute, but to purpose and contrive what shall be executed, and by whom ; and then, the Execution, though it be by the same Divine Essence, yet, it is by reason of a second and third property, which is natural to it ; according to which, God, that is *One*, is also *Three* ; *One* in Nature and Spirit, *Three* in Properties and Operation ; a Spirit after such an incomprehensible manner as is known fully to himself alone, having three distinct inspiring Properties, whence he gives being to his own Name, or to him that he purposeth within himself, shall bear his Name, and give the sight and knowledge of his essential Glory and Likeness, unto the understanding of others, as his own mouth, that is set up, to utter and deliver the *lively Oracle* of his Eternal mind.

This Person, whom God from Eternity hath designed to this high
and

and great Office, *is he*, whom we mean, when we expres him under the Title of *the Mediator* ; the *Wisdom* and *Power*, or *Understanding* and *Will*, that **God hath the image** of, within himself, from all Eternity. As it is *in him, it is himself* ; one that is *with him*, as *brought up by him*, that is *daily his delight* ; and whose *delight* also is in the habitable parts of God's Earth, and with the sons of men ; The Wisdom and Power of *God's Essence*, in the form of the highest Understanding and best Will, purposing to manifest it self, and build it self a house in some other nature, wherein to well, and therewith to converse, whether upon terms of *pure Justice*, or *free Grace* ; and so, to make himself either a *sojourner for a season*, or *an home and in-dweller*, as his place of *Rest for ever*.

And by the *setting up of this building* in the Person of the Mediator, as the Root and Foundation of all intercourse between God most high, and the work of his hands in both Creations, let us see the fruit and great benefit which comes to men, as he himself describeth it, *Prov.* 9. 1, 3. For, *by this means* the *Beasts are killed*, the *Lamb is sacrificed*, the *Wine is mingled*, or, the pure *fruit of the Divine Nature* is so *tempered* and prepared, in its manifestation and day-break upon the Creatures understanding, *by the first mixture of these two natures in the Person of the Mediator*, that it *becomes fit drink* and *sutable meat for all such, as are to feed at this Table of the Lord*.

From hence it is evident, that God is to be looked upon by us, as under one Consideration, in his own, proper, simple, absolute and incomprehensible Essence, wherein he is known, and perfectly enjoyed by none but himself, in the most blessed Trinity ; and under another Consideration, according to what he hath eternally purposed, and actually made himself to be, in the Person of the *Mediator*, wherein only he can be seen by the Creatures making it unlawful to own any other image, form, or likeness of him, *Exod.* 20.3, 7. or *to bow down* **to it, or** *worship it* ; forbidding unto Angels or Men, all the *Imaginations of God*, which they are apt to feign of him from the device of their own hearts, as the *Object of their Worship*, upon this very ground, because he hath one by him that he hath made the *Angel of his face and presence*, whom he hath employed to bring them out of *Egypt*, and who was seen by *Moses* in the Bush, and shewed Himself to the Church or whole Congregation of the People in the Wilderness, when they tempted him, in setting up and worshipping a *molten Calf*, of their own invention, new and *strange gods*. This to do before his face, and to own (besides him, that was the face and mouth of God amongst

amongst them) would be a *great provoking*, which he told them should *not go unpunished :* This caused God to say, *Thou shalt have no other Gods besides*, or before *me* ; that is, not only *not in my sight*, but *not in preference to him*, that I have given to you, as *my face* and *mouth*. Provoke him not, for *my Name is in him* ; intimating with-all, that herein they were the more inexcusable, because they had him with them and amongst them. In him the light of God's Glory was shining forth as in God's own face and very similitude, speaking his Mind by his own mouth ; and he was to be incarnate, that the same Word might be near us, *even in our mouth and in our heart, to bear it, and do it.* This is the Prophet, like unto *Moses*, which God said he would raise up unto them, out of, and from the midst of their Brethren.

Let us then acknowledge this great Mystery of the Father and the Son, *distinguishing what God is by Nature and Essence, from what he gives himself to be, in the Person of the Mediator*, the only begotten, *that lieth in his bosome ; who yet is also his Messiah*, whom he sends and makes his Substitute, by way of his in-dwelling Deity and Presence, for the performing of all his pleasure in both Worlds.

The *Trinity* is the *head, and immediate cause of the being and fulness*, which is set up in the *Person* of the *Mediator*, whom they *not only inspire with each of their Names and Similitudes*, but *make him a Vessel of meet use, to convey the holy Oyl, in* the way of a twofold Ministry, *and Pipe to both Creations* ; He therefore became incarnate, that he might make use of no other spokesman, immediately to interpret and declare the Mind of God unto his People, than the *Son of man glorified*, of which we have the *lively Type,* (*Exod.* 4. 15, 16.) in the Office of *Aaron* to *Moses*, shewing that *Aaron* was made the *mouth* to *Moses*, and *Moses* the *mouth* to *God* ; *Aarons* Office of spokesman, figuring out that of *Christ's Manhead*, and *Moses* his, that of *Christ's Mediatorship in spirits before his Incarnation ;* upon which occasion God promiseth there, in the Type, that which he ful-fills in Spirit and Truth, in Christ's Person. For, as *Moses had Commission to speak to* Aaron, *as God's spoksman to him ; so hath the Spirit of the Mediator to* Jesus *the Son of man.* And as it was *Aaron*'s Office to be *spoksman to the People ;* so is it the Office of Christ's Man-head, to be *the spoksman of Him* that *Moses* typed out, that *great Prophet*, the *Angel of God's Face and Presence ; and to be to him the Interpreter and Declarer of God's Mind*, and signifier of God's Commands *to all in both Worlds.* Christ (as he is the Son of man)

is

is to himself (as he is the Word of God) instead of a *mouth* or *Prophet*; And Christ, as he is the *only Begotten*, or *Word of the Father*, is *instead of God*, most high unto his own Manhead; answerable to the Promise, made vers. 15. and *thou shalt speak unto him*, and *put words into his mouth*, (meaning *Moses* to *Aaron*) and *I will be with thy mouth, and with his mouth, and will teach you*, (that is, both of you) *what ye shall do.*

Here we see (and may see it with Admiration, as the Queen of *Sheba* did in *Solomon's* Temple, which was the Type) *the Glorious Ascent into the House of God*, and the *gradual access* which by *one spirit*, we have *through Christ* unto the *Father*. I would have you **know**, saith the Apostle *Paul*, 1 *Cor.* 11. 3. *that the head of every man is Christ, the head of the woman is the man, and the head of Christ is God.* Christ that is the head of every man, is the head of his own manhead ; and therefore was Christ *God's Angel, Messiah*, or *sent-one*, before he was *Man* ; and had for his Head, the *one God and Father of all things.*

How God is the Head of Christ, we have shewed. The blessed *Trinity*, is the Father to that only begotten One, who is the *hidden Wisdom, ordained before the World was*, to our glory ; The *Angel*, that is, the *Messenger and Mediator of God's Covenant*, of whom he commands us to beware *(Exo.*23.21.*)* and to obey his voice ; *Provoke him not*, sayes he, *for he will not pardon their Transgressions ; for my Name is in him.* What can be more plain? The most high God hath his *Messiah*, his *Angel* or *sent-one*, invested with his Majesty and Power of Command, whose Voice must be obeyed as the Voice of God, it being his Office, to be *instead of God* to his Church. What he binds is bound, what he remits is remitted, for the Name of God is in him ; He is in likeness and truth, so near to God, that he is *God's equal*, the *true Michael*, that is second with God in the Throne : and yet, he that is found in the Form of God, *and accounts it no robbery to be equal with God* ; doth not disdain to have also his Equals, *the man*, that is, *his fellow*, the *man of his right-hand*, whom he hath made strong for himself.

With the most knowing *Jews*, the acknowledgment of Christ in this his heavenly and spiritual being before his incarnation, was most usual and avowed. The Angel that redeemed *Jacob*, Gen. 48. they call the *Divine Majesty*, owned for *God*, and for *Christ*, that was tempted in the Wilderness ; whose Voice, say they, is to be obeyed, as the Voice of the living God ; and his Office is, to be the Leader

and

and Guide of the *true Israel*; the great Prince, that is the Presence and Majesty of God, and the Lord and Ruler over all the Earth as well as Heaven, all that is therein being governed by his hand. Unto Him the pure and simple Essence of God is the Father; and he is set up from everlasting, the *Father* and *Root*, whence that *chief Branch* springs, that is *Jesus the Lord and Christ*, in the capacity of *Son* to this *Father*, *who must reign till all things be subdued under him*, that is, *all inferiour Rule, Authority* and *Power* whatsoever, that *officiate*, or ought to do so, *in his right*; But when that is done and finished, then shall this *Son* also himself, *be subject unto Him*, that is, his **Father**, that raised him from the dead, and put all things under him, *that* **God** *may be all in all*.

This occasioned Christ whilst he was on Earth, to say, *Joh.* 12. 28. *Father, glorifie thy Name*; speaking therein to God the Mediator; to Him, whose Office is, *to be to him the Mouth of God*; from whom, he receives the lively Oracles to deliver to his Church; as it is written. *I will declare thy Name to my Brethren; in the midst of the Church will I sing Praises unto thee.* And again, *I will put my trust in him, even in him who wrought in Christ, when he raised him from the dead, and set him at his own right-hand of the Majesty on high*, or in the heavenly.

This made Christ say, *when I am lifted up, I will draw all men unto me*; that is, mediately, and in order afterwards, to resign them up unto his Father, and give up all his interest of Rule in them, unto him; unto whom, as he is his Equal, (for, saith he, *I and the Father are one*) So also he is *his Servant*, and hath his *Office of Ministry under him*. For, the end of Christ's Ministry is, *to unvail the Glory of his Father*, and to *shine with him as second in the Throne*, which he prefers much before the drawing of all men to himself, to depend and rest on him only, and not on the Father, in and through him, as all those do that rest in the knowledge of Christ according to the flesh, and behold not that vail rent, upon his spiritual Cross, in order to *live to him, that died for them, and rose again*.

By what we have already shewed, we have, or may have, the sight of him who is the Holy and Invisible One, from whom, as from the Head, all Natural as well as Spiritual good doth flow.

2. The next thing propounded, is, to set forth the *two distinct Branches* and *Administrations of this Headship*, exercised by Christ, as he is the Son of Man glorified, ministring the Inspiration, Anointing and Image of God, which is given according to the Principles

C   and

and Law both of the *first* and of the *second Covenant.* The influence and effect hereof upon all rational beings, whether Angels or Men, in their mutable estate or immutable, doth proceed from Christ, as he is the *second Adam,* that *quickening Spirit,* who is *Lord from Heaven* ; And hereof he hath his living and undeniable Witness in the Hearts and Consciences of his Subjects and Followers, from the beginning of the World to the end thereof.

1. The *Headship* which Christ exerciseth by the *first* of these Ministries, is that of *Supream Natural Lord and Sovereign over all Creatures* ; by the *breath of whose mouth they were made,* Psal. 33. Rev. 4. 11. and *redeemed by his Blood,* Rev. 5.9. So that his right of Rule to them and over them, is indisputable, and their obligation for duty and service to him, indispensable and perpetual. The Angels that fell, are charged (*Jude 6.*) *with defection from, and rebellion against this their Prince and Sovereign Lord,* leaving and deserting him who was their appointed Habitation, and Object of Worship and Duty by the very Law of their Creation. And, unto the same Disobedience and Revolt from Christ, was the first *Adam* tempted, who was subjected at first to none but God. While God the Mediator ruled, and man obeyed, all went right : For God being most perfectly wise and just, could not erre in commanding ; but man, though innocent, yet being free and mutable, was capable to be tempted from his Obedience, as it fell out. *Satan,* that by his disobedience had overthrown himself, knew thereby the way how to overthrow man. He perceived God could not be corrupted nor tempted to unwise or unrighteous Government ; And, if neither King nor Subject could have been corrupted, the Kingdom must needs have stood. But, he quickly found, man was *frail,* though *holy,* and had not yet attained to his incorruptible estate, though upright, and was therefore capable to be wrought upon, and corrupted in his mind, from the simplicity that is in Christ. Man would be as God, have no guide but his own understanding, hating that just restraint, which was needful as a bridle, to be put upon him, to keep him from falling, and which God provided to offer to him, as the means to remain innocent, and pass out of his mutable into an immutable holy state, without sin. But this would not go down, nor be born ; The resignation of his Will, and absolute resolution of it into the Will of his Sovereign, by believing, who required it for his good, would not be hearkened unto. He could not, or would not, or would not think he was such a fool, as stood in need of being so absolutely at the will and dispose of another, when as yet
he

he was his own man, free to continue under the guide of his own self-rule, a thing very beautiful and good, as he thought, to be put into practice. This was the Choice God had given unto man, in this his righteous mutable state, either to trust to his own guidance for the ordering of his steps, according to the Rule set before him, and the conditional Terms of the Law of Nature, and first Agreement or Covenant made with him at his Creation ; or else, to distrust his own Wisdom, as insufficient to be his guide, and his own power of Will, that was mutable and uncertain in its best state, and thereupon commit and resign himself, through Faith, unto the guidance and power of his *Natural Head, Lord* and *Sovereign,* to do, as by the sight of Faith, he should find him do, and cleave close to him, whatsoever he should go before him in.

The first of these, the *first man determined himself in,* and in that Act, chose for his whole seed as well as for himself, who, if God pleased, might have been then concluded by it, without any new offer of Grace made unto them, or their ever being brought to so fair a tender again. But so far was God the Mediator from applying himself speedily to any severe course of proceeding against the *first Adam* and his Posterity, that sinned with him in his loyns, as that he takes this occasion to renew his *first Offer,* upon the experience Man now had of trusting to his own wisdom and strength. God freely of his own accord, makes a Promise to man, of a Redeemer that should come in his own Nature, and be made flesh, to recover him out of his sinfull corrupted state, and bring him and his Posterity once more, into *a state of Reconciliation with God,* that what the Law could not do, in that it was weak through the flesh, might be done *by God's sending his Son in the likeness of sinful flesh, who by the sacrificing of himself, condemned sin in the flesh, that the Righteousness of the Law might be fulfilled in all such, as walk not after the flesh, but after the Spirit.* And here, behold the Righteousness of God, which is, and declares it self by the Faith of Jesus Christ, unto all, and upon all, that believe, making no difference ; but *as all have sinned, and come short of the Glory of God,* in the Act of our first Parents disobedience ; So all should be restored and brought into a capacity of being justified freely by his Grace, through the Redemption that is in Jesus Christ, and made the Righteousness of God in him, against all that can be objected by the Malice of Satan, or from the Justice of God's Law, that hath been broken, and must be satisfied, either by the person offending, or some other, proper to make *Atonement by his Obedience,* in the im-

p::ation

putation whereof we may be accounted *righteous,* **as by** the Act of *disobedience* in the first *Adam* we were made *sinners.* **This** is done by the *Redemption* which is wrought for *all men,* **and** *forgiveness of sins through the Blood of Christ,* either *conditionally* or *absolutely,* Col. 1. 20, 23. Hereupon, God expresly and sincerely declares, he *desires not the death of a sinner,* having sent his only begotten Son into the World, that *all should live through him,* and *none perish or die* in their sins, *for want of a possible and sufficient Remedy*; even him, whom God hath fore-ordained and set forth, *to be a Propitiation through Faith in his Blood, for the remission of sins that are past.* And this is so far from making void the Law or first Covenant between God and man, that it doth establish it, and much clear up the Justice of God, in exacting the Debt of Obedience and Allegiance due to him from **Man,** according to the Law, when so much Clemency and Forbearance hath preceded, and an *Act of Oblivion* freely and of Grace hath been passed, the benefit whereof is conditionally extended unto all. Hence it is, that the Office of giving and putting in execution the Law of God, as it is a Ministry that works wrath, is committed by the Father unto Christ, as he is the Son of Man ; First, *to dispence Judgment with Mercy, great patience* and *long-suffering* ; and afterwards *without Mercy,* as that *fiery Indignation,* which is reserved for *wilful* and *hardned sinners.*

This Christ doth plainly intimate, *Luke 12. 10.* where he saith, *Whosoever shall speak a word against the Son of Man, it shall be forgiven him ; but unto him that blasphemeth against the Holy Ghost, it shall not be forgiven.* For what else can be the meaning of these words, but that Christ would have his Disciples know, that *Judgment* was first committed to him, as he is the *Son of Man,* made the chief Officer and Dispenser of God's Justice, whether *distributive* or *revenging,* the exact Rule whereof is given and contained in the Law of Nature, or Covenant of Works ? The Transgressions against this Law **are capable** of remission and forgiveness through his Blood, the Intercession whereof *speaks better things than that of Abel,* and prevails for gifts *even to the Rebellious,* so that they receive not God's grace, nor take his Name in vain : if they do, he will not hold them guiltless, nor continue any longer to extend to them the benefit of his Sacrifice. Secondly, Therefore Judgment was committed to him without Mercy, in reference to such sins, by which the doers of them *blasphemed* and *resisted the Ministry* he was intrusted with, of giving the Holy Ghost, or inspiring the hearts of the Regenerate with the

new

new Name, and that *saving knowledge of God,* which is communicated according to the *Law of Faith,* and of the *new and everlasting Covenant.*

This is the Royal Office and Dignity, which *Jesus,* as the Son of Man, is exalted unto, by the personal union which he hath with the Word, being *made a meet Minister,* in all respects, *through his Death and Resurrection, to dispence God's sovereign Justice,* and *to execute Judgment and Equity, according to the Law of Nature, renewed and confirmed in his own Blood.* Herein he is *King of Kings* and *Lord of Lords,* the great and Universal Monarch, that is appointed *Law-giver* and *chief Judge* in Heaven and Earth, to and over all Natural Beings, whether *Angels* or *men,* and is the rewarder of every man according to his works, with the same measure that any man metes unto another, he measures out unto him again ; and strictly doth insist upon, and require that which is just and due to be paid unto God or man, by the Law and Principles of the first Covenant. He therefore hath the Gifts and Abilities, incident to that Communion with God, committed to him to dispence, being the Head of God's *distributive,* as well as his *revenging Justice,* and will make it appear, that *he desires not to reap where he hath not sown,* nor to gather where he hath not first strewed, and dispersed abroad in his bounty and liberality, none being a more chearful giver and lender of his Goods than He, looking for nothing again where there is no ability to pay, not happening through our own default.

This is the Ministry which worketh *Wrath,* that is to say, contracts a debt of Punishment, and of the Curse, to every one that joyns issue with God upon the terms of this Covenant, and continues not *in all things written in it, to do them.* And although by this *Ministry,* and that *from Christ himself* as he is the *Son of man,* there be *a life* and *communication of God's Image given,* which, in it self considered, is pure, holy, righteous, *spiritual,* and *good* ; yet, it is but upon such terms, that it may be again withdrawn and revoked by the Giver, if he please ; or may be corrupted or forfeited by the Receiver, and so end in death and wrath. The proof of this was seen at first, in the Fall of our *first Parents,* and is since, in *all the Children of Perdition,* who, after all their great and high enlightnings and clensing from all their old sins, fall into a relapse that is *irrecoverable,* so as to become *trees twice dead,* finally to be pluckt up by the roots and burned.

It is *Christ* in the exercise of this *his first Ministry,* that we intend, when we say, that he is the *Lord of Nature,* and *Fountain of all Ju-*
stice,

stice, upholding a powerful and lasting Witness of himself *in the very Natural Conscience*, where he begets and sets up that knowledge, which declares God *Just*, and the *Justifier of him that either is perfectly* righteous *in his own person, with the righteousness that his Law requires* ; or, that (in default thereof) is *righteous in another*, that God hath given to be *made a Sacrifice for them, that they thereby might be made the Righteousness of God in him* ; such, as he is willing to accept on their behalf, and to reward, not of *Debt*, but of *Grace*.

In one of these two wayes it is for all men to seek to be justified, to answer the end of the Law, and to receive the reward of it : But as to those, that neither in the one nor the other of these wayes, desire to approve themselves, and be found righteous, they are justly convinced of all, and shall be judged of all, as meet objects for God's revenging Justice, to be shewed upon them as the Judgement that is final, after which, no place is left for Mercy. So then, in and by this Ministry, that begins in Justice *distributive*, which is founded in God's bounty and liberality, by which he giveth to all their *being*, *life* and *motion*, and filleth the desire of every living thing ; and which endeth in *avenging* and *punishing Justice*, *upon mercy* and *bounty abused*, (as the known natural Principles of all Law, and righteous Magistratical Government) God manifests himself the Fountain thereof, in the Person of Christ the Mediator. And in this kind of knowledge of God, and obedience to his Law, all mankind are and must be conversant whether they will or no ; and are to shew themselves, either his obedient Subjects, whom he countenanceth, protecteth, and rewardeth, in their well-doing ; or his rebellious and disloyal Subjects, over whom he will glorifie himself in his avenging Justice and dispensation of Judgment at last, without Mercy.

A remarkable example of this we may see in the Case of *Jacob* and *Laban*, Gen. 31 44. *Laban* a Righteous man (at least pretending to it, in his appeal to the God of Justice) conversing with God, in and under the Law of Nature, and what of God is to be known under that Ministry, saith to *Jacob*, Come now, after all our difference and unkindness, thou shalt see I will deal righteously with thee, and put thee to the proof who shall be found more righteous, thou in thy way of serving God, or I in mine. Let us strike a Covenant, I and thou, and let it be for a Witness between me and thee ; Let Him whom I know and serve by the Light and Law of Nature, and whom thou servest by a higher Law and Light, that of Faith, (which doth

not

not destroy, but establish the Righteousness of the Law) let him, whose eye only seeth, and before whom we cannot be hid, (either from his knowledge or his vengeance) watch and mark our carriages, in pursuance of our Covenant and Agreement; and accordingly be a Witness, for, or against us, upon the breach thereof. Unto this *Jacob* chearfully agreed upon his Principles, and *Laban* upon his. In which, it is evident, that the same God and Christ may be conversed and walked with, upon differing Principles; and that righteous Agreements may be upheld and maintained by those that own and call Christ to witness, as he is the *Sovereign Minister of God's Justice,* whether their knowledge of him be according to the *first* or *second Covenant,* in both which Christ comes forth, as to his Communications and enlivening Presence in the hearts of the sons of men; which is the point that we are now upon, and have cleared in the first branch of it.

The Second (being that which consists in a *knowledge* and *manifestation of God,* that is *beyond and above Nature,* that which man in his natural make, at best, reacheth not, or hath a mind or will to receive) is more difficult to be expressed, and when expressed, to be understood. For after this manner God is not seen or communicated unto any, but in a secret and hidden way, which he makes not common, but reserves for peculiar kindness to those that find grace in his sight, upon their coming, as *Esther* did, into the inner Court, to have this golden Scepter held out to them, by promise, or else they die. God's first Voice and Manifestation of himself unto the Creature, speaks and declares him (as we have shewed) to be just, in a way of Law and righteous Government, which he exerciseth over his Creatures. He is their Sovereign, they are his Subjects, in order to receive the reward of Love, or of Wrath : That which this Second Voice ministers and speaks, is that Love, and the knowledge of God in it, which he spreads abroad in the hearts of his good and loyal Subjects, after the proof made of the Loyalty and stedfastness of their Love to him ; *Not that they love him first, but of his own Will they are begotten, by the Word of Truth, into this Love of his, which comprehends them, long before they apprehend it, and God in it.* But he that shall come, will come, and will not tarry.; if by Faith we are taught to wait for him, *Whom, having not seen, yet, we love,* or, have secret cleaving to, and earnest longing after : *In whom, even whilst we see not,* but find out selves altogether in the dark, and at a loss, *as to what may be seen and known of him by natural Light and Reason ; yet, believing, and having thereby given us the evidence of things, unseen by the na-*

tural

tural eye, they become so real, and are made so certain to us, as we rejoyce with joy unspeakable and full of Glory. We could do no more, were we at the end of our Faith, and did see, as we are seen, as we shall at the compleat Salvation of our Souls.

From him then, that is thus the Love and Joy of the believing Soul, that is to say, *Christ,* the Minister of the Spirit, and giver of the holy Ghost, and that new Name which none know but they that have it, is this Second kind of Knowledge of God, and Communication of Life from him, that we desire to open and lay before you.

You have already heard that Christ is the only begotten of God, as he is the Building and Sanctuary, which he that is the builder of all things, sets up in himself, for his own use, as his Temple and speaking-place, where to give and whence to deliver his lively Oracles and Inspirations, of both sorts, with which he fills all things. In this Heavenly Habitation, God records his Name, and hath the place of his Throne and of his Footstool, with which he will dwell and tabernacle among his People for ever.

Again, By this workmanship and heavenly building, *Christ* the *Mediator* hath a *Creature-being* given unto him *in spirit, before the World was,* and is he who was before all things, and *by whom all things consist* ; is the *Angel of God's Face and Presence,* that is *by God* and *with him :* First, *As his chief Messenger and Servant, his Messiah*; and then, *as his Spouse and Equal, that lies in his bosom, knows all his secrets,* and is retained *in the most intimate bond of spiritual marriage-union, that is possible for Creature-nature to be taken into with God, even by personal union, as the body is with the soul.* And thus Christ is found, even as a Creature in the form of God, and is called *Michael,* God's Fellow and Equal, after such a manner, as the body is to the soul, both making but one person.

Now *Christ,* as he lies in the Father's bosom, and is the Spouse to the blessed Trinity, is a higher manifestation of God, than he hath sent out from God, as the *Messiah,* that bears God's Name only by figure and representation, as his single Image, which yet speaks truly what God is, and as fully as the Creatures first vessel of Receipt and Measure, knows how to bear and receive ; but doth not speak out all God's fulness, nor shew the Original it self, whereof it is the figure and character, which in its single standing and appearing out of God, as a thing distinct from God, and not at the same time known to have any abode in him, after that intimate manner of union and conjunction, before-mentioned , the finite and short-sighted understanding of the
Creature

Creature is ready to imagine that manifeftation and fight of God's Glory to be all that is to be known and inherited of God ; And to defire, as the *Ifraelites* did, (*Exod.* 20.) in the Perfon of *Mofes,* as the Type, that *God would not add to fpeak more,* or fhew forth his naked and unvail'd glory to them ; but they would content themfelves to hear God fpeak under the Vail, which *Mofes* had put upon his face, and not look out after any higher attainment. When God had fpoken once, and fhewed the Creature as much of himfelf as it could take in by its firft make and conftitution of being upon natural Principles, he proceeds to declare his purpofe to fpeak again, and *form a hearing ear* and *feeing eye, proportion'd to his fecond voice,* adding this kind of hearing and fight to the fame Creature-being , (whofe firft Principles of Knowledge and Will, are too fhort and weak to bear this *Voice*) called in Scripture, the *fight and hearing of Faith, that muft be mixed with our natural Principles, as their ftability and confummation,* and have the place of *guide to them,* and *Lord over them,* that the Scripture in this fenfe may be made good, that *the elder. fhall ferve the younger.* The Root of this *Second fight of God,* is wrought out in Chrift, as he is the *only begotten* that lies in *God's bofom,* and from thence is made the Minifter and Giver of what himfelf firft receives and enjoys. So that now, fuppofing the *Spirit of the Mediator,* (that is the *only begotten* and *firft-born of every creature*) to be the *Root of all natural Principles and Perfection,* as he is the *Meffiah,* and the *hearer* and *obeyer of God's firft Voice* (of which we have already fpoken) we are now to know, that God proceeds to make the fame *only Begotten,* to have being and abode in him, as his peculiar poffeffion and choiceft object of his Love, in the relation of his Spoufe and Confort. He is formed and prepared hereunto, by becoming him that is made able to *hear, receive* and obey *God's Second Voice,* his higheft, moft excellent, and fulleft manner of *manifeftation of himfelf to Creature-underftanding, with power* in the difpenfation of the fulnefs of time, *to become Man,* made *of a Woman, under the Law,* and afterwards *raifed up from the dead,* and made to *fit down on the right hand of the Majefty on high* ; working out the fame work in *Jefus* his Servant, the chief and principal Branch, which is firft wrought out in himfelf, as in the root and head of all natural and fupernatural perfection. It is then a kind of *working over the Creature again,* out of its firft frame and conftitution of being, into a frame and conftitution *much more excellent and capacious,* a ftate *incorruptible,* never needing, nor being fubjected to change of any kind, afterward,

D

which

which the first building upon natural principles, doth, and did need.
This *working over*, or *re-building the Creature* again, called in
Scripture *Regeneration*, is not simply *restoration* or *confirmation*, conveying immutableness to the first Principles, and no more; but it is
quite a *new Creation*, that takes down of the first building, as much
as the Builder pleaseth, and leaves no more of it standing, than what
is consistent with, and grows up into perfect harmony, use, and ser-
viceableness to and with the new addition and enlargement that is
made, not destroying the first Image of God in man.   This *rebuilding work* then produceth not a total anihilation of the *natural being*,
but brings upon the life and manner of operation that flows from *natural principles*, such a cessation as amounts to a kind of *death*, at least
to a *bitterness* more than *death it self*, rendring it impossible for the
Creature to live or move any longer unto sin and evil; and quickning
it, and raising it out of this dead state, into the greatest freedom to, and
stedfast perseverance in all kinds of good that is imaginable, as that
which becomes most natural and delightful, the contrary thereunto
most grievous and disquietful to it.

This *Second Life*, which accompanies Salvation, and brings Immortality to light, is a kind of life from the dead, that the natural
beings of Angels and Men are begotten into, by being made meet
Temples and Subjects for the Holy Ghost, in a state of life eternal, by
a union with God that can never be dissolved. Angels therefore as
well as Men, are called *Children of the Resurrection*, Luke 20. 35, 36.
as they are brought into a state never to change more.

Hence it is, even amongst these *Children of the Resurrection*, that
the *immortal life*, wherewith they are quickned by Christ, as he is
the giver of the Holy Ghost is of two sorts, as to the degree and
measure of the glory thereof. First, Such, *wherein Men and Angels
are equal:* And the Second, *Such, wherein some Men are made in
such manner Christ's Equals, the Lamb's or Bridegroom's Wife* that
lies in *his bosom, that they are the Angels superiours,* and are made
joynt-heirs with Christ, of that Name, which he hath obtained, *better
than that which is the Angels food,* that *Word of God's mouth* that
they live upon. So that now, when we speak of Christ, as the *Author
of life Eternal, in this second sort of Ministry,* wherein the natural beings of the creature are, as it were, wrought over again and rebuilt,
we would be understood, that *there is a birth of this Immortality,
which amounts to the giving of the Holy Ghost, in the single portion
of it,* and also *in the double portion of it,* as we shall distinctly open

in

in its place; both being distinct from that *pure, holy, righteous life of Nature* that was at first given by *Creation,* or afterwards renewed by a *Restoration* and kind of *new Creation of qualities,* but falls short of *true and saving Regeneration,* properly and rightly explicated and made known ; by which the *natural frame and make of the natural soul and spirit of man,* is in a manner wholly altered and changed, and much for the better, because it is raised out of its *frail, mutable, wavering,* as well as *sinful, natural-state,* into a *strong, stable, immutable posture of mind,* in *Righteousness* and *true Holiness,* as a *Rock and Stone,* that *the Gates of Hell cannot prevail against.* This further Gift and Grace of God, though it be the end of Man's Creation, and that which God, as the reward to those that are obedient under the first Ministry, doth promise and hold forth, in a way of Promise, yet is conditional, and so, that which in Justice God need not confer upon any that perform not the Condition, but by their sin do forfeit it. And therefore it so happens, that all who inherit this Blessing, are made receivers of it, by Promise, and by a second and new Agreement with God, which he enters into with them, in regenerating them, and makes them new Creatures, thenceforward to serve him and live to him, in newness of Spirit and Life.

3. We now come to shew, according to the *Third* Particular proposed, who those be that are Christ's *Anointed Ones* and *Witnesses,* under both his fore-mentioned Administrations, and the Anointing it self, which is given, by the one and by the other.

Christ is, as we have shewed, the *Original and primitive Pattern of all Perfections* ; the Works, that were finished from the beginning, known to God from all Eternity, and actually wrought and set up from Everlasting, in the Mediator, through that Eternal Wisdom, which was by God, as one brought up with him, *Prov.* 8. and whom he possessed in the beginning of his way, before his Works of old, ere ever the Earth was. And what is true in Christ, who is *not only the Root, but the chief and principal Branch,* hath its Witness, and is declared in the Work which he begets, and shines forth in, amongst his Members, knit to him, by an abiding or indissoluable union ; all that are Branches in this *true Vine,* whose Fruit is such as is *cheering,* both to the *heart of God* and of *Man* ; that is to say, of Man considered in his higher or lower attainments, and growths, up into the knowledge and love of God, as he is Man, and no more, partaking of the Spirit of God by measure ; And, secondly, of Man, made the only Begotten of God, that lyes in the bosom of the Father, and is

anointed

anointed with the *Oyl of gladness above his fellows,* which Christ's exalted Manhead is, and that after such sort, as not to have and inherit the dignity of it to himself, single and alone, but *as* the *Head and Husband to that General Assembly of the First-born,* whose Names are *written in Heaven,* and *have right to the double portion.*

The right opening of this, is the great Key to all our practical and experimental Knowledge of God, which is found amongst the dispersed Seed of God, that are either of the one or other birth, Children of the *first* or *second Covenant,* in every Nation, Tongue, Language or Form, truly fearing God and working Righteousness, and therein accepted of God, either through Faith, or with that common acceptance declared, *Gen.* 4. *If thou dost well, shalt thou not be accepted?* whilst in the mean time they may be great strangers unto, if not much prejudiced against one another, for not walking together in one and the same way of Profession and external Communion.

Give me leave then, to distinguish this Seed of God into *Four sorts:* Two, that are *Witnesses unto Christ's first Ministry,* as he is the Author and Restorer of the *Law and Principles of pure Nature,* and is the *dispenser of God's Image,* and *the manifestation of his Will, upon the terms of the first Covenant;* And other *two,* that are *Witnesses unto the truth of Christ's second Ministry,* as he is the *new Creator, that regenerates and makes over again his first work anew,* is the *Author of Life from the dead,* and *bringer of Immortality to light;* which is not done by the first Covenant, nor can be; but, by this *second knowledge* and *Image of God,* begotten and wrought, by, and according to the tenor of *the new and everlasting Covenant.*

The first sort of Witnesses we shall speak unto; and rightly to have the knowledge of them, we must yet further consider Man in his first make, and in the primitive constitution of being that was given to him in his state of Innocency before sin entred: So as to enquire, upon what terms Man then stood with God, and in what respect he was pronounced *good* in God's eyes, and might be said to be accepted of him.

Man then had the *perfect knowledge of God* and *of Christ, as his Creator and Law-giver* (for God created all things by Jesus Christ; by the Word of God's mouth, in the Mediator, did all things live, move, and had their being) so that what might be known of God, even of his *Eternal Power and Godhead,* by the things that were made, that is, by the means of any created beings, visible or invisible, it was *manifested in man,* and was *shewed to man, by that mixt, com'*

poun-

pound being, which was given him, of an *intellectual* and *sensual* or *animal Soul*, which furnished him with inward and outward senses, proportioned for such a *knowledge*, and which were retained *in due subjection* and *subordination* the one unto the other. From such a prospect and survey of things, as Man at first was fitted to receive both from within and without him, the *invisible things of the Godhead* were clearly seen by him, rendring him without all excuse, being thereby instructed in the duty of his *obedience* and *subjection* to the *Law of God* under which he was made, to the glorifying him as God ; which as God expected and required from man, so he owned a liking and acceptance of from man, with whom he treated, and agreed upon the terms of his *personal obedience*, and *entire observance of all his Commands*, and *continuance therein.*

Three things man in this state, might, and did experimentally find in himself.

First, *The light and manifestation of God's Mind and Will, as a Law within him*, called in Scripture, *The Candle of the Lord, the Oyl with which God furnished the Lamp of man's spirit, which he was to take care, that through his default he did not let it go out, nor diminish ; but quicken and renew it, as it should need, by such means God instituted.*

The second thing which man experienced, was, *the life of a rational and intellectual Soul ;* that is to say, *a superior part in the same Soul, affording the use of inward senses, that by keeping open and awake, he had, as it were, an intercourse with the spiritual and invisible beings of Angels, and saw the intrinsick natures of the Creatures.*

And thirdly, *He found also, a brutish nature, of which he was compounded and made, which furnished him with the use and operation of outward senses, by which he might go abroad, and walk up and down in converse with earthly things and inhabitants : The fountain of these outward senses, his inferior part, to be in his soul or spirit. With these he came to perform, and put in execution, that which the superior and directive part of him, judged right and fit to be done.*

This was the inward and outward order of actings, that Man at first was created in, with a freedom to make use of this Light within himself, (which God, as a Talent, had committed to him to imploy according to his will) and rely upon his guidance and the sufficiency of it, to attain the end God set before him, in the way of his *perfect obedience,* and keeping out the entrance of sin, or else upon the sense of the *instability* he might discern in these Principles of *Freedom,* that

leave

leave him alone and to himself, and the *Insufficiency* to continue by the power of the *Grace* received in well-doing, against all resisting and deceiving temptations, to chuse rather to make resignation up of this his Freedom, wherein he was at his own guidance and dispose, in exchange for a better and more *perfect Freedom*, that is to say, in order to be intirely at the will of another, and the leading influence thereof in all things, even of such another, whose service is *perfect Freedom*, and who should be as Surety for the performance of the duty to God's Law, and secure us from the penalty of the Curse therein threatned against the Transgression thereof, which was pointed out to *Adam* in the Tree of Life, as *John* interprets by the Promise, mentioned, *Rev.* 2. 7. *To him that overcometh* (which is done through Faith) *will I give to eat of the Tree of Life* or Immortality, which is fed on by Faith ; through the power of which, the entire resignation of our will, into the leading and rule of the Spirit and Will of Christ is onely wrought, and of which w: shall treat particularly in its proper place, though this small touch of it is needful here : But the choice which Man made, was, to lean to his own understanding for his guide, and to trust to the use of his Freedom, which gave him to be at his own dispose, as sufficient to encounter with and resist all Temptations, and upon the first encounter failed and miscarried, and let in Sin, Death and Wrath upon himself and all his Posterity, as the sad Consequence of that Fact of his.

  To be then upon these terms, as *Adam* was before his *fall*, personally righteous, and finding *acceptance* with *God* whilst we stand in such *Obedience* and *Righteousness*, is an Effect which *Christ* in his *first Ministry* doth produce in the *hearts of men*, making them in this respect the *first sort* of the *four Witnesses* we have before-mentioned, and which, though we have been considering of them in the Person of the first *Adam* before the *Fall* ; yet by the same Rule and Proportion, the *Witness* is still the same, whether it be communicated originally at mans *Creation*, or else by *renewal* or *restauration* again after the *fall* by the *same hand* and *Ministry* which first gave it, which *Christ* may do if he please ; and that he hath done is most obvious and undeniable from the experience we have had of late years, within these Nations, in a sort of *Professors* and *Witnesses of Christ*, that do exactly go upon this bottom of *Personal Righteousness*, wrought by the Principles of *pure Nature*, *renewed and restored within them*, which they assert may be held *in perfection whilst we are here in the body*, and by which we may, as by the *Light within us*, perfectly

sub-

subdue our brutish nature, and keep under the body, though all this be accompanied with *mutability*, and the *acceptance* which they find with God is according to their works, whilst they do well, *otherwise sin is at the door*, and the punishment according to the same. This sort of Professors of the Name of Christ, rise so high in their Testimony concerning him, as to call him, *The glorious Sun of the soul*; the *Searcher through of all darkness*; the *Wonderful Power*; the *Incomprehensible Wisdom, and Immutable Holiness*; a thing that is invisible to every fleshly thing; the one individual Spirit of Brightness, that created all souls; and are so dazeled with the Beams of this Glory, (all which he truly is) that they overlook him too much according to his Humanity, and see him not as he is the Son of man, in whom Redemption is wrought for us, and the Atonement for sin made by the price of his Blood, the benefit whereof they have, whether they confess it or not: These are they, that *by the Candle of the Lord that is lighted within them* (the work whereof is written in their inward parts) though they be not so much *hearers of the Law by the Ministry of the outward Word*, yet do they shew themselves *doers of the Law by the power of the Light* that is *within them*; *doing*, as it were, *by Nature the things contained in the Law, and so not having the Law*, outwardly considered, *are a Law to themselves, shewing the work of it written in their hearts*; and *by keeping the Righteousness of the Law, do judge them, who by the Letter transgresse the Law, and do feel Peace and Comfort in their works*. In this manner did the *Centurian fear God* and *work Righteousness*, Act. 10. before he heard those words from *Peter*, that instructed him in the knowledge of Christ's Death and Resurrection, and the Peace that comes to the Soul by his Blood, unto the Remission of sins; by whom all that believe are justified from all things, which they could not be justified from by the Law of Nature or Works. These ought not to be denied place in this rank of Christ's Witnesses, whereof we have been speaking, since they own and declare themselves to be *fearers of God* and *workers of Righteousness*, upon these first principles of it which *pure Nature* teaches and plants, where-ever it is renewed and restored from the hand of Christ's liberality and bounty, to put the Receivers of it to the tryal, how far they will shew their faithfulness in the measure committed to them, and in what readiness they are to put these Talents out in the way of exchange to get more, and not to rest untill they obtain that state which is immutable. It therefore greatly concerns such to look to their standing, which is very slippery and un-

certain, and take heed lest they fall ; and to think soberly of themselves as they ough: to think ; and not affirm, as they are apt to do,
that their Witness contains in it all that Christ is : lest otherwise,
when they come to be weighed in the ballance of the Sanctuary, they
be found at last to *deny* more of Christ than they *confess* of him : Nor
are they to exalt this part of the Ministry of Christ, which is but the
beginning against that fuller fight and knowledge of him that is still
to be revealed ; but this one thing they should do, *Forget that which
is behind, and press forward to the mark of the prize of the high
calling which is in Christ* : And although it be a commendable thing
in them, even upon their Principles, to spread the knowledge of Christ
in all the dark corners of the world, where the Scriptures and written
Word of Truth are not heard or received, the effect of which labours,
with God's blessing, may be the heightning and refining man's nature,
and purging it from filthy lusts and prophaness, teaching them to fly
from the Wrath and Vengeance which awaits evil-doers ; Yet this is
to be done in subserviency unto, not in opposition against the right
knowledge and powerful Preaching of the Scriptures, those Divine
Oracles which God hath preserved for the great benefit and use of his
Church in all times since the first writing of them, By these are witnessed the righteous Principles and Actings according to the Law of
pure Nature, wherein Man was at first created, and may so often as
Christ pleases, be again received in by that Light with which he enlightens every man that comes into the world, whereof Christ (as we
have shewed) is the Author and Dispenser ; and under this first Witness all these are to be comprehended, who approve themselves *doers
of the Law, men that fear God and work Righteousness in every Nation,* in such manner as God accepts, though as yet they have not attained to the knowledge of Christ by the outward Ministry and hearing of the written Word.

But as these are such who pretend, to be *doers of the Law by a
Light within* them, without dependance upon the Ministry of the
written Word, by a Teaching of the Word, as it is spoken inwardly
to the mind by Angels, who are entrusted with it, *Heb.* 2. 1. So there
is a second sort of Witnesses unto the same Principles in substance, that
is to say, to the life of the Image of God in pure Nature, wherein man
was at first created, as it comes again to be renewed and restored with
power in the soul, by the knowledge of Jesus Christ, and the Redemption that is by his Blood through the Ministry of the written
Word, and the operation of the Spirit of Christ in the use of those

Ordinances

Ordinances and Institutions of Worship, which he hath appointed and revealed in the Scriptures, according to the several measures of their growth up into this knowledge of Christ, and faithfull walking with him therein, under the variety of Profession and Forms of visible Worships that are extant, in that which is acknowledged or witnessed to be the visible Christian Church; which, by the preaching of the Gospel, upon the Ascension of Christ, and the Ministry of his Spirit poured forth in the primitive state of it, came to be raised up by God's visiting the *Gentiles,* to take out of them a People of his Name, that he might substitute unto himself as another *Israel* and *holy People* and *Church* of visible Professors of his Name, in the room and place of the *Jews,* and the old Law and Form of Worship that had been in practice among them, *Rom* 11. which made *James,* in *Act.* 15. 16, 17. apply the words of the Prophets, unto this new Christian Gentile Church, which sayes, *After this I will return, and will build up the Tabernacle of David, which is fallen down, and will build again the ruines thereof; and I will set it up, that the residue of men might seek after the Lord, and all the Gentiles, upon whom my Name is called, saith the Lord, who doth all these things.* Now amongst the visible Members of the Christian Church (as evidently appears, *Gal.* 4.) there were a Generation, that under the Name of *Christians* and *hearers of the Gospel and Ministry of the Spirit, according to the New Testament,* chose still to retain the Principles of the Law and first Covenant, as the ballance of all their Faith, Obedience and Worship, desiring to be under the Law and Dominion of it, and to cleave to the upholding and doing those things, which, according to the Judgment of the Apostle *Paul,* made them *debtors to the whole Law,* and stuck them clear off from the true Principles of Grace, that are by the **Law** of Faith, and of the new and everlasting Covenant; and of this, they gave but too clear a proof, in that they gloried in something that was on this side the Spiritual mind, which is set upon things that are above, and which ought to be died unto by the Doctrine of the Cross, unto which they shew themselves the declared and zealous opposers.

Not, but that in words and profession these pretended as much to own the Principles of Free-Grace, and of the New-Testament, as any, and have their approach to it, at least, when they please themselves, some more and some less; but, when they are brought to the Tryal, they quickly shew that they are not able to endure the bridling and restraint which the New-Testament puts upon them, by the Doctrine of the Cross of Christ, to the crucifying that wherein they de-

E

fire and affect to glory, from which they are excluded by the Law of Faith and the New-Creature, as we shall shew in its place ; So that in Truth, that which these *second sort of Witnesses* have in their eye, is not the being and life of the New Creature, but the restoration of the *old Adam* in his primitive, righteous and holy state, into which they grow up and are found for the life of their holiness ; and upon that bottom, as a qualification to entitle them to all the Promises, and their abode and continuance in Fellowship and Communion with Christ, and Interest in his Death, for the Remission of sins ; They do experience such acceptance from Christ, and are in themselves so certain of their good Estates to their Eternal Salvation, that they will not endure to hear, wherein they are in a mistake, nor that it is possible for them to be better.

Thefe do indeed excel the *first Witnesses* in the doctrinal part of the knowledge of Christ, confessing him in that great part of his Priestly Office (which the others see not) as he bare our Transgressions, and made Atonement for the sin of mankind, by the Sacrifice of himself ; in the benefit of which Sacrifice they find their outward *peace* and *joy* more than in their *righteous works* ; nay, when as to the *light* and *evidence* of their *Sanctification*, they are at a loss and in the dark ; they have an adherence to the *blood of Christ*, as the propitiation for their fins, and his intercession on their behalfs to the Father, for the obtaining new strength against Corruption, and the renewal of their former peace and comfort; which experience the *first sort of Witnesses* are strangers to, or see no need of, but account themselves Justified as well as Sanctified by the inward purity and perfection which they have attained with power over the *brutish* and *sensual Nature*, that they are more careful and able to *keep under*, than this *second sort* are.

Neverthelefs, The *Oyl* which is given from *Christ* under this *first Ministry* in either of these respects before-mentioned, is that *Annointing* that through the frailty and weakness of the *Vessel* that receives it, is not abiding, but at the best is but as a sojourner, that finds not in these hearts the *new man*, that is the place of its rest, *Isa. 66.* and though it be used by *Christ* to trim the *Lamp of the spirit of man* with, when renewed and restored to the *obedience* and *subjection* that is required by the Law of God, in any degree and measure of sincerity or chastity of the pure *Lamb*-like and virgin Spirit, yet being only in the *Lamp*, where it spends and consumes, and must be duly renewed, and by a frame of heart meet to receive it, and cheerish

it ;

it ; or elfe being grieved and quenched, it fuddenly departs : Hence
it is, that amongft thefe *two Witneffes* under this *Anointing* , which is
from *Chrift*, and the operation, good, righteous, holy, and fpiritual,
and the *change* made by it, true and real ; there are fuch a number of
vifible Profeffors that prove Hypocrites, Apoftates , and fall away
from the Grace and enlightening they have felt and experienced, deceiving both themfelves and others, being not able to hold it out in
the day of Tryal, nor to perfevere and endure to the end ; without,
on the other hand, ftumbling on the *ftumbling ftone*, and becoming
prejudiced againft any higher and further growths up into Chrift : or,
on the other hand, through fear of lofs by Perfecution, are terrified
from well-doing (with amazement) or, are bought off from it with
the reward of *unrighteoufnefs*, as *Balaam* was ; and as *Demas* who
embraced this prefent World.

And the Reafon of this, as to the *one* as well as the *other fort* of
thefe *Witneffes*, is, becaufe that is wanting to them which fhould *fix*
them, and make them *unchangeable* in well-doing, and caufe them to
be *Pillars in the Houfe of God* that never *go out* more.   That they are
partakers of *righteous Principles*, and are qualified with *Power* to
work *Righteoufnefs*, and this from prefent *annointing* and *impreffion*
of the *true and right Spirit*, is not, nor ought not to be denied them :
They may be *Virgins*, and have *Lamps well trimed with Oyl frefh and*
full, and yet not *able* to *keep this Oyl from fpending and going out*, nor
prevent their own being to *feek* for *want of it*, when they fhould
have the *greateft ufe* of it. And indeed, the *firft fort* do confefs as
much, and own their *Righteoufnefs* to be *mutable*, and they no longer to have certainty in it, than they can ftand in the *Obedience* ; and
that their ftanding or falling, may be or may not be, as they give their
free affent or diffent to the *Good* and *Evil* that prefents it felf to them.
But with many, under the *fecond fort of Witneffes*, it is not fo ; for
they faften upon the *Righteoufnefs of Chrift*, *that is wrought in his*
Perfon, *as that which is unchangeable in it felf*, which it is, if they do
but rightly apply it, and hold it upon the Tenure of the abfolute and
better *Promifes* which are by the *new Covenant*, whereof they make
no doubt but they do.   And as to their *Sanctification*, they have the
Law for their *Rule*, which in it felf is Moral and Perpetual, and fo
they believe all real and true *Conformity* to it, wrought in their *hearts*,
muft alfo be, although their *hearts* be not yet made that *good foyl*,
that *where it hath received the Word*, *and retained it for a feafon*,
are not prepared to keep it for ever, *and to bring forth fruit with that*

patience, *as will lose all other things, rather than ever be prevailed
with, to let it go.*

From both these *sorts of Witnesses, Christ* is Preached, and *Righteousness* made known and Propagated in the World, and a Testimony kept up against open Looseness and Prophanness, Atheism and Idolatry ; and by these Spiritual Traders and Merchants in the Traffick of Christ's Goods and Talents of the Common Gifts and Graces of his Spirit, there is by some, a right & good use and approvement made, so as they are at last perswaded to put them to the Exchangers for their Lord's Advantage, and their own benefit ; being willing to purchase the *one Pearl* of great price, which is obtained through *saving Faith* and *Regeneration* ; for many of these *small Pearls* that in the Day of Proof and Tryal, will not endure : And those that do *eat and drink unworthily of this Table of the Lord,* notwithstanding the many wonderful things they do in his Name, *he will profess he knows them not,* but let them see, they *have eat and drunk their own damnation,* and *left themselves wholly without all excuse :* And therefore, both these degrees and growths up into Christ Jesus, as branches in the *Vine,* that after real union, must either by better husbandry applied to them, come to receive a fastening in and with the Root, that cannot be shaken nor dissolved, or else prove *withered branches,* at last that upon tryal are only fit for the fire ; Their great care and business should be to make their Calling and Election sure, and from evidence which cannot fail nor deceive, experience that the Root bears them, and not they the Root.

And thus we come to the Consideration of the other *two sorts of Witnesses,* that are the *standing Plants and Olive Trees in the House of God,* which are planted by the *Fathers right hand,* and none whatsoever can pluck up. In the former I have spoke to, Christ *dwells as in his Tents and mutable habitations,* who in that respect are called *Temples of the Holy Ghost,* that may so be defiled, that God may destroy and cast them out of his sight for ever ; but these we now come to describe, do Constitute that *Mount Zion* that cannot be moved, that *Heavenly Jerusalem,* which is made a quiet *habitation,* a place *of everlasting Rest,* a *Tabernacle that shall not be taken down* (as the first must, in order to be new built in the Regeneration) *not one of the Stakes thereof shall ever be removed, neither shall any of the Cords thereof be broken* ; but there the Lord will be for ever, a place of broad Rivers and Streams that shall spring up into life eternal, and that from the lowest Ebbs, at first no higher than the Anckles,

becom

become still ascending, not only to the heighth and stature of man in his fullest perfection, but also above it, till it come to be a River to swim in, a River, pure and clear as Cristal, that proceeds from the Throne of God and of the Lamb (the Son of man glorified) in the midst of the street; and on either side whereof is the Tree of Life, or those who live and feed upon that incorruptible Fruit.

The work which is wrought by Christ in and upon the *two first sort of Professors of his Name,* is that which seals them and binds them fast up in the bundle of life unto the Redemption that is eternal, and makes them to give witness to what Christ is and doth in his *second Ministry,* as he sends the holy Ghost, the Spirit of Truth, which abides in them that are made Receivers of him, under an Obligation, *never to depart from them, nor suffer them to depart from him ;* that is, he that stablisheth us in Christ, pouring out that Anointing which sealeth us with the Seal of the living God, as with the Name of our Father in our forehead, the effectual calling of whose Name upon us, by working in us, and making us fit Vessels to receive it and bear it, is our Adoption, and that manner of admitting us unto the right and dignity of Sons, which makes us heirs according to the Promise.

And this is done by Christ, not as Creator, and the Giver of the Law and Life of pure Nature upon its first Principles ; but by Christ as he ministers that Spirit of Truth, which is the Inspiration before-described, that proceeds from the Father and the Son, by the operation of the holy Ghost, or third Person in the Trinity, whose work is Perfection and consummative of what is already in being, by the Creation and Operation of the Son or Eternal Word ; and yet causeth so great an Alteration in the natural being of man, taken at his best, from what it was before, and that so much for the better ; with respect to abundance and immutability of that which Nature it self **calls** *good and righteous,* that it justly deserves to be call'd a *new Creation,* or *Regeneration,* that gives a new Creature *Being* and *Life* far excelling the *first,* and much differing in glory from it. To evidence this,

Let us consider Man in the righteousness of his Natural being, wherein he hath a right understanding of God's mind (in what is required by the Law, which he consents and agrees to, as that which is righteous, and holy, and spiritual, and good) and a will to put it in execution, as that which, in the doing thereof, he doth but his duty, and which he is obliged to by G O D, and his own voluntary Engagement, and to continue therein under the danger of the
Curse

Curse upon failer. Here the Command is a Lamp, and the Law is Light, to instruct man in his Duty ; and the Spirit and Mind of man, keeping to this Light, and walking up to it, and faithfully in it, is in a good and perfect state, by God approved and justified ; so that there be but a continuance in it : And this Christ seems to acknowledge to him that put him the Question, *Luke* 10. 25. *What shall I do to inherit Eternal life ?* In the Answer he gives, bidding him do that which is written in the Law, which sayes, *Thou shalt love the Lord thy God with all thy heart, with all thy soul, with all thy strength, and with all thy mind ; do this, and thou shalt live :* Where then lies the difficulty ? what is it that is yet wanting ?

The difficulty lies in man's part, whereof he is not enough sensible, and the want is, that of a Guide and Surety, to set and to keep man's spirit right in the doing of that which the Law requires, in the manner God prizes and most esteems : For there is a way that is right in man's eyes, even in yeelding obedience to the Law of God, wherein man glories, and is puffed up in himself, but hath no praise from God ; and this is from that spring and principle of activity which is seated in the freedom of Will, which is natural to man in his first righteous Nature, and was found in him before his Fall, and is capable of Restitution since, nay, is actually restored through the benefit of his Death, more or less in every man, by that common Light and Grace which Christ doth no more withhold from any man, than he doth his Rain from raining upon the Just and Unjust ; but in way of further bounty, doth confer in large proportions where he pleaseth, a distribution of his Goods and Spiritual Gifts, in which he causeth the Receivers thereof to differ one from another, according to the use he intends them unto. By which enriching of man's nature upon this his restored natural bottom of a free active righteous spirit, according to the Law, whilst the primitive mutability is still continuing with him, he is so far from being made a New Creature and truly regenerate (as is but too generally conceived) that nothing but passing under the new Creation-work, translating man out of his primitive natural freedom and activity, into an activity and Freedom of another kind, is capable to hinder this first freedom from engendring to bondage, and the righteousness accompanying it, from failing and ending in the death of Hypocrisie and final Apostacy ; which made Christ, in *Joh.* 8. 31. to deal so plainly with the *Jews*, that in this wavering spirit were for the present such as passed currant for Believers, and were so called by the Evangelists ; but Christ knew they were not of continuance, and so told

told them, ver. 31. together with the Remedy which he had by him for the cure of it. For they stood in need to be made free by the knowledge of the Truth; or rather, to be known of him that is True; the Son that abides in the house for ever, who is able to bring them into that state of freedom, that shall make them *free indeed*, with an impossibility ever to be imbondaged more, or to serve sin as their lord and master.

This mutable state, wherein man did at first receive God's Image by Creation, and doth in the way of Restoration again partake of it, by vertue of the Ministry of Christ's first anointing and comforting Presence, in which he takes up his habitation in the soul, as a sojourner and passenger, although there be given that knowledge of God's Will and Mind to man, which is true, and as perfect and full, as the Vessel that takes it can bear; yet the weakness of the Vessel is such, that it is like the wave of the Sea, tossed with every wind when temptation arises, and is either of it self apt to mistake and misunderstand the Rule given him to walk by, or to close and fall in with a false deceitful spirit, transforming himself into the Image of Righteousness, and imbrace him for the True one: for whatever Image of God that which is a meer Creature, and no more, is found in, the old Serpent knows how to imitate and personate the same, in the very likeness wherein it shines forth in Christ's own Person, and with the same to seat himself in the hearts of his followers, as in the Temple of God, and to shew himself as far as that will go, for proof and demonstration that he is God, to the imbondaging and carrying captive by this deceit, all that receive not the Truth in the love of it.

Whereas the Image and Knowledge of God, and of his Will, which is given by the Truth, or by his coming into the Soul, who is the true *One*, doth anoint and impress the Soul, with that Name of God, which doth exclude by the very Nature of its evidence, all possibility of falshood, deceit, or uncertainty, as doth the Dayes-spring of Light to the natural eye, which by its self-evidence assures it, It is that Light wherein is no darkness at all, but is able to distinguish it self, as that which is separate from the darkness of every counterfeit and false representation. This comes only by the Law of Faith, and true Regeneration, that Gift of the Holy Ghost, as he is the Second and better Comforter, the Spirit of Truth which the World neither doth, nor can receive. Christ therefore calls himself *the Truth,* as he is the receiver and giver of this Anointing, as these *Rivers of Living Waters* flow from him, that fail not, but are a well-

spring

spring unto Life Eternal, as it is written, *Joh.* 7. This spake he of the Spirit, for the Holy Ghost was not yet given, that is in this Ministry, and by the means of Christ's Manhead, because Jesus was not yet Glorified. Jesus was a man, and the most perfect righteous natural man which ever was, the form of which is made in him Incorruptible, having its first mutability fixed, by being subjected and made a Servant, though the elder, unto a New-spring of Light and Divine Birth that was added to him, as he became the engrafted Word, and wherein he and the Father are One, and not he, but the Father doth the work; Therefore he sayes, in *Rev.* 1. 18. *I am he that liveth and was dead, and behold I am alive for evermore, and have the Keyes of Hell and of Death.*

According to this pattern of man's Natural Perfection made in Christ incorruptible, and brought forth in perfect subjection and subservency unto, and agreement with a more excellent birth of Divine Glory, which Christ's Man-head is exalted unto, (in which he is according to his Man-head, He that is above all, one with the only begotten, that is in the Father's bosome, and hath the highest and clearest *sight* of God, beyond that of Angels themselves) It is, that all Regenerated ones that are made heirs of the Spirit, in the single portion thereof, are built up, and are Temples of the Holy Ghost, an everlasting Habitation of God, through the Spirit.

And because the same Jesus, that after this first pattern of humane Perfection which is in him, gives only the Witness that he is a meer and perfect man : and in the exalted and more heavenly state of Manhead which he also hath, as he that God the Father hath sealed and admitted to the sight of his own shape and very similitude, hath by Inheritance obtained a more excellent Name than the Angels, and must also give the Witness of what he is, and in what Glory he lives, as he inherits the Spirit in this double portion thereof : Therefore by the same new creating Power, which he is intrusted to administer, as he gives the Holy Ghost, he produces this second sort of new men, and adopted Children heirs according to the Promise, upon whom Christ poures out his Spirit, not only by the measure, and pattern, or Rule of the first Creation, but above it and beyond it, according to the proportion that his own glorified Manhead hath obtained it in its highest exaltation, admitting them into the same bosome of the Father with himself, wherein he is as the only begotten ; into which bosome, and most intimate vision of God : neither do the Angels nor first sort of Heirs and Children of the Son's Kingdom ever arrive, but

is

is reserved to be dwelt alone in by this Seed of *Abraham* God's friend, that are made Christ's peculiar Possession, consisting of a select number of his choice Favourites and Friends that he Redeems from amongst all other men; to make as the *first fruits* of his *Creation* to God and to the Lamb, who are joynt-heirs with him of the double Portion, and co-habit together with him in his Father's bosom, where they see and Inherit his Glory in the Naked and Primitive purity, which it hath in the Breast of God himself; Experiencing as well what the Gift of the Holy Ghost is, when it is God's Name poured out above measure, as well as by measure; that which *Paul* had some taste of, whether in the body or out of the body he could not tell, upon his being caught up into the *third Heavens,* to the hearing of things, impossible for him to utter in his Bodily state, nor others to receive.

And if thus we understand the *third Heavens,* as indeed we ought, then the finding out the other *two next* below them, will not be difficult, since the *second Heaven* is that wherein are the Angels and Spirits of Just men made perfect, upon the laying down the Body; and the *first,* that Presence of Christ and knowledge of his Name, which he vouchsafes unto his Church and particular Saints, in the converse they have with him here below, in the Body, which *Paul* doth also call *a Heaven,* Phil. 3. 20. where he sayes, *Our Conversation is in Heaven*; meaning by the *walking* with Christ in Spirit, as well as *being* and *living* in it, whilst we are here in this World, in which Christ is able, and doth appear to our Bodily sensual part, before its change, and putting on that which is Incorruptible, as it must do; and Christ's manhead thus considered, as it makes this *threefold Heaven,* was lively represented and described by the form of building; God caused the *Ark* to be built up, in *Gen.* 6. 16. where the directions that are given, do require *Noah* to make it of *lower, second,* and *third stories,* or *heights,* one above another; like the *outward Court,* the *Body of the Temple,* and *Holy of Holies,* or *inmost* part of the House, which God commanded also in *Solomon's Temple*; and both not without signifying this great Mystery in the glorified manhead of Christ, by the Spirit and Presence whereof, he makes a *threefold Heaven,* and way of converse, with the Sons of men, under the threefold degrees of Light and Glory, that from his Face, and by the Spirit of his Mouth are given forth, and hath answerable Hearers and Receivers.

F

1. That

1. That *Administration of the Light of pure Nature*, the effects whereof upon the hearts of the Receivers, produces healing and restoration of the wound made by sin, and renews a like frame of Spirit in man, as to the kind of it, wherein he was at first Created, and is still exercising his first mutable and wavering Principles, that in time of tryal fail, and so end in Apostacy and Death, through the weakness and fault of the Vessel, not of the Liquor, or Oyl which is poured out, into these Lamps, that in his own Nature is Incorruptible, but is suffered to leak out by these broken and frail Vessels.

Secondly, The *Light of pure Nature and right Reason*, fixed and made incorruptible through Faith and Regeneration, whereby the former frailty and leaking of the Vessel is perfectly cured, without changing the fashion of it, any further than what is requisite to bring it into subjection and obedience to a supream Judgment and Will, given as its guide and surety, to sustain and influence the actings thereof throughout.

The *Third*, is the *Light of Divine Love*, which he that dwells in, dwells in God, and is in the Light, as He is in the Light, beholding divine beauty in its original, where it is most attractive, and binds up the Judgement and Will of the beholders into its own likeness, most willingly, and irresistably, transforming them into the thing beloved.

This is the *Love* which casts out fear, and all torment, in the cleerest evidence, and greatest assurance that the Creature can possess : And by this Love it is, when not seen, that Faith works, and the Spirit of Adoption, crying, *Abba, Father* ; that Spirit and Presence of the Son that is sent into our *hearts*, which we are knit into by an inseparable *union*, and the *Soul* is formed thereby into the likeness of him that doth beget in either of the two last degrees of Light and quickning before-mentioned : Both which do beget that *Seed of Life in the heart that is immortal*, the *Princely prevailing conquering Seed of Believers, that are the true* Israel *of God, to whom all the Promises are sure* ; this is wrought by the coming of the *Son* in *Spirit* into the *Soul*, there to beget and form his own likeness in our Understanding and Will, the making us know him that is true, and that we are in him that is true, either according to this *lower* or *higher birth* of himself, of which he calls us to partake, and so become Witnesses thereof in our selves, and unto others.

This

This then, is the knowledge of the Truth which we are to understand, doth make the Adopted Children of God free, with another and better kind of Freedom than that wherein man was at first Created in that mutable and Primitive state of purity. And what this Freedom is we shall shew, that is so worthy to be obtained and sought after, in exchange for the other. This Freedom consists in the witnessing every respect which is wrought in the Understanding and Will of man by Regeneration and Divine birth, of the one or other sort, to render them of entire use and service, unto that higher and superiour Will in the second *Adam* the Lord from Heaven, that is made and given of the Father, to be a quickning Spirit unto them in a twofold capacity ; First, of their natural Head and Sovereign, whom they are to serve as in relation of Subjects to their King and Lawgiver, and therein fulfil and answer the very end of the Law of Nature, and actually become those righteous persons against whom there is no Law that can take hold of them to punish them, or take the least exception to their perfect Righteousness, that have given to them a constant and perpetual Will to do right to every one, and love the Lord their God most intirely, by influence from their Head, who in this respect is the common Parent to both the sorts of Children, whom he makes free Citizens, and Inhabitants of the *Heavenly Jerusalem*, his own glorified man-head, which is the Mother of us all.

But, secondly, Christ, the *second Adam*, comes forth also in another Headship to the *second sort of these Children*, which is, that of *Husband and Bridegroom*, gathering them up into a state of higher Love and Duty than that of *Servants* and *Subjects*, and receiving them unto more honorable use, in familiarity, intimacy, and a kind of equality, comprehending the Love and Duty of *righteous* and *faithful Servants*, but in respect of the nearness of relation and union, becoming much the more excellent and transcendant. The Inspiration and holy Anointing which flows from Christ in this *twofold Headship* of his, into the hearts of these his Members, hath that effect upon them, as joyns them to him *in unity* and *agreement of spirit*, (or of *judgment* and *will*) and so entirely possesses them & engrosses them in the *service* and to the *use of their Lord*, that it leaves them at no liberty to be at the use or service of any other, but *in subordination to his will*, which excludes sin and all evil, esteeming it their greatest happiness thus to be bound up in a way of love, delight, and entire obedience in the Will of their Head, their *second Adam* and Lord from Heaven. Hence they experience that they are not their own in any thing ; for, *it is not they*

that

that live, but *Christ liveth in them,* and with his Princely prevailing Influence, as their Head, is their *infallible Guide* and *firm Security* in all their operations, giving them such an abiding and growth up in all things, into him, in an entire resignation and obedience to his Will, as co-workers together in every thought, word and work, that they cannot miscarry, nor shall ever be hurt by the *second death,* but shall be rewarded with those pleasures that are at his right-hand and at his left, in his Kingdom for evermore. And although this *most perfect Free-dom,* which is obtained by this binding and conjunction in unity and agreement of spirit with Christ, be esteemed by the Possessors of it of price inestimable, yet it is the greatest bondage and cross that can be-fall a wicked heart, and is that which is reserved by Christ to be their torment for ever, (in the end, which will be given by him to his *first Ministry,* in the hearts where he is finally rejected) from whom, after he is departed and withdrawn for a season, as if they should never hear of him, (as indeed they shall not to their comfort) yet they shall to their terrour and sorrow be made sensible of him, by the fast-ning which he will make of his Darts of enlightnings into the minds of the wicked, as sharp Arrows and a *gnawing Worm* that shall never dye, when by the breath of his mouth he shall kindle a fire of Con-viction and self-judging in their Conscience, together with the just sence of his Divine Vengeance, they can no longer flee nor escape from.

But, on the contrary, the truly regenerated souls are made willing and exceedingly pleased to draw in this yoke with their Head, to see with his eyes, and act by his quickning in all they do, and to put on with him this lowliness, meekness and purity of spirit, which feeds on that which is incorruptible, and is with God of great price, so great, as no righteous workers have his praise and blessing, but these, who are properly *Christ's Mystical Body,* the *Branches* that abide in him, and whose Fruit is permanent unto Life Eternal : and this Body or Church of invisible Saints and spiritual Worshippers of the true God, even whilst they are in their Wilderness and suppressed state, Christ, the great Overseer of their souls, doth feed with Teachers af-ter his own heart, and is not wanting by an outward Ministry under him, to feed and refresh with Oyl, the Lamps of all sorts that he makes use of as his Witnesses, and bear his Name, whether according to the knowledge of his Will, that is revealed in the *first* or in the *second Covenant* ; that so he may, by upholding such an Office under him, edifie all that are under his Charge, as he sees occasion, and is agree-

able

able to the condition the Church is in, whether of restraint or freedom from the Powers of the World.   By those which Christ puts into the Ministry of his Spirit under him, we are to understand such a
he gives his *Unction* and *Mission* unto, as he is the Head of Nature
or of Grace, and from their own Experience are made able to minister the knowledge of Christ in his *healing and restoring work*, or in
his regenerating and New-creation-building, before described ; giving
their Witness *according to what they themselves have received of
the Spirit in the three distinct Dispensations of it*, before expressed ;
in the first of which, because of the mutable state of the operation
thereof, both in themselves as well as in their hearers, they that are
eminent Preachers unto others by the excellency of Gifts with which
they are anointed and that from *Christ*, may nevertheless themselves
be found at last *Cast-awayes*.   But, in the other two, they which experience the *Anointing* thereof, become Pillars in the House of God,
that never go out more, and may obtain the highest Order and Rank
of Ministry in the Church, even that of *Apostles*, in the same way as
Paul himself did, by such a Spiritual Light of Christ, as he sayes,
1 Cor. 9. 1. *Am not I an Apostle? have I not seen Jesus Christ
our Lord?* And as thus the Apostolical Order came to have being in
the Church, by the immediate sight of *Christ in Spirit*, as we see in
Paul's Case, which comprehends in it all other the inferiour Ranks of
Ministers, whether *Prophets*, *Evangelists*, or *Pastors* and *Teachers* ;
So there are of these inferiour Ranks (to the *Apostles*) which hear and
receive the knowledge of the Gospel, and the holy Ghost, either
from the *mouths of the Apostles*, and by the *laying on of their hands*, as
did the *Evangelists* ; or by other subordinate instituted means ; that
is to say, either inwardly, onely by the *inspiration of Angels*, thereunto sent and authorized by Christ ; as to *Philip* in the case of the
Eunuch's Conversion ; and to *Abraham*, and the *Patriarchs* after
him, four hundred years together, before the written Word was
given, and who, before the Incarnation, were made use of to give
the Law, which is there called *the Word spoken by Angels*, Heb. 2. 1.
Or secondly, by the communication of such Gifts, for interpreting and
opening of the written Word, as we find in the Church of *Corinth*,
and this by such Prophetical Gifts, as not only the Officers did partake
of, to fit them for the Ministry ; but, secondly, the very Members of
the Church also shared in, for the common edification of the Body.

So, that, either by *inward Inspiration from Angels, under Christ* ;
or, *by the witnessing Spirit of Christ immediately*, which is the Spirit
of

of Prophecy ; or, *by Gifts of Abilities in a more ordinary way, for the interpreting and opening the Scriptures* , Christ hath alwayes had his Labourers in his Harvest.   And all these several Degrees in the Ministry, as they are found in subordination, subserviency and agree-ment one with another, in their place and differing measures, do make sweet harmony, and redound to great profit in the Church. But if they break their Ranks, and the interiour exalt and lift up them-selves in preference above, and opposition to the superiour and greater measures, these then corrupt and set up for themselves, or are made use of by him that knows how to transform his ministers into Mini-sters of Righteousness, to advance his Kingdom, and turn bitter and implacable Enemies and Persecutors of the Womans Seed, and true Spiritual Worshippers.   Let it not then be said, that to be against the Ministry in this last sense, is to be against all Ministry , especially such who acknowledge *Christ* the Chief Minister and great Or-dainer of God's Worship, and all those to be his Ministers that have Unction and Mission from him, in all the Orders and Degrees of them, wherein they are acknowledged by the Scriptures, whom God hath pleased to make use of to bear the Witness committed to them during *Antichrist's* Reign, in a *suffering, sackcloth, prophesying state,* which will not lose its fruit, but *become a sweet savour of life unto life in them that are saved,* and *a savour of death unto death in them that perish.*

We now shall proceed to the next Enquiry, which is, *Who they are that in Principles are opposit to these two Anointings, and the Effects of them ; and declare their Enmity by their continued War, in the posture of our Enemies or dissembled Friends, both making up but the same Kingdom of Darkness, which since Christs coming is called* Antichrists?

Righteousness and *Truth* are the two supporters of Christ's Throne; with the first, God enlightens and quickens the natural beings of An-gels and men, who in their mutable and uncertain state are possessors of Righteousness in purity and perfection ; whilst they are and may be strangers to Truth, that is, firmness and certainty, which is as the Crown and Top-stone to the first Building.   And therefore the Light of Truth, (which is a clearness in the Judgment, that had a right discerning before, that doth fix it and ascertain it beyond all possible doubt and contradiction, and the activity of Truth, which is a sted-fastness and pressing forward in the Will, wherein may be found righ-teous operation before, to run in that race, and never fail nor faint) is

most

most necessary to follow and succeed, where the first goes before, as that which is its consummation and final perfection.

In the breast where these two Lights meet, imbrace, and kiss each other, there is the true *Urim* and *Thummim*: the Divine enlightned mind, which makes all those wherein it is found, free Citizens of the *heavenly Jerusalem*, and beloved Children and Subjects of *Christs Kingdom*; As it is written, *Joh.* 3 19, 20, 21. *Light is come into the world.* Light in both these respects, is come to dwell with us in our own nature, when *the Word was made flesh*, and *to be amongst us, in our mouth and in our heart, to hear it and obey it.* Whence it is that this is said to be *the Condemnation of the World, that Light is* thus *come in* the person of our Redeemer *the second Adam, and men have* notwithstanding *loved Darkness better than Light*, because of the *contrariety* that is in the *evil deeds* of men unto the *very nature of Light*, which *makes manifest and reproves them*, and from thence contracts hatred from evil men, very unjustly, who love not to be discovered in their wickedness, nor to be under censure and reproof for it; but perfectly hate thus to be discovered and judged: and that is at bottom the quarrel and rise of the enmity between the Subjects of these two Kingdoms, of *Darkness* and of *Light*.

Hatred and enmity against the Light of *Righteousness* and *Truth*, which shine forth in Jesus Christ, as in the head, and in his Witnesses and Children, as the members; in what hearts soever they are found, are in general the opposit Principles we are now speaking of; and the Root or Cause whence those spring, is from the love that such hearts at bottom do bear unto evil, that is to say, to unrighteousness and falshood, which they prefer and adhere unto before the Light of the Image of God, which is wrought out in Christ and in his members.

Of these *lovers of Darkness more than Light*, we are to consider; Either, first, such as are born blind, and are already darkned in their understandings, and alienated in their wills by evil works, dead in trespasses and sins.

Or, secondly, such as have their Light freely restored to them again for asking, and, however, so much of it, as may make them sensible of the need of more, and to discern the means of their perfect cure.

Or, thirdly, Such, as, after their first Light restored, are offered the gift of a better sight than ever they had at first; which shall not only enlarge what they had at first, in their primitive purity, but preserve

ſerve it in an endleſs life, without any poſſible danger ever to loſe it more.

For the firſt; It is the condition of all Mankind in general, and was the effect that followed upon the ſin of our firſt Parents, by which door Death entred and paſſed upon all men, becauſe in them all had ſinned. Nor did this befall the Children meerly or principally becauſe of ſin, as if that were the end that God had in it; but, that the works of God's Grace ſhould be manifeſted thereby: For, no ſooner did the diſeaſe and wound appear, but God had provided a Phyſician and healing Medicine, which declared the Caſe, as yet, (which Man was in) not ſo deſperate, but he might be reſtored; and not only ſo, but have an additional ſight given to him, that ſhould make him ſee better than ever he did before.

For the ſecond; It is alſo that ſtate which is common to all that have ſinned, and upon whom Death hath paſſed, as to the alienation of their minds from the Life of God; whoſe teeth are ſet on edge by the ſowr grapes that were eaten by our firſt Parents, and therefore by way of free gift are reſtored by the benefit of the Ranſom paid by the Redeemer on their behalf, to ſuch a degree of enlghtning and renewed Righteous Life, as is a Lamp or Candle lighted in the ſoul of every one that comes into the World; in which *little,* they are put to the proof of their faithfulneſs, how far they care or deſire to hearken to it, or not; that which is the work of the Law written in their hearts by Chriſt, as a Record and Witneſs againſt them, if it be ſlighted and abuſed, whereby there is a Witneſs ſet up in the very natural Conſcience, as a light in a dark place, that is ever *accuſing* or *excuſing,* as the action done doth deſerve. To this *Light in the Conſcience,* which is the *Law within us,* muſt every one ſtand or fall, as to matter of information or proof how that ſoul hath ſhewed it ſelf in this ſtate, whether a lover of *Darkneſs* more than of *Light;* for, this will either ſhew it ſelf our Friend or our Enemy, as we behave our ſelves in receiving of its inſtruction, and following its guide, and ſubmitting to its reproof; For, he that is faithfull in the leaſt, is to be preſumed he will be faithfull in much; and he that is unjuſt in the leaſt, will be alſo unjuſt in much; So that Chriſt may truly and juſtly ſay to ſuch, *If they have not ſhewed themſelves faithful in the unrighteous Mammon, or uncertain Riches, who will commit to their truſt the true Treaſure?* And thence it is, that all thoſe who in this ſtate of proof and tryal under this firſt diſpenſation of *Light,* declare themſelves Enemies in a fixed Rebellion, and hardning againſt the

Teaching

Teaching and Dictates thereof, they plainly shew that they love the *Disease* better than the *Remedy*; and had rather continue *blind*, than have their *sight* and *limbs* restored, to use them as they ought, and by the *Law* they are obliged to do, for running with *delight* and *continuance in the race of God's Commandements*; and had rather *perish in their sins*, than *believe in Christ*, and by *believing, be freed and saved from the wrath that is to come.*

The *Natural Conscience* in this sense corrupted, heardned, and become unreclaimable, by *refusing Reproof, and perfectly hating all those that set about their recovery and restitution out of this their bondage, under what ever Name or outward Profession of Religion, and Divine Worship it be found in,* doth afford the *first sort of Subjects,* whereof the *kingdom of Darkness* doth consist; a Region like to that where *Abraham* (coming in his Travels) did pronounce, *The fear of God is not in this place*; nothing of *Conscience* was there owned or practised; but the Contrary, of open *Prophaneness* or *Idolatry.*

The *Third state* is that which is not of such general extent, but a more peculiar condescention and effect of *God's bounty and good will to some sinners beyond others*, in admitting them to a *farther and higher proof than the former,* and therefore doth vouchsafe them a *greater measure and gift of the Spirit, and work of Restauration, out of their natural blindness, and death*; for, *with a mighty hand, and a stretched out Arm, and with many Signs and Wonders, he brings them, as he did Israel of old, out of the house of Bondage, and by the Angel of his Presence, saved them from the hands of their Enemies, and offered to lead them into the state of rest and immutability, which he had prepared for them*; and therein did propound *to give them a better sight, and fuller fruition of himself, than in the way of meer Restauration they could attain unto.* For, as to the *Restauration* and *Freedom* out of *Egypt,* God's Work was perfect, and a just and right God he had shewed himself to them; nevertheless, they that were new come to have the use of their *sight,* and their *feet* again *to be washed with Water, and anointed with Oyl,* and when they were *in their blood,* God bid them *Live, and made them again living Souls*; yet, like an unwise and foolish People, they very evilly requited this bounty and goodness of the *Lord,* and of the *Rock* that *begat them,* and of the *God* that *formed them* they were very *unmindful,* and proved themselves *a very froward and provoking Generation, Children in whom was no stedfastness, nor that cared to use*

G *the*

the means to be made so when it was offered ; but they rebelled and vexed his holy Spirit : that is, as *Steven* interprets it, *They blasphemed and resisted the Holy Ghost, and refused the Teachings of that Ministry, by which the Truth is conveyed in the love of it, which would for ever free them from the power and dominion of sin, and for ever fix them in the Kingdom of Christ, and make them Pillars in God's Temple, never to be removed.*

These are *they,* that because they say they *see,* or have *sight* enough already, and neither *need* nor *desire better,* therefore *their sin* remains, and is a *sin unto death* ; for which, *God swears in his wrath, they shall never enter into his rest.* The *light* of their *eye* upon this, becomes *evil,* and hates those that *see clearer* and *better* than themselves, and cannot endure to hear of *new lights* that go beyond theirs, or that is upon the *encreasing* more and more unto the *perfect day.*

In this *evil mind,* there is a lusting to *Envy* against the *true heirs,* and a saying in the *heart, Come, let us kill them, and the Inheritance shall be ours :* which so far doth, many times, transport them, that they *become* the *bitterest Enemies* to God's *choicest Saints* and *dearest Children* ; and *when they kill them, they think they do God service* ; and *when they cast them out, and make them as the scum and off-scouring of the World,* they say, *Let God be glorified* ; these are *they* that are neither *hot* nor *cold,* but under whatever *forms of Godliness* and *different perswasions* they may be in *matters of God's Worship,* do give their strength to the *common Enemy* of the *true Saints* ; and though they can no more *cleave the one* to the *other,* than the *Iron* to the *Clay,* yet *they both* can fit at *one Table,* devising the destruction of the *true Israelites,* and take up their *places* in the *Feet* and *Toes* of the *great Image,* that *figured out* the *universal Kingdom of Antichrist.*

These are the *Two opposite Principles,* unto the *Two Anointings,* and the *effects of them* in and upon the *truly Regenerate ones.* In these Principles *Satan lodges and dwells,* as in *his seat* and *suitable habitation,* in *the hearts of his Children,* who is the *Father of all Unrighteousness and Deceit* ; these *flow from him* as from their *Fountain and Well-head* ; and *he* is their *Countenance, Protection, and Propagation,* for the *encrease* and *enlargement* of his *Kingdom of Darkness.*

By the means of this *Two-fold hatred* that *Satan* begets in the *subjects of his Kingdom,* against *the Light of God's Glory shining in the*
                                                                Face

Face of Christ, and *in the witness of those that are the Members of his Mystical Body here on Earth,* he blows up a continual War, and *keeps on foot a fixed Enmity between the subjects of the one, and of the other Kingdom;* and the *Enmity* is still *the same in effect,* whether it be *open and allowed,* or *dissembled and hid;* the *hatred* and *opposition* is not the *less* in it self, but the *last* of the two is the worst, and most dangerous.

This he Heads, with a *visible* Power, as well as sowes the Seed of it *invisibly,* in the *Children of his Kingdom;* and either by *violence* or *fraud,* or *both,* hath never *failed* from the beginning of the World to this day (by the wise permission of God) for the *bruising of the Heele of the Womans Seed in the Head and Members*) to shew himself the God, or chief Potentate and Ruler, in and over the whole World : And so influence, in such manner, all the visible Rule and Authority, whether *Civil* or *Ecclesiastical,* that is exercised on Earth, and is supported by humane Wisdom and Power, centring in the foresaid *Principles* of *hatred* and *prejudice* against *Christ and his Kingdom,* that he hath ever got the better of it, in the *eye of flesh and blood,* over the *true subjects and servants of Christ ;* and hath as much as is in him, *slain Christ's Witnesses, and kept them under in a most oppressed and dispersed condition.* Of this, the Seed of *Abraham,* beginning in *Sem,* and so downward until *Christ's* Incarnation and Death (and as the Consequence thereof, the rejection of the Seed according to the flesh) were the living and known examples in their dayes, what Servitudes and Captivities were they not exposed unto, and did they not undergo ? And at last the very visibility of their own Church and State, was wholly defaced and lost, though both of Divine Constitution, and supported not only with divine Laws, but with the visible signet of the Divine Presence ; and by whom was this People (upon whom the Name of God was called) brought under, persecuted, and suppressed, but by those who were foretold by *Dan. ch.* 2. and most lively represented and described by that *great Image,* which was the subject of *Nebuchadnezzar's* Dream, that none but *Daniel* could rehearse and interpret, signifying the Persons and their Successors, that should be found possessing the Universal Empire, and Command of the World, during the continuance of those known *Four Monarchs* that have followed successively one after another, according as they were fore-told and charactered out some thousand years ago, and are now standing upon their last legs, the time drawing on apace, when the *spiritual seed* of the same

Abraham,

Abraham, shall be made *heirs* even of the World, by *Faith* ? and what was done by *Abraham*, in Figure and Type, as to his Conquest over the *Four Kings*, Gen. 14. must have its accomplishment in Reality and Truth, by those of his *seed*, that are the *true Israel* in Spirit, who by the Spirit of Life entring into them at the appointed time, together with the Charge committed to them, of pouring out the *seven Vials* of the *last Plagues* of God, shall bring the final *downfal* and *destruction of those Four Monarchs*, and in and with it, of the *Kingdom of the Beast, and of Antichrist* ; and bring *home again*, and receive the true *Lots* that have been *sojourners* in the *Sodom* of *this World*, *all this time under the Power of their Oppressors*.

And as it did befal *Israel* after the *flesh*, that were *Abraham's Natural Seed*, under the *three first Monarchies*, and *part of the Fourth*, (our Saviour suffering *Death* under the *Roman Empire*) so are the *Scriptures* very plain and express (if considered with a *spiritual eye*) that the *Israel* after the *flesh*, that have been *adopted into the room and place of the former*, and (though *wild by Nature*, yet) *engrafted upon the same Stock and Root of the good Olive Tree, the true anointed One*, that is *the Father of many Nations*, as he is the *Second Adam*, whose *standing is by Faith*, that if they *exalt themselves*, and become *hardened, and resist the Ministry of the Holy Ghost* (as the *Jews*, that were their *Predecessors*, did) *Christ* will then make it appear (also in the Case of these *latter Jews* (who say *they are so*, but having *not the Spirit and Nature of true Faith in them, do lye, and deceive themselves as well as others*) that it is *not they* that *bear the Root*, but the *Root that bears them*, who therefore can *cast them off*, as he did the *others* ; and once more not only *shake the Earth*, but *the Heavens*, although called *Christian*, to make way for that *Kingdom of his that cannot be shaken*, whereof we have already shewed ; and how nigh this is accomplishing, and is even at the very doors , we shall have occasion to make mention of more particularly, as the next and last Particular we are to speak unto.

For an *Introduction* whereunto, let me only mind you of some few things that the Apostle *John*, in his Book of the *Revelations*, layes before us on this behalf, declaring first the things that were to befal the *Heathenish Roman Empire*, and *the Church of God abiding under its Protection*, *during the time of the first Six Seals*, which by Computation continued till somewhat more than four hundred years after

Christ ;

Christ; about the end of which period, that *Empire*, as *Heathen*, dissolved, and a *new face of things*, *in Church and State*, *rose out of it*, *at last*, *for so much as concerned that part of the World*, *which thereupon in Name became Christian*.

And because the *Spiritual part of the Church* at that same time began to be most *suppressed*, being forced to fly from the *fury of the Serpent* into a *wilderness-state and condition*; therefore the visible Constituted Frame of *Civil* as well as *Ecclesiastical Power*, called *Christian*, were represented unto *John*; The *First*, under *the seven-headed and ten-horned Beast that came out of the Sea*; And the *Second*, under the *two-horned Beast that came out of the Earth*, answerable to what was under other similitudes, intimated of them in the *Iron Legs*, and the *Feet* and *Toes* of *Nebuchadnezzar's Image*, *part of Iron, and part of Clay*; Whereby the *Iron legs*, are the *Civil Power* as it became Christian, and retaining still the Reliques of the *Roman Empire*; and by the *Feet*, *part of Iron and part of Clay*, is meant, the *Ecclesiastical State and Power*, partly Papal, and partly Reformed; *as an earthly Jerusalem yet visible*, *and both enemies to the Jerusalem that is above*, *and yet not very good friends between themselves*, *whose continuance is measured out by the time of the six Trumpets*; that is to say, in the exercise of these three distinct Powers under the Name *Christian*; the one, *Imperial and Magistratical*; the *other*, *Spiritual and Ecclesiastical*; in the *two Horns and branches of it*, pretended unto, of Divine Right and Institution; or whether it be more diffusive in a Collective Body of Church-Rulers; and as more particularly it is expressed to last twelve hundred and sixty Prophetical dayes; that is to say, years, in the 11, 12, and 13 *Chap.* of the *Revelations*; and by comparing what is spoken and described in the foresaid *Chapters*, with *Chapter* 17, concerning this Constitution and Face of the Christian Church and State, that was fore-seen to rise up out of the dissolution of the Heathenish Roman Empire, and the driving into the Wilderness the Spiritual part of the Church, made up of those who are said, for the heavenliness of their Principles and Converse, to be those that dwell in Heaven, *chap.* 12. *vers.* 12. and *chap.* 13.6. It seems very plain, that upon the Disputes that was likely to arise in the Christian Ecclesiastical State and Government, upon the bottom of the Papacy and Rule in the Church, by one universal visible Head under Christ, here upon Earth, as one of the Horns belonging to the second Beast, by *Daniel* called the *Little Horn* (mentioned single, because he was most Potent, and for a long time was

able

able to uphold his Authority without any considerable cruelty and division that was visible) But in process of time, the separation and division happened, as *John* (in mentioning of the two-horned Beast) did fore-tell, there would alwayes be within the bowels of the visible Church of the outward Court-worshippers, a more and a less corrupted and backsliden part , the one of which compared with the other, would or might be likened to the *earthly Jerusalem,* in the temper it was in when Christ was upon Earth, for *persecuting the Prophets,* and *killing the Heir himself* when he came amongst them ; As the other might be to *Samaria* and the worshippers of *Jeroboams Calves,* after that he had headed the ten Tribes in their defection, not only in the Civil State, but from the Purity of God's visible Worship, kept up according to God's Ordinances. This latter being the lively resemblance of the *Papacy,* and all that acknowledge the *Papal Authority,* as the *chief Ruler* and *Head* of the visible Church throughout the several States and Dominions of the Christian Empire ; the other figuring out the *Jerusalem* that now is, and *is in bondage with her Children,* distinguishing her self from *Popery* on the one hand, and from them that dwell in Heaven, as the true Citizens of the *Jerusalem* that is above (the Mother of all those that are Heirs according to the Promise) on the other hand : accounting the one *Babylonish, Antichristian* and *Heretical;* and the other *Schismatical* and *Erroneous, Fanatical* and *Blasphemous.*

And because the *Woman,* as the Apostle calls the *earthly Jerusalem,* (which was amongst the *Galatians* in his dayes, as being in bondage with her Children to the Law and worldly Rudiments, that perish in the using, *Touch not, taste not, handle not,* as Objects of Divine Worship, which feed most the outward senses) doth make a very fair shew in the flesh , *having the Form of Godliness, but denying the Power of it ;* and withdrawing from, and disowning the Children of the Promise, that are of a more heavenly birth, and of the free Woman : Therefore we shall find this sort of Professors described by *John* in his 1 Epist. 2. 19. *They went out from us, but they were not of us ; for if they had been of us, they would, no doubt, have continued with us,* and not have made a manifest distinction of themselves from us ; that is to say, from being *followers* (1 Thess. 2. 14, 15.) *of the Churches of God, which in Judea are in Christ Jesus ; that are the Circumcision in Spirit, and have no confidence in the flesh;* For which cause sake, the *Thessalonians,* in adhering to the primitive pattern, which shewed it self in those Churches, did *suffer the like*

things

things from their own Country-men, the *Jews*, among whom they lived, as those Churches of God in *Judea* did from the *Jews* there, *who both killed the Lord Jesus, and their own Prophets*, and chased out the chiefest of the Apostles from amongst them; *and they pleased not God, and are contrary to all men*; forbidding, under pretence of too much familiarity with the Heathen and prophane World, that the Gospel should be preached unto the *Gentiles*, whereby they might be saved, every way filling up their sins, and bringing wrath upon themselves to the uttermost.

This is the Woman which *John* saw in *Rev.* 1. that was *drunk with the blood of the Saints*, ver. 6. *and with the blood of the choicest Martyrs of Jesus*; at which he wondred with great admiration, as little expecting to find what he saw, or to reade that name written upon her forehead, which he did, of *Mystery Babylon the great, the mother of Fornications and Abominations of the Earth*; *with whom the Kings and Inhabitants of the Earth commit Fornication*, and have been made *drunk* with it: For at last her false, unchaste, whorish spirit to her Lord and Husband, is discovered and made manifest, by the open rejection of him in his Members, and by the Combination and Conjunction which she is found in with the *seven-headed* and *ten-horned Beast* and his *Adherents*, under the *Papacy*, thereby to make War with his *Witnesses* and slay them, and expose their dead bodies to *shame and reproach* in the streets of this *earthly Jerusalem*; who for her exceeding Apostacy and fierce Enmity against the true Temple-worshippers, is spiritually called *Sodom* and *Egypt, where also our Lord was crucified*; and though she have strengthened her self, as one that *sits upon many Waters*, and who is the City *that reigns over the Kings* (or chief eminent Persons, men of Name) *of the Earth*, which the Children of the *earthly Jerusalem* are; yet (sayes he) *God determines to bring her to Judgment*, and, in order thereunto, the Instruments he will employ therein, are the several Potentates and Kingdoms, that have given their Power to the *Papacy*, who, at the time appointed, shall find it their Interest to agree and become of one mind, in hatred of this *Whore*, or unchaste Spouse of Christ, that sitteth upon Peoples, and Multitudes, and Nations, and Tongues, and shall therefore combine together *to make her desolate and naked, and shall eat her flesh, and burn her with fire*; For God hath put it into their hearts to fulfil his Will, in this Judgment, which they are to execute, as *Nebuchadnezzar* formerly did upon the earthly material *Jerusalem* in his days; until which be fulfilled, they shall agree and hold together, giving

joyntly

joyntly their Counsel, Authority and Strength in support and maintenance of the Beast, that is the first and chief Horn of the two-horned
Beast, which is the *Papacy*.   And how to give a right interpretation
of the things in this 17th Chapter, but by this Key, deserves our very
serious consideration, according to the usual understanding of the
Papacy to be meant by this Whore, which is not denied to be a part
of *Babylon*, and a chief part, and to be also a Whore and Mother of
Fornications; but she is so *openly* and *avowedly*, not secretly and under the shew of Reformation; and there is not any mystery or secret
in it, to find her out, as there is in the other case.

We come then in the last place, as the Conclusion of the whole, to
shew what Word and part of his Counsels, contained in the Promises
and Prophecies not yet accomplished, the Lord is now fulfilling in
these present dispensations of our day; and this, by the comparing
Scriptures with Scriptures, and observing what gradually hath been
fulfilled since the time of Christ's Ascention to this day, and what
signs he hath before given of the times wherein we now are.

There is nothing more positive and express in the Scripture, as may
appear by what hath been already mentioned, (and for which many
particular Texts might further be alledged) than this, That there is a
*Kingdom of the Everlasting Gospel, which neither can nor shall be
shaken, that must be brought upon the stage here in this World*; which
shall stand firm as a Rock against all opposition, and come forth as a
stone cut out of the Mountain without hands; that must break down
the visible heads, which the Serpent hath kept up in and over the
whole Earth, for these many thousand years together; by the means
whereof the true Children and Heirs have been kept out of their Possession, and have been necessitated to a Witnessing and Prophesying
condition in a way of Sufferings, and of utmost cruel dealings and
oppressions from their implacable Enemies; to whom it hath been
given to make and continue War with them, till the course of Sufferings be finished.   Of this *bitter Cup*, the Captain of our Salvation
drank the deepest draught, and had the greatest share; And lest we
should think he had put an end to the Sufferings of his Members by
one Death on the Cross, he dealt plainly with his Disciples in this
point, both before his Death, and also during the forty dayes he spent
upon Earth after his Resurrection; for, when the two sons of *Zebedee*
had hopes to have seen him in his own Person speedily in his Kingdom, before his Sufferings, and were desirous the one to sit at his
right hand, and the other at his left, in that day of his Glory and
                                                                    Power

Power, he intimates to them immediately that there is a Preparation requiſit to be wrought in all that ſhall be thought worthy of that dignity, which is, *to drink of the ſame Cup, and to be baptized with the ſame Baptiſm that he was baptized with*, according to that true and faithful ſaying, *If we die with him, we ſhall live with him; if we ſuffer with him, we ſhall reign with him.* And ſo, when all the Diſciples together, a little before his Aſcention, *Act.*1.6,8. asked him, ſaying, *Wilt thou at this time reſtore the Kingdom to Iſrael?* his Anſwer is in effect this to them, That until *Iſrael's* witneſſing-work be over and finiſhed, that muſt prepare them to Rule, and ripen their Enemies for the Judgment and Deſtruction appointed unto all ungodly men, that muſt firſt precede; the reigning-work, which they too much looked for, and thirſted after, would not come, nor the dayes of it begin. Now this witneſſing-work, which is to be finiſhed by the true *Iſrael* of God, as the needful and requiſit Preparation of you to Reign, is, *What is to be wrought in them upon their own hearts*; and, *what is to be wrought by you as a Teſtimony born and given to the World on God's behalf.*

And the latter of theſe is uſually made uſe of by God to accompliſh the former, *ſince all that will live godly in Chriſt Jeſus* (ſhewing forth the Vertues of Him, that hath called them in a holy and good Converſation, ſhining as Lights in the World) *muſt ſuffer Perſecution*, and are ſure to be hated and oppreſſed by the World and Powers of it, by all wayes and means that may prove their Faith and Patience. And theſe Tryals, which thus give proof of their Faith, do cauſe Patience to have its perfect work in them, till which, they are not thoſe meet veſſels fitted for their Maſter's uſe, as that he will dignifie them to appear ſeated, as on his Throne, in their hearts; and thereby qualifie them with a Power of Rule ; ſo, as at their word, and by their prayers, all things ſhall become poſſible to them; *What they bind on Earth, ſhall be bound in Heaven*; *and what they looſe on Earth, ſhall be looſed in Heaven:* For greater works than Chriſt himſelf did when he was in the fleſh, they ſhall do, becauſe he is gone to his Father.

Secondly, The witneſſing-work is not only to be wrought in them, to prepare them, in mind and body, to be meet veſſels for the uſe of their Head (by them to ſhew forth his Wiſdom and Power, to the glorifying of God in their ſpirits, and in their bodies, which are his;) but the Light of it muſt be given out, and born in the ſight, and for the profit and good of others, if the fault be not in themſelves that should benefit by it ; unto whom the favour of the knowledge of Christ, ministred by his faithful Witnesses in their several places, and callings, will prove in the issue, either a *favour of life unto life*, or of *death unto death*, according as either it is received and valued, or rejected and expelled. *No man* (saith Christ) *when he hath lighted a Candle, putteth it* in a secret place, neither *under a Bushel, but on a Candlestick, that they that come in may see the light :* which Scripture is interpreted, 1 *Cor.* 14, 24, 25. where the instance is given, in meeting of the whole Church together, *in one place* ; that is, as many visible Saints and Believers as could well hear one another, in the place they assembled in for their common Edification. In which Church-meeting they were as a *Golden Candlestick*, that did in such manner hold forth the shining Light of Christ's Truth and Holiness, to those that came in, and were lookers on, and were not of the Society, that by the Spirit of Prophecy, which in and among them of that particular Church was exercised, it so fell out, that whoever came in, desirous to learn and be instructed, *he was convinced of all, he was judged of all,* and the secrets of his heart were so manifest, that falling down on his face, he worshipped God, and went out and reported, *that God was in them of a truth.*

This is then the second sort of Witnessing-work which by Christ was intrusted to his Disciples and Followers, to be exercised and imployed in, according to their several places and callings, till his return, in the day wherein he is to come and judge the World in Righteousness, that is, take an account, who they are that have acquit themselves as they ought to do in their witnessing-stations and callings, and what fruit their witness had, how it took place in the hearts of others among whom they conversed, and what returns they met with from a wicked and ingrateful world for all the labour of Love and Service they shewed amongst them : Of all which, Christ intends to take a formal and judicial account at the time of the end that is set by him to this witnessing-work, in his witnesses, that upon this employment, Prophesying in sack-cloth, were to continue as in constant war and violent persecution from the Powers of the world for twelve hundred and sixty years together. At the end of which time, the Judgment or time of Wrath is to come ; not that which is the final Judgment and Wrath of the great **Day**, but a like proceeding of God towards the World, in pleading with it by Fire and Sword, upon the finishing the Testimony of his Witnesses, as he did by Water upon the first World, where he made a visible distinction *between the Wicked* and *the Righteous*, and between

tween them that truly *fear God* and are sincere, and them that *fear him not*; but are tainted and corrupted with Hypocrisie and Apostacy, as is plainly expressed, *Rev.* 11.18. *And the Nations were angry, and thy Wrath is come, and the time of the Dead*, or the Cause of thy slain rejected Witnesses, *that they should be judged*, and an Inquisition made after their Blood, and the hard usage they have met with in the World, in order now to receive Countenance and Reward for their Sufferings, according to the nature of them, and the condition and place in which they gave their Witness, whether they were *Prophets* or *Saints*, *that fear God's Name*, *small or great*; and to yeeld Vengeance and Destruction to impenitent and hardned Sinners, that they may no longer *corrupt the Earth*.

And therefore, as in this place we may see, Christ lighteth up his Candles in the World, of all sorts and sizes, and indeed in all places of it from East to West, and hath given the Light of his Glory and Kingdom, as that Testimony which is appointed to be given and preached in all the World, as a Witness to all Nations; and immediately after this is finished, then the End comes, the End that God will manifest of his patience and long-suffering which he hath exercised towards the *World*, in forbearing to avenge the Cause of his *Elect*, which hath been night and day crying to him, *How long, Lord, how long?* which in this day of his Wrath he will avenge, and that speedily, and *cut the work short in Righteousness*.

And because we have said, the Candles or Lamps which God lights up in the World, for this his Witnessing-work, ever since his Ascention to this day, (according to the Commission he gave to his Disciples, *Act.* 1. 8. and in them to all his Saints small and great that fear his Name (as we shewed before) are of several sizes and kinds, it may not be improper to declare them.

As first, Their Witnessing-Lights may be such as are in publick Office and Place in the visible Church; and so are either those that are in the Ministry, or those that give their Witness, as the Body of some particular Congregation, that own themselves in the sight of the world as a Golden Candlestick; or some particular Church-Assembly of visible Saints in order and practice of the Gospel, according to their measure and light. And under this first head will fall all sorts of Principles and Professions of Godliness, that make the Rule of the Word and Spirit of God, (*the Ballance of the Sanctuary*) the Standard by which they desire to regulate themselves in their Doctrine, Worship and Conversation, what-ever difference in Principles, or Ministry, of the knowledge of Christ they are under, as hath been before opened and distinctly spoken unto.

Secondly, Their Witnessing-Lights may be Publick Persons, with relation to their Office in the Magistracy; For it is *by me,* saith Christ, that *Kings reign, and Princes do Justice* : So that in the administration of pure and impartial Justice, as a Magistrate, in whatever Place and Calling we are set by God, and a lawful Appointment from men, we keep on the right way, without turning on the right hand or on the left, for fear or favour, discovering a just mind, that is, a constant and perpetual, or unchangeable will, to do right to all, whatever discouragement, opposition and hatred we meet with in doing our duty. This is a Light before men, which Christ will own in the day of his appearance, to have been for his Service, and shall not go without its due reward.

Thirdly, There are also the same witnessing Lights in the lesser sphears of every man's particular station and calling, which shine forth in a personal, righteous, and blameless conversation; or where their vote or consent is given, in reference to the good of the Church or State, or to the private Rule which every Master and Head of a Family is by Christ entrusted with in reference to his own Children and Family, who are under his charge, and not so much at their own dispose as his, who hath a right over them by God's Law and man's; and by the duty of this relation, every man may be somewhat directed, even by the world, what he is, and what Witness he gives, in the measure of the Knowledge and Light of Christ he hath received; and shall accordingly be taken notice of, and judged by Christ, in the day of his Judgment, ministring Perdition to ungodly men : In this little, a faithfulness to Christ is expected, and that according to the measure of Light received, and the Anointing we are under, of which there hath already the several degrees and kinds been made known.

The use therefore that Christ makes of this Light in the world, that these several wayes he makes to shine like Lightning from the East to the West, from *Jerusalem* to the utmost ends of the Earth, is, as to the world, to leave them without excuse, and ripen them as white fields, to the harvest of his just Vengeance, when the time is to put in his Sickle. And as to the Witnesses themselves, to bring upon them a time of refreshing and rest from the presence of the Lord in the sight of their very Enemies, where a Table shall be prepared for them, and their Cup shall be made to overflow.

This then being the Testimony that must be finished, and these the
Witnesses.

Witnesses in their several Places and Callings, who have been imployed in bearing and giving their Testimony in the World ever since Christ's Ascension ; the course whereof hath had its progress from East to West, and is now come to these utmost ends of the Earth. The Scriptures do with great clearness, as to the present dispensations of our day, teach us three things.

First, That this Testimony is now upon its finishing point in the World, and upon these times are brought all the concurring and forerunning Symptoms and Characters thereof.

Secondly, That the time of the End, that is to say, the fore-told-of day, in which Christ is to judge the World in Righteousness, so as to make up his Jewels on the one hand, and gather them as his precious Fruits into his Granary ; and to kindle an Oven of his fiery Vengeance, to burn up the VVicked root and branch, and gather together the Tares to be burnt in unquenchable fire, is at the very doors, and ready to open it self upon us, as the day of Redemption to the Good, and Terror and Amazement to the Wicked.

Thirdly, That this Day shall begin with the Rising of the VVitnesses, clothing those that then shall be in the World, with such a Ministry of Power and Glory, as shall qualifie them to discharge their several *Witness-bearing Duty*, before specified, with great applause, and good reception from the World. God permitting none to stand before them that make resistance or opposition, which shall be as a necessary fore-running dispensation for Christ's Personal Manifestation and Rule on Earth *a thousand years* ; but by these *Saviours* that thus shall be brought up upon *Mount Zion*, as *a Stone cut out without hands* ; *New Heavens and a new Earth, wherein dwelleth Righteousness*, shall be constituted, and the *four Monarchies* utterly broken to pieces and destroyed ; and the *Kingdom of Antichrist*, and the *Beast*, brought to final ruine and destruction.

The very mentioning of these three Particulars, without alledging particular places of Scripture, will bring them to your mind, which teach and speak expresly concerning the truth of them, and the matter of fact it self, as to what progress and course this witnessing-work hath made from *Judea*, where first it was lighted, step by step, into all Nations and Kingdoms all the World over, who have been acquainted with these VVitnesses, and have seen their Light shining in these Golden Candlesticks, and can give an account how from time to time they have been put out and removed from one place to another, till at last the bodies of these two Prophets are found dead in the streets of

the

the *earthly Jerusalem*, and *spiritual Egypt* and *Sodom*, if they might be suffered to be put into their Graves; and surely it is not without great wisdom that these Witnesses are called *Two*, considering the *two* distinct Ministries of Christ which they bear witness unto, and how each Ministry hath *two*, out of whose mouth it receives its Justification.

But further. That this Testimony is upon its finishing point, let us enquire whether the last slaying of the Witnesses, declared by the sight of their dead bodies (*Rev.* 11.) fit to be put into their Graves, be not already before our eyes. The right opening and understanding whereof is of great use, as a key to many other most considerable and difficult Scriptures. These *two Witnesses*, as they justifie Christ's second Ministry, the knowledg of him in spirit, are the Saints in their invisible Church-state, fled into the Wilderness, from the violence and rage of Persecution, which Satan stirred up against them by the visible Church, and Powers of the Civil Rule & Government, called in for assistance.

How these *Witnesses* are two, we have shewed, being the two Orders of Believers, which Christ's Mystical Body hath been ever consisting of, though rather mystically figured out, than appearing as they are, in the truth and brightness of their proper Glory, as Heirs of the Spirit of Promise in the single and double portion thereof.

These in their Spirit, Nature and Principles have been disowned, persecuted and slain, by the visible Church, (as much as in them lies) by exposing of them to the utmost of bodily sufferings and harms; and this from the time that the visible Church hath degenerated, grown Papal, and been defended by the *ten horns* of her Civil Government in the Western Empire of the World; and the sharpest and most bitter Enemies to these two Witnesses are the Reformed part of the visible Church, who declare their ripeness to be rejected by Christ, and have the flood of the Papal Power and Tyranny let in upon them, as they hate and reject the heavenly Seed and spiritual part of the Church, and can find opportunity to go back again into Conjunction with the Corrupt part of the visible Church, to hinder the growth of that which is Spiritual, rather than to go forward and become one with it. So that it might be made appear in the whole progress the Gospel hath made from East to West, the Reformed part of the Church never lost ground, nor was swallowed up again by the Papal, till it self first took up its stand, as to going on forward, and refused to be more Spiritual and Heavenly, being fiercer enemies hereunto, than any other whatsoever. And the greatest demonstration of this, is given in the last act of this Enmity that hath been acted, and is yet

in

in acting to the last slaughter which is to be made of the Witnesses in order to expose their dead bodies in the open streets of this *Earthly Jerusalem*, where they are as spectacles to be seen *three dayes* (that is, years) *and an half*, by them of Peoples, and Tongues, and Kindreds, and Nations, headed by the Papacy, who shall not suffer their dead bodies to be put in their graves by the Inhabitants of the *earthly Jerusalem*, who were willing enough to do it, as exceedingly joyed at the sight of their dead bodies, but shall rather chuse to quit those dead Carkases in way of contempt from any further prosecution of them ; and instead thereof, apply themselves with the strength of their whole Party, to strengthen and besiege the *earthly Jerusalem*, in whose streets the dead Carkases of the Witnesses are to lye (in a way of open reproach to be gazed upon) and shall make a gathering against it (as *Zach. 14. 2.*) as to battel, so as the event of it shall be the taking of the City, and the utter ruine of that part of the visible Church, distinguished from the other by the Name of *Reformed*; which when it happens, will be a *Fourth sign :* and by conjecture, this work is already begun, and materials for this Siege, are not only in readiness, and the Design laid, and the Parties agreed, that are to undertake it, but the open Defiance to the Battel is given, and both sides fixed in their resolutions to abide the issue, which will not exceed the term of *three years and an half*, before it be fully decided. Upon which decision, that, according to *Dan. 2. 43.* is to happen between these two parts of the visible Church, immediately after they find they cannot pitch upon the way of piecing up together against those that dwell in Heaven, though it be both their interests, and that they earnestly desire and labour it. Nay, this *Mount of Olives*, on which this second pair of Witnesses, or visible part of the Church Reformed are, that shall (*Zach. 14. 4.*) *cleave* also *in the middest*, as not being able to hold longer together, or to fasten the one to the other ; *and the one part shall go toward the East*, into down-right Popery ; *the other unto the West*, at the vastest distance, and greatest contrariety one to the other that is imaginable ; so as half of this Mountain of visible Saints in Name *shall remove North*, deeper into the Apostacy ; *and the other half South*, nearer to the Heavenly Jerusalem ; And in this state of things, when the *Iron* shall break the Kingdom of the *Clay* to pieces ; And again, that Kingdom of *Clay* shall divide and remove, one half to the East, and the other to the West, causing a most terrible Earthquake, as in the dayes of *Uziah*, at which time (of this Earthquake) the tenth part of the Papal Sea, shall make a final defection from

from her ; and *the Lord my God shall come, and all the Saints with thee*; that is to say, He shall Muster up his Heavenly Troops, and take to himself his great Power, in which he shall begin to reign, by the executing of his Wrath and divine Vengeance upon his Enemies, in the pouring out the *seven vials*, which *is the time of the end*; that is to say, of ending the 1260 years for the two Witnesses Prophesying in Sackcloth, and the Womans remaining in the Wilderness, and the time when the rising of the Witnesses doth begin, and *that Saviours shall come upon Mount Sion, and judge the Mount of Esau spiritually*, as the ten Kings shall judge them outwardly, and give the flesh of the Whore to be torn in pieces and burnt with fire. These, with others that might be alledged, are the characters and signs, to prove the first particular, that the Testimony which Christ declared so long ago, was to be given by the Preaching the Gospel of the Kingdom in all the World, and unto all Nations, is upon its finishing point.

The Second, which is the ending of that Dispensation, and the beginning of a new one, by the pouring out of the *seven vials*, to the utter destruction of Antichrist's Kingdom, and the cutting out the stone without hands, in preparation to the perfect deliverance of the Church out of *Babylon*, and the compleat bringing them out of their Captivity, in order to the actual Restoring the Kingdom of *Israel*, is that we shall likewise give some short discovery of.

Two things are comprehended in the Restoring the Kingdom to *Israel*; First, *Israel* it self, the true Inhabitants and Citizens of the *New* and *Heavenly Jerusalem*, must be restored to a Kingdom, that is a visible incorporated Society of Subjects, relating to the true *David* their King, as their Soveraign and only Law-giver, disclaiming all other reigning or exercising Dominion over them.

Secondly, Over *Israel*, thus restored to be a Kingdom, Christ will shew and own himself visibly their King, and the Universal Monarch over the whole World, who at that time shall be one Commonwealth of *Israel*, and Children of *Abraham*, under one of the *two Covenants*, yielding either true or feigned Obedience ; if not out of Love, yet from the fear of Wrath & Divine Vengeance, begun to be revealed and poured forth upon all the Disobedient. For no sooner shall the Vials begin to be poured out, but the time is come of *Christ's Wrath*, that is to say, when he shall come forth in the visible execution of his Royal Office and Power amongst them, in the hands of his undoubted Officers, executing Judgment upon all that shall withstand his Peoples Freedom, and coming out from under their former

Servitude

servitude and bondage under the Kingdom of Antichrist, and this in order to restore *Israel* unto such a constitution of a Kingdom which Christ is to exercise over them, during the space of a thousand years.

And therefore that which first begins this new dispensation, called *the time of the end,* is the rising of the Witnesses by an extraordinary pouring out of the spirit, *as the latter rain,* which like *Life from the dead* shall enter into them and set them upon their feet, and qualifie those in office amongst them, as their Rulers in State or Church, with a like and greater power than was given in the Type and Figure, to *Moses* and *Elias,* at whose word the earth was smitten with visible plagues and curses as often as they saw cause to promote the end for which they were sent and employed; and so it must be again, in a much more glorious dispensation, thereby to restore and constitute *Israel* into a Kingdom, in despite of all opposition; which plainly evidences, that such a dispensation as this, is necessary, as that which must be preparatory and conducing to give the actual being and constitution of a Kingdom, to a People that are found in so great and universal a state of servitude and bondage, far beyond that which *Israel* was in, to whom *Moses* was sent to bring them out of *Egypt. Therefore behold the dayes come, saith the Lord,* Jer. 23. 7, 8. *that they shall no more say, the Lord liveth which brought the Children of Israel out of the land of E- gypt, but the Lord liveth, which brought up, and which led,* (a parallel dispensation to *Moses* his bringing them up, *and leading them as a horse in the Wilderness,* Esay 63.) *the seed of the house of Israel out of the North Country, and from all Countries whither I had driven them, and they shall dwell in their own land.*

The spiritual seed of Israel, driven in the time of the *Gentiles* into the Wilderness, and kept slaves to the highest degree, during the reign of Antichrist, must have a time of gathering and bringing up into their land under their own King, and the Nation that hath kept them in bondage, God himself must and will judge more signally than he did *Pharaoh* and the *Egyptians*; by which means this stone that hath been fallen upon, and suppressed for so many hundred years, even these fixed, unmoveable, chaste followers of the Lamb, must rise and stand again upon their feet with great power and authority, so as they shall not onely be a burthensome stone for all people that burthen themselves with it, Zach. 12. 3. to the cutting them in pieces, though the people of the earth be gathered together against them; but *vers.* 5, 6. *In that day saith the Lord, I will make the Governours of Judah like an hearth of fire in a sheaf, and they shall devour all the people round a-*

I

bout, on the right hand and on the left ; and *Jerusalem* shall be inhabited again in her own place, even in *Jerusalem*, and the Lord himself shall defend in that day *Jerusalem*, and he that is feeble amongst them shall be as *David*, and the house of *David* as God, as the Angel of the Lord before them ; so as the Governours of *Judah* shall say, there is strength to me, and to the Inhabitants of *Jerusalem*, in the Lord of Hosts their God.

I know it is and will be Objected, that these places refer to the conversion of the *Jews*, that are the natural seed of *Abraham*, which are expected to be first received again, as Life from the dead, before these promises shall be accomplished. In Answer to which, I shall only say, There will indeed, upon the rising of the Witnesses, that seed of *Abraham* appear and be made manifest, that are the true and proper *Jews*, a Nation advanced in love and glory from God, above all other Nations and People, of which an account hath been given before; and then it will be found, no other *Jewish* Nation are to be eyed, but as they fall within and are comprehended amongst the *Gentile* fulness of those Nations that are to be saved.

FINIS.

THE
Face of the Times :

WHEREIN

Is briefly difcovered by feveral *Prophetical Scrip-*
tures, from the beginning of *Genefis* to the end of the
Revelation, the RISE , PROGRESSE, and ISSUE of the
ENMITY and CONTEST , between the SEED of the
WOMAN , and SEED of the SERPENT , to the final
breaking of the Serpent's head, in the total and irrecoverable Ruin of the MONARCHIES of this World, which
have been fpirited, influenced, and headed all along by
him, for the bruifing of the Saints Heel (or killing of
their Bodies) for the Teftimony of Jefus, which by them
hath been given forth in the true Spirit of Prophefie.

The Defign of this Writing, is,

To ALARM the World, and awaken up the prefent
Generation of God's People in it, to a more diligent and curious obfervation of the prefent Signs of the near approaching
day of the Lord, that they may be more carefully minding
and doing what moft concerns them, by way of preparation
thereunto.

Seeing that all thefe things fhall be diffolved, what manner of perfons
ought we to be in all holy converfation and godlinefs, looking for and
hafting unto the coming of that day of God, (which will come as a
thief in the night) wherein the heavens being on fire, fhall be dif-
folved, and the elements fhall melt with fervent heat ? 2 Pet. 3.
10, 11, 12.

Printed in the Year, 1662.

THE

Face of the Times.

IT was the saying of Christ to the Generation he conversed with, while in the flesh, *Ye hypocrites, ye can discern the face of the skies, but can ye not, or how is it that ye cannot discern the signs of the times?* Why do you not set your selves to observe and spel out the meaning of God's providential voice, given forth in harmony with his written Oracles, by the Judgements which he is now executing in the earth, as to that most pertinent and concerning Truth, *The near approach of the day of the Lord?* It will surprize and overtake the wicked that are in darkness, as a thief, and exceeding dreadful will it be to them. But the Children of Light and of that day, are required *to lift up their heads, when they see the signes thereof,* (however dismal to their fleshly part) *for their Redemption draweth nigh,* Luk. 21. 25, 28.

God is still working and carrying on his designes in the world, on the behalf of his People, as also over-ruling all the contrary actings of his and their enemies, in pursuance of his decree, published at passing that sentence upon the Serpent, *Gen.* 3. 15. *I will put enmity between thee and the woman, and between thy seed and her seed; it shall bruise thy head, and thou shalt bruise his heel.*

In the latter branch of this sentence, (which was first put in execution) God declares himself as to sundry particulars, which do summarily and fully contain his design and work throughout all ages of the World, till it be accomplished, and the Mystery of it finished, as he hath declared unto his servants the Prophets, *Rev.* 10. 7. Then the Saints Turne will come, to act his part in pursuance of the

former

former branch of the Decree, for bruising of the Serpents head, and giving an incurable wound to all his adherents.

There is indeed a great mystery in the managing of this war, which God declares he hath founded in the enmity set by him between the seed of the Woman and seed of the Serpent. Matters are so contrived in the most wise designe of God, that the seed of the Woman must suffer first, and be on the losing hand, (as to any outward quietness and fair dealing that they are to expect in this world) for a long tract of time, wherein the headship of this world, the Empire and Government of the whole earth shall be, as it were, in the hands of the evil one, who shall be very much permitted to dispose of the powers of it, to his own instruments and creatures. But at the sounding of the seventh Trumpet, this time is to end, and be no longer. Then the seed of the woman must break this headship, which Satan for so long time hath exercised over the whole world, and destroy all those worldly Kingdoms that have been managed under his influence, to their prejudice. *Then Judgement will be given to the Saints of the most High. They shall take and possesse the Kingdom for ever, even for ever and ever,* Dan. 7. *Then the Kingdomes of this world shall become the Kingdoms of our Lord and of his Christ, holding of him as their visible head, who is and was and is to come, and will take unto himself his great power for that purpose.*

The particulars which are summed up, (*Gen.* 3. 15.) concerning the nature of this war, and the manner of managing it, (explained since by time and the history of things in the Scriptures) are these,

1. Let Satan do his worst, and make all the Power and parties he can, amongst the Sons of *Adam*, yet God will have a Seed in the World, called there the seed of the woman, that shall be in a state of fixed enmity and war against him and his seed.

2. For a long tract of time, Satan shal not be chained up nor restrained from using all his skill and power, by himself and his instruments, for the doing of his utmost in a way of war, to ruine, destroy and prevail against the Seed of the Woman. For this end he shall be permitted to have the subordinate exercise of the Empire and visible Government of the whole world, to be given and bestowed as himself will, for the strengthening his interest, and encouraging of those that will be his creatures, and fall down and worship him.

3. The contrariety of mind and principles between these two seeds, will

will be so fixed and unchangeable, that they will never give over contesting and fighting one with or against another, whatever it cost them, till the heel of the one be fully bruised, that is, till the sufferings of Christ yet behind in his body mystical, and every member thereof, be accomplished, by sustaining loss in the flesh, even to death it self; and the head of the other fully broken, that is, till the headship and visible Government of the World be wholly taken out of the hands of Satan and his instruments, and reassumed by Christ into his own hands, and the hands of fit and meet Ministers and Officers under him.

4. After a long time of patience under bodily sufferings, not loving their Lives unto the death, the seed of the Woman shall at last certainly and fully overcome the seed of the Serpent, tread Satan and his kingdom under foot, for ever and ever. The principal means they shall rely upon for the bringing of this war to a good issue, is the way of overcoming by the blood of the Lamb, (or force of Christs intercession, whose blood cries for vengeance against his enemies) as also by the word of their Testimony (freely and boldly given forth by them in their very sufferings, whilst worldly Power stands on the enemies side) which shall have its effect upon friends and foes, as a savour of Life to the one, death to the other, a sweet savour to God both ways, prospering in the thing whereto he sends it, and performing all his pleasure, 2 *Cor.* 2. 15, 16. *Esay* 55. 11.

Pursuant to this counsel and decree of God, (declared, *Gen.* 3. 15.) he hath wonderfully and signally preserved the seed of the Woman, unto this very day. He hath given them being, preservation and protection in the midst of all enemies, and in despite of all their rage and opposition. He hath carried on his C A U S E, and upheld righteousness on the side of his People, whatever disguises, reproaches or blemishes have been endeavoured to be put upon it, by the Devil and his adherents. The miraculous preservation of the Womans Seed, the Scriptures distribute into three principal Branches, which distinguish the whole tract of time allotted to them for their sufferings, into three great Periods and seasons, wherein the seed of the Woman hath received variation, as to the outward form and dispensation of things, though in mind, principles, and spirit, they continue still the same, in and under all these Changes.

The first appearance of the seed of the Woman, in order to enter the list with the Seed of the Serpent, we find in the line of *Adam*,
which

which he begat of *Eve*, the Mother of all living. *Abel* the firſt Martyr died before he had any iſſue, or means to propagate it. God ſupplied that defect in the line of *Seth*. In this new line is carried on the decreed enmity between the two ſeeds, till the Flood came and ſwept away (in a manner) all mankind, from off the face of the earth. At that time the firſt war ended. But the foundation and matter of a new war, in this kind, is contracted into, and found even in the family of *Noah*. The firſt war, begun in *Adams* line, and continued in *Seths*, was (in a way of God's juſt judgement upon the whole world) brought to an end by the Flood. The ſeed of the Woman was now narrowed and diminiſhed into *Noahs* perſon and two of his ſons. The ſeed of the Serpent was contracted into a leſs room yet, the other ſon.

This *Epocha* of 1656 years, from the Creation to the Flood, is in Scripture diſtinguiſhed as one great period of time and revolution of things in the world, relating to this war between the two ſeeds, and the event of it. It began in and with the Patriarchs, in the perſon of *Abel*, whom *Cain* that was of that wicked one, ſlew. It continued all along with the Patriarchs and their day on earth, who lived every one of them hundreds of years : And it had its period in that univerſal miniſtry of God's wrath and vengeance upon the whole world, which in Scripture is called, *THE DAY OF THE LORD.*

The ſecond appearance then of the ſeed of the Woman and ſeed of the Serpent alſo, we find in *Noahs* family. From the matter and fuel, contracted into this narrow compaſs, does the fire of the war between the two ſeeds break forth a-freſh, and another world (as it were) and ſtate of things, diverſe from the forme, under the government of the Patriarchs, is brought upon the Stage. This new and differently ſtated war, ariſes and is occaſioned from the differing minds and principles, found in *Noah's* three ſons, *Sem, Ham,* and *Japhet*. The flood having deſtroyed all the families of the earth, ſave *Noahs* onely, the Government of the World came hereby to receive a conſiderable change, becauſe the Right of the Empire of the whole world was now by Gods Providence devolved upon the family of *Noah*, and in particular, upon himſelf in perſon, as the right heir of it. After him, it came to *Sem* and his line, by God's ſpecial deſignation, though *Japhet* were the eldeſt.

In *Noahs* three ſons, as in type, the three ſorts of principles and mindes, which influence this ſecond world of mankind, are deſcribed, and (as I may ſay) perſonated, to the life. Theſe three principles diſtinguiſh all perſons deſcended of *Noah's* family, throughout the whole world, into three ſorts of Inhabitants.

The

The same method does *John*, by way of allegory hold, (*Rev.* 12. 12.) calling one sort of them, *Inhabitants of Heaven*, or those that dwell *and have their conversation in Heaven*, corresponding in their Principle and way of Life, with the *Jerusalem that is above.*

Another sort he tearms, *Inhabitants of the Earth*, or *those that dwell on Earth* ; the tribes of the Earth, or citizens of the earthly *Jerusalem.*

The third are *those that dwell in the Sea*, or are found in a state of *deep darkness*, and *alienation from the Life of God, casting up mire and dirt, as raging waves of the troubled Sea,* (Esay 57. 20.) living in that open heathenisme and prophaness, that the greatest part of the world chuse to abide in, notwithstanding the offer of Liberty made to them, by the ransom paid on their behalf in the blood of the Redeemer.

1. The mind that shews it self in the first sort of these *Inhabitants*, is that which was in *Sem* ; a holy, spiritual mind, *set upon things above*, or *in heaven, at Christs right hand.* This, when it comes to operate, is that active, living Faith of the new creature, *which works by love.* By this Faith, or in this spiritual mind and principle of Life and operation, *Abel offered unto God a more excellent Sacrifice than Cain*, Heb. 11. 4.

2. The mind that discovers it self in the second sort of inhabitants, (those that dwell on Earth, citizens of the earthly *Jerusalem*) is that which was in *Japhet*, as a middle wavering state, perswadeable either to good or evil; either to leave the earth and love of seen things, and to ascend and dwell in the tents of *Sem*, in order to be fixed and set on things above, or else to cleave unto things seen, in affection and desire, and thence to descend, and draw back to perdition, apostatize and lodge in the heathenish principles of *Cham*, and so partake of his curse as well as sin. Those that thus decline from the wavering spirit and principles of *Japhet*, to the prophane state of *Cham*, are noted in Scripture to be such as *having known the way of righteousness, do turn aside from the holy command*, and so come to have their lot amongst those that *are twice dead, and pluck'd up by the roots, whose latter end is worse than their beginning.* For upon such a fatal backsliding, such an irrecoverable fall in their own persons, they come to be fixed in evil *and bound up with the fallen Angels in everlasting chains under darkness, unto the judgement of the great day,* 2 Pet. 2. 20. Jude, vers. 12. and vers. 6.

This wavering spirit of *Japhet*, considered singly in its own sphear and activity, (as neither advancing towards the tents of *Sem*, and

K

things

things above ; nor declining to the heathenish and prophane state of *Cham*) is that spirit which properly constitutes the *Israel* after the flesh, in distinction from the true *Israel* of God, or Circumcision of the Spirit, on the one hand ; and the heathenish uncircumcised Nations, on the other, whilst God kept up the war in the line of *Abraham*, or seed of *Israel* according to the flesh, till Christ's incarnation. For in *Abraham's* line, deriving from *Heber* and *Shem*, did God renew and maintain the war with the Seed of the Serpent, and continued it till his signal rejection of that line, and utter cutting them off from being any more a Nation and People of themselves, at the last sacking and destruction of *Jerusalem*, after the death of Christ, by the hand of *Titus Vespasian*.

3. The mind that declares it self in the third sort of Inhabitants, who dwell in the Sea, or in the depth of alienation from the life of God, (without any sense or feeling of that which is morally and naturally good according to the Law, hating and despising God's image in any kind, where-ever it shines forth) is that which was in *Cham*. For *this* was he cursed and judicially fixed in his bondage, as a servant of sin, resembled by that servant under the Mosaical dispensation, who for refusing his freedom when offered, was bored thorow his ear, in token of his perpetual servitude, *Exod.* 21. 6.

1. The first sort of these Inhabitants are heavenly, having a mind and principles fix'd in that obedience of Faith which is acceptable, and by entring into God's Rest through Faith, do become unmovable in the right way of working Righteousness, wherein they attain the end of their hope, that is, *the salvation of their souls*.

2. The second are earthly, unfixed either in good or evil, wavering between both, having a mind sometimes serving the Law of God, and sometimes the law of sin. These, however they may draw near to God with their words and tongue, their heart is alienated and at a distance from him ; at least, may be, for ought they know, notwithstanding the form of godliness they live in. For they are not able to make a true and certain judgment of themselves, till they partake of that Anointing from above that can teach them all things. This is that only that will enable them to keep the word of Christ's patience in the day of their tryal. Without this Grace extended to them, and possessed by them, they will become Apostates, forget they have been washed from their old sins, and will shew themselves at last the most hardned and bitter resisters of the holyGhost and Power of Godliness.

3. The third are like the Sea, foaming out their own filth, and they are constant and fixed therein, having minds and consciences
seared

seared and made harder than the nether milstone, in works of darkness. Being past feeling, they have sold themselves to work wickedness. Peradventure sometime they may be made a little sensible of the sting and penalties of the Law, so as to make some slender acknowledgments and feigned professions of obedience and subjection thereunto, (the Devils also believe and tremble) but no hearty or sincere repentance from dead works, or pure obedience of love, springing from the spirit of Adoption, and appearing in a steady amendment of life, is to be found in them. Yea, they are by God himself judicially hardned, and unchangeably fastned in their own chosen wayes of darkness. They give themselves up to work all uncleanness with greediness, and God gives them up to vile affections, to take their course, and fill up the measure of their abominations, till he see time to strike them once for all.

The first and last of the above-named minds or principles, are the two extreams, in the one or other of which, the middle or second sort of Inhabitants (that are in the wavering, changeable, contending state, with whom God is striving by his Spirit) will come at last to be unchangeably fixed. The perfect and righteous state which Man was at first created in, was this middle, wavering and unfixed state of perfection which was at first, and upon renewal thereof is again capable to be guided by the Spirit of God (through Faith) into a higher and better, or to be tempted and seduced by Satan into a lower and far worse.

The sinful state likewise into which mankind was plunged by the first transgression and fall of Man, is not fixed, or made immutable and desperate, until a new proof and tryal be made of all men. In order to this, by vertue of the Blood of the Redeemer, and through observation of the Rules appointed by God for recovery out of the Fall, a restitution to the rectified Principles and Righteousness of our first Creation, is in Christ most certainly attainable by every sinner, without exception. For by Christ's Blood there is remission to be had for all sins past, and a new tryal is propounded and set before every one for time to come, upon the terms, and according to the tenor of God's conditional, or absolute Covenant. Hence it is the War arises, and the Enmity is set, or comes to be fixed between the two seeds, each serving, as it were, for the proof and tryal of the unmovableness of one another, either in good or evil.

Through this was occasioned the quarrel between the seed of the Woman, and the seed of the Serpent, growing up out of *Noah's* family. The usurpation of the universal Government of the World in

K 2   favour

favour and assistance of the Serpent's seed, was attempted and pursued by *Nimrod* and his successors. Afterwards it came into *Nebuchadnezzar's* hands, and by *Daniel's* interpretation of that prophetical Image of worldly Monarchy that *Nebuchadnezzar* saw in a dream, the continuance thereof in his line and three other successive branches of Universal Monarchy in the lines of the *Medes* and *Persians*, *Grecians*, and then *Romans*, was foretold. All these have been the inheritors of *Cham's* spirit, upholding a heathenish state of Idolatry, Ignorance and Prophaness, against the Kingdom and Obedience of Christ, kept up and witnessed unto, all along, in and by the line and seed of *Abraham*, from *Sem* downward, to the last sack and utter ruine of the Temple and City of *Jerusalem* under the *Romans*. The chief memorables in this space of time, that concern the opposit interest to these worldly Monarchies, were the eminent Call of *Abraham*, *Isaac* and *Jacob* to the Faith, the giving of the Law, the building and rebuilding of the Temple, the long continuing of the Prophetical Office in the Jewish Church, Christ's Incarnation, Ministry, Death and Resurrection. About forty years after the Resurrection of Christ, *Jerusalem* is destroyed by *Titus Vespasian*, and there ended the second great Period and Revolution of this War, that was managed between the two seeds. All along this second War, the seed of the Serpent was possessed of the Universal Monarchy of this World, had all the countenance and assistance which that could afford. The main visible Protection vouchsafed by God on the other hand, to his Church and People, was continued in the line of *Abraham*, accounting from *Sem* downward, unto God's judicial rejection of that seed of *Abraham* according to the flesh, upon their crucifying the Lord of Glory.

In this second War, we find the seed of the Woman bruised still in the heel and coming off with loss. Yea, upon the winding up of this second great Day or Period of time, (wherein the Prince of Life was by wicked hands put to death, and the whole Nation of the visible Church of God on Earth, rejected, and their Worship prophaned and destroyed) the Devil might seem to himself and others to have come off compleat conqueror. But the War is again renewed by the Serpent and his seed, against the seed of the Woman, who are repeated and brought forth again by the Regeneration, from amongst the very heathenish Nations of the World, that were not before accounted by God as a People of his, but given up, as it were, to the dominion of Sin and Satan.

This third War had its foundation laid in the Incarnation, Death
and

and Refurrection of Chrift, who (though a Son) was taught obedience by fuffering, and in the condition of a fufferer obtained the victory. *Through death he deftroyed him that had the power of death, that is, the Devil.* And *by tafting death for every man, as became the Captain of our Salvation, he was made perfect through fufferings.*

This way of fighting and overcoming the Devil and Sin, was a great myftery till then, and the moft unlikely of all other, ever to break the Serpents head, and difpoffefs him and his Inftruments of their worldly Thrones and Powers. Yet in this way of the Crofs, by the blood of the Lamb and the word of their Teftimony, do the true Witneffes of Chrift manage and carry on this third War. One thoufand two hundred and fixty dayes, that is, yeares, have bin alotted them for prophefying in fackcloth, in a perfecuted, wildernefs condition. Then they are to rife out of their graves, ftand again upon their feet, and prophecy with power. 'Tis paft all difpute, that the conqueft muft fall on the fide of the Lamb and his followers, at the ending of this third great feafon and revolution of time, wherein the feed of the Woman hath ftill been on the fuffering hand. The end of their fuffering feafon will be, when the feventh Trumpet begins to found, immediately after the effect which the pouring forth of the Vials fhall have upon the Beaft and his kingdom.

This is the Rife, Progrefs and Iffue that is given unto things in the third Age of the World, called *Chriftian*, that was made to fpring up and have its being out of the deftruction of the Jewifh World, *Rom.* 11. 11.

The cleer view and profpect of things in this Chriftian World, (both as to the Civil and Church-government, as alfo the War between the two Seeds, brought on again and continued) was given by Chrift unto the Apoftle *John*, and revealed to him by his Angel in the Book of the *Revelation.* For there we find the period that muft happen alfo to this third World, and to the Heavens and Earth, or the Civil and Church-ftate appertaining to it, and carried on under this difpenfation, in order to give place to a world to come, which is yet to fucceed. This World to come, will be of a more heavenly and fpiritual Conftitution, as to the general ftate and frame of things, which is to be brought forth by Chrift's fecond appearance, upon the fpirits and bodies of men, on this fide their compleat and utmoft glorification. The final afcending up to the Father, to fit down at his right hand, is after this world that is yet to come (or the thoufand years Reign of Chrift with all his Saints on earth) fhall have had its courfe.

Unto

Unto the risen state of Saints, when they shall begin to come forth in their victorious posture, and unresistable power of Faith and Prayer, doth the Prophet *Hosea* seem to refer, *chap.6.verf.2,3. After two dayes* (sayes he) or *great seasons of Affliction and Suffering* (already described) *he will revive us, by the WORD's being made Flesh, and the day spring from on high therein visiting us.* This (*Hab.3.2.*) is called a reviving the work, or preserving it alive in the midst of the years of Wrath and Oppression from the Serpent and his seed, that was yet to be under-gone for the space of 1666 years after Christ's birth, as will appear in its proper place. *In the third day* (sayes *Hosea*) that is, at the end of it, when the Witnesses are to arise, *we shall live in his sight.* By following on to know the Lord, we shall perceive that his going forth in this his third great revolution of time, hath been as the morning, shining more and more unto a perfect day, and that his coming to us (according as hath been by him purposed) in his *first* and in his *second Appearance*, will be as the *former and latter rain unto the Earth.*

The *former rain of Christ's Spirit*, in the season of his first Appearance, began at the day of Pentecost, in visible gifts and distributions of the holy Ghost, dividing to every man severally, as himself pleased. By this means he raised up a Ministry that formed and laid the Foundation of the Primitive Church. That Church was upheld in its original purity, more or less, as long as they kept the Word of God's Patience, and withstood the opposition made against it, after a right manner, by the blood of the Lamb, and by the word of their Testimony, in the giving whereof, they loved not their lives unto death. This appeared, all along those hard and cruel Persecutions they under-went, until such time almost as *Constantine* came to the Empire.

But to avoid Persecution, Christians then began to mingle Interest with worldly Powers, and (to please Governours) took their rest in the outward Court, some out-side form of godliness, so as that which we call Christian Religion, became the Religion of the Empire (or of the body of the Nation unto which it was received) as commanded and compelled by the Laws of the State, and power of the Sword. This practice commenced and bears date about four hundred years after Christ, from which time little of the *former rain* hath fallen upon such visible or state Christianity, in their Publick and National Meeting-places of Worship. That *rain* became then *hidden Manna*, the peculiar food and refreshing of the Woman and her seed in the Wilderness, where she is nourished for a time, and times,

and

and half a time. From about the time that Christian Religion hath been made National, and in the Rules, Ordinances and Doctrines thereof, been embodyed with the Laws of each Nation in the Empire, and so enforced by the Civil Sword, those that truly keep the Commandments of God and Testimony of Jesus, have been driven into a state of desolation, persecution and dispersion, and are so to continue and be warred upon, forty and two Months, by the Earth and her Inhabitants on the one hand, and by the Sea and her Inhabitants on the other.

Both these sorts of Inhabitants and Enemies of the Church in the Wilderness, do make up and constitute but one great City or incorporated Society of the Serpents seed, spiritually called *Egypt* and *Sodom*, under the headship of worldly Government, as it arises out of the Sea. This worldly Government is still but the same fourth Beast and universal Romane Empire, in Principles of opposition to the Kingdom of Christ and Seed of the Woman, as before. It seems indeed to be now healed and reformed with the shew of Christian Religion, under the headship of Church-Government and coercive Power arising out of the Earth, or apostate Principles of the worldly Church, departing from the Primitive Power, Purity and Patern ; retaining still something of the form of Godliness, but denying the Spirit and Power thereof.

The *first Beast* carries the *second*, and is willing to be *rid upon by it*, finding great benefit and advantage by having the *Whore* upon their *back*, for the propagating of servitude, and rooting out of the earth the pure and chaste Principles of the Primitive, Apostolick, Catholick Church.

Thus the War is managed between the *two seeds* in this *third day*. Towards the latter end of this day is our lot fallen, who are at present alive in this world. But before the period, and shutting in of this day, the Sufferings of the Womans Seed shall have an end. Then, that Ministry of the Spirit shall come in, which is compared to the *latter rain*. This is that which shall break the Serpents head, utterly tread him, his kingdom and followers under foot. This is that, which (by the pouring forth of the seven Vials of the wrath of God upon the kingdom of the Beast, to the utter ruine and destruction thereof) will prepare the way for the coming down of the *new Jerusalem* out of Heaven, as a Bride adorned for her Husband, and so, for the thousand years Reign of Christ on Earth. At the beginning of that Reign, Satan shall be chained up, and there shall be no more Sea, or prophane worldly-Interest, and beastly Government left.

In

In the *evening-time* of this *third day* or age of the World (wherein we now live) it shall be *light*, by the coming on of the Kingdom and Reign of Chrift, with all his Saints, *Zech.* 14. 5, 7.

This then that we have been defcribing, is the third fignal feafon or great revolution of things in this world, wherein the fame War that was from the beginning, hath been, and ftill is carrying on between the two Seeds, under the name of Chriftian, or of Chrift's followers. The Seed of the Serpent, under pretence of being for Chrift, do prove at laft univerfally againft him, moft fhamefully and wickedly rejecting him, and falling in with the kingdom of Antichrift, in direct oppofition to his Kingdom. This they will do, notwithftanding that he hath been gracioufly ftriving and contending by the Miniftry of the Gofpel, to work the whole World into a ftate of Obedience and Subjection to the Righteoufnefs of his Scepter. For this end hath he been many hundred years giving forth the light and glory of his Gofpel and Kingdom, from the Eaftern parts of the World to the Weft, and fuffered himfelf all along to be caft off, and his Members to be oppreffed and troden under foot, by degrees, in one Nation and Country after another, till at laft it came to thefe Weftern parts, and was fpread from hence in *America*, which with thefe Nations we live in, feem to be the laft piece of Ground this Quarrel is to be fought out in. Yea, and probably this is the time as well as the place, wherein the Witneffes are finifhing their Teftimony, being the laft that are fignally to be flain by the Beaft, as the proper accomplifhment of that Prophefie, *Revel.* 11. 7. The Beaft is represented here as generally in his afcendant pofture, being gratified with fome remarkable Rife in his affairs, as a lightning before death, to enable him for the accomplifhing of this great counfel of God that is to be acted upon the dead bodies of his flain Witneffes, within the three years and half before their rifing again and ftanding upon their feet. Then they are to enter upon the fecond part of their Prophetical Miniftry, compared to that of *Eliah*'s in *Ahab*'s time, and that of *Mofes* in *Egypt*, when at their word they fhall fhut Heaven that it rain not, have power over Waters to turn them into blood, and to fmite the Earth with Plagues as often as they will.

By them alfo Heaven fhall be opened, and a fuller and more excellent difcovery of Chrift in Spirit miniftred, than ever yet hath been. Amongft them fhall be found thofe feven Angels, or Officers of the Church, to whom fhall be committed the pouring out of the feven golden Vials, full of the wrath of God. Thefe Vials contain a like univerfal Miniftry of Wrath and of the Judgement of God by
Fire,

Fire, upon ungodly men, as was brought by Water upon the old World in the dayes of *Noah*. This miniſtry of wrath by Fire, ſhall put a period to the third ſtate of things in the world, as that by Water did unto the firſt. Out of the deſtruction of the preſent World and frame of things, by this fiery miniſtry of God's wrath, is the thouſand years Reign of Chriſt to ſpring up, in that Kingdom of his that ſhall never end.

And here bear with me in giving (by way of digreſſion) ſome few broken Notions, in order to the better and more diſtinct opening of Chriſt's Kingdom, which we ſhall find (*Luk.* 17, 20, 21. and *chap.* 19. 11, &c.) to be diſtinguiſhed into a Twofold ſtate ;

1. *A Kingdom inward.* The *Kingdom of God is within you* ; and is the dominion of God in the Conſcience and Spirit of the Mind. This Kingdom ſtands not, nor comes in or with any outward obſervation, but is the commanding, ruling Principle of Life in the true Saint, as a Law written in his inward parts. Chriſt's Kingdom, as thus conſidered, is intended, (*Rev.* 11; 1.) where it is called the *Temple of God*, or the *inward Court*, and thoſe that worſhip there, glorifying God in their Spirits. This Kingdom of Chriſt is capable of ſubſiſting and being managed imwardly, in the minds of his People, in a hidden ſtate, concealed from the eye of the world ; By the Power thereof, the inward ſenſes or eyes of the mind are opened and awakened, to the drawing them upward to a Heavenly converſe, catching and carrying up the Soul to the Throne of God, and to the knowledge of the Life which is hid, with Chriſt, in God. Thoſe that are in this Kingdom, and in whom the Power of it is, are fitted to flye with the Church into the VVilderneſs, and to continue in ſuch a ſolitary, diſperſed, deſolate condition, till God calls them out of it. They have VVells and Springs opened to them in this VVilderneſs, whence they draw the VVaters of Salvation, without being in bondage to the Life of Senſe, and the objects depending thereon, as *touch not, taſte not, handle not*, which periſh in the uſing.

2. But Secondly, *Chriſt's Kingdom is alſo outward* ; appearing to ſenſe, and to the eye of the ſenſual or inferiour part of the mind, which works only by bodily organs, judging by the ſight of that eye, and the hearing of that ear, whoſe life is in and by the body, conſiſting in bodily exerciſe, and is therefore compared (*Revel.* 11. 2.) to the *outward Court*, and the VVorſhip thereunto appertaining. This is the Dominion of God in the Conſcience alſo, though but in the inferiour or ſenſual part of the mind, where it becomes a Law in our Members, to put in execution and perform the Law of the Spirit of

L   our

our Mind, that so our very bodies may become the Temple of the holy Ghost, and we may be able to glorifie God, not in our Spirits only, but in our Bodies also, as clean Vessels and earthen Tabernacles, upon which may be written, *HOLINESS TO THE LORD*, *Zech.* 14.

Now the Kingdom of Christ comes not properly to appear in outward shew and visibility, but as it shines forth in this lower and earthly part of the Soul, witnessing the Dominion and Power of God to be there as a Law and commanding Principle, in, and over the outward man. With respect to this kind of its Appearance, in affecting and influencing the bodily part of man, and becoming the Life thereof, it is capable to come forth in a Power and Glory that is *corruptible, fading, and that wears away*; as also in that which is *incorruptible and abides for ever*. The first of these is meant, (1 *Joh.* 3. 1, 2.) where 'tis said, *Now are we the Sons of God, and it doth not yet appear what we shall be: but we know that when he shall appear, we shall be like him*, (or have the like appearance with him) *for we shall see him as he is*. The Sons of God are not yet in the proper appearance of *his Sons*, but do bear the form and appearance of the *fleshly man*, to the *making a fair shew in the flesh*: They have their Treasure but in an earthen Vessel, unredeemed from its present bondage unto corruption. But the time is hastening, when they shall in Spirit shine forth as the Sun in its strength, in the Kingdom of their Father, and their very bodies shall be as the Firmament, transparent, and of service to unvail the glory of the inward man, and not cover and disguise it, as now they do.

But, alas! *This fair shew in the flesh*, which may also be made by those that are strange Children, passes with most for the Kingdom of Christ, even yet in these last dayes, some crying, *Lo here*; and some, *lo there*; according to that form of service and divine worship they are perswaded in their minds, is according to the Rule of God's VVord, though it be but that only which appertains to the *outward Court*, which is given up by God into the hands of the *Gentiles*, to possess and tread under foot at their pleasure. The Heavens hereof are passing away with a great noise, and these worldly Elements are melting apace; As a Vesture they shall be folded up and changed, they shall perish and wear old as a Garment, whilst Christ's inward and spiritual Kingdom shall remain, and in its due time come forth in an appearance that shall be lasting and unshaken for ever. VVherefore we receiving this Kingdom, which cannot be moved, let us hold fast, and have Grace, whereby we may serve God acceptably, with reverence and Godly fear. *For our God is a consuming fire.*

But

But to return, and apply our selves to the subject we were on before, which is, To give the view of what Word God is fulfilling, and what part of his Counsel he is executing among us, in this our day. The Heavens are now black over our heads, the Sun is turned into darkness, the Moon into blood, and mens hearts are failing them for fear of what God is bringing upon the Earth. Great distress is in the Land, and upon the Nations ; Wrath is coming upon that People, who say they are *Jews* and are not, but shall be found liars. The Sea and the waves also, will roar; the prophane heathenish party of men will be in great perplexity too.

Surely, the Figtree, and all the Trees are shooting forth ; and after this cruel, sharp Winter that is (and for some space is yet to be) upon us, the Summer approaches that will make amends for all. Great cause there is for the Sons of God to lift up their heads, as foreseeing that their Redemption draws nigh.

In this point, the Book of the *Revelations* will be every day more and more opened, to give us light and instruction, the Providences of God helping much every day too, as to the interpretation thereof, together with the Spirit of Truth, that dwells and lives in the hearts of Saints. Through mercy, the Lord who is that Spirit, hath not been wanting in his Teachings of this kind to a poor Worm in my present solitude and bonds. I shall have occasion to tell you by and by, that there appears cause to me of dissent from Mr. *Mede*, as to some applications that are made by him in his learned Commentary on that Book, when I come to speak of some particulars concerning the Witnesses, and their twofold time and state of prophesying.

1. Their *thousand two hundred and sixty years prophesying in sackcloth, in a persecuted wilderness state.*

2. Their *prophesying in power and glory, during the space of the pouring forth of the seven Vials of Wrath, as a fore-running Eliah-like Ministry, preparatory to Christ's thousand years Reign on Earth.* Yet, as to that which Mr. *Mede* calls his great Key for the opening of that whole Book, to wit, his *Synchronisms* or Contemporations of things, which he finds to agree and fall out together in the same age and time, I exceedingly reverence his Judgement, and look upon him as one that hath most happily found out the hidden order and method, used by the holy Ghost in that Prophetical Book.

This method being once known to the very rational judgment of man, that may be exercised upon the matters contained in that Book, they are thereby rendred much more easie and intelligible.

Let us also take it for granted, (as that which is the common

judgment

judgment of thofe that acknowledge the Scriptures) that in this Book of the *Apocalypfe*, are contained and revealed, in an orderly method, the things which were to fall out in the courfe of God's Providence, and wife ordering of matters for the good of the VVomans Seed, during the third Day or Age of the world. This day reaches from Chrift's Afcention (or departure into a far Country) to God's bringing again this his only-begotten Son into the world, that every tongue may confefs, and every knee bow to the honour of his moft glorious Name. Then fhall he, in the quality of Univerfal King, as well on Earth as in Heaven, enter upon and keep the poffeffion of his Kingdom, againft all Ufurpers and Oppofers whatfoever.

This fpace of time between Chrift's Afcention to Heaven, and Reign on Earth, is meafured out in three great and diftinct Sections or Divifions, in the Book before-mentioned, as Mr. *Mede* takes notice; and every of thefe three are again made to contain in them feven Sub-divifions of that portion of time that is allotted unto each of them. Hereupon Mr. *Mede*'s own words are, *The order of the Seals, and in them, of the Trumpets, is certain and undoubted, to wit, the fame, which the number to every one afcribed doth point out,* 1, 2, 3, 4, 5, 6, 7. *The reft therefore of the Prophecies in that Book, being compared firft between themfelves, and afterwards with the Seals, by way of Synchronifm, the Order of the whole* Revelation *will be evident.* This Affertion of his I take to be moft clear.

He therefore begins with that notable *quaternion* of Prophecies, which are fo very remarkable, by reafon of the equality of their times.

1. The firft is, the Prophecy of the VVoman's remaining in the VVildernefs *for a time, times, and half a time,* or 1260 *dayes,* as is there more manifeftly declared.

2. The fecond is that of the feven-headed Beaft, reftored and ruling forty two months.

3. The third is of the Court (or of the holy City) trodden under foot by the Gentiles.

4. The fourth and laft, is that of the *two Witneffes, prophefying* 1260 *dayes,* that is, years.

Now although (as Mr. *Mede* well obferves) the character of equality of times will not be fufficient to evidence that they are the fame times, but may be before or after, yet by other characters which that Book affords, to make out the demonftration, it feems very clear. Thefe other characters he brings (as well he may) out of the twelfth Chapter, where 'tis plain, that when the Dragon is caft down by

Michael

Michael out of Heaven, the VVoman escapes from his presence into the VVilderness, *ver.* 6, and 14. The Dragon being angry that he had failed of his attempt to destroy her in Heaven, repairs to his earthly weapons, and applies himself to make war with the VVoman and with the rest of her Seed, to wit, those which she should bring forth in the VVilderness, *ver.* 17. And for this purpose he gave his Power, his Throne, and great Authority to the ten-horned Beast, out of the Sea ascending, *Chap.* 13. 1, 2.

By *Chap.* 11. it appears, that the times of the Beast and of the Prophecy of the VVitnesses are equal, and that they are finished together at the end of the sixth Trumpet, which shews they began and held on together, the whole space. The twelfth *verse* shews the Ascention of the VVitnesses into Heaven, which puts a period to their mourning Prophecy, as also that great Earthquake (wherewith the Imperial City being overthrown, the Kingdom of the Beast comes to be abolished) noted by the very moment in which the second Woe, which is under the sixth Trumpet, went out. On this, the third Woe is quickly to ensue, at the sounding of the seventh Trumpet. In that very moment of time that the Witnesses, (whom the Beast ascending out of the bottomless pit had slain, being at the point of finishing their Testimony in sackcloth) were revived by the spirit of life from God entring into them, and ascending up into Heaven, the same hour the tenth part of the City fell, by means of the great Earthquake.

Then matters are brought to that pass, that the seventh Trumpet sounding, all the Kingdoms of the World become our Lord's and his Christ's. In the same moment also, the Wrath of the Lamb comes to be poured out by the Ministry of the Vials, and the Temple of God is to be seen in Heaven, *ver.* 15, 19.

The great Harlot, or *mystical Babylon* (chap. 17.) is of the same time with the *seven-headed* and *ten-horned Beast*, as are also the *hundred forty and four thousand sealed Ones, being Virgins*; these are of the same time with the Whore of *Babylon* and the Beast.

The period of the Tyranny of the Beast, and of this Company of the sealed Virgin-Saints, is at the coming forth of the multitude of Palm-bearers. For, out of what tribulation could they come, but of the Beast's persecuting the Saints? Therefore they leave the Tyranny of the Beast behind them, and are of one Mystical Body or Church with the *sealed Ones*, and have been under the same Persecution with them; but are Saints of an inferiour rank and station to those that have the priviledge and dignity to be sealed with the Name of the Father in their foreheads, *Chap.* 7.

The

The *two-horned Beaſt* hath contemporized with the *ten-horned Beaſt*, (Chap. 13.) The *Whore* with both, and all theſe *three* with the *Woman in the Wilderneſs*, the *treading under foot the holy City*, and *the Witneſſes* (mean time) *mourning in ſackcloth.* The company alſo of the *ſealed Virgins*, and the company of *Palm-bearing Virgins*, brought from under great tribulation, into a ſafe and bleſſed ſtate, (though no mention be made of their being ſealed) theſe (as to the ſeaſon of their tribulation under the perſecuting Beaſt) contemporize with the *Whore* and the *Beaſt*. All theſe contemporize one with another, and fill up the ſame ſpace of time. After this, ſucceeds the Miniſtry of the *ſeven Vials*, at the Riſing of the *Witneſſes*, and the moment of their aſcending into Heaven. This will come to paſs at the beginning of the ſounding of the *ſeventh Trumpet.* Then the triumphing ſtate of the *Witneſſes* will come on. The power of the *Keyes*, and the pouring forth of the *Vials of God's Wrath upon the Kingdom of the Beaſt*, will be viſibly committed to them , and the time of the *Beaſt's* and *Babylons inclining to Ruine*, or the *viſibly declining ſinking ſtate of both*, will fall in together with this Diſpenſation of the *Vials*, to make way for the *Marriage of the Lamb*, and the *coming down of the New Jeruſalem out of Heaven*, to be ſeen as the Tabernacle of God amongſt men here on Earth.

The remaining difficulty then is, to fill up the firſt of the three great Sections and Diviſions of time, before-mentioned, to wit, the ſpace which had an end put to it by the Womans actual flight into the Wilderneſs. This began, when *John* received this Prophecy in the Iſle of *Patmos.* Mr. *Mede* very judicially ſummeth it up in theſe three Particulars.

1. The value and preference which is put by God upon the ſtate of the Church, as it anſwers to the *inward Court* of the Temple of old, comparatively with thoſe who in their ſpirit, principle and way, anſwer but to the *outward Court* thereof, and the Worſhip appertaining thereunto. The former have the true inward Circumciſion of the heart in the ſpirit, *whoſe praiſe is not of men, but of God.* The latter are thoſe, who, at beſt, have but the Circumciſion of the heart in the letter, which labours to ſhew it ſelf in ſuch outward Circumciſion of language and practice, as may ſerve to keep up a ſhew or form of Godlineſs in the ſight and to the well-pleaſing of man, whilſt they are at an utter diſtance, even in their hearts, from the very life and power of Godlineſs, that ſprings up from the new nature, that is found in the true Circumciſion, which worſhip God in the ſpirit, and anſwer to the *inward Court.*

Paul

Paul takes notice of this in his time (*Gal.* 4.) where he diſtin-
guiſhes between an *earthly Jeruſalem,* that is in bondage with her
Children, under the Covenant of Works or Dominion of the Law,
and a *Jeruſalem above,* which is free, and is the Mother of all that
Seed of *Abraham,* who are Heirs according to the Promiſe. Theſe
are deſcribed (*Rev.* 12.) by *the Woman clothed with the Sun that hath
the Moon under her feet, and upon her Head a Crown of twelve Stars.*
This figurative deſcription ſhewes the Glory of the City *Jeruſalem,*
as it is *above, inward and in ſpirit,* who with her Children is in freedom, under the Covenant and Dominion of Grace. The ſame is
alſo ſignified by the *inward Court,* appointed to be meaſured by the
Reed of God, in diſtinction from the *outward Court,* which is not
meaſured, but abandoned and given up, as it were, to the power of
the *Gentiles,* to be by them troden under foot, and defiled.

2. In this ſame ſpace of time, falls out the impregnating of the
Woman, or her growing Great, ready to be delivered of a Man-
child. The principal care of the Apoſtles, and other Teachers, who
ſucceeded in their Spirit, in the Primitive Church, (deſcribed under
the repreſentation of the ſeven Churches of *Aſia,* and the Angels or
Officers appertaining to them) was, to be doing what had the moſt
conducible tendency to the haſtening and forwarding this birth of the
Man-child, which the Dragon oppoſed, diligently watch'd to hinder, reſiſt, and (if poſſible) to devour, as ſoon as born.

3. The ſeven-headed Dragon's lying in wait, and managing the
battel againſt *Michael* and his Angels, about the aforeſaid birth, muſt
needs contemporize with the *two* fore-mentioned Particulars. All
the *three* do therefore fill up the firſt ſpace of time, or age, ſucceeding
the Apoſtles, meaſured out by what is contained in the *ſix firſt Seals,*
and was fore-told to *John,* as that which ſhould happen both to the
Church and World, until the Womans flight from the Dragon, after
this great battel in Heaven, and retiring into the Wilderneſs, there
to be nouriſhed of God, her appointed time.

Theſe *three* are the immediate Antecedents of thoſe things, which
have been ſhewed to contemporize under the *ſeventh Seal and ſix
Trumpets* ; that is to ſay, the diſtinguiſhing between the *inward and
outward Court,* with the Worſhip and Service appertaining unto each ;
Secondly, The impregnating of the Woman : And then *Thirdly,* The
battel hereupon ariſing in Heaven, or within the Primitive Church,
and continuing a long time, till at length the Man-child comes to be
born. Then the Dragon loſes his credit and authority in the Church.
His ſubtilty in accuſing and laying falſe imputations on the Brethren,

(the

the truly pure and spiritual part of the Church) is detected. Hereupon, he is cast out into the Earth, confined (as it were) to the *outward Court*, and the Worshippers and Service belonging to it, as the only matter for him to work upon, for the increase of his Kingdom by the number of Hypocrites and Apostates, drawn by him out of the true Church. They were in truth never of it, though for a while they were in it. At length, they find it their interest to make a Separation from it; being sensual, and not having the Spirit, they can no longer endure those that have it, and that shine forth daily more and more in the Life and Testimony thereof. The old Dragon became hereby necessitated to manage and prosecute the War with the earthly Weapons only of worldly Power and Government, in a way of outward force and compulsion, exercised by the power of humane Laws, and of the civil Sword. This Power and Sword, the corrupt, sensual, and malignant Church (founded and consisting in the worshippers and service of the *outward Court*) getting into their hands, or engaging it on their side, by mingling Interest with worldly Governours, committed Whoredom, like *Tyre*, with all the Kingdoms of the VVorld upon the face of the Earth, *Isa.* 23. 17. Yea, this Beast with *two horns*, so influenced, encouraged and back'd the *ten horn'd* Beast, that he became thereby fixed and engaged, in his Mind as well as Power, to continue and carry on the War, *forty and two months* longer, against the Woman and her Seed, and to blaspheme God, his Name, his Tabernacle, and them that dwell in Heaven.

Thus in brief Heads have we seen how the two first great Sections or Divisions of time, in the *third Age*, are filled up, to wit, the space from *John's* receiving the Prophecy of them in the *Isle of Patmos* to the end of the first battel, or war, made in Heaven, and (as the issue of that) the catching up of the Man-child unto God and to his Throne, and the Womans actual flight into the VVildernefs, and from thence to the rising of the VVitneffes, which puts a period to the suffering feafon, alloted to their Prophefying in Sack-cloth. And as to the third and last Section of time, it is that which is measured out by the founding of the *seventh Trumpet*, and the pouring out of the *seven Vials*, which begins with the beginning of that *Trumpet*, and continues till the *Whore* be judged, *Babylon* sunk, and the whole Kingdom of the *Beast* for ever ruined and destroyed. This makes way for the marriage of the Lamb to be celebrated here on Earth, and so, for the coming on of the Kingdom of Christ into the actual exercise of a visible ruling Power and universal Empire over the whole VVorld, for a *thousand years*.

Having

Having thus had a view of the diſtinct periods of time, together with the matter of the Propheſies, which were to be fulfilled in and under each of theſe diſtinct Revolutions, it will yet much prepare and help our uuderſtandings, rightly to diſcern and look into the Myſteries of this moſt excellent Book, if once we can but arrive at a ſatisfactory opening, and interpreting (at leaſt, in ſome chief particulars·) the things which are ſignified under many of the Figures and Allegorical Expreſſions, made uſe of throughout the whole Prophecy. For Example : Let us conſider theſe ; *The ſeven Churches and the Angels of them : The Throne in Heaven : The ſealed Book : The Woman : The Dragon and his Angels : Michael and his Angels : The Man-child : The throne and ſeat of the Dragon's Power and Authority : The outward and inward Court : The Floud, iſſuing out of the Dragon's mouth : The diſtinguiſhed Inhabitants of the Heavens, of the Earth, and of the Sea : The 144000 ſealed Virgins : The Palm-bearers: The Remnant of the Womans Seed, that keep the Commands of God and have the Teſtimony of Jeſus : The ſeven-headed, ten horn'd Beaſt : The Beaſt's Image : The two horn'd Beaſt : The falſe Prophet : The Whore : Myſtical Babylon : The great City that rules over the Kings of the Earth : The Number of the Beaſt's Name : The two Witneſſes ; their hidden or obſcure Propheſying in Sack-cloth ; their glorious Appearing and Propheſying in Power, and in a Wonder-working Miniſtry, like to that of Moſes and Eliah : The Kingdom of the Beaſt, and his aſcent out of the bottomleſſ pit : The ſlaying of the Witneſſes, at the finiſhing of their Teſtimony, or perioding of their Sack-cloth-Propheſying, and their lying Dead in the ſtreets of the great City, ſpiritually called Sodom and Egypt : The Witneſſes riſing and aſcending up into Heaven : The coming of the Wrath of the Lamb : The ſight of Heaven opened, with the Temple and Ark therein contained : The Harveſt and Vintage : The marriage of the Lamb : The coming down of the new Jeruſalem out of Heaven ; to be as a Tabernacle of God amongſt men on Earth, all the Kingdoms of this World becoming the Kingdoms of the Lord and his Chriſt.*

The Charge given *John*, by him that was dead and yet liveth for evermore, the Amen, or everlaſting Truth of God (*Rev.* 1. 18, 19.) was, to write ; *Firſt*, The things which he had ſeen, in the deſcription of the fulneſs and excellency of Chriſt's Perſon, exhibited to him, *verſ.* 12, 17. *Secondly*, The things which are, or the ſtate of the Church in his time, as it had for its chief places of abode, thoſe principal Cities in *Aſia*, by name expreſſed, (*chap.* 2d. & 3d.) together with the Repreſentation in them, (as in Type and Figure)

of

of the state of the Universal Apostolick Christian Church, which was
to continue under the seven distinctions of time, contained under the
seven Seals, under the last whereof, *six* of the *Trumpets* were (as
'twere) included. There was that also found in those seven *Asiatick*
Churches, that did typically represent the decrease and sinking down
of a great Party in the visible Christian Church, into the Apostasie
foretold in this Book of the *Revelation*, until the very time of the rising of the Witnesses.

Thirdly and lastly, *John* was Commanded to write the things
which shall be hereafter, or which were to succeed that present state
in which the then seven Churches were, at that time, respecting as
well the Corruption and Apostasie, coming upon the face of the Primitive Church, as the continuance of it, with countenance and support from worldly Powers, till the sounding of the *seventh Trumpet*.
These things that shall be hereafter, (when time shall be no longer,
or when the Mystery of God shall be finished, and all persons and
things shall appear plainly and manifestly as they are) amount, in
general, to the Constitution and Concerns of that glorious state
of the Church, which is to be from thenceforth, for evermore.

To proceed then to the Explicating of many of the chief Allegorical Expressions in this Book of *Revelations*.

    1. By *the seven Churches in Asia*, let us understand, as in type,
the state of the Christian Church, characterized and described (as
Brightman intimates) under the distinct periods of time, held forth
by the things done, during the *seven Seals*, which reach to the sounding of the *seventh Trumpet*.

    2. By *the Angels of the seven Churches* are to be understood,
not only or principally, the Officers or Persons ministring, but rather
the Light of the Gospel in its distinct measures and degrees, administred according to the nature of the times and seasons, which the
things done under the *first six Seals*, did occasion. For upon the rejecting of that, there was caused a gradual and successive removing
of each *Candlestick* out of its place, and the Church sinks down at
length into an universal Defection and Apostacy, as to the visible
part of it. This renders it, in its concluding and final state, so
naucious and loathsome to God, that he resolves *to spue them out of his
mouth,* **and** *reject them for ever.*

To confirm this, ⬤ find each Church to consist of *two* very different sorts of Members ; *one*, that are spiritual, prepared with spiritual senses, or eares to hear what the Spirit sayes to the Churches :
the *other*, though they have the name and credit of Church-members,

yea,

yea, and in procefs of time, the greateft vifible Power and Sway in it, faying they are *Jews* or right Heirs of Promife, yet are they not fo, but do lie. They are indeed of the Synagogue of Satan. They came out from the fpiritual and better part of the Church, as no longer able to joyn, and go along, or keep pace with them, in their heavenly Life and Converfation. Being fenfual, and having not the Spirit, they feparate from the true fpiritual worfhipper, feeking their upholding and maintenance in this or that Form and Way, from the Powers of the World. And having once got worldly Power and outward ftrength and force on their fide, they refolved to perfecute and make War upon the better and more fpiritual part of the Church, with earthly Weapons, and by compulfion of the Civil Sword.

3. *The Throne in Heaven*, defcribed in the *fourth Chapter*, is the Seat which God hath made for himfelf, in the Creature-being of Chrift the Mediator, as his own Sanctuary, from whence to iffue forth all his Authority and Power, decreed to be by him exercifed, whether in Heaven or on Earth, in the capacity of Head and univerfal King over all the works of God's hands. He that fits on this Throne, is the fame that (*chap.* 19.) is cloathed with a Vefture dipt in blood, and whofe Name is called the W O R D of God. He is faid (*chap.* 5. *verf.* 6.) to have *feven horns*, and *feven eyes*, which are the feven Spirits of God, fent forth into all the Earth ; and this, by his being made flefh, and by his Death and Refurrection, in which he fhewed himfelf the true Sanctuary, which God pitch'd, and not man. This had been, in type, from the beginning, a moft glorious high Throne (*Jer.* 17. 12.) defigned from all Eternity to be the Throne and the place of the foals of his feet, whofe Name is the W O R D of God, in order to dwell in the midft of the Children of *Ifrael* for ever, and bear unto their fight and enjoyment the clear and compleat vifion of the invifible God.

4. *The Book* (chap. 5.) written within, and on the backfide, *fealed with feven Seals*, as it is part of the Vifion given to *John*, is a defcription of the inward and hidden meaning of the matter of this Prophecy, whether as to that which more efpecially concerns the Affairs of the Church, or that which more generally relates to the Affairs of the World and the Empire thereof. The *feven Seals* with which it is fealed on the back-fide, do intimate the dark and myftical movings or difpenfations of Gods Providence, that the feven-fold diftinction of time, under the *feven Seals and Trumpets* fhould produce, as the method and way that Chrift would take to open and

M 2   make

make known the inward writing, and to give so plain a Vision of it, *that he that runs may read it.*

The matter of this Prophecy, as it peculiarly relates unto the Church, contains in it the Church's progress and growth up in all things into Christ her Head, according to the purpose of the Father, which he purposed in Christ Jesus before the World was, and this, in despite of all contradiction, or opposition, from the Serpent and his Seed. In this respect it is, that (*chap.* 12.) the Man-child with which the Woman was in Travel, comes at last to be born, and seated on high, above the reach of Satan, as to any hurt that he could do unto it. In the end, it becomes a Mountain, filling the whole Earth.

As the matter of this Prophecy doth more generally relate unto the World, that lies in the wicked one, and holds of the Serpent, as of its universal Head and Ruler, it contains the wonderful workings and contrivances of God's Providence, in favour of his Church, and in rendring to every one according to their works, filling those that are of the World with the wayes of their own chusing. By this means, his worst enemies are taught and made to acknowledge his Justice and long-Suffering towards them, in and under all. His steady Counsels lead to the certain and final treading of all his Adversaries under foot, and to the exalting of the horn of his Anointed, who is both Lord and Christ.

5. By *the Temple of God*, and the Altar, and them that Worship therein, appointed to be measured, (*chap.* 11. 1.) is to be understood the right Worship of God, as well with respect to the object of it, shining forth in the Person and Spirit of Christ, inwardly known and conversed with, as with respect to the worshippers themselves, who are such only as are qualified with spiritual senses, rendring them meet for such Duty and Service, which they are called to the performance of in their Spirits, and with their inward man. But that which consists in the outward and bodily exercise, described by the *outward Court*, is given up, to be suppressed and troden under foot by the *Gentiles*, for 1260 years, *verf.* 2.

6. By *the Holy City* is meant *Jerusalem*, the City of the great King and Living God, the incorporated Society of Inhabitants or Citizens, that stand in relation to Christ, as his Subjects and Servants, under the obligation of one or other Covenant, that is conditionally or absolutely. Those that are his Subjects but in the conditional Covenant, are Citizens whose Names are only written in the Earth, who (upon tryal and proof) do not remain so. Though they say they

are

are *Jews*, they are not, but do lie. Yea, they evidently difcover themfelves in the end, to be the very Synagogue of Satan. But thofe that are the Subjects of Chrift, abfolutely, or in and by the new and everlafting Covenant, eftablifhed in all things and fure, they are fuch Citizens, whofe Names are written in Heaven, among the living in *Jerufalem*, where they become Pillars in the Houfe of God, never to go out more, being found in a ftate of Life and way of converfe with, and worfhipping of God in Chrift, wherein they are fecured from final Apoftacy and Defection.

7. The *Earthly Citizens*, or the Inhabitants and Children of the *Jerufalem* on Earth, do prove at laft to be as great enemies to their King, as any among the heathenifh and prophane World, when once they revolt from his Scepter, disjoyn and feparate from the fpiritual and better part of the Citizens, whofe Names are written in Heaven, or in the Lamb's Book of new-creature Life, in a character that is indeleble, and by vertue of that Covenant which cannot be broken. And their great Defign (when once actually feparated from the true fpiritual Worfhippers) is, by the calling in of ftrength and aid from the prophane World, to tread under the holy City, even the very Heavenly *Jerufalem*, and fo to keep it under, that it may never come to have any Credit, Authority, or Power in the World.

Thefe *Citizens and Inhabitants of the Heavenly Jerufalem*, are defcribed (*chap. 7.*) by thofe *that are fealed with the Seal of the Living God*, and are either a Company certain, and numbred, making up the 144000 there mentioned ; or elfe, a Company and Society of *fealed ones*, that in comparifon of the former are numberlefs, and of a more large and univerfal extent, called (by way of diftinction) *Palm-bearers*.

The firft fort of thefe *fealed ones* do anfwer to the 24 Courfes of the *Levites* of old, who were given unto God, inftead of the firft-born. They ftand in a peculiar relation to, and dependance upon the great High Prieft, as their Head, and do properly conftitute and make up that Affembly of the firft-born, whofe Names are written in Heaven. Thefe are a Kingdom of Priefts, reprefented before the Throne, by the four and twenty Elders.

The fecond fort of thefe *Citizens and fealed ones*, do anfwer to the whole Congregation of *Ifrael*, diftributed into their four parts and ftations, round about the Ark, at a greater diftance from the Throne, a Kingdom of common Subjects, and lefs priviledg'd Children than the former. Yet, thefe latter fort of men fhall be recounted as well

as

as the former, to have been born in her, whom the Moſt High doth eſtabliſh, *Pſal.*87.5.

Thus, *Pſal.* 49. there is notice taken of *high or noble men,* and *of low or common men.* Theſe two Orders are eminently found in a ſtate of perpetuity and continuancy, in Chriſt's own Kingdom. Both of them have their original and foundation in the Manhead of Chriſt, who is one manner of man, as *he bears the form of a Servant, like unto us* earthly men, *in all things, ſin only excepted.* In this capacity he is conſtituted King over the whole Earth. But he is another manner of man; as he is called and made an High Prieſt after the Order of *Melchiſedec,* without Father, without Mother, without Pedigree or Deſcent, having neither beginning of dayes, nor end of life. It is therefore ſaid of him in this ſecond ſenſe, *Conſider how great this man is, unto whom even the Patriarch* Abraham *gave the tenth of his ſpoyls.* And again, the ſame Apoſtle (*Heb.*5.11.) teſtifies, *that of him he had many things to ſay, that were hard to be uttered, ſeeing they were dull of hearing,* and ſlow to diſcern the diſtinction of that excellency and perfection which ſhines forth in Chriſt's own humane nature, in the twofold reſpect which we have mentioned.

8. By *the Two Witneſſes* then, we are hereby taught to underſtand thoſe *two ſorts of Citizens,* or *Inhabitants of the Heavenly Jeruſalem* ; the word of whoſe Teſtimony is, according to this their twofold and diſtinct birth, which makes them Kings or Prieſts with Chriſt, or both ; that is, joynt or co-heirs with Chriſt, in the dignity and perfection of his Manhead, in one or both of theſe Conſiderations of it. This is intimated, (*Iſa.*43.10.) *Ye are my Witneſſes, ſaith the Lord, and my Servant* (Chriſt) *whom I have choſen ; that ye may know and believe me,* or be one in Judgment and Will with me , *and underſtand that I am he. Before me there was no God formed, nor ſhall be after me.*

And they are called *Witneſſes,* not only becauſe they know and believe him, and are one in Spirit with him, as he is a glorified earthly man, and a man alſo that is *Michael,* God's fellow ; but as they Prophecie in Sack-cloth, or in a ſuffering ſtate, not loving their lives unto the death, rather then ceaſe to be Witneſſes and to bear their teſtimony to the Truth, when called thereunto, under the greateſt contradiction of ſinners.

9. By the *Woman* (chap. 12.) *clothed with the Sun, &c.* who being with Child, cried, travelling in birth with a Man-child, and pained to be delivered, is meant the true *Sarah,* or ſpiritual Womb of Chriſt's dead body, (*Rom.*7.4.) which lawfully diſcharges us from the Covenant of the Law, or obligation to act ſingly by the activity

it

- it gives, *that we should be married to another, even to him who is raised from the dead, that we may bring forth fruit unto God*, as quicken'd into a life and activity much more excellent. There is therefore set before the eyes of our Faith, the Law of the Spirit of Life that is in Chrift Jefus, rifen from the dead, for us hence-forward to be conformed and live unto, as that birth of manly perfection, which shines forth in him, who was crucified indeed in weaknefs, but was raifed in power, or a man of Power, in whofe hands all Power in Heaven and Earth is intrufted. And thofe who become one, in conjunction of Spirit with him, by the new and everlafting Covenant, are with him caught up to the Throne of God, in the one or other capacity (before intimated) of the two forts of Citizens, that by the new birth are members of the *Heavenly Jerufalem*, and of the remnant of the Womans Seed, that keep the Commandments of God, and have the Teftimony of Jefus.

: The great Conteft and Battel which happened between the *Witneffes* on the one part, (comprehended under the name of *Michael and his Angels*) and the *Serpent and his brood* on the other, was, as the one were Friends, and the other Enemies, to the Crofs and Death of Chrift, and as the Judgmen, Opinions, and Practifes of the one or other made void, or elfe eftablifhed and advanced the Myftery and Efficacy of the Crofs and the Law of it, which thofe that obferve and follow, *peace will be upon them, as on all the Ifrael of God.* In this Quarrel the *Witneffes* do fight under the protection and bleffing of *Michael*, their Head; as the other do under the fupport and encouragement of the *Old Dragon*, their Head.

10. By the *Old Dragon* we are to underftand the Spirit that rules in the Children of difobedience, who is (for the prefent) Head and chief Ruler over the World, as managing the univerfal Scepter thereof, by Chrift's permiffion. The Enfigns and Characters of this Empire (according to Scripture phrafe) is *feven heads and ten horns*, intimating the nature, as well as perfection and univerfality of that worldly Power, which is exercifed by the *Old Dragon*, in waging war againft the *Woman and her Seed*.

This War he is capable to manage, either as *an Angel of Light, and a falfe Prophet in the Church*; or as an *univerfal Monarch and Governor in the World*.

In the firft Capacity, as this *Dragon* transforms himfelf into an *Angel of Light*, and Minifter of Righteoufnefs, he works with all Power, Signs, and lying Wonders. As *Jannes* and *Jambres* withftood *Mofes* and *Aaron* in their Commiffion, fo do the Serpent's Seed

in

in Sheep's clothing and Chrift's own likenefs, refift the *Witneffes* in their Teftimony, and oppofe the Inhabitants of the *Heavenly Jern-falem*, by pretending a greater Friendfhip to Chrift, and conformity to his written Law, in all their words and actions, than the true Seed of the Woman, having indeed the form of Godlinefs, but de-nying the Power and Spirit thereof.　After this manner did the *Dra-gon* and his *Angels*, in the Primitive Church, fight with *Michael* and his *Angels*, to prevent the birth of the Man-child, and to keep up the Credit and Authority of the Law, and their following after Righ-teoufnefs in the Principles, and upon the terms of the firft Cove-nant, in oppofition to the Miniftry of the Spirit, according to the Promife and Tenor of the new and everlafting Covenant.　This battel continued, in the Primitive Church, about four hundred years, and came at laft to this iffue; Satan was caft down out of Heaven, upon an evident difcovery of his deceitful workings and lying won-ders, in the Teachings and Infpirations which came out of his mouth, as a falfe Spirit and Prophet, fo that he was not able, fingly this way, to bear up any longer againft the Power and Demonftration of the Spirit of Truth, in the mouth of the Saints, but found himfelf neceffitated to refort to his earthly and worldly Weapons, the Power of the Civil Sword, that fo joyning both his Interefts together, that of the Magiftrate and falfe Prophet, he might grow up into fuch a formidible pofture, as is mentioned, (*Chap.* 13. 4.) where it is faid, *Who is like unto the B E A S T, or able to make War with him ?*

This pofture the Apoftle *John* beheld the *Dragon* putting himfelf into, when the *feven-headed and ten-horned Beaft* arofe out of the Sea, and the *two-horned Beaft* out of the Earth.　Both of thefe together do become the Seat or Throne, to which the *Dragon* gave up his Power and Authority.　The firft of thefe two Beafts receives him, as the old, unclean, prophane, heathenifh Spirit; they that are meant by that Beaft, are ftill the fame in Principles, as before, only out-wardly baptized into the name of the Chriftian Profeffion or Religi-on, when Chriftian Religion became the Religion of the Roman Empire.　Thus was that Beaft healed of its former Wound, when *Paganifm* was deftroyed and pull'd down.

And becaufe the bare name of Chriftian Religion, or out-fide Profeffion thereof, without fomething of real Reformation and Pow-er of inward Principles, was not of credit or authority enough, to advance Antichrift's Kingdom, therefore the Miniftry of the Law or firft Covenant (even the knowledge of Chrift according to the flefh,

as

as it is capable to ferve the Serpents Seed for a cover and vail of their enmity againft the Crofs of Chrift, and Power of his Refurrection) doth fpring up over the head (as it were) of the firft Beaft. This fecond Beaft, or branch of Antichrift's Subjects and Kingdom, with two horns, like the Lamb, but fpeaking as the Dragon, chufes rather to joyn Intereft with the firft Beaft, than to fuffer the Citizens of the heavenly *Jerufalem* to come out of their Wildernefs-condition. Yet this earth or miry clay, cannot (when all's done) cleave heartily and thorowly to the heathenifh prophane Spirit of the firft Beaft, but at laft is preyed upon by it. This Earthly *Jerufalem* is unexpectedly furprized, and overflowed as with a flood, by that prophane Intereft it ventured to call to its affiftance againft the true Seed of the Woman, in which refpect it is faid that the Earth helps the Woman, the wrath of the prophane party of Antichrift's Kingdom, or of the ten-horned Beaft, being chiefly fpent and poured out upon that Profeffing Party that make up the fecond, or two-horned Beaft.

11. By *the Inhabitants of the Heavens, of the Earth, and of the Sea,* (chap. 12. 12.) are meant, *Firft,* The Citizens of the heavenly *Jerufalem,* who are under Grace ; *Secondly,* The Citizens of the earthly *Jerufalem,* who are under the dominion and curfe of the Law ; And *Thirdly,* The prophane Party who live under fin, moving therein, as in their Element, paft feeling, by reafon of the blindnefs and hardnefs of their hearts. This ftate of Sin is neverthelefs not unchangeable, nor thofe that are Captives under it, in a condition irrecoverable, for Chrift died to redeem men out of it.

12. By *the feven-headed and ten-horned Beaft,* arifing out of the Sea, is to be underftood the Empire, or Governing Power of the World, in whofe hands foever it be found, as it is made the Seat and Throne of Satan, and promotes the Intereft of the Devils Kingdom in corruption of manners, and prophanefs, even by the countenance of humane Laws, or at leaft in the execution of them.

13. By *the two-horned Beaft,* arifing out of the Earth, we are to underftand the Ufurpation of the Prophetical Office of Chrift, by a falfe Spirit, or the faid Office as deceitfully executed in a private Spirit of felf-byaffed Reafon, in disjunction from the Spirit of the true Head, undertaking to counfel and lead men in the interpretation of the written Word, or other evident fignification of God's Will. This, once joyned with worldly Government and Power, (made its vaffal and ridden by it) is that Spirit and Principle for promoting of worldly Religion, which is founded in, and fupported

N by

by humane Laws, under the Name and Form of Christianity. The two-horned Beast and the false Prophet are therefore the same, as by comparing *chap. 13. verf. 14.* with *verf. 20. of chap. 19.* is most clear. And the ten-horned Beast is wont also to be called the Image of the Beast; where ever therefore the Beast and the false Prophet are mentioned together, (as they are, three times) there by the name of the Beast is meant no other but the ten-horned Beast; as by the false Prophet, the two-horn'd. Contrarily; where, with the Beast we find coupled the Image of the Beast, (as *chap. 14. verf. 9, & 11. chap. 15. verf. 2. chap. 16. verf. 2. chap. 19. verf. 20. & chap. 20. verf. 4.*) there, by Beast is to be understood the false Prophet; and by his Image, the seven-headed and ten-horn'd Beast, as restored. For this Beast, seeing he acknowledgeth the false Prophet as his Restorer, and suffereth himself to be guided by him, as his supream Lord, (*chap. 13. verf. 12, 14, 15.*) he is (not without cause) called his Image, not as representing or bearing the similitude of the two-horn'd Beast, but he is the Image which the two-horn'd Beast, speaking like the Dragon, did restore, and which he challengeth for his own. To justifie this; that very Image of the Beast, which the false Prophet did give life unto, did cause that whosoever would not worship the Image of the Beast, should be slain. To conclude, of the self-same is the Image of the Beast, and the Name or Number said to be, *chap. 15. 2.* The Name and Number seem not to be called the Name and Number of any other Beast, than of the two-horn'd, as of the principal Founder and Lord.

14. The *Number of the Name of the Beast*, being said to be the Number of a man, signifies that it is the sensual part of man's Wisdom or Reason, become devilish, by joyning in combination with Satan in his revolt from his true Head, and in exercising enmity against all Righteousness, upon one account or other.

This *sensual part of man's Wisdom* savours and minds Earthly or seen things, and delights in corporeal fleshly objects, whether actually corrupt, or only corruptible. This is the Wisdom that is prevalent with the generality of men in the World, according to the Principles of which, the Empire and Government of the World is managed, and the judgment and interpretation of the very Law and Word of God is made, for the Rule in matters of Faith and Worship. This Wisdom is in its best estate, unstable and unfixed, so as from the top and height of its honour, there is suddenly a being made like the Beast that perishes, and so a falling short of the true Rest. This was the case of the first *Adam*, who was created on the *sixt day*,
and

and whose unstable perfection is therefore numbered by *six*, thrice repeated.

This *sensual part of man's Wisdom*, is the executing or performing Power of the Soul, in reference to the dictates and enlightnings that declare themselves in the intellectual and angelical part of the mind, which many times serves and approves the Law of God, whilst the sensual part serves and obeyes sin, and as with a Law of common consent from the Members, opposes and resists the good and right Rule which shines forth in man's intellect, and which we call sound or right Reason. But as this sensual part, in its movings and actings, holds agreement and is in conjunction with the intellectual part, as its Ruler and Guide, following the dictates thereof; so far the actings thereof are sound and right, holding conformity to the Law of God. Thus even the sensual part (as subject to the right dictates of the intellectual) is it self a Rule unto humane action, and is the principle and foundation of righteous Magistratical Government amongst men. Now when this Principle in Magistrates, ceases to be any longer found in a state of down-right *Paganism*, and comes to be healed and restored out of darkness and prophaness, by receiving of the Scriptures or written Word of God, (opened and interpreted by such as pretend to be commissioned and gifted for that purpose) unto which it owes its healing and restoration, it doth by way of acknowledgement receive and set up that prophetical Office, in an administration, countenanced by humane Laws and the Magistrates Power. Where-ever this kind of Magistracy is, in both the branches of it, both Civil and Ecclesiastical, (setting up for themselves and their own Interests, in their own wills, in disjunction from Christ and his Spirit, the true Head, and in opposition to the Remnant of the Womans Seed, and their testimony in word and action) there is the Kingdom and Seat of the Beast and Antichrist, leading the People over whom it is exercised, into servitude both of Soul and Body. This is that Principle and Power, that after the limited time of 1260 years, must fall and be taken out of the way.

15. By *the Witnesses Prophesying in Sack-cloth*, are meant the true Circumcision in Spirit, who Worship God in Christ Jesus, and live in a through-resignedness of mind to him that is risen from the dead, who is the Spirit of Truth which is given them by the Father to be their guide, of whom and of whose Testimony they are not ashamed, what ever disgrace it be in, or however rejected by the Government under which the Providence of God hath placed them. They do therefore own it as their Principle, and make it their practice, to

bear

bear and suffer under such worldly Powers and Governments, in Faith and Patience, whatever befals them for their Testimony's sake, without attempting to resist the Powers that are, to disturb their peace or give them any just cause of offence.

They are called *Witnesses*, because of the word of their Testimony, which they forbear not to give in the worst and most suffering times, whatever it cost them. And they are *Two*, described by two Candlesticks, or Societies of Believers, and two Olive Trees or Sons of Oyl, because through Faith they are the receivers of the Anointing which comes from the Holy One, and is Truth and no Lie. This Anointing proportions it self in its Gift, either according to the measure it finds the Nature of man capable to take in and possess, without any new addition of a distinct, superiour capacity and reception; or else gives forth its self in a vast and boundless communication, wherein it is capable to flow forth into man, and to form in him an answerable Reception thereunto, (beyond and above that capacity and measure of knowledge and discerning, which is proper to man in his first make or building) to the extending and enlarging the intellectual part of man's Being, into a more abundant fruition of God, in a superiority to that of Angels, even to a joynt inheriting, seeing, and enjoying of God with the exalted humane Nature of the Son of God, in that Name which he obtains above Angels, and wherein he is more excellent than they. At this more excellent Name of Christ, as it originally shines forth in Christ's own Person, every knee must bow, and every tongue confess, to the glory of God the Father.

These two sorts of Saints are in most intimate Union and inseperable conjunction with the Lord that Spirit, who is the Son of man glorified or justified in Spirit, and who hath the gift of the Anointing, in both the respects before-mentioned. The one sort of these Saints as well as the other, do with open face behold (as in a glass) the Glory of the Lord, whether that, wherein he is perfect man, or that wherein he is more than man, the man that is God's Fellow and Equal, and so Superiour and Head to Angels, Principalities and Powers, ascended far above all Heavens. And they are changed into the same Image, respectively, whether of the one Glory or of the other, by the Spirit of the Lord, or the Lord the Spirit.

These *Two Witnesses* do live and abide in their Principles and word of their Testimony, when their persons die, and they have put off their earthly Tabernacle. For the Witnessing-work is carried on in a succession of new Witnesses, brought upon the stage of this World,

one

one Generation after another, during the time declared of 1260 years, whilst they are appointed to prophesie in Sack-cloth. And when that suffering season of theirs shall have an end put to it, (as it must) the like two Companies and Societies of Saints (spirited with the same Principles, that these sackcloth or suffering Prophets are of, both of them making but one Church and House of the Living God) shall be quicken'd and rais'd up in Power, by such a Redemption wrought in and upon their bodies (even here, in this life) from the bondage of Corruption, as is called the *Adoption* of the body, *Rom.* 8. 23. This Adoption or Redemption of the body, on this side the Resurrection, will hold proportion very much, with Christ's Transfiguration. This state of the body is prophetically described, *Dan.* 12. 3. where we are given to understand that the bodies of the Saints, or of those that are wise, shall shine as the brightness of the Firmament, and their Spirits as the Stars for ever and ever. For into such an intimate relation and conjunction, will Christ, as he is the Head of Angels, take and adopt the Spirits of Angels, and men regenerated, with himself, and with one another, as by his own influence on the Spirits of Saints, and by his and the influence of their own Spirits on their bodily or sensual part, to reduce their bodies into so near a relation to, and conjunction with the Life of their Spirits, and Christ in Spirit, as will raise and advance them into a heavenly frame, and render them meet for so great a glory of Spirit, or eminent exercise of spiritual Life and Power. This will be a glory of the body, not before known, as a common and general dispensation, since the World began, nor yet hardly so eminently experienced even by those few choice Types and Shadowes of it, *Enoch,* *Moses* and *Elias,* or others. This is that state of body, or of the very outward-man and sensual part of the Saint, whereby Christ will be glorified in his Saints, and admired in all those that do believe.

A LETTER

A LETTER

OF

Sir *HENRY VANE,*

To his LADY, from the *Isle of* S C Y L L Y.

My Dear Heart,

THe Wind yet continuing contrary, makes me desirous to be as much in Converse with thee (having this opportunity) as the Providence of God will permit ; hoping these will come safe to your hand. It is no small Satisfaction to me in these sharp Tryals, to experience the Truth of those Christian Principles, which God of his Grace hath afforded you and me, in our measures, the knowledge, and emboldned us to make the profession of. For surely by this Fiery Tryal, which is from God appointed to try us, no strange or unusual Dispensation of God hath happened to us, differing from that which all his Servants and Prophets from the beginning of the World to this day, have found also to be their Lot : Nor is it other, than the Condition (as I may say) and Law, that all those must come under and submit unto, that will approve themselves Christ's Disciples indeed, *Luk.* 14. 26, 27. And it is no small Mercy, that the greatest Extremities we have already under-gone, and which do as yet threaten, have found that strength and rooting of the Grace and Love of Christ in our Hearts, which causes us not to despair of being made more than Conquerors in the end, without desiring those Conditions of peace, (*vers.* 32.) which are not consistent with our being such Disciples of Christ, as will cheerfully (when called to it) forsake all they have, in love to him, and subjection to his Will.

Why should Christ ask us, *Whether we be able to drink of the Cup he drank of, and be baptized with the Baptism he was baptized with ?* Was it not, to intimate, *That if we die with him, we shall also live with him ;*

him; *if we suffer, we shall also reign with him,* and have it granted to us *to sit down with him, on the Throne of his Glory, our very Enemies beholding?* What would it be less, even in this world, if he should but please to cause, upon this occasion of our Suffering, that the Spirit of God, and of Glory, should rest upon us, and bring forth his Kingdom within us, in Power, giving us that Mouth and Wisdom that will make us mighty in word and deed; that Faith, to which all things are possible; that Spirit of Supplication and Prayer, that he will alwayes hear and immediately answer? God's Arm is not shortned; doubtess, great and precious Promises are yet in store, to be accomplished in and upon Believers here on Earth, to the making of Christ to be admired in them. If we come not to live here, in the actual fruition and full accomplishment of them, (as they will be experienced by Believers, even on this side the death, or full change of their mortal body) yet if we die in the certain fore-sight and embracing of them by Faith, this will be no small blessing.

This dark night and black shade, which God hath drawn over his Work in the midst of us, may be (for ought we know) the ground-colour to some beautiful piece, that he is exposing to the Light. His Sons must be manifested and evidently distinguished from those, who say they are such and are not. There is a glory to be revealed in them, unto which their Suffering is made the needful Preparation; and this is called the Redemption of the body. In that day, the tabernacling of God in men shall be visible. Their very bodies shall be the Temple of the Holy Ghost. In them, as his Sanctuary, will God dwell for evermore, whence shall be given forth such visible signs of his extraordinary Presence, as shall render it past dispute, to the sight of every man, that God is in them and with them of a Truth.

This state of entire resignedness and subjection of our bodies to our Spirits, and of our Spirits unto Christ, the Father of them, shall certainly be brought to the view of the whole World. The eyes of those that see them, shall acknowledge them; and the ears that hear them, shall bear witness to them, that they are the Seed and Off-spring, which the Lord hath blessed.

Our body, thus considered, as capable of such advance and honour, is not meerly the outward case or shell, that must return to dust, but includes also the bodily, organical state of Life, or that souly, animal Life, which the Spirit of man exercises in conjunction with his mortal body. In this kind of Life it is, we see, hear, and speak, have the exercise of our Senses, after a distinct manner from Angels and intellectual Substances, in a way of operation in-

feriour

to be awakened by the Father of Spirits, and come forth in a superiour way, even of natural life, received by man in his first creation, to act as out of the body, or without the use of bodily organs, as an equal or associate to the very Angels. Now because the bodily and inferiour powers of our mind, are the instruments of that converse we are subjected to in these dayes of our vanity, so that if we will be sociable, it must be by the use thereof, the Apostle *James* comprehends all the action of these inferiour powers by the sensible organs we make use of in the exercise thereof, under the name of the tongue, when he saith, *If any man offend not in word, the same is a perfect man, and able to bridle the whole body.* To bridle and regulate the tongue, order all the language, action, and expression of the animal powers aright, is to bridle the whole body, under the government or ruling authority of the Mind or Spirit, considered in its superiour and angelical kind of life and acting, as out of the body, or above and without the use of bodily organs. The Mind or Spirit of man thus considered, is as the Pilot that turns the Ship about, whithersoever he listeth. If it well and truly exercise its governing power, it causes the animal life in all the operations and affections thereof, to obey its dictates and commands, however fiercely driven by contrary Winds, false Doctrine, any corrupting violent influences of Devils or men upon it, and fetches it off from whatever tumultuous disorder, its own sensual lusts and passions are ready to run it into, *Jam.* 3. 2, 5.

To be partaker of the Redemption of the body, is to be made this perfect man, which is taught so to live and act, from right, spiritual Principles, as not to offend in word, through the Power actually conferred on him and exercised by him, for the bridling of the whole body, in the sence above declared, and for the keeping it in subjection to the Spirit or angelical part in him, in righteousness and true holiness.

This taming of the tongue, or subduing of the bodily part in us to the spiritual and intellectual, is a work of no small difficulty, a thing that is not to be purchased but at a dear rate. It may cost us all that

we

we have, and no ill bargain neither, since by our words it is that we shall be justified, and by our words we shall be condemned. For until we have brought under our body, and reduced it into a fixed subjection and entire resignation to our Spirits, let us boast never so much, that which is perfect is not yet come; even that perfection which in a very eminent degree shall be experienced by the Saints here on Earth, on this side the grave, and during their continuance in the mortal body. This, for ought I can discern, will be the product of the present sharp and fiery Tryals, that God hath brought upon his People all the World over. After they have suffered a while, and the same Afflictions have been accomplished in the rest of their Brethren that are in the World, they may so far have the work of Patience perfected in them, as, in this sense, to become perfect and entire, wanting nothing, and to shine forth as so many bright morning stars, and fore-running signs of the near approach of the brightness of the Day of Christ's second coming. This God hath set before the eye of my Faith, as the mark for the price of the high Calling of God in Christ Jesus. This is that perfection, which by conformity with Christ in his Death, and fellowship with him in his Resurrection, is in a most eminent degree attainable, before our dissolution and the putting off our earthly Tabernacle. It shall be so far attained by the Power and Glory of Christ, that is to be revealed in us, that it shall not much fall short of a very Transfiguration. And the state of the then glorious Church will be no less than an Heaven upon Earth, in the new Heavens and new Earth, wherein dwelleth Righteousness. This glorious state of things we look for, and therefore are or ought to be hasting a-pace, unto the coming of that Day of God.

Yet, when I say, until we experience this kind of perfection in Power in us, that which is perfect is not yet come, my meaning is not, that the incorruptible Seed and Principles of this very perfection are not already seated and rooted in the inward man and in the Spirit of the Mind, so soon as we are regenerated, and that Christ is formed in us, dwelling in our hearts by Faith. Thus it is, that we are all glorious within. Thus the Kingdom of Heaven is within us, liken'd to the hidden Treasure, which when a man hath found in the field, he keeps it concealed, till he hath sold all that he hath, and bought that field. Faith, which is the substance of things hoped for, and the evidence of that Glory which doth not yet appear, is not unfitly expressed, when it is called *a light shining in a dark place*, that is, in our bodily and sensual part, which continues so for a long time

O   after

after our new birth. But thofe that are all glorious within, muſt have their time of manifeſtation, and be made all glorious without alſo. The outward-man of the heart, and the *outward Court* of the Temple, muſt come to be meaſured, and be of account and eſtimation, in the ſight of the World. Then the whole body ſhall be full of light, having no part dark, as when the bright ſhining of a Candle doth give thee light.

This is the Perfection which is near us, even at the very door, ready to be teſtified and witneſſed unto, after another manner than thoſe do pretend to, who are for the ſubjecting and keeping under the body, but by thoſe mutable and wavering Principles of Perfection, which amounts but to that viſibility of Saintſhip, which is the ſubject of Apoſtacy, yet hath hitherto paſſed for currant Coin. Nor would I have it thought, that I have already attained the powerful practice of this holy Duty and Perfection, but it is much in my deſire, aim, and hope. The difficult Circumſtances I am in, and that I am ſtill more and more every day caſt into, by God's wiſe-diſpoſing Providence, to the ſequeſtring me from the World, and with-holding all ſenſible Comforts from me, ſo much as he doth, make me, in ſome ſort, confident it is for a good end, and that out of love and faithfulneſs I am made to drink of this bitter Cup, the better to help forward this neceſſary work in me, and upon me, wherein conſiſts the glorious Liberty of the Sons of God. If I may have and enjoy this, it would ſeem a very little matter to me to be in outward bonds, baniſhment, want, or any other afflictions. Help me then (in all your ſolicitudes and cares about me) to what will further and advance this Work in me.

The Lord grant me and mine to be content, if he deny us to live of our own, and will bring us to the daily bread of his finding, which he will have us wait for, freſh and freſh from his own Table, without knowing any thing of it before-hand. Peradventure there is a greater ſweetneſs and bleſſing in ſuch a condition, than we can imagine, till we have tryed it. This may add to my help, even our making little haſte to get out of our Troubles, patiently waiting till God's time come, wherein he will open the Priſon doors, either by Death, or ſome other way, as he pleaſe, for the magnifying his own great Name, not ſuffering us to be our own chuſers in any thing, as hitherto hath been his way with us.

And why ſhould ſuch a taking up Sanctuary in God, and deſiring to continue a Pilgrim and ſolitary in this World, whilſt I am in it, afford ſtill matter of jealouſie, diſtruſt and rage, as I ſee it doth, to
thoſe

fal me, I account belt of all. And till then, I defire to be made faithful in my place and ftation, to make confeffion of him before men and not deny his Name, if called forth to give a publick Tefti-mony and Witnefs concerning him, and to be herein nothing terrifi-ed. What then will the hurt be, that I can or fhall receive by the worft that man can do unto me, who can but kill the body, and there-by open my Prifon door, that I may afcend into the pleafures that are at Chrift's right hand, prepared for thofe that teftifie and openly difcover their love to him, by not loving their lives unto the death. Surely this will prove better, than to prefer fin or evil (fo much as in appearance) unto Affliction and the Crofs, which Chrift would have me take up daily and follow him in.

If the Storm againft us grow ftill higher and higher, fo as to ftrip us of all we have, the Earth is ftill the Lords and the fulnefs thereof ; he hath a good ftore-houfe for us to live upon. There is nothing more deftructive to us every way then the uncertainty we are in.

God can, and (if he think fit) will chalk out fome way, wherein he may appear by his Providence to choofe for us, and not leave us to our own choice. And being contracted into that fmall compafs, which he fhall think fit to reduce us unto, we may perhaps meet with as true inward contentment, and fee as great a mercy in fuch a fe-queftration from the World, as if we were in the greateft outward profperity.

I know nothing that remains unto us, but like a toffed Ship in a ftorm, to let our felves be toffed and driven with the Winds, till he that can make thefe ftorms to ceafe, and bring us into a fafe Haven, do work out our deliverance for us. I doubt not but you will accor-dingly endeavour to prepare for the worft.

March 7. 1661.
62.

F I N I S.

ERRATA

ERRATA.

In the Epiſtle to the Reader.
Page 1. line 30. leave out, *if,* and *now.*

In the Epiſtle General.

Pag.6.l.9.f.*well,*r.*dwell.* P.7.l.30.f.*manhead,*r.*manhood.* (the ſame word is ſo miſprinted all along, and to be ſo corrected) P.8.l.23.f. *their,*r.*your.* P.10.l.39.leave out, *or would not.* P.15.l.17.f.*or,*r. *nor.* & l.37.r.*ſee him not.* P.21.l.30,31.leave out,*the fountain of theſe outward ſenſes, his inferiour part, to be in his Soul or Spirit.* & l.37.f.*his,*r. *its.* P.23.l.17.r.*much as hearers.* P.24.l.22.f.*and,*r.*which.* l.23.leave out,*in.* P.25.l.9.f.*of his,*r.*for his.* P.26.l.10.f.*are,*r.*ſeem.* l.40.f.*duly,* r.*daily.* & f.*by,* r. *find.* P.27.l.9.f.*other,*r.*one.* & l.40.leave out, *not.* P.28.l.6.f.*by,*r.*amongſt.* P.29.l.7.f.*firſt,*r.*laſt.* l.25.f.*perfection,*r.*perfective.* l.29.r.*to the.* P.30.l.22.f.*his,*r.*Chriſts.* l.28.leave out,*which.* P.33.l.13.f.*nor,*r.*or.* & l.23.f.*by,*r.*thereby.* P.34.l.8.f.*his,*r.*its.* & l.28.f.*into,*r.*unto.* P.35.l.7.r. *witneſſing in every reſpect.* l.39.f.*their,*r. *the.* P.37.l.3.f.*a,*r.*as.* P.38.l.27.f.*our,*r.*open.* P.43.l.14.f. *ſo,* r. *to.* l.37.f.*Monarchs,* r.*Monarchies;* ſo p.44.l.8. P.45.l.14.f. *whereby,* r. *where by.* P.48.l.25.f.*heads,*r.*headſhip.* & l.35.f.*one,*r.*his own.* P.52. l.23.f.*directed,*r.*diſcerned.* P.53.l.21.f.*duty,*r.*duties.*

Many other obſcurities through the miſtake of words, and miſplacing of Points, have happened in the *Printing of this General Epiſtle,* by reaſon of the ſeveral *difficulties* that attended its *Publication:* It being twice taken in the *Preſs,* and *two Preſſes,* well furniſhed with *Materials,* taken away in the doing of it.

Errata in The Face of the Times.

Page 64. line 26. for *forme runder,* read *former under.* P.70.l. 33. f.*unto,*r.*into.* & l.37. leave out, *or.* P.78.l.36.f.*o,*r.*or.* P.95.l.10. f. *doubteſs,* r. *doubtleſs.*